I0612609

ANGEL DESCENDED

THE AWAKENED BOOK 6

MATTHEW S. COX

DIVISION ZERO PRESS

Angel Descended
The Awakened Book 6
© 2014 Matthew S. Cox
All Rights Reserved

DIVERGENT FATES
—NOVEL—

Cover Art by Jackson Tjota (Tjota.deviantart.com)

Interior art by Ricky Gunawan (http://goweliang.deviantart.com)

Cover layout by Alexandria Thompson (www.gothic-fate.com)

ISBN (ebook): 978-1-949174-34-2

ISBN (print): 978-1-949174-35-9

The Awakened Series

Prophet of the Badlands

Archon's Queen

Grey Ronin

Daughter of Ash

Zero Rogue

Angel Descended

CONTENTS

A DEVIL'S BARGAIN

Mamoru

Obligation weighed upon Mamoru's mind as he gripped the ancient gunslinger's hand and met the man's unflinching gaze. Paper-thin skin wrinkled at the corners of red eyes, accompanying an anticipatory smile. In contrast to his frail appearance, the elder had an iron grip. Not a trace of sweat appeared upon him. Mamoru clutched the gloved fingers with committed strength, a single, curt nod cementing his acceptance. His sister lay at the precipice of death. He would not allow her blood to stain his hands, no matter what price this man before him asked.

Carrion-scented air slipped from the old man's broadening smile.

Sunlight shimmering on the ground behind the old man brightened, reducing the rickety figure to a silhouette, a black distortion in the wavering heat. A whispery rush of thousands of voices in the distance built from a tiny prickle at Mamoru's eardrums to deafening chaos. Cries of rage and terror swirled around, underscored by an unearthly roar that gained in intensity until he could not help but raise his free arm to shield his face. At that instant, the devouring tumult ended with the fury of a massive explosion—leaving behind only the stillness of the desert.

Mamoru lowered his arm, and the old man was gone. He relaxed, glancing about at the open desolation, rotting semis, and the ruins of Hank's Truck Stop. No sign of the old cowboy remained in the swirling dust, not even boot prints.

Relentless sun battered the ground, creating a standing wall of heat that thickened the air and brought a scratch to his throat. Somewhere, metal rattled in the wind, the only noise aside from the faint whistle of the breeze. His gaze settled on his right hand, still outstretched as if in the act of shaking. A thin layer of pale brown silt coated his palm. He curled his fingers into a fist.

"For Sadako."

The voice was Mamoru's, though he had not spoken. He took a knee at his sister's side. Her petite figure lay cocooned within the arrangement of straps and cords he'd rigged to secure her to the door he had scavenged from the crashed shuttle. Worry had left him, replaced by contained aggression. He opened her stifling black sneak suit, ignoring his discomfort at her lack of undergarments. Sadako didn't move, moan, or react to him as he undressed her.

Aware of its value, he bundled the high-tech garment and placed it next to the bottled water below her feet, at the end of the aircraft door. Dark purple and red blotches covered most of her skin, from neck to thigh. She shouldn't have been breathing, but breathe she did.

He jogged across the sweltering blacktop to what had once been the restaurant portion of the truck stop. The crumbling remains of an ancient Peterbilt slumped by the door, like a buffalo that had dragged itself to the edge of a watering hole to die. He rummaged inside the restaurant for a few minutes, finding a tattered yellow curtain, once white, that he could use to cover her. He ripped it from the rod and hurried back to her, tucking the coarse fabric into the cords to hold it in place.

Her labored breathing had faded to a noiseless rise and fall of her chest. One narrow line of dried blood cut across her dust-caked face, a trail from her nose to her right ear. He rested his hand on the side of her neck, detecting a slow, but regular pulse. Her expression held calm, as though she rested peacefully rather than clung to life by a feeble thread. Snapshots of the crash flickered to mind as he stared at a face full of innocence. Asleep, she looked like a child to him. He remembered her screaming, remembered the smell of sparks and smoke, and the awful noise she made when her body careened into the console.

The old man has saved her... somehow. Mamoru stood, squinting into the west. *The angel must burn.*

Only his sister's life mattered.

Mamoru gathered a handful of the scuffed wires he had rigged to the door and stood. He pulled the cable over his shoulder and held it tight against his chest, leaning forward into a determined march in defiance of the early morning sun. Scraping metal and the rattle of plastic bottles followed close behind. The door-turned-stretcher slid with ease over the parking lot and out onto abandoned road. He glanced back every so often; Sadako's hair fluttered in a sad excuse for a breeze, her chest rising and falling with regular breaths.

She no longer worsens. He set his jaw tight. Nothing about this felt *right*, but everything about it was his fault. Mamoru let his head sag, staring at his boots flashing in and out of view along the pockmarked paving. *This confidence is not of my heart.* Sadako would live; he knew but did not understand how—or how he could be so certain of it. What sort of *Akuryō* had he given himself to? Mamoru closed his eyes, ignoring the bite of the cabling in his shoulder.

It didn't matter. Sadako would not pay for his mistakes any more than she already had.

🐍 🦅 🐚 🌙 🏺

HOURS LATER, MAMORU HESITATED, SQUINTING AT A METAL BUILDING PAINTED teal. White block lettering spelled out 'East Mountain Pumping' along one wall. A strange feeling lingered in the air here, attracting his gaze to a distant patch of charred ground. The *chi* of this place had shifted out of balance.

"Something happened here. The death of many. Do you sense it, Sadako?"

She continued sleeping, showing no reaction.

He glanced to his left, down a four-lane highway heading into a shallow canyon, toward the setting sun. An inexplicable urge tugged at him, beckoning him in that direction. He dropped the cable and sagged to a seat at the edge of the highway, spending a few moments of rest brushing hair out of her face. He rummaged among the supplies he'd packed on the tail end of the door in search of water and food. Mamoru drained a bottle in one continuous pull and tossed it aside. A packet of raw OmniSoy came next, forced down his throat by a stone-fisted squeeze. He shivered at the flavorless slime.

Sadako didn't wake at his attempt to give her a drink. It worried and reassured him at the same time. He poured water little by little into her mouth, holding her head in such a way that she swallowed out of reflex. It seemed unlikely she'd be able to ingest OmniSoy in her condition. Mamoru squinted to the west.

Have I done the right thing?

The question formed in his mind but never made it past his lips. Surely, she would say no. She would rather die than see him suffer the claws of a dark spirit. Even after he'd failed to save her from the Nippon Shōgyō-Kumiai, she still regarded him as family. At the back of his mind, a cluster of voices whispered, as though a conversation went on in another room among at least a dozen people of varying age. Muted and indistinct, he couldn't make out most of the words, though a handful pierced the fog.

"He needs you," said what sounded like a young boy.

"Burn them all," rasped an elderly voice.

You were only ten, Mamoru, said Sadako, in his head. *I do not blame you.*

"Had I been a proper son and trained as Father asked…" He clenched his fist in shameful rage. "I could have killed them all, even as a boy."

His knuckles creaked on the wire as he gathered it against his shoulder.

"They all deserve to die," said an unfamiliar woman.

"We can kill them, too," added a creepy little-girl voice.

Who are you? Why are you in my thoughts? Mamoru shut his eyes, shaking with the effort to clear his mind.

"We are they who seek vengeance," responded a chorus. "You are our instrument."

Fear and doubt drowned in the onrush of noise. The ancient gunslinger's knowing smile stretched the right side of Mamoru's mouth. He would save Sadako this time, no matter what it cost him.

SCRAPING METAL ECHOED BACK AT HIM FROM THE SCRUB-BRUSH-COVERED WALLS on either side of the highway. He had been walking for what felt like days without sleep, though his body did not demand rest—as if he could go on forever. The pain in his fingers from gripping the cable had long ago faded to numbness. This road would take him to his destiny. He knew it without a doubt. Mercifully, the chorus of vengeful voices had silenced themselves. They had seemed satisfied at his willingness to do whatever it took to protect Sadako.

Mamoru lifted his gaze from the road when he sensed a change from uphill to level. A scattering of small huts and trailers to the right looked abandoned for many years, reclaimed by shrubs and small lizards. Straight ahead, the road descended into the carcass of a once-great city. Southwest of the old metropolis's center, a built-up section less than a quarter of the size of the outlying ruin glowed with artificial light. A fortified, two-story wall made from slabs of metal and stacked cars packed between old concrete buildings glowed like an oasis in darkness. Shadows walked behind coils of razor wire, following a walkway that encircled the settlement.

He squinted at it, watching the movement of what could only be guards.

They would be of no consequence.

His heart swelled with relief at the sight of the place where Sadako would be saved. He forced himself to a brisk walk, grunting each time the stretcher-sled dragged him to one side or the other. The downhill grade took the weight off his shoulder and let the next half-mile or so pass in a blur. At the bottom, the tops of the reinforced concrete wall simmered like a gargantuan bowl filled with light. Half on autopilot, half too weary to change course, Mamoru lumbered ahead into the ruined city.

The night shifted around him. Spots of red and yellow—eyes—appeared in the darkness for seconds at a time before vanishing. Once, a dark grey wolf advanced enough to show its face, bowed its head, and backed out of sight. Whatever other creatures lurked in the alleys and shattered windows seemed fearful, or perhaps reverent, and did not approach. An inexplicable sense that these creatures 'escorted' him rather than hunted him confused and worried him in equal measure. The scuttles of paws and quiet breaths of animals followed for several blocks, never advancing close enough to be more than sound or shadow.

A pair of large towers atop the wall marked what appeared to be the main gate, a pre-war auto parts store on one side, an unmarked white cinder block building on the other. The two-lane road between them stopped at a massive concrete slab marked with bloodstains and bullet gouges. He marched straight toward it.

Scuffing from Sadako's improvised stretcher on the road eventually drew the notice of the figures upon the wall, causing a cluster of silhouettes to gather on the near side. At the chirp of modern firing circuits arming, he stopped and held up his left hand.

One of the men fiddled with something for a moment before Mamoru took a powerful flashlight beam in the face. The man let off a cry of surprise, followed by a series of curses as he fumbled with the light until the figure next to him, likely a woman, grabbed the flashlight away from him and trained it on Mamoru, though she was kind enough to keep it out of his eyes. The spot of light lingered on him for a few seconds before moving to Sadako and back.

"How'd you make it through the ruin?" asked an older-sounding man with a heavy Spanish accent.

"I walked," said Mamoru.

Sadako emitted a weak moan.

"Ain't likely you made it in one piece, what with draggin' wounded behind ya." Another shadow figure spit. "You either damn lucky or damn foolish."

Mamoru suppressed the growing urge to kill the man for his insolence. "My sister is dying. I seek the one known as the Prophet."

The sentries went quiet. Soon after, murmuring spread among their ranks, and a droning mechanical whine erupted, loud in the still air. The concrete gate rose upward at a laborious pace. When it opened high enough for a man to duck under, four figures emerged and approached.

A woman led them, five foot nothing and dark skinned. Her clothing, aside from an armored vest, looked typical for the Badlands, though the compact assault rifle not quite aimed at him came from the modern world. She'd shaved the sides of her head, leaving a pad of tight, curly hair on top.

Three men behind her muttered at each other in Spanish and fanned out into a horseshoe around him. One used a smaller flashlight to get a better look at Sadako. Mamoru kept his gaze on the woman, his expression one of weariness.

She glanced him up and down. "What's your story?"

"Our shuttle crashed."

"What the hell's a shuttle?" muttered a man in the back?

She raised an eyebrow. "You two the only ones to make it? What happened?"

"Everything failed all at once. We could not stay airborne."

The men exchanged glances, though whatever they worried about, they kept to themselves. One made the sign of the cross.

"You armed?" asked the woman.

Mamoru indicated his katana. "Just this."

"Only a sword?" The woman chuckled. "You got some set on ya, I'll give ya that."

"*La mujer se ve herida; traigala adentro rapido,*" said the man squatting by Sadako.

Mamoru tensed at the sudden realization someone had gotten close enough to touch her without his notice. His almost preternatural awareness of his surroundings had failed him. Was this fatigue or had the *Akuryō* done something to him?

"He said your friend looks bad. I'm Sergeant Simms with the Watch," said the woman. "Welcome to Querq. Come on; let's get her to the hospital."

The three men slung their rifles and moved to the corners of the improvised stretcher. Mamoru took their cue and traded the wire for a grip on the metal. They lifted together and carried her in the gate, over steel plates covering the roadway. Simms advanced ahead, occasionally walking a few steps backward to watch him. He avoided eye contact, feeling certain she didn't trust him. A faint moan from his sister erased his worry of what anyone here thought of him.

More figures atop the wall shifted to the interior side to observe the procession. He couldn't see them but knew somewhere between six and eight rifles were at his back. Mamoru let the Watch lead, keeping his eyes locked on Sadako's face, hoping she would last another few minutes.

2

CHILD OF LIGHT

Althea

Unease permeated the strange, shifting world crafted from slices of centuries long gone. Althea held onto Aurora's hand, shying away from a phantasmal horse-drawn carriage that appeared out of nowhere and thundered past in a fury of spectral neighs and hoof beats. A pair of riders chased it on horseback, firing pistols but always missing. The slower of the two locked eyes with her, and the bandit's greedy anger gave way to a pleading look.

Before she could speak, the woman pulled her onward. Aurora seemed to glide forward with little effort, equal parts flying and walking. Althea's toes touched down every few seconds as their travel consisted of great bounding leaps in a world devoid of gravity. None of the scenery made sense; trees, warped and bent, hung at unnatural angles, superimposed over the astral shadows of the modern world.

A baleful wind whipped across the gaping windows of a far-off city, but the breeze washing over her lacked the fury of its distant kin. Whenever they stopped, tattered inhuman silhouettes coalesced out of the distant fog, whirling to fix her with malicious, yellow eyes. Althea shrieked as they charged, but Aurora leapt high into the air, pulling her along before the monsters got close.

The pair came to a halt in the central street of a long forgotten town. Althea clung to Aurora's arm, looking around for the angry shadow people, but none appeared. Buildings fluttered like a mirage. Drawn in tones of sepia and black, the world shifted, seeming to drift closer and farther even though they'd stopped. Gaunt, withdrawn faces hovered in dark gaps where alleys should be, peering past spidery fingers clutching crumbling brickwork. The road beneath her feet had no temperature, neither warm nor cold, and the constant light wind made her miss the towel she'd left behind in the real world. Then again, something told her clothes wouldn't have done much to lessen the chill of this place.

Althea clung to Aurora as if to let go would be her doom. They had departed the awful city some minutes ago where Anna's friend had been hurt, and stood among the astral echo of a town that no longer existed. While Aurora looked around, presumably to get her bearings, Althea glanced at the specters watching them, a look of concern in her eyes. Their dress varied from the ancient (cowboys she recognized from stories) to the modern scrap clothing of the Badlands. Most of them looked to be from the same section of pre-war time as fitting the town. Something about this place felt familiar, yet she couldn't recall ever having seen it before, not even in dreams. One man continually shouted to the others insisting something called 'Vietnam' was a mistake and 'our boys' needed to be brought home. Althea tugged at Aurora, trying to run to the man; if she could cure his sons of 'Vietnam,' she had to try.

"It's alright, child." Aurora pulled her close, telepathic voice soothing. "These won't hurt you. They're not like the others. You cannot help them."

Althea looked from one to the next as they shied away from her stare. "What do they want? Are they ghosts?"

"Aha. There it is." Aurora gestured at the distance. "That way. Yes, mite, ghosts would be one way to put it."

Old shops and cars blurred into smears of coffee brown and cream as Aurora pulled her along. Their walking pace felt casual, though the world flew past. Althea put a hand over her stomach to quell a twinge of nausea. Wisps of darkness slipped from spaces between objects, forming into pleading, hopeful faces, staring at her.

"Why are they all watching me?"

"They think you're here for them."

Althea tugged on Aurora's arm until she stopped and stared up at the woman with wide, glowing eyes. "Can I help them? I want to."

Aurora ran her free hand over Althea's head, patting. Once again, the woman's silken voice flooded her thoughts despite her lips not moving. "No, mite. What they need is a bit beyond you. They're waiting to get out of this place."

"Oh." Althea stared down at the road. "I'm sorry."

"It's not your fault. You've got a certain energy about you they can feel. They think you're something else."

Althea remembered the old man in Dr. Ruiz's clinic. "Like that man in the hospital?"

"I wasn't there, mite." Aurora smiled.

"A man had a dark sick in him." Althea traced a finger around her chest. "Around his air bags. He was almost at death. When he saw me, he asked why I made him wait. He knew I was coming."

"Oh." Aurora nodded. "Yes. He mistook you for something else. A type of spirit that helps the dead go to where they belong. The same as these poor souls are doing right now."

Althea stared down at her chalk-white self. This place made her look far paler than natural and covered her legs with goosebumps. "I'm not a spirit, and he did not go to death."

"Aye, but he expected to. Come on, then. I promised I'd take you right home before anyone missed you."

Thoughts of the warm bed waiting for her chased away the sorrow of being unable to help these people... whatever they were. Althea bit her lower lip, casting a somber gaze upon the crowd of ethereal figures collecting in a nearby alleyway. A woman seemed trapped in the driver's seat of a car, presumably where she'd died, and screamed for help. Althea got one step into a run toward her before Aurora jerked her back by the arm.

"There's nothing you can do for her. Don't run off. If you let go of me, you could get lost here."

Althea pouted at the trapped woman as Aurora pulled her once more into a gliding leap. Minutes later, the terrain flattened to blurry desert racing past them. The shadow-city streaked off into the distance, a mass of black vapor swallowed by the smoky horizon behind them. The open ground southwest of Querq appeared familiar, but not the dozens of military vehicles scattered about a field strewn with smoking mechanical parts and burning craters. Grey-tinted shades of soldiers, judging by their clothing, staggered about. A few moaned, while others, still lost in the throes of war, fired spectral echoes of rifles at other spirits in different clothes. Others lay on the ground, injured and wailing.

All at once, every one of them stopped what they were doing and shifted to face her. Most cast pleading glances, though a few regarded her with cold animosity. Something deep in their vacant eyes sent a shiver down her back and made her clamp her arms around the woman guiding her. Aurora's skin pressed to hers felt icy, like something not even alive.

"A-are you dead?" Althea shivered.

The woman leaned her head back and laughed. "Not the last time I checked."

"Why are you so cold?" Fear beat discomfort, so she continued clinging.

"Why do your eyes glow blue, or why are mine all black? It just is."

Aurora sprang upward again, pulling her into the air. They glided over an afterimage of before-time Querq, its streets packed full of confused citizens. Althea closed her eyes, holding on, unable to bear the sight of so many dead people. A strange sponginess engulfed her, a sensation she remembered meant they'd gone through a wall. By the time the touch of soft carpeting met her feet, grief for all the dead overwhelmed her, and she cried quietly to herself.

"Shh," whispered Aurora. "Do not worry, Althea. Most weren't real ghosts."

"What?" Althea sniffled and looked up, finding herself at home, in the bathroom. "They're not?"

"No, mite. Think of a holo-disk, the way it records data..."

Althea's blank stare stalled her.

"Bother. You've no idea what a holo-disk is, do you?"

Althea shook her head.

"It's just an imprint of things that happened. An image of trapped emotion, not people."

"Oh." Althea stooped to grab her nightgown from the rug, but her fingers went through it.

"One moment." Aurora closed her eyes and a look of concentration settled on her features.

The walls ceased wavering. Color spread over the sepia, and the once-neutral air became warm and dry. Aurora let go of her hand and patted her shoulder. Althea's arms had once again taken on their usual suntan. Her companion, however, remained whiter than snow.

"Thank you for helping Aaron. It was very brave of you to come with me to the city."

"I couldn't let him die." Althea gathered her nightgown, clutching the warm fabric against her chest. The chill of the astral world left her teeth chattering. "Is Querq safe? Is my family safe? Will the bad find us here?"

She waited in silence, staring at the black square of window, dreading the answer. When the anticipation became intolerable, she glanced back over her shoulder.

And found herself alone.

Althea closed her eyes and swallowed her fear, gathering a sense of resolve in her heart as she slipped into her nightdress. *She* would make sure her home remained safe.

She exited the bathroom and crept down the hallway of mismatched walls: wood paneling, green wallpaper, yellow paint, and beige wallpaper surrounded her in various sections as Father had repaired the house. His heavy snoring emanated from his half-closed door. She hurried past it and tiptoed up to the room she shared with her sister. Taking the knob in both hands, she tilted her entire body to turn it with excruciating slowness in an effort to remain quiet. The door eased open without creaking. She peeked in the gap, smiling at finding Karina still asleep—unaware she had been out of the house. Althea padded across the moonlit room to the bed and crawled in, snuggling under the blanket against her sister. After what seemed like hours on the other side, she adored the feeling of being close to a warm body and wrapped in blankets. Karina muttered in her sleep and slipped an arm over her. Althea tried to hold still, but Karina opened her eyes a moment later.

"Where'd you go?" she whispered. "Your feet are so cold."

Althea pondered the degree of lie in saying 'to the bathroom' or 'someone was hurt,' and remained quiet, trying to think of how to answer.

"Thea?" Karina opened her eyes. "Is everything all right?"

"Yes," she whispered. "A man was hurt. It's long. I did not want to give you the worry. Can I tell it in the morning?"

"Okay."

KARINA GOT THE FULL TRUTH THE NEXT MORNING WHEN THEY WOKE. HER reaction was everything Althea expected. The clingy part didn't bother her, but her sister's fear made her feel guilty. By the time they had dressed and started preparing breakfast, Karina had calmed. Althea grinned and made silly faces during the meal, but kept her promise to the powers that be. She attempted to use the fork no matter how frustrating it got.

After they ate, she collected the dishes, but Father shooed her out of the kitchen since it was his turn to clean them. Karina rushed past on her way to the door, headed to the fields where she worked. Althea set about some of her morning chores, sweeping the downstairs hallway. She made it out onto the porch before Father, having finished the dishes, embraced her from behind.

"Go, play a bit. The broom will be here later."

She let him take it from her and hugged him. "Are you going patrol?"

"In the evening. The city people are showing us things today. How to work some of their machines."

Althea shivered.

He kissed her forehead. "It is what it is, Althea."

Nervousness surrounded him. She clung tight to his chest. "I will not let them take me away."

Father relaxed, squeezed her shoulder, and trounced down the steps. Althea followed, holding his hand until he reached the place where the outsiders wanted to make adults go to school. A number of the Watch filtered in, as well as the men who ran the water purification system. Althea lingered in place, accepting a number of pats and hugs from passersby, staring at Father until he disappeared inside. She couldn't walk for any significant distance without someone running over with a small cut, blister, or sprain, but at least no one tried to pray to her or kiss her feet anymore.

Corinne called out to her from across the street, balancing a basket of clothes against her side to free an arm for a wave. She looked much better than the day they pulled her out of the creek.

"You're coming, right?" yelled Corinne.

"Yes, we are." Althea's eyebrows drew close together.

She wondered why everyone made such a big fuss over showering a baby. Perhaps because she thought it silly. It seemed far easier to give them baths. That the event coincided with Corinne's twentieth birthday caused all the women of the town to want to make a major celebration of it.

Althea pondered the unusual sensation of boredom as she wandered to the next cross street, where she stopped and lost a few minutes watching ants scurry about.

At the next corner, a man and a woman in Division 0 uniforms waved at her, though she looked at them only long enough to return a polite smile before glancing away. They reminded her too much of the bad city, and they —as well as their magic toys—didn't belong here. Distrust, rather than dislike, kept her at a distance. She contemplated crossing the street to avoid passing close to them, but felt guilty about it and kept going straight. They fawned over her for a little while before she found a polite opening to get away. Two blocks later, she cut across a front yard, arguing with herself about if the Many had made them come here.

The city police had brought strange devices with them, which most of the adults adored. Althea frowned at the memory of grown men acting like ten-year-old boys celebrating their first successful hunt. They also brought that 'electricity' thing to Querq, but she feared the evil of that horrible metal city would soon follow, creeping into her home. Everyone there had been so angry all the time, so hurried. No one smiled at anyone there. They all kept their heads down and rushed to wherever they wanted to be. She would not let that happen here.

Althea paused, crouching by a wooden plank fence, and looked back. The black-clad figures both watched her, chatting away. Sunlight glinted from their silver belts, making her squint. She sensed curiosity and pity from them, but nothing like what she'd expect if the bad old man sent them here. Content they meant no harm, she ducked through a gap between boards too small for an adult into a grassy space where a crowd of smaller children played.

They welcomed her, unconcerned with the age difference. Althea felt most at ease among the little ones. While the kids her age and older weren't as fearful of her as the Scrags had been, they treated her with an uncomfortable reverence. The five-to-nine-year-olds didn't care she was—or had been—the Prophet and let her into their midst as an equal. Father said, as he always did, to give the older ones time. For now, she joined the chaos of little bodies running in circles, kicking a soft pearlescent orb about. She laughed, hiking her annoying shin-length dress up to her thighs so she could run. As soon as the ball got close enough, she kicked it toward the largest cluster of children she could find in a split-second search.

"No, wrong way!" a boy yelled in Spanish.

All of them laughed at her. She couldn't help but giggle at their shocked faces.

"You gotta kick it that way," said an olive-skinned girl of about nine. "You're on our team."

At that point, Althea noticed roughly half the children had scraps of red cloth tied around their heads. Since she lacked one, the team without them had claimed her.

Their game involved two groups, each trying to get the ball to go between a pair of buckets they called a 'goal.' Granted, with the majority of the participants being six or seven, her initial assumption of random kicking hadn't been too far off the mark. It didn't take her long to figure out each 'side' got a 'point' whenever someone on that team managed to get the ball to go between the pails. She didn't want to exploit her size advantage, so she let her teammates have the ball whenever she could, though one girl—Esmerelda—was bigger than her despite being a year younger.

A few weeks ago, Althea had run off into Old Querq to help Santiago, Diego, and Pedro. She'd found some people who had come from the modern city looking for her. They wanted to kidnap her too, thinking her property that belonged to one of those 'corp-rations.' They said she had been born eleven years ago—not twelve. Regardless, everyone continued to mistake her for being ten.

Althea locked eyes with her, both of them taller than the swarm of screaming children running around. As luck would have it, they wound up on opposing sides. Esmerelda did not possess Althea's hesitance about using size as an advantage and plowed down a handful of six-year-olds on her way to the goal, knocking them aside. One boy burst into tears after landing on his face.

"Hey!" yelled Althea.

The larger girl came right at her, likely expecting she'd have little trouble knocking aside a girl as scrawny as her. Althea braced her stance and caught Esmerelda by the shoulders, letting the ball go bouncing past.

"Stop it."

Esmerelda blinked in shock, surprised Althea had the strength to halt her. She recovered in seconds, grabbing Althea by the arms and wrestling them around in a circle. Wailing from the kids she'd run over rose up in the background. The din of gleeful screaming faded to quiet as the others realized something was wrong.

"Don't be mean," said Althea, grunting with exertion. "They're little."

A ripping sound came from Esmerelda's lime green dress and her left shoulder slipped out. She snarled and shoved, trying to use her weight to force Althea over backward. Althea twisted and widened her stance, giving up ground, but maintaining balance. Strange elation came on; this girl—hostile though she was—treated her like any other kid living in Querq. When Althea loosed a giggle, Esmerelda roared and shoved her away. Althea stumbled to the side, barely ducking a hasty punch before the other girl tackled her, pulling her hair while sitting on her.

The little ones gathered around, not one of them making a sound. In the distance, an older woman yelled, "Knock it off."

Still laughing, Althea brought her arms up to protect her face, allowing the bigger girl to hit her a few times in the body.

"Stop laughing at me!" screeched Esmerelda, fist cocked.

"Esmerelda! Behave yourself," shouted a different older woman.

A chorus of oohs came from the small kids.

Althea peered between her forearms at the bulging eyes behind the hovering fist. She grinned. Esmerelda pounded her on the arms twice, failing to get her knuckles past them to Althea's face.

"Don't laugh at me!" Esmerelda jumped to her feet and grabbed two handfuls of Althea's dress, pulling her up off the ground.

Althea wrapped her arms around the larger girl in a tight hug. "It's okay."

After one half-hearted punch to Althea's undefended ribs, Esmerelda sagged, gasping for breath. "You're weird. What's wrong with your head? You like getting your ass beat?"

"No." Althea stopped hugging her and leaned back to smile. "No one ever hits me. I like the normal."

After two seconds of gazing at glowing blue eyes, Esmerelda seemed to realize what she had done. She trembled, gasped, and covered her mouth with both hands. Her emotion shifted from anger and confusion to terror in an instant.

The azure light in Althea's eyes flickered brighter as she muted Esmerelda's fear, replacing it with calm and stalling her trembles. "It's okay. Please don't be scared of me. I want to be—"

Esmerelda flew into the air with a squeak, kicking and screaming. A tall, stocky man hauled her up by one arm. Spanish scolding ran by too fast for Althea to pick out every word, but she got enough to understand he was terrified what his daughter's attack on the Prophet would mean for his family. The Badlands swarmed with legends about how bad things happened to those who mistreated her, though the truth had a far less magical explanation: those who had taken her as a slave soon found themselves under attack by other bandit groups who wanted to own her. Here in Querq, her home, those legends did not apply, especially to a girl her age fighting over a game of kick-the-ball.

Two middle-aged women, who had been watching over the kids from a nearby porch, ran up behind him, yelling at him to calm down. Althea rolled to her feet and advanced.

"Please, stop. It's okay." Her soft voice drowned under his tirade.

The man gripped Esmerelda by both forearms, shaking her and screaming until she burst into tears. All the small children scurried back to a safe distance. When he drew back his arm to slap the girl, Althea pounced on it, startling him. The two matrons pried his hand away from Esmerelda and got between them.

"I don't want you to punish her for hitting me." Althea held on until he relaxed.

"She struck you," said the man. "You are the Prophet."

Esmerelda sniffled and straightened her posture, trying to salvage some dignity back from the crowd of children watching her cry.

Althea shivered at the word. "Please don't call me that. I'm not a thing you own. This is my home. I *want* people to treat me like a person. I'm not mad at her."

He looked down on Esmerelda. "You see how nice she is? You attack her, and she's the one feeling bad? Shameful. You apologize right now and pray nothing happens to us."

"I'm sorry, Papa. I didn't see she was the…" Esmerelda choked on the P word, staring at Althea.

"Be sorry to Carlos, Sophia, and Henry." Althea waved at the small children Esmerelda had shoved to the ground.

Esmerelda sulked over to them and muttered an apology before her father ushered her away. The matrons gathered the children to the porch and handed out small pastries and milk. Althea joined them, and within a few minutes, the tension evaporated. The awkward feeling of being a child as well as a caretaker crept over her, and she excused herself when the small ones settled down for a late afternoon nap.

Althea meandered to the end of the block, pausing on the curb at the corner and rubbing her bruised ribs. She closed her eyes and concentrated on the minor injuries while pondering the oddity of her finding comfort in violence. Of course, the bigger girl hadn't been trying to kill her or even inflict real harm. Scrag children fought like that all the time, practice for when they were older. No one had ever dared strike her before and it made her feel normal in a way she didn't realize she craved until she experienced it.

Querq had eroded much of her wildness. The thought made her grin at the memory of Father calling her feral.

With the last of her bruises gone, she opened her eyes and resumed wandering. The town square had many strange things in it since the City Police had arrived. Gleaming silver cubes with wires as thick as her arms crisscrossed the street. They radiated an eerie feeling of power, though whether she sensed something real or merely feared the horrible city, she couldn't tell. She gazed up the length of a metal pole, topped with a cluster of light-making things high off the ground, dormant while the sun shined. Upon noticing the wire less than a foot from her toes, she edged away.

Two of the scary flying cars huddled against the wall of the building the Ravens had let the City Police bring to Querq. Althea eyed them warily, not wanting to move fast enough to attract their attention. She sidestepped, staring at the glistening, black vehicles, sparing only faintest slivers of attention downward to keep from stepping on a wire. She couldn't tell if the metal beasts were asleep or acting like they hadn't seen her.

"Hello, Althea," said a man behind her.

She screamed, jumped, and whirled about. A pair of Division 0 officers had come up close enough to touch her: a man in shiny black armor and a girl not much older than Karina in a clingy cloth uniform. If not for their city clothes—and the violet streaks in the girl's hair—their darkish skin would've let them pass for Querq natives.

"*Hola, me asusaste,*" said Althea, in a wavering half-whisper.

The woman pulled a small device out of a case on her belt and glanced at it before leaning toward the armored man. "We scared her, Kev." She smiled. "I'm sorry." Light appeared above the device. "*Lo siento.*"

"I have the English words." Althea peeked at the two cars, neither of which had moved.

"She speaks English?" The woman raised an eyebrow.

"You didn't read the report," said the man. "Mostly English, but she throws in Spanish when she doesn't know the right word."

"I'm not dumb." Althea studied her toes.

"We didn't mean to scare you. What are you so frightened of? Is something bad going to happen?" The man sat on a nearby crate, also black and covered with those strange markings that spoke to the city people.

"I don't want to wake them."

"Wake who?" asked the woman.

"Them." Althea pointed at the slumbering cars.

The woman made that *aww* noise Althea had grown tired of, while the man burst out laughing. Between the two of them, her nervousness gave way to indignation. She folded her arms and glowered at the road.

"Sweetie, those are patrol craft," said the woman. "They're not alive."

"They went flying alone two days ago. No person." Despite her mood, the memory of it added a fearful whine to her voice.

"It's remote recall." The man tapped a finger to his left forearm. "There's a computer in here that I can use to make the car drive to where I am. We all have it. They won't eat you."

Althea blushed. Had he sniffed her surface thoughts? "Com... puter?"

"Wow, look at her eyes, Kev." The woman stooped closer. "I'm sorry, do you mind?"

"Would you care?" Althea sighed and opened them as wide as she could. A wave of embarrassment radiated from the woman, making her regret the snap of petulance. "Sorry. I don't like it when people think I'm"—she smiled, thinking of Esmerelda—"weird."

"Oh, sweetie." She took Althea's hand. "You're not weird. You're very special. Why do you want to be out here, working for these people? Isn't this the same thing that always happens to you?"

She let the woman hold her limp arm, wanting to yank back, but feeling it pointless. "I liked helping people. I didn't like the cages and leashes. I hate being tied."

The woman made that *aww* noise again.

"This is my home." Althea cast a sidelong glance at all the technology scattered throughout the courtyard. Someone had left a bright red plastic cup on the still-standing leg of the broken, ancient statue. "This 'city stuff' is wrong to Querq."

"We're not going to take over." The man summoned his most reassuring smile. "You need to read the reports, Jess. Command is concerned about corporate interference if Althea's talents become known. Besides, Director Carter herself indicated this was the healthiest place, psychologically speaking, for her to be. She did not seem likely to acclimate to the city."

"What?" said Althea. "It's psionic, not psi-co-lodge-amy."

"*Aww.*" The woman hugged her. "She's adorable!"

Althea weathered the embrace, despite feeling mocked by it. The teen launched into the usual barrage of questions the new arrivals always hit her with, but her companion cut her off.

"Jess, everything you're asking is in the report. You were supposed to read it. Admin is too lenient. If you get into I-ops, you'll need to learn 'orders' aren't a request."

"I'd rather talk to her." Jess looked her up and down. "She's so thin. Does the metabolic drain of accelerated healing affect her body when she's inducing cellular regeneration on someone else?"

"That wasn't English *or* Spanish," mumbled Althea.

"Seems that way," said the man, though Althea couldn't tell if he answered her or his partner.

"I'm a healer like you." Jess squeezed her hand. "Sort of. I can only fix myself. I wonder if you can teach me how to help other people."

Althea looked down, rubbing the back of her neck with her free hand. Memories of collars, shackles, and cages raced around in her mind; a spongy sensation wrapped around her brain from the man intruding on her surface thoughts. She looked at him. "Bad people will want to take her. I shouldn't try."

Kev reached out and put a hand on her shoulder. "We're here to make sure nothing like that happens to you ever again. I know it will take you time to believe us, but the city isn't all bad."

"Oh, there's no rush. I'm not sure it's even possible. We know so little about you," said Jess.

Althea fidgeted. "You don't want to be a Prophet." She remembered staring up at clouds, lying in a pool of other people's blood while the escaped slaves fled Vakkar's camp. That man had seemed stunned she chose to stay, but didn't argue for long. Going with those people would have doomed them. "You don't want it."

"I'm sorry for making you sad." Jess squeezed her shoulder, then looked up at Kev. "Besides, the report said it was due to her being 'Awakened,' whatever the hell that means."

"You read—?"

"Of course." Jess laughed, gave Althea a quick hug, and walked away.

She stood in place, staring at the two police officers as they crossed the courtyard, slipped past the cars, and disappeared into their building. The man radiated annoyance, but not anger.

Two members of the Watch walked by, holding their modern rifles as if they were magic relics bestowed upon them by some ancient deity. Althea returned their greeting and moped off down the closest street. Corporations would try to take her, as the raiders had, except the corporations had fancy magic guns and armor, too. For the Badlands, Querq seemed a nigh-impregnable fortress. Against people with city weapons, what chance did they have?

Yet again, Althea worried her presence brought doom upon those she loved.

Her spiraling mood came to an abrupt halt three blocks later when the farm came into view.

No. I will not let them take me. She had forgotten herself again. Her power would protect her and everyone in Querq. Rage simmered at the thought of someone trying to abduct her. Fancy city rifles wouldn't do much good if the people holding them were sobbing their eyes out, or wetting themselves at the sight of her, or filled with adoration.

With renewed contentment, she skipped up the dirt path toward the farm, arriving amid the rows of vegetables at the same time Aldo crested the far hill, behind his rickety, squeaking lunch cart. The old man wheezed and groaned, but considering his age, he was lucky to be walking at all. Althea raced to his side, ducked under his arm, and took hold of the push bar, absorbing the burden from the old man's grip.

"Bless you, girl," rasped Aldo. He let go, but left one hand on her shoulder, following her to the spot by the water valve where everyone ate. He stuck his fingers in his mouth and let loose a whistle that made her clamp her hands over her ears. "*Almuerzo!*"

People emerged from the garden, gathering around and forming a haphazard line. Althea helped him dole out empanadas and rice to everyone, before taking a plate for herself and curling up next to Karina on the half-height wall ringing the farm. Aldo slid a folding chair off the side of the cart and sat on it, taking his portion last.

"What are you doing today?" asked Karina. "Where's Den?"

"The Ravens gave him a job."

Karina snickered. "Yes, with the Watch. They let him do what he asked. He'll be fine. Father is with him."

"I learned a game with the small ones today." Althea nibbled on the corner of an empanada as she described the ball and goals.

"What happened?" Karina stopped eating. "I know that look."

"I got into a fight."

Karina laughed.

"I did." Althea traced a line in the dirt with her big toe. "I didn't start it. Esmerelda was hurting the small kids, so I got in her way. She got mad and hit me."

Karina lowered her fork, her smile fading to a look of concern. "Tell me what happened."

Althea recounted as best as she could remember.

"I'm going to speak to her father." Karina set her plate down and fawned over her. "Are you okay?"

"You don't have to. He saw it. He was gonna hit her, but I asked him not to; she's only ten."

"She's twice your size."

"No." Althea stuck her tongue out. "She's a little taller."

"And double your weight."

"It's okay. It didn't bother me."

"Fighting?" Karina gasped. "You liked it?"

"No, I did not like the fight, but it made me forget about being... you know."

"You're not the Prophet." Karina ruffled her hair. "You're Althea."

She leaned against her sister, feet tucked under her atop the wall, and ate with a big smile.

A grating metallic squeak from the top of the hill drew her attention to a mushroom-shaped house made of mismatched metal plates. The Water Man emerged, still ponderous and fat, but less so than the first time she had seen him. Ornry, the brown-and-white pit bull, ran circles around him, tail wagging. She grinned at the faces he made while trundling down the path. Sweat rolled off his head by the time he reached the food cart, but he seemed to enjoy his newfound mobility. He went to the valve and filled a metal mug, which he chugged before refilling it.

Ornry bee-lined to Althea and licked at her legs until his master went toward Aldo, at which point the dog bounded to the Water Man's side, begging for food. Aldo set a plate of meat scraps on the dirt, barely getting his hand out of the way before the animal inhaled it in two quick snaps of his wide jaws. The dog licked his jowls and looked up, his expression obvious in the sentiment of 'That's all? Where's the rest?' The Water Man tossed him an empanada. Ornry snapped it out of midair and continued to stare expectantly upward.

The big man settled against the wall to Althea's right, his broad grin renewing her good mood. She reached out and put a hand on his arm, earning a sideways look as he bit into one of the pastries, filling his beard with tiny flecks of dough. Althea linked her senses to his life-shapes, finding no trace of sick within him. When she opened her eyes, he hadn't moved at all since she'd touched him, not even to chew once.

She leaned back into Karina's side, smiling.

He had difficulty faking his curmudgeonry as he grumbled. "Damn. Now I gotta warsh kid-germs offa mah arm."

"I'm glad you're feeling better," said Althea, before brushing the last of her rice from her plate to her mouth.

The Water Man relented with a chuckle. He thrust out his upper lip, making his walrusine moustache dance, and appraised the patchwork lengths of copper tubing hanging over the plants. "Aye. Got to 'bout half the leaks already. Ought'a be done by end 'o the month."

"It's good to see you outside," said Karina.

"Mmm." He mumbled into his food.

Ornry bounded over and assaulted Althea with a flapping tongue. She let off a squeal and dropped her plate, which being empty, only distracted him for a second.

"Behave," yelled the Water Man. "Sit."

The dog curled up against the wall between them. Karina stifled a groan as the others formed a procession past the cart to return dirty plates on their way back to the fields. Several refilled their water jugs and reclaimed hand tools they'd rested on the wall.

Althea slid to the ground, skritching Ornry all over. The dog moaned and wriggled, trying to expose his entire belly all at once. It didn't take long for the Water Man to finish eating. He looked around as if to make sure no one was watching him and winked at her before plodding up the long, curving path back to his control room. Ornry stayed put until the screech of a metal door echoed over the farm. He bounded to his feet and zoomed up and inside before the Water Man closed it. Althea spent a moment watching Karina work, wanting to spend time with her, but not wanting to get her sister yelled at for 'idling,' whatever that meant. When Aldo grunted with the cart, she hurried to his side.

"I'll push it."

The old man smiled at her. "Bless you, child."

❦ ❦ ❦ ❦ ❦ ❦

FATHER HAD RETURNED HOME LONG ENOUGH TO EAT, HEADING BACK OUT TO the wall less than twenty minutes after walking in the door. Althea and Karina had agreed to handle cooking dinner and dishes in his place, since the Watch demanded more of his time, splitting it between learning and patrolling. Althea gathered the dishes from the table while Karina ran water in the sink. She carried them to the counter, confused at the strange expression on her sister's face. About to ask what was wrong, she let out a yelp when she noticed an undulating mass of white foam where water should be.

Karina could contain herself no longer and burst into laughter.

"What's in the sink?"

"Soap."

Althea swiped at it, catching a blob of suds. After making a face at the strange weightless substance, she sniffed it.

"It's liquid soap, from the city."

"*Eww!*" She flailed her hand, throwing suds everywhere.

Karina laughed too hard to speak for several minutes until the deepening pout on Althea's face pulled the rug out from under her mirth. "Oh, Thea. It's not going to hurt us."

"I don't want them to make Querq like the city. Then everyone will be bad and no one will smile anymore."

Karina rubbed her back. "They are bringing us small things to make life easier. It is not the same as making our home into a city."

She frowned at the foam and stared past her reflection on the window. At the hour, Querq should have been too dark to see anything but blackness outside, but the magic lights the police people brought were bright enough to light up the street behind the house, stretching a long shadow from the water pump.

They washed the dishes in relative silence, and by the time they finished, she felt better. No eerie feelings came over her when she thought about her family. With the chores out of the way, Karina went out onto the back porch and sat at the top of the stairs. Althea followed, taking a seat one step down, directly in front of her, with her arms draped in her lap. The city used to appear black and white, Althea's version of 'dark.' Now, smears of color intruded everywhere.

Karina spent a moment raking her fingers through Althea's hair before going for the brush.

"Did you try to play with the older kids when you were done helping Aldo?"

She let the brush pull her head to the side with each stroke. "Yes, but they wanted to pretend fight each other. I didn't like it."

"They won't do that all the time, and avoiding them won't help."

"I know."

Karina jumped at sudden banging on the front door.

Althea curled her toes over the step and sighed. Why did people always get hurt when she had time with her sister? "I should go."

"Althea?" Den's voice filled the house. The pounding stopped, and heavy footfalls on floorboards became louder.

Karina pulled the brush through Althea's hair once more. "I'll go with you."

They stood together as Den rushed onto the porch behind them. He looked so different in a white 'tee shirt' and 'jeans,' as Father called the strange garments. However, seeing him with shoes that matched felt the most odd. A few days' worth of stubble darkened his face and made him seem older than his fifteen years.

"Althea, Dr. Ruiz asks for you at the hospital. A woman is hurt, almost dead."

She offered an eager nod. "Let's go."

3

HIGH NOON BLACK

Aaron

Tangled strands of wire dangled from a sparking gouge on the underbelly of a huge advert bot, evidence of a recent collision. Aaron cringed at the amount of damage. The poor bastard who hit it had probably died when their car landed fifty stories down. The hulk meandered along between hovercar lanes, a lazy whale surrounded by impatient minnows.

A thirty-foot tall hologram of a woman's head below the enormous bot flickered in the rain, flashing an overacted smile after sipping her NuOrganix genuine coffee. Yellow letters circled around the gargantuan cup, proclaiming, 'A taste like Earth intended.'

The hovercar jostled in a sudden gust that also caused the neat line of traffic in front of them to sway upward and left. In a manner of seconds, individual vehicles regrouped into their usual, linear flow. Aaron sat with his back as much to the wall as the seat, dividing his attention between Anna, beside him, and Talis in the passenger seat. Archon, seated in front of him, drove. He'd directed the woman to the front. While Aaron was grateful not to have to sit next to the bitch, the black cloud over Anna's head deepened at her being relegated to the back seat. Aaron had tried to shoot her a 'see what I mean' look, but she refused to make eye contact.

Talis glanced back at him, strands of fine, long dreadlocks pulling over her shoulder. Cockiness, a trait well suited to her high, regal cheekbones, fled when she met his stare, leaving her quivering. He glanced away before she did, finding her cowering uncomfortable. Having a woman, even one he wanted to kill, cringe like that made him feel like a bastard. He found it much easier to kill the person who destroyed your life when they were arrogant.

Of course, he knew she faked it. At least, bullshit seemed the most likely explanation. Sure, his peculiarity with invasive mental abilities scared her to death, but her rapid change from haughty to simpering reeked of an implanted trigger. Hypnotic suggestion, as the database called it, a psionic's ability to embed a conditioned response into a subject. Aaron suspected Archon programmed her to feel extreme fear at the sight of him, though there remained a tiny chance of the woman's terror being genuine.

What luck he'd had to find her only to have Archon recruit the bitch. So what if she's Awakened too? No amount of apologizing would ever bring Allison back, and Archon expected him to work *with* her? To pick up and leave Earth, stuck on a stolen spacecraft for who-knows-how-long with someone he'd spent months fantasizing about murdering.

The man really is daft.

He stared at Anna's hand; small and pale, she'd whitened her knuckles on the edge of the seat. Unlike the PubTran, Archon's Halcyon-Ormyr had lush, padded seats covered in leather that had never mooed. Aaron considered reaching out and putting his hand atop hers, though perhaps such a show of affection in the same car with Archon would be unwise. Lucky enough the man hesitated at peeking into his brain. It seemed even 'the most powerful telepath in the world' didn't know for sure how dangerous Aaron's mind had become.

Almost three hours after leaving the abandoned starship plant, Archon peeled away from the hovercar lane and turned east, descending to the fortieth floor and slowing from their cruising speed of 320 mph to a casual 110. The Navcon in the center of the dashboard beeped and flashed red.

"Warning, you have entered Sector 10079. You are *ten* miles from a dangerous area. Warning, Sector 10081 is disavowed. Recommend alternate flight path."

"Anna, how do you shut this bloody thing off?" asked Archon.

"I can't reach it from all the way back here, luv."

Aaron swore the car got ten degrees colder.

"You would have preferred I put these two in arm's reach of one another? We would have arrived with one left alive."

"I'd say I'm not the one with impulse control issues, but I'd be lying." Aaron flashed a saccharin smile at the rearview mirror.

The gleaming surface of silvered windows sliding by changed in the blink of an eye to shattered and twisted ruins. Archon descended further, to the third-floor level, and slowed to a veritable standstill of forty miles per hour. Rag-clad people watched them from nearby office towers; some peered with curiosity, others threw bottles, and some aimed handguns. Aaron leaned forward, raising an eyebrow at a mostly flat corporate campus that seemed to be their destination.

Whatever corporation had owned Sector 10081, a five-mile square that showed up black on the Navcon, had used most of the area to create an artificial park-like environment. A cluster of buildings, the tallest a mere ten stories, bore obvious signs of missile strikes and had few intact windows. Two adjacent towers, each a humble six stories, sported several gaping holes tunneled all the way through them, large enough to accommodate a hovercar.

Aaron whistled at the graveyard of cyborgs littering what had once been a grand reflecting pool. Few were full-conversion bodies; most of the dead had one or both arms replaced with crude cybernetics, and sometimes legs as well. The human parts had rotted away decades ago, leaving ghastly metal framework behind.

The burned out shells of police vehicles, older Lunar Motors 200 series hovercars, suggested the last time the law set foot here had been over a century ago. Aaron shuddered at the thought of flying a patrol craft without any armor and actual glass windows. Compared to modern police vehicles, it would've been like driving a PubTran car into battle.

"I thought you said you had a power station," said Aaron. "This looks a bit more pastoral than I expected."

"We *had* a power station," Anna mumbled, rubbing the front of her neck.

"Indeed," said Archon, a frown audible in his voice. "Your former associates discovered the place. Perhaps it was not grey enough to keep them at bay."

Anna trembled and covered her face with her hands. "Bugger the station, James. You almost died."

"Yes, well... We shan't be having that problem here." Archon brought the car in for a quiet landing in front of the tallest building. "The authorities have a rather useful aversion to these places."

"The disavowed areas aren't as bad as people think," said Talis. "Cops avoid them because the people can fight back there."

"Try livin' out there without your tricks, luv." Aaron winked. "You'd not last a weekend."

She glared over her shoulder again but cringed away as soon as they made eye contact.

"Can I trust the two of you to mind yourselves?" Archon swiped at the dashboard, powering the car down. "It would be best if you remained inside the campus wall."

Talis wasted no time hopping out of the car, and rushed into the middle building without looking back.

Aaron cringed at the sour air that greeted him outside. It surprised him to catch the occasional whiff of carrion, given how long the rotting cyborgs had been left where they'd fallen. He squinted into the foul breeze toward the doors of the shorter office tower on the left. People moved around inside among tents set up in the lobby.

"The lodgings are not quite as luxurious as we possessed at the power plant, but I assure you, they are only temporary." Archon started for the door, but paused. "Feel free to look about. Take any open room you care for on the seventh floor."

"Right." Aaron glanced at the far side of the courtyard, past a field of broken robotics and exposed human bones. Two figures bearing submachine guns walked a patrol. Neither looked older than twenty. He glanced at where Anna had been, but found her trotting after Archon toward the doors of the main building. "Right, indeed."

Anna paused with a hand on the frame, her pained stare lingered on him for a few seconds before she hung her head and went inside. Aaron leaned on the luxury hovercar, rubbing his nose in an effort to acclimate to the stench. Long shadows stretched over the artificial lawn, warping the half-human remains in a macabre shadow play. Gunfire sounded in the distance, too far away to be of immediate concern. He shifted his weight onto his feet and wandered along the road passing between the central and west building. Strips of artificial grass lined both sides, interrupted by the occasional charred shaft where a decorative tree had been. Glass from innumerable destroyed windows crunched under his shoes, diverting him to the false turf before he ruined them.

Old missile strikes scarred the east-facing wall of the shorter structure, leaving a wide-open gap into the lobby. Inside, the tents glowed in the late afternoon sun from the opposite side of the building. A trio of Asian girls armed with handguns rounded the far corner of the building, chattering away in what he assumed to be their native tongue. As soon as they saw him, they stopped and stared, their conversation halted. The oldest in the middle, perhaps sixteen, raised a battered NetMini, her face lit by the tiny screen. The shortest stared at him, and the telltale poke of a surface thought read followed.

Muscles in his back tensed; he concentrated on his ride in with Archon, hoping the images of their leader driving him here would transcend the language barrier. The middle girl yelled at the one to her left, who ceased peering into his brain. They scurried past him, offering deferential micro-bows, before scurrying out of sight via a gap in the smashed wall.

He wandered in after them, glancing around at a small army of young people who ranged in age from tweens to early twenties, the majority skewing toward the lower end. One boy, a few weeks away from needing his first shave, concentrated on a chrome skull sitting on the ground at the center of a circle of seated teens. The cyborg head twitched and floated upward, rotated, and settled back to the floor.

The man's raised an army of children.

Aaron ducked a jagged piece of rebar and walked inside. To the right, another group of teens sat wherever they'd decided to drop, cleaning weapons. Two men moved among them offering instruction. One spoke in Greek-accented English, the other lectured a pair of twin blonde tweens in Russian. The sisters disassembled their pistols and cleaned them as if they'd been doing it for years.

Sporadic gunfire continued out beyond the end of the abandoned corporate campus, accompanied by the occasional thud of a small explosive. He wandered among the tent city, peeking here and there at surface thoughts. Most reacted to his eavesdropping, and the ones who didn't show a physical reaction had a sudden shift in the content of their heads. Everyone in the building he checked out possessed psionic talents in one form or another, though few seemed to have any level of real potency. About a third dwelled on their being smuggled into the country, brief images of a harrowing journey played out in their minds. The remainder dressed and acted like a mixture of runaways from the local area, as well as East City, with a fair number of refugees from Britain.

Aaron's head shook in disbelief by the time he reached the far side of the 'camp.' A plain door offered access to a gravel-filled tract behind the building where the husks of four large air handlers sat idle. Older members of 'The Awakened' gang lounged about on the ductwork and glanced up with curiosity and suspicion. A black-haired twig of a young woman peered over a Flowerbasket inhaler at him and winked.

He looked up at the lack of stars. *What the hell is he doing? Kids and street punks.* Aaron pinched the bridge of his nose and ran over in his mind a few scenarios of how this whole mess could go completely and horribly wrong. If, as he claimed, Archon's goal was to leave Earth and take the 'unwanted and oppressed' psionics with him, it might be worth considering. On the other hand, if the government got spooked and pushed Archon enough to start a war…

The echo of a sniffle derailed his train of thought and drew him to the far side of the decrepit HVAC systems, where a vent cover lay askew on stained gravel. The unmistakable sound of a crying child echoed from within. He squatted and looked into the emerald eyes of an olive-skinned girl of about eight. Most of her face hid behind a dingy green dress drawn taut across her knees.

"Hi there," said Aaron, smiling. "It's probably not very safe for you to be in there."

She stared at him.

"Come on then, where're your parents?"

Gravel crunched to his left, drawing his gaze to the sylph with black hair walking up to him.

"You are wasting time with that one," said the woman, a strong Russian accent to her voice.

"Am I then?" Aaron leaned on the air handler.

"You are new here, yes? I am Iliana."

"Aaron."

"You are. She does not know the English." Iliana stooped at Aaron's side, speaking a few hesitant words in what he assumed to be Arabic.

The child half-whispered back in the same language and tried to scoot deeper into the duct.

"She is afraid of soldiers. Whenever there is shooting outside the wall, she thinks they come for her."

Aaron blinked. "Why would soldiers be after a little girl?"

"She can hear the thoughts of someone else. Is against law in Iran; for this, they would shoot her like dog in street." Iliana tapped three fingers to the side of her head. "She does not know she is far away. Most of us come here in box. No windows."

"Parents?" Aaron levitated a few pieces of gravel, sending them into an orbit around his hand. The girl smiled and crept forward.

"I do not know." Iliana shifted her stance, all her weight on one leg. "She does not talk much. She came with group, only person from Middle East."

Aaron let the stones clatter back to the ground as the girl crept out into the air and ran to the woman's side, muttering.

According to his NetMini, she asked "No soldiers?"

"They can't find you here," said Aaron. Seconds later, the device in his hand repeated it in Persian.

She smiled.

"Hey," said Iliana. "You're one of them, aren't you?"

"Not anymore."

The woman raised an eyebrow. "I didn't think you could stop being Awakened."

"Oh." Aaron stood, scratching at the side of his head. "That. Yeah. I suppose I am."

Another girl rounded the corner, wearing a baggy jacket and a tattered pink tutu over worn-out black leggings and combat boots. She looked to be about fifteen with curly dark hair and a permanent frown molded onto her face. The instant she spotted Aaron, the bad mood draped over her worsened, and she honed in on him like guided ordinance. She passed by the three of them, giving him the evil eye until she could no longer do so without turning.

"Hey Liss," said a tall young man in a high-collared coat. "Hear you ain't the top TK dog anymore."

"Fuck you, Jinx," said the teen. "He's a fuckin' cop."

"Yeah, and a cop gets past Ark. Sure thing, chica." Jinx blew a kiss at her.

"Yeah," added a pudgy boy wearing a set of gaming goggles. "This one's real Awakened, like the big man."

The girl shrieked in anger and raked her hand into the air. The heavyset teen lurched forward off the ductwork. She thrust her palm up and he sailed skyward, halting about thirty feet off the ground above her.

"I *am* Awakened, shit for brains. Normal telekinetics can't lift your fat ass without meditating."

Iliana leaned closer to Aaron and whispered, "Melissa is, how you say, touchy?"

The chubby kid whimpered and pedaled his legs in the air. Jinx found the situation hilarious, laughing himself to tears. Iliana gathered the small girl and hurried her into the building.

"That don't mean nothin'," said another dark-skinned teen, peering up from her NetMini past a curtain of tight curls. "Terrence can lift him, and he ain't Awakened. Reboot ain't *that* fat."

"Terrence gotta concentrate for a minute to do it," snapped Melissa, shoving Reboot another twenty feet higher and gliding him around like a kite. "He can't move him this fast." She glanced up at him. "Still think I'm faking it, asshole?"

Reboot shook his head. "N-no, no."

"The new guy's more powerful," said Jinx, picking at his teeth.

Melissa flung Reboot into him, denting the sheet metal ducts and silencing most of the compound in the wake of a rolling *boom*. She whirled on Aaron, alone by the dead HVAC unit, and pointed. "You and me, right now."

Aaron held up his hands. "Sorry, kiddo. I draw the line at eighteen."

"Fuck you!" she screamed, flinging her arms out and toward him.

Aaron braced, absorbing her telekinetic assault with his power. Her attack carried a lot more strength than he'd expected, but holding her back didn't strain him much. In his time with Division 0, he hadn't run into another telekinetic as strong as this kid, so perhaps her claim of being Awakened had some merit. Melissa grunted, her face twisting with effort. He groaned, more for her benefit than from the exertion.

She let go, panting, and snarled. "That's not what I meant, asshole. Fuckin' nasty. You're old enough to be my dad."

Aaron tapped a finger to his lip. "I'd 'ave been fourteen. I suppose it's technically possible, but—"

Melissa let off the bastard offspring of a swear word and a scream while reaching toward an empty dumpster near the building. The thousand-pound container zoomed at him in a straight line. Rather than waste the effort to catch it, he nudged it off course, letting it slam into the wall behind him. The second echoing *boom* drew the attention of everyone inside the tent city. Faces as young as six and as old as forty appeared in the windows, with another group of teens lining the second-story.

Reboot moaned, regaining consciousness, and pushed himself up off Jinx, who wheezed. Blood trickled from the heavyset kid's nose.

Aaron held a hand up to Melissa. "Not much of a sense of humor, eh?" He peeked at her surface thoughts, but she blocked him out in seconds, glimpsing only a sense of dread that the others would ridicule her for being weak.

Spectators cheered, some for her, some for him, others at the duel in general. She dragged the dumpster off the wall, flinging it at him a second time when several voices in the crowd referred to her as 'the bitch.' This time, Aaron stalled it in midair, earning *oohs* from the younger ones.

Melissa growled with increasing desperation as she attempted to force the container into him. Aaron raised an eyebrow as he found himself almost working to hold it at bay. His jaw tightened with genuine effort. Without warning, she ceased pushing and pulled back. With their combined powers pushing it, the dumpster rocketed off over her head. She emitted a growl of exertion past clenched teeth and steered it around to come back at him.

Again, he stalled it in midair.

"Ha ha, Liss! You're losing," shouted an anonymous boy.

"Fuck!" she yelled, her spike of anger launching the dumpster out over the wall.

Seconds later, a slam of crumpling metal and crunching glass conjured the image of it striking an old, dead car a block away. Melissa held her arms up like claws, attacking him directly. He responded in kind, entering a telekinetic tug-of-war.

They lifted each other, whirled about in circles, and hit the ground, skidding apart. He wagged an eyebrow at her, responding to her attempts to grasp his body with her power. Each time the sense of tightness built up, he fended her off with small telekinetic jabs to her sides… like an older brother tickling his kid sister.

Minutes passed in a silent staredown, tense for everyone except Aaron. Melissa flexed her fingers, squinting, waiting for him to flinch. Aaron glanced sideways at the spectators lining the ground floor windows. A small African boy sitting on the windowsill grinned at him.

"Does anyone else fink this would work better wif a tumbleweed or two driftin' by?"

She caught him off guard with a hard shove at his shoulder, which sent him stumbling backward. He expected the subsequent tug at his feet, and levitated himself at the same instant she pulled, flipping in place and landing upright.

Aaron flashed a devil's grin and seized all hundred pounds of her in a telekinetic grip. Despite her frantic attempt to resist, she glided upward, kicking, gasping, and grunting as she strained to oppose his power with hers. As soon as the look on her face went from anger to fear, he set her down. Melissa collapsed to all fours, out of breath. Aaron acted winded.

"Well, looks like a bit of a stalemate." He smiled.

She raised her head to glare at him, still gasping for breath, her sour face no less venomous than when she'd first come around the corner. *You're fucking with me.*

He kept his expression neutral, responding to her telepathic message in kind. *Look, those bastards'll give you no end of shite if they think you lost. If we stalemate, they'll have nothing to say.* "Two Awakened, it's a draw."

Melissa's entire body trembled, perhaps with rage, though tears ran down her cheeks. *I don't need your fucking pity! I'm not a child.*

He dusted his sleeve off. *I've seen you do the floaty gun thing, remember? That's not easy to pull off.*

She stood, fists clenched, but kept her head down so no one else could see her watering eyes.

I'll take a dive if you want. Aaron flashed the smile that sent a hundred panties to the floor. *I don't much care what they think of me.*

Fuck you and your fucking cop... shit! Even her telepathic voice blurred with the sound of crying. Melissa sprinted into the dark courtyard, the crunch of boots on gravel diminishing with distance. A hundred yards or so later, she jumped the wall of the dry reflecting pool and darted among the ancient skeletal cyborgs.

"Guess the princess is pissed she couldn't take you down, old man," said Reboot. "Word is you stuffed Archon."

"Archon? Feh. He's not telekinetic." Aaron glanced at the point Melissa had leapt the wall before the shadows took her. He tugged on his suit jacket to set it straight on his shoulders. "He only dabbles."

4

A QUEEN'S RANSOM

Anna

Converted from what had once been an executive office, Archon's new bedroom lacked much of the odor of the surrounding environs. Two disc-shaped bots the size of dinner plates worked their way around the carpet in an ongoing war with stink. The front space, likely once where the executive assistant's desk stood, had become the holo-vid room, complete with a couch and bar. The actual office, four times the size of the front room, housed the bed as well as an attached bathroom with electronics that some of the more technically-gifted psionics had coaxed back to life.

He hadn't spoken much in the elevator, only enough to tell Talis to choose a room on the seventh floor before continuing to the ninth. Anna stepped over one of the chrome discs, fervent in its mission to suck the dirt from the century-old rug, and followed him into the bedroom. He went straight to his desk, booting up all six terminals with one wave. Whatever had happened with Mamoru had gotten under his skin.

I'm rather tired of him taking it out on me whenever something goes pear-shaped. She huffed, staring at him for a moment before removing her long coat and draping it over a narrow chair by a faux-onyx conference table. The starship factory's chemical taint still permeated her clothes, and she wasted little time before shedding them and padding to the bathroom.

Despite a screen full of errors and warning icons, the autoshower worked as if new. Anna shut her mind to the world at large, concerned that a device held together by a psionic gifted with machines would be twice as vengeful if her emotion ran away with itself while she stood naked and wet inside it. Her distrust of the tube reminded her of Althea's first encounter with one, mistaking it for a cage. Anna laughed briefly before it struck her as more sad than funny. The girl had been as frightened as Twee had been when the CSB nabbed her.

Why did I do that to her? I'm no better than Gordon. Anna let her head hit the acrylic tube with a *clunk*. She straightened when the spray ring descended and moped while the machine went about its task of cleaning her before blasting her with whirling hot air.

At the precise moment her toes touched the plush white throw rug outside the tube, an echoing *boom* rumbled outside. She scurried to the bathroom door, peeking out into the bedroom to ensure no one had wandered in to have a meeting with Archon. Seeing him alone, she walked out.

Archon glanced up from his work at her nudity, offering a momentary smile as she crossed to the bookshelf serving as a dresser. One of Aurora's white satin bathrobes sat at the top of the pile and provided sufficient attire for the time being. On Anna's smaller frame, the fabric hung to her knees. She stopped at the reassembler to generate a cup of Earl Grey and carried it to a violet and black divan along the window behind the desk, where she reclined. Decaying buildings, streaks of black across a dingy amber sky, made the window look like a huge painting of the apocalypse.

Images, maps for the most part, as well as several faces, flickered in and out on the holo-panels surrounding him. Anna sipped her tea in silence, watching him swipe and claw at the intangible screens.

"Are you attempting to seduce me from my work, my dear?"

Anna studied the irregular blob of light wavering on the surface of the tea. "Perhaps. Are you still cheesed off?"

He tilted his head back, staring down his nose at one of the maps. "Do you know what the worst part about Mexico is?"

"The heat?" Asked Anna.

"No, my dear. The Mexicans." He glanced at her for a moment and shook his head. "At least the ones in uniform. Superstitious bunch, the lot, still taken with all that religious nonsense. They don't know well enough to leave their betters alone."

"Betters?" She sipped her tea.

"Psionics. Good grief, Anna. How long have we been doing this?" He pulled his glasses off and rubbed the bridge of his nose. "Are you feeling unwell lately?"

"Aside from havin' to spend all my time around an Arsenal wanker, just peachy keen."

"Really? You have found it that distasteful?" Archon raised one eyebrow. "You seem rather fond of him."

"He thinks he's the cat's whiskers, he does." Anna smirked. "He *is* charming, but I see it. He just wants to get in my knickers." She thought back to the afternoon she'd spent with James by the lake in County Gwynedd and found herself grinning at nothing.

Archon coughed, rubbing his nose. "I did not find that the least bit humorous."

"Oh, James. It was a pisser. You should've seen the look on your face. The way your hair stood—"

"So you have not the least bit of an infatuation for him then?"

Anna shifted from reclining to sitting on the edge of the divan, elbows on her knees and leaning forward. "Don't tell me you've never looked at Lauren."

"How could a man not? The woman has less modesty than one of the Bard's nymphs."

"Well then, don't get on me for lookin' at 'im." Anna swirled the tea around. "Nothin'll happen, James. He might have a pretty face, but he's not the sort to lift a girl out of the gutters an' give her a life back. Besides, I'm not a cheat." Warmth flooded her cheeks. "Do you know he was tweakin' the stone? Telekinetics... in Frictionless. They didn't even fine him!" She gestured at the wall. "He's corrupted the records for centuries, killed the careers of at least three goaltenders and—"

"They let him get away with it," said Archon, sounding bored.

"Yes!" Anna jumped to her feet.

Her enthusiasm faded at the smirk twisting his goatee to the side.

"Of course they did. If they let it out he was one of us, there would've been riots."

"It's still not right." She plunked herself down, pouting. "An' 'ey, if you're worried about that, why'd you keep sendin' me to be with him?"

He lost a struggle to suppress an amused smile. "Worry is not the proper term, my dear. I am amused." Anna turned red. "I am starting to understand where Lauren's idiosyncrasies originate from. Knowing the outcome ahead of time, and watching everyone scramble to forge their own destinies, all the while knowing it futile, is rather entertaining. I find it rather like observing ants. No matter how many times you shake the sand, they keep building tunnels, as if they cannot fathom the futility of their toil and the inevitable outcome."

"Did you just call me an ant?"

He chuckled. "I suppose you could look at it that way, but you are the most beautiful ant in the farm."

She glared, not knowing how to take his meaning. "You didn't need Lauren to tell you that I love you."

"Of course not, Annabelle. Her saying it merely reinforced what I already knew."

The rightmost terminal emitted a *bee-oop* noise and spawned a sub-screen half the size. A square-jawed man's head appeared, with short, white-blond hair combed back over his head and round-lensed black glasses.

"Alles ist bereit. Wir erwarten unser zahlungs."

Archon's gaze dipped to words scrolling along the bottom of the image.

"Of course. Within two hours."

His voice repeated itself, faint from the other end of the communication, speaking German.

"Ein behagen, Herr Mardling."

Anna tilted back the last of her now-tepid tea. As soon as the communication pane faded away, she stood. "Where are we going?"

Archon took a credstick from one of the desk drawers and plugged it into the side of the silver terminal bar. A small pop-up window appeared containing the letters ICFC, the logo of InterTrust Commerce Facilitation Corporation. Both C's resembled three-dimensional carved glass and rotated as the terminal synchronized with his account. Soon, a thin metallic bar scrolled across the underside of the screen with a sliding tab control. Archon touched one finger to it, pulling to the right until the number hit ₵200,000. He unplugged it and tossed it to her.

"Two hundred thousand credits?" Anna blinked. "What's this for?"

"The Syndicate is helping us with our little logistical problem."

She almost dropped the empty mug. "Syndicate? Are you daft? I've been in the company of those people; nothing good will come of getting involved with that lot."

"They have quite a bit of experience moving people through hostile territories, my dear."

"Exactly how many girls do you think they diverted for their own purposes?" She fumed, pacing back and forth. "You don't know what those bastards are capable of."

Archon couldn't help himself but chuckle. "I think you have that last bit backwards." The mirth faded from his face fast enough to send a chill down her spine. "They are quite dependable, given our arrangement. Be a dear and retrieve our new compatriots?"

"You aren't coming?" Anna glanced at the credstick in her hand, feeling revulsion at the cyan numbers on the side. Giving money to *those* sorts of people felt contrary to everything Archon prattled on about improving lives. "Are you absolutely certain about this, James?"

He faced his terminals again, pointing at one bearing a street-level map of a location not part of either raised city. "I am afraid I have a conflicting appointment on my schedule. I need to pop over to Mexico City for a short while."

"Whatever do you need down there?"

Anna walked to the shelf, letting the robe slip from her shoulders and gather around her feet. A pang of sorrow crawled up her arm when she grasped a bundle of black lacy underthings. The same style of smalls James had gotten her that night years ago—the first underwear she'd owned in years. She clutched them to her chest and glanced to her right so James couldn't see her reddening eyes. *What did I do that he's treating me like this?* Her mind raced, searching recent memory for what she'd done wrong.

Archon set his elbow on the chair arm and rested his temple on three fingers. "Certain instabilities in the local climate have necessitated my meeting with a Vice President of Citizen Management and his directors."

"They killed Martinez?" Anna tugged the panties in place and slipped into her bra, turning her back to him. "James, would you mind?"

He glanced in her general direction; the bra cinched itself behind her back. "No, Cortez. Martinez has been dead for six months. It is becoming quite bothersome. The Council isn't terribly different from elected politicians. Ready for the highest bidder to give them their opinion."

How romantic. Does he not want to be near me? She adjusted her breasts and the straps but couldn't find comfort. Silence filled the room, save for the electronic *bip-bip-bip* of his selecting holographic buttons on one of the displays. A plain shirt and baggy, fatigue-style pants, both black, made her feel like a CSB commando without the firearms. She wasn't in the mood for fashion and passed over her knee-length, high-heeled boots in favor of more utilitarian military ones. After shrugging her coat back on, she turned toward the door, but found Archon in the way, close enough to touch.

"Cripes!" she yelled, hand over her heart. The room lights, as well as the desk terminals, all flickered. "Are you trying to make me brick it?"

He put a hand on her shoulder, drawing her into a gentle embrace. "Forgive me, Anna. The business with the ship has me out of sorts. All these people are counting on me. You have done nothing wrong."

She rested her head against him, reassured by his breath warming her hair. "You had me worried."

He held her for a few minutes, gently swaying side to side. "I wish we had more time. Once we are away from this horrid little sphere, we will have all the time in the galaxy. I suspect you might even grow weary of my company."

"James." Anna looked up at him. "Don't be silly."

She leaned up and kissed him, eyes closed, clinging as if he'd brought her to the precipice of a cliff. Something seemed different, as if he *tolerated* her affection more than *craved* it. She shut it out of her mind, blaming the distraction of everything going on. Archon had work to do; the ship—the key to their whole plan—had gone missing, almost a hundred psionic refugees had set their hopes on him, and now they had the matter of Aaron and Talis within strangling distance of each other.

Yes, I suppose he does have reason to be distracted.

"Be careful, Anna. They'll meet you by the Sentinel Corporation wharf in Sector 9881, more or less due west from here." He gave her another kiss, a brief peck, and wandered back around his desk. "Forgetting something?"

Anna followed his gesture to the credstick sitting by the empty tea mug on a small table adjacent to the divan. Before she could walk after it, the one-inch fob glided through the air to her.

"It's a wonder telekinetics aren't all enormous." She tucked the small fortune into her coat pocket and walked out. "Don't have to leave your bloody chair."

⚖ ✤ ▦ ◍ 🕮

MUCH LIKE THE AUTOSHOWER, A COUPLE OF MECHANICALLY INCLINED PSIONICS had coaxed the main building's elevators into working. Anna felt certain no conventional technician could find a reason for the thing to be functional, nor did she trust it when Archon wasn't there to 'catch' it should it plummet. She strode past it to the stairwell, trying not to look at any of the hundreds of bullet holes in the cinder blocks. Aurora, being Aurora, had told her when they first occupied the place that local gangs used the building for 'gaming.' By that, she meant they shot each other, like a video game, only with real bullets, and for no other reason than being bored and finding it fun. They used small guns and wore armor, but accidents were common.

The stairwell made for an 'excellent level' as Aurora claimed one of the ghosts said.

An eerie sense of being watched dogged her as she rushed down the switchback stairs. All her life, certain places felt *wrong*. Thanks to Aurora, she now believed them haunted. Apparently, all psionics had a degree of sensitivity to the presence of spirits that came as a side effect of one's brain being opened to power. Fortunately, only a few could see or speak to them, and Anna *never* wanted to be an astral sensitive. If any sort of deity existed, she'd want to thank them for sparing her that.

Faint sniffling echoed off the bare walls from below. The sound gripped her with dread as her thoughts ran away with all manner of horrible explanations for why the sound of a crying child existed in a place like this. *Bugger me. I am not hearing ghosts.*

At the bottom of the second-floor landing, a reedy girl in baggy pants and jacket sat against the wall, head forward over her knees, long, dark hair cascading over clunky boots two sizes too big. She looked about fourteen or so, close enough in age and size to Faye to slap Anna with the hand of guilt. *What now?*

"Oy, are you alright?" Anna stopped. "You're alive, yes?"

The girl looked up and sniffled; violet smears ran from both eyes down her cheeks. "Huh?"

"Kim, right?" Anna crouched. "What happened?"

A tint of rouge spread over the girl's cheeks at being caught crying. "I'm sorry, ma'am." She shivered as sadness traded places with fear.

Anna made a show of looking around. "Stop. I'm not as much of a bitch as everyone thinks. Are you all right?"

"I lost my gun," she whispered, cringing.

"Oh." Anna rolled her eyes. "Is that all? Don't worry, we'll get you another."

"You're not going to kill me?"

"Kill you?" Anna blinked. "Why on Earth would I do that?"

Kim drew her hands over her face, shivering. "For fuckin' up."

"Kinnel... what the devil are you kids talking about at night?" Anna took Kim's hand. "We're trying to protect you. The last thing I, or Archon, want is for anyone to get hurt."

Kim sat up straight and gathered her hair behind her. "What happened to Althea?"

"Althea?" Anna blinked. *Why is everyone obsessed with that child?* "I... Umm..."

"Piotr said we had to leave the station because of her." Kim shivered. "He said you killed her 'cause she tried to fight Archon." Her gaze fell to the ground, and her voice to a whisper. "I thought she was nice."

"I..." Anna gasped. "No, Kim. I did not kill her. As far as I know, she's still alive. And aye, she *is* nice. Too much so."

"Where is she?" The girl's mood brightened. "Is she coming back?"

"I doubt that. She and Archon had a disagreement, plus the little primitive didn't much like the city."

"Why? Archon's gonna save us all. Why would she want to leave?"

"Uhh." Anna fidgeted with her coat. "I don't... I mean, she's too..."

"Innocent," said Aurora from the first-floor landing. Much to Anna's relief, the woman had covered herself with a clingy white dress. Skimpy beat nothing. "Sometimes the things that must be done for the greater good seem distasteful in the short term."

Kim drew her knees up to her face. The fear Anna commanded from the rank-and-file as Archon's right hand paled in comparison to the wave of unease Aurora elicited.

"Right, well. I've got an errand to run." Anna stood. "You're better with this sort of thing anyway."

Aurora smiled.

The girl stared at her, eyes pleading and red. Had Anna been anyone other than the supposedly short-tempered lethal second-in-command, the girl might have attempted to hide behind her to get away from the creepy astral-clairvoyant. Instead, Kim went rigid and trembled, like a child caught between a tiger and a lion.

Anna hurried down the steps, not paying much attention to Aurora's attempt to be soothing and explain Althea's absence away as her being 'too delicate' for her own good, and 'too nice' to understand it was okay to hurt people who wanted to harm you. At Aurora's claim Archon 'felt awful and let Althea go home' when she begged to go back to her family, Anna scowled and shoved open the door to the lobby.

If only.

She stomped through the azure glow of the 'command center,' where all the people with mechanical aptitude worked on a mixture of terminals and cyberspace decks. The look on her face sent a pall of tense silence over the room, spreading from person to person and leaving them frozen. One boy jumped out of his chair, abandoning his terminal to hide under the table. A number of adults on break from perimeter security made it a point not to look at her and found their rifles quite interesting.

"What?" she snapped.

Everyone jumped.

"I'm *not* a witch!" she shouted, waving her arm at them. Holo-panels and portable lights faltered and recovered. "Go on, do whatever you were doing. Be happy. Smile or something."

A flea farting would have been deafening.

"Kinnel," she muttered, storming out to the courtyard. People being frightened of her was nothing new, but having other psionics react to her as if the Angel of Death had walked in got her gut aching. She hesitated as the automatic doors slid closed behind her, glancing over her shoulder at the room full of worried faces. Althea's sad, pleading stare flooded her mind. *How many of them believe I murdered that poor child? I'm not that mean, am I?* She tried to remember Twee's grateful smile after she'd rescued the girl from the CSB. No young people looked at her like that anymore; they all ran the other way and hid.

Anna took two steps toward Archon's gold Halcyon-Ormyr before she stopped. "Drat. No. That won't work. I'm probably picking up more than three people." For the second time in five minutes, everyone in the lobby startled when she walked in.

"Randall?"

An athletic man over by the 'security team' sputtered coffee and tried not to drop his rifle. "Y-yes, ma'am?"

"Would you be a dear and bring the van around?"

He leapt up and sprinted down an interior hallway. Anna crossed her arms and leaned on the wall, pondering the sudden thought they might not be so much afraid of her as afraid of Archon. *Don't be foolish.* Anna's smile further tensed the room. *He's a teddy bear inside.*

5

EL TÍO DE LA MUERTE

Kate

Vulnerable points in the green-tinted metal wall lit up with thin red circles as the targeting system in Kate's helmet identified them. The heavy exo-armor suit thudded across the ship's cargo hold, feeling much like a wearable leather couch due to the padded interior. She thumbed a button on the side of the huge, boxy rifle in the suit's articulated metal hands to launch a spray of six mini-missiles from her shoulders.

The explosion rumbled the floor; for a brief instant, the sensation of carpet on her backside broke the illusion of being in a thirteen-foot-tall mechanized battle armor. Car-sized spider bots swarmed out from the smoking hole left by the barrage of missiles. Her vision exploded with a mess of blue and red HUD rings over each target.

Kate opened fire with a rifle as big as a human body. A hail of 55mm slugs swatted leaping spiders from the air, detonating them into sprays of parts. One dropped from the cargo hold roof onto her back, knocking the exo to a knee. She rolled with the impact, crushing the bot with the weight of her suit before the laser-tipped mandibles could burn holes in her helmet.

"Odd targets, one through fifteen, fire," said Kate.

From the ground, she fired the rifle at bots on the left side while the micro-missiles operated on automatic, singling out targets given odd numbered designations by the system. One by one, her attackers flew to pieces, but they kept on charging, electronic brains incapable of fear. She fought her way standing, punting two more out of the way, and ran for the bulkhead door.

The passage she hoped to be a way out turned into a dead end. Ten feet from the cargo hold, the ship ceased existing—a starfield full of debris was all that remained of the front half of the *ISS Excelsior*.

"Shit!" she hissed. "How do I always fucking forget this?"

She looked back at the unending swarm of murderous robots, then out at the infinite blackness. This run had been her fourteenth attempt at this level, and so far, every time, she died here. A glimmer of light caught her eye in the distance, drawing her attention to a hole in the side of a chunk of hull floating by. The opening used to be a corridor before the *Excelsior* broke apart.

"Son of a bitch." When she looked directly at it, the suit's electronics calculated the distance at three hundred and forty meters. "Fire boost!"

Four thrusters in the suit's back ignited, hitting her like a Gee-ball defender determined to earn a penalty, launching her in a calculated drift toward the distant opening. Spiders spilled out of the breached hold behind her, but she didn't dare fire her cannon lest the recoil send her spinning to oblivion. One of the robots widened its mandibles as it glided nearer. Kate stared at the approaching hole, squinting when unfiltered sunlight peeked over a large hunk of debris with a blinding flare.

Time froze.

Kate, the spider, the sun, even the tiny flecks of starship debris all stopped moving at once.

"What? Bullshit! I'm not dead. This has to be what you're supposed to do here!" Kate's scream fogged the visor.

Neon green words appeared in the stillness: ‹Incoming call.›

"Dammit!" She grumbled. "Fine, fine. Pause."

The senshelmet shut down, reducing the space battle scene to blank darkness and releasing its hold on her neuromotor control. She lifted the flimsy plastic visor away from her eyes and found herself once again in her apartment, sitting cross-legged on the floor. A mess of wires connected her two-day-old white-and-pink Yume Koujou game system to the helmet, the only thing on her. On the far side of the apartment, the Vidphone warbled, indicating an inbound call.

"Who is it?"

The Vidphone ringing stopped long enough for a familiar voice to say, "El Tío."

She let her head loll back onto the sofa cushions. "Answer."

A hologram of her former benefactor faded in as if sitting in the recliner at the right side of the couch. As soon as he took on the appearance of being solid and real, he raised an eyebrow at her.

"Kate. They told me you'd gotten over your little issue."

She lifted the helmet off and set it in front of her on the rug. "I did."

"And yet you're still naked."

"Makes the game more real. Less conflicting sensory input. Besides, I'm home alone." She got up and walked to the bedroom. El Tío vanished from the chair and shimmered into view standing to her left. He waited, not quite watching, but also not quite averting his gaze, as she put on a robe. "I hope you're well."

"I am as well as can be expected. You don't look very happy to see me."

Kate glanced at the grandfatherly figure in the dark coat and black fedora, unable to help but feel guilty at the standoffishness she radiated. "I'm sorry, El Tío. So much has happened to me. It's hard to adjust." She smiled, tying the satin belt closed while walking closer to the digital ghost. "I will never forget what you did for me."

He took a long pull from a Nicohaler made in the shape of a cigar. "I never doubted that."

"You were always good to me." She gazed wistfully at his shoes, hoping he could see the sincerity on her face.

"So it's true then, you wound up with the police?" He chuckled.

"Division 0. Psionic police. They don't care about your business."

"I need you again, Katherine."

"Need? I'm... I can't do that anymore."

El Tío's image took a step closer. "I am sorry to intrude upon your idyllic new life"—she cringed—"and remind you of dark times, but no one else can handle this. The job is a psionic."

Her mind raced for a way to say no to El Tío. Such a thing was generally considered impossible at best, unhealthy at worst. The reality of having to 'repay' his generosity for the rest of her—or at least his—life settled in her gut like a puddle of ice water. He'd found her living naked in the streets at fifteen and given her a lifeline: the heat-shielded NetMini that projected hologram clothes. He'd provided the education that lifted her up from a feral wild-girl to a functional member of society, fed her, protected her, and perhaps had even become fond of her somewhat like a father.

All she'd had to do was kill whoever he asked her to.

She couldn't bear to tell him she felt more grateful to a little ten-year-old blonde girl with glowing blue eyes. That child had freed her of the curse, and let her join the world instead of stand outside watching it.

She sank to the floor at his feet, staring down.

"El Tío, please forgive me. I can't do what you ask. They are watching me. If I resolve a job for you, they will... They said they'd forget everything in the past, but I don't know if I can keep doing it."

"Kate," he said, half-whispering. "I am aware of your special circumstances, and believe me, I would not ask if it was not a last resort. This individual has already cost us significant amounts of money and has spat in our eye on multiple occasions. He has killed and humiliated our associates and is responsible for the death of Julian Cray."

If this guy can get to someone that high up... Kate gasped. "Cray's dead?" *Good for him, bastard.*

"Yes. Tseng as well. The mark is psionic, and you are now a police officer who hunts psionics. We can help you arrange it to look justifiable. The old men are willing to pay you two million."

She gathered the robe tight around her body and stared at the floor. El Tío had taken her in, protected her, but what had he asked in return? He had hardened her, made her a killer, and destroyed whatever innocence remained in her heart. The face of David Ahmed appeared in the back of her mind, smiling at her. How would he feel if he knew she considered doing what the Syndicate wanted? What form could El Tío's disappointment take if she said no? She clutched her hands over her heart, cringing at the sensation of tears sliding down her cheeks. Her life seemed a continual process of finding herself trapped in untenable situations.

"W-who is it?"

El Tío's hologram took a datapad from his coat pocket and held it up to the device recording him. The face of a blond man in his later twenties appeared on its screen, hovering above the shoulders of a Division 0 uniform. "His name is Aaron Pryce."

Kate wheezed as if a hand squeezed her throat shut. He wanted her to kill a cop. The Syndicate considered succeeding in a hit on a police officer the only way to redeem oneself after a betrayal, but doing such a thing and walking away alive never happened. El Tío may as well have put a bullet in her head himself. They didn't expect anyone to come back from those jobs. Her eyes burned red as she found the desperation to look him in the eye.

Her body shook with sobs; the person most like family wanted her to die. "I'm sorry..."

"Shh." He stooped, intangible fingers brushing over her head. "You have not gone astray, little one. This is not *la penitenza*." He smiled. "Mr. Pryce is no longer on the roster. He is out from the shadow of their protection."

Somewhere in the back of her thought process, the figure of two million credits spun around in a chaotic mess. She was certain he'd mentioned a price that high but found it as scary as the concept of the job. Money like that would get noticed. If not by Division 0, by *them*.

Her fingers brushed at her throat, remembering the cold metal stunner. Tears stopped, replaced by the calculated calm of a plan. "This is not a good idea, El Tío. Please, hear me out."

He leaned back, head tilted. "They will give you medals for this, Kate. The man has already killed several other officers. We're not sure what is driving him, but he's clearly out of control. My sources tell me he is a wanted man. In an unusual turn of events, the wants and needs of the police are parallel to mine."

"It's more than that." Kate rested her hands in her lap. "I didn't agree to join Division 0 to run away from you."

El Tío's mouth curled into a weak smile. "No? Yet you do not wish to help me. What can these *lawmen* offer you that I cannot?"

She bowed her head. "I mean no disrespect. I was detained by C-Branch."

His lips peeled into a thin line. The energy in his mannerisms drained away into the same place the color in his cheeks went. Whatever arrangement the Syndicate had with the National Police Force held no sway over military intelligence.

"David said the police could protect me from them. They're the people who created me, and they want me back." She fidgeted. "I did not want to lead them to you. Even if Division 0 can't protect me forever, whatever happens to me will not affect you."

He paced back and forth. "Military intelligence…"

"I was scared and alone. You took me in and protected me. I love you like family, even though I had to kill."

"You never told me it bothered you."

Kate looked up at him. "It didn't… then. My loyalties have not changed, but there are some things I just can't do anymore." She blinked the last of the tears away from her eyes, struck by a sudden mental image of Althea smiling at her. *What did that girl do to me?* She ran her hands up and down the sheer sleeves of the robe.

"I would not ask this of you if I had another choice." He flickered out of existence and reappeared at the door with his back to her a second later. "I never found the time to take a wife, but I would have been proud to have you for a daughter."

She twisted around to look at him, savoring the feeling of the plush cream-colored carpet between her toes. "What of C-Branch?"

"They do not bother with our business." He sucked on his Nicohaler, face aglow for three seconds in reflected orange light. "Will you take the job if it is the last I ask of you?"

The disappointment in his voice sounded too much like it would be the last time he saw her alive. "I will always be loyal, but I can't hide everything from the telepaths. They won't let me get my hands dirty without consequence."

"Your arrangement of convenience with the police could wind up serving our purposes. Agreements can be made, even with them."

Kate stood and glanced at the clock. David would be there any minute to pick her up. She'd never be able to hide her guilt from him. She'd have to hope this Aaron Pryce was as bad as El Tío said and on everyone's shit list.

"I understand. I'll do what I can."

El Tío took one last pull from his Nicohaler; his hologram disintegrated into columns of whirling black and cyan pixels as he hung up. She stared at the last of the tiny black squiggles seeping into the carpet and closed her eyes. Seconds later, an eerie chill passed over her.

Happiness would not be hers for long.

6

THE WAR WITHIN

Mamoru

Sadako lay in the hospital bed, her expression the same peaceful calm it had been since the old man vanished. The local doctor, Ruiz, had been in long enough to perform a cursory examination. Whatever he had seen with her had alarmed him enough to rush out of the room.

Crinkles in the white sheet deepened and faded as she breathed. Mamoru clasped her hand, his mind swimming with rage at how limp and lifeless she felt. The crash replayed itself in his mind in an endless loop, yet he could not find any explanation for the sudden failure of every critical system. If something had shot them down, he would have felt the impact against the hull. If someone had sabotaged the computer, he would have sensed it happening and overridden it with ease. He had not detected other aircraft close enough to engage. Surely, the military would have been aware of his theft of the shuttle, but they wouldn't have bothered chasing him into the Badlands; they would've waited for him in the west.

Even the orbital particle cannons the government denied having would have been noticeable as a burning lance piercing his body, tactile feedback an often unpleasant side effect of his mental link to machinery. *No, the shuttle simply decided to drop dead in the sky.* Having no target for his anger frustrated him beyond measure. Someone had tried to kill him, and may yet still succeed at taking his sister's life, and he could do nothing in the name of vengeance.

As much as he tried to summon sorrow over the life of servitude forced upon her by his failure, his emotion found only the handhold of rage. The

NSK had stolen her childhood because he had been weak. Mamoru sighed and bowed his head. The repeating shuttle crash gave way to the memory of trees rushing past as he chased his little sister's screams.

He stood at her bedside and lifted her arm, touching the back of her hand to his forehead. His thinking mind wanted to shed tears for what had happened to her, but the well held only blood and a need for revenge. Mamoru shuddered, face twisting as hate wrenched his outward calm.

"Stay with me, sister, or I swear upon our father, the entire world shall cry for your suffering."

Her fingers twitched as if to curl around his, the motion enough to feel but not see. He squeezed her hand with as much care as he could muster, and laid her arm back at her side. The sound of a metal door banging open out in the hall got him to his feet.

"Where?" asked a child.

"Be careful," replied a deep voice.

Dr. Ruiz's hard shoes echoed closer. "Room nine."

"Althea, wait," yelled a teenaged boy.

Mamoru faced the door at the approaching *pap-pap-pap* of bare feet on the polished hallway. All the fury swirling in his heart condensed beneath the surface of an outward calm. A wisp of a blonde girl, maybe ten or eleven, rushed into the room and stared at him. Her eyes glowed with an inner light like fireflies, but azure instead of yellow, her irises a deep sapphire. She skidded to a halt two steps in, staring up at him. The look of concern on her face faded to one of worry and then of anger.

The sight of her started a war of awe and discomfort in Mamoru's heart. All at once, he felt deep respect for this scrawny child and a stark sense that her presence here defied the natural order of the world, as if her mere existence offended the kami. Her eyes narrowed to a distrustful squint and flared brighter for an instant. The inexplicable urge to destroy her slid from his consciousness, a shadow careening back down the well from whence it had climbed. His numbness evaporated; worry flooded into the void, sending him to one knee fighting the urge to weep like the ten-year-old version of himself who could not save his sister.

A sienna-skinned teen in a white shirt and jeans caught himself on the doorjamb as he ran in and stared at him over the girl. "Althea, be careful. We don't know him."

The girl moved closer. "The woman is hurt."

Her simple statement of fact triggered a wave of dizziness that blurred the room. Whatever force had so focused his thoughts toward hatred had receded. *Sadako is dying.* The girl moved past him, a blur of a white dress glided by in his peripheral vision. A massive figure obscured the doorway, too muscled to seem real, watching the girl.

"Help… my sister." Mamoru's words came slow and raspy, with the great effort necessary to cloak sadness from his voice.

Dr. Ruiz jockeyed side to side behind the huge man, unable to get into the room. The child scurried to the bed and grasped Sadako's arm. Mamoru stared at her back and the upwelling of gratitude disintegrated, collapsing to a blind desire to kill. *Why do I wish to harm this child? She wants to help Sadako. This makes no sense.*

His right hand moved to his katana; his left hand followed, trying to stall it. *Sadako.* He would not fail his sister again.

"Althea!" shouted the boy, rushing at him.

The aggressive motion allowed reflex to smash his concentration. His blade leapt from the scabbard, a clean stroke aimed right for the girl's neck. The boy jumped between them, flinging himself into the blade to keep it away from her. The katana cut him across the back from left to right, breaching both lungs. He screamed and collapsed to the floor, his limp legs buckling under him. Red seeped down his shirt, expanding in a puddle.

Mamoru readied another strike at the girl, who still had not reacted, apparently lost in meditation over Sadako. Again, the idea that she helped his sister stalled him. The effort to hold back the *Akuryō's* killing urge made him shake where he stood. The huge man charged, roaring like a wounded beast. Instinct brought the katana around, but the giant ignored the blade stabbed into his side. A fist as large as Mamoru's head smashed into his chest, launching him off his feet into the wall. The strike knocked all the wind from him and cracked a ronin-shaped outline in the cinder blocks.

Dazed and unable to breathe, Mamoru blinked at the katana still protruding from the titan's breast and fell forward like a plank. Somewhere in the fog reality had become, a little girl's scream broke the silence.

The big man grunted, and the clatter of metal came from the left. Hands seized Mamoru by the shoulders, hauling him into the air. He punched the giant in the chest, as close to the bleeding wound as he could, but the man disregarded his attack and hurled Mamoru across the room. Before he hit the wall, he concentrated on hardening his body; white energy flames crept down his arms as power coursed through his bones. The throw embedded him in the wall, his body crushing an opening in the cinder blocks deep enough to support his weight.

The giant charged.

This time, Mamoru rolled out of the way, leaving the man to bury his arm up to the elbow in the wall. Dr. Ruiz stared in horror at Mamoru for two seconds and ran out of sight into the hallway. His leap for the discarded katana ended in midair as a meaty hand closed around his shin, and swung him up and over before driving him into the floor. Mamoru weathered the hit with a burst of psionic effort reinforcing his bones.

As soon as Mamoru sat up, a massive fist careened into his face, spreading a spider web of pain around his skull and flooding his senses with a loud *crunch*. His body crossed the room in under a second, sliding along the floor into the wall. Rage bloomed; his smashed skull crackled and shifted under his skin, mending itself. Mamoru couldn't tell if his fear came from fighting a man who could crush him with one hand, or from the power of the *Akuryō* within him.

He rolled away from the monster's grabbing fingers, getting to his feet as another punch caught him in the middle of the back. Mamoru sailed across the room again, crashing chest-first against the wall. He bounced away, landing on a table and smashing a tiny vase on his way to the floor. The giant sprang, forcing him to roll to avoid it. Mamoru scrambled upright, cringing as ribs knit back together, and circled around behind, using the seconds it took the ogre to find him to alter his power from reinforcing his body to making it stronger.

More flames erupted from his shoulders and spread down his arms, casting the room in wavering shadow. Mamoru caught the man by the wrists, both of them growling as they wrestled and knocked furniture around. The stalemate surprised Mamoru for only a second. No longer hesitating, he released a guttural noise from deep within his throat and twisted. A fleeting memory of the stunned look on Caiden's face when the boy watched him rip armored doors apart appeared in his mind.

His strength, boosted beyond even that of a cyborg, hauled his opponent off his feet. Mamoru let his movements flow with the weight. In a move half jiu-jitsu throw, half brute force, he tossed the man as hard as he could. The giant crashed through the cinder blocks, raising a cloud of dust and shaking the entire building. Upon a pile of rubble in the next room, the huge man lay dazed and moaning. Strands of pre-war electrical wire dangled from the top of the hole, swaying back and forth.

Mamoru had pushed himself too far. His body throbbed with a dull ache from forehead to toes. He staggered to his sword and struggled to pick it up before whirling about, looking for the girl. She knelt by the wounded teen with both hands on his back. The boy gurgled bloody foam from his lips, staring into space with no consciousness behind his eyes. Her tear-streaked face warped with anger as she let off an unintelligible scream.

Every muscle in his arms twitched and tightened. The undulating ripple crawled up into his shoulders and seized him by the throat. Mamoru wheezed but found himself unable to move to grasp at his neck. Force like that of a titan strangling him cut off his ability to breathe. His arms creaked as his body turned against itself, twisting bones in ways they were not meant to bend. The innocent little girl staring at him had changed. Her visage filled him with dread unlike anything he had ever experienced. Deep inside Mamoru's head, a roar of terror rang out in a polyphonic voice many octaves too low to come from anything human. He needed to get away from her—it—at any cost, but his legs refused to obey.

Consciousness slipped. Grey hazed the edges of his vision. He felt himself falling and focused his last aware thought toward his sister.

You don't want to hurt me. A little voice echoed in his mind as the horror crawling under his skin ceased. *That is not why you came here.*

Mamoru's vision cleared. The child stood, leaning her weight forward on one leg in a threatening posture he'd have found humorous if not for the undercurrent of dread her presence triggered within him.

Her eyes widened. "You! Why are *you* inside that man?"

Mamoru raised an arm to shield his face. "*Otasuke wo negaitai!*" He staggered for the door, dragging his katana. "Please... help." He crashed into the doorjamb, one arm and his head out in the hallway. It took every ounce of his willpower not to run screaming from the *thing* staring at him. Why had he tried to kill the person who could help Sadako?

"*Sumimasen...*" He slipped away from the door, into the hall. "I do not know why I have done this."

The hospital melted into a haze of running, lights, and shouting men. A sharp crack, perhaps a gunshot, rang out behind him. White fire licked over his back as he forced himself to run faster and faster. Streets and people blurred by. A metal staircase flashed, bright lights streaked overhead, voices shouted, sparks appeared with the *ping* of bullets glancing off plastisteel. The stairs led to the top of a wall, but he kept going straight. Running became falling. Darkness and starlight filled his vision. He hit the ground boots first and rolled into a somersault back to a run. Dust puffs blew up everywhere, the continuous crackle of gunfire behind him.

Mamoru surrendered to the terror of what dwelled within the city, running blind into the night. Despite the wall surrounding the settlement and every building in between, the creature in the guise of a little girl seemed to stare right at him.

7

MERCY FOR A SHADOW

Althea

Althea scowled at the doorway, her glower softening as Dr. Ruiz pulled himself upright with the help of the doorknob. The stranger had bowled him over on his way out as if he didn't even see the doctor standing there. Warm blood slicked the ground at her feet. Shouts and gunshots outside faded into the night. She dropped to her knees and wrapped her arms around Den.

Her mind linked to his life-shapes and she focused on the great bundle of white roots down the center of his back. The sword severed them around where they passed the heart, turning the tendrils below that dark. Althea had seen raiders suffer similar cuts. Without her help, the wound would have left Den unable to use his legs. She shuddered from the amount of effort it took to force the hairy threads back together, despite the relative smallness of the damage from a thin, sharp blade. The stringy shapes had always been difficult to mend.

Once she finished restoring his 'back root,' she turned her attention to the hasty closure of his air bags she'd managed to do while Shepherd fought the outsider. Compared to the backbone, it felt easy. Den moaned and moved while she chased the last of the blood-shape out of his airbags.

"Althea," he wheezed.

"Amazing," muttered Dr. Ruiz. "You reconnected his spinal nerve."

"What?" She looked up at him.

"The police said your abilities represent an enhancement of the body's normal healing capabilities, but at an order of magnitude faster. Nerves don't usually regenerate, or if they do, it takes decades."

"I don't understand." Althea pouted.

"It's not important right now."

Den rolled over and sat up.

"Can you move your legs?" Dr. Ruiz helped him balance.

"Yeah." Den wagged his feet back and forth. "What happened?"

Althea draped herself on him and burst into tears. "You saved me."

Den patted her back, rocking her as Dr. Ruiz made his way through the hole to the adjacent room. She sniveled, clinging to Den, feeling grateful as well as guilty she had gotten him hurt.

"I'm sorry," she whined.

"It's not your fault," Den grumbled. "Where did he go?"

"It wasn't him." Althea switched from hugging to holding his hand and sat back on her heels. "The Many was inside him. That man wanted me to help his sister. The bad ones made him fight. He was sad."

"I'm going to kill him." Den jumped up.

"You can't." She looked up. "The bad part isn't a person. I told it to go away. He's already gone."

Sporadic gunfire outside tapered off to silence. A few shouts sounded far off, likely at the city wall.

Den scowled at the bed. "What should we do with the woman?"

Althea blinked at him, hurt he'd even ask such a thing. "It is not her fault. That man loves his sister, and she did not try to hurt anyone. It would be wrong to punish her for what the Many did."

"I will find him." He started for the door, but she held on, sliding on her knees in the blood until he stopped.

"No. I don't want you to get hurt. He is stronger than Shepherd." She glanced at the hole.

Den growled.

She squeezed his hand. "Why do you feel shame? You protected me."

His face flushed red and he stomped in a circle, away from her attempt to hug him again.

She stared at the blood on the floor—Den's blood—and wept. "I'm sorry. It's my fault he came here."

A surge of embarrassment radiated from him. She reached for his hand, but he gave her a wounded look and ran out, almost colliding with a man and a woman from the Watch as they rushed in.

"Althea," said the doctor, "Shepherd's hurt."

She crept over and peered into the hole. Shepherd lay on his back on the other side, blood covering his face. Althea clambered past the breached wall, tracking bloody footprints to his side. Her hasty attempt to stop caused her to slip and fall on top of him. He grunted.

"Careful," whispered Dr. Ruiz. "He's probably got a concussion."

Althea spared a second to give him a confused stare before putting her hands on Shepherd's bare arm. Her worry faded as concentration took over, and his life energy filled her awareness. Cracks marked a number of his bones, including his skull, but she sensed nothing wrong within his mind-shape. Thin black lines faded from the white as she forced his bones to knit. Her nose scrunched and a soft growl slipped past her teeth while she struggled to keep fragments of bone from scratching his brain on their way back into place.

Once everything felt right, she released the link and collapsed over his chest. A moment later, his huge hand pressed into her back and patted.

"Ouch. That had to be a damn doll. Skinny bastard was tough... and strong."

His deep voice vibrated in her chest, bringing a smile. Shepherd took a few breaths and got up, cradling her in his arms. She caught herself about to nod off and whined.

"I'm not finished."

He carried her into the hall. "You need rest."

"She is going to die."

Shepherd set her back on her feet when she started wriggling. Dr. Ruiz gave her a worried look as she stumbled over to the bed. The woman's life felt weaker than it had moments before. Althea swayed in place, clinging to the mattress to keep from falling over. She crawled up onto the bed, lying next to her and cradling the limp arm. No sooner did her fingers make contact than an unsettling chill crept over her. A tainted presence permeated the woman's body, one she recognized out of instinct as belonging to the specter that visited her in the garden.

Althea closed her eyes and opened her mind to the foul energies swirling around in the stranger's body. The blood-shape had seeped into places it should not be, and many of her bone-shapes had become collections of splinters rather than solid. Several of the other blobby parts in the center looked burst as well. The darkness concentrated around the areas most damaged. Her initial assumption—that it fed on the pain—proved untrue. The instant she forced the evil substance out of her, the woman lapsed into convulsions as all her inner bits failed at once.

Power coursed down Althea's arms. Every bone in her body throbbed from overextending herself. Her attention leapt from one shape to the next, trying to repair each one a little bit at a time to keep any single blob from quitting altogether. The woman's heart-shape wanted to give up and go still, but Althea commanded it to keep going. Pain snaked up her throat. Warmth spread over her mouth, blood running out of her nose. Time lost meaning to the urgency with which she funneled her energy into the fragile woman next to her.

As soon as she focused on the crushed bean-shaped lump in the woman's lower back, the heart-shape started quivering like a lump of jelly Shepherd had just punched rather than how it should move. It stopped cold a second later. Althea redirected her attention to the heart-shape, nudging it back into motion, though it refused to keep a steady beat. Blood leaked inside her from too many breaks. She closed damaged blood-tubes like a cat chasing a panic-stricken roach: chest, arm, leg, neck, chest, and around again. The heart-shape throbbed in an unnatural, erratic rhythm and stopped again. Althea dared not break concentration to yell for help, emitting a telempathic pulse of distress instead.

She got the woman's heart beating again, despite the stabbing pain in her own. Her lungs burned as though she had been running for hours. When a new hole pierced a thick blood tube in the woman's arm, Althea wanted to scream in frustration. Fluid entered the woman's body from that point; it took Althea a second to realize Dr. Ruiz must have put a needle in. She continued sustaining the heart while pushing herself to keep the other blobs together. Eventually, the incoming liquid bolstered the blood presence enough to lessen the strain on the heart, though it felt too thin. At Althea's urging, the woman's body created more blood.

With the reassuring presence of a regular heartbeat, Althea resumed forcing the purple bits as close to the way they were supposed to look as she could while fighting the growing urge to pass out. Several frantic moments later, the woman's life no longer seemed in danger of detaching from the body at any second. She still needed help, but Althea could summon nothing more. The link collapsed, and she managed to open one eye for a fleeting second. Father and Karina hovered over her.

"I don't understand."

Father put his hand on her forehead. "Shh, child. Don't try to talk."

"Evil... but it... helped."

The room blurred to darkness.

Sunlight upon her eyelids chased away sleep, though her leaden limbs refused to move. Althea lay for a while, awake but still. The bed did not feel like the one she shared with Karina. The strange smell in the air told her she remained at the hospital.

"What happened to her?" whispered Karina. She sounded close by.

A chair creaked past the foot of the bed as Father spoke. "Ruiz said she worked too hard. She will be fine."

"It is almost noon." Karina ran a hand over Althea's head.

She opened her eyes; her weak smile banished the worry from the face hovering over her. Althea reached up to touch her sister's cheek but froze at the sight of a plastic tube connected to a needle in the back of her hand. Frightened by the presence of something stuck in her, she grabbed at it, but Karina caught her hand.

"Dr. Ruiz said it will help you. You get hungry when you help people, and you did too much last night."

"It's food?" Althea stared at the IV.

Karina shrugged.

"Food goes in the mouth, not the arm." Althea frowned. Her stomach made its protest audible.

"I will get you something to eat." Father got up and walked to the bed, holding her other hand. "You gave us a scare last night."

"I'm sorry. The bad man was here."

"He got away," said Father, anger clear in his quiet voice.

"No. Not that man. The old man from the garden. The Many." She sat up. "He was inside."

Father and Karina exchanged worried looks.

"Stay with her." He patted Karina on the back and went out.

Karina fussed over her, using a damp cloth to wipe dried blood from Althea's nostrils and off her face. She smiled, enjoying being cared for, until she noticed the late-morning sun outside.

"You're late!" Althea clung to her sister's arm. "You're going to get in trouble."

"It's okay. They know." Karina held Althea's hand in both of hers. "They let me skip today so I could be here for you. Dr. Ruiz said you are going to be weak for a while."

"I'm not hurt." Her stomach growled. "Just hungry. Where's Shepherd?"

"He's working. The man's unstoppable."

Althea smiled. "Did the woman wake?"

"I don't know." Karina glanced behind her as Father walked in.

He set a plate of empanadas and leftover bacon from breakfast on the table near the bed. The scent of the food overpowered her disinterest in moving, and she swung her legs over the side, whining at the soreness all throughout her body.

"She woke for a short time, but only enough to mutter in a strange language." Father's serious tone broke into chuckling.

Althea hadn't realized how feral she'd gone on the food until he laughed at her. She stared from the fork lying on the tray to two half-eaten empanadas, one clutched in each hand. Her voice echoed in her thoughts, making a deal with the ancestors that she would always use the fork if they allowed her to return to her family. The sight of the untouched utensil terrified her. Both pastries slipped from her hands and she covered her mouth, ready to burst into tears.

"Althea?" Karina sat next to her and put an arm around her back. "What's wrong?"

"I promised." She sniffled. "I'm sorry! I didn't mean to. I don't wanna go away."

Father's face reddened and his lip quivered. Karina squeezed her. Althea blinked at him. The emotion radiating from him was part love, but mostly the urge to laugh. Her confused expression punched the last crack in his attempt to hold it in, and he guffawed. She sniffled away a few more tears.

"Oh, Althea," he said. "No one will take you away because you didn't use a fork."

"I didn't listen when Karina told me to use it, an' then I got taken away. I promised if I could come home I'd always—"

Karina picked up one of the empanadas and held it to Althea's mouth. "It's okay to eat these with your hands. We don't use forks with everything."

Father's laughter grew infectious, and Althea giggled.

◦ ⚔ ▦ ◦ ◎

ALTHEA HID BEHIND THE DOORJAMB, RUBBING THE BACK OF HER HAND WHERE the needle had been, watching the strange woman sleep. They had moved her to a different room, one without blood on the floor or a massive hole in the wall. She edged away from the door and took a step in, but Karina's hand on her shoulder held her back.

"You need to rest."

Althea looked up with a worried expression, whispering, "I have to make sure she is okay."

Karina relented and walked with her to the woman's bedside. Althea reached out, held hands with the sleeping figure, and closed her eyes. Numerous small fractures marred her bone-shapes, though she looked in far better condition than the previous night. Without the urgency of imminent death making her rush, she noticed thin, dark lines in the woman's arms and legs—metal inside the body. She was too exhausted to purge that and figured she should probably ask the woman before removing the metal. Althea shivered. Some of the city people *liked* having that stuff inside them. That, she would never understand. One by one, she mended the last of the tiny hurts. Calling again on her power so soon left her winded even from the minimal amount of energy needed to seal the cracks. She checked for broken blood tubes, found none, and let go.

Althea held on to Karina's arm for stability and followed her to the door. After a lingering glance at the poor woman on the bed, she let her sister guide her out of the hospital and back home. Karina insisted on an exception to the one-bath-a-week rule since she had dried blood all over her, which she feared would bring sickness. Althea hovered close as Karina hung two buckets over the fire to warm them. Father said they could have baths whenever they wanted once the Water Man got around to giving them one of the magic tanks—strange machines the city people offered that provided a constant supply of hot water without the need for fire.

Althea scowled at the thought of the 'city stuff' infiltrating Querq. She liked things as they were, but offered no protest as she followed Karina to the bathroom. By the time she sat armpit deep in warm bathwater, her stomach growled again. With no real food ready, Karina left her to wash while she fetched some baked treats from a neighbor. Soon, Althea nibbled on cinnamon cookies while her sister washed her hair.

They spent the rest of the day together, free of chores or farm work, resting in the shade of the porch and talking. Karina tried to introduce her to the concept of dolls, but Althea didn't see the point in tiny wooden or cloth people.

"Better to care for a real baby who can grow up," she said.

Karina found that hilarious and laughed, which got Althea giggling.

With the approach of evening, they marched inside the house and got to cooking dinner. Althea still felt hungry, as though the big lunch, cookies, and two whole, raw potatoes hadn't existed. With the focus of a task distracting her from thoughts of her family, worry crept in. She squeezed and rolled the tortilla dough, glancing out of the corner of her eye at Karina chopping vegetables at the other side of the counter.

"Have you seen Den?"

The knife stalled. "No… I thought he was out with the Watch."

Althea closed her eyes and grasped the agate arrowhead hung around her neck on a leather cord. Her flour-covered fingers tightened around it while she concentrated on him. She felt nothing, which could mean good and bad. Good because the lack of alarming feelings suggested safety, bad because it offered her no information. Light from her eyes sent shadows dancing on the wall as she plucked a small wad of dough away from the larger mass and mashed it flat with her hand. After getting it as round as she could, she stood on tiptoe to reach for the handmade rolling pin behind the sink.

"I thought he was at the hospital."

Althea worked the roller back and forth over the lump. "He is angry with me."

Karina put the knife down. "He... what?"

"I told him not to chase that man because he is stronger than Shepherd."

"Oh." Karina put a hand on her shoulder. "He's a boy. He doesn't understand. He thinks you called him weak."

"I didn't!" Althea whined. "I have to find him."

Father's boots thudded over the porch.

"He'll be okay, Thea. It's just his pride. You didn't do anything wrong. Come on, we need to finish. Father's hungry."

Althea's stomach rumbled. She looked down at herself.

"And so are you." Karina poked her in the side.

"Okay." She managed a weak smile and set aside her worry.

ALTHEA AWOKE ALONE IN BED, DRAWN TO CONSCIOUSNESS BY THE SCENT OF eggs and bacon. Sunlight bathed the room in warmth. She sat up, feeling as though a weight balanced atop her head, and rubbed her eyes, which protested being open. She grasped the nightstand to steady herself and felt her way to the dresser. After a moment to ensure she wouldn't fall if she let go, she pulled her nightgown off. Approaching a state of sleeping-while-standing, she swayed side to side in front of the chest of drawers.

She tugged at the handle and took the last folded dress on the left side. The old chest cloth Den had given her sat on the wood beneath it. In truth, it had only been three months since she had worn it, but it felt like another lifetime. Weary arms draped the clean dress over her head and let it fall around her. Althea didn't bother threading her arms into the sleeves and trudged from the bedroom to the kitchen downstairs.

Her guilt at sleeping in faded at the sight of Father cooking. She hadn't left Karina to do it alone after all. Karina gasped. Father chuckled. Althea didn't understand what they found so funny until the cold chair at her bare backside told her the dress had tangled at her neck like a scarf. Too tired to care, she slumped over the table.

Karina rushed over and pulled the garment down, dressing her as if she were a three-year-old. Althea remained limp and tolerated it. Father set a dented, blue metal mug next to her.

"You look like you could use that, Thea."

She sniffed it. Bitter steam assaulted her nose, making her scrunch her face up. "What is it?"

"Coffee," said Father.

"Father!" Karina took the mug. "She's too little for coffee."

"Heh." He grinned. "I had my first cup when I was ten."

"And look at you," said Karina.

He mumbled at her in Spanish, grinning despite sounding as though he complained. "Put milk in it."

Althea sipped it after Karina softened and cooled it with a generous portion of milk. The flavor caused a mild grimace, but it was hardly the worst thing she'd ever tasted. She propped her cheek up on one hand while battling her omelet with a fork. The way Father mixed tiny bits of bacon into the fried potatoes made her want to lick the plate, but she insisted on chasing down each little scrap with the utensil.

"Where is Den?" Althea glanced at Father.

"Because of his injury, we are letting him rest. Dr. Ruiz said he shouldn't do much for at least a week."

"He'll be okay, Thea." Karina patted her on the back as she passed on her way to the sink.

Father stood, gave each of them a kiss on the cheek, and left for the day. Karina got started on the dishes without her. Althea rushed to finish the last of her breakfast, figuring scraping the food to the edge of the plate and into her mouth with the fork counted as using it.

After dishes, Althea walked her sister to the farm area, hovering at the wall for a few minutes until she could no longer see her among rows of tall corn stalks. She fidgeted with the agate pendant, wondering where Den could have gone. When worry got the better of her, she pushed off the chest-high wall and scurried down the street, guided by instinct rather than thought.

🜚 🜍 🜛 🜔 🜕

THE GARDEN, THE ONLY EXPANSE OF GREENERY ANYWHERE IN QUERQ ASIDE from the farm, would remind Den of the place he once called home. Warm water shimmered on the sidewalk leading up to the old stadium. With each step, the coarse texture of worn concrete emerged from beneath a slime of algae. Althea moved to the door, peering into the dark, eerie hallway full of old pushcarts containing pipes, machine bits, and canisters of powdered chemicals the Water Man had called 'food' for the garden.

Inside, thick, humid air saturated with the overpowering fragrance of plants caused Althea to break out in a sweat. She ran on the balls of her feet to the interior door and crept along a walkway of loose metal sheets, which led down past a tiered atrium full of hydroponic tanks. The Water Man told her that long ago, the place had been full of seats where people used to watch 'games.' She thought it quite silly to think anyone would trade pay-things to see grown men play with sticks and a little ball.

The walkway clattered with each step, no matter how quiet she tried to be. At the bottom, she stepped into the shin-high grass surrounding a small grove of fruit-bearing trees.

Wariness gripped her, tensing the muscles in her back. This place should be peaceful, but something hung in the air—something that did not belong here.

"Den?"

Her tiny voice echoed in the cavernous space, startling several blackbirds in the rafters beneath the opaque, white dome. She cringed, raising an arm at the sudden noise, but sighed at the sense of normal animals.

"Greetings, Althea."

As soon as the gravelly voice came from the cluster of small trees, her heart leapt into her throat. Her toes gripped the dirt as she turned her head to the right, finding the decrepit old cowboy standing a few paces away from her, gazing at a fallen orange in the grass.

His black, wide-brimmed hat obscured his eyes but not his seaweed-colored smile. His hands hid in the pockets of a long, leather duster coat, which fluttered about his boots. Under his stare, white crept over the surface of the orange before a dusting of corroded-copper green took its place. The fruit deflated, withering into an unrecognizable lump.

The sour smell of fermented, rotting orange crossed her nose. She wrinkled her face in response, trying not to breathe. Althea stared at him, at once wanting to tremble in fear and scream with anger.

"Leave us alone."

The figure straightened; the brim of his hat pulled away from red, luminous eyes. "You surprise me, child. I thought you were trying to kill that woman."

Her conviction faltered with regret and she stared at the ground. "She had bad inside her."

He feigned a gasp, removing one hand from his pocket to cover where a heart would be. "I'm hurt. I was only trying to help her."

Althea looked up, her face stern. "Bad can't help."

"Can you say she would have been alive had I not?"

"I don't know what you just said."

He frowned. "Do you think she would be alive without my help?"

As confusing as it sounded, he had a point. The condition of that woman's body should not have let her live. "I..."

"Don't understand." He approached, taking care to place his boot on the fetid orange, crushing it into the ground.

She stepped back, cringing at the awful squish.

"We agree that I destroy, yet that piece of fruit becomes part of the earth and feeds the next crop. In destruction, I make life."

"You kill people. People don't grow out of the ground." Althea set her stance, refusing to back away further. "You want to trick me."

He stopped at arm's length, smirking down at her with an expression part way between sneer and smile. Contempt, disgust, and fear swirled around him.

"You're afraid of me?" She tilted her head.

"Of course not. You're a pitiful little child who doesn't understand the way the world works." His breath carried the reek of the dead, making her cough.

"I understand you are bad."

"You only exist because of me," said the man.

Althea clenched her hands into fists. "I don't believe you."

"Well." He shifted to the right, gazing at hanging grapes overhead. "Perhaps in some form, a girl that resembled you would have existed, but would not have been *you*. You've come to destroy me. I cannot let that happen."

She started to lower her gaze, but acting demure had only ever gotten her into trouble before. How many times had she simply surrendered to being taken prisoner, when all the while she'd had the power to protect herself? "I don't want to hurt you. I never wanted to."

"You are an awful liar." He edged away. "Why else would you be here? They are so obsessed with *balance*." The word rolled off his tongue with contempt thick enough to feel in the air.

The odor surrounding him—charred flesh and rot—watered her eyes, but she took a step closer. "I don't know what you mean. All I want is to help people."

"If not a liar, a fool." He backed up another few feet. "Do you expect me to believe you don't know what you are?"

"I'm Althea." She nodded as if to underscore the point.

"Nauseating," he muttered, drawing the word out into a grating throat noise. "Are you really that blind?" His eyes flared from red to orange.

Dark vaporous smoke welled up from the ground at her feet. The air gathered around her legs like syrup, crawling up and over her skin with a clammy wetness, over her arms, heading for her throat. Her body tensed with revulsion as if she'd stepped barefoot in dog poo. At the instant she wanted it gone, a wave of energy issued forth from her, flattening the miasma outward in a widening disk away from her.

"Part of you *is* human." The man seemed to fight his trepidation to lean closer. "Fascinating."

"What did you do to me? Where's Den?"

"Do not worry. Merely a curiosity. Perhaps you would agree to a truce."

Althea blinked. "I'm not lying."

He gazed into the distance, letting off a sigh that leaked smoke between his teeth. "Not truth. Truce. *La tregua*. We stop trying to destroy each other, and we both get what we want."

"Oh." She smirked. "I do not want to kill you. You are all all angry. I can feel your sadness, and I'm sorry you died. It is okay for you to be angry that you died, but if you hurt others, you're the same as the people who killed you. I want to help you."

She reached out a hand.

He bared his teeth with a cringing sneer. The glow in his eyes brightened, and the air filled with the roar of a thousand voices crying out in anguish. Smoke obscured the garden, trees and plants replaced with before-time skyscrapers awash with flame. Gunfire rang out everywhere, interspersed with spikes of emotion. Random flashes of anger, anguish, panic, and a terrible desire for revenge came out of nowhere. A deep scraping sound like a boulder dragged across the sky went overhead, following a vision of a before-time flying war machine. Objects fell from it, blossoming into great clouds of fire, anguish, and death.

Althea collapsed in a heap, arms crossed over her face, trying to fight off the pain of a young boy who had watched his mother die in a hail of bullets. The whooshing noise ended with a powerful explosion that rattled the dome. Expecting pain, she screamed, but the symphony of war had stopped, leaving her cry echoing over silence.

She peered between her unfurling arms, finding herself alone in the garden. Althea eased herself upright, trembling from the emotional echoes of terror, suffering, and agony still hanging in the air. A wisp of sweet rot from the stepped-on orange teased at her nostrils.

"Why?" She yelled, moving in a slow turn, searching for any sign of life among the trees and corn. "Where did you go?"

Only the distant sound of dripping water answered.

"Den?" She yelled, her voice echoed until the garden fell silent once more.

Head down, Althea trudged along the wet, mossy path to the exit.

NO SIGNATURE REQUIRED

Anna

The dull thrum of heavy tires might have lulled Anna to sleep if not for the way the flat-faced van created the illusion of floating above the street. She pondered the paradox of how 'flying' seven feet off the road made her more nervous than a hovercar at fifty stories.

Randall hadn't said much more than "yes, ma'am" since they'd started the drive to the wharf. Blue light from the console painted his already dark face in harsh shadows and glare. He'd made no attempt to peek at her mind, though whether it came from his fear of Awakened or something else, she couldn't say. Kinetics like him sometimes lacked telepathic ability.

She'd seen him shoot pills out of the air for fun. If this went south, it would be good to have him along. Her face soured. Why didn't Archon send that new empath? Then, they wouldn't have to give money to a criminal organization. Was Archon afraid of the Syndicate, or too lazy to put forth the effort to control them? Perhaps he didn't trust Talis either. Again, she looked over at Randall. His nervousness might as well have been a glowing NanoLED tattoo across his forehead calling her a horrible bitch.

"I didn't kill that girl."

He nodded, though remained as tense as before.

Anna glanced at the automatic weapon he'd left on the seat between them. To keep herself distracted, she focused on it until threads of amber light appeared to her wherever its circuitry carried power. She plunged her awareness into it, mapping out the path from the battery in the pistol grip to the tiny metal dot that sparked the rear end of the propellant in the chamber. Her mental wandering along the wires leading to the ammunition counter came to an abrupt halt when the van bounced over a bump. She held on to the door to keep from winding up on the floor as Randall hit the brakes a few feet away from a sliding security gate.

A man in a black raincoat and sunglasses leaned against the non-moving part of the barrier holding a full-length assault rifle. *I'll never get used to that.* Even after five years in the UCF, the idea of civilians carrying firearms felt wrong. Worse was how brazenly he held it, pretending to be some manner of soldier. Archon had made sure all of them knew firearms were legal over here. Guns that threw bullets could be owned by anyone over eighteen—lasers, not so much.

"What do you want me to do, ma'am?" asked Randall.

"Please stop calling me that. I'm no one's grandmother." She pushed a button on the center console. The passenger door let off a hiss, slid an inch away from her, and glided backward into the wall. "I'm not even twenty-nine yet."

"Yes, ma—miss?"

"It's alright if you call me Anna, you know. We're not in the damn army." She clung to the handles around the doorframe, managing a somewhat graceful descent via a built-in boarding ladder. With her boots on the ground, the seat cushion hovered higher than eye level. "Bloody hell. Did he have to steal the biggest one?"

Randall tapped his fingers on the wheel, saying nothing.

Anna approached the sentry, confirming via surface thought read he worked for the Syndicate. She allowed a little concentration, searching for cybernetics inside him. "Pardon the delay, we hit a traffic snarl. Some idiot decided to steer a motorbike into the PubTran tube and hit an oncoming taxi."

"Ouch. One less dumbass in the world." Amber threads shimmered down his right arm, highlighting wires, as he raised it and banged on the metal wall twice. "Ivanov got called away, but there is no problem"—the gate shuddered, grinding open with the labored whine of a small motor—"provided you have the money."

She smiled, enjoying the ironic feeling of being less afraid of him for having so much cyberware, and flicked her thumbnail on the credstick in her coat pocket. "I do, and there won't be any issues from our side so long as all of our guests are all accounted for."

Anna walked around him, slipping past the end of the still-moving gate. The guard followed her across an empty parking lot in front of a small three-story office building bearing the logo of Sentinel Corporation. The hulking silhouette of an intercontinental cargo ship blackened the sky beyond the roof. She gathered her coat close about her neck, already shivering from the sound of the wind on the ocean before she got past the corner and stepped into a stiff, salt-scented breeze.

Two hundred yards of open metal tiles, scattered with coils of heavy chain and stacks of boxes, separated her from the wharf. In the shadow of a wheeled loading crane, a box big enough to be the trailer of an articulated cargo transport sat on the ground behind three men. Two had dark skin, while one looked like he'd emigrated from Sweden only hours ago. She moved up to a brisk stride, eager to get out of the sea breeze as soon as she could. Randall crept along behind them in the van.

Anna smirked. "When did the Syndicate start issuing uniforms?"

"Huh?"

"You've all got the same coats and glasses. If you're trying to be inconspicuous, it isn't working."

"Hmmf." He shook his head, grumbling.

The blond man concerned her the most, due to his massive size and lack of embedded sources of electricity. Still, she sensed plenty of juice in power lines underfoot, should the need arise. Anna walked right up to him, showing little sign of intimidation despite the top of her head coming up to his swollen pectorals. He'd obviously had work; he looked too perfect.

"*Guten abend, fräulein,*" said the blond. He seemed amused by her blank stare. "Forgive me. Good evening, Miss. I am Ulrich, your point of contact."

Anna's discomfort at dealing with the Syndicate showed on her face. "There should be fourteen, correct? There better not be any missing."

"We have honored our end of the bargain. Besides, there is no market for young girls with"—he tapped himself on the head—"gifts. The clients who"— the man stifled a cringe—"favor that sort of thing often have secrets they do not wish eavesdropped."

Anna scowled. *If selling thirteen-year-olds to executives bothers you so much, why do you work for them?* "Let's be on with it then."

"The money?" he asked, eyebrow raised.

"I'd like to see them first."

"Of course." Ulrich glanced at one of the men behind him. "Open it."

"*Si,*" said the shortest, still a head taller than Anna. He waved a hand at the door, summoning a holo-panel with a ten-key pad. After he fed it a code, the entire cargo box resonated with a heavy clank.

Two men each grabbed one of the half-doors and pulled them aside with a grating metal-on-metal screech that launched an explosion of pigeons off the wharf in the distance. One feeble LED bulb, swinging naked on a wire in the middle of the container, illuminated a group of bedraggled people. The stink of bathroom buckets rolled out, watering Anna's eyes and making her cough.

"*Raus,*" said the blond man, waving his arm in a beckoning gesture.

Four women, the oldest about Anna's age, the youngest barely eighteen, moved first. They each took hold of small bags and approached the open end, fear plain in their eyes. A pair of Middle Eastern looking men followed who seemed happy, smiling at Anna as they stepped into the glare of a pole-mounted light. One held his arms up as if to embrace the sky.

Eight figures remained huddled in the dark—all kids. After a moment of fearful staring, two preteen girls in the outfits of British schoolchildren were the next ones brave enough to emerge, dirty and disheveled, clutching backpacks. Their rumpled skirts looked as if they'd been wearing the uniforms nonstop for weeks. Long, raven hair obscured the face of the taller girl while the other wore her straw-blonde hair clipped up. They didn't look related but clung to each other as if siblings.

It's all right, said Anna, telepathically. *We're going to protect you.*

They brightened at hearing a familiar accent in their minds and hurried over to her. One of the Syndicate men caught them by a hand on each backpack, halting them in their tracks. He forced them into the forming line by the rest, half carrying them by their schoolbags like kittens. They stared at Anna as if to ask what they did wrong. She narrowed her eyes at the man.

"It'll be alright, give us a moment. Apparently, I have to pay for you first."

"Come, come, Anna. You are paying for their passage. This isn't the middle ages." Ulrich's perfect teeth showed from a used-hovercar-salesman's smile.

The girls took their place near the women, eyes downcast and on the verge of crying.

Anna squinted at the taller girl. *Did they hurt you at all?*

No, Miss. Just kept us locked in that horrid box for over a month.

"Tell me again why you shipped them on a bloody boat?"

Ulrich made a clucking noise with his tongue. "I thought you understood how these things worked. No one really uses boats anymore. Much less scrutiny."

Four boys, whispering amongst each other in Russian, got up and ambled to the exit. Unlike the others, they showed no trace of fear. They all had the look of a hard life: gaunt faces, lanky bodies, and hollow eyes that made Anna wonder if they'd killed. The oldest couldn't have been more than fourteen, the youngest about eight. All of them tried to read Anna's surface thoughts.

She let them in, enough to see images of the tent city and other people like them, trying to make it seem welcoming. Their suspicion diminished but remained. One of the boys, about twelve, glared a challenge at her as he passed.

Anna looked at the line. "There should be two more."

Ulrich offered an exasperated sigh to the short man.

"*Paren de esconderse y vengan aquí.*" yelled the thug. "*Rapido.*"

Whimpering emanated from the back of the container, the cavernous metal lent an eerie echoing quality to the sound. Anna took a step closer. One of the Syndicate men leaned forward as if to block her, but thought better of it and stayed out of her way.

"What?" She scowled at him. "It's not like I'm going to stuff them in my pockets and bugger off." After brushing past him, she grasped the frame. "Hey, come on out. It's okay."

The short man whispered, "They don't know English."

Dingy cloth, no doubt used as bedding on the long trip, shifted. Two faces of dark brown, a boy and a girl of about ten, obviously siblings, peered out at her. Anna covered her mouth, gasping as two barefoot, forlorn children struggled to emerge from their nest. Long, black hair hung down to their thighs. Their clothes seemed little more than rags ready to disintegrate at any moment, a plain white t-shirt and jeans on the boy, a moth-eaten peach dress on the girl. Both both had bright orange handcuffs on their wrists as well as ankles, the restraints around their wrists kept snug to their bodies by a length of chain around their waists. The girl made eye contact, her frightened expression easing back to one of hope. Her brother kept his gaze down. Together, they shuffed along, barely able to move, secured like violent serial killers in miniature. They tried and failed to hold hands, chains clicking as they shuffled in tiny steps toward her. That anyone even manufactured cuffs so small broke Anna's heart.

"What the devil are you people doing?" Anna yelled. The augmented thug closest to her experienced a convulsion. "Is *that* necessary? They're *children!*"

Ulrich held his hands up. "It is not our doing. That's how they were when we acquired custody of them. Mexican police do not take risks with psionics. You should be glad our people down there got to them before they were shot."

"You've had them for five weeks and you left them like that?" shouted Anna. The overhead light flickered, causing all the refugees to cower. "What sort of animals are you people?"

"That isn't our concern." Ulrich popped a breath mint into his mouth. "We were paid to bring them to you alive. This isn't first class, you know. Besides, they seemed keen on running away. Think of it as extra packing material... so they didn't get damaged in transit."

The siblings halted two feet away from her, shivering and out of breath from the effort it took to get there. The girl whispered in Spanish to her brother. Anna caught enough to understand the girl had felt her surge of anger and had become frightened, worried that they'd done something wrong. The boy shrugged and mumbled back. He stared up at Anna, a trace of curiosity in his eyes. Since the girl had reacted to her emotional state, Anna assumed her a telempath and tried to project concern.

Up close, the marks of healing bruises showed on both of the round faces staring up at her. Anna kept her expression stoic, but at her upwelling of pity, the girl's hopeful smile returned.

Twisting her wrists in the rigid binders, the little girl whispered, *"Yo también los odio. Duelen."*

Anna crouched and touched the bruises on the girl's face before shooting Ulrich a dark stare. "Your people didn't do this, did they?"

"La policía do not have the psionic inhibitors." The short man gestured as if striking the boy with the butt end of a rifle. "So they hit them if they think they're trying to make eye contact."

Anna hissed. She grasped the cuff around the boy's wrist. A glint flashed across the words *'Gestión Ciudadana Tijuana'* stamped in the orange-painted plastisteel. Chafing and bruising reddened his skin where the metal touched it. At the sight of dried blood on the children's wrists, a spike of anger radiated from her, sending a spark into the ground.

The cybernetic arm of one of Ulrich's men flapped in a spasm in time with a faltering lamp overhead, forcing him to grab it with his other hand.

"It's alright. I'm going to take those things off you. Sorry if it zaps a bit."

The short man translated and the boy relaxed. His sister stared at Anna with adoration.

A hand grabbed Anna's shoulder, pulling her upright before she could concentrate on the electronics inside the restraint. The man who had met her at the gate nodded sideways at the blond man.

Ulrich cleared his throat. "Do you have our payment?"

A sound like a rifle shot echoed over the wharf as an inch-thick spark connected Anna's shoulder to the chest of the man who'd grabbed her. He sailed off his feet, sliding to a halt fifteen feet away, twitching and moaning. Tiny sparks snapped from his limbs to the metal ground.

All four Russian boys dove flat on their chests. The siblings tried to backpedal, but the handcuffs around their ankles tripped them up and they fell seated.

"The next one of you cretins to touch me won't be getting back up. Am I clear?" Anna threw the credstick to Ulrich with a contemptuous snarl. "I can't believe you people. You're not transporting cases of synthbeer. These are *people.*"

The Viking-in-a-suit raised a hand, stalling the other two from drawing their weapons.

Anna pulled out her NetMini. "Translate, Spanish." She took a knee by the shivering children. "I'm going to get those things off you, please hold still."

Her words repeated from the device. Both kids still appeared terrified but nodded. The girl struggled, trying to brush hair from her face, but couldn't raise her hands from her waist. Anna looked away before her anger could burn out the electronic locks.

"Yo también los odio. Duelen," said the girl again. Anna's NetMini said "I hate them too. They hurt."

Typical for ACC hardware, the electronics in the restraints were cheap. Anna had little trouble bypassing the logic module that processed the code entry and feeding current right to the little motors that opened the cuffs and released the chain around the kids' waists. The boy rubbed his nose hard, like he'd been needing to do it for a long time. As soon as Anna freed her, the girl leapt into a hug and squeezed the breath from her lungs.

"*¿Es usted mi mamá ahora?*"

"Uhh…" Anna patted the girl on the back. "I wouldn't make a very nice mum, but I'll protect you."

The girl grinned at her. Soft brown eyes filled with hope stared up at her, squeezing her heart in the iron grip of guilt. The boy clung on her other side. She held them awkwardly for a little while until Ulrich broke the silence with a harsh clearing of his throat. Both kids jumped away. They continued beaming up at her, which didn't make her guilt any less unwieldy. Red marks from the binders on their skin sent a second ripple of anger down her arms, pushing sparks around her coat.

"Two from Ukraine," said Ulrich, gesturing at the four women. "One from Moscow, one Dresden." He waved at the men, then the boys. "Two from Iraq. Four from Russian farm country. Those boys should be a great asset to your cause. They grew up in the resistance, basically soldiers already. They know how to shoot." He motioned at the British girls. "Those two came from your friends in the CSB. Detained within days of each other, from the same school even."

Taken from their parents…

The schoolgirls shivered. Anna's mind ran away with visions of the CSB giving them the same treatment she got. Anger boiled inside her at knowing Archon had already killed Agent Gordon; she wanted to do it again. The little monster in her head roared and an overhead light exploded, sending trails of burning shrapnel in all directions. Refugees screamed. Once again, the four Russian boys dove to the ground. The twelve-year-old glared at her as if he wanted to hit her for scaring him twice.

"These two," said Ulrich, gesturing at the siblings. "Not a lot of information. The Citizen Management people in Mexico hate being in Mexico, so they're even less motivated than normal. Records are spotty down there, but it looks like they were street urchins. Probably got caught using their powers to take advantage of people until they got reported."

The boy looked up at her with watery brown eyes and muttered. His voice repeated itself out of her NetMini, in English.

"I understand small English. We were poor. Papa gave us to the police for the reward money when he saw us do magic. They were mean to us. Kept those things on us the whole time. Hit us if we looked at them. We had to stare at the floor."

His sister spoke a touch above a whisper, her voice timid. English followed from the NetMini a second delayed. "A man came to the jail. He shot the police and took us to put in that box."

Anna jammed the NetMini into her shielded handbag as fast as she could to protect it from her barely contained rage. She had the distinct urge to make someone scream, and fast lost the ability to care who absorbed the brunt of her wrath.

"A pleasure doing business with you," said Ulrich.

"I'm surprised you didn't fill the container," Anna muttered.

Ulrich bowed. "We do not deal with such things in the UCF. Strictly off-world. Too many complications here. Your laws seem to favor media ratings. 'Rescuing' prostitutes makes for great video."

Anna scowled. "They're not my laws, and they're not called prostitutes when you *sell* them. Prostitues get paid."

The smoking man moaned and flailed his arms, trying to stand.

His associates closed the container while a third man climbed into the crane.

Anna took the brother and sister by the hand and approached the rest of the people in the line.

"Did you buy us?" asked one of the British girls, sniffling. "What's to become of us?"

"No, we did not." She looked at them each in turn, weathering a barrage of telepathic pokes. NetMini held aloft, she spoke in a slow and even tone. "This country is more tolerant of psionics than where you are from. Detestable as they are, these men have a lot of practice at transporting people out of sight of the authorities. Archon does not plan to keep any of you against your will. You are all free to go wherever you choose; however, we would like you to join us. We can offer you a safe place to stay, food, and the company of others like us. Archon will take us somewhere we do not have to hide what we are. Where we can be free of the prejudices of the unenlightened, and embrace our gifts."

The handheld device repeated her words in Arabic, Spanish, Russian, and German.

Everyone looked at her, but no one spoke.

"Come on then." She motioned at the van.

Four rows of seats made for a tight fit, and the air conditioning had no chance of purging the stink of fourteen people in dire need of new clothes and showers. The Iraqi men chattered incessantly while sporting huge grins, pointing around at everything and everyone as if seeing Earth for the first time. The Russian boys took the furthest rear bench, scanning the area as if expecting an attack at any second. Anna settled into the passenger seat, glaring out at the Syndicate men putting the cargo box back on the ship it came from. *What is wrong with people? How can anyone be so cruel?*

Perhaps Archon had a point. This world offered no solace for psionics.

ANNA CREPT DOWN A DARK HALLWAY PAST A LARGE INDUSTRIAL BATHROOM where tattered plastic sheets floated like phantoms in a faint breeze. The taste of rusty metal and unknown chemicals settled on her tongue with each breath and a tingle of unease ran down her spine, an eerie feeling that supposedly meant something *else* was in the area with her. Of course, it could only be the presence of the abandoned power station around her. Such places seemed to have a dark energy all their own. She found the quiet as unsettling as it was oppressive and wondered how many real ghosts watched her.

I wish Aurora never told me that feeling meant ghosts.

Sometimes she found it impossible to differentiate a psionic sense of otherworldly energy from simple nervousness at being alone in a decaying industrial building. Maybe this time, the eerie tingle grasping at the back of her neck came from a mundane case of nerves.

Anna paused at a mangled metal door, half torn from its hinges. Althea's memory stared back at her from inside with the not-at-all-scary rage of a little girl who didn't get her way. At the time, she'd found the child petulant and annoying. Someone with so much ability to help them, but all she wanted to do was go home. Like a child, she couldn't see all the good she could do for so many people and demanded her own want.

Of course, they *had* kidnapped her.

The office-turned-bedroom remained—aside from the ruined door— exactly as they'd left it. Anna hadn't been back since she scraped Archon off the grating of Cooling Tower One and got him into the hovercar only minutes before dozens of Division 0 patrol craft swarmed the place. *How exactly did they find us? Were we infiltrated?*

She sat on the bed, jostling a pile of datapads and several stuffed animals. A blue, cartoon bunny glimmered into view.

"H is for happy. Can you say happy?"

"Sod off."

"You're getting closer. Good try! Try again." The rabbit flashed a big grin. "H is for happy can you—"

Anna touched the screen by the power icon and the ten-inch creature vanished. She stacked the six datapads on the Comforgel slab and traced her fingers over the topmost one. For no reason she could think of, the datapads made her sad, as if the gift she had brought the child had been unwanted.

"So much for educating the savage."

Some part of her had looked forward to spending time with the girl, helping her go through the lessons on these pads. Maybe she sought some sort of absolution for leaving Faye behind in the UK by offering a wing for Althea to hide under. Why did it bother her so much the girl wanted nothing to do with her? Aurora thought she had projected Faye's resentment for her leaving England onto Althea. *Bah. Faye has parents; she didn't need me.*

"Why did I even bother coming here?" She gazed up at the scorched vent cover, feeling a new wave of guilt. How had she gone from helping one young girl escape a secret government prison only to turn around and abduct a different one? "Maybe she was right."

Anna gathered the datapads under one arm, and the stuffed animals under the other. No sense letting them rot here.

A block of sweet coated in a bit of sour. Aaron's voice whispered in her thoughts. She hadn't wanted to kill the techs in the Timmons-Orben building. Archon had seemed indifferent to it, mostly bothered by the inconvenience of it taking longer to steal the data in a way that didn't require killing people. How could he be so cold to the world at large, but so charming to her?

She squeezed the damp stuffed animals, wondering if her offering had made Althea any happier here. Perhaps if she'd had the nerve to give them to her rather than sneak them in while the girl slept, she would have received them better. She frowned at the floor, grumbling to herself internally about all the sappiness and wasted time. Despite that, she collected the toys and took them.

I'd better get out of here before I'm noticed.

Anna trudged back out the way she'd entered, pausing at the doorway of the former command room with its large, silver table. A twinge of old pain stabbed her in the hand. The bloodstained chopstick still sat on the floor, molded over from a puddle of rainwater. James had used it to prove his point. He'd been so blasé about it, as though ramming a wooden rod through her hand had been no more severe than asking her to demonstrate knitting.

Rats scurried from the alcove behind James' chair, where the computers had been. How they'd ever gotten everything out of here before the authorities carted it off would likely remain a mystery. Then again, perhaps they didn't. He had influence everywhere, it seemed. Maybe the police had been the ones to do the moving for them.

She felt foolish, carrying the datapads and stuffed animals from the bowels of a ruined nuclear power plant. The combined value of her armload was under three hundred credits. Why had she risked detection to retrieve things so easily replaced?

I suppose I missed this place. Five years was a long time to live in the same digs, even if it was a shithole.

FOLLOWING A LONG SHOWER, ANNA DONNED A KNEE-LENGTH VIOLET SLEEP shirt and flopped on the floor at the foot of the king-sized Comforgel pad. As alien as the black zone corporate campus felt, it was an order of magnitude more posh than the power station. She clutched a stuffed green dinosaur with a stubby yellow horn to her chest while staring at her NetMini on the carpet at her left. It had been a few years since she'd spoken to Faye and at least six months since she'd tried to call Penny. The last time she'd seen her best friend on the Vid, it felt like looking at a complete stranger. Penny seemed to remember her, but the conversation rambled as if she spoke to someone she'd gone to school with twenty years ago and hadn't seen since, not someone who'd spent many harrowing years on the streets at her side.

Of course, what did Penny care now? She had a cushy job with the university. She'd moved out of Coventry tower to a proper apartment in the heart of London, and even Spawny seemed to have scrubbed up.

Staring at the NetMini wouldn't make it call anyone.

At the sense of not being alone, Anna cringed to the side, using her body to conceal the stuffed hybrid dinosaur/unicorn.

"Oi, sorry. Catch ya flickin' the bean?"

Aurora.

Anna went florid crimson. She wasn't sure what would be more embarrassing, getting caught touching herself or hugging a stuffed animal.

"Oh, just a plush." Aurora laughed. "The way you flinched, I thought you were four fingers in."

"Must you?" Anna snapped. She slammed the toy to the floor and crossed her arms.

"Oh, are you having a slumber party?" Aurora padded over, standing toe to toe. "We could paint each others's nails!"

"Stop."

"No, really." Aurora crouched, reaching for Anna's foot. "You've got none on."

Anna glared at the wall. Aurora's attempt at cheering her up only reminded her of a life she'd never had. "What do you want?"

"Testy. Well, I'd be that way too if I rooted for Manchester."

"Hmm." Anna picked her eye with her middle finger. "What's the occasion? I've seen you twice in three days and both times you have clothes on."

"Oh." Aurora waved dismissively at the empty desk on the far side of the room. "James thinks it's indecent with all the small ones around."

Anna made a 'gee, you think?' face.

"The match is about to come on. Thought you'd care to watch it." Aurora tilted her head, stooping to the side until her shin-length blonde hair touched the floor. She reached forward and pinched Anna's cheek. "Who's a dreary Daisy?"

"Will you stop?" Anna yelled. "For fuck's sake, I'm not six."

Aurora fixed her with a stare and tapped one foot. "Says the wee lass curled up 'round a plush."

Two minutes later, Anna sighed. "Do you think we're doing the right thing?"

"What, watching Manchester lose?"

"Fuck you."

"Won't James get jealous?"

"You're incorrigible!"

"I know." Aurora winked. "Offer stands if you change your mind. It'd be a thrill if you shocked my naughty bits a little while—"

"Stop. I know you're not serious." Anna slid her heels in close and rested her chin on her knees. "I mean with the whole people smuggling thing and leaving Earth."

Aurora sashayed around and sat on the bed behind her, one foot on either side. "You know"—she massaged Anna's neck and shoulders—"I've got an enormous strap-on that says I might be serious."

Anna giggled. "Stop it."

"You're so tense. Relax." Aurora kept quiet for a moment. "I think James has honorable intentions. Those people would have been far worse off had he not arranged for them to be smuggled out."

Kneading hands threatened to put Anna to sleep right there on the floor. "Why the cargo boxes? Those Syndicate bastards left two children in handcuffs for weeks, shipping them from Mexico to Europe and back. And not just cuffs, they had them trussed up like spree killers pumped full of Lace." She fumed, making the lights flicker. "Why didn't they send them straight here? Why all the clandestine nonsense? It's not like this country has a problem with immigrants. They *want* to steal all the people they can from the ACC."

"James doesn't want the authorities picking up on a large influx of psionics." Aurora worked the massage down over Anna's shoulders onto her arms. "They'd suspect something was up."

Anna thought about the bedraggled refugees, wondering how much of their suffering had been because of James. *Oh, get off it. So they had a 'orrible boat ride. If not for him, they'd be dead.* The roaming massage derailed Anna's train of thought. "Lauren?"

"Yes?"

"That's my breast you're squeezing."

"I'm well aware of that, dear. Cute little things you've got. Shall I get the toy? It's a real stonker."

Anna grabbed her friend's wrist and guided the hand back to her shoulder. "Are you trying to kill James? Do you've any idea what he'd do if he walked in on *that?*"

Aurora laughed. "You know, to get a picture of his face it would almost be worth going through with it. He is getting old, though; it might be too much for his heart."

"You're awful. He's not *that* old." Anna chuckled into a wistful sigh. "Do they all really think I killed her?"

"I doubt it. Besides, they're more afraid of me than you."

Anna leaned back, gazing up at the onyx-eyed face hovering over her. She couldn't remember when hearing a voice but never seeing the woman's lips move had stopped unnerving her. "When we leave Earth, who will help the ones stuck in those places? I doubt we'll be able to smuggle them into space."

"There's no point in worrying about that." Aurora rolled off the bed, skipping toward the door. "So, coming to watch the match?"

9

LEAD ME TO TEMPTATION

Kate

Avast expanse of desert scrub raced past the window. Kate fixated on the stretched shadow the hovercar left on the ground forty meters below, imagining it a patch of liquid slithering over every rock and bush that zipped by. She almost forgot she stared at an ultra-high-resolution display on the inside of a two-inch thick armored panel and not a window. Every so often, the outside world faltered with lines of static. David didn't notice it, but Kate twitched each time it flashed. She would have preferred more sleep; five hours spent trying to track down Aaron Pryce had proved a massive waste of time. His records checked out. He *had* killed several Division 0 personnel, in a violent telekinetic blast that also inflicted significant damage to the medical facility, and a pickup warrant had been issued for him along with an extreme caution warning.

She leaned away from the door, sliding her hand onto his leg.

Tactical Officer David Ahmed shot her a startled look and chuckled before directing his attention forward. "What's got you so nervous? I thought you got over your fear of flying."

"It's not the flying that bothers me, it's the sudden stopping."

The latest generation video hardware in the driver side door recreated the sunlight outside so well it made her squint, even as it highlighted his chiseled nose and lean cheekbones. If she didn't know better, she'd swear it felt warm on her face.

"We're not going to crash." He glanced at the side for a second. "We're only doing 310. Even if the collision avoidance circuitry somehow failed and allowed the car to go straight into the ground at our current speed, the high-impact survival system would protect us."

"Oh, that's reassuring. So we don't die on impact, our unconscious bodies suffocate in a car full of hard foam."

He glanced at her with a fading smile. "Now you're starting to worry me."

She folded her hands in her lap. "You've heard the stories about machines failing out here, haven't you?"

"Oh, is that it?" His grin returned. "Some presence out here hates technology and makes it fail? I wouldn't worry too much about that. It's just a bunch of scary stories the artifact hunters circulate to scare competition away. The fewer people coming out here, the more they can sell their junk for."

Three thin bands of static climbed Kate's window. She watched them scroll up and disappear at the top. Foulness seeped into her memory, the stink of the decrepit priest's breath.

"You're genuinely scared." He flicked on the autopilot and took her hand. "What is it? Is there something out there?"

"Static on the window."

David squeezed her hand. "It's probably interference from a radiation cloud. There were some small-scale nukes used in the war."

"I've met him... *it*." Kate looked down at his hand. "It's real. Whatever it is feeds on hate and suffering. It doesn't want people to leave. I think it... possessed me or something the first time I went to Querq. I don't remember much but being filled with hatred. I wanted to kill everything... especially Althea. That... *thing* hates her for some reason."

"You shouldn't hold on to so much guilt. It was an external influence."

Kate cocked an eyebrow at him, almost smiling. "An external influence you just said doesn't exist."

He tapped his boot.

She wondered if getting into a relationship with an empath would prove to be a blessing or make for many infuriating arguments. The widening grin still hovering at the edge of her vision brightened her mood.

"You're worried it'll happen again."

"Yeah." She let her head fall back against the seat. "If it doesn't kill us in a crash first."

He gripped both control sticks, easing their speed down to a lazy 250 mph and gliding nearer to the ground. "I'll keep you close. If I feel anything happening to your emotional state, I'll warn you." He looked her in the eye. "Remember, external influence on emotion is all about feeling. You can overwhelm it with rational thought. Remind yourself over and over that something is *forcing* you to feel a certain way, and you can fight it off."

"Okay." Kate scooted to her left as far as she could, and leaned over the center console to rest her head on his arm. The position wound up awkward, but not intolerable. Whoever designed patrol craft to be half again the width of a standard car obviously never had a romantic interest in their partner.

"This is why they don't let couples ride on duty together."

"Mmm." She rubbed her head into his shoulder like a cat. "Good thing we're off duty."

She gazed out at the onrushing terrain, well aware her lack of worry was David's doing—and didn't care.

⁂

David's voice nudged her awake. "You might want to sit up; we're about to land."

"Right when the dream was getting good," she muttered underneath a yawn as she righted herself in the seat and stretched.

Querq raced toward them, a patch of life and color among the scar of an ancient city. He slowed, lining up on a path to the square at the center of town. From this height, the remnants of the statue in the courtyard looked like a broken toy soldier, one of those little green men snapped off its base, leaving half of one leg standing. A pair of prewar pickup trucks, with machine guns mounted in the beds, flanked it on either side.

He tapped a button on the console, and mechanical whirring vibrated the patrol craft. Ground wheels extended from behind their protective shrouds, which retracted out of sight. The mechanical whine stopped with a near-simultaneous *clunk* as all four locked into place. David circled once and brought the car to a midair standstill before easing it straight down onto the tires. A blast of air from their landing knocked a red, plastic cup off the broken stone leg.

Kate's contentment evaporated at the sight of empty walls and uninhabited streets. No signs of activity existed anywhere. "David? Something's wrong. Where is everyone?"

He shut down the drive system and hit the door release, ducking under the rising gull wing to get out faster. In her rush to follow him, she tripped over one of the two-inch thick power cables spider-webbed throughout the courtyard and landed on all fours. Under one of the old trucks, three grown men huddled together weeping like boys with a monster in their closet.

"That's strange," said David. "I wonder where they went."

"Found some." Kate sat back on her boot heels, gesturing at the truck. "This looks like your job. I think they're afraid of the patrol craft."

The men calmed and glanced at each other. As if under a silent pact never to speak of what happened, they crawled out, recovered their rifles, and stood. Kate, still kneeling, looked from them to David as he walked over. Along the wall, men and women emerged from hiding places and went about their business as though nothing had happened. The distant wails of terrified children rose into the air, crying out for mommy or daddy.

"Or, maybe not." Kate accepted David's hand and let him pull her upright. "Did you do that?"

"No," he whispered. "They snapped out of it on their own."

Behind them, several townspeople emerged from their homes. Some carried laundry on their way to the creek bed. Others chatted with neighbors. Some collected panic-stricken kids. Various exchanges along the lines of "What's wrong?" and "I dunno!" repeated with different families.

"Think it's Althea?" asked Kate. "Did she do this?"

David exhaled, raising both eyebrows. "If there's an empath capable of fear-bombing an entire town, it would be her. If she did, we'd better keep a lid on it. If Burckhardt finds out she can make six hundred people shit their pants at once, he'd want to weaponize her."

Kate laughed, despite feeling guilty about doing so. "Why are the little ones still scared?"

"They're scared because they don't know why they were scared. Everyone else is brushing it off out of embarrassment." He winked at her. "What happens in Vegas..."

"What?"

"Never mind. I watch a lot of old videos."

She took his hand, pulling him along down the nearest street. "We should find her."

"It's probably nothing," David said. "Some other kid probably snuck up and startled her and it radiated."

"How can you be so sure of that?"

"It's not continuous. The telempathic effect seems like a radiant burst. Quick, instantaneous, and already over. If she was in danger, it would still be happening."

"She could also be hurt." An odd sense of protectiveness took root in her mind. She *had* to make sure Althea didn't need help.

Kate jogged up to a light run, flashing reassuring smiles at disoriented townspeople. A few blocks later, a streak of white darting down an alley caught her eye. Kate sprinted after it, entering a narrow passageway packed with trashcans laden with plumbing scraps and one unimpressed black goat. She took a hard left at the end, exiting to a wider street where a handful of townspeople and more goats wandered about with no sense of urgency. The clattering of metal behind her announced David's ungainly encounter with the junk.

Three blocks to the left, Althea darted out of one alley, zoomed across the street, and disappeared into another.

"Althea!" yelled Kate.

The girl backpedaled into view and stared in her direction. As soon as they made eye contact, an overwhelming sense of gratitude washed over her. Her mysterious need to protect the child swelled. Kate waved, beckoning her closer, and shut her eyes. *She did something to me. Why do I want to twist the head off whoever scared her?*

"Kate." The child's voice sounded nearby.

Her eyes snapped open. Althea had approached close enough to hug, standing with her arms at her sides. Clean tear trails marked her otherwise dust-covered face, though she seemed more worried than sad. Kate couldn't resist the urge to embrace her, as though she'd been reunited with a long absent daughter.

"Are you okay?" asked David, hand on Kate's back. "That doesn't feel natural."

"I'm sorry." Althea's voice sounded meek and mousy. "I don't know what I did."

Kate's mood leveled off. She let go and wiped her eyes. "I'm glad you're okay."

David looked back and forth between them for a moment, tapping his chin.

Althea's calm broke to worry. "Have you seen Den?"

"No, kiddo, I haven't." Kate looked the girl up and down, relieved at no sign of injury. "Did something happen to you?"

"The Many was here."

"What?" asked Kate.

"Umm, Aurora called him the sen-shins." She stared at the ground. "In the garden."

David looked confused.

Sentience, Kate said, telepathically to David. *I told you it's real.* "What did it want?"

"He is scared I want to kill him." Althea twisted her big toe into the dirt. "He lied. He says we help each other. He doesn't help; he hurts. I'm afraid he's hurt Den."

"This sentience," said David, "did he attack you?"

"He showed me scary things. War machines in the air dropping fire, and people dying." Althea looked up at him. "It makes him angry that I am happy."

David gave Kate a knowing look.

"Maybe I shouldn't be here?" Kate shivered, finding the thought of separation from Althea as painful as it was strange. "He fed on my rage, wanted me to be the queen of his hell." She looked at her hands. "My power's only good for hurting people."

"That's not true." David grinned. "You can put fire out as easily as start it... you could be Querq's fire brigade."

"Funny." She poked him in the side, but couldn't help smiling.

Althea leaned up and put a hand on Kate's cheek. "You don't have the angry anymore. He cannot reach you."

She did something to you similar to what she did to that big guy, Shepherd. From what I understand, he tried to kill her too. It's a lingering telempathic imprint, something we haven't ever seen before. I'm not strong enough to dislodge it, but you don't seem to mind.

David's voice in her mind sent warm tingles down her back. Coupled with the emotion she felt from Althea's touch, it brought tears of happiness.

"Why are you crying?" Althea tilted her head. "You give off happy."

"Sometimes that happens." Kate sniffled and gathered herself. "I don't want to be a risk."

Althea let her arm fall to her side and smiled. "You are not alone anymore. The bad man has nothing to hold you with."

"Thea?" called a young woman over a row of houses.

The child faced the direction of the voice, stood on tiptoe, and yelled, "I'm here!"

A girl of about sixteen, with long black hair and dark skin, rushed out from an alley. Dirt and mud spattered her coral-orange dress and bare legs. Two dandelions fell out from behind her ear as she ran over and wrapped her arms around Althea.

"I thought something happened to you. Everyone went crazy for a minute." The older girl glared at Kate. "What do these people want?"

Althea shot a deliberate look at the girl. The teen's glower softened as a shift in her expression gave away a telepathic conversation. "This is my sister, Karina. This is—"

"I know who she is. She tried to hurt you. Now she is a police? She is on the wrong side of the cage."

"Karina!" Althea poked her sister in the side. "It was the Many. I mended the hurt. She is our friend now."

Kate squeezed her hands into fists, feeling like the orb of a Gee-ball game. The false priest had manipulated her emotions one way, Althea the other. El Tío, while by no means mystical, had pulled her strings to work her like a puppet as well. She had always been someone else's pawn, a reed bent in the wind to please the people around her. At six, she had burned the little wooden blocks to make the men in white coats smile. At sixteen, she had burned living people to make El Tío happy.

Would she ever be in control of her own life?

Althea's frail arms encircled her with a hug, startling her out of her inner debate. "Don't be sad. Karina wants to protect me."

A lump in Kate's throat wouldn't let her speak, so she patted the girl on the back and offered an apologetic glance to Karina. The older girl's hostility had weakened to suspicion, but trust still seemed a ways off.

Althea looked up at her with a smile weighed down by worry. She took Karina's hand and they walked off together.

"So," said David. "Crisis averted. Whatever that... sentience made her see hit her hard enough that she radiated her fear over Querq."

"You're not worried about the boy?"

"I doubt he's in danger. The girl is mildly clairvoyant. I don't think she could be so calm if something threatened him; worry would gnaw at her and not let go. At least, from what I understand about clairvoyants with strong emotional ties."

Kate stared eastward at the ruins of the Old City, squinting against the breeze. The dark spaces within the crumbling ancient high-rises seemed to gaze back at her. "I hope you're right."

"Of course I'm right." He leaned in and kissed her on the lips. "I'm psychic."

10

EVERYONE'S EYES ARE BLUE

Aaron

Sleep had been fitful on a bed of sofa cushions in a room once used as some middle manager's office on the seventh floor. Iliana's late night visit in a tank top and red panties hadn't helped Aaron sleep. She'd brought him some blankets and offered to keep him warm. He wondered what had come over him, not jumping at the chance to take the nineteen-year-old sylph up on her offer.

Aaron couldn't stop thinking of Anna, despite her still-obvious attachment to Archon. Perhaps the quiet desperation in Iliana's eyes had gotten to him, the barely-contained fear that at any moment the military would find them. Living seconds away from an imagined death tended to loosen one's knickers. The way he'd tried to soothe the little girl hiding in the vent endeared him to her.

Aaron rubbed the crumbs from his eyes and stared in a daze at the decomposing, grey drop ceiling. He almost remembered saying she didn't have to have sex with him to make him like her. She'd gone wide-eyed at that and flopped down next to him, chatting about her life growing up in the region around Prypiat, Russia. Her family had been part of an experiment; her parents hadn't even met before they were assigned to each other and forced to have four children.

Half-awake, Aaron retained bits and pieces of the story: soldiers bothering them at all hours with strange, painful injections, dragging her and her siblings off in the middle of the night, and testing for evidence of psionic ability. The eldest, Leonid, took to it and had turned into a little drill sergeant by the age of twelve. When the other three decided to run away, he almost got them arrested. Aaron didn't know if she'd embellished her stories of crawling through the sewers of a Russian city with an assault rifle as a nine-year-old for pity, or if she'd needed to open up to someone.

He didn't bother looking into her thoughts last night, and she'd gone by the time he awoke.

After a stretch, he gave up on going back to sleep and got up. Since his 'apartment' consisted of a one-room office without a bathroom, he stumbled down the hall outside to the men's. Someone, likely the same people responsible for the working elevators, had installed a portable autoshower in one of the stalls. He'd have to put on the same two-day-worn suit afterward, but he couldn't resist the lure of hot water and soap.

AARON FOLLOWED HIS NOSE INTO THE LOBBY OF THE WEST TOWER, AMID THE tent city housing most of the psionics Archon had collected. More than half looked younger than eighteen, and the youngest of them either stared shell-shocked at the walls or clustered in small groups speaking languages other than English. Most of the older teens seemed local and wore tattered jackets with spray-painted, lopsided capital As on their backs. He'd come to realize they all referred to themselves as 'The Awakened,' essentially a gang. They seemed able to use the word interchangeably referring to either the collective or to an individual of greater power. The teens seemed to know the intended meaning—the gang or someone like him—at an instinctual level he couldn't quite grasp.

Maybe I'm just too old.

People stared at him as he stumbled over to a line waiting by where a woman and two men cooked on portable hot plates. He didn't bother trying to figure out how they had obtained cases of expensive vat-grown chicken, fish, and hydroponic vegetables. Chances are, the room held at least a half-dozen suggestives, likely far more than that.

"It is!" squeaked a young girl.

Aaron glanced in the direction of further squealing, cocking an eyebrow at a pair of tween girls clinging to each other and pointing at him. Their matching outfits screamed British schoolgirl.

"Oh, bloody hell." He tried not to make eye contact.

The pair rushed over, both clutching their NetMinis, one pink and one white, to their chests. He forced a weak smile, a bit embarrassed at all the attention after so long, especially with everyone in the room staring at him. Aside from the girls, everyone else looked confused and wary. They wore rumpled uniforms: stained white shirts, navy skirts and coats with the same red shield on the breast pocket. A rather unpleasant odor wafted from their clothes. That both girls had attended the same private school raised an inkling of suspicion in the back of his mind. He wondered how long the CSB had been monitoring them, or if they had a hand in their existence—as with Anna.

"Aaron Pryce?" asked the younger one. "I'm Meredith. I'm a massive Arsenal fan!"

"Yes, yes," chirped the other. "I'm..." Her eyes fluttered.

"Oh, please don't faint." Aaron smiled and steadied her with a hand on the shoulder.

"Lucy," the older girl whispered, shaking.

"T'was such a kick in the bollocks about your leg," said Meredith.

Aaron chuckled. "Were you even old enough to watch a match when I last played?"

Meredith looked downcast. Plates and small objects on the table around the cooks rattled. "Mum would always have it on. I wanna go home."

"We can't!" whispered Lucy. "They'll lock us away."

Aaron glanced at the imminent poltergeist. "Telekinetic, what?"

"Aye." Meredith sniffled.

"Me, too." Aaron grinned at her.

"Really?" Meredith's face lit up.

Lucy did the math right away; her mouth hung open.

He winked at her. "Just a little nudge 'ere and there."

"Can we 'ave your siggie?" Meredith bounced up and down, holding her NetMini up.

Aaron fished his device out of his pocket, opening an app he hadn't touched in years. He waved it past the kids' handhelds and all three of them chirped with the transfer of a digital autograph. The girls' devices played a ten-second version of 'God Save the King' in stereo. They gripped them tight to their chests and squealed again before scurrying back to where they had been sitting.

The line moved, leaving him on the opposite side of a folding table from a short, black man with a shaved head who nudged three hunks of chicken around a pan. Seasonings had left the meat somewhere between orange and brown, studded with tiny fragments of leaves and garlic.

"Something wrong?" asked Aaron, at the man's perplexed look.

"Why you not eating with th' others like ya?" His accent had a trace of French.

"Others like..." It dawned on him he meant Awakened. "Oh, right... I wasn't aware we had separate kitchens." He figured *that* the more likely reason everyone had been staring at him. A big shot associating with the little people. "Is it a problem?"

"No, sir. Just unexpected." The man handed him a plate: chicken, something green, and sliced yams. "You are welcome here. A nice change."

Aaron fought the urge to roll his eyes at the thought of Archon. "I'm not so puffed up."

Nervous chuckles spread out among those close enough to hear. Aaron took his food and wandered to the nearest open table, sitting opposite a pair of well-tanned men in ragged clothes who burst into rapid conversation in Arabic, of which he picked out his name and 'Frictionless.' After a few minutes, they got their excitement under control and switched to weak English. The men preferred to cheer for the Iraq National team, though due to having different leagues, they wound up not being direct rivals. The men respected his career, feeling honored to be in the presence of a 'big celebrity' and managed a pleasant—though frustratingly slow—conversation about the nuances of the game.

After eating, Aaron spent the next hour and change wandering around, getting a look at the layout of the facility. The west building housed non-Awakened psionics, mostly the younger ones, as well as a small number of ungifted relatives or friends who'd refused to be separated. The first two floors of the central tower were home to the gang members—Aaron couldn't help but think of them in that way—who had been with Archon the longest. They made up the bulk of the 'security team,' and all but two looked old enough to vote. One man sat in the corner of the grand lobby, between a pair of plastic bamboo plants in four-foot tall onyx vases. He looked like he'd worn the same white suit and black dress shirt for months. Shaggy black hair hung down to his belt, and he had the vacant stare of an avant-garde rock star who'd hit the Nightcandy a bit too hard and couldn't come back from his high.

Aaron drifted in the direction of flashing light, crossing the lobby to lean against the wall by the door to an old conference room. A giant table with rounded ends, large enough for thirty people, lay covered with dozens of net decks and terminals. At least a hundred holo-panels floated above it, varying in size and angle as if an explosion of light tiles had frozen in time. The operators were young, ranging from eleven to fifteen, except for three twenty-something men at the far end of the table who appeared to be in charge of the 'tech team.' None of them had plugged in via wires. A few of the kids used helmets, though most linked to the hardware by touch, psionic communication between brain and machine.

Most of the screens showed star charts and database entries listing the attributes of various colonized worlds. He watched them scout potential new homes for a while, mesmerized by the shifting screens full of high-resolution images depicting colorful planets. The biggest holographic display threw off enough light to tint the walls. Deep azure saturated the conference room as an enormous water-covered planet raced forward to fill the forty-inch panel.

He shifted out of the way of a grumbling teenaged girl carrying a large canister of self-heating soup in one hand and a spoon in the other. Her head wagged about to music pumped into her skull via earbuds, and she sang along in either Korean or Chinese. Aaron rolled flat against the wall to let her pass. She went over to the catatonic man, sat cross-legged next to him, and squeezed a button on the side of the metal cylinder. Twenty seconds later, the smell of chicken and mushrooms reached him.

Aaron raised an eyebrow as the girl removed her buds and put them in the man's ears. She set the soup on the floor with the spoon balanced on top and placed one of his hands on the bare skin of her thigh between a skirt and red-ringed leggings. After a moment, the girl faded into a trance and the man blinked and looked around.

He took the canister, opened it, and spooned soup into his mouth with a jerky, robotic motion that fit the image of a horror-vid zombie. Aaron wandered closer, hands tucked in his pants pockets, and an amused smirk on his face. Two sets of surface thoughts dwelled in the man's mind: a male presence stuck in an endless loop of crippling sadness, and a chipper female voice mentally singing along with the lyrics. The man seemed aware of the sound but too depressed to care about it.

"Hey," moaned the man. "You're that new guy, right?"

Considering the despondent sod looked like a burned out British glam-rocker, Aaron assumed by the Asian accent, the girl 'drove.'

"Aye. I'm Aaron. What happened to this poor bastard?"

"Little miss angel." Soup dribbled down his chin. "She dropped some kinda big-ass sadbomb on Donnie. Archon tried to fix him, but he went from crying his eyes out twenty-four damn hours a day to staring into space in silence. Too bad Pixie killed her for being a little bitch, woulda been nice if she could unfuck him. I'm *so* done with making him eat."

Aaron exhaled. "That's a neat trick."

"Astral projection, not a big deal. Lucky me I'm the only one here who can do it. 'Cept the queen of the freak show, and this is below her." Donnie jammed the spoon into his nose. "Dammit, Donnie, eat already. Possessing people is such a pain in the ass. They should make fuckin' Aurora do this. She wears people like clothes. So easy for her."

"You sound jealous."

"You're not the one sitting in someone else's loaded adult diaper."

Aaron winced. "A fair point. Maybe Aurora could ask her to fix him. Oh, by the by, Pixie didn't kill that sprog."

"Yeah, right."

"She rather saved my scrawny ass the other day." Aaron rubbed his thigh.

"No shit?" Donnie attempted to shrug. "For someone supposed to be so sweet and innocent, she worse than killed him."

Aaron tapped his chin. "Now what would make her do that?"

"The hell should I know?" Donnie shrugged again. Another spoonful missed his mouth.

"Telempathy isn't my thing, sorry." An unpleasant thought made him snarl. "Maybe that other bitch could help, only problem being she doesn't *help* anyone."

"The one you wanna kill?" Donnie gave up on the spoon and drank from the canister. After a heavy gulp, he moaned. "Hot, ain't it? Stop fucking fighting me then, asshole."

"You know about that?" Aaron chuckled.

"Everyone knows about that, and how you're some kinda walking apocalypse so we're not s'posed to do anything to your head."

"Yeah, well…" Aaron sighed. "We all have our problems."

Motion from the corner of his eye drew his gaze to the front door. Melissa emerged from an interior hall and stomped across the room, arms folded tight across her jacket, head down, and boots clomping. Everyone got quiet as she bee-lined for the entrance.

"I'd say talkin' to Talis about his problem is better than sittin' in shite, but I'm not so sure. Either way, your choice." Aaron waved. "Nice meetin' ya, but I gotta run."

He rushed to the doors, jumping through the glass-less metal frame into a strong, cold breeze outside. Melissa had stopped at the corner of the building, staring into the west tower at the tent city. She hovered at the edge as if afraid to get close enough for anyone inside to notice her. Aaron jogged to a halt about ten paces away, letting his feet land loud enough to announce his approach.

She glanced over her shoulder at him; her initial casual dismissal became a double take and a glare when she recognized him.

"What do you want? Go away."

He stuffed his hands in his pockets and took a few steps closer, summoning his most disarming smile. "I wanted to apologize for last night. I didn't mean to patronize you. Figured you'd look better to your friends that way."

"I don't want your fuckin' pity." She ran around the corner, trailed by a waterfall of dark, curly hair.

Aaron chased her over a series of yellowing spots from a row of exterior lights protruding from the second story. She kept going past the far end of the building, darting across the false grass in the 'park' area in the south-central part of the corporate campus. Her foot caught on the lip of the dried out reflecting pool, but she spared herself a fall with a telekinetic push and wound up pulling a superhero flight to the other side. Aaron vaulted the edge, shoes clanking over brown metal patterned with silt.

The girl spun around, jogging backward long enough to lift and throw a chunk of stone in his general direction. Shiny black marble from what had once been a field of artistic obelisks careened over his head and thudded into the ground. It seemed a deliberate miss to distract. He continued pursuing as she sprinted off, heading for the wreckage of an old parking deck, collapsed decades ago.

"Melissa, wait," he yelled.

She ducked around the back end of a crushed police hovercar, past shattered pieces of metal in the ghastly likeness of human body parts. Aaron followed, careful not to step on anything sharp as he made his way past the car and into a maze of smashed vehicles and the toppled remnants of the parking deck.

He paused where a metal torso and arm protruded from under a concrete slab, crushed into the front end of a six-wheeled military transport. The cyborg's skull, stark white bone, had blackened in trails down the front where fluids had long ago leaked from the eyes, nose, and mouth. Narrow rods of dust glowed in light leaking from bullet holes in the floor of a flipped police car. Her fleeing shadow disrupted similar rays at the far end of a corridor formed by debris.

What the bloody hell am I doing? Aaron slowed to a halt, panting.

Seconds after she cornered at the end, a frightened scream echoed back.

"Bugger." He swallowed his fatigue and ran.

Melissa had stopped ten feet from the turn, hands clasped over her face and trembling, her gaze locked upon a massive human form forged from black plastisteel. Gothic pauldrons flanked a blood-red skull with luminous green eyes. The figure looked like a techno-nightmare reconstruction of a medieval knight that likely would have stood fourteen feet tall had he not been sheared in half at the waist. Dark ichor stained the dusty metal ground, a starburst-shaped blotch spread outward from the torso. The man had been dead for at least fifty years, but the cybernetic eyes seemed to hold more than simple electronic light. In the odd way that psionics tended to do, Aaron *felt* like the thing still watched them.

Aaron's shoe scuffed over grit as he stopped, startling another scream out of Melissa. She stared at him, lost to a momentary convulsion, and gasped.

"T-tell me that was you."

He leaned on a hunk of shattered concrete covered in tire skid marks, trying to catch his breath. "What's that?"

"You made that… that… *thing* move." She pointed at the huge cyborg.

"Sorry, luv. You're either seein' things or it's a ghost."

She whimpered, glanced at the corpse, and eyed the narrow space between Aaron and the wall. "It's dead."

"Precisely why there'd be a ghost. I didn't believe in that sort of thing either till I started reading some of the files my former compatriots kept." Aaron shoved away from the slab and stood in the center of the only way out of the dead-end alcove. "I reckon there's probably quite a few of them, and if the condition of the bodies is any clue, they're probably rather cheesed off."

"That's not funny." She risked a step closer to him. "That thing moved."

Given the eerie feeling in this place, Aaron wouldn't put it past truth. "Stop running?"

She glared defiance at him for a moment before a creak of metal made her yelp and jump.

Aaron looked away from the dead cyborg. Even he thought the skull had tilted. "Probably the wind, luv. Maybe there's still a bit of charge in the power cell."

She edged closer. "Why are you chasing me? You like little girls or something? Sorry asshole, I don't put out on the first date."

Her attempt to sound accusatory struck him as sad. "You know what?" He shrugged. "I honestly don't have a clue. I seem to keep stumbling on people who need help. What are you doing here?"

"Running away from you." She folded her arms, trying to look tough, but another creak from the old 'borg left her shivering.

Aaron didn't much care for it staring at him either. "I mean here." He waved at everything. "With Professor Tweedbeard."

Melissa let out an involuntary giggle. "Are you a cop? No bullshit."

Aaron took his wife's nameplate out of his pocket. "I haven't entirely decided yet, to be honest."

"What's that?"

"All I've got left of me wife." He held it out to her.

The girl seemed to lower her guard and moved close enough to read it. "Allison?"

"Aye." He let his arm fall limp at his side. "Your boss' new pet made me... uhh... yeah."

"You don't gotta say it. Sorry." She leaned against him, several handguns under her coat obvious as hard lumps. A shiver rattled her as a labored metallic squeak came from the hulk. "I swear that thing is fucking moving. Can we, like, go somewhere else?"

"What are you doing here?" Aaron backed up, letting her out of the dead end. She scurried around the corner away from the ghoulish sculpture. "Your parents were well off, weren't they?"

"Fuck 'em." She scowled. "They threw me out 'cause I was a freak that kept calling poltergeists. Dumbasses thought it was ghosts."

"Runaway subconscious manifestations are pretty common among telekinetics during hormonal changes."

"You still sound like a damn cop." She jabbed him the side.

He leaned on a bent pole wrapped in chain link fence, dotted with holes showing signs of laser melting. "Talis is Awakened. I couldn't resist her suggestion. Something broke in my head when I shot my wife. Now, the bean doesn't react well to being poked. Department telepath killed himself when he pushed it too hard."

"Fuck…" Melissa looked up at him. "You killed a cop?"

"Technically he killed himself, but yeah… a couple. They're not too happy with me right now."

She sat on a coffin-sized chunk of scorched concrete studded with yellow reflectors. "They kept trying to abandon me at the dorm. I hated it there. It was like prison… showering with other people, forced schedule, locked in our rooms at night."

"Bollocks. They don't lock the doors."

Melissa blushed. "They do when you, uhh… do bad shit."

The sound of groaning metal made them both jump and stare at the corner, expecting the legless titan to drag itself after them. After a moment of tense silence, she breathed into her hands and shivered.

"So you ran away?"

"Yeah." She kicked her heels against the block. "Got into a gang, got pretty wrecked on SoCal." Her face scrunched up as if she were about to cry. "That was good shit. I want more. I didn't think about anything but happy."

"People die on that junk." He moved to sit next to her and pulled the hair off her face. The corners of her eyes had turned red. "You're what, fifteen? You've got too much life to throw away."

Melissa drew her knees up to her face, hooking her boot heels on the edge. "I was so happy. I can't even explain it. Nothing mattered. When I was tripping, everyone had long, silky blonde hair and bright blue eyes like a Jamaican ocean. There was this music, too. Always, music, faint in the background. I couldn't tell you what song, but it was always there." She rocked side to side, humming. "No parents, no laws, no pain. I was happy and mellow all the time. I miss it so bad. They detoxed me, but I'd still kill someone to get more."

"It's hard to find that stuff. They caught the only guy making it. Fascinating really. He combined a synthetic hallucinogen with clever short-life nanobots programmed to stimulate certain regions of the brain to create specific hallucinations and emotions."

"Dr. Kushing thought the world was circling the drain. He wanted to take away the pain before we went down."

"You knew him?"

She shrugged. "I helped him sell the shit." Five handguns floated out of her jacket and hovered in the air around her. "Mostly I played guard." The weapons glided back to their holsters. "I think I shot some people, too, but I didn't mean it. I was hallucinating."

Melissa hid her face behind her knees and shivered.

Aaron glanced at her surface thoughts; hazy memories played out of her experiencing a pastel-colored reality filled with smiling blue-eyed, blonde people straight out of an idealized suburban utopia. The tenor of the scene changed without warning. Blithe happiness gave way to dread as black blood seeped from the walls and bubbled out of storm drains. All the smiling people hunched forward, becoming a legion of shadow-faced figures with glowing eyes and the same perfect blonde hair. Melissa ran, but couldn't get away from them. The bright flash and scream startled away his telepathic link.

"Oy, that looked like a bad trip."

She nodded, sniffling. "When I woke up, I saw so much blood. I ran away. I don't remember much. I was all kinds of fucked up."

"Withdrawal."

"No shit." She smirked at him. "Aurora found me. Said I was Awakened and they wanted me."

"So you came here?"

Melissa stared at him, mouth open. "Have you seen that bitch?"

"Aye." Aaron grinned.

"Fuck, no. She's freaky. I ran home." She got quiet. Aaron waited for a few minutes, until she eventually continued, albeit with a begrudging expression. "Mom and Dad weren't too happy to see me, but they let me stay. I was shitting bricks about what happened, sick from the drugs. You know, I actually did whatever they told me to do like the perfect little preppie daughter they wanted. It was nice for a little while... I almost thought they loved me." She made a gagging face. "Fuckers kicked me out a week later, saying I was too dangerous to be around. Mom was afraid she'd 'catch the psionics' and Dad thought I would kill him the next time we argued."

She spent a few minutes trying not to cry and failing.

"Melissa..."

"Fuck them. They don't want me."

Aaron squinted into the smog overhead, eyes drawn to glowing patches where advert bots flew in the distance. Her story sounded all too familiar and more than a little suspicious.

"You sure you're all right?"

"Yeah." She wiped her face. "Tell anyone I cried and I'll rip your nuts off."

"Not a soul." He held up his hand as if being sworn in. "I promise."

11

THE PRESENCE

Mamoru

F ar above in the sky, a hawk's cry broke the silent veil of dreamless sleep. A steady but mild wind blew over Mamoru from the right side. He drew a deep breath, holding the flavor of Badlands dust in his nostrils for a minute before letting it out. His fingers squeezed the handle of the vibro-katana at his hip, its presence assuring him all remained right with his world.

Mamoru sat up and squinted at the shimmering horizon. Everything took on a blue tint, an aftereffect of the sun beating upon his formerly closed eyes. A lone tumbleweed bounced lazily past his boots. He frowned at his once-black coat and pants, which had become closer to light brown with a coating of fine sand. The skeletal remains of Albuquerque darkened the ground to his right, distant enough to where he couldn't differentiate the resettled interior where that *thing* resided from the ruins surrounding it.

The mere thought of it shot a pang of worry down his spine. That the creature resembled an innocent girl caused a sliver of guilt to taint his loathing. It made little sense. He remembered an overwhelming need to destroy the false child, yet at the same time, it seemed wrong to do so. The journey from the city to where he had collapsed had vanished from his memory. Only a trace of mortal dread remained. Looking at the city, even from this distance, made him uneasy.

Thoughts of Sadako brought a sense of peace in knowing she would live, as well as the weight of obligation. Dust lifted from his palm as he studied it, recalling the handshake. He must fulfill the oath he had sworn.

Despite sleeping on the unforgiving earth, nothing ached or cramped, and he stood with ease. He took another great breath and looked over his hands. A sense of power swam through him, beyond anything his chi had ever done. The west called, and he did the only thing he could—he walked.

The desert sands bore the occasional marks of habitation: tire tracks, footprints, large paw prints, and inexplicable serpentine trails that sent his imagination racing with visions of massive centipedes. Over the course of several hours, he sensed the presence of living things nearby, yet only once did he see anything. A hulking figure—part man and part wolf, with bright red eyes and patches of shining chrome grafted into its ebon fur—lingered at the corner of an old trailer barely long enough to make eye contact before it slinked behind cover.

It had bowed its head, ever so slightly, as if deferring to its master.

Feeling as though creatures shadowed his every step, Mamoru marched westward until the sun weakened in the sky. A collection of pre-war houses altered his course into what had been a small town. He walked down the main road, the only paved one in the area, glancing into the broken windows of several dwellings, a tavern, and a pizza shop before halting at an intersection. At the far corner, several children explored what had once been a hardware store.

Six small figures climbed over the rubble of a wall. A Hispanic boy of about thirteen led the way, holding a well-worn spear. A tattered brown skirt lapped at his legs as he stepped with care around snarls of rusting rebar. Behind him crept a blonde girl with a dark tan, carrying an ancient compound bow painted with green camouflage and loaded with a handmade wooden arrow. An electrical cable tied around her waist acted as a belt holding up a threadbare hand towel for a loincloth. Metal bits attached to various leather bangles on her forearms and shins sang in the breeze. Another boy, a year or two younger than the leader, clutched a crowbar as if expecting to have to smash something at any second. His pants appeared to be made of animal hide, with fringe along the sides of the legs.

Another blond, a boy, walked fourth in line, perhaps the archer's brother. Green fatigue pants, cut down to shorts and sized for an adult man, ended in tatters at his shins. He carried a crossbow made of old machine parts welded together, as well as a knife in a sheath tied to each leg.

A second girl of about nine, with sienna skin and ankle-length black hair, followed him. Aside from a coating of dust, she wore only an anklet of polished copper wire and a beaded leather cord around her neck, from which dangled a cluster of small leather pouches. She carried a prewar handgun, which she kept in a two-handed grip aimed down and to the right while navigating the broken concrete. Mamoru found it amusing to watch a child walking like a soldier.

Were the weapon not real, he would have thought her adorable.

The youngest boy lurked at the end of the scouting party, guarding a pair of olive drab duffel bags big enough for him to sleep in. His single item of clothing consisted of a cracked, olive drab, bug-eyed gas mask, from which a metal box dangled down to his stomach on a ridged hose. He looked about seven or eight and had no weapons. Despite the shaded lenses, he noticed Mamoru before any of the others.

After three seconds of staring, the boy urinated where he stood.

Once the stream stopped, he let off a yowl, muffled by the mask, and ran out of sight toward the oldest boy with the spear. The other Scrag children froze in place. All of them—save for the girl with the pistol—trembled. She cautiously stepped to a taller chunk of debris and faced him without fear. The boy with the crowbar hid behind it as if it would protect him. The blonde girl raised her bow, but the one Mamoru assumed to be her brother pulled her arm down.

Mamoru knew they were Scrags—primitive tribal villagers—out scavenging, but did not understand how or why he knew this. That part of him connected to the Akuryō sensed the presence of adults nearby, parents, he assumed, due to the way the gas mask boy kept edging in that direction. The soreness in their feet, the hunger in their bellies, and the terror in their hearts called to him. Something dark and deep within his mind reveled in it, demanding blood, wishing to feast upon the agony of their parents when they found bodies. However, the part of his mind that still existed as Mamoru, separate from the dark spirit, felt pity, and abject horror at the idea of harming children. A battle within his thoughts brought sweat to his brow. He wondered how savage a world would have to be for parents to send kids that young hunting on their own.

Mamoru wanted to protect them, but *he* sought pain.

They are connected to this place like the creatures. The girl who is not afraid senses the Akuryō.

After a moment, the children disappeared into the rubble in search of nooks and crannies too small for a grown raider to chase them. The girl with the pistol remained, standing with her head held high, staring right at him. Small fingers smeared marks like war paint in the dirt on her chest and face. She dipped her fingers in a pouch and added black smudges to the markings. Her whispering voice carried to him on the wind, which he should not have been able to hear from such a distance. Spanish words left her lips, which he did not comprehend, though her intentions came to his mind with clarity: she spoke a sign of reverence and a plea for his favor.

The little girl addressed him as 'He Who Watches,' and acknowledged his mastership of the land. She did not fear what the others had sensed within him. This girl knew, and she bowed to him with fealty. The *Akuryō* inside him smiled.

This one is strong.

Mamoru, the part of him still Mamoru, had no interest in harming a group of children or the adults who would come at the sound of screaming. The girl's show of respect slaked the *Akuryō's* need for anguish. He nodded to the tiny shaman and walked away. A chiding feeling crept up his back, turning his stomach. These people endured this harsh life of primitivism, unaware modern society still existed. Postwar hell had become their world, and they had no desire to leave it. The girl who had prayed to him weathered her unforgiving life in contentment. For that, *he* would watch over them.

Dead people could no longer suffer.

Ten paces away, he glanced back over his shoulder. The armed girl stood straight and tall, feet together, hair billowing to the side in the wind, as proud and confident wearing only dust as she might have been in samurai armor. She bowed, crouched, and climbed down out of sight amid the debris. He grumbled, remembering his distaste for the Red Planet. The Badlands embodied everything he hated about Mars and then some: desolate, dusty, devoid of comfort, and far beneath his station.

Darkness came hours later, though his body craved neither rest nor sleep. He did not feel hungry or thirsty, only driven. At night, the sounds of creatures intensified, yet still, none dared show themselves. The whole time he walked, the sense of being *escorted* by the strange denizens of this place followed him. Genetic wartime experiments gone awry, as well as crazed, degenerate humans, were common urban legends of the Badlands. Some of the stories had even reached Japan. From everything he had heard, he expected to need his blade drawn at all times while traveling. Yet, it seemed as if the land itself embraced his presence.

Mamoru walked, never slowing, even as the sun rose and set again, his direction guided by an inexplicable calling. Moments before the sun set for the third time on his journey, he spotted the remains of a small settlement. Once darkness fell, a weak, pulsating light throbbed in the center of a five-building town. Elongated shadows spread outward over the scrub, littered with the rapid motions of crawling insects. He kept to the dark, behind a leaning wooden building that had the look of a tap house.

At the center of the 'town,' eleven people arranged themselves around a metal barrel-turned-grill. One man in a torn pink dress and combat boots tended the meat, which appeared to be some manner of prairie dog. He mumbled a song in mockery of a French chef while adjusting the carcasses over the fire. A medieval-style sword, at least five feet in length, hung from a rope sling across his back. His bright red Mohawk brought to mind a rooster.

Others sat on the ground—two in the bed of a rusted pickup truck with no tires left on its wheels, and one hovering over a deathtrap buggy, tinkering with its engine. The mechanic noticed him and pulled darkened-leather goggles off his eyes while smearing a greasy hand over his bare chest. His stitched-leather pants looked ready to fall off from the weight of tools and parts crammed into the pockets.

Laughter and howls of celebration faded as the crunch of Mamoru's boots on dirt captured their attention.

A woman, dirty brown hair down to her waist from the half of her head not shaved, appeared in the doorway of the building closest to the buggy. She held her chin high as though she ruled this place and balanced an ancient pump shotgun over her shoulders. Two sashes loaded with red plastic shells crisscrossed her otherwise bare chest over a necklace of animal teeth. Black tatters, leather as well as cloth, hung around her waist forming a thick skirt that draped over combat boots too big for her. At least three machete handles protruded from the scraps.

She regarded Mamoru with barely-contained hostility. A sneer tugged at the scar crossing her cheek below the right eye.

The rest wore a patchwork of random items: skirts, pants, sneakers, even 'armor' made from old sporting pads or pieces of tire. All bore a multitude of weapons, mostly blades. Another woman sat up from the bed of the pickup, her leather vest covered in dried blood and bullet holes. Wild hair exploded from her scalp like an out-of-control shrubbery, shrouding bright green eyes fixated on him with a zealot's lust. She bowed in supplication, shuddering as if his mere presence had driven her to the brink of ecstasy.

Mamoru glanced at the woman in the doorway, a smile forming on his face at her desire to hurt him. An assortment of items, many stained with blood, littered the floor of the structure behind her.

Raiders.

A minute passed in a wordless standoff. Only the adoring wild woman made noise, whispering a mixture of English and Spanish. She wanted him to 'take her' and did not seem to care if he interpreted it sexually or murderously. Mamoru frowned, his distaste at her behavior fed by knowing his denial would cause her greater torment. He, or whatever it was he had made a deal with, would leave her to her pathetic pleas. The faintest eye contact between them seemed enough to communicate a sense of 'you are not yet worthy.'

She crawled backward out of sight, hiding behind the two marauders seated on the tailgate.

The raiders' shotgun-toting leader snorted and backed into her building. The others kept wary glances on him as he approached the grill. Mamoru helped himself to one of the skewered creatures and nodded at the cook.

"To your pleasure," said the large man, his eyes vibrating with eagerness.

This one had come to the Badlands seeking the *Akuryō*. He had given up on the false society. Images of battle, conquest, and fire filled Mamoru's mind. He smiled.

"Wilma," he said without understanding why.

The man bowed.

Mamoru wandered away into the dark, gnawing on the charred meat.

None of them made a move or a sound until he was well enough away not to notice.

For two full days more, Mamoru walked across the desolate sands of what had once been Arizona without stopping. The farther he got from the heart of the Badlands, the weaker the presence in the back of his mind became. Late afternoon on the fifth day of his journey, the gleaming shape of West City engulfed the horizon. Endless miles of chrome-silver plastisteel buildings caught the sinking sun, shimmering as if the gods had spilled molten metal over the land. He almost felt like himself, though still the burden of obligation tugged at his soul.

Mamoru marched on, ignoring the fatigue gnawing at the mysterious endurance that had sustained him thus far. When the sun set beyond the city, the blinding expanse of metal faded to shadows. Receding daylight gave way to the glow of technology, and the horizon lit up once more: high-rise spires with racing streams of flying hovercars and advert bots laced among them.

The NetMini in his coat pocket chirped, indicating it established a connection to the GlobeNet. An hour or so later, his boots clanked up a ramp leading to the metal wall blocking the city off from the Badlands. He stopped three paces from a massive gate, large enough for two semi-trucks to pass abreast, and waited for someone inside to notice him.

Minutes later, a head-sized orb bot glided over the top, settling down to eye level with him. Blue and green laser lines crisscrossed his body as it orbited him, scanning. After a minute, it whirled about and zipped over the wall. To the right of the gate, a person-sized door opened, revealing a muscular woman in blue Division 1 police armor. She showed two signs of trust: her helmet was off and her pistol remained in its holster, though her hand rested on it. A rectangular strip on her chestplate bore white letters reading 'PO2 Charles, C.'

"Nice night for a walk?" she asked, raising an eyebrow. No doubt she glanced over the false citizen identity profile he'd created when he first arrived in the UCF.

"My vehicle suffered a minor mechanical problem." Mamoru offered the shallowest of salutatory bows. "I am also in need of new clothes, a bath, and a proper meal."

"C'mon in, Mr. Haruko." She moved out of the doorway, gesturing at him to enter. "We'll get you on your way soon. Entry screening should only take a few minutes."

Mamoru smiled and stepped inside.

12

DOMINOES

Aurora

A great rolling curtain of fire rose up behind a tidal wave of junk, devouring gleaming towers of silver glass and plastisteel as it drew closer. The deafening inferno roared, louder than the explosions of crashing hovercars. Fragments of shattered glass rode by on a concussion wave. Aurora stood naked and calm in the center of the street, a stark white body among millions of people screaming and running. She stood her ground against the onrushing conflagration, squinting into the flame-heated wind whipping her long hair into a curtain of gold.

Half-molten advert bots careened out of the sky, smashing into the crowd of terrified citizens and falling like fireballs into the glass walls of hundred-story buildings. The ground in the distance buckled with a second concussion wave, rising several stories skyward before plummeting down with the collapsing city plates toward the earth. Panic-stricken men, women, and children rushed through her intangible body, showing no reaction to her presence. The deep rumble of West City falling back to the earth swallowed the screams of thousands.

Century towers careened away from her into the expanding maw, the enormous skyscrapers tumbling like stripped trees out of sight. The devastation halted inches from her toes; time itself ground to a standstill. Aurora glanced at a plump fireball swelling up from the ground hundreds of miles north. Her gaze climbed, following a trail of smoke that pierced the clouds. With the grace of a ballerina, she tiptoed over the buckling slabs of metal, hopping over individual, free-floating chunks of frozen destruction like stepping stones in midair. At the apex of the curve, she peered over the edge. Cars, buildings, and people hung suspended in mid-fall, raining toward the natural ground seventy-five meters below the artificial city surface.

One man had wound up in perfect position to stare right at her, outstretched hand begging for help. She closed her eyes and pressed both hands to her face.

When she looked again, she found herself face down on carpet, sprawled like a murder victim in an abandoned office building. Deep in a 'black zone,' no artificial light broke the darkness covering the world outside. Aside from their compound, electricity didn't come within eight miles of Archon's new base of operations. Some of the more technical-minded psionics had gone deep into The Beneath to tap a line for power, but she preferred it dark like the rest of the decaying buildings surrounding the campus. It almost reminded her of the cabin at County Gwynedd, how the darkness of night could be so completely enveloping without the pollution from millions of electric lights, advert bots, and civilization.

A moment of concentration changed the perfect blackness to wavering tones of sepia. Her eyes glowed with black light, peering into the astral world to illuminate the living one.

One foot remained in her hazard-orange sleeping bag, though the sofa cushions she'd arranged beneath it had gone askew. She pushed herself up and pulled her knees under her, sitting back on her heels and rubbing her face before stretching. It never got easier, watching horrors-to-be. Alone, without a judgmental eye upon her, Aurora curled into a ball and wept. From a single person's untimely death to an event like the collapse of the entire city, she would never be 'grateful' for her gift.

"Bad one, eh?" asked a growly male voice.

Her tears switched off.

"I've 'ad worse." She said, not looking.

A man's head, with shaggy brown hair and Hispanic features, floated around in front of her. He had no body—merely a length of spinal nerve fibers trailing him like a serpent. His empty eye sockets filled with roiling black smoke. The head hovered to her side, nerve bundle swishing like the tail of a happy dog.

"Have you been behaving yourself?"

He gasped, feigning shock.

"Enrique...," she said in the tone of a scolding parent. "You gave Melissa nightmares."

"*Si*. I only messed with *esa pequeño niña* a little." He grimaced, spine-tail going limp. "She getting too close to *mi cuerpo*."

Aurora stood and dusted carpet lint off her skin as she walked. "Anything interesting going on?"

The floating head trailed her across the repurposed office to a small hot tub in the corner of a private bath. "No. Is more of the same. One or two of the little ones, they see me and scream. I don't speak no Russian or whatever. An' that creepy one chased me for an hour."

"The one with the giant rag doll?" asked Aurora.

"*Si. Algo está muy mal con esa chica.*" The floating head shifted side to side, making the spinal nerve wiggle. "Something very wrong with that girl."

She ran the water cold and climbed in, soaking up to her neck. It didn't refresh her like the creek in the wilds of Wales, but a tepid soak beat nothing.

"*¡Ay, caramba!*" yelled the floating head; the nerve cord contracted in a squiggle. "I'm a spirit and that's makin' *me* freeze."

"Sorry." She stuck her tongue out at him. "Feels warm to me."

"You said you was gonna help me with this." Enrique wagged the tip of the spinal nerve about like a gesturing hand. "How I get my shit back?"

"You should've thought of that before you had them lop your head off and put it in a giant robot."

He hissed. "*Puta*, don't yank me."

"You've not got a todger to yank."

The head raced about in a circle for a few minutes, cursing and muttering in Spanish, before coming to a halt right in front of her face.

"Oh, fine." She rolled her eyes, not that he noticed. "When you died, you were just a head encased in metal. Since that's how you see yourself, that's how you exist as a spirit. All you've got to do is think the rest of you back into existence."

"What's the trick?"

"No trick. Just want. Picture yourself as you used to be, and desire to appear that way." She closed her eyes again and tried to get comfortable.

The spectral grunts and groans of a constipated-sounding ghost echoed amid drips of water falling from the faucet.

"You're going to strain yourself."

"It ain't workin', *chica*."

Aurora put one foot up on the end of the tub and crossed her ankles. "Getting angry won't help. In fact, you'll not be able to do anything until you are calm. Try to remember yourself before you went and got all that metal."

The head's eyes bulged.

"Don't tell me you're in a hurry?" She laughed, cold and haughty. "Have somewhere to be?"

He grumbled and snarled. After a moment of impotent glaring, the hovering face sagged as though he hung his head in resignation. "Calm, eh?" The spirit glided away, into the wall, muttering.

"Yes, well… I suppose that's the trick to it."

She stopped concentrating on Darksight, and let the room go black. Water lapped at her neck and ankles, threatening to lull her back to sleep. A knock at the door disrupted her peace a short while later.

"It's not locked." She concentrated on the Astral realm, letting her body slip past the veil. A blast of ice washed over her as gravity lost meaning. The water collapsed to fill the space she had occupied with a loud pop, creating a tall spout. She floated out of the tub like a sylph on the wind, gliding into the main room, where Archon fumbled at the wall for the light switch, which took him a moment to find. After the lights came on, she hung in midair, laughing at his clueless expression as he searched, looking right past the space where she waited.

When his confusion took on a sense of irritation, she drifted to his side and landed on the toes of her outstretched foot, slipping back into the normal world. The sensation of the change slid over her body as though she tore through a thick sheet of hanging plastic from a comfortable, cool world to one of stifling warmth. Her hair gathered at her back, tickling her calves.

Archon shifted, his polite sideways stance affording her a bit of modesty she couldn't care less about.

"I was in the bath." She took her time picking among the assortment of robes, dresses, skirts, and leggings on the floor with her toe.

He stood with his back to her, muttering. "What is going on, Lauren?"

"Whatever do you mean?" She got her foot under the edge of an aqua satin robe and lifted it to her hand.

"Are you here to help or hurt us?"

"James," she said, sounding hurt. "How could you even ask that?" She folded the floor-length robe closed over herself and tied the belt in a loose knot. "You can look now."

Archon faced her after a hesitant peek to confirm she had dressed. "I did not think I was unclear. I am confused as to the nature of your intentions with us. Are you here to help or are you here to hinder us?"

She pushed the memory of the standing wall of fire out of her mind. "You'll have to be a bit more specific than that."

"You could have warned me of our difficulties with the ship."

"What makes you think there are difficulties?" She padded to the desk, sat next to a portable food assembler, and crossed her legs. "Tea?"

"That would be lovely." He moved to the end of the desk. "Do you see me gathering everyone to go to the starport? The bloody thing is missing."

"Mamoru knows where it is." Beeps punctuated the silence as she poked buttons on the machine. "Simply because it isn't here *right now* doesn't mean it won't ever be. I assure you, the ship *is* coming."

He grumbled, accepting the mug she handed him. Aurora smiled at the face he made, as if surprised she'd prepared it as he preferred—no sugar and heavy on the lemon. She set about making a second cup for herself, idly swaying her dangling foot back and forth.

"What color do you think I should use?"

"Pardon?"

"Toenails."

He choked on his tea. "Can you for once adhere to the topic at hand? What is going on here? May I remind you that you informed me there was zero chance Anna would be a problem."

"Aye." Aurora sipped her creamed tea through a smile. *Zero indeed.*

"She has gotten a bit too comfortable around that Pryce fellow. The girl always was a bit too soft inside to do what needs to be done."

"Still on about that office job? You'd have had us kill the lot of them?"

"Regretful, but, it would have saved months of cleanup work."

Aurora tilted her head. "You don't think it would've stepped up the police response? Even factoring out questions of moral decency, it may have proven more expedient at that moment, but the aftereffects would've been bothersome."

"They were only mundanes, not a lick of gift among the lot." Archon sipped his tea and sighed. "Sooner or later, her empty sentimentality is going to cause a problem."

"You may be right about that bit." Aurora held her cup with a daintily raised pinky finger. Red in Archon's cheeks signaled a direct hit of her mockery.

"What do you see coming? Will we have any further issues?"

"'Ang on a minnit. Let me fetch the scrying ball."

"Droll."

"It doesn't work like that, James. Significant things come to me when they come. Sort of like a disinterested boyfriend."

He made a gurgling noise. "Must you turn everything into an innuendo?"

She flashed a wicked grin over her tea. "Does it make you uncomfortable?"

Archon opened his mouth as if to answer, but only glared.

Aurora lowered her arm, cradling the warm mug in her lap and staring into it. "James, you got the CSB off my back and gave me a place to stay when no one wanted the freak around."

"I think of you like the troubled younger sister I never had." He spent a moment studying the surface of his tea. "Have you seen anything recently?"

"Nothing that means anything to us."

"Well, I suppose that bodes well." Archon glanced at the coal-black windows. "I see you have not been sleeping soundly either. Should I be concerned?"

"Visions of the future are fickle things. I see endpoints, probable endpoints at that. Small wrinkles in between don't make themselves known unless something serious goes wrong. Most future sight links on an emotional level. You know precognitives who can see the fate of total strangers are rare."

"Such a pity."

"What, that I'm a cold, heartless, ghost of a woman with no emotional ties? A mostly-blind precognitive?"

"No, Lauren. A pity your gift is so rare. I loathe having to constantly ask you to search such ugly dreams."

She gazed at her lap, brief flashes of long-ago panic flashed across her mind. A little girl whose parents screamed at the sight of her. A child who panicked and etherealized out of her clothes when the soldiers came for her. Authorities dragging her away like some kind of criminal. Days spent in a featureless cell until she realized she could leave whenever she wanted.

"I've done everything I can to help you, but there's something you have to accept."

"And that is?" He raised an eyebrow.

"Some futures will come to pass whether you want them to or not." She looked him in the eye. "You don't seem to want to accept that. I tried to tell you taking Althea against her wishes was going to end badly for you. I honestly thought she'd have let..."

His expression hardened. "I suppose you cannot see everything. It was a gamble I needed to take. The benefits far outweighed the risks."

"If she wasn't a child... Don't press her, James. Please." Aurora slipped off the desk, set her mug down, and put a hand on his arm. "I'm still certain she will watch you die."

Archon failed to conceal a shudder. "Well... Of course. She is a child. I expect she will outlive me."

"I half want to say she'll choose to *let* you die, but I can't fully believe she would do that."

He closed his eyes, sighing irritation out his nose. "I would rather prefer it if you would tell me who I can trust and who my enemies are."

"James." Aurora leaned in close enough to kiss him. "Your biggest adversary is your own refusal to adapt, compromise, or..." She leaned back, stood, and wandered to the window; the dark rendered it an onyx mirror, her body a milky ghost upon its surface. She hovered there a few seconds, smiling at him via reflection.

"Or what?"

"Or look over the edges of tall buildings."

Archon blinked. "What?"

She threw her head back, laughed, and slipped between worlds. The chill of the Astral realm cascaded over her front as the smoothness of satin slid down her back. Leaving him there to stew in the confusion kept her grinning.

She glided through the glass as though it had no more solidity than a diaphanous spider web. Without a passenger along, she flew high and fast, blurring over the terrain of the city, the Badlands, East City, the ocean, and countryside in a matter of minutes. The journey made her think of Althea's wide, innocent eyes. For a few seconds, she regretted that a person so pure would be caught up in the approaching storm. She found it curious that she'd never once been tempted to mess with that girl. Her usual habit of adoring it whenever she made someone squirm didn't apply to her. She'd only ever felt pity toward that child, laced with a tinge of admiration—and guilt over playing a role in her experience with Archon.

After all that mite's been through, this little shitstorm shouldn't change her. Aurora bowed her head. *I hope.*

About an hour after leaving Archon, she glided into a dense wooded area. Three men in chain mail armor, bearing swords and shields, paused to give her wide-eyed stares as her feet settled upon a soft bed of dirt and leaf detritus. The one in the middle held up a cruciform broadsword and bade her return to hell.

"I'm not a witch, you dolt. Also, you're dead. You've been dead for over a thousand bloody years. If you haven't found your god yet, I doubt you're going to."

She stepped out from beyond the veil. Noonday sunlight and green washed over the sepia-toned trees as her body reappeared in the living world. A short distance ahead at the end of a stone path, a tiny cabin sat in the tranquil forest shade of County Gwynedd, Wales.

Aurora smiled at the warm glow of firelight flickering in the windows.

13

A FEW YEARS YET

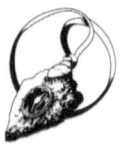

Althea

Late afternoon sun made the flower-patterned white curtains over the kitchen sink glow with comforting warmth. Althea took a handful of diced chicken from a bowl and spread it over a tortilla shell, added a ladle of sauce, and a sprinkle of cheese. After rolling the enchilada into a log, she placed it in the tray waiting for the oven. Karina appeared behind her in time to grab her wrist when she attempted to sneak a bite of chicken.

"Wait for dinner." Karina hauled a pot of water onto the stove.

Althea rubbed her foot up and down her shin, trying to scratch an itch on her sole since she had to keep her hands 'food clean.' She grabbed another tortilla and laid it flat. "That's silly. I can't eat before I eat?"

"It's rude." Karina opened the oven door and set up the kindling.

"I tried to talk to Den today, but he ran off." Althea kept her gaze on Karina, sneaking a blind grab at one of the bowls and stuffing a few pieces into her mouth while her sister wasn't watching.

Jalapeño.

She turned red and whimpered, unable to spit it out, lest her thievery be discovered.

"He'll be okay." Karina left the fire to grow and walked behind her to the other side of the L-shaped counter. "Jalapeños are hot."

Caught.

An upwelling of guilt stalled when Karina laughed and patted her on the head. Althea coughed on the peppers, eyes watering, but managed to swallow them before Karina handed her a cup of milk. She sent a distrustful glower at the strange new box in the kitchen that made things cold, fearful it would bring the evil of that awful city with it.

"This water doesn't look safe."

"It's milk."

Althea blinked at it, an expression of horror spreading over her face.

"From a cow." Karina blushed.

"Eww." She scrunched her nose.

Karina laughed. "Some of the things you eat, and you're making that face at milk? Go on, it'll help the spice. Besides, you've already had some in the coffee the other day."

Althea stared at her, horrified. "It came out of a cow?"

"You've never had milk before?"

"No." She pouted at the cup. "Sorry for sneaking food."

"It's fine, Thea." Karina rummaged the cabinets in search of seasonings for the rice. "Electricity is going to make our life better."

The fire in her mouth made her doubts regarding the suspiciously cold milk seem unimportant. After a tentative sip didn't taste horrible, she tried not to think of it being made from a cow and gulped it down, holding the last mouthful on her tongue to cool it. Karina took over assembling the enchiladas. Althea stood close at her side, eyeing the bowls of makings.

"You'll ruin your appetite."

Althea grinned, twice reaching for a bowl with no real intent to take anything, and twice having Karina grab her hand. She continued the game until Karina, laughing, ushered her away from the counter.

"Enough. Would you please get some wood?"

"Okay." Althea swung her arms in an exaggerated walk to the back porch door.

She stared at the knob, remembering the fear she once had at going outside alone, as if a horde of raiders waited to ambush her at any second. A little nervousness returned, but she opened the door with confidence in herself and marched out onto the back porch. Even her slight weight sent *thuds* through the house with each step on the old boards.

The pile of firewood sat at the left side, up against the wall where the rotting frame of old screens had collapsed outward and the air carried the scent of fresh-cut wood. Even in split logs, it continued to want to grow. Pieces at the bottom, idle longer than the rest, had threaded tiny roots into the floorboards and sprouted a few leaves. None lasted long; the ancient magic that kept them growing only lingered for a few days before it gave up. She suspected it had something to do with whatever chamán had caused the trees to grow in the desert a few miles southeast of Querq. Father called it 'technology' from before the war, and once told her the trees they cut for wood grew back in a matter of weeks.

Althea shook her head. *Father doesn't understand magic.*

She squatted next to the pile and selected a few pieces, laying them across her lap. The wind picked up, causing the walls to creak. A *clap* came from the flimsy excuse for a door by the porch steps that clattered in its frame with the gusts. Althea disregarded the noise, balancing a third log atop the first two. Not until the floorboards shifted under her feet did she realize someone had snuck up behind her.

The logs went tumbling away as Althea whirled around, falling back against the woodpile, butt on the floor. Her panic never quite made it to a scream; expecting a kidnapper, she found herself staring up at the wild-eyed face of Esmerelda. The younger, though larger, girl radiated fear and anger in almost equal amounts. Small, round welts covered her face, arms, and legs.

Althea raised an arm, hand up. "I don't want to fight."

"Take it off me." Esmerelda's tone wavered between demand and plead.

"What?" Althea scrambled to her knees and reached for the other girl's hand.

Esmerelda leaned away. "The curse. You put bad on me for hitting you."

"Who did this to you?" Althea radiated calm, altering the girl's mood.

"Please." She scratched at her arm. "It hurts. I fell off the pipe and hit a nest of bees. The bad luck curse. Yesterday, I shut my hand in the door. Papa told me not to come here, but it hurts *so* much. They stung me all over."

"Sit still."

Shivering, Esmerelda ceased backing away whenever Althea reached for her.

Althea grasped the girl's arm and concentrated until her consciousness linked to Esmerelda's life essence. Tiny disruptions in the girl's skin appeared, too many stings to count, as well as threads of liquid toxin swirling around the blood-shape. It took little effort to force her skin to mend itself and collect the venom to be purged.

"I did not put bad on you." Althea opened her eyes. "I am not angry."

"Take it off." Esmerelda bit her lip and squirmed, crossing her legs.

"I… When you hit…" Althea furrowed her brow. She couldn't think of how to explain feeling happy at being treated like a normal person while at the same time not enjoying being hit. Rather than stumble with words, she projected the emotion into Esmerelda. "Go make water. You must let the poison from the bees out."

As the other girl ran off down the street, Althea re-gathered the firewood. While picking up the fourth log, she spotted a fat, white grub wriggling along the surface. She grabbed it with a squeal of delight and jammed it in her mouth, lifted the wood, and used her butt to push the door open. Karina blinked at her as she walked to the stove.

"What took so long?"

Althea tried to look innocent. *Esmerelda got stung by bees.*

Karina's concerned look at the telepathic message faded to playful suspicion. "What's in your mouth?"

She attempted to smile without opening it.

"Thea…" Karina tapped one foot.

"Grub." She opened her mouth in an over-wide grin, showing off bits of half-chewed mash.

"Ugh." Karina cringed away.

Althea dropped the wood and clamped her hands over her mouth to prevent her laugh from spraying bug guts all over the kitchen. Still giggling, she set the wood in the stove and backed away, flopping on one of the chairs to let Karina tend the fire.

"You don't need to eat bugs anymore." Karina pulled on the handle to open the flue.

"I know. I'll ruin my ap-tight." She swung her legs back and forth, eyes downcast, but smiling.

"No, you'll ruin mine." Satisfied the rice could be no further along until the water boiled, Karina pulled a chair close and sat. "Did you have fun today?"

Althea nodded. "Yes. Juan and the others let me go with them."

"About time. What did you do?"

"We went swimming in the pond behind Water Man's house, and then we went hunting after food."

"Hunting?" Karina got up to tend the rice pot as it reached a boil.

"Looking for trade-things to give Beard. Treasures in the old city."

"Althea…" She almost dropped the spoon. "It's dangerous outside the wall. You shouldn't be out there."

She stared down. "I know, but Sophia and Manuel are in the Watch and they said it was okay. Sophia said the bad stuff hides in the day."

"I don't want you doing that again, understand? *They* are seventeen… it's okay for them to go scavenging, but you are too little."

Althea bit her lower lip. "Henrietta broke her foot when she fell. Manuel got bit by a dog. Tim got stuck with a piece of metal when a wall fell on him; it came out his back." She stared at the floor, legs no longer swinging. She thought back to the arena at Vakkar's factory. "I guess that's why they wanted me to go with them. They did dangerous because of me."

Maybe they didn't like her as much as wanted her there to fix hurts. Her mood bottomed out.

"Ay… they brought *all* of them? Those kids aren't old enough either."

Karina shook her head. "It's not your fault. You had no reason not to believe them. I'll ask Father to speak to them."

"Speak to who?" asked Father from the other side of the house.

His boots thudded closer, muted by the threadbare carpet in the hallway between the kitchen and the front door. Althea ran to him, waiting for him to hang his jacket and hat on a peg to the right of the archway before flinging herself into a hug. He squeezed her and shifted her under one arm to open the other for Karina.

Karina walked with her arm at his back, rambling on about Juan and their trip outside. He took his seat and set his hat on the corner of the table.

Father echoed her sister's statement of her being too young, adding, "Don't go off like that again unless someone will die if you don't... and even if that happens, make sure someone comes and lets me know."

"Yes, Father."

Althea looked down at the floor for a moment before helping Karina bring the food to the table. After they each had a plate in front of them, Karina and Father got to eating, but Althea stared at her baked enchilada. The same dish as the first food she'd been given here. The sight of it caused her to remember her old life, and she choked up at how happy she felt.

"What's wrong, Thea?" asked Father.

"It is what you gave me the first day I was here." She flashed a mischievous smile. "Should I eat it like a dog?"

Karina giggled.

Althea grinned and battled with the knife and fork, which had gotten easier to use, though she made a show of failing at it. "Can Den stay here? There's rooms."

Father studied the ceiling for a moment. "You like this boy?"

She offered an eager nod.

"In the kissing sense," said Father, fidgeting.

"Oh." Althea shook her head. "I'm not old enough for wifeing yet."

Father lapsed into a coughing fit. Karina looked away.

"No," said Father. "Most definitely not. If he were to stay with us, the town would consider him your brother... and that would be..."

"Inbeading?" asked Althea.

Karina's head hit the table with a thud; she hid her face behind folded arms. Althea looked confused by the strong embarrassment radiating from her.

Father chuckled, coughed again, and hit himself in the chest twice. "It's only inbreeding if..." He paused, drumming his fingers on the table for a moment. "You know, it's not important." He loosed a dry chuckle. "If you still fancy him when you're older, you two will get a home of your own. Like

Corrine and Carlos. You've got a good few years yet before you need to worry about that. Don't waste time worrying now. Be a child."

The thought she would someday no longer share a room with Karina brought warmth to the corners of her eyes. She thought back to the way she felt when Den had kissed her: strange and warm and scared all at once. Never in her life had she known such a sense of safety and security as she felt here in her *home*. Would she ever want to give that up to be with Den? It seemed so far away and silly to think about, but both Father and Karina appeared to believe she would. She let the fork drop from her hand and stared at the half-eaten enchilada.

"Althea?" Asked Karina, sounding nervous. "Did you see a bad vision?"

"No."

"Why do you look about to cry? If you two marry, that would be happy."

"If I'm with Den, we wouldn't have the same room anymore." Althea sniffled.

Karina reached over the table to hold her hand. "In a couple years, you'll rather share a bed with Den than me."

"Nuh-uh," muttered Althea.

Father found his plate beyond fascinating at that moment.

Karina glanced at him and winked at Althea. "*Tomará tiempo.*"

Worry kept Althea's smile from expanding to a grin, but she giggled at Karina's imitation of Father.

14

HATE, LOVE, AND FIRE

Kate

Tumbleweed's had the usual crowd of people for the hour, a handful too old or frail to work. A heavyset man behind the bar, shaved bald save for a frizzy salt and pepper beard, glanced up with a smile as Kate and David made their way to a table. Her snug, grey, long-sleeved shirt and loose-fitting, blue pants made her feel as out of place among the locals as her Division 0 uniform would have. All around her sat people in tattered flannel, ripped jeans, and handmade boots.

The pair got the suspicious-curious stares outsiders often did when invading the world of those who spent most of their waking hours in a tavern, though no one seemed hostile. David left her at the table to stop by the bar; his uniform—and the E90 on his hip—pulled every eye off her. The laser weapon cast a rhythmic blue light from tiny LEDs along the sides of the barrel, a point of glow sweeping back and forth from tip to end. Two old men stared at it like cats ready to pounce on a mouse, mesmerized by the moving spot.

Kate smoothed her shirt and studied the Spanish phrases and names cut into the old wooden table. She wondered if the locals would stop staring at her if she went tribal, full on loincloth and spear mode. *Nah, I'd rather have a sword.* If nothing else, going off the grid again would be a way to avoid El Tío. Even with David around, the dread of the job she'd begrudgingly accepted kept her from feeling happy. Not being able to find Aaron Pryce had given her some reprieve. That he showed up in the system as a wanted fugitive had calmed her dread that the Syndicate gave her the job as a death sentence, but made her fear being caught in a murder plot and losing everything this second chance might offer.

She glanced at David's back. He'd leaned his right elbow against the bar, making easy conversation with the man she assumed to be Tumbleweed. David had that ability, exactly how much of it came from his telempathy she couldn't say, but everyone he met seemed to like him. So far, he had limited his use of psionics on her to lifting her mood whenever she remembered needing to kill Pryce. He relied on concerned glances and long, pointed stares to get her to open up.

How can I tell him I've been asked to do a hit for the Syndicate? Much less on a cop. Kate picked at a deeper carving where Juanita and Lucinda swore their eternal love for each other. How long ago had that happened? The table could've predated the war given its condition; the two lovers may well have been centuries dead.

David startled her out of her daydreams by setting a glass of orange liquid in front of her. She looked up and smiled before the pungent sourness of alcoholic citrus assaulted her nose.

"It was either that or the 'rust water,' which I assume to be their version of beer. Figured I'd err on the side of caution." He sat.

Kate sipped enough to get the taste on her tongue. Fizziness carried a war of sweet and bitter, tinged with more than a little alcoholic burn. "Wow, this stuff..."

"Yeah, we'd better pace ourselves." He took a sip larger than hers and grimaced as it went down.

The *crack* of pool balls breaking and scattering around a table in the back made her jump.

"Okay, it's been days. What's wrong?" David gave her that imploring look she found so irresistible—somewhere between begging puppy and dashing pirate.

She stared at the fizz bursting on the surface of her drink, knowing she couldn't lie to him. He'd sense it. Deception had never been her strong suit. Fire fixed her problems more easily. Unlike lies, she didn't have to remember ash piles. "I still feel lost. I can't stop thinking about when you found me. Two seconds later, and..."

"Is that where all that guilt's coming from?" He let off a faint sigh. "Kate, you don't need to be with me as some kind of 'thanks.' If you're not—"

"No." She reached across the table to take his hand. "No, no. It's not like that. I'm not with you out of some guilt thing. I—"

"That Esteban fellow?"

"No." Kate laughed. "*That* was desperation. Twenty-five years old and I'd never been touched. I don't mean *touched*. I mean anything... holding hands, someone grabbing my ass, kissed. I feel different about you, David. I want it to be perfect."

"Take your time." He squeezed her hand, smiling. "You are worth waiting for."

"Hah." She laughed. "I'm as broken and fucked up as they get."

His face twisted into a doubting smirk.

"I'm afraid of chasing you off." More guilt.

"So what's bothering you then?"

Kate took a mouthful of the pulpy concoction, coughing from the sensation of so much at once. "Maybe after two more of these, I'll be able to enjoy it." She thumped herself on the chest and coughed again, eyes watering.

"Aye," said a sixtyish woman in a flannel dress. "Takes getting used to."

I've been alone for so long. Everyone who's ever tried to help me has always just wanted something. She stared into David's brown eyes. *What'll I do then? Kill a cop and hope the man's as dirty as El Tío says?* "I told you about my past."

David's expression hardened, as if bracing for bad news. "You did."

"Paul found me at a Cyberburger. I must've been a sight. Fifteen, naked, stuffing my face with hamburger meat like some feral creature. They saw me roast the manager."

"You had a perfect mixture of innocent appearance and lethal ability."

"Yeah, something like that. They wanted me to kill for them, figuring half the time I could get in as an underage sex toy. It didn't take long for them to figure out why that wouldn't work, so I just did it the old-fashioned way."

He sipped his drink. "I can't say I'm happy about what you had to do, but you *were* a child being exploited by someone in a position of trust... sort of. This El Tío assumed a quasi-parental role over you, and you had a strong need to please him. Perhaps you were afraid if you upset him, he'd cast you out."

Kate held her glass with both hands on the table, spinning it in a series of quarter turns with her thumb. "At first. When I got a little older, I was afraid he'd kill me if I didn't do what he wanted. I'd seen him get angry at those who he felt betrayed his trust." She looked up, forcing herself to make eye contact. "I... wasn't all truthful with you before."

David summoned his best 'it's okay' face.

"When you first interviewed me, I said everyone I killed had been dirty. That wasn't completely true. Two of the people hadn't done anything other than want to change employers. Though, both did steal secrets when they left. One was a geneticist. His begging didn't bother me at the time." She shifted her jaw, avoiding eye contact with David. "I saw him like one of the bastards who created me."

"How do you feel about it now?"

"I wish I'd stayed in the wilds and never come to the city. After I woke up

here, after Althea did whatever she did to 'fix' me, all the guilt hit me at once."
Kate's eyes watered, though she resisted the urge to weep. "I wasn't on the
outside anymore. I didn't destroy everything I touched."

Her gaze fell into her lap. David scooted around the table, pulling a chair
with him so he could sit next to her. She leaned on him, shuddering with the
battle to keep her composure. His arms holding her felt *wonderful*.

After a moment, he leaned closer and touched heads. "You're supposed to
feel better now. Your guilt is getting stronger."

What if he decides to turn me in if I tell him? She shied away to the right, no
longer able to hold back the tears as she saw the look on his face. "I-I can't get
away."

"What?"

"He called me. El Tío. He wants me to do another favor for him." She
shivered. The truth hovered at the tip of her tongue like a venomous kiss. Her
voice dropped to a weak whisper. "The job's on a cop. A Zero."

His arms tightened around her. "You should've said something sooner.
When we get back to the city, we can file a report and Div 9 will take care
of it."

"You mean kill him."

He seemed less than thrilled about the idea, but nodded.

"But..."

"If he cared about you, he wouldn't have put you in this position. Any
sense of loyalty you have to that man is misplaced."

"How is Division 9 killing him any different than what he had me do for
him? Besides, he says the guy has gone rogue, and the government wants him
dead, too."

"A fugitive?" David blinked. "Who?"

Kate glanced around to make sure no one eavesdropped. "Pryce. Aaron, I
think. He said I was a last resort, tried to sound all sympathetic to my
situation. They haven't had much luck doing it themselves because he's
psionic. Apparently, some kind of badass since he's killed two dozen
enforcers and one of the higher-ups already. They want me to handle him."

He rubbed her shoulder. "If the Syndicate is trying to kill him, they're
either out of their mind with rage, or this guy is really disavowed. Nine would
be all over them if they put a hit out on a cop otherwise."

"What should I do?" Kate shivered as soon as she asked. She hated herself
for the lapse of independence, trusting someone else—and a man at that—to
take control. That wasn't the kind of woman she had ever been nor cared to
be. Still, this entire situation made her feel like a little girl trapped in a tank,
surrounded by scientists who wanted to kill her. Then again, man or not,
she'd longed to have someone she could confide in for years. "If he did go

rogue, maybe I should do it. It'll get El Tío off my ass and might score some points with the brass."

"If." David shifted as she leaned more of her weight into him. "No matter what, he was still one of us once. You shouldn't hunt him down like a dog."

"I'm not exactly good at the whole 'subtle' thing. Besides, if he's been able to stay a step ahead of the Syndicate, I shouldn't give him a chance to kill me, too."

"You're scared."

"Yeah, I am. Been a while. It's easy to be fearless when you don't care if you survive and have nothing to really lose. I guess I'm a cop now. Doing a hit for the Syndicate seems like a one-way ticket to a small room at best, constantly looking over my shoulder or dead at worst." She snuggled into him. "I don't want to die."

David's kiss lingered on her lips for minutes. After he leaned away, he smiled. "I can't tell you how happy I am to hear that."

KATE STROLLED DOWN THE STREETS OF QUERQ, HOLDING DAVID'S HAND. MOST of the locals kept a cautious distance from the pair. Small children ran over to get a closer look at David's 'light gun,' while a handful of adults returned grateful nods for the help the 'city people' brought to Querq. More than a few remembered her initial arrival and gave her the evil eye. She looked down, accepting the guilt their stares held.

She smiled at everyone, wary and welcoming alike. They crossed most of the city and stood in the shadow of the west wall, by a long row of small houses made from the back ends of ancient trucks. Everyone who lived in one of the trailer-dwellings was single, mostly men. Along the inner side of the street, old storefronts still bore the logos of their former franchises. Large windows left obvious the internal barriers erected to separate the commercial spaces into individual homes. Quiet pervaded the street. Aside from a handful of elders, the people who lived in this part of town had gone out to work at that hour.

A woman with long black hair and dark skin pushed a glass-paned door labeled 'Subway' open with her backside, carrying a large plastic crate full of dirty clothes. Her cream-colored dress stopped an inch above her knees, and a silver ring around her left second toe gleamed in the sun. Sandals made from old tire rubber scuffed on the paving as she passed, and she offered a bashful smile at the two of them.

"They seem so happy here," said Kate. "Like they don't care at all they're living in the stone ages."

He glanced up at a man clanking along the metal walkway atop the outer wall. "It does have a certain rustic charm. No pressure of an office job, no traffic, no alarm clock, no taxes, no rat race."

"No real hospitals or GlobeNet access."

"You grew up in the wilds." David slid a hand around the small of her back. "Would you miss the net if you never knew what it was?"

She watched the woman round the corner at the end of the street, headed to the gate to take her laundry out to the creek. Memories flickered in her mind of living alone in the wilds, unaware of such a thing as cities, cars, or technology. "I suppose not. I didn't really need it back then, but I got lonely."

"That's unusual. Most feral children I've read about had to be dragged, kicking and screaming, back to civilization. Even the ones we found in disavowed sectors or living in The Beneath. Usually takes quite a bit of therapy and patience." David rubbed his head. "Ugh, this one boy with mind blast we found in the grey. He was... difficult."

Kate shrugged. "Guess I have wolf blood. I wanted to be social."

Shepherd went by, carrying a Fubox power cell on each shoulder. The man lugged the three-foot cubes as if he carried hollow plastic toys. He watched her as they passed; a trace of unease narrowed his eyes.

"He doesn't trust me." She found herself leaning into David.

"Althea's influence has left him overprotective. Besides, he doesn't distrust *you*; he distrusts whatever influence sent you here in the first place."

David must have sensed the fear rising in the back of her heart. His arm tightened around her.

"I don't trust me here either." She bit her lip. "She did something to me, too. I've never had a kid, but whenever I look at her, I understand how a mother gets when their child is threatened. I'd melt down the whole city to protect her."

He stared into her eyes. Odd feelings cascaded over her brain, as though ghostly fingers stroked it beneath her skull. The sensation weakened her knees, and she held on to him to keep from swooning to the ground.

"Shepherd exhibits similar psychic imprints. You both tried to kill her, though I'd venture to say she found him more frightening based on the depth of the mark. As a guess, I'd say it's some kind of panic-driven instinctual response on her part. In your case, I think she made you feel parental to give you something to help you resist that anger. Like a rock in the middle of a river you can cling to in order to avoid being swept away with the current."

"She wanted to make sure we couldn't bring ourselves to hurt her." Kate smirked, unsure how she felt about being 'programmed' to like the girl, even if she owed the child so much.

"It's primal," said David. "Strong and simple. I don't think she put a lot of premeditation into it. A child's id screaming 'don't kill me' is about the extent of it."

"Thanks. I didn't feel guilty enough about that already. Now, all I can see is her staring at me begging for her life." Kate rubbed her face.

A large, white goat walked by dragging a scrawny boy of about eight along by its leash. He yelled, *"Parar! Cabra tonta!"* and tried to set his heels on the pavement. It pulled him off his feet, but he refused to let go, despite his shorts sliding down to his knees as it dragged him.

Kate cracked up giggling.

David made a sharp clicking sound, which attracted the goat's attention long enough for him to influence its emotion and make it stop. The boy leapt upright and fixed his pants before seizing the animal by the collar. He grinned at them, waved, and led the goat away, muttering scolding things at it in Spanish.

"I'm starting to like Querq." Kate waited for another member of the Watch to clank past on the wall overhead before kissing David on the lips. "Do you think we could spend a little more time here?"

"There aren't a lot of officers eager to get stuck out here."

He leaned in about to kiss her, when a loud wooden crash echoed from the far end of the street, followed by clattering metal. Whatever sight greeted him when he peered over her shoulder left him laughing into the crook of her neck.

"Cabra tonta!" yelled a small boy.

15

NOT SO FRICTIONLESS

Aaron

C hildren squealed and screamed four stories down, chasing an improvised frictionless stone that one of the technokinetics had managed to cobble together from parts scavenged in the yard. As they had no armored boots, they'd covered the thing with padding. Aaron leaned against the railing on the patio of a former employee lounge. He chuckled at the spectacle of it, as though a group of ruffians had decided to gang up and abuse an ambulatory pillow.

Gunshots snapped in the distance every so often, followed by the occasional *clank* of something hitting the exposed girders of a nearby building. Only the two English girls, the new arrivals, showed any reaction to the shooting, ducking and cowering behind a central air unit. The rest disregarded it as background noise. Many of the ones from Europe had grown up with war always in the distance.

Shadows moved within the darkness of the ruined offices high up on a tower across the street. The denizens of the black zone, lured by the echoes of playing kids, came to investigate. Except for one almost fully augmented man covered in metal plates, they took cover from the security detail taking pot shots at them with submachine guns.

One of the Russian boys handled his weapon like a trained soldier, despite being only fourteen. Most of his bullets hit the aug in the chest, not that they did much other than make the armor plated man laugh.

What is Archon thinking putting all these people in the middle of a disavowed sector? This won't end well.

A brief peek at the aug's surface thoughts relieved Aaron to a point. He had no interest in the small ones, he wanted women—plus whatever weapons, food, and expensive shiny shit he could steal.

A casual tug with telekinesis pulled the man clear of the window, floating him over the street eleven stories down. The cyber-ganger flailed and kicked, releasing a half-human digitized scream. Aaron squinted up at him, sending a telepathic message:

Oy, Mate. If I was you, I'd leave well enough alone. Nothin' in here for you but a bad day getting worse.

He flung the guy back into the office, unconcerned with how gentle a landing he provided. Hopefully, an aug's fear of psionics would keep him away for the long term. Aaron resumed watching the game, surprised at his utter lack of missing the limelight.

"It is good to see them in high spirits," said Archon, from behind.

Aaron glanced back. The Lord of Tweed hovered in the door to the lounge area, amid a patch of shadow. Above him dangled the remains of a light that had been shot out years ago and never repaired. Archon stepped over a permanent green-black stain seeping from a dead food assembler, weaved among a few round, white tables, and joined him on the patio.

"Aye."

"I realize you are unhappy with my bringing Talis here." Archon paused to let him respond, though he said nothing. "You must understand we all have to make concessions for the cause."

"Aye." Aaron narrowed his eyes, looking past the game to the rotting cyborg corpses forty yards behind the more distant goal. "She didn't know Allison was my wife, right? No harm done."

"Sarcasm does not suit you." Archon offered a professional smile. "You have every right to be angry; however, consider what she has done for you."

Aaron shot him a glare.

"Of course I do not mean your wife. You are Awakened now, because of her."

"A great bag of wank." Aaron slouched over the railing. "You know I'd rather have her back."

"Rumor has it a certain child has brought back the dead." Archon lifted an eyebrow. "Is it true?"

"Rumor has it you're an intelligent man," said Aaron. "What the bloody fuck are you doing bringing children into a black zone? Do you've any idea what would happen here if the locals kicked in the wall?"

Archon waved dismissively, raising his nose to peer down at the game. "They will not be here long. Every one of them is gifted, but alas so few are

Awakened. They may look like schoolchildren, but they can protect themselves."

"They shouldn't have to." Aaron stood as if to walk away.

"A moment," said Archon. "Might I ask what your intentions are toward Anna?"

Aaron froze. What he wanted and what Anna seemed open to were quite different things. He couldn't get the image of her pleading stare out of his mind. Every time he tried to sleep, every time he closed his eyes, she'd be there in his mind. Two women haunted him, neither of which he could have.

"Something amiss?" asked Archon.

"Anna reminds me a bit of my wife." Aaron squeezed his hands into fists and stared into the distance. "That's all. She's made it abundantly clear she belongs to you."

That word, *belong*, made him want to cringe, though Archon cracked a smile. For all his highbrow ideals, he seemed little more than an alpha wolf marking his territory. When they had kissed at the starship factory, Archon appeared to have all the emotional investment of someone selecting what coat to wear. Aaron hid his feelings from his face.

"Anna is rather fond of you, chap. After the life she had, she could certainly use an older brother."

Or father. Aaron kept that to himself. The man would've been around seventeen at the time she'd been born. It was a wonder Archon hadn't invaded his thoughts; surely, he couldn't be so powerful as to be able to do that without him noticing. *No, he's still smiling.* "Aye."

"Keep her safe for me, would you? I fear I must depart again for a few days."

"You just returned." Aaron raised an eyebrow, though he could in no way claim disappointment at the man's imminent absence.

"I have become aware of a section of the Venezuelan resistance movement with an unusually high number of gifted individuals. I am meeting with some of their Citizen Management chaps to see about an arrangement."

"An arrangement?"

"Indeed." Archon strolled for the door. "We protect the psionics from execution, and they have one less resistance cell to worry about."

"How is it you go in and out of ACC territory without batting an eyelash?"

Archon paused by the ruined food assembler. "Simple. I am not a UCF citizen. I am a subject of the King, with tenured credentials at Oxford traipsing about on droll educational forays. Ten minutes of explanation is all it takes to bore them to death."

His tweed coat billowed around as the man strode away.

Aaron stared at the empty doorway in disbelief.

LONELINESS DROVE AARON FROM THE ABANDONED BREAK ROOM TO AN HOURS' worth of roaming the grounds. Most of 'The Awakened' gang kept their distance. Already, rumors of the bad reaction he had to mental psionics had run the gauntlet, as well as whispers that he'd gone easy on Melissa in their 'duel.' Anna had made the mistake of talking about him catching the elevated walkway that almost fell on them, something she theorized even Archon couldn't have done, and it got overheard.

His wandering eventually brought him to the sixth floor of the main building and he followed the sound of all-too-familiar music, *God Save the King*, to a room at the corner they had converted into an entertainment area. A sofa and two reclining chairs sat over the outline of a massive L-shaped desk, permanently stamped into dark carpeting. Broken, decrepit, imitation Roman statues lined the walls among fake plants. Aaron assumed this had once been some executive's corner office.

A 120-inch holographic screen filled the room with bright light and the cheering of a stadium full of Frictionless spectators. Anna sat draped on a small couch, clad in a long Manchester United t-shirt. Her sock-covered feet rested on a glass coffee table, ankles crossed, ass an inch away from sliding off the edge of the cushion. Aaron smiled at her bare thighs. She likely had panties on as well, though he couldn't tell by looking, and rather liked to imagine the contrary.

Aurora perched cross-legged on a huge reclining chair, apparently scavenged from a nearby apartment building. She leaned vulture-like over a massive bowl of popcorn in her lap. Aaron felt far more comfortable around her when she wore clothes. Like Anna, she had on an oversized tee shirt, plain white, save for a sketchy cartoon of a psychotic-looking bunny rabbit with bloodshot eyes dragging a bloody cleaver beneath the words 'I feel fine' scrawled in childlike handwriting.

Seven other people lounged on an arrangement of cushions to the right of the seats. Five children played some manner of holographic board game with an older teenaged girl likely assigned to watch them. A sapphire-haired young man hovered at her side, no doubt tolerating the youngsters to impress his girlfriend.

With a blue and red flash, team logos for Arsenal and Manchester appeared, showing their win-loss stats for the year thus far. Arsenal's three and seven made him cringe. Fortunately, Manchester hadn't been undefeated, though he still expected no small amount of teasing since they'd gone eight and two.

"I didn't think you cared much for sports," said Aaron, glancing at Aurora.

"I don't." She tossed a single piece of popcorn up and caught it in her mouth. "I do love watching Anna get all lathered up about idiots running about chasing a metal ball."

"Those *idiots* are an important part of our society," said Anna, a little louder than necessary.

"Hey. I used to be one of those idiots." Aaron moved around the sofa and sat next to Anna.

He landed hard enough to cause her to slide forward. Her shirt rode up, disappointing him by revealing black lace panties. His telekinesis arrested her fall, and he set her back where she'd been.

"Careful!" She swatted at him. "Were you this clumsy on the field?"

"Easy," whispered Aurora. "She gets petulant during the games. Especially if Manchester is cack-handing it."

"I thought that was normal for them," mumbled Aaron.

"Shut up," whined Anna, frustrated at the lack of anything in arm's reach to throw.

"See?" Aurora laughed.

"The dedication of our fans is legendary." Aaron helped himself to her snack, levitating a small train from the bowl to his mouth.

Aurora narrowed her eyes at the thread of pilfered popcorn, a playful look of mock anger.

Players lined up on the screen. Seconds later, a shiny metal sphere of pentagonal panels descended from high above, settling to hover a foot off the ground between them. Aaron remembered the tension of those few seconds; one tiny telekinetic nudge could guarantee Arsenal first possession. At the blare of an electronic horn, armored boots blurred into chaos, scuffing and clicking. The stone, an orb of metal riding a cushion of glowing yellow light, rocketed away from the tangle of bodies, zooming toward the Manchester Goal. Individual panels opened and closed as it rotated, creating the illusion that the same trio of tiny ion thrusters remained pointed down.

Anna fumed. "Sodding idiots!" She sat up. "Does it take an act of Parliament to give you first possession for once? Twenty-two fecking percent."

Aaron opened his mouth, but Aurora waved at him and mouthed 'no.'

Ten minutes later, neither side had scored, but the orb had been closer to Manchester's goal for most of it.

"You're adoring this, aren't you?" Anna squinted at him.

"What's that? Your lack of pants?"

"No, dammit, Arsenal toying with us." She froze, staring at him for a moment before looking down at her bare legs. "I..."

"It's been a few years since she had an audience," said Aurora.

"Oh, both of you can go to hell." Anna scooted upright on the sofa, pulling the shirt down to the middle of her thighs. "Is it a crime to want to be comfortable?"

Aurora shrugged. "That's what I keep asking."

Postlethwaite, Arsenal's current all-star striker, broke away with the orb and ran uncontested toward Manchester's goal. Anna forgot all about her modesty and jumped to her feet.

"No, no, no!" she yelled. "Sons of bitches, they're just standing there! Catch him, you pack of wankers."

"Cooper and McQuillen always did have lead in their asses," said Aaron. "Even when I played."

"They've gotta be old men now," whispered Aurora.

The yellow-clad Postlethwaite nudged the orb sideways and jumped over a slide tackle from a man in blue.

"Fecking Lerwick! You idiot. Postalwaste *always* jumps!" screamed Anna. She whined at the shrinking distance between the orb and the goal. "Un-be-fucking-lievable."

"Postalwaste?" Aaron chuckled.

The kids on the far side of the room, except for one of the young Russian boys, all stopped paying attention to their board game. The true reason for their presence in the room showed by the amused looks on their faces as they watched her lose her mind.

"You better knock that bastarding thing, Patel." Anna pointed at the Manchester goaltender, who had a look on his face akin to a deer staring down an onrushing starship.

"He's new," said Aaron. "What's he, nineteen? He's going to choke."

"Stuff it!" yelled Anna. "Patel! Block that fecking stone!"

Postlethwaite ran in an arc, faking right and kicking with his left leg. Small ion thrusters in his boot heel fired, punting the 'stone' in a pin-straight line. Patel leapt at it, pulling his knees to his chest, deflecting the eight-pound sphere with his armored shins. A pair of Manchester defenders caught up and recovered it on the rebound.

"See!" Anna stuck her finger in Aaron's face. "Without your cheating, they can't score."

His cheek smushed into his hand, one finger up along the side of his eye. "You're quite beautiful when you're angry."

Anna stood statue still, save for a faint twitching in her upper lip. A moaning sound emanating from the crowd five seconds later made her look at the screen. A stocky blue-uniformed figure lay dazed near the center of the field; once again, Postlethwaite had the stone moving for Manchester's goal.

"Howsham, what the bloody hell are you doing?" Anna jumped up and down like a nine-year-old pitching a tantrum. "You know you've got a bloody glass skull."

"Is she this... animated when they're winning?" He leaned around her to wink at Aurora.

"About the same, with less screaming." Aurora pinched the air. "A skosh less."

Anna dropped to her knees, arms outstretched, raging at the screen. Postlethwaite ducked two defenders and appeared to slip and miss, right boot kicking over the ball while attempting to take another shot on goal. The thruster on his errant boot swept him off his feet, lifting him skyward.

Anna leapt up, starting to erupt in a cheer of "Yeeeee," which could've been 'yes' or 'you sodding idiot', for all Aaron knew.

Before she could get more than a single syllable out, Postlethwaite's diagonal backflip brought his left leg around and in contact with the orb, sending it at a wild angle Patel never saw coming. His 'missed kick' proved to be intentional.

Postlethwaite ate artificial grass as the orb skidded into the goal area, setting off a nuclear war of flashing lights, buzzers, sirens, and flickering holographic ghosts all over the stadium.

All the energy sapped out of Anna, she flopped back on the sofa. "Well, lucky little shit."

"That wasn't luck," said Aaron. "He meant to do that. Runaway firehose. I hate the taste of turf by the way."

"What?" She squinted at him.

"They call that maneuver the 'runaway firehose' 'cause of the way the player flips around... like a—"

Anna pouted. "Sod it. Go ahead, get it over with."

"What?"

"You know you wanna say it." She stared down at her socks.

He leaned close, whispering. "You're beautiful when you're sad."

She blushed, gawped at him, and shoved him sideways into the couch. Aaron laughed. The celebratory flashing ceased and another eight minutes of back-and-forth doldrums passed, but at least a few spectacular wipeouts kept it entertaining. Anna got riled up again when debatable hand contact on the part of an Arsenal player earned a ruling of accidental. They reset the play, but she bellowed for a penalty as the cameras zoomed in on McManus, the Manchester head coach, who screamed at the ref.

"I really don't understand all the fuss," said Aurora. "They're just running from one end of the arena to the other, over and over. What's so damn exciting about that? If I wanted to watch a pack of wankers traipse about in circles getting nowhere, I'd go observe Parliament."

"There's less blood here." Aaron gestured at the screen.

Anna settled into a simmering stare at the holo-panel. Occasionally, she'd mutter the name of a player like an oath.

What's the deal with all the kids? asked Aaron, telepathically.

Aurora munched on popcorn. *Take what we can get, mostly. We had about forty locals, but most of them were teens when we started. Early twenties now. James has been bringin' em over from London whenever he can, but things are changin' back there. Softening up a bit. Most of the new arrivals are from ACC territory. Much easier to smuggle kids out of those places... and not a lot of psionics get to grow up if they stay there.*

Aaron glanced at the side of the room. The Russian boy, twelve if that, looked like he'd crawled straight out of a war zone. Tattered clothes, too-large boots, even a pistol in a belt holster. He stared at the game board like Kasparov reincarnated, plotting his next move. When the older girl and her boyfriend lip-locked, and the other kids occupied themselves laughing at Anna throwing a fit, he reached up and moved three pieces.

Aaron couldn't decide if he should laugh, scold him, or feel pity.

Is this what they want? He lifted an eyebrow at Aurora.

For a lot of them, it's 'leave Earth or die.' She tilted the bowl toward him, offering more popcorn. *They'll be all right.*

Aaron raised an arm to shield his face as a three-pronged assault left the Arsenal goaltender confused. Alastair Morgan punted one in to bring the game to a tie. Anna leapt several times as if trying to see if she could reach the ceiling. Hall and Sivakumar, who had distracted the goalie, hoisted Morgan up and carried him back into a crowd of cheering players.

"See that!" she yelled. "We don't need telekinetics to score!"

"I was waiting for that," he mumbled.

Anna held both arms up, letting off a long "Woooo" while falling backward onto the sofa.

Aaron's devilish grin earned a sidelong glance, and a few seconds later a full on stare.

"What?" Anna squinted at him and checked to make sure her panties weren't showing again.

"I was just thinking," he said. "Alastair isn't the only Morgan to breach the defenses of an Arsenal player."

"We've scored at least twenty—" She got a bit of color in her cheeks and sank back to her seat. "Aaron..."

"Yes, Miss Morgan?"

"That's not fair." She picked at the hem of her shirt. "You know I can't think like that. If things were different..."

Aurora shook the popcorn bowl, trying not to smile.

Red filled the room as the image on the screen changed.

"Oh, bloody hell," muttered Anna. "Damn adverts. They were in the middle of a play."

"Middle of running about like fools," said Aurora, earning a scowl.

A short Hispanic woman in a sea-foam green blazer and white frilled collar stood in front of a burning structure surrounded by desert scrub. Fire suppression bots orbited the wreckage, spraying trails of white chemicals from above while men assaulted it with hoses from the ground.

"NewsNet brings you a special report, live from the town of La Lobeña, Mexico."

"Sod the special report," yelled Anna. "They can't do this. A thousand channels and they have to pre-empt Frictionless? If I wanted news, I'd have on the goddamned NewsNet."

The reporter spoke in Spanish, with English words scrolling along the bottom. "Hours ago, Security Forces raided the church of Saint Michael the Purifier in the outskirts of the quiet, law-abiding town of La Lobeña." She gestured at the building behind her. "The fire broke out as personnel with the Citizen Management Office engaged gunmen loyal to the presumed-dead Fernando De la Cruz, former leader of the congregation. Born as Fernando Medina, he was known in and outside Mexico as a vocal proponent calling for the purge of all psionics as embodiments of the Devil. What a shock it was to this reporter, and no doubt all of Mexico, when evidence came to light that his fire-and-brimstone preaching was little more than a front to disguise efforts to provide equipment and refuge for local anti-establishment rebels.

"Due to the quick actions by local citizens"—the camera panned back to a smiling man, woman, and three young boys—"the law-breaking pastor and his traitorous group of rebels cannot threaten the safety and security of any of our beloved citizens."

Aaron ignored the rest of the woman's ramble about how the 'loyal family' would be rewarded for their patriotism by reassignment to higher paying, more prestigious careers that qualified them as 'citizens.' He put a hand on top of Anna's.

"What?" She stopped glaring doom at the NewsNet feed and looked at him.

"Archon was just in Mexico."

"Yes, so?"

"Don't you think it's a bit suspicious?"

"I suppose." She waved at the screen. "Come on, then. We get the point. Back to the game."

"Hey," yelled the twentyish girl watching the kids. She pointed at the Russian boy. "I saw that. You're cheating."

He gave her a defiant look that said 'do something about it.' "Play to win or do not play."

The other kids fidgeted.

"Alexi, that's not how we play games." The woman tried to sound stern. "Put the pieces back and apologize to everyone."

"You do not care of game. You want to make the sex with him, like whore, in front of us." Alexi folded his arms as if to underscore his refusal to uncheat.

The woman gasped and slapped him. "Don't you dare talk to me like that, you—"

Her shouting lasted only long enough for his little brain to process that she'd struck him. He blinked, and punched her square in the nose, knocking her over backward. Her blue-haired boyfriend responded in kind, slugging Alexi in the head hard enough to send him sliding away from the game board. Smaller kids screamed and scurried for cover as Alexi sat up with a bloody nose and pulled his gun, shouting in Russian.

Before he could fire, or the young man could shit himself, Aaron's telekinetic yank tore the pistol out of Alexi's hand. The woman emanated a faint pulse of psionic energy and sprang upright, a motion blur that whisked Alexi off his feet and pinned him against the wall. She glowered at him for two seconds with a cocked fist and punched a hole in the cinder blocks next to his head. Aaron caught the floating handgun.

"What did you call me?" growled the teen.

Alexi stared at the hole in the wall inches from his cheek. He squirmed, but couldn't budge the fist that held him off the ground by the shirt. He lapsed into a panic, kicking and thrashing, still shouting in Russian, though he had taken on a pitiful mewling tone. Aaron skimmed his surface thoughts; in his mind, he saw a huge soldier in crimson armor holding him against the wall, raising a pistol to his face. Bodies littered the ground behind the man. Though he couldn't understand the stream of Russian thoughts, his fear of using psionics showed clear. He thought if he tried to act normal, they wouldn't kill him.

The boy had been part of the Russian Resistance.

A little Hispanic girl ran from the room, screaming.

The blue-haired teen put a hand on his girlfriend's shoulder. "Calm down, Dana."

"You called me something," Dana muttered. "Say it again."

"Dana..." said the older boy, "he's just a kid. A bastard, but a kid."

Alexi kicked her in the stomach, but she didn't budge; he grimaced as if he'd hurt his foot.

A hair-thin lightning bolt leapt from Anna's hand to the far wall, with a sound like a rifle shot.

Everyone cringed.

"Sack it, the lot of you." Anna glared. "Put him down."

"Ma'am..." Dana set the boy on his feet and backed away. "He was gonna shoot Saph."

"Saph did punch him in the head," said Anna. "Look at his bloody nose."

"Do you mean that in the British sense of bloody or the literal sense?" asked Aaron.

Alexi wiped at the smear of red on his face and backed away from both of them.

"He's unstable," said Dana. "He needs to be watched, and he shouldn't be allowed to have a gun."

The news broadcast ended; the screen again showed the Frictionless match, now at 2:1 in favor of Manchester. Anna's right eye got bigger than her left and she made a series of cat-having-a-hairball noises.

"Relax." Aurora winked. "We can download the uninterrupted stream when it's over."

"It's not the same." Anna paced about and whined for a few seconds. "It's not live."

"What difference does it make?" Aurora sighed. "Look. You sit down. I'll deal with the brat."

Aurora's body dissipated in a cloud of wispy fog, which leaked out of her empty shirt as the fabric fell flat on the chair. Alexi let off a startled yelp, arching his back as though someone had poured ice water over him. A moment later, he adopted a feminine stance.

"There. All set. I'll just walk the little blighter down to James's office and that'll be that."

Dana and Saph looked about ready to faint. The three children who hadn't run from the room all cried at once.

Alexi, rather Aurora, rolled his eyes. "Yeah, yeah. I scare the shite out of children." He looked down at himself, feeling at his ribs. "I think I'm going to make sure this little bugger eats first, though. He's all bones."

Anna and Aaron's heads turned in sync as the twelve-year-old boy wandered out.

"I'll never, ever, get used to that," said Anna.

Aaron checked the pistol, hit the magazine release, and cleared the round from the chamber, catching the little orange block out of midair. "What did you expect, giving children firearms? Has Archon completely lost his mind? Even 'ere in the UCF they require eighteen years old."

"With parental permission in the home," muttered Aurora from the hallway.

"Oh, we didn't give that to him. He 'ad it with 'im in the cargo box." A streak of yellow drew Anna's attention back to the screen. "Fuck you, Postalwaste. God dammit. No!"

2:2 tied game.

Anna fumed.

He raised an eyebrow at the caseless round in his palm. *Orange propellant?*

That's ACC-made. "The operative word there being had. Why didn't anyone take it?"

"This *is* a black zone," said Saph. "Somethin' gets over the wall, you rather he have nothin' to defend himself with? Never thought he'd go schizo on us."

"Looking after psionic children is a lot like trying to control a room full of tiny, angry drunks with minimal impulse control and access to high-grade weapons." Aaron rubbed the bridge of his nose.

"Fucking run you wankers! Dammit Heathcomb, move your ass." Anna shrieked incomprehensible made up words as two Arsenal defenders cornered a Manchester striker.

"I don't wanna get shot," whispered a little voice from inside cabinets near the disrupted board game.

Aaron settled into the sofa, with Anna freaking out on his left and Archon's bad, bad idea all around him. He stuffed his hand into his pocket, rubbing Allison's nameplate while thinking back to what he'd told Melissa: that he hadn't decided yet about still being a cop.

P'raps I ought to make up my mind. What'cha 'fink, Alli?

16

A PROPHET'S DOUBT

Althea

Holographic shapes hovered in midair over the thin slab of transparent plastic. Althea sat sideways with her feet up on Father's tattered old sofa, staring at the three little symbols. Frustrated, she glanced up at the ceiling, wondering what Father had asked Karina to help him with that kept her away so long.

The smell of dinner still lingered in the air. Beams from handheld lights waved amid the darkness of the living room windows. Two of the city police walked by out front, small dots on their belts glowing like azure fireflies. Althea took a deep breath, snuggling deeper into the cushions and again staring at the 'word' in front of her. Archon had given her similar things to 'civilize' her, but this time, Father had *asked* her to use them. She wanted nothing to do with the big city full of angry people always in a hurry. He thought she should learn how those strange marks on things talked to people. 'Reading' seemed useless, but she would do it to make her family happy.

"Sat," she said.

"Almost," replied a voice reminiscent of a kind, older woman.

An image of a cat appeared, walking around the word. It stopped and meowed at her, blinked, and sat on its haunches.

"*Gato*," she said.

"English please."

Althea furrowed her brow and thought it over. "*The* gato."

"Try again, you're getting warmer."

Her knuckles whitened on the sides of the finger-thick plastic slab. Few things had ever made Althea as angry as this thing, but she knew it was a mere object. She mulled for a few minutes, staring at the blinking C at the far left.

"C-cat?"

"Correct," said the elder. The first letter grew large, and the others disappeared. "What letter is this?"

"Cee. It should be a kay. Cee is like ess. It's the top half of an ess, so it should be like a shorter ess sound." Althea frowned at the cartoon kitty, thinking this 'reading' thing would never make any sense. It constantly broke its own rules.

Another word appeared with four letters. Beneath it, what appeared to be a mound of earth.

"*La tierra,*" said Althea.

"English please," said the female voice.

Althea's eyes watered. She wanted to throw the thing across the room, bury her face in the cushions, and sob. She bonked herself on the forehead with it twice, sniffled, and stared at it.

"Earth."

"You're getting warm. What else is earth sometimes called?"

"*La tierra,*" mumbled Althea, staring at the four-letter word floating above her knees.

Tears slipped away from her eyes and ran over her cheeks. Father would be disappointed in her.

"Try again. You can do it." The word glowed and flipped over. "It rhymes with hurt."

Now the thing made fun of her. How could something unalive make her feel so bad? She stared at the word, trying to sound it out. She recognized the *D* from dog but had no idea what the straight line after it meant. She squinted at it, wondering if it should be a U instead.

Imagining the 'i' to a 'u', she said, "Durt."

"Very good."

"This is wrong," Althea whined. "What is that?" She poked her finger at the hologram, impaling the letter 'I.'

"I," said the voice. "One of the five primary vowels. *I* is usually pronounced with an *ih* sound as in 'fit,' but can also represent *ur* as in 'dirt', and sometimes *i* as in 'dine.'"

"I'll never remember this." She flung the datapad onto the cushion beyond her toes. "I hate this thing. Why can't a person show me?"

Althea wrapped her arms around her legs, gathering her knees to her chest and sniffled, pouting.

The pad, ignorant of its new location on the sofa, displayed another word.

Three letters, with an animation of a forkful of food going into a cartoon child's mouth.

"Eat," grumbled Althea.

"You got that on the first try. Excellent."

Why did it feel like it made fun of her again?

Thuds crossed the ceiling. A moment later, Father descended the stairs. Her tears stopped in an instant at the sight of him. A lime green blazer with gold buttons at the ends of the sleeves practically glowed in the dark. Under it, he wore a pink button-down shirt with a bolo tie but still had on his jeans and boots. Odder still, a strange chemical smell followed him. Sensing anxiety on him, Althea moved to her knees and leaned over the sofa back.

"Father, what's wrong?"

He sucked in a breath and approached, ruffling her hair. "Nothing is wrong, *cariño*."

"You're scared." Althea reached out and took his hand.

Father chuckled at the concern brimming in her eyes. "It is nothing to worry about. I will be back in a few hours, but you should be asleep by then."

She hugged him, suppressing the urge to gag on the odd smell. Althea felt confused by his strange mixture of eagerness and dread but said nothing as he walked out. Karina crouched near the top of the stairs, peering under the level of the ceiling at her.

"How is your schoolwork?"

Althea grumbled as she rolled off the sofa to her feet. "I don't like this." She picked up the datapad, turning it over in her hands in search of how to make it go dark. "It isn't alive, and it makes me angry."

"Why?"

Althea stared at it. "It calls me dumb, and makes fun of me." Unable to find the off switch, she trudged around the sofa to the stairs.

Karina took the device, and had about as much luck finding a means to turn it off. Out of desperation, she held it up and said, "Off."

It went dark.

Althea followed Karina to their room and pulled her dress off over her head. "If they want me to learn the reading, why can't a person show me?" She took a soft, cotton nightgown from the peg on the inside of the door and wriggled into it.

Karina changed as well and got into bed. "The city police are busy."

"That is why they are all angry." Althea crawled in next to her sister. "They don't have time for people, so they use machines to do people things."

Karina reached over her to turn off the small light on their nightstand. Color faded to black and white, save for a tiny patch of blue where the ceiling reflected the glow from her eyes. She lay flat on her back, thinking. The 'lectric lamp was a new addition to their room, and not a welcome one. Many of the small children feared the dark, but Althea felt protected without light, when only she could see. The city police had told her some astral sensitives could peer half-into the spirit world to see in the dark, and somehow, she had developed a similar ability that remained on all the time. Her description of it merely being without color had baffled them, as their understanding of 'Darksight' made her think of how everything looked when Aurora took her 'behind the curtain.' In the dark, Althea saw the world without color, not full of wavy walls, strange whispers, and eerie shadows. She felt foolish, thinking of dozens of times during her years of captivity where she could've used that to escape had she not been so obedient. She could have eluded raiders who couldn't see. Althea frowned at the 'lectric lamp near the bed. It reminded her of the giant, modern city in the west.

It had never truly been dark in that awful place; she'd never felt safe.

Her mind strayed back to their conversation about Den. She scooted closer to Karina, not ready to give up the safety of *her* bedroom. Conflicted emotion kept her awake. She liked Den in ways that felt confusing—exciting and scary at the same time, but the idea he would take her away from her family worried her the most.

"Mmm." Karina emitted a soft moan. "Stop fidgeting."

"Sorry." Althea lay still. "Why was Father dressed funny?"

Karina yawned, stretched, and laced her fingers behind her head. "He's got a date."

Althea looked at Karina with a confused expression, making her squint from the bright blue light so close to her face.

"Date means he's going to Tumbleweed's to spend time with a woman."

"Who?"

"Her name is Alejandra. She arrived with the other one who wanted to kill you."

"Kate didn't want to hurt me. The Many made her do it." Althea swished her feet back and forth under the blankets. "Why was Father afraid? Is she gonna hurt him?"

"No, Thea." Karina laughed. "He likes her. Father is probably worried she won't like him."

"Oh." She smiled. "He is not so sad now."

"She is not my mother, but if she can make him happy, I guess it's good." Sadness.

Althea rolled on her side, putting an arm over Karina's chest and snuggling. "Sorry."

They lay in silence for a while. Karina's sense of loss for her mother waned after a time, replaced by love for the family she had left. Althea closed her eyes and tried to sleep, but could not settle her roaming mind. She had a loving family, a safe place to live, and no one had tried to kidnap her in a few months. Her sense of contentment worried her. Every time she had felt safe or happy in the past, something had followed soon after. Whenever she'd found a settlement that treated her well—even if she had to put up with worship—it would only last a few weeks before raiders came, and she'd spend another few months in chains or a cage. A brief moment of sleep came bearing dream memories: her vision of a sad Karina in the fields when Archon had taken her away. Fear that someone or something would take her away from her family built and brought tears. Althea curled in a ball and concentrated on not letting her feelings leak out over Querq.

She sniffled and cried.

Her sister stirred, dragged back from sleep by the sobbing girl. "Thea? What's wrong."

"I'm too happy."

Karina tickled her on the stomach. "You don't sound it."

"I *am* happy," wailed Althea. "Something bad is gonna happen, 'cause whenever I'm happy something bad always happens."

"Oh, Thea." Karina sat up, pulling her into a tight hug. "It's okay." She shivered. "You didn't get a vision did you?"

"No." She sniffled, wiping her eyes. "I'm scared. I was dreaming of you when I got taken to the city. I saw you working on the farm, crying." A few sobs interrupted her. "I wanted to tell you I was alive, and I yelled your name. You ran off like you heard me."

Karina's eyes watered as well. "I remember. I *did* hear you, quiet like you were far away. I don't know why, but I knew you were alive and needed help. I ran home, thinking you might be there, but you weren't. I told Father." She rocked Althea back and forth. "He thought I was so sad I imagined it."

"I'm sorry."

"The city police arrived a few days later. They said they found you and wanted to know who her father was."

"I told them I had a father and a sister." Althea grinned.

"We went with them because I heard you call me that day. I knew you needed us."

They held each other for a few more minutes before they lay back down. Althea shut her eyes again, trying to sleep. Another dream came, of Nalu dragging her by the arm to the green beast.

"You cannot kill without hesitation; you are a burden here," said Nalu in the dream.

The world changed to the courtroom. Querq's council of judges rose into the air over her, their black robes stretching them into giant, demonic ravens. Hector's awful wild-eyed face glowered from the shadows as he shot Karina.

"Nalu has wrong. I would hurt someone to save your life," whispered Althea.

"Thea?" Karina's voice woke her. "You are having a bad dream."

Light from Althea's eyes covered Karina in a bright azure glow, making her sister seem darker. "Nalu shut me inside an old machine because he said I could not protect myself." She smirked. "I was too afraid until the Ravens almost sent me away."

"You shouldn't dwell on such bad memories."

Althea smiled. "It is not a bad memory. It is when I knew I was home. When I felt how sad you were to watch me leave, I knew I couldn't let them send me away."

"If there is such a thing as fate, it owes you a little happiness after all you have been through." Karina stroked Althea's hair. "You are so innocent. All you want to do is help everyone. It is about time the world is nice to you back."

Karina poked her in the side.

Althea poked Karina in the side.

Karina tickled her on the stomach.

Althea attacked Karina's ribs.

Soon, the blankets lay askew and they rolled around in a tickle fight. Despite Karina's weight and size advantage, Althea's subconscious control over her body gave her strong muscles, and the battle stalemated. Their laughter got louder and louder. Soon after they both collapsed, breathless and sweating, three heavy slams hit the wall.

Father was home—and trying to sleep.

Both girls gasped and covered their mouths.

"*¡Lo siento!*" said Althea.

"Go to sleep," murmured Father, from behind the wall.

Althea sat up and gathered the blankets, flopping back down and cuddling at Karina's side. Her urge to giggle grew as they stared at each other. The more they tried to keep still, the more irresistible it became, until both of them burst out laughing again. Seconds later, they held their breath, grinning and dreading another bang.

Father's mood must have been good, for he didn't hit the wall again. After a few minutes of grinning at each other, the hilarity faded, and they settled down to sleep.

THE DEVIL'S LITTLE SISTER

Aaron

A small corridor full of dead vendomats led up to a large cafeteria that could have served thousands of employees. Archon's army of disgruntled, disenfranchised, psionic teens jostled about in search of places to sit. Older recruits preferred to eat alone, either in the tent city or at the places they stood guard, and the youngest of the refugees were still too new to the country to brave going outside.

They segregated themselves into small groups: a few of the youngest teens sat together at one table. Two geeky-looking boys distanced themselves from everyone else, busy with some manner of hovering electronic device. Aaron chuckled at how much like high school it looked, if students carried fully automatic weapons.

He leaned against the archway at the edge of the light, flicking his thumbnail over the side of his NetMini. When the British schoolgirls entered from the far door, Aaron edged deeper into the dark. So far, no one had noticed him there. If those two saw him, they'd go fangirl and ruin any chance he had of accomplishing what he hoped to do.

The pair huddled together as they walked to the Czechoslovakian man who'd wound up in charge of the industrial-sized food assembler, another item the mechanically inclined psionics brought back from the dead. The girls seemed somewhat less afraid of him than they did the world around them, flashing polite smiles before hurrying off with their trays. The taller one, Lucy, he thought, glanced in his direction, but appeared not to notice him. Jet-black hair shadowed green eyes set in a face so downtrodden, Aaron had to bite his lip to resist the urge to send a comforting telepathic message. Meredith, the younger girl, led the way to a table apart from everyone else. They sat stooped like starved hyenas over their food, wary stares aimed around the room as they ate.

One did not need to be psionic to know they pined for their families.

At last, the object of his hunt appeared: Melissa. She stormed in from the courtyard double doors, which appeared to open on their own. The clatter of a thin plastisteel frame with no glass silenced the cafeteria. Except for the boys with the gadgets, every eye in the room focused on her as she stopped by the 'cook.'

Whispers started as soon as she passed by. Aaron only caught a few snippets: if she's Awakened, why's she still in here with us? Did Aaron go easy on her? She's such a bitch. Don't look at her or she'll start a fight. Melissa glared at the room; fourteen food trays flipped onto their owners all at once.

"Get outta my fucking head, you assholes!" Melissa screamed, fumed, and glared at the man trying to hand her dinner.

She took the tray and stomped along a row between two empty tables. Aaron raised his NetMini and lined up the green corner markers around her face. The second his thumb touched the button to capture a scan, a woman cleared her throat behind him.

"Am I interrupting something I'd rather not know about?"

Anna.

He didn't flinch. Image capture in hand, he swiped his finger at an app he hadn't touched in months—the National Police Force Reference Database. He flashed a half-grin. "What is it you think you're interrupting?"

"She's fifteen." Anna, standing behind him in the dim corridor, folded her arms. "It's not bad enough you humiliated her in front of everyone the other night, you're lurking here like a nonce?"

Text popped up in a frame next to Melissa's picture. He furrowed his eyebrows. "Please tell me you don't honestly think that."

"I was hoping not." Anna let her arms drape at her sides and her expression softened. Light from the room behind her made her white pixie cut glow. "So, what is it then?"

"You ever 'ave this naggin' feeling just gnawin' at the back of your mind?" Aaron pocketed the NetMini.

She glanced at the noisy room. Watching Meredith and Lucy seemed to darken her mood. "Aye. You're 'avin' doubts about all of this, aren't you?"

Aaron moved closer, gazing into her sapphire eyes. "Tell me you don't?"

"They're better off here." She glanced down. "It's not perfect, but it's better than getting killed, or shut up in some CSB laboratory. You think those girls would be happier with little bombs in their brains?"

I think they'd be happier with official asylum. Before his willpower could falter to the point he tried to kiss her, he took her hand. For a few seconds, he found himself admiring the softness of her skin. "Come on. I need to see something, and I think you should see it as well."

Anna stumbled along behind him, struggling to keep up with his longer strides. "Where are you going in such a rush?"

"You think James will mind if we borrow his car?"

"What? You're not serious."

"I am." He stopped at the door, still holding her hand. "Take a ride with me?"

"What are you doing?" She looked down at her bare legs and sock feet.

"Trying to help."

Her head snapped up. Eye contact. Aaron felt his eyelids closing a little, his weight shifting forward, his lips parting ever so slightly. Anna looked as though she didn't much mind the thoughts forming in his mind. Their noses glided past each other. Millimeters from lip contact, they both froze.

"Let me get dressed at least."

Her whisper floated into his mouth. Aaron glanced aside and down, nodding. "Right. Aye. Knickers would be good."

Her face went pink. She gave him a playful shove and trotted off. Aaron grimaced, cursing under his breath for slipping. Something *was* wrong; if he pushed too hard, he'd lose her. Granted, he hadn't meant to push. He trudged to the main lobby, not bothering to open the glassless doors on his way to lean against the gold Halcyon-Ormyr parked in the courtyard. A small version of Melissa's face glared at him from his NetMini. Her anger had become that little thing nagging at the back of his mind.

Aaron glanced up at the tower, hoping Anna trusted him.

🐌 🦞 🍖 🐚 🐛

THE HOVERCAR LET OFF A FAINT HISS AS ITS WEIGHT SETTLED STRAIGHT DOWN onto its wheels. Aaron opened one eye, casting a hesitant glance at the stationary vehicles all around them. A hundred and two stories up, clouds flanked the roof parking deck on all sides. According to the 3D holographic Navcon map over the dashboard, they'd arrived at the address he'd programmed in.

"Oh, that's quite enough," said Anna, from the driver's seat. "Sod it."

"You nearly hit four advert bots and some manner of flying sushi boat." He pointed to a small bit of salmon stuck to the windscreen in front of his face. "It's a bloody miracle we didn't get forced down."

"This thing's got a bit more power than I'm used to. You know how it is at home. I never touched one of these bloody flying things till two years ago." She glared at him. "If you're going to brick it, you can walk back."

"No, no… it's just that I've been trying to limit my near death experiences to one or two a week."

What started as a snarl turned into a giggle at the expression on his face. "You're incorrigible."

He sighed. More than anything, he wanted to hold her. Right there in the car, on this roof parking deck, right now, he wanted to kiss her. The weight of the NetMini in his pocket dragged him back to the reason they'd come here.

"What're you thinking?" she asked. "I'm not sure I like that look in your eye."

"I was admiring how beautiful your eyes are, if you want the honest truth, and I need them to see something."

She blushed.

Before she could remind him she loved Archon, he got out. "Come on."

Aaron crossed the parking area to the elevator hub, Anna following at an awkward distance. She remained silent on the ride down to the forty-eighth floor. Lifeless brown carpet, neat, clean, and bland, stretched a hundred meters out to a four-way corridor framed by pale green walls with glowing clamshell-shaped lights of frosted plastic every three doors. He went to the eleventh apartment on the left, and stopped, facing it.

"Follow my lead." He pushed the doorbell.

"What are you doing?" Anna whispered.

"Just follow along."

He tapped his foot for a little over a minute and brought up a blurry image of a Division 0 ID on the physical screen.

The door opened, revealing a bleary-eyed man in his middle-to-late forties. He had a little paunch inflating his powder-blue sweater, and the telltale crimp of a senshelmet compressed his bushy, receding hair.

"Can I help you? You know I'm still at work right now."

Aaron held up his 'badge' for an instant as he started talking. "Tactical Officer Pryce, Division 0. This is Agent Postlethwaite, with Investigations. Do you have a minute to discuss your daughter, Melissa?"

You are a bastard. Anna's voice echoed in his mind.

The man backed away as Aaron invited himself in, fighting the need to smile, still talking fast and loud.

"We're looking into her recent disappearance, and wondering if she has tried to make contact with you or your wife." He pulled the NetMini out of his pocket, flipping to the panel showing the results of his search. "You would be Mr. McKay? May I call you Ken?"

Anna followed, hardened eyes fixed on Aaron. *Postlethwaite? Really?*

"Uhh." Ken scratched his head, worsening his already horrible hair. "Is this gonna take long? We haven't seen her in a while."

A woman's voice came from the right. "She ran away again?"

Her mother, a forty-something version of Melissa, emerged from a beige hallway. She had the same fiery presence and black hair as her daughter.

"Please, one at a time." Aaron smiled at the father. "What can you tell me about her?"

The man rambled on about how dangerous she had become: getting into drugs, worshipping the devil, planning to murder them in their sleep. Aaron ignored most of the words, telepathically delving into the man's mind instead. His thoughts gravitated to every screaming match they'd had in the last months of her living at home, before Division 0 had taken her the first time. In her father's memory, Melissa's eyes glowed red and smoke curled out of her lips as she snarled. Aaron concentrated, burrowing deeper into the man's thoughts. A feeling as if he had head-butted a gelatinous mass spread over his face. For an instant, he saw a sobbing Melissa pleading with her father not to hate her—the man remembered her screaming how much she hated him.

An implanted memory.

"… so we let you people take her before she killed us," said Ken.

The woman glared. "And a lot of good that did. Can't you people hold on to your criminals?"

Aaron glanced at Anna. *Read his mind. Something's been done to him.*

She squinted at him, but turned her attention to the man as Aaron approached the mother. He peered at a collection of finger-sized holo-bars on a bookshelf; pictures of Melissa at various ages glimmered above them. At ten, she smiled and looked innocent, but in the next photo dated a few months after, she stared at the camera with a 'please don't hate me' expression.

That's when they discovered her 'gift.' He brushed aside a twinge of guilt. When Aaron's talent had manifested at eight, his father had been enthralled like a giant child given a wonderful new toy. He kept insisting that Aaron do things, and found it brilliant. His mother didn't even bat an eyelash, commemorating his psionic firsts the way the parent of an ordinary boy might've made monuments to any other milestone in their son's life. Yet this girl hadn't received anything but fear from her own family.

"Mrs. McKay," said Aaron. "Your daughter has run away from the dorm again. Home is the first place she'll likely go."

The woman's strong presence crumbled in seconds. She trembled, as if he had told her half of West City wanted her head on a pole. When he dove into her thoughts, images of poltergeist-like activity surrounded him. Eerie echoes of a screaming girl came from everywhere at once. Aaron broke out in a sweat, trying to force his way through the sense of falsehood. What had been knives floating around in search of parental throats became books, holo-bars, and stuffed animals.

Aaron decided to take a chance. "Melissa wasn't trying to kill you."

"Of course she was!" yelled the mother. "She had her coven here that night. They were waiting for us to go to sleep so they could slit our throats."

Mrs. McKay slumped to her knees, sobbing. Images in her memory showed Melissa sneaking up on her while she lay in bed. The white sleep suit Melissa wore flickered between a snug knee-length garment and a long, hooded black silk robe that covered everything but her head and toes. Her daughter's face shifted as well, a ghostly, superimposed grin of demonic glee hovered over an expression of fear. A group of specters, other faceless teen girls, vanished and manifested in time with Melissa's robes. In one blink, a frightened daughter came looking for comfort; in the next, seven devil worshippers closed in, daggers eager for blood.

"It's not real." Aaron gasped for breath. "You've been tampered with."

"You people haven't helped us one bit," said Ken. "We sent her to you as a frightened child, and now she's a bloodthirsty psycho."

"You should leave," said the mother.

"Ken. Look at your wife. She's trembling. Does that seem like the woman you know? If she's anything like Melissa, she's not afraid of a damn thing." Aaron squeezed his fists tight. "To the point of stupidity."

Sweat beaded along the man's forehead as he glanced at his wife. His mind knew Aaron had a point, but something else in there pushed him to doubt. Anna put a hand to her mouth, eyes widening with shock at what she appeared to see in his thoughts.

"You sense it, don't you?" Aaron looked at her. "False memories."

"Christina," whispered Ken, reaching for his wife. "She'll be coming for us."

"What's going on?" asked the woman. "I saw things. Those other girls were appearing and disappearing. The robes too. I—"

"They weren't real. A fabrication. Your daughter was coming to you for help." Aaron focused psionic energy into Christina's mind, battering at the telepathic imprint. It felt as though he chipped at a boulder with an icepick. Heat filled his lungs from the exertion. "Think about your daughter. Your little girl. She still loves you." A tremor of vulnerability rattled the stone inside her brain, but not enough to dislodge it.

Anna intercepted Ken as he moved to grab Aaron by the shoulder. "I'll need you to stand here, sir. Need I remind you this is an official investigation?" *I thought you got sacked.*

Aaron cringed, trying to balance his psionic war with the incoming telepathic message. He found a sliver of spare concentration to reply. *Get... picture... young.*

Her stare flicked from him to the shelf full of small vases and holo-bars.

She ran to it and back, holding a transparent image of Melissa, around six or seven years old, up to the woman's face. Anna's mental voice crept into Christina's mind, a telepathic message mimicking the plea of a little girl.

Mommy, help me.

His right leg twitching from the strain going on in his mind, Aaron let off a surge of power. Anna's imitation of a child worked like a prybar, letting him get 'under' the implant and rip it loose. Images, sounds, and feelings exploded in the woman's consciousness as the past six months returned to the way she had truly lived them.

Aaron staggered backward until he fell onto the sofa, panting and gasping, as exhausted as if he'd iron-manned a Frictionless match without any intermissions or even water. Christina continued to tremble, though it seemed a product of anger rather than implanted fear. She stared at Aaron until Ken broke the silence.

"Look, you bastards in black have done enough damage to our family. Our daughter's gone insane, what more do you want from us?"

"She's not insane, you idiot," screamed Christina. "Something's happened. You... we were so fucking stupid." She glared at her husband. "Don't just stand there gaping at me. We have to find her."

"You want to let that creature back into this house?"

Christina slapped him.

"Hold on, Ma'am," said Anna. "It's not his fault. Same thing's been done to 'im as you."

"Are you really with the police?" asked Christina.

"Yes," Anna replied, quick enough to seem convincing.

The woman folded her arms. "What's with the accent?"

"I'm originally from Britain. What, never heard of immigration?"

"Oh. Sorry. Should I offer you tea or something?"

Aaron cackled. "That would be nice."

Ken took an aggressive step closer, but Aaron levitated him across the room and dropped him in a recliner.

"Need a minnit to find me breath before we do that again. Those boots aren't regulation are they?"

Anna glanced at her past-the-knee blue faux-suede high-heeled boots. "I don't rightly know. The commander's never made a big issue of it before. I think he fancies them."

"You believe me now?" Aaron lifted an eyebrow. *How many people you think he's done that to?*

Her face reddened. *You don't honestly think James did this? Why would he?*

Aaron smiled at Melissa's mother as she handed him a glass of iced tea. "Thank you, so very much." He gulped down half of it before stopping for air.

Ken jumped up and made it one step before he floated back into his seat.

Christina blinked.

"Stay put, mate," said Aaron, before looking at Anna. *Because, Anna... He wanted Melissa. The girl's Awakened. Precious to him, but she had a home. They needed some help handling her, but her parents* do *care for her. He had to sever that connection to get her. She'd never have joined him if she had a home.* "Mrs. McKay, we'll 'ave your hubby right as rain in a moment. Whoever altered your memories is quite powerful. It took a lot out of me to get rid of it."

Anna shook her head, closing her eyes. "No..."

Of course, it's him. Apparently, I'm Awakened. That makes my abilities, what was it, an 'order of magnitude' stronger than other psionics?

Anna nodded.

It stands to reason my telepathic abilities should far outstrip a psionic that wasn't Awakened, yes?

Anna frowned, though she nodded. *Aye.*

Then who else could've left an imprint that's such a ballache for me to dislodge?

Tears gathered in the corners of Anna's eyes but didn't fall.

Aaron finished the tea, handed the empty cup to Christina, and stood. *How many people do you think he's done that to, eh?*

No. Anna grabbed his arm, fixing him with a glare. *You're being paranoid. James wouldn't do that.*

He pulled her over to the chair where Ken cowered. *No, I suppose he wouldn't do it with everyone. Only when there was an Awakened he rather wanted to have on his side, and something got in his way. If it's a question of what he is willing to do ... Look at what he 'as Talis doin' at the starport.*

Anna cringed, shuddering. "T-that's different."

"What is?" asked Melissa's parents, in unison.

"Oh." Aaron flashed a disarming smile at Christina. "The nature of the implant. One moment. Agent Postlethwaite... would you mind giving me a hand?"

When Christina looked at Ken, Anna jabbed him in the ribs.

Aaron grunted. "We'll be out of your hair in a few minutes."

The woman stood behind her husband, hands on his shoulders, staring at Aaron. "Where's my daughter?"

He rubbed his side, grimacing. "We're working on that, ma'am."

A THOUSAND STEEL CLAWS

Mamoru

S team whorled along the surface of the water. Mamoru reclined, alone in a large hot tub in the bathroom of a two-thousand credit a night hotel. The distractions of the city, of once again being within civilization, had drained a day out of his life. His return to the world of cyberspace had been nothing short of transcendental, an exiled god returning to the kingdom of his creation.

Despite his rush of rekindled power, he had been cautious. His influence over the digital world made padding his credit statement trivial. He'd added enough to brush off the cost of the room and four gourmet meals. Three showers, eighteen hours of sleep, and two bottles of imported, unfiltered sake had almost erased the Badlands from his soul.

He relaxed in the slow churn of water jets, gazing at droplets of condensation gathering on the grey-white tiles. Need lurked at the back of his mind; he had something to do. Urgency seemed unnecessary since he had hidden the ship well enough. A day or four to enjoy civilization again seemed a well-earned respite from the primitive mess.

When he had gone to the terminal to order female entertainment, he hesitated, thinking of Nami. That which was not Mamoru, yet dwelled within him, savored the emotion of her finding him with another woman, yet he could not bring himself to betray the woman he had been too afraid to admit his feelings to. He had not thought of her since the crash. Consumed by worry of Sadako, his mind never strayed from its focus for his sister's safety until he had confronted that horrible creature disguised as a little girl. Her blue-glowing eyes bored from his memory into his soul, torturing him with her very presence. Timid, fragile, innocent—all lies. *Concern.* "Hah!" His laugh echoed in the warm humidity. *She has concern only for destroying us.*

The journey from Querq to the city had passed in a blur. As best he could remember, he'd wandered alone in the desert for days. Nothing about it felt real, as though he'd staggered away from the crash and twenty minutes later found West City. Here, safe in the warm bath, he allowed himself the pain of remembering her.

"Nami-chan," he whispered.

"You have a guest," said a soft, female voice.

A hologram shimmered into view above the tub. A woman, only a year or two removed from being a girl, stood in the hotel hallway outside his door. She had the build of a runway model wrapped in a plain black coat. Her a delicate nose and high cheekbones conveyed a look of bored resignation. Porcelain skin reflected luminous violet NanoLED tattoos, a glowing raccoon mask of blacklight eye shadow. Half-inch gemstone spheres clung to her earlobes, matching the candy red of gleaming high-heels held on by a lattice of finger-thick tendrils winding up her legs to the knee.

The fourteen-inch tall figure showed no reaction to his nakedness, a clear sign a one-way observation camera created the hologram.

Nami's face appeared in his mind. *I do not remember sending for this woman.* His arm emerged from the water to rub his forehead, sending warm trails down his face. "Inform the woman she has come to the wrong room."

"Thank you, sir," chimed the AI room attendant.

He settled into the tub once more, eyes closed and trying to remember what had become of his woman. *His* woman. *Slave?* Mamoru cringed. Nami had been his servant. His possession. *No.* He had never thought of her that way. It felt wrong. The Nippon Shōgyō-Kumiai had made a slave of his sister when she was only eight years old. How could he do the same to another person?

Mamoru looked up at the delicate flutter of cloth crumpling to the floor.

The slender woman from the hallway stood over him, wearing only her high-heeled shoes and earrings. No hair hid her womanhood from his eyes. She held her arms slightly apart, as if showing herself off. In person, she seemed even younger. Seventeen if a day.

"I hope I am to your liking."

Red serpents receded from around her calves, withdrawing back into her shoes, which she kicked aside.

Mamoru put a hand to his brow, at once averting his eyes and rubbing the beginnings of a headache out of his temple. "You are quite beautiful and quite young."

She clasped his wrist with both hands, delicate fingers caressing his skin. He found himself captivated by her small breasts as she knelt beside the tub and pulled his hand against them. Emotion, at last, appeared on her blank face —a hint of a smile, perhaps at his awkwardness. Her chest felt neither warm nor cool.

"I'm Chloe," whispered the girl, "but you can call me whatever you like."

Her hands dragged his down her stomach, toward her sex. She grinned. Continuing to hold his wrist in her left hand, she leaned over the edge and reached underwater to caress his cock.

"Your eyes say no," she cooed. "Your body has other ideas."

Mamoru pulled his hand away before she could push his fingers inside her. "Stop. You are too young. I have a—"

"You're not wearing a ring." Chloe closed her narrow fingers around his length. She placed her left hand on his chest, sliding it up to his shoulder. "You aren't doing anything wrong if you're not married."

Mamoru cringed inside, ashamed of his body for its reaction. *What is wrong with this girl? She is too forward. This is improper.* He shuddered, grabbing the hand that stroked him. She continued rubbing up and down, her wrist too slippery to halt. "You do not need to do this. S-stop."

"I am yours, Master. To do with as you will." Her sudden switch to Japanese almost stopped his heart.

The hand between his legs became a vice; the hand on his shoulder slid over his throat and crushed. Crimson light shone from her eyes. All the strength left his legs as she dragged him by the genitals deeper in the tub so his head slipped under. Whirring, the high-pitched whine of water jets grew deafening; distorted blobs of ceiling lights danced around the placid face of the girl trying to drown him.

Paralytic agony between his legs left him disoriented. He couldn't decide which arm to grab first, the one crushing his throat or the one strangling his manhood. His surroundings vanished in a flare of whiteness and full-body pain that made the squeezing hand seem trivial. Lightning arced from the drain to his back, creating a dazzle of ice blue flickers glinting on the shiny cream-colored tub.

Chloe convulsed and her grip weakened. Instinct kicked in. Mamoru's mind channeled psionic energy into his muscles, empowering his body against the electrical assault. Flames of psionic energy burst along his back and shoulders. He swung his left arm forward, knocking her hand away from his crotch, and his right arm up, catching her in the abdomen. Mamoru screamed in pain from the electrical arcs raking over the small of his back as he rolled and flung her into the wall.

Tiles cracked on impact, a clattering rain fell with her into the water.

Mamoru dove over the side, away from the deadly bath, landing on his hands and knees upon the thick, black bath-rug. He let his forehead rest upon the sopping wet mat, gasping for air, and grabbed himself to make sure everything remained attached. Inches to his right, the plastic clunking and banging of Chloe's convulsions thudded within the tub. Water splashed over the edge onto him. Her screaming gave way to a horrible, digitized warbling noise, followed seconds later by silence.

Only the faint buzzing of electricity remained.

"Ngh." Mamoru groaned, still holding himself.

He sat back on his heels, panting, catching sight of his crimson face in the mirror. Behind him, a small fire flickered in the middle of the hot tub. Chloe's body draped in the water, her hair fanned out like ebon seaweed. Perfect white teeth showed between her parted lips. Flames sputtered out of her chest, between her breasts, where a hole the size of a fist revealed metal ribs. Acrid fumes watered his eyes with the stink of molten plastic and singed silicon.

A doll.

It made sense now why he had felt so awkward. She did not radiate any chi, a body with no sense of presence. Mamoru frowned, took a deep breath, and forced himself to his feet, twisting to examine the red lines zigzagged over his back and shoulders from the electrical arc.

The buzzing crackle of runaway electricity ceased. Chloe continued to smolder. Dense, black smoke wisped from the ends of the flame. A malfunctioning artificial concubine was one thing, but he had not ordered it, and to have the hot tub short out at the same instant defied belief. Mamoru leaned against the sink, his legs still not thrilled about the prospect of bearing all his weight. He stared down at his bruises, contending with a momentary worry he might no longer be able to produce an heir.

Someone tried to kill me.

With anger, his pain faded. He'd lost his Matsushita Oni deck in the crash and had not yet thought to replace it. He thought of only one explanation: the Nippon Shōgyō-Kumiai, Sadako's former masters, had somehow discovered he had freed her and come for him. He stared at the vibro-katana, dormant in its scabbard on the bed by the clothes he had set out before his bath. If the NSK sought to make an example of him for defying them, he would wipe them from the face of Japan.

Mamoru reached for a pair of black boxer briefs, still brand new in plastic. A hundred pound naked body landed on his back before his fingers touched it. Wet arms the size of a teenaged girl, but imbued with the strength of a large man, closed around his neck. The dry crust of burnt plastic scraped at his back.

A sheath of glowing white energy covered his arms as he channeled psionic energy into physical power. He seized the doll by the elbows and wrenched downward, tearing the left arm off at the shoulder and flinging the machine to the bed in front of him.

Chloe kicked into a back flip, rolling off the far side of the Comforgel pad. Mamoru dropped into a fighting stance as she sprinted around the end and rushed him. He leaned back to avoid a spinning kick and drove his fist into the side of her head as her body came upright again. The hit sent the lithe artificial body careening into the air. Graceful flight ended with a loud *crack*. She hit the wall and fell onto a wide chest of drawers.

When she sat up, a sleeve of artificial skin gathered loose about her neck, exposing a metal skull with a fist-sized crater below the missing left eye. Six-inch blades sprouted from the fingertips of her remaining hand. Mamoru used his power to accelerate his body and mind; reality sank into slow motion, reducing Chloe's charge into an ungainly shamble. His grip closed about the handle of his sword, drawing it with such force the scabbard did not slide upon the bed.

The doll raised her hand, claws gleaming. Bright white flames rippled along his arms, deafening in the slowed world. Mamoru brought his blade down onto the doll's right shoulder. Three eruptions of sparks and light came from inside her chest in the blade's wake. The hypersonic edge met little resistance on its way to her left hip. Two halves of torso went in different directions, collapsing in a heap before catching fire.

Mamoru relaxed his power and time returned to normal. His rush of adrenaline dissipated, leaving fatigue in its wake.

Cutting this abomination down had been as easy as performing *Tameshigiri* on a *goza* target. The artificial body hadn't split as cleanly as a rolled up straw mat, twitching and sputtering dark green fluid as well as blue sparks. He loosened his grip on the rubberized handle, allowing the vibro-inducer to quiet, and the blade to cool. He took a knee, touching the defunct automaton on the side of the head. A moment's concentration allowed him to attune his psionic talent for machinery to the fallen doll and know its every circuit.

Mamoru closed his eyes and found himself as a suit of gleaming white samurai armor standing in a small room with walls of black onyx squares separated by bright blue lines. Ornate picture frames of gleaming silver surrounded rectangles of plain black. The largest of the 'paintings' contained a swirling vortex: a standard depiction of a wireless uplink to the GlobeNet. A Comforgel pad, also black, rested atop a chrome slab. Chloe sat at the end, whole again and naked.

"System failure. Personality construct designated *Chloe* has been backed up to a removable neuro-memory module. System shutdown in fourteen seconds due to power core failure."

Fourteen seconds? An eternity in here. "You are sub-sentient?"

"Novo-Aram Waif series, Type 4. I am a semi-sentient Class 2 doll. My primary function is entertainment. I am not considered self-aware by the AI Sentience Act." Her head changed in an instant, from facing forward to staring over her left shoulder at him. "I am owned by Mercury Onyx Incorporated. An entertainment services company."

"Who sent you to this hotel room?"

"That data is unavailable." Her eyes became pools of chromatic light. "Memory recording jumps from 21:02 PST to 21:58 PST."

"Display 21:00 PST, today's date."

A video panel stretched open in the middle of the room, four feet past the edge of the bed. It expanded to cover the entire rear wall and filled with an image of a row of small berths, like twenty metal coffins stood on end. Each bore the nude figure of a person, three female to one male. At the left edge of the view, racks of clothing lingered as a blur. The view came from Chloe's eyes as she lay in her bunk, awaiting 'work.'

"Play," said Mamoru.

The image became video, though the only indication it moved came from a changing time display at the lower right corner. At 21:02, the time display leapt to 21:58, and the image shifted to Mamoru's nakedness as viewed from the floor of this hotel room.

Mamoru grumbled. "Reconstruct missing time segments from I/O ingress buffer."

Chloe's hollow eyes shifted to deep green light. The virtual holo-panel displayed a copy of this room, with the doll seated as she was before him.

"Play, half speed," said Mamoru.

At 21:01, two black tendrils emerged from the swirl in the large painting, pulling it wider. The samurai armor floated closer to the screen, gazing into the cold yellow eyes of an enormous Onyx-scaled dragon as it pulled itself into the tiny room.

"Stop."

He stared at the creature. The C-branch network AI. The Black Dragon construct.

Nightwing.

"Mercury Onyx offers a reward of five thousand credits for the return of my memory backup."

"They can get it themselves."

Chloe faced the GlobeNet uplink and raised her arm. A white butterfly appeared in a flash of pixie dust and took flight. It disappeared into the hole a nanosecond before the azure glow in the gridded walls faded. Mamoru released his link and returned to the real world.

He slid the blade into its scabbard and leapt into his boxers and pants. A two-inch thick disc-shaped carpet maintenance bot slid out of a trapdoor in the wall. He assumed it headed for the puddle of doll 'blood' in the carpet and ignored the machine until it zoomed into the side of his ankle. Mamoru let out a yell.

The complimentary food assembler hummed to life.

"I am sorry, sir," said the placid female voice of the room attendant. "I am afraid your death has been unfortunately delayed. Emperor Suites regrets this inconvenience and will take all necessary steps to ensure the rest of your murder is pleasant and free of inconvenience."

He staggered to the side, managing to leap onto the bed before the disc bot could ram his other anklebone. White foam seeped out from the gaps in the reassembler door.

"What is that demon of an AI doing?" He muttered, not expecting an answer.

"Food assembler has generated a complimentary dinner, sir." The attendant sounded cheerful.

"What dinner?"

"Successful synthesis of organophosphorus compound, formula $C_4H_{10}FO_2P$."

A loud *click* came from the room's door.

Mamoru didn't like the sound of that, and pulled on his shirt, coat, and boots without bothering to fasten any of the clips or buttons.

"I apologize for the confusion," said the placid woman, her voice warping into a deep masculine sound laced with the scrape of metal on metal. "You might be more familiar with the term Sarin."

Mamoru held his breath, grabbed the katana by the scabbard, and ran to the door. Disc bots whirred underfoot, trying to trip him. The first one he saw and avoided, the second got under his left boot as he watched the first. It accelerated, flinging his foot out from under him. He whirled his arms, preventing a fall with a graceful spin down to one knee.

"I cannot explain what you did within the net." The voice of Nightwing rumbled the ceiling on speakers never meant to handle such bass. "In this world, it is *you* who are the worm."

Holo-projectors in the ceiling created a wide panel screen along the left wall, a rectangular hole in reality rimmed with dark smoke. The shape of a great ebon dragon glided closer, as if peering into a window from another world.

Mamoru drove his fist into the next disc bot to make a run at him, crushing it in a shower of sparks. He sprinted to the exit, still holding his breath. Not even bothering to try the controls, he drew his sword and sliced it along the edge where the door slid into the wall before punting the loose slab of Epoxil to the ground.

Out in the hallway, he gasped for air. Two housekeeping dolls ran at him from a distant intersection. Again, Mamoru tapped his kinetic power and plunged the world into slow motion, taking their heads before they could lay a hand on him. Every light went dark. Muted shouts of angry guests cried out from various rooms as he felt his way along with a hand on the wall.

He decided to skip the elevator.

The stairwell proved uneventful except for a steady assault from fire-suppression hoverbots. He made it to the lobby covered in foam, ignoring the four receptionist dolls that rose from their seats to chase him, and ran outside.

For three blocks, Mamoru sprinted, all but unnoticed by the pedestrians despite his bare chest and drawn sword. He stopped at an intersection out of instinct, due to a red light. With a moment of quiet at last, he buttoned his shirt, cinched his coat, and stooped to fasten his boots.

Lights washed over him.

Mamoru's head snapped up. A PubTran taxi came at him on the sidewalk, accelerating. Bodies slid up and over its hood as it plowed into people. A young couple inside screamed and banged on the door. Mamoru shot a burst of psionic power into his legs, amplifying his strength. He leapt straight up as the tiny car rocketed past him and t-boned a much larger sedan waiting for the light. The PubTran's windows flashed white in an instant from impact suppression foam.

He landed amid thirty moaning people. Before he could mentally process what happened, a man behind him screamed. He spun; an advert bot careened out of the sky, headed right at him. Driven by Awakened kinetics, his muscles launched him sideways as the coffin-sized hover-bot, still displaying advertisements for lingerie, crashed into the screaming man.

A fine red mist painted everyone and everything within thirty feet. The demolished advert bot must have sensed all the injured people nearby, for as ruined as it was, it had enough power left to switch its failing holographic displays to offer medical products.

Another PubTran car, this one riderless, attempted to drive diagonally across six lanes of traffic to get him, but a huge cargo transport intercepted it by chance, crushing the little car like a synthbeer canister.

Mamoru sprinted. Every ten to fifteen seconds, another advert bot made a suicide dive. He sliced orbs the size of bowling balls out of the air, tapped his power for superhuman sprints to avoid the larger ones, and flung himself through a window to evade a thirty-foot long billboard display that fell like a stone straight down when its thrusters cut off.

The ground shook from the impact, which caused the electronics store he'd invaded to go dark. Customers screamed and ran in all directions, hands up to shield their faces from the rain of sparks falling from above. Mamoru rushed outside among the crowd, breaking to his left as soon as he could. His gift pushed him up to a forty-mile-an-hour sprint.

Tens of thousands of PubTran cars trying to get to him in defiance of traffic safety caused widespread snarls and brought ground vehicles in southeastern West City to a halt. Mamoru ran atop the stalled cars to avoid the slowdown of other people in his way.

Already, the NewsNet displays at almost every street corner as well as flying overhead bathed the area with reports of unexplained malfunctions of the PubTran network. A short, bald, man in a shiny metallic-maroon coat came on and announced that ComTec International was not to blame for a spate of advert bot crashes. He reassured the public that the hacker or hackers responsible would be found and prosecuted.

Chaos followed him for miles. By the time he'd run himself to gasping, the confident man from ComTec had been backed into a panicked corner when Kimberly Brightman, the public face of the NewsNet, remarked at how easily hackers could take over his company's robots. He blurted without thinking, blaming hostile action from the Allied Corporate Council, and thus started a wave of paranoia about World War Four.

Three blocks later, the NewsNet panels erupted with debate after debate. Everyone wondered if this strange behavior signaled the beginning of international aggression. The ACC, the only other superpower to remain aside from the UCF, had been a simmering rival since the end of the Corporate War. Everyone waited for the shooting to start again, but no one had ever dared suggest it imminent.

Still stranded in traffic, people got out of their cars to watch what they all believed to be the end of civilization. No one much noticed the Japanese man running over traffic and swatting an unending rain of advert bots out of the sky with a seething hot vibro-katana.

He wanted a hovercar but didn't trust it to be more than a deathtrap at that moment. As much as he loathed the thought of it, the Badlands would be the safest place for him. He growled. Mamoru would not let a mere *program* beat him. It was right. Out here, in the real world, he *was* weak. The only way to destroy a beast like that would be to confront it where he could kill it.

A woman's amplified voice barking at people to remain calm made him abandon the elevated walkway of stranded cars and duck down an alley. Red and blue flashing lights at the end cast a larger-than-life silhouette of a female figure on the grime-stained wall of a hundred story residential tower.

A short woman with dark brown skin in blue Division 1 armor stood beside a police hovercar half on the sidewalk a modest distance from the alley. She had parked by a blasted-out window, damaged when a PubTran car had driven through it into the counter of a Chinese takeout place, likely following the most direct path to wherever Mamoru had been at that moment. Her silver visor was up, exposing her face. A wireless connection carried her voice from her helmet to loudspeakers on the patrol craft at her side, encouraging the crowd of onlookers to go on about their business.

He ran up to her, skidding to a halt a few feet away.

She spun toward him, one hand on her sidearm, one raised. "Easy, citizen."

"Where is the closest grey zone?"

"What's going on? Did you dose an illegal chem?"

"No. A dragon is trying to kill me."

She looked at his sword, at his face, and pulled her gun. "Drop the knife."

He sighed. "I don't have time for—"

A rounded bulge in the patrol craft's roof above the passenger seat split open, exposing a three-foot-long laser cannon, which rose on a strut and pivoted toward him.

The officer glanced over her shoulder at the mechanical whirring. "*¡Dios mío!* What in the..."

Mamoru's arms lit with a brilliant psionic glow as he pushed himself to the limit of his ability. The officer's motions slowed to a veritable standstill as he lunged forward, diving into a somersault under an intense blue-white laser blast. The turret swiveled after him. To his accelerated perception, the whine of its actuators sounded like the dire groan of stressed metal warping. His leap skimmed past the range of its motion, ahead of it by less than a second. Mamoru sailed over the car, severing the weapon from its strut with a quick slash as he passed. The laser cannon fell onto the armored windshield with a *clank* before sliding onto the hood.

The astounded look on the officer's face told him she'd seen him disappear and reappear on the other side of the car. Or, perhaps she had simply never seen a Japanese man covered in white flames before.

"Grey zone. Where is the closest?"

She pointed without a word.

He ran, keeping to narrow alleys as often as possible to limit the angle from which aerial assault could dive on him, yet Nightwing's thousand steel claws grasped at him for sixteen miles. Visible decline in the surroundings had never been so welcome a sight. The energy simmering along his shoulders, his psionic power bolstering his endurance, kept people away or staring—either suited him fine. Deep in the blighted ruin of a grey zone, where no advert bots dared to go, Mamoru felt safe.

His security lasted about a minute.

A flash of sparks overhead made him look up a split second before a dog-sized advert bot smashed into the ground two feet to his left. A chance encounter with a fourth-story cable run between two buildings had altered its dive enough to cause it to miss. Mamoru stared at the wreckage, willing his heart to beat again.

I need a deck. I cannot go to a store with this chaos around me. He stumbled on, barely able to remain upright. *I cannot order one; it will override the delivery—*

Mamoru felt like a fool.

At last, he realized how Nightwing followed him. He jammed his hand into his pocket, clasping his NetMini, and forced it to power down. His psionic influence over technology was faster than the long-winded 'safe' power down sequence. In the span of a quarter second, it went dark. *Now* he could take a moment to gather himself. He stumbled across the street and into an abandoned building. Walls of bare grey concrete surrounded him, lit only by the pale glow of a faltering streetlight outside.

Why does fate deny me the comfort of civilization?

He stood in the middle of crumbling ruin, head bowed, breaths ragged. Sweat dripped from his nose, appearing as dark dots on the dusty floor between his feet. This place offered a small degree of solace for now, devoid of cameras, technology, or others who would interfere in his affairs.

Mamoru trudged over to a pile of debris, and sat to rest.

The strange presence in the back of his mind returned, calming him.

Soon, *they* would get their revenge on this city for its insolence.

Soon, everything would burn.

19

TACTICAL TRAINING

Kate

Kate had signed on the proverbial dotted line less than a week ago. David knew the things she had done for El Tío, and yet they still welcomed her, even issued her an energy weapon. They had no guarantee she'd cast aside her old life. Officer Aaron Pryce hung over her, a boulder suspended on a thread with no good way out from under it. The look on El Tío's face when he'd asked her to kill that man made her think he already expected betrayal. Misplaced guilt sent her to the terminal. A little digging in the open warrant database confirmed what her former employer said. Division 0 had Pryce listed as a rogue operative, wanted for questioning —and considered extremely dangerous. She bowed her head, desperate to think of a way she could make El Tío happy without getting herself killed or locked up. Nothing came to mind, and she needed to report in soon.

With a sigh, she got up to put the rest of her clothes on; command would probably object to her showing up in underwear and socks. The holo-panel at her desk terminal shut itself off when it sensed her move away.

The woman staring at Kate from the mirror looked like a stranger. Less than two months ago, the thought of wearing clothing of any kind seemed an unattainable dream, and a police uniform hadn't even been on the list. The snug Division 0 blacks, shiny silver belt, and heavy shin-high boots felt more like a Halloween costume than reality. She took the E-90 laser pistol out of its holster and smirked at the warped, skin-toned smear her face became upon its mirrored housing.

I can't believe they trust me with one of these.

She rubbed her thumb between the soft, rubberized grip and the smooth silver plastic.

I don't even trust me with this.

A patch of iridescence on the trigger reminded her of the ten-minute instruction she'd been given about the security interlock. This weapon would only work with *her* finger on the trigger. Anyone else trying to fire it would get a nasty shock. She didn't let her finger get anywhere near it. Merely looking at it made her nervous. Kate let the air out of her lungs and slid the weapon back into the holster.

She stared at the total stranger wearing her face a moment longer. *Not quite what I wanted...* A smile teased at her lips as she rubbed a hand over the material covering her stomach. *But I'll take it.*

She walked toward the apartment door. "I'm leaving, Andy."

"Understood," chimed a subdued male voice from the ceiling.

The windows along the rear wall went from clear to amber, darkening until they approached black.

"Shall I prepare a meal for you at six?"

She sighed. "Yeah, David's in the East for a few days for some inter-coastal cooperative exchange."

"What would you like?" asked the ephemeral voice.

"Surprise me."

The door hissed closed behind her.

She encountered no one in the corridor outside, or the elevator, or the lobby of her apartment building. When she emerged on the street, she hadn't prepared herself for the reaction of pedestrians. The uniform she thought silly had a profound effect on anyone who bothered to peel their eyes away from their NetMinis long enough to look at her. Backs stiffened, conversations got quieter, some walked faster, and a small minority offered tentative smiles. Most had fear in their eyes. To her surprise, no one ogled her, despite the snug fabric.

Confidence welled up inside her.

The sense of being isolated from society was nothing new; however, she much preferred standing proud in her uniform than sneaking bare-assed around the alleys of a black zone hoping no one saw her. Not that she'd been ashamed, but getting seen always wound up ending in one of two ways: accidentally burning someone who wanted to help her or not-so-accidentally melting the face off a thug.

At the edge of the sidewalk, she used her NetMini to summon a PubTran taxi.

They'll issue me a damn laser pistol before training, but no department car until I'm on the roster. She grumbled. *Guess it really is all about the money.*

Kate folded her arms, grinned at the crowd giving her a comfortable distance, and gazed up at the stream of hovercar traffic while waiting for her ride. A basic search by inexperienced hands in the police database found no activity on Pryce's registered NetMini for months. She'd expected that. No different from any of the people she'd hunted for the Syndicate. Anyone with at least a quarter of a functioning brain got a burner NetMini. Her mind went in circles trying to think of where to start hunting for someone even the cops couldn't find.

A few minutes later, a little teal-and-grey car pulled to a halt in front of her.

Not quite half way into the ride, her NetMini chirped with an incoming call. She answered without looking and went rigid as the face of El Tío appeared in hologram.

"I hope you're not slipping, Kate. I expected some news by now."

A sudden feeling of not deserving her uniform made her pick at the snug fabric. "I've been looking… the man's a ghost. Zero can't find him either, and they've got clairvoyants hunting for him. None of my gifts help me find people. I have to do that part like everyone else."

The air inside the car dropped ten degrees. She'd have thought it psychological if her breath hadn't begun to fog.

"Perhaps you need a little… assistance."

Her heart pounded. "I'm sorry, El Tío." Desperation added an uncharacteristic whine to her voice. "I'm doing everything I can… he's not in the city. I've been looking everywhere. I—"

"Calm yourself, my girl." The old man smiled. "Not everything I say is a veiled threat. I meant assistance, not *encouragement*. We know he's using a false personal identity. If we isolated his PID code, and only you knew it, you could find him before he knew he was compromised."

"Yes, El Tío." Her knuckles whitened on the NetMini, but she kept her shame out of her expression.

His holographic head collapsed into a tiny point of light and vanished. She stared at the inert device for a minute without moving. Something white bobbed in her field of view. A bare foot, the color of clouds. Kate's head snapped up; she let off a yelp at the suddenness of no longer being alone in a moving car. A nude woman with calf-length lemon blonde hair sat on the rear-facing seat, smiling at her. Onyx eyes glimmered with mirth.

Aurora.

"Oh, shit." Kate flattened herself against the back of the car, hands poised to conjure flames. "What the fuck do you want?"

"Calm down, dear." Aurora winked. "All I wanted to do was take some weight off your mind."

She let her arms down, squinting. "Did he send you to find me again? He tried to take over my brain. Next time I see him—"

"Shh." Aurora grinned. "Your former employer's got you by the short and curlies. Yes, I'm aware you don't have any. I'm rather fond of that style myself. It's only a turn of phrase."

Kate blushed.

The snow-skinned woman smiled. "Don't bother wasting another moment worrying about Pryce."

"What?" Kate looked up.

Aurora vanished in a cloud of silvery glowing fog.

"Fuck…" She shied away from traces of luminous smoke collecting in the curve of the seat and around her boots. Raising her legs, she cringed against the wall in an effort to get away from the mist.

A faint spectral laugh swirled around the car, though she couldn't tell if she'd only imagined it.

THE PUBTRAN LET HER OFF AT THE POLICE ADMINISTRATIVE CENTER TWENTY minutes later. The place thrummed with more activity than Kate had ever seen in one place. Holographic panel signs floated overhead, displaying directional arrows to help people find their way. Division 1 had the largest entrance, where two parallel corridors led straight into the facility opposite the door. Another sign pointed to the right for Division 5 and 6 barracks. Beyond that, a plain metal door flanked by a pair of men in long, brown coats bore a large numeral nine. As soon as she glanced at it, she remembered David mentioning them 'dealing with' El Tío. Kate looked away, feeling guilty at the mere thought of being indirectly responsible for his death.

She trudged to the left side of the main concourse where a large zero marked a pair of sliding glass doors. Behind them, a blinding white corridor led deeper into a side wing. Kate found it amusing that police officers, including huge men in heavy armor, reacted to her much like the civilians had. Most moved or looked away. Some tried to pretend she wasn't there. Their surface thoughts betrayed their distrust of psionics; rumors had left most of them merely nervous, though a handful reacted with genuine terror. A number of men stared at her, not concerned enough about her psionic abilities to resist the desire to admire her skin-tight pants. One even seemed shocked that a 'psionic girl' could be so beautiful.

Score one for the assholes in lab coats. Exotic Russian goddess? Check.

She got bored about halfway to the entrance to the Division 0 wing, stopped eavesdropping on brains, and pondered learning the language—mostly to mess with people.

Another redhead sat behind a plain desk at the end of a short hospital-white corridor with lights glowing from all four corners. She seemed a little older, perhaps in her early-to-mid thirties, and wore her hair much shorter than Kate, off her shoulders.

"Good morning…"

"Kate." She held out a hand.

The receptionist leaned up and stared at Kate's chest. "Tac Officer Solomon?"

"Oh, yeah." Kate smirked at her nameplate. "Still not used to this whole saluting thing."

"Robin." The woman accepted her handshake with a wink before glancing down at her one-way holo panel. "It's not as bad here as the rest of the force. You'll want to head down that hallway to the right. Looks like you've got a couple of light days ahead of you. Fourth door on the right, Lieutenant Drake is waiting for you."

"Thanks." Kate started for the hallway.

"Kate?"

She paused four steps later and glanced back. "Hmm?"

"Is it true?" whispered Robin. "That you're off the charts?"

"Well, that could be taken more than one way." Kate offered a sultry wink. "I'll assume you mean my pyrokinetics."

Robin blushed.

Kate summoned a fist-sized blue fireball over her palm, willing it to fly in an orbit around her hand for a few seconds before letting it dissipate. Robin made a face like a child awestruck by a magic trick.

"Seems I've gotten someone's attention at least." Kate stared at her hand for a few seconds, not sure how she felt about the police being so blasé about her life as an assassin. *Maybe they're not so different from the Syndicate after all.* "I should go."

"Best of luck to you, and welcome to the team."

The hallway followed a gradual curve to the left. A tall, thin man with pale skin and battleship-grey hair looked down his nose at her as they passed. She twisted around to continue staring at him with an expression of 'what?' After a final, pointed glare, he walked off at a sharp stride. A door on her left slid into the wall with a faint hiss, revealing a boy of about ten in a smaller version of her uniform. Instead of a utility belt with a gun, he had a hovering cart with various electronic devices on it as well as a box of tools. His nameplate and rank insignia were silver, rather than the matte black she'd seen on everyone else.

"Hey," he said, not really looking at her.

"Hi. Aren't you a little young? What the heck are you doing wearing a uniform?"

"Cadet Gutierrez. I'm a techno, so they let me fix terminals and whatnot as a break from school. I live in the dorms." He looked up with sudden alarm on his face. He, too, stared at her chest.

Kate felt awkward until she realized his attention focused on her name tag.

"Oh, whew." He slumped. "I thought I'd forgotten to salute an officer again."

She glanced at the empty hallway where the older man had last been. "Is that bad?"

"Not really since I'm just a cadet. I'm not enlisted yet. Worst I'll get is extra homework." He looked up, shrugged, and trudged off.

She continued to Lieutenant Drake's door, marked by a plain silver rectangle with the name in black letters. It opened automatically as she approached, letting her into a small office. A large virtual window displayed a view of a nature preserve that bathed the room in false sunlight tinted green from trees. Shelves lined the wall to her left as well as the one behind the desk, filled with a mixture of trophies, plaques, holo-bars bearing pictures of smiling children, and a number of ancient, physical books.

The man behind the desk glanced up at her, eyebrow raised as if questioning her for walking in without knocking. His hair, buzzed short, existed as little more than a black smudge on already-dark skin. Where her nameplate had a sword impaling a large zero, his had a shield with a zero carved into it. David had mentioned it meant something significant, but she couldn't place what.

"Morning. I'm Kate... Uhh, Tactical Officer Solomon." She fidgeted, not sure what to do with her hands after he ignored her offer of a shake. "I'm new."

Lieutenant Drake leaned back, pursing his lips as if appraising what he saw. Her attempt to read his surface thoughts met initial resistance, as if she'd walked face-first into a soft bubble. Perturbed, she pushed past it with relative ease. Indignation at her intrusion disintegrated, awe and fear at how easily she'd overpowered his telepathy filled in the space it left behind. Annoyance rattled around in his surface thoughts at whoever had failed to train her to salute officers, but it shifted to alarm at how casually she eavesdropped on his mind.

"Officer Solomon. Stop that at once." Lt. Drake gestured at a chair facing his desk. "I understand you're a bit of a feral rescue, so I'll forgive you this time."

Kate sat and crossed her legs. "I'm not that feral anymore. It's been about ten years since I ate a deer with my bare hands."

"Still, I see there are some nuances of ethics you have not been brought up to speed on. As a representative of Division 0, it is considered unethical for you to invade the secrets of everyone you meet. You are to refrain from using telepathy on others, *especially* individuals outside of Division 0, unless to do so represents an immediate and imminent need in the line of duty."

"Why? It's not like they'd notice."

"Precisely. Look, Officer Solomon. I understand due to the nature of your early life, knowing the motivations of everyone you meet as quickly as possible became a survival instinct. The rules have changed. Not only is there your legal status as an officer of the law, one of the responsibilities of our division is to safeguard psionics in the eye of the public."

"PR bullshit." Kate frowned.

"To a point. If you feel threatened or feel that a life hangs in the balance, by all means, use every talent you have at your disposal. The policy is intended to dissuade casual eavesdropping. Besides, telepathic evidence is not permitted to stand during Inquests."

"Okay." Kate held back the urge to roll her eyes. "I think I can handle that."

His demeanor softened, and he smiled. "I noticed your lack of a salute when you barged in. Have you not been given the rundown on ranks?"

"I've had a lot on my mind lately, sir. Who's ass to kiss hasn't been very high up on my priorities."

"Fortunately I'm not as hung up on it as some are"—he chuckled, tapping his nameplate—"but you'll notice the shield. A shield signifies the wearer is part of Investigative Operations, or I-Ops."

"Oh, right. David mentioned that. Detectives, right? All officers."

"Correct. The first rank, Agent, is technically an officer, but they lack command authority. As a member of the tactical squad, you are enlisted personnel. General rules of military etiquette—"

"Yeah, I got it."

"...dictate you should salute, and not interrupt, officers." His mirth vanished for a moment. "We do try to maintain a certain sense of decorum."

"Sorry. This is all... It's a lot to handle. I'm used to fending for myself. If I can be honest..."

"Please do." Lt. Drake laced his fingers, elbows on the desk.

"The only reason I agreed to join was because you guys can keep C-Branch off my ass. I don't really feel the whole '*sir, yes sir!*' routine. It's better than what I was doing, or going back to living wild... and it's definitely better than being a government lab rat, but I'm not sure I'll ever be able to wrap my brain around the gung-ho thing."

He grinned. "Give it a few months, Solomon. It kind of grows on you. You're not used to being part of a team ready to take a bullet for you. Lone wolves sound sexy, but they die alone."

Kate's thoughts returned to sitting in a blasted-out building staring down the barrel of her own gun. She gazed into her lap. "Yeah..."

"Look, Solomon, that's enough gloom. Today is your first official day as a

Division 0 officer. I'm not going to blow sunshine up your ass. The next few weeks will be boring. You're going to get started on some dry, but necessary stuff including a lot of classroom instruction. Since the nature of Division 0 does not lend itself to large training classes, everything is on sim. For the next thirty-two work days, you'll be flat on your back wearing a helmet."

"That sounds kinky."

He coughed. "Far from it. You'll be taking classroom instruction via virtual reality. Some of the modules are solo, others may include other new recruits from all over West City as well as the east coast."

"Okay, a month of nine-to-five. That sounds doable."

"I have a good feeling about you, Solomon. Based on your file, I half expected you to be grumbling about wasting your time in a classroom instead of running around blowing things up."

She offered a one-shoulder shrug. "I've gotten that out of my system."

"That's good to hear." His voice sounded somber. Dark brown skin turned pale grey in the castoff light of his holo-terminal as he switched screens. "Your psych profile says you killed people when you were only seven. Is that true?"

"Keep reading. I didn't have 'requisite intent' or whatever they called it. I was just a child who didn't want to die. I wanted the 'bad men' to go away. My brain did the rest on its own."

"Your evaluation seems rather remarkable given your life."

Kate looked at him. "What should I do? Waste my life sobbing in the corner and sucking my thumb? Jump at every shadow? I could wallow in it and let it control me, but that's not what I want to do. Shit happened, so I dealt with it. I tend to be direct."

"Officer Ahmed mentioned he had to influence your emotional state to forestall suicide." Lieutenant Drake raised an eyebrow. "Yet, the department evaluator raised no red flags."

Dammit, David. That's going to haunt me. Why did you have to tell them that? She shut her eyes and sighed. *Probably thought it would help me to get it out. No more secrets, right?*

"Officer Solomon?"

Her eyes snapped open. "It was a situational thing, sir. C-Branch locked this fucking thing around my neck that I couldn't get off. Any time I tried to use my abilities, it zapped the shit out of me—literally. I was in a black zone with like two bullets left, I didn't have the protection of being too hot to touch anymore, and I did *not* want to get found by a gang of crazy augs. My back was against a wall. I didn't think I had any way out."

"I see."

"Tell me you wouldn't eat a bullet to avoid being gang-raped... or cannibalized... or both. Possibly at the same time."

He held up a hand. "Valid point. Forget I asked."

Kate kneaded her hands. "Sorry, I... I wasn't in a good place there. I don't like to think about it. I am over it. I haven't come out of a nightmare and killed everyone within fifty meters of me in at least a month."

His expression went slack.

"Sorry, I guess I have an inappropriate sense of humor too. Coping mechanism."

He exhaled. "Please try to be careful of that. The world as a whole is on eggshells about psionics, and comments like that could be problematic."

"Okay. So what now?"

"Well, as I said, you have about a month of classroom time ahead of you. That, of course, represents the equivalent of what conventional instruction can do in about eighteen weeks. Bear in mind you will experience a bit of fatigue. Time passes differently in cyberspace. Depending on the network and hardware involved, it can be anywhere from five to twenty seconds in net time for every one second in real time. We include simulated sleep breaks to help the brain cope, but you will get the equivalent of two-point-eight days of classroom training to every one real time day."

Okay, maybe this will *suck.* She nodded.

"After that... or possibly interrupting it at some point depending on scheduling, you will be going with a group of Division 1 trainees for ISCOT. You'll be headed to Fort Armstrong with the 11th Training Brigade."

"ISCOT?"

Lieutenant Drake sighed. "Initial Soldier Combat Orientation Training. You and about two dozen Division 1 recruits will be attached to a basic training platoon of the UCF Marine Corps where you will run the same boot camp as soldiers. Of course, unlike the Division 1 personnel, you are considered activated with Division 0 and have full police powers. Granted, those powers are limited on a military installation, but you would have jurisdiction if a psionic event occurred."

"Wait? Marines?" Kate shifted. "Military intelligence has to be all over that place. What if they try to grab me?"

"Two things." He lowered his voice. "You are fully authorized to defend yourself by any means necessary. Second, one of the few perks Division 0 enjoys is the belief that other aspects of the government have secrets only because we haven't tried to go digging yet. As you are one of ours, they know we would come looking. As tantalizing as your 'weapons project' is to them, they have other things they'd rather the world not learn about."

Kate relaxed a little.

"It is full military training, as your position as a Tactical Officer is a front line role. Since you've grown up as a civilian, I assume you are not used to mixed bathing facilities?"

Kate laughed.

"Solomon? That wasn't a joke. Do you have issues with an utter lack of privacy?"

She cackled for another minute. When she recovered, she wiped her eyes, unable to stop grinning. "I thought you read my file?"

"Oh." He tapped one finger on his desk, momentarily unable to look her in the eye. "Oh, that's right. Do bear in mind during the boot camp that your rank of Tactical Officer I is laterally equivalent to Private First Class. Despite being in a different branch, their command staff will expect proper decorum. Far more than we do here."

"Nice recovery."

Lieutenant Drake stood. "I'll walk you to the training room. From now until you are assigned a patrol craft and partner, I will be your first point of contact and your immediate superior. If you need anything, have any questions, or run into any difficulties, come to me first."

"Okay."

"Solomon…"

"Yes, sir." She saluted.

He smiled and returned her salute. "That's more like it."

LIEUTENANT DRAKE WALKED WITH HER TO THE END OF THE CURVED CORRIDOR outside his office and past another set of transparent doors. Three lengthy hallways and one elevator up later, he stopped at a white metal door bearing the words 'Training 03' and swiped his hand past a dark metallic panel. The door opened with a muffled squeak, revealing a rectangular room about 200 feet long. On each of the longer walls, a row of twenty shining chrome slabs, covered with segmented black pads and headrest cushions, occupied alcoves.

Raised floor tiles clicked and clunked with the weight of technicians in see-through plastic lab coats over dark blue jumpsuits bearing Division 2 markings. Thick wire bundles ran from each station into the space below. Each platform looked like the bastard offspring of a chair and a bed, with the addition of thick nylon straps by the forearms, waist, and ankles.

A tech approached, a thin Asian man about her age. "Welcome, Officer Solomon. I am Jun. I'll be running your modules today." He gestured at one of the stations.

Kate raised an eyebrow at the straps, leaning closer to Lieutenant Drake. "I thought you said this wasn't kinky? Am I supposed to get undressed now?"

Jun dropped his datapad.

Lieutenant Drake coughed. "Think of them like seatbelts. They're only used during advanced combat training sims. Sometimes, the neural inhibitors intended to transfer brain activity into the virtual world lapse, and trainees will punch, kick, or flop about in the real world. You won't need to worry about them today unless you get a strong urge to punch a figure lecturing about policy and procedure."

Jun chuckled nervously. His obvious effort to avoid looking anywhere near her breasts left him staring into her eyes with a manic smile.

"I might." Kate rubbed her face with both hands. *Yeah, this is going to blow.* "Lieutenant?"

"Yes, Solomon?"

"Do you know what my assignment will be when I 'graduate?' What are the chances I could get posted in Querq?"

"What is Querq?"

"The Badlands outpost."

"Oh, that." Lieutenant Drake raised both eyebrows. "It's unusual to have someone asking *for* that assignment. Just about everyone else is scrambling to beg off it. I suppose if you actually want to go out there, it'll probably happen for you… but, it's too early to say."

Kate walked over and sat on her training station. The thick faux-leather pads radiated coolness through her thin uniform. For a moment, she perched on the edge, letting her feet sway back and forth.

"Most trainees remove their utility belt and boots for comfort," said Jun. "There are lockers." He pointed to the inside of the alcove that covered half of the thing she'd spend eight hours a day for the next thirty-two 'sleeping' on.

"Whatever," muttered Kate.

She stashed her belt, boots, and left forearm guard with all its electronics in the locker and hopped back on the table. Jun hovered behind the headrest holding a sleek silver helmet with a wire bundle coming out of the side. Once she settled in, he slipped it over her head and walked to the wall opposite the locker. A bank of holo-panels surrounded him with slabs of light. He poked at them, causing the glow to shift and flicker.

"When you are comfortable, pull the visor down. There's a small sliding switch in the middle of the helmet."

Kate figured she'd already gotten as comfortable as she could. She reached up, found the knob, and slid it downward. A black visor-shaped shield covered her eyes and made everything dark.

"Relax like you're going to sleep."

"Yeah, I know the drill. Been spending a lot of time with my Yume lately."

"Nice, what game?" asked Jun.

"Requiem Excelsior."

Beeps and *boops* emanated from nearby. "Oh, I loved that one, but the third map was *so* annoying. Took me a month to figure out I had to boost across open space to the other half of the ship."

"Right? Ugh. I hate that level."

"Okay, starting the sim now. Try to relax. And there are no aliens in this one." He chuckled.

Jun's muted voice sounded far away. Kate took a deep breath and tried to relax. A wave of vertigo came and went, as though she'd fallen down into the chair/bed. She jerked upright, yelping from the sense of plummeting, and found herself seated at a desk in a university-style classroom.

A brilliant point of light, at about head level appeared, split into two, and traced the outline of a humanoid figure entirely of silver wireframe.

"Good morning, Officer Solomon," said a voice neither male nor female. "I am Gnosis version 6.331. I will be your instructional guide for the foreseeable future. At this time, for maximum comfort in your learning experience, you may customize me to your liking. Please select male or female."

Kate stared up at the white drop ceiling tiles and beige aluminum strips. Someone had decided to make the room look like a pre-war school, even down to a chalkboard with actual chalk. Well, actual in a virtual sense. She shut her eyes and pinched the bridge of her nose, not wanting to deal with that particular philosophical conundrum. David had been a perfect gentleman so far, but the mere thought of him stirred something in her nether regions. She didn't want to be stuck alone in a room with a man for days unless it was him.

"Female."

The wireframe changed its proportions to a female outline. Floating control bars allowed for the adjustment of height, body thickness, breast size, hip size, and a thousand other conceivable ways to tweak appearance. Kate had trouble thinking of any woman in her life whom she had admired or had felt the least bit motherly to her. Althea came to mind first, but the AI wouldn't let her make it short enough to be a child, never mind how awkward it would be to have an eleven-year-old professor. Kate played with the controls.

By the time she finished, Pixie, almost, stared back at her.

Getting her out of a C-Branch facility was the second best thing anyone had ever done for her. Kate propped her chin on her palm, elbow on the desk, wondering what had become of the woman. She couldn't help but feel a bit bad for her, shivering at the memory of when Archon attempted to overwhelm her mind.

"Confirm settings?" asked Gnosis 6.331.

Something seemed off.

"Can you do a British accent?"

The virtual woman walked to the chalkboard. "Aye. Right, let's get on with it, shall we?"

20

EXTERNAL INFLUENCE

Aurora

The skyline of West City shimmered with an uncountable number of small lights moving within a permanent haze of violet and indigo. Rain fell straight and strong, filling the windless night with a continuous hiss Aurora found soothing. A veritable lake had gathered on the roof, deep enough to cover her feet. The textured surface mimicked thousands of pea-sized stones adhered together, like walking on a massage.

Rivulets of water ran down her bare skin, streaming off her breasts and outstretched arms. Long abandoned by civilized people, Sector 10081 remained quiet, unusually free of gunfire. Even the augmented crazies and fringers sought cover from the heavy rain. At least ten miles in all directions separated her from the still-functioning parts of West City and all the associated noise of it. Not even advert bots ventured here.

A pleasant forest it was not.

However, she did find it preferable to the abandoned power station, or that dreadful hotel in East City. She peered over the edge, watching a pair of young men patrol the grounds. A small spectral army of mutilated cyborgs followed them, still clueless why their guns wouldn't fire. A huge man rushed at the teens, pale, bare-chested, and with two black metal legs connected to a rebuilt, mechanical pelvis. He rounded a nine-foot-long sword, slicing it through both of them in one swing.

The boys reacted with mild shivers, enraging the giant even more.

Aurora laughed. She always found new spirits amusing.

She moved away from the edge, allowing herself the amusement of dancing in the rain. The only thing that would make the night perfect would be a colder downpour. For the better part of half an hour, she pirouetted, swayed, and leapt about like an amateur ballerina. Maybe someone watched her from one of the distant broken high rises. Imagining the thoughts a voyeur would have made her laugh. She glanced around as she continued, hoping to spot a pair of eyes on her.

Moments later, she got her wish as a man in a long, green trench coat emerged from between two massive air conditioning units. Baggy black pants, military fatigues with too many pockets, clung to his legs in front. A sheen of moonlight made them look wet. Unkempt, curly dark hair hung to his belt, obscuring a dingy t-shirt stained with blood. Sunken eyes fixed her with a malicious stare, unblinking as he strode right at her. His heavy boots didn't disturb the water.

Aurora stopped dancing, leaving her arms above her head for a few seconds to accentuate her chest. "What's the matter, Theodore? You look angry. Aren't you enjoying the view?"

Theodore walked through a waist-high metal box by a broken obelisk transmitter three times his height. His legs coalesced back out of vapor as soon as he cleared it.

"Well, what is it?" She lowered her arms. "What's got you in a bad mood then?"

"No luck. I think your fucked up eyes are losin' their mojo. Far as I could tell, that Flatline shithead couldn't find a trace of the kid's mom. Say, how old did you say the girl was?"

"Hah." Aurora lost the ability to speak for a moment, trying to contain the laugh. "First of all, she's far too young, even for you. Secondly, if I were you, I wouldn't provoke that one."

"Oh, what's she gonna do? There's only one person I know who can do anything to me more than scream, and we're best friends." He started to smile at her, but wound up sighing. "You could at least *act* uncomfortable havin' me stare at your tits."

"What about your friends? The old ghosts?" Aurora sauntered past him, taking a seat on the electronics cabinet by the antenna in a rather immodest pose. "Is this better?"

"You mean The Kind?" Theodore's eyes darkened. She grinned at her small amount of revenge for all the women he must have tormented over the years. Her utter lack of embarrassment seemed to anger him.

After a moment of staring, he rushed at her. A weak scintillating glow swept over his hands, and he grabbed her by the throat. Other than being icy, he felt solid. An instant of concentration pulled her bodily across the veil. The color of the world around her washed out to tones of sepia and the rain ceased touching her. A steady breeze blew from the south, pushing her long hair to the right. Theodore took on a luminous, transparent appearance that flickered bright with every small motion, as if an intense spotlight only shone on him.

"If you wanted to touch, all you had to do was ask, Theo." Aurora winked and grabbed his crotch.

"Gah." He jumped back. "What the fuck?"

"I'm here." She hopped down to her feet, hands on her hips. "Are you sure all you want to do is cop a feel?"

"Fuck you." He stomped around in a circle.

"That's the offer." She twirled some hair around her fingers, pouting. "Where are you going?"

Theodore stopped with his back to her, hands clenched into fists. "You know I can't. No spirit can."

She almost felt bad. Almost. Of course, she knew that. "Pity. Did you do that little favor I asked of you?"

"Yeah, yeah." He glanced at her. "You're a freaky bitch, you know that?"

Aurora held her hands up, as if innocent. "So I've been told." She slipped out of the astral world. Water around her feet burst into splashes as if she had stomped, hard.

"None of The Kind know thing one about it. We felt the blast about eleven years ago, give or take a couple months. Was like the wall between the… the…" Theodore held his hands out as if trying to grab a word.

"Planes?"

"Whatever. I ain't understanding that esoteric bullshit. Planes, dimensions, realities… whatever. I guess that works. Anyway, this ripple came wobblin' through the veil, makin' everything all blurry and shit, right? We figure, was a lot of people probably died in one shot for that to happen."

"Well, if by a lot you mean about twenty-three, then yes. The ripple was something else. It wasn't what they were attempting to do, but they managed to open a portal to another realm, rather than a faraway point in this one." Aurora tapped a finger to her cheek. "Granted, it stayed open for less than one fortieth of a second. Long enough for something to slip in."

"How the hell do you know that?"

She smiled. "A girl never tells her secrets."

"Bullshit. You ain't no *girl* with tits that size."

"Oh, fine, killjoy. I had a nice chat with Dr. Hitesh Rao. He's the bloke what designed the thing that exploded. In return for my assistance in coaching him on the fundamentals of his new ghostiness, he explained it. Most of it went straight over my head, but I got the crucial bits." She leaned back, enjoying the rain on her nakedness for a moment. "Poor man still doesn't believe he's dead."

Theodore shrugged. "Couldn't find shit. No trace, no one saw her, nothing. She ain't alive, she ain't dead. Like she just stopped being. My guess is she got ganked out there in the nowhere and got a ticket to the silver door right quick like."

Muted clanking mixed with the sound of the rain.

Aurora slouched. "Darn. Oh, well, I should've guessed. You might want to disappear in a moment."

"Whatever for?" Theodore leaned toward her. "Tired of disappointing me already?"

"James is on his way up here."

"Oh noes." He feigned cowering. "Not *James*. Must be bad if you sensed it before it happened."

"Suit yourself, and no, I can hear his boots on the stairs."

"Did you just try to roll your eyes? You do realize they're like... all black. Rollin' em doesn't do any good 'cause no one can fuckin notice."

Aurora held up two fingers.

"Two?" Theodore blinked. "Two what?"

"Oh, bloody hell. Fecking Americans." She switched to a middle finger over her shoulder as she walked away. "There, does that about do it?"

"I think I'll stick around to watch you squirm."

"You'll be waiting awhile, Theodore."

She wandered to the edge and gazed once more upon the city. Rusty hinges squeaked. Archon grunted, forcing a door that long ago stopped working on automatic. Aurora enjoyed a few more minutes of rain while Archon crept across the roof. The sound of clattering upon sheet metal grew louder. The oddity of the noise made her look; a dented five-foot square slab of rolled steel hovered over him, performing the function of an umbrella.

"Good heavens, Lauren." Archon made displeased noises while examining his shoes. "Do you have any idea how much these cost?"

"I don't, but I'm sure you will educate me any moment."

Theodore, looking disappointed, sank into the roof.

"Why are you traipsing about without a kit?" Archon raised an eyebrow. "It's raining."

"If you don't know me by now, dear. Why are you wearing clothes?" She glanced at him for a second before a distant zooming red light caught her eye.

He tilted his head at her in astonishment, mute for a few seconds. "Why am I... It is what people do."

"Well, there you 'ave it." She admired herself. "Given the downpour, I'd rather not be stuck in a sopping wet kit."

"Forget it. Your wardrobe choices are the last thing on my mind at the moment. Where is my ship? Did you think it would be amusing to watch me fume when Mamoru toddled off with it?"

"I'm clairvoyant, James—not omniscient."

"So you have no idea if some dogsbody across the alley is about to take a pot shot at us?"

"Of course I do." Aurora gazed up past rain at the roiling indigo smog. *He'll never understand.* "Unless I rather loathed the person, I'd see it a few seconds to a minute beforehand. The more emotional investment I've got in their survival, the more forewarning. Remember when Gordon slipped your control and tried to pop Anna in Lord Thompson's office? Now"—she held a hand up as if stopping traffic—"before you go off on a ramble about the one percent of the one percent that gets precognitive visions about total strangers, yes, I do. However, that does not mean I see every little bloody detail months ahead of time. If someone's going to blow up a PubTran bus, I won't know if he decides to stop for a quick wank on his way there."

"A three thousand foot long starship going missing is hardly a trivial detail." Archon's improvised umbrella shuddered as some of his rage leaked into his telekinetic grasp. "How could you fail to see that? I have been trying to convince myself you are not deliberate in your sabotage."

She pivoted; the rain running over her cheeks made a good stand in for tears on her pouting face. "James… You know I could never act against you."

He fidgeted, shifting in a futile attempt to keep water out of his overpriced dress shoes.

"I suspect some manner of external influence has altered the course of Mamoru's destiny."

"External influence?" He blinked. "Explain to me again, in as much detail as you need, how exactly you failed to see this coming?"

"If I didn't see it, chances are it will wind up being ultimately meaningless." She gazed out upon the city over dark towers dotted with spots of light, an obelisk garden standing amid drifts of glowing smog. The quiet somberness made her kick at the water like a child playing in a puddle.

"You have seen the ship's arrival then?"

A shiver ran down her back. The soft violet light in the mist shifted to a torrent of liquid flames in her imagination. Skyscrapers faltered and toppled. She closed her eyes to stop the vision. "Yes."

He put a hand on her shoulder. "Something is bothering you."

Aurora looked at him, for an instant pondering seeking solace in his arms. The concern in his eyes *might* have been for her; more likely, he worried for his dreams and what her sudden drop in mood meant for his plans. Of course, it was rather difficult to lie to a man who made a living at it.

She steeled herself and put on a plastic smile. "Not everything comes to pass exactly in the manner I foresee it."

"You saw something." His tone darkened.

"That external influence I mentioned. Something wants you to fail. Perhaps Mamoru's sister found him."

"Nonsense. The woman is not even psionic." He scoffed. "She is of no concern."

"Well, I suppose that leaves the 'sentient Badlands drivel.' Of course, you don't believe in that."

"Perhaps you should find a proper bed and sleep with thoughts of our starship dancing about in your mind?" He gestured at the metal floating overhead. "This racket is unbearable. You are certain he will turn up then? With the ship?"

"Mamoru will bring the CSS Angel here." She refused to look at the city, afraid of confronting her estimation of possible versus probable. "Without a doubt."

21

SOFT ON THE OUTSIDE

Anna

The fourth time Anna pushed her finger into the unlit metal panel above the stenciled numeral ten, it occurred to her she hadn't gone anywhere because she kept mashing the button of an elevator that had been dead for years. As if the collapsing ceiling, dangling wires, off-the-rails doors, and knee-high junk piled inside hadn't been enough of a clue. She stood in silence, vaguely aware of the seep of water trickling down her back under her clothes. Her gaze shifted to the puddle of rainwater by the glassless doors at the front of the lobby.

The darkness outside felt like a metaphor for the shadow devouring her life. Water patted to the floor around her; the short sprint from the car to the door had left her soaked to the skin. The wetness felt unreal, as did her presence here. At any moment, she'd wake up somewhere else, perhaps back in Coventry Tower. Maybe she had never made it out of Agent Gordon's interrogation chair and she already floated at the banks of the Thames, the usual fate of a Cov.

Maybe everything from the moment she awoke handcuffed to a chair to now had been a dream playing out in the instant between a bullet to the head and death.

Anna looked at her hand, finger still extended to the inoperable button. A droplet gathered on the knuckle of her middle finger and fell. The *pat* of it striking the floor shocked her with the force of someone clapping in front of her face. Aaron repeatedly reminding her of his doubts about Archon had not had one one-thousandth the effect of looking into the thoughts of a woman made deathly afraid of her own child. When Aaron broke the implant, the cascade of guilt came back over the telepathic link and left her speechless. Someone had programmed Melissa's parents to hate her: to want her out of their house.

Why?

She cringed, hearing Aaron's voice in her mind. *He wanted her.*

Someone had programmed Deacon Bell to confess to Old Bill. Someone had programmed Talis to grovel before Aaron. *No, it can't be.* Anna shivered, wondering what *someone* had done to her or her friends. Her mind slid backward down a tunnel of doubt, landing in Plonk's flat. Anna felt naked again, her hands fixed behind her in cuffs with Archon's angelic face floating in front of her. How *heroic* he seemed; gallant James Mardling there to save the poor, wretched girl, fallen back upon her old vices.

What vices? She blinked, returning to the now. *I'd been on drugs, hadn't I? What drugs?* Her mind grasped at open air searching for the word. How could she forget the name of the thing that had almost killed her? James's glowing face told her she didn't need to worry about that nasty stuff anymore.

Anna snapped out of her daze and an uncomfortable weight settled around her shoulders. She ducked past the broken elevator doors and left a trail of water down the hall to the stairwell. When she reached the second story, a metal squeak preceded a hollow slam echoing off the bare walls. Her mind lifted bits and pieces of the past, matching the sounds to similar noises from her days in Coventry Tower. The Angry Ones bursting in looking for a place to crash, younger kids playing, older teens fighting over chems and food, and East End Boys kicking on doors to see which flats had an appetizing young woman.

Lights flickered overhead.

She shied away from the faltering bulbs. That aspect of her mind that messed with electronics whenever her emotions strayed from calm had been the reason she'd tried the drug she still couldn't remember the name of. The drug had suppressed her power, allowing her to hide as a normal, but she had been overconfident. Rather than controlling herself, using it only to stay undetected, it had consumed her entirely.

Another door thudded closed somewhere near the top of the vertical shaft. She trudged along, trying to make sense of how so much of her past seemed to have ceased existing. On the fifth floor, she remembered a man she used to live with as a child. He'd worked for the government, assuming the role of her caretaker and posing as her father for the neighbors' benefit. The memory of his face summoned a legion of tiny sparks spider-crawling over the cinder blocks. A secret government agency killed her mother and left her in the custody of a man shitless about psionics and who knew fuck-all about them.

What sense did that make? Why would a man so terrified of her power stay there and use alcohol to cope, rather than quit?

How could he not have known what he was getting into?

As much as she tried to hate him for beating her, her mind summoned only indifference at his death. A few fleeting pangs of shame lapped at the edges of her heart, as if wondering why she wanted this shouting, drunken, father-impersonating, intelligence agent to love her. She thought of Aaron's wry smile but remembered the concern in the rest of his face.

I have to know.

Her stride picked up speed; she covered the last few stories fast enough to get her heart racing. At the tenth floor landing, Anna paused to glance at a trail of water from the roof access to the interior hallway. Cold wind forced its way in around the broken excuse for a door, making her squint as she crept over. Outside, Aurora frolicked naked in the rain.

The mere sight of her made Anna shiver and gather her coat with a squish.

Anna frowned at the wet footprints. *I wonder what bad news she gave him this time.*

The air grew mercifully warmer the deeper into the corridor she walked. She tried not to pay attention to the clingy, wet clothes wrapped around her as she hurried along to their living space.

At the sight of a small hand slipping out and grasping the edge of the door, she halted a few paces away. Alexi pushed the faux cherry wood slab to the side and stepped into the hall. He looked bored and lonely. The boy took a step into the hall before he noticed her and jumped with a start. His ice blue eyes no longer held the angry vitriol they'd brimmed with in the lounge, and his clothes looked more or less new: a burgundy sweater with beige slacks and plain black sneaks. If not for the lack of an emblem on his breast, he might have been off to a private academy. His whole posture had changed, all the aggression gone.

The boy pulled unkempt dirty-blond hair away from his face and smiled. "Oy, sorry mum. I didn't see ya there."

Anna blinked at his English accent. "Alexi? Are you alright?"

"Who's Alexi? Are you nutters?" His eyes narrowed to a squint for a moment before he laughed. "Oh, you're takin' the piss."

His innocent smile made her feel sick to her stomach. She couldn't reconcile this boy with the growling, homicidal ragamuffin Aaron had to disarm.

"Uhm…" She looked over his head, into the room she shared with James. "I might be a little woozy from the weather. I must have you mixed up with someone else."

"Aye, there's a right lot of us, aren't there?" His grin broadened. "I'm so happy Archon found us before the Met got us." He leapt into a hug, sniffling. "They would'a separated us."

After clinging for a moment, his fear lessened. The boy took a step back, wiped his face, and smiled again. "Is it okay if I go hang out with my friends?"

Numb, she nodded, unable to speak. *Why is he asking me that?*

"Thanks, mum!" Alexi gave her another brief hug before running off to the stairwell.

Anna stumbled into the room, slid the door closed behind her, and peeled her coat off. She draped it over the back of a chair by an unused table on her way to James, who sat behind his desk. Absorbed in his work, he didn't react to her. She remained silent, dripping and staring at him like a puppy that had wandered in from the rain.

"You should take those wet things off before you catch your death," said James, not looking over.

"What happened to Alexi?"

"He is Alastair now." James continued fiddling with holographic models of buildings.

"James." A trace of whine added to her voice. "I'm serious."

"Are you asking what happened to the boy he used to be? Why he was so aggressive and angry?" James tapped a finger on the desk. "Let me see. Alexi was pressed into combat at the age of ten when the Russian Resistance swept up his family. Suspicious neighbors reported him to the authorities for being psionic. He watched the authorities kill his grandparents and drag his mother off to who-knows-where. That sort of experience tends to leave a mark." A long, virtual building slid sideways across the holo-panel, as if adhered to James's finger. "Or, perhaps his mind shattered when he had to take refuge under three dead men, one of whom was his oldest brother. Their mission to steal food had met with unexpected complications, and he had to crawl under corpses and play dead while Citizen Management troops walked within inches of him.

"Now that you mention it, I think what truly made the lad homicidal was what the older boy kept doing to him at night when no one was there to hear him cry out. The Resistance made their homes in old sewers, you see, and their bunk was all the way at the end of a cistern, in the dark. A few weeks after he turned eleven, he shot the other boy at point-blank range and dragged the body into the mire." James finally peeled his glare off the holo-panel and made eye contact. "He learned that guns fix problems. Tell me Alexi would be happier than Alastair, and mean it, and I shall put him back the way he was."

Tears streamed out of her eyes. "You can't just make awful things go away." She folded her arms, shivering in the air-conditioned space. "What will happen when whatever you did to him breaks down? What will he do if his memories return?"

He raised an eyebrow, almost scoffing. "Breaks down? Indeed. You must have mistaken me for a normal telepath. I rather think he need not worry about that. Now that the boy's demons are no more, he can focus on strengthening his abilities. He had blamed his gift for what happened to his family and not used it since. You did, of course, see how happy he was on the way out? He is quite fortunate that I care so much for our charges."

"Why did you make him British?"

James chuckled. "The amount of psychological trauma in that boy required I construct an entirely new personality. I had to use what I knew. Of course, I built on the similarities. *Alastair's* father left because he could not deal with a psionic child. He and his mother lived on the streets around Coventry Tower. He spent his days roving with a pack of urchins, living a carefree life of begging and playing like something out of a storybook. He remembers the time fondly, if not a touch blurrily." He swiped his thumb across the screen, laying down a road made of metal tiles.

"What game is that?"

He smiled. "I am designing our future home. A quaint little village."

"Please tell me you'll not call it Jamestown or something droll."

He frowned.

Teeth chattering, Anna slipped out of her boots and wet clothes before moping over to the autoshower tube. Alexi's—or Alastair's—smiling face haunted her as she thought about what James had done. Was he better off? If it had been her, would she want to remember something like that? She had been fortunate, due in large part to Penny, not to have suffered any sexual abuse on the streets of London. At least, not until she'd started working for Mr. Blake—but that was her own fault, and she'd been an adult by then.

"How much of my past did you rearrange?" Anna's voice echoed in the tube; she had to yell over the building whirr of the machine.

I cannot hear you over the device, dear.

His voice in her mind, clear despite the noise made her jump. She shifted around to peer through the steam-covered plastic at him. *How much of my life is your dream?*

James smiled. *Your life is all I dream about, my dear.*

Hot soap distracted her for a moment, purging the stiffness of cold, rain-soaked clothes from her muscles. She let off a moan that could've been confused for sex, and let herself enjoy it.

Relax, Anna. We can converse when you are no longer frozen. He crossed to the food assembler, winking at her before tapping the controls.

Anna lost herself in the warmth of a shower for a while. Fifteen minutes later when the tornado of heated air ceased, she hesitated with three fingers on the door handle, dreading the temperature outside. Her breath echoed in the closed tube and the foggy cylinder grew opaque. James got up from his desk, rushing over with a long terrycloth robe in hand. Torn between adoration and doubt, she emerged and allowed him to wrap the garment around her, winding up with her back to his chest.

"Something still bothers you."

"I'm not sure it's right to just erase a bad memory."

"What harm could come of it?" He raised one hand in a half-shrug. "It is not as though he has anything to gain from remembering other than pain. The other boy cannot harm him further, and Alexi had the shame of what happened to him and the horror of murder weighing on his innocent heart."

Something gnawed at the back of Anna's mind. What had happened to the boy struck a nerve she couldn't remember having. Mr. Blake left her locked naked in a stripper's cage overnight as punishment for 'not dancing well enough.' The scene replayed in her mind. He staggered in the next morning, like the arrogant king of the underworld, and yelled at her for lazing off the previous day. The cage door squeaked open and he reached for her, brandishing a truncheon. He wanted to teach her a proper lesson on how a whore should behave. Anger overwhelmed her and she pulled all the electricity out of the sound system, through the cage and out her arms. Blake had turned to a cinder in the middle of Bristol City.

Killing him shouldn't make her feel dirty and worthless. Why, then, did the image of his sneering, fat, face make her want to curl up and hide? *Something's missing.*

"How much of what I think I remember is real?"

He rested his chin on her shoulder. "You were quite determined to destroy yourself on some street chemical. I decided to spare you that."

"Is that all?" She couldn't stop thinking about Alexi. "That boy wasn't even the same person. What if someone speaks Russian to him?"

"Oh, drat. I forgot to erase that." James made a pensive face. "I suppose he'll know it, but not know why he knows it. I can clean it up later if there is a problem. Honestly, can you call him a person the way he was?" He rubbed her shoulders. "He was little more than a shell, ready to lash out. Think about it, Anna, he was about to shoot someone because they would not let him cheat at some silly game. *Alastair* is much happier."

He refused to use his powers. That's the tragedy to James. Anna tensed for an instant, expecting a response from her idle thought, but he hadn't been eavesdropping. A psionic who wouldn't use his powers couldn't help 'the cause.' How much had he changed her? Even at her life's lowest point, she never imagined herself capable of kidnapping a young girl. At the time, it had been what Archon wanted—and so she did it. Without Althea in front of her, the idea didn't bother her much. The guilt had existed only as long as she stared into those sad, glowing eyes. The silly child hadn't even hated her for it. *She told me I was sad inside.* Had Aaron been right? A wistful smile lingered for seconds on her lips at the memory of him calling her a block of sweet coated in a bit of sour.

"How much of me did you change?"

James let his hands slip off her shoulders. "If you must know, I did manipulate your environs to a degree for your own benefit."

She spun to face him, mouth agape. "James..."

"The problem with addicts, my dear, is that they are seldom capable of realizing the state they are in. Without my intervention, it is doubtful you would still be alive." He caressed her cheek. "That, my dear, would have been a tragedy."

Anna tensed.

"The mere thought of a woman as beautiful as you suffering as you did, fills me with rage."

"You don't sound very angry." She glanced down at her toes, peeking out from under the crumpled robe.

James raised a hand, catching a floating cup of Earl Grey. Behind her sounded the *ka-chunk* of the food assembler door closing. He guided the cup into her hands.

"I have nothing to be angry about. You are here, healthy, and safe."

Smelling the tea reminded her of her 'father's' loathing of the flavor. Once, in a drunken haze, he had mentioned he couldn't stand it because it had been her mother's favorite. *It doesn't make sense he hated it because it made him think of her. Why would a CSB operative care?*

"There are things that don't make sense in my head anymore." She sipped the tea. "Why would the man claiming to be my father detest this tea because my mum fancied it?"

James glanced upward, tapping his lip while thinking. "There could be a few reasons. Perhaps the man had been minding her detention cell and had to fetch it for her every day. Your mum was gifted as well; perhaps she did something to him in her escape attempt."

Images from the information Mamoru had discovered replayed in her mind. A blonde figure sprawled face down, shot in the back. Anna had been a toddler when the CSB murdered her mother in the street like a common criminal. The woman hadn't even been armed. Emotion weakened her legs, and she found herself leaning into James for support.

He cocked an eyebrow.

"Why did they kill her, James?" Anna sniffled. "She was only twenty-three. What possible threat could she have been?"

"Paranoia seldom shares a bed with logic or reason. She knew about their breeding project. Even if she had no intention to do so, she could have gone public."

She pushed herself to arm's length. "Did you make me think fondly of you?"

"Annabelle…" He wiped a tear from her cheek with his thumb. "It hurts to hear you ask such a thing."

Her glare didn't soften.

"No, my dear. I never forced you to have feelings for me. In fact, I attempted to talk you out of it. Do you remember me assuring you that you did not need to offer yourself as some manner of gratitude for my assistance?"

"I…" She looked down at his chest. "Yes. I've the oddest fondness for black lace underthings now."

"You went a few years without."

She looked away. "I didn't have the credits to spend on them."

"The least I could do was offer you basic dignity."

He had given her dignity. Her worst memory was the shame she felt when he found her at Plonk's flat. The chem merchant had tricked her into kinky sex in exchange for drugs, and refused to let her leave after because she didn't fuck him 'good enough.' He wanted his money's worth. *If James hadn't found me, I could still be leashed to that bastard's bed.*

Anna squinted. That didn't seem right either. Plonk was many shades of scumbag, but a rapist? Certainly not. She could see him keeping her chained for a little longer than she wanted as a tease. Kidnapping her didn't fit the memory of the man.

"If you are having second thoughts about us, Anna… You should not feel obligated." He held her hands and smiled. "It would pain me to lose you to that Arsenal bloke, but if that is where your heart lies…"

"You didn't make me love you?" She looked up into his eyes.

"Of course not, my dear. I use my gift to help people, not harm them. Forcing a person to love someone they do not is the greatest trespass I could imagine."

Anna let her head lay against his shoulder. "I am confused."

He swayed side to side, comforting her with an arm around her back. "This world has no place for our kind, Anna. There is no excuse for the way you have been treated. I would do anything to bring your mum back, but it is far beyond me. All I can do is offer you the stability you have always deserved, but never had."

She slipped her arms around him, feeling no less confused about everything going on. The promise of stability called her like a siren song. James did have a point. Alexi would be better off forgetting everything about his horrible life. If all James had taken from her was the worst memories of being a drug-abusing exotic dancer, how could she hold that against him?

Anna leaned up on tiptoe, and kissed him.

James closed his eyes and pressed his lips tight to hers. She didn't resist as he walked her to the edge of the large Comforgel pad.

He leaned back long enough to whisper, "Are you certain this is what you want?"

"*Mm-hmm.*" She stretched out on the bed, tugging the knot out of the robe's belt.

♌ ⚼ ⛢ ⚴ ♎

ANNA'S DREAM OF BEING A CAPTIVE PRINCESS CHAINED BY THE WRISTS TO A dungeon wall while watching an armored knight slay faceless beasts on his way to save her faded out to her lounging in bed with her arms over her head. Sunlight at the side of her eyes pushed sleep farther away. Cologne and the ambiance of a recent shower scented the cool air caressing her bare skin, except for her left leg tucked under a sheet up to her thigh. The Comforgel pad radiated heat from below. Anna let out a soft moan of protest at being awake. To her right, the sound of a belt buckle rattling hinted at the reason for her consciousness.

When she reached to wipe her eyes, her arm stopped short after an inch with a metallic rattle. She opened her eyes and tugged, finding her wrists fixed together around a post in the headboard by blue, furry handcuffs. *That explains my dream.* Pink-furred cuffs with longer chains attached her ankles to the far corners, keeping her legs wide. Anna remembered the previous night and grinned. She stretched, shuddering with the wonderful feeling of tension evaporating. Afterward, she went limp, glancing to the side at James in the middle of getting dressed.

"You fell asleep rather fast. Did I wear you out?" She bit her lower lip.

He smiled over his shoulder at her and took a necktie from the shelf. "I am getting old, and you are impossible to resist."

"You're not old. You're forty-five. Blimey, I can't believe you left me like this all bloody night." She swished her feet back and forth. "Planning on having another round?"

"I do not understand your fascination with being restrained." He knotted the necktie and strolled to his desk. Imitation leather creaked as it absorbed his weight. "For a woman who loathes feeling helpless, it defies logic you derive pleasure from it."

"Not a clue." She absentmindedly pulled at her wrists. "I used to hate it when clients did it to me at Bristol's. Maybe I always hoped someone would save me or something."

"Could be." Holo-panels popped open in front of him, forming a curtain of light. "Some think that people in positions of power secretly crave submission."

Anna laughed. "I wasn't exactly in a 'position of power' when you found me."

"Indeed, but it is still who you are. You protect yourself when you have the presence of mind to do so. Bloody CSB. I cannot see why you let them frighten you into ruin."

"Probably because they're the military, James. Not to mention sneaky. I might be deadly, but I'm not much of a spy. I had to hide." She stared at the ceiling for a while, thinking about her life before James. The handcuffs proved distracting. She writhed and squirmed, wanting but unable to touch herself. After several frustrating minutes, she craned her neck to peer at him. "Care to go again?"

"Perhaps."

Anna tried not to think about sex. The plain metal cuffs had no electronics. It had been her idea since it would not have given her the same sense of excitement if she could let herself out whenever she chose. The longer he left her there, the more she grumbled about that decision. Was he teasing her? James didn't seem fond of that sort of play; in fact, the entire handcuff thing had made him uneasy at first. He found it strange she enjoyed it, and it had taken a few weeks of asking to get him to agree to it. A twinge of shame followed the memory of Constable Brown. How broken had she been that she'd felt a thrill even there?

"James, do you think it odd how things happened in London?"

Beeping from the terminals paused. "How do you mean?"

"Well, Ol' Jack, Spawny... and even Penny seemed so hostile out of the blue." Anna stared at the pink fur around her pale ankle. *Like the way Melissa's mother had been 'adjusted.'* She couldn't bring herself to mention that to him yet. "It doesn't feel right."

"You know how things are over there. The whole bloody country wets their knickers at the smallest mention of psionics. Once the reality of what you were sank in, it got to them. Even dear friends may not be willing to suffer a military interrogation." He leaned to the right to peer at her between two floating screens. "Did you forget those children from Orkney? The boys' own parents handed them over to the CSB because they didn't want to be arrested."

Anna's sense of vulnerability slipped from arousal to unease. She twisted and pulled at her arms and legs. "I think I've 'ad enough for now. Do you think the CSB threatened them?"

James waved his hand over the terminals, shutting all the screens down. "Possible, but they are perfectly safe now. Before we left, I made some adjustments. You need not worry your pretty little head about it."

She watched him cross the room to the bookshelf-turned-wardrobe, from which he took his suit jacket. "I'd like to bring them with us. Penny and Spawny. It's bad enough being across the ocean. I don't like the thought of never seeing them again."

He fixed three buttons closed and adjusted his tie. "I imagine that would be their choice, yes?" James walked to the exit. "Sorry to pop off like this, but something urgent has come up. I shall return soon."

The door slid closed behind him.

"James!" She rattled the cuffs. "Where are you going? Let me out! This isn't funny anymore. What if someone walks in?" After a second to listen for his return, she shouted, "At least cover me up!"

Footsteps in the hallway outside grew faint.

"James!"

Anna stared down the length of her body, past her toes, at the door. For five or so minutes, she made faces at the ceiling, whistled, tapped her foot on air, and tried to remain calm. The handcuff key on the nightstand to her left mocked her with a glint of sunlight. So close, but so far. *What's he getting on about? Does he think I enjoy this?* She grabbed and pulled on the metal strut in the headboard, but couldn't break it. Despite knowing she lacked the strength to snap the chains, she tried. The Comforgel pad sensed a rise in her body temperature and automatically backed off the heat. *Is he angry with me? Oh, no.* She shivered. *What if he was looking at my thoughts? Does he know how much I doubted him? He did seem cold this morning; what if he's going after Aaron?*

She glared at the restraints, which seemed to grow tighter the more she fought them. *If I get out of these, I'm going to drop them in the rubbish.*

"You win, James. This isn't fun anymore."

Anna blinked as a sense of relief washed over her. *That's it! He never cared for kink; he must be trying to make me loathe it.* If he read her mind and saw the depth of her doubts, he would not have left it unmentioned. Anna shivered. He'd not batted an eyelash at impaling her hand with a chopstick for a simple demonstration; what might he do to her if he thought her loyalty faltered? His attempting some manner of reverse conditioning made the most sense. *He could just say he doesn't like it.*

A child's voice giggled out of the air vents.

Oh, no. Please, no. Don't let someone walk in here now, especially not a little kid. How the devil would I explain this to a child? Buzzing came from Archon's desk terminal as her embarrassment peaked.

Anna bit back the urge to scream for James, fearing someone she'd rather not find her in such a predicament might hear and come to see. Minutes passed in silence until the urge to relieve herself became hard to ignore. *Shit. I will never forgive him if he makes me wet the bed.* She struggled, kicking at her legs in hopes of breaking whatever James had locked the other end around.

Despite the rattle of the solid bed frame offering little hope, she fought until she ran out of breath.

Angry, she flopped limp and panting.

Yeah, captive princess, right.

Anna ticked off a list of people who she could tolerate finding her tethered starkers to a bed. Alas, her first choice was in England, Penny. Aurora would laugh, but wouldn't make a big deal of it. However, she would tease the hell out of her in private. Anna grumbled. Aaron would make a *huge* deal of it and probably work in some lame Manchester joke... but the more urgent her need became, the less she cared. Some of the security people might not be *too* bad, but they never went up to the tenth floor unless called.

"Fuck... Fuck... Fuck..." She thrashed. "He's going to be gone all bloody day."

Staccato pops in the distance signaled the usual turf wars between black zone gangs. Muted whirrs from distant hovercar traffic leaked past the din of the younger psionics playing their version of Frictionless in the courtyard. Warmth crept over her face at the thought of any of them finding her. Anna leaned her head up and stared at the door, growing angrier by the minute. No amount of squirming or struggling helped. She could only wait, or risk shouting and making things worse.

Buzzing came from the Comforgel pad, startling her from furious to nervous.

"Oh, bloody... if this thing catches fire, I'm..."

She closed her eyes and tried to meditate away her anger as well as the intolerable discomfort in her bladder. The game outside provided a mild distraction, but after the third set of cheers went up for a goal scored, she couldn't take it anymore.

"Lauren?" she yelled and banged the cuffs on the headboard to make noise. "Lauren? Anyone? Can anyone hear me?"

After a moment of silence, she let her head flop back on the pillow and sighed at the ceiling.

"Shit."

22

A CHOICE THAT'S NOT

Althea

Warm sunlight lit up the opaque white panels of the garden's dome. Althea reclined in the grass with her head on Den's shoulder, ankles crossed, and a blue-winged moth perched on her big toe. He'd not wanted to go swimming with the other older kids since the mood he'd been in since the attack hadn't changed much. Aside from his duties with the Watch, he had kept to himself. She reached over and held his hand in the grass at her side. Birds gathered among the orange trees, tweeting and darting about in pairs. She gazed up through the crisscrossing vines, watching birds flit about.

His emotions remained dark, and she couldn't understand why he felt embarrassed and ashamed. She thought back to the moment they shared in the seed room when she had snuck away from the tribe to warn him. He'd done that awkward thing where he pressed his lips to hers; it would've been strange if not for the love radiating from him at the time. Officer Ahmed thought her too young to even touch lips with a boy, though Karina and Father thought it cute. She still didn't grasp the point of it, but it made Den feel happiness and love. Maybe the city police man had been right and it made no sense because she hadn't become old enough to understand.

Althea picked at the grass with her free right hand, trying to untangle her feelings. Being with Den here in Querq didn't nag at her with the same worry she'd felt back with his tribe. The idea he had only pretended to like her to gain more power as chief by joining with The Prophet wouldn't matter here.

He liked her for... because.

She smiled. Few people besides Father and Karina treated her like a person. Even in Querq, most kept her at arm's length like a goddess they feared offending—except for the smaller kids who never heard the stories of the Prophet. Perhaps that explained why she spent so much time with hem. Her sister said the day would come when Althea would rather share a bed with Den. She squinted at him, making a face as though she'd tasted something sour. No way would she ever want to be with a boy more than her own family. Besides, she didn't want to abandon her sister. Nothing made her feel as safe or as happy as having Karina's arm around her at night.

Of course, if Karina thought that way about her and Den, the day may come she wanted to have a man in her bed. Would her sister choose a boy over her? Althea smirked, jealous over a person who didn't yet exist. Worry played games with her stomach, and she swished her feet side to side. The moth ignored her motion, its wings twitching as it adjusted its balance. She grinned, remembering how happy she had been to see Den when the Watch found him. Zhar thought he'd forget her, but he hadn't. He gave up his home, his status as Chief Braga's son, and walked across the Badlands to find her.

Althea squeezed his hand; the moth flew away when she scooted a little closer to him.

She suspected Den wanted to spend time with her here in the Garden since the green plants reminded him of home, where there had been forest. Real forest, not the same unnatural growth of trees in the desert around here. She smiled at the memory of when they'd had a moment together, leaning against the wall while Jake recovered from the bonedog attack. She liked being with Den. She stared at the moth, corkscrewing off over the grass, wondering what the boy might be doing now. Most of the people in the old tribe had been afraid of her, and Palik's jealousy had been far from subtle.

Den shot upright, left hand on the grass behind him, poised to leap to his feet. He cast a hard glare at the trees while reaching for the handle of a knife on his belt. Althea sat up as well, searching around for what had spooked him. She fidgeted, uneasy at how the bad man always seemed to torment her whenever she came to the Garden.

Althea glanced at him. After a second, he shifted his eyes toward her. His dour expression softened but remained dim. Worry chased her grin away. When her concerned expression had no effect, she tickled under his arm. He grunted and pushed her hand down. At that, she reached up and used two fingers to force his mouth into a smile.

He grasped her by the wrists and pulled her hands to his chest.

"What's wrong?" She tilted her head.

"You don't need me."

She furrowed her brow. "Need you?"

He turned his gaze to the plants overhead. Althea wanted to make him look at her, but he kept her hands trapped. She emitted a playful snarl like an angry, tiny dog and pulled at her arms. The corner of his mouth curled, though he still avoided eye contact.

"Den, please." She whined. "Don't quiet me. Your feelings are bad. Please talk."

"Thea…" He sighed. The sense of shame surrounding him grew.

"I'm sorry." She sniffled. "Did I do the bad?"

"Don't cry." Den finally looked at her.

An overwhelming sense of humiliation radiated from him. He let go of her hands and folded his arms over his chest. She moved to sit cross-legged, but her white dress didn't offer the same freedom her old skirt did, so she wound up tucking both legs to her right.

Her lip quivered. "Why do I make you have shame? Do you not like me now?"

"I *do* like you. A lot." He threw some small bit of plant matter he'd been twisting between his thumb and forefinger off into the grass.

She bit her lower lip. "Why are you having angry? I thought it was my fault."

"You didn't look in my dreams?"

Althea shook her head. "Karina says it's not nice to listen to the thinking of people unless I don't trust them." She stared at the ground between them. "I don't wanna do the bad."

He kept quiet a moment, his mood twisting to anger. "When that man tried to hurt you, I wanted to protect you, but all I did was get hurt. If I had done nothing but watch, it would not have mattered."

"You saved my life. If you only watched, he would have killed me." She shivered. "The evil was inside him. He threw Shepherd like a little boy. He was no *man*."

"The many-man?" Den calmed, a trickle of fear dampened his rage. "The chamán spoke of such things, but I thought it a story to scare small children… Like you."

Althea's head popped up to glare at him. "I'm not small children."

"You're a kid. And you're small."

She stuck her tongue out at him.

He chuckled. "You believe those stories."

She gave him a raspberry. "You *saw* those stories. The big wolf that bit you. It was The Many."

"You didn't really kill it. It got up and dragged itself away when no one was looking." He frowned.

"No." Althea scooted closer and clung to him. "It turned into dark and flew away."

His fear grew as he squinted into the distance, searching his memory. "I… didn't see tracks."

She cowered away from the cornstalks where the old man had first appeared. "It made the bonedogs attack us. It hates me and I don't know why."

He stared at her for a long moment. "It is darkness… if it exists. Darkness does not need a reason to hate."

"Now you sound like a chamán."

"When we found you"—Den brushed the hair out of her eyes—"you were weak and scared."

Althea tried not to remember the feeling of metal locked around her ankle. Perhaps the sentience made her see it, but her mind jumped right back to when a band of marauders had kept her tethered by a chain to a peg in the ground at the center of their camp. Nalu, Den, Palik, and a large party of Seekers from the tribe had hunted them down to repay an ambush. As always, she prepared herself to change owners. Althea rubbed her right bicep, where Nalu's hand had squeezed when he'd shoved her into the cage. The same cage they'd dragged her back to the village in.

"Palik wanted to kill me."

Den tightened his arm around her back. "He thinks himself bigger than he is. He will never be a true chamán. He was jealous."

"You saved me from them, and you made the happy with Braga, and he let me out of the cage."

He stroked her hair. "You are not the same frightened girl. No one knew you had such magic. Why did you let people take you?"

She rested her cheek on his shoulder and swished her right foot back and forth in the grass. "I had the scared. Mystics who can take people's minds are burned. I had the stupid too." She scratched at an itch on her left shin, displacing a small beetle. "It took me long to learn I should protect myself."

"You do not need me to protect you." He spun a dandelion around between his fingers. "You protected me. I am the wife."

Althea put a hand on his heart, staring into his eyes. "You *did* protect me… That man would have hit me with his sword if you didn't get in the way. You saved my life."

He stared down. "I stole time. I'm only good enough to get killed in one swing."

She leaned up on her knees and bent closer, touching foreheads. "I was touching that woman's life-shapes. I did not see him. You"—she raised her head, making eye contact—"saved me."

Den gazed into her eyes for a second before looking down. "Anyone can jump on a sword. I should be able to protect you."

She lowered herself back to sit at his side but left her arm around his back.

"You can protect me when it is not the…" Her brow furrowed as she tried to work out the English word. "Sentience."

"What is a sen-shints?"

"The Many. The ghost woman called it a sentience." Althea frowned. "She made me do the saying again and again till I saids it right."

"I wanna kill it because it tried to hurt you."

"You can't. No one can. It isn't a man." She sat up straight. "You can't kill hate with hate. Make stronger, only. Strong does not matter with psionic."

"Psionic?" He cocked an eyebrow.

"The magic. The ghost woman said it was named psionic." She raspberried at nothing in particular. "Made me do the saying of that a lot too."

Den thumped himself in the chest with a fist. "I am a warrior. I must protect my wife."

She gave him a fearful look, not convinced that being wifed could be anything other than horrible. Images of raiders dragging screaming women away for wifeing came and went in her memory, followed by the aftermath: bruises, bleeding, and crying. She would never let *anyone* do that to her… even Den.

Althea pondered for a minute. Felipe and Luisa must have done the wifeing as they had a baby. Luisa loved him. None of the slaves she had seen wifed loved the raiders. Of course, none of the raiders had ever touched lips with those women the way Den had with her. Althea didn't understand, nor did she much care to ask why he did that—it felt too strange.

Althea pulled her hair back over her shoulders. "You can protect me from not psionics and not the sentience."

"Why can't I protect you from psionics?" He tickled her side.

She squirmed, giggling. "'Cause, mystics… umm, psionics don't care 'bout strong."

"I think they do."

"Nuh-uh," she said, in a singsong.

He sighed. "You want me to feel better, but you are wrong."

"*Dance,*" said Althea, her eyes flickering brighter for an instant.

Den clambered upright and hopped around in a circle, acting like a chamán trying to summon wind and rain. He glared at her, unable to stop his body from obeying her psionic command.

Althea planted her elbows on her knees and rested her chin in her palms. "Psionic don't care about strong."

He grunted and growled for about two minutes until the effect wore off. Den looked furious, but she sensed playfulness in his heart. With a wild roar, he ran at her. Althea leapt to her feet and sprinted off giggling, hiking her dress up to open her stride. She weaved among the thin citrus trees and raced toward the corn stalks.

"You *better* run!" he yelled, stifling a laugh. "When I get a hold of you..."

She darted left, finding the warm, wet grass slippery under bare feet. Waving one arm to keep her balance on a turn, she jumped a low-lying irrigation pipe. He cleared it with ease, pushing himself until he closed within a few paces. After a quick glance over her shoulder, she bounded between rows of corn, arms raised to shield her face from whipping leaves. In another eight strides, she made a sudden swerve that brought her back to open grass. Den overshot and almost fell.

"You're gonna get it." He grumbled.

They ran in a wide arc around the clearing at the center of the garden dome. Althea giggled as she found it easy to stay ahead of him. Eventually, his intermittent 'threats' lost steam. Frustration emanated from him. She peeked over her shoulder, finding his face a mask of grim determination. Althea grinned at the sudden idea perhaps she should let him catch her. She took a few more strides before swerving left and heading for the edge of the orange grove. In the middle of the open field, she 'tripped' and slid. Den pounced, and they rolled over each other a few times. Althea wound up on her back, hair splayed in the grass, with Den on top of her. She bit her lip, not sure what to make of the way his smile made her feel.

He tried to hide his fatigue, but sweat gathered at the tip of his nose. "You're not... even breathing hard."

"You are big and heavy, and I run a lot."

"Heavy?" He attacked her sides, tickling.

Althea squealed and squirmed, unable to get away from him without boosting her strength. She grabbed at his arms, gasping pleas to stop between peals of laughter. After a moment, he let her up and flashed a weary smile. She lay still in the grass, her hands dangled over her chest like a duck with two broken wings, and tried to breathe between lingering giggles.

"Sorry." He smiled. "I shouldn't be jealous of your magic."

Laughter eased to a broad grin. "I know you like me." She let her arms flop to the side. "You left your home to find me."

He reached over, lifting the green agate arrowhead pendant from her chest. They both stared at the light glinting off the rough facets.

"I told you I would find you." He rubbed his thumb over it and let it fall. "I'd do it again."

"When a Seeker gives such a thing to a girl..." Althea bit her lip, nervousness rising. "You want to wife me?"

He plucked a dandelion from nearby and tucked it behind her left ear. "Your father said he would throw me off the wall if I asked you to marry before you had sixteen birthdays."

She cocked her head at him, eyebrows together. "I only have one."

Den laughed. "No, I mean your birthday has gone by that many times."

"Oh." She smiled at a passing butterfly. "Karina is sixteen."

"It is good to see you happy."

She squeezed his hand. "I am sorry you left your family."

He rolled on his side, facing her. "Braga was angry when I refused Yala. He demanded I take her as a wife or I would be cast out."

Gloom enshrouded him.

She propped herself up on her elbows. "You are sad for leaving."

"No." He twirled another dandelion between his fingers. "That is from when I thought I would never see you again."

"I am glad you found me." Althea twirled a bit of hair around a finger, wondering if he would want to do the lip-touching thing again.

Her smile proved contagious.

Den grinned. "I hope you will feel the same in five years."

She poked him in the side. "I'm twel—" A sigh escaped her. She'd spent a long time thinking herself twelve years old, but the 'corporate' people who tried to trick her into going with them believed she'd been born eleven years ago. It annoyed her that they didn't know anything about her mother despite hunting the pair of them for years. Though, they could've been lied to. Just because *they* believed it didn't make it true. "What if I'm twelve? Five years is *seven*teen."

He held his hands up. "Your father said five years, or I get thrown off the wall."

Althea grumbled. Five years was a long time, almost the same amount of time she had spent a captive. As best she could remember, she'd been six when the Wagon Man took her from the village by the lake, but she might've been five. She glanced at the arrowhead, its weight upon her chest minuscule but noticeable, wondering how five years of freedom would change her. Again, she thought of Karina suggesting she'd want to share a bed with a boy.

"Bleh."

"What?"

As she opened her mouth to say 'nothing,' a rustle in the cornstalks made her whip her head about with a gasp. Den sat up, following her gaze.

Something moved in the plants. Her old feral instincts kicked in; she flipped over onto her hands and the balls of her feet, ready to hide or sprint. She did not sense the presence of the Many but crept backward nonetheless.

"Be calm." Den put a hand on her shoulder. "One of the goats probably got out of the pen."

Althea glanced at him for an instant, but startled again at the noise in the leaves. To make him feel better, she shrank behind him, her body language asking for protection.

Den jumped up. "Wait here."

She grabbed his leg with both hands. "Don't."

When he kept walking, she scrambled upright and followed. He drew a ten-inch knife from his belt and held it to the side.

"Who's there?" yelled Den.

Aurora emerged from the cornstalks, wearing a skirt and skimpy top made of leaves. She sauntered closer, her expression neutral. Den raised the knife, pointing it at her.

Althea grasped his arm and pulled it down, clinging. "No, she is not a danger."

"Hello, Althea. This must be Den." She winked. "Sorry for scaring you, but it took me a moment to work these things into a garment. I didn't want to give the poor boy a blood imbalance, and I'm sure you prefer this to me wearing him."

He leaned back. "I hear her speak, but she is not speaking."

"She speaks psionic." Althea looked back and forth between them. "What? Why would you hurt his blood?"

"Oh, my... you are so precious." Aurora laughed. "I meant all his blood would rush to one particular place."

She scrunched up her nose. "Huh?"

Den shifted his weight into a combat stance. "I hear her voice but her lips do not move... is this a spirit?"

"She just does that," whispered Althea.

"Is someone hurt?" Althea frowned at the grass. "Do you need me to go to the bad city again?"

"No, child. Not yet."

Althea exhaled with relief.

"The police will ask you to help them." Aurora paced a circle around them. "They will want to take you into the city."

She shivered; tears gathered at the corners of her eyes. Den grasped Althea's hand.

Aurora stopped in front of her. "If you do not help them, a great many innocent people will die. The police will not make you stay there."

"Okay." Althea gazed at the ground, crying in silence. "I will help."

"Oh, Althea." Aurora ran a hand over her head. "Why are you crying?"

"I don't like the city. Everyone there is bad."

"If they're all evil, let them die," said Den.

"They are not all evil." Aurora's voice took on a soothing tone. "It is a different life they lead. Jobs, worries about money. They are all in a hurry, and don't have time to care about a person they don't know."

"What will kill them? How can Althea stop it?" Den edged in front of her, shielding her from the strange woman.

"Evil," said Aurora. "Althea's presence is necessary to prevent millions of people from dying."

"Is that more than a hundred?" asked Den.

"Quite." Aurora smiled.

Den put his knife away, pulled Althea into an embrace, and glared at Aurora. "Will she be hurt?"

Aurora gazed at the dome, her attention diverted for a little while by a swirling mass of sparrows congregating at a hole. "It is difficult for me to know such things for sure. I have not yet seen anything that would make me believe so, but there are no guarantees."

"What is garan-tees?" asked Althea.

"Promises. I cannot promise that you will not be hurt." A momentary bit of sadness took Aurora. "Or even killed. I do know you are crucial to saving a great many innocent people from the folly of an idiot."

"Archon?" Althea glared at the corn. "Asshole."

Aurora giggled. "Indeed, though this is not entirely his fault."

"Okay." Althea pulled away from Den, balled her hands into fists, and took a deep breath. "I will go when they ask."

The solemn look on Althea's face brought the woman to tears. She went to one knee and took her hand. "You are unlike anyone I have ever known. So selfless. You do not deserve the life you've been given."

Althea looked down. Something stirred deep within her, and her sadness evaporated. "The Sentience. It is him. I do not have sad for my life. I have met Karina and Father and Den. If my life was different, I would not have known them, and I would not be here to help Querq."

"You're infectious." Aurora dropped her hand and stood. "Kim was asking after you. She couldn't believe you distrusted Archon."

"She likes pancakes." Althea hoped the nice girl hadn't gotten in trouble because of her. "I drank the syrup and she laughed. Is she okay?"

"Yes, she is fine." Aurora smiled. "You've gotten her doubting him too."

"I don't want him to die either"—Althea stomped—"Tell him to stop."

Aurora's body imploded in a cloud of fog, leaving her leaf-garments hanging in midair for a second before they dropped. Her voice echoed from thin air. "You've already seen how well the bloke listens to me."

The pair stood in silence for a moment, staring down at the leaves. Althea took Den's hand and pulled him along behind her as she crossed the field toward the way out. Warm, wet moss squidged under her feet upon the sidewalk, the slimy layer giving way to the coarseness of stone beneath it.

He jogged to keep up. "Where are you going?"

"Home. I want to be with my family for as much as I can."

23

DEFENSELESS

Aaron

A wall of old vertical blinds tinted the late morning sun to a soft, orange-tan glow. Aaron laced his fingers behind his head, finding the bed of sofa cushions quite comfortable given his expectations. His new arrangements made the blown-out Comforgel pad in his last place seem like the block of gummy snot it was.

No wonder Darwin didn't use it.

Weight shifted over the grey-blue drop ceiling tiles as something crawled overhead. From the sound of it, the critter could've been the size of a five-year-old child.

"Oi, who's there?"

The motion ceased.

"S'awright, not in any trouble."

After a moment, motion resumed.

I suppose I should get used to rats in the walls. Little bugger might not speak English.

Without a set schedule, Aaron felt no great urgency to get out of bed. If he got up, he'd feel the need to confront Melissa about her parents. He wasn't sure what he dreaded more, having to destroy a teenaged girl's image of her savior and hero, or dealing with Archon if she decided to race home to the family she obviously wanted. Not moving offered a much easier and far more appealing option.

He closed his eyes. "Bugger me."

"I rather lack the appropriate equipment," said Aurora. "If you really want, I suppose I could put on a—"

"Please don't finish that sentence."

"So what are you doing this morning?" The sound of her voice circled from behind him, near the window, around to his feet.

"I've set myself to the task of setting a new record for *extreme* sofa-cushion surfing. I'm also multitasking with some procrastination."

Her voice kept circling, approaching his head. "You can open your eyes, you know."

"That would involve effort. Besides, you're naked, aren't you?"

"There's no need to be polite on my behalf." She sounded as though she knelt right over him. "It doesn't bother me if you stare."

"What if it bothers me?"

"You fancy men?"

Aaron opened his eyes. Sure enough, a large pair of snow-white breasts dangled over his face. "Look, they're very nice. Lovely actually, but I know you're not here to 'ave a shag."

She sat back on her heels and pulled her hair behind one ear. "You're a grump today. Perhaps I can cheer you up."

"Still not interested." He closed his eyes again.

"Not like that. *Now* who's the one with dirty thoughts? Get up, twit. You need to get upstairs to the executive office right away."

"Whatever for? I'm perfectly comfortable here."

"Well, it's your loss if you don't go. I'd hurry if I were you. Certain types of chances don't come 'round so often."

The woman vanished in a cloud of silvery fog, which seeped down into the floor.

Aaron flung the blankets away and sat up. After a moment of staring at the door, he stumbled over to the desk where he'd left his clothes, scratching his ass as a brief homage to Darwin.

"Great and bloody Hell. Archon wants to see me." He muttered in the voice of a petulant schoolboy as he stepped into his pants. "I suppose I should go straight away before I get in even more trouble."

He hissed through his teeth. Probably wanted to give him the Nth degree for dragging Anna off to see Melissa's family. Aaron's joviality died in an instant.

Shite. She was beside herself on the ride back. What did she say to him? "Fuck…"

Aaron ran out the door trying to pull his suit jacket on and button his shirt simultaneously. He gave up on both tasks and sprinted up the stairwell up to the tenth floor and the atrium with the ostentatious sculpture, an explosion of cubes from a cracked silicon slab. Three doors led out of the receiving area for the company's top executives, now home to little more than rats and whatever trash Archon's little army had left behind.

A doll in the image of an Asian woman sat behind the desk facing him, its artificiality obvious by the gaps at the corners of the mouth and eyes, and the creepy sense radiating from skin that didn't look right. The doll didn't move; it hadn't so much as twitched for decades. As old as it looked, it likely had a power cell rather than a fusion core or had run off the building's electricity.

He jumped the desk and ran toward the office of the CEO, the space Archon had appropriated as his. Aaron slowed as he passed an executive conference room and a private elevator.

I've no idea what I'm walking into. He squeezed the comforting presence of the E-90 under his coat. *Archon would hesitate to invade my mind.* The gun came out. As soon as his finger touched the trigger, azure dots swished back and forth on both sides of the housing, making the walls glow. Two steps later, he hesitated.

This won't look good if I walk in there with a gun out. Shit, what if he's done something to Anna?

Metal clattered in time with Anna grunting.

Aaron stopped breathing. *That bitch. She tried to trick me into running in on them fucking.* He stomped back to the stairs.

"Hello? Can anyone hear me? Is someone out there?" Anna yelled.

"Sorry. Aurora's being a pain in the ass."

"Aaron?" The distinct sound of chains rattled. "Aaron! Please! Oh, feck, hurry up."

His mind conjured all sorts of horrible images of what Archon had done to her when she'd confronted him with the truth about Melissa. It didn't prepare him for the scene waiting for him when he burst in the door, E-90 raised.

Anna lay naked on the bed, arms cuffed to the headboard, pink furry shackles around her ankles chaining her legs apart to the corners. The Comforgel pad beneath her glowed from orange to yellow in an endless, mesmerizing shift. A grinning azure faerie tattoo marked her milky-white skin up and to the right of her sex. Muscles in her legs tensed from her futile effort to close her legs against the restraints.

He looked straight at the floor. "Uhm... Now, that I wasn't expecting. You're as defenseless as a Manchester goal."

She grunted as if straining. "Dammit, Aaron, let me out! Shoot the chains."

"What happened?" He looked up, shocked at her lack of comeback for the jab at her team, and put the E-90 back in his coat. "I can't. It'll go through six floors at least. Too dangerous."

Anna writhed. "Hell if I know. James just up and buggered off, leaving me like this. Come on, shift your arse and get the damn key. It's on the nightstand. I'm about to burst."

He tried to hide the amusement in his grin as he approached the nightstand. "Now why do you think he did that?"

Her face turned pink.

"Did he think you'd like it?"

Pink darkened to crimson. "No. Not this time." Anna thrashed. "Fecking hell. I'm not as helpless as I look. I can still zap the smile off your face. Let me out!"

Aaron swiped the key, leaned one knee on the Comforgel pad, and stooped over her. He fumbled at the furry shroud in search of the keyhole. Anna whined and made faces as she squirmed, as if pulling on the cuffs would make it easier for him to open them.

He watched her face for a moment. "You *are* enjoying this, aren't you?"

"No, you twat. I'm about to piss all over myself. I've been like this for hours." She looked away, voice trembling. "Reminding me where I came from, I suspect."

"Hold still." He squeezed her arm, offering a reassuring smile.

She went a still as she could manage, save for a persistent bouncing of her right leg. As soon as he got one side open, she flew upright and grabbed herself between the legs. Aaron dropped the key on the pad between her knees and turned his back. Anna whimpered as she bent forward to unlock her ankles. A steady stream of whispered cursing emanated from her as she struggled to reach with an overfull bladder.

Moments later, she rolled off the bed and loped across the room. He stifled a laugh as she rushed to the CEO's huge private bathroom, still with handcuffs dangling from her left wrist and in too much of a hurry to care about clothes.

She didn't even bother to close the door.

Aaron meandered across the room, stooping to pluck a robe from the floor along the way. He leaned near the ornate arch with his back to the wall and made appraising faces at the robe until her relieved moaning subsided.

"When Aurora told me to get up here, I thought you'd confronted him. I was honestly expecting a much worse sight."

"I started to, but he made everything sound so necessary." Her voice echoed from within a chamber of faux-marble walls. "I can't believe he left me fixed to the bed like that. I got sick once when I was in the gutter. Bastard of a manager locked me in the cage overnight."

"You must've been quite a handful if they kept you in a cage." Aaron chuckled.

"Dancing cage, twat."

"Oh, yes. That's much better. I didn't think those could lock."

"They usually don't. Blake was a miserable shit and modified them. I expected something like that from him, but James? He's never been cruel to me before." Metal rattled; she sniffled as if wiping her face. "Wait, no. I'm wrong."

"Do I want to know?" asked Aaron.

"Put a chopstick through my hand. Needed a guinea pig to show that little girl what a stimpak does."

A wave of heat rose inside him. Archon didn't care about her at all. He saw her as a tool, a possession. "You remember what I said about friends turning on you?"

The clicking of metal approached the door. Aaron held out the robe without looking. She took it.

"You've already seen everything there is to see. You don't need to be so polite."

"The tattoo is cute." Sensing she'd tied the garment around herself, he looked up with a smile. "Aye, but it wasn't exactly by choice. Tryin' to make it less embarrassing for ya."

Anna looked exhausted but happy. She held up her left arm, cuffs dangling. "Not the most mortifying thing that's ever 'appened to me. Twice you've come to my rescue, innit?"

Telekinesis fetched the key from the bed to his hand, and he took the cuffs off her. "This is hardly on par with getting tossed out the window of The Spire."

Anna shivered. "Maybe not, but I was starting to doubt I'd ever get off that bed. It's strange… I was only there for a few hours, but I thought I'd never get free."

Aaron held her bruised wrist, letting the restraints drop. She smelled of sweat and plastic, her short, white hair matted to her head. "From the cuffs? Or from him?"

"He… saved me from the gutter." Anna stared out the window. "I'd be dead if it wasn't for him."

"Is that true?"

She glanced up, sapphire eyes brimming with fear, doubt, and pain. Her mouth opened and closed twice, but she didn't come up with anything to say. He couldn't pull away from her forlorn expression. Anna looked so small and vulnerable. She'd been the only reason he'd gotten this far in over his head. In that moment at the starship plant, he knew he couldn't let her face Archon alone. His fear, of her running off in a panic if he said the wrong thing, had held him back long enough.

He ran his fingers over the mark on her arm. "You're quite beautiful when you're lost and confused. I'd rather like to get to know the real Anna."

She stared at his hand touching her for a silent moment. "I don't even know her anymore."

"Look inside. She's waiting for us both." Aaron almost kissed her when she made eye contact again, but hesitated at the static tingle crawling up his arm. "You're tingling."

"I..." She pulled away.

Aaron's heart skipped a beat. *Too far. Idiot!* "Anna... I—"

"I need to go to London." She sighed at herself. "And I need a shower."

He leaned on the wall to avoid falling over, watching her scramble to collect an outfit before racing back to the bathroom and hopping into the autoshower.

She hesitated before closing the tube door. "Aaron?"

"Hmm?" He stuffed his hands in his pockets, gazing at his shoes to give her some privacy.

"Will you go to London with me? I'm not sure I can do it alone."

He pursed his lips, grimaced, and tapped his foot. "Aye. It's been too long since I've been to a decent chippery."

24

PENNY AND SPAWNY

Anna

Without thinking about it, Anna reached over the armrest and grasped Aaron's hand as a familiar skyline filled the windows of the shuttle. Forty-nine minutes after leaving West City, she found herself staring at the unmistakable black scar where Coventry tainted east London. They flew too far away, and too high up to pick out the tower from the murk. A gradual descending turn brought the buildings closer. Far off to the north, the glimmer of a handful of private hovercars dotted the green, well away from the city and King William's paranoia.

A man in a teal and grey PubTran jumpsuit, a flight attendant, made his way down the aisle trying to sell last minute drinks and snacks.

Anna didn't look at him, and had only a vague awareness of Aaron's polite "I'm fine, thanks."

Minutes later, the shuttle glided to a graceful stop in midair and settled in for a landing.

"You look surprised to find the city's still here."

She smiled at him, though worry weighed her down. "I can't believe it's not raining."

"It's not that bad." He winked. "You probably just remember it raining all the time because you were in an awful situation."

"So you're saying the four days a week of rain is a metaphor in my memory?"

"Something like that." Aaron glanced to his right, over the aisle, and out the opposite windows. "You're sure we'll not run into any... difficulties?"

"We shouldn't. As long as we don't go making a scene." *It's not like the CSB made a habit of publicizing what they did to us. Old Bill wouldn't know us to look.*

Aaron gripped her hand tight. Whether he tried to comfort her or searched for reassurance, she couldn't tell. "Aye. Not plannin' on scene-makin', are we?"

"No," she whispered.

Once the crowd in the aisle had thinned, Aaron stood and moved to let her go first. She accepted his hand, climbed out of her seat, and led the way to the boarding chute. A line started at the security gate and backed up all the way into the shuttle.

Unlike the UCF, the transportation authorities of Britain had a problem with personal firearms. Anna fidgeted as they went from waiting on the shuttle to waiting in the docking tube. Every time the line moved another twenty-six inches forward, she had to fight harder to keep her nerves in check.

In the terminal, five uniformed officers of the Metropolitan Police Force stood in a row, flanked on either side by robotic attack dogs. Matte black armor and red-lit eyes gave the false canines a demonic presence, though Anna didn't feel the least bit of concern for them. In fact, they reassured her. Two handy power sources to draw upon if things got hairy. The gaze of the three men and two women in black armor worried her more. She hadn't set foot in London in five years, but she worried one of them might remember her. Of course, a constable relegated to guard duty around Coventry wasn't likely to be at Heathrow. That place held undesirables on both sides of the law. Police had two ways out of that job: enduring it until retirement or quitting.

Dying, the obvious third option, seldom occurred. Even the East End boys appreciated the irony of watching them suffer out the tattered end of a career shot to shit. That sergeant seemed like a nice man. *I wonder what he did to wind up there?*

What's wrong? The sudden intrusion of Aaron's voice in her mind almost made her scream.

She whirled on him, a momentary glower became a stare of pleading. *I don't trust constables.*

Even psionic ones? He feigned a wounded expression.

All five of the cops drew rifles on a middle-aged man when an alarm went off.

The man shrieked and held his hands up. "It's a museum piece! It hasn't worked in four hundred years."

She buried her face in Aaron's chest. *Oh, shit. Please tell me you left your gun behind.*

He patted her on the back. *You tell me. Your face is mushed into the pocket I usually store it in.*

When their turn at the desk came, Anna went rigid, expecting hands to roam her every curve. Much to her astonishment, the guard waved a detector around without making contact.

Oi, I'm a Proper now. She flashed a nervous smile. *Don't reckon they'd respect me if they knew I was 'gifted.'*

Twenty minutes later, Anna held back the urge to sprint as they cleared the checkpoint and made it to the street outside the terminal building where an army of autocabs waited. She darted into the first one she could find.

"Good afternoon," said a pleasant male voice. "Welcome to Britain's Autocab. Please state your destination."

"Grandpoint, Oxford, please," said Anna. "Nine Marlborough Road."

Aaron got in and pulled the door closed.

"Sixty-one credits," chimed the voice.

She swiped her NetMini over the reader embedded in the wall and folded her hands in her lap.

"You know, we spend an awful lot of time in taxis," said Aaron.

Anna laughed. "Aye. Seems."

THE AUTOCAB WHIRRED TO A HALT OUTSIDE A FOURTEEN-STORY RESIDENCE complex a short distance from a bend in the Thames. False red bricks covered the first four floors, after which plain plastisteel ran the rest of the way to the roof. Anna followed Aaron out of the car and approached the gate. She couldn't make up her mind which would be worse: finding things to be as she expected, or finding something done to Penny's head. After taking a deep breath, she entered a tiny front yard and trotted up the six steps to the main entrance, a locked door.

Anna put a hand on the mirrored panel containing the ImDent reader. Since she lacked an implanted identity chip, it didn't do anything. She concentrated on the electronics within, and a rush of energy swept over her. The building's wiring drew itself in as traces of scintillating amber threads. She focused on the door mechanism and zoomed her view in, as though she stood on the printed circuit board. It took only a moment to feel out the line that would cut power to the magnetic locks, and she pulled energy away from it.

The door opened from its rubber seal with the sound of a kiss.

"Bloody..." muttered Aaron. "You're a technokinetic too?"

"No." She pulled the heavy door aside and ducked in. "It's all circuits. I don't have to defeat the security system. I skip right over it. Ultimately, it comes down to which wire needs power fed to it to work the lock. Or, in this case, turned off to free the magnets."

"I get the feeling you've done this before."

She pushed the elevator call button, folded her arms, and offered a wry one-eyebrow-raised smile. "I used to be a bad girl."

"Really? You?"

Anna spun about, backed into the elevator, and waited for the doors to close. "Not *that* bad. I did some freelance work for some people. Personal protection, infiltration, snooping… corporate espionage mostly. I wasn't a hitter or anything."

"Fascinating."

"Of course, if you ask again, I'll deny mentioning that."

"Right."

Why did I admit that? She tapped her foot. *Next thing you know, I'll tell him about dancing.*

"And now you're blushing…"

Shame collapsed under the weight of anger, mostly at herself. "Don't ask."

Aaron's attention followed a crawling spark among the control buttons. "Wouldn't dream of it."

Anna stormed down the plain pea-green hallway decorated with holograms recreating ancient oil paintings of pastoral fields, lakes, and forests.

"Good grief," said Aaron. "Do you think they've a committee of little old women who approve all the décor?" He mimicked an elderly woman's voice. "Sorry, my dear. This piece is not boring enough. It simply won't do. Take it away."

Knots of nerves in her gut unwound a little at his joke, but not enough to let her laugh. She stopped at the fifth door on the left and pushed the buzzer before she could think about what she was doing.

"Minnit," called Penny's voice from the other side.

"Aaron?"

"Aye?"

"Stand behind me and hold my arms."

"Why?"

"So I don't run when the door opens."

He did. She let herself lean into him a little. *Am I betraying James?* A twinge of nausea slid around the pit of her stomach as she thought back to the look on Aaron's face a few hours ago. There she stood, naked save for a handcuff dangling from her arm, and he stared into her soul as though he wished he could reach inside her and peel away all the pain she'd ever felt.

James never looked at me like that.

The door opened.

"I'm sorry, I wasn't expecting visi—" Penny Dhara froze, mouth open. "Anna?"

She'd gained a little weight since they'd last met, but was still a far cry from heavy. Anna had always seen her on the verge of starvation. At or perhaps a smidge past optimal weight, she looked like another person entirely. She seemed... alive.

Anna cried despite her smile. "Penny... you look great."

"Come in!" Penny all but dragged her in the door.

Her apartment was done up more or less like an ancient English grandmum lived there, save for a few touches of Indian art. The scent of clove and incense hung in the air. A desk against the far wall glowed with a half-dozen holo-panels open to various documents. Small bits of kitch dwelled in the various spaces of an open shelving grid between the kitchen area and the living room.

"Wow." Anna took it in. "You're doing well."

"Aye. Busy as anything. Administrative work for the University." She lowered her voice to a conspiratorial whisper. "I cannae believe what they're payin' me too. Feels like I'm gettin' away wit something, but... I am workin' my ass off."

Anna couldn't resist any longer and grabbed her friend in a crushing hug. "I'm sorry I was away for so long. Things've gotten complicated."

"I'm glad to see you're okay. The way you ran off... I thought you'd gotten yourself into a mess. Sit." Penny waved at a table. "I'll put up some tea. I had the strangest idea you'd gotten cheesed off and never wanted to see me again."

"Pen! How could you ever think that?"

The woman shrugged on her way into the kitchen.

Anna wandered in a spinning gait toward the table, happy and jealous of her friend for having so 'normal' a life. This flat was a world apart from their lodgings at Coventry Tower. She lowered herself into a chair as if unworthy of touching it. Aaron joined her. She studied the marks her boots had left in the plush beige carpeting until her friend returned with a kettle, three cups, and a plate of Tim Tams.

"Seems the job suits you then?" asked Anna.

Penny poured them each a cup. Aaron took one of the chocolate-covered treats, bit off both ends, and proceeded to suck his tea through the chocolate crème inside it. Anna's nerves kept her from chuckling at him.

"Aye. 'Tis easy work, but honest. Spawny doesn't know what to do wif himself these days. I still can't believe you're back. Takin' an awful risk, aren't ya?"

Anna ran her hands over her knees, expecting to wear holes in her dark leggings. "I'm not *back*. I had to ask you something. Do you 'ave things in your memory that don't seem right? Like going from as good as my sister to being shitless of having me around?"

Penny smiled. "Oh, he's not doing much. Still hasn't found work." She leaned close, lowering her voice. "Not that he's trying."

"Pen. That's not what I asked."

"Oh, these are brilliant." Aaron grabbed another Tim-Tam. "It's been years."

"I mean, it's not like he's really got to work. I make enough for us to live. Quite nice, actually."

"Penny!" Anna yelled, reaching over the table to grab her friend by the wrist. "Listen to me."

The woman blinked. "Well, you don't 'ave to shout. I'm right 'ere."

"Miss Dhara, if I might have the pleasure of your attention for a moment." Aaron set his cup down and folded his arms on the table.

Anna clutched her hands into fists, gripping her coat as Penny's placid smile faded to an expression of worry. The woman who had been the reason she survived to adulthood looked like a complete stranger.

Aaron's face reddened; after a moment, he let off a constipated sigh. "It's bloody strong this time."

"Oi, Pen, I'm back," Spawny yelled from the small corridor between the living room and the outer door.

Boots clunked, cloth ruffled, and a closet door slid closed. He appeared a few seconds later, still in a shredded mesh top, slashed up black military fatigue pants, and the same boots he'd always worn. Five years hadn't made much of a difference; he still looked like a holovid star about to die from a chem overdose.

"Gah!" Spawny stared at Anna. "Shit! We're fucked! Pen, get the hell out of 'ere."

Spawny's mad scramble for the door became a midair flailing fit when Aaron levitated him in place. He screamed as if natives prepared to hurl him into a volcano as a sacrifice to Pele. Penny glanced back and forth between Aaron and Anna, looking clueless. A few seconds later, she broke out in a cold sweat.

"Pix?" Penny covered her face with her hands. "Why am I feeling so afraid of you right now? I don't like it."

"Tell 'er to get the feck out of here!" Spawny howled.

"Keep your hair on, mate," said Aaron. "You've been conditioned to mess your trousers at the sight of her."

"Wot?" Spawny froze in midair, approximating a surrealist sculpture of a human dancing.

Aaron moved Spawny to a sofa on the far end of the room. "Mental programming. Someone's put a trigger in your mind what makes irrational fear come out of nowhere at the sight of Anna."

"You speakin' feckin' English or wot, mate?"

Aaron pinched the bridge of his nose and grumbled. "Someone bloody mind-zapped you to act like a feckin' schoolgirl in a horror vid at the sight of her."

"Oh." He sniffed and adjusted his mesh shirt. "I'm not an idiot."

The scrawny man clutched the end of the sofa arm, trembling. Bloodshot eyes surrounded by overdone dark makeup locked onto her, as though he would bolt for the door if she so much as twitched.

"Bezzy mates," Anna muttered at the carpeting.

Spawny's mouth hung open. For a few seconds, a low noise gurgled out of his throat before it built into a voice. "Aye. I said that, didn't I?" He grimaced and bit his knuckle, but continued trembling.

Anna glanced up expecting to find an 'I-told-you-so' smug grin on Aaron's face. Instead, his eyes held regret and concern. Her lip quivered. The corners of her eyes grew warm. Anna steeled her jaw, intent on not breaking down in front of everyone.

"I'm not sure if I can fix this." He scratched his head. "I don't exactly know my onions when it comes to telepathy."

She reached into her purse with shaking hands, fumbling for her NetMini.

Aaron cocked an eyebrow.

Anna clutched the device as if her life depended on it. "I need to call someone."

25

HOW TO FLATLINE A DRAGON

Mamoru

A mound of small concrete chunks had proven to be a more comfortable bed than Mamoru had anticipated. Rapid gunfire interrupted his rest, accompanied by an incoherent roar muted by the walls. A feline return to consciousness held no trace of grogginess. Only his eyes moved as he scanned the room. Pale bands of light leaked in from fist-sized holes in the front wall, illuminating dust. The stink of mildew permeated everything about the place. Voices, male and female, screamed taunts and threats between bursts of automatic weapons fire. A roar answered, followed by the straining sound of warping metal.

The brazen shouting gave way to screams of terror.

Mamoru brushed dirt from his coat with casual swipes of his hand and stood. Outside, a tremendous *crash* rocked the street before the building shuddered, knocking a cloud of dust from the walls and ceiling.

"Noah! I'm stuck!" A female voice degenerated into shrieks of pain.

"Die fucker!" shouted a man, an instant before a long barrage of gunfire drowned him out.

Cracks and gaps in the front wall lit up with a flickering azure glow. Dull clanks, fleshy thuds, and the sharp snaps of bullets striking concrete rang out. A few puffs of powder burst from the wall. Ricochets hit the floor behind him.

A deep male voice chuckled outside.

Mamoru strode among the hail of fragments and stray bullets without flinching, even as something whistled by, inches from his ear. Plaster crunched under his boots down the length of a short hallway with a destroyed bathroom off to the right. A rotting corpse, too far gone to recognize any trace of the person it had been, sat on the toilet and leaned against the wall.

"Suck this!" shouted a different male voice.

The *boom* of an assault rifle went off outside.

Intent on ignoring the local conflict, Mamoru emerged from the opening where a front door had once been. Fifteen or so meters to the right, a punk with fluorescent orange hair stood in the middle of the road, mouth frozen open in a war cry no one could hear over his erupting rifle.

The crushed remnants of a land car lay upside down against the wall. A girl with snow-white hair and a glowing red NanoLED tattoo of a 'spray-painted' raccoon mask on her face slumped against it, screaming and sobbing. Her left arm looked pinned, and crushed, between it and the building.

Mamoru regarded a second street punk with a raised eyebrow. Six thumb-wide ponytails hung down to his waist from his otherwise shaved head. Tiny silver cones studded his eyebrows as well as the curves of his ears and ran in two rows down the length of his nose. He rattled a small submachine gun, attempting to remove a stuck magazine.

On the left, a nine-foot tall behemoth foamed at the mouth. Dark blue plastisteel, a banded metal torso, showed beneath his shredded clothes. His arms and most of his face gleamed metal. The punk with the rifle kept firing, though the bullets seemed only to damage the monster's coat and baggy sky-blue pants. The aug's eyes, lens tubes with red light inside, rotated clockwise and extended a half inch forward at the same instant a flap opened on his left shoulder. Mamoru continued walking, disregarding the scene.

A tiny rocket leapt from the mechanical shoulder, passing close enough to Mamoru's face for the exhaust to singe his cheek. It plunged into the chest of the punk with the rifle, sticking like a fiery crossbow bolt. The teen stopped shooting and gawked at it as the propellant burned out and trailed dense white smoke.

Blood seeped out of his mouth with a nervous laugh. "Holy shi—"

Boom.

Bits of flesh flew in all directions; everything from the base of the ribcage up ceased to exist. The rest of him remained upright for a second before falling over backward. Mamoru reached up and touched his middle finger to a chunk of gore sliding down his cheek. He appraised it for a second and flicked it away.

The girl wailed and grunted, slapping her free hand on the car.

Mamoru took a step forward. *I will need a new coat.*

"Die," growled the huge aug.

A second shot leapt from the implanted launcher, headed at the next closest target—Mamoru.

White flames rippled down his arms as psionic energy flooded his body, accelerating his reflexes to the point time dragged to an almost-standstill. Mamoru twisted and leaned under the crawling cigar-sized rocket. He continued the spin, grasping the projectile and guiding it around in a curve. When he relaxed his ability and time returned to normal, an orange streak flew from his hand to the behemoth's chest, where it detonated on impact.

The blast knocked the aug back a step and left a two-inch sparking hole on his right pectoral, surrounded by a wider char mark. Mamoru stood within the loop of a thin smoke trail resembling a lasso, staring at the man, waiting.

Screaming behind him subsided to soft whimpering.

"What the fuck was that?" muttered the punk with the jammed submachine gun.

"Pain," roared the aug. He glanced down as though he'd spilled mustard on himself, picking at the sparking hole. "Make hurt. Smash!"

Mamoru sank into a combat stance as the psychotic cyber-junkie rushed at him. Eighteen-inch blades sprang out from the closed fists of his metal arms. Grunts and inhuman moans accompanied his first swing, an overextended right arm aimed for Mamoru's neck.

Time crawled again as Mamoru accelerated, boosting speed and strength beyond even what the cyborg could attain. Once more, Caiden appeared in his mind. The elevator doors had surprised him as much as the boy. Had his powers grown, or he had been holding back?

Mamoru would not hold back anymore.

He grasped his vibro-katana, yanking it from its sheath and severing the aug's right forearm with the motion of the draw. A sparking metal hand, and the blade it clutched fell. The crazed man twisted to bring his left arm around in a low arc, slashing for legs. Mamoru's upswing cut the mechanical limb with ease. Squealing metal roared from the war between hypersonic blade and armor-grade plastisteel. Sparks shimmered as metal separated in slow motion, the edges heated to glowing by the passing vibro-katana. The aug's forearm sailed into the air, vanishing into the fifth story window of an abandoned building across the street.

Before his opponent could react, Mamoru whirled into a spinning, horizontal slash that severed the cyber-freak's body at the waist. The instant his blade cleared the far side of the target, he released his right hand's grip, leaving the weapon in his left. The white flames rippling across his shoulders intensified; he focused as much energy as he could into pure strength. Time leapt back to normal as he completed the spin and drove his fist into the aug's chest.

The metal torso blurred into a silvery, bloody smear. Two blocks distant, a muted *crash* blew dust out of the windows of a building. Hips and legs remained, a perfect cut left the top as smooth as ruby glass.

"Whoa…" said the remaining male punk. "That was ruinous, man."

Mamoru sneered at the legs and put his sword away. The glow along his arms faded. "Where can I find a deck?"

"Uhh…" The boy stopped fighting with his weapon and shrugged. "Notta fuckin' clue, man."

"Hey," said the girl, in a weak rasp. "Somebody help."

"Mmm." Mamoru walked straight away from where he'd slept, the punks on his right, the still-standing legs on his left. A tiny whisper at the back of his mind tried to make him care about an injured girl, but the darkness devoured it.

"Dude, you can't fuckin' leave Ferret like that? You launched that crazy motherfucker… holy shit."

Mamoru kept walking. "I must find a deck."

"Noah," whined Ferret. "It's gettin' fuckin' cold. I… I don't wanna metal arm."

"Wait," Noah called after Mamoru. "I can help. Sorta."

Mamoru stopped, but didn't turn around. "I am listening."

"I dunno about sellin' you a deck, but I can take you to a guy that's got a shitload of 'em."

"I assume you will ask me to help your friend in exchange."

"Uhh, yeah man, seein' as how you not doin' it to be like… the right thing to do and shit."

"I will assist your friend once we speak to this person." Mamoru faced him.

"No way, man. She's gonna die before that. Her whole damn arm is salsa-fied. We gotta get her outta there first."

A low growl rumbled deep in Mamoru's throat as he frowned.

"You think I'd fuck with someone who did *that*." He gestured at the remains of the aug.

Distrust or not, time and options were limited. "Do not betray me."

Mamoru approached and rested his hand on the end of the car. Ferret looked into his eyes for only an instant before she cowered and jerked at her trapped limb. He stared at the bloodstain seeping into the fabric of her sleeve and shoulder. The raccoon mask across her pale face glowed the color of maraschino cherries.

What does she see in my eyes? What am I?

Wisps of energy burned down the lengths of his arms, bringing strength. Mamoru pulled the car away from the wall with little effort. Ferret fell on her side and dragged herself away as fast as she could crawl. Her left arm dangled limp and useless.

The *Akuryō* frowned at her.

Weak.

She whimpered, kicking at the ground to push herself along.

Pathetic.

Ferret risked a glance back at him when she had crawled a few meters away, but raised her good arm over her face in a defensive cringe. Her tears caught the glow from the cybertattoo around her eyes.

Mamoru frowned at himself. *Still a child.* He forced his way out from under the *Akuryō.*

"Give me a credstick." Mamoru extended a hand toward the punk.

Noah edged closer, offering him a small black device as well as his gun. "Take it… take them both."

"I am not a thief."

He held the credstick in a closed fist, opening his mind to the electronics inside. Soon, his vision changed to the virtual world created by the tiny one-node network inside the device. White samurai armor hovered in a small space behind a painted yellow line near a huge, round door. A guardian construct made to resemble a man wearing a banker's suit sat behind a desk at the edge of a vault. It looked up at him, ready to destroy the credstick if it sensed a hacker's tampering. Mamoru's will brought program code into being, changing zeroes to ones. The vault space behind the guardian filled with glowing coins, the cyberspace equivocation to money. Unable to process psionic influence, the guardian remained wary, but did nothing.

Mamoru opened his eyes, once more in the black zone. A faint trace of charred meat crossed his nostrils, no doubt the effect of his vibro-katana on the aug. He tossed the credstick back to the boy. The balance of two million and change credits nearly made him faint.

"Bring her to a hospital. I will fill it to ten million if you can bring me to a deck." Mamoru sat on the wrecked car. "I shall wait here for you."

"Yeah man… Don't go anywhere." He held up the credstick as if it were a holy relic, stuffed it in his pocket, and helped Ferret to her feet. "Soon."

Mamoru closed his eyes and tried to meditate as the teens ran off. Peace eluded him while the weight of his obligation burned deep within.

Noah returned three hours later, without Ferret. He didn't mention her, nor did Mamoru ask. Without word or ceremony, he waved Mamoru to follow him and jogged off along the broken-down streets of the black zone. Six blocks later, he ducked into the hollow shell of a four-story building and headed for the basement, where a pile of debris concealed a hatch in the floor.

The ladder on the other side led below the level of the street, into maintenance tunnels embedded within the city plates. Weak rectangular LEDs along the ceiling gave off barely enough light to identify walls by virtue of faint metallic glints. Noah checked his NetMini every so often, leading the way for what felt like twenty miles of subterranean corridor.

"Where are we going?" Mamoru's attempt to whisper seemed thunderous in the quiet.

Noah jumped. "Shh. Nasty shit lives in—"

Mamoru smiled.

"Yeah, right. Yell if you want, you'd probably mess the Feeders up. There's a deck jockey down here, calls himself Flatline. Dude came back from the dead. If anyone can help you, it be him."

Ten minutes later, Noah pointed at a ladder back to the surface. "We're here."

They emerged in an alley behind a hundred-story residential tower. Judging by the sour, metallic smell in the air, a bad part of town. Mamoru grasped the wet traction coating on a surface that hadn't seen a ground car in a decade and vaulted out of the hole. None of the buildings in immediate view appeared smashed or crumbling. Fringers lounged or roamed about, male and female, from young teens to sixties. The ones who moved kept their heads down and their hands in their pockets. Those who lounged on chairs, trash canisters, or the ground, seemed mentally absent.

Noah kicked the hatch closed and jogged to the back door of a crumbling building that declared itself the 'Triumph Hotel' by way of shimmering gold holographic letters. From the look of it, blight had triumphed. Mamoru coughed on the taste of burned meat and trash in the air.

A slender Asian boy, ten years old, in a baggy, dingy jacket and pants glared a challenge at them, daring them to try something, as if he knew he could take them on.

Noah scurried past the kid and went inside. When the boy locked stares with Mamoru, a strange tingle glimmered in his eyes. A sense of energy, of feeding on the misery all around him, empowered him. The boy's angry glare morphed into a knowing smile. Darkness fed darkness. He shoved off the wall and walked away. Mamoru slithered out from under the eerie presence sharing his mind, haunted by the sight of the boy sauntering into the dark.

"Coming?" asked Noah.

"Yes." Mamoru lingered a few seconds more, staring at the alley where the boy had vanished, and strode inside.

On the thirteenth floor, Noah knocked on the door of apartment thirty-seven. Two minutes of silence passed before a whirr in the ceiling drew Mamoru's attention to a metal eyeball watching them from a ventilation grating.

A man's voice murmured from behind the door, bleary as if he'd recently come out of a deep sleep. "I don't work for Yakuza anymore."

"Hey, dead man," said Noah. "This guy ain't Yak. He's some void-walkin' freak show from planet WTF. Sharded the Titan, and blasted him orbital. Dude ain't even aug."

"The hell you dose?" asked the crackling voice.

"Nothin'. Fuckin' Titan lost his shit and pasted Zak. Almost stomped on Ferret too. Check the vidcap I sent on ahead."

Another minute of silence passed.

"You are dosed out of your shit to bring that motherfucker to my pad. Get the fuck out."

"This boy claims you are a man of some supposed skill," said Mamoru. "I fail to see the truth of it."

"Hah. Already punched my ticket once. Not lookin' to do it again."

"I seek your assistance in the GlobeNet." Mamoru sneered at the wall for having to say that. As much as he hated admitting it, referring to his last meeting with Nightwing as a draw was at best a stretch of the truth. Mamoru had tricked the AI into fleeing, but if they met again, it would be wise to his trickery. "I wish to slay a dragon."

Noah tapped his foot for three minutes, casting awkward glances from Mamoru, to the apartment, to the hallway they'd entered from.

The door whipped open with a rush of air scented in beer and underarm. A pallid man in black silk boxers with rows of lime green skull-and-crossbones down the sides teetered like a flesh scarecrow backlit by a rectangle of bright neon. Metal studs emerged from his temples, mounting points for a ViewPane, cybernetic eyes for those who didn't want to give up their real ones. He leaned his noodle-thin arms on the doorjamb, tilting his head at Mamoru like a dog not quite sure what to make of something. Behind him, numerous holo-panels flashed with a thousand colors, a churning rainbow of epileptic proportions. Short grey-black hair hung at uneven lengths, as if it grew at different rates depending on where on his skull it emerged.

An odd sense of anger washed over Mamoru at the sight of him, twisting his expression. Something about the way this man *felt* offended him, as if some manner of loathsome energy had saturated him, and he still reeked of it. The other presence inside reacted with primal instinct, urging Mamoru to kill. With great effort, he resisted—for the time being.

"A dragon?" Shadowed grey eyes stared, unblinking. "You're either Cat-6 or got a death wish."

Mamoru smiled. "That much anger only comes from a man who has lost." His mind detached from his outward affect. *How can I know this? I am no telempath.*

"Lost makes it seem like I was stupid enough to try and take one on."
Flatline rubbed the left side of his neck. "I wasn't an idiot. I was too slow."

"I can smell your desire for revenge." Mamoru moved to within inches of
the man. "This dragon has made itself a nuisance. It impedes me."

"That was you?" Flatline blinked. "The whole fuckin' city went haywire
yesterday. NewsNet's havin' a damn feeding frenzy. They're wailin' about
ACC infiltration, terrorists, corporate takeovers… Why's a mil-spec AI
chasing you down?"

"I almost killed it."

Breath flavored with cheap synthbeer and peach Nicohaler vapor
infiltrated Mamoru's nostrils as the scrawny figure leaned closer. "Horse shit.
You ain't even got a jack."

Mamoru's hand flew to Flatline's neck. The man grabbed his wrist,
scratching and pulling, too weak to dislodge it. Luminous energy exuded
from Mamoru's shoulders, and the world twisted into a blur of color. His
power connected his mind to the cybernetics in the man he held. Seconds
later, he embodied the suit of floating samurai armor in a dingy office ripped
from an old noir detective vid.

Flatline, six inches taller and ninety pounds of muscle heavier, sat behind
an old wooden desk lined with bottles of whiskey and shot glasses. He had his
feet up and leaned back in his chair like the king of the world. A cigar perched
at the edge of an ashtray; the creep of an ember threatened to cause it to tip
and roll away at any second. To the right, three women, each the spitting
image of Aurora, lounged on a divan. One in red lace lingerie, one in black,
and one in only her skin.

Mamoru glanced at the trio.

"Wank bank," said Flatline, no trace of apology in his voice. "Body's still a
bit weak for the real deal… it's a tide-me-over."

"How do you know that woman?" The armor loomed over the desk.

"She asked me to find someone." Flatline blinked. He sat up in the chair,
feet hitting the ground with a sharp *clap*. One hand on a gun under his coat,
he squinted. "How the fuck did you do that? You're in my NIU's PVN."

"What?" Red eyes appeared in the hollow helmet, angling down in an
irritated scowl.

"You 'spect me to believe you almost killed a dragon, and you don't know
what I said? You're a deck jockey, right? Neural interface unit? Private Virtual
Node?"

"I am aware of the concepts, not your abbreviations. I am not a traditional
operator."

He grasped one of the whiskey bottles, lifting it to examine the small bit of
software that simulated liquor. If someone consumed it in cyberspace, a signal
passed along a wire to the brain stem triggering the same chemical reactions

as real alcohol. Liquid sloshed as he turned the bottle over in his armored gauntlet. Mamoru desired the program to change. It melted into a blob of unrecognizable silver goo, which took on the shape of a pink rabbit. Mamoru set it on the desk, where it hopped around.

Flatline stared at the rabbit. "You changed my JDsoft into a damn Netßunny? Ugh, that bitch is so annoying." He froze. "Pause. Did you just rewrite a Soft in an instant?"

Mamoru folded his arms in the virtual world inside Flatline's headware. He released the connection and folded them in the real world. "Yes. Is that enough of a demonstration?"

"Whoa." Flatline held his head as he staggered back inside. "Fuck yeah, that's tripped. 'Mon in."

Noah opened his mouth.

"You may go," said Mamoru without looking.

Noah closed his mouth.

Mamoru took one step into the apartment, but stopped, holding out a credstick. "Your payment."

"Thanks, man." Noah snatched it and sprinted off.

Six cats hissed in unison as Mamoru entered. Two calicos, two tabbies (one grey and one orange) an all-black, and an all-white cat glared at him for seconds before disappearing in an explosion of furry streaks. Mamoru ignored them, stepping over wires across the rug. In the back of the living room, a four-foot tall obsidian rectangle stood atop a wheeled base. Bright azure lines traced along seams on its sides and at its flattened corners. A nest of two-inch thick wires ran from it to a metal desk. Another pair of the same cables led from a power splice on the wall. Eight net decks, four on the desk itself, formed a ring around Flatline's throne. Stacked shipping boxes and a rickety wooden nightstand held a pair on either side.

The place held an overall dinge. Powder blue walls had darkened as if someone sprayed them with still-wet tar. Every so often, the smell of beer farts gave way to two-week-old Chinese leftovers lurking somewhere in the trash. Mamoru didn't even want to touch the *air* inside this place.

Flatline fell into his chair. The black and white cats leapt into his lap, both staring at Mamoru as their human stroked their fur. "Meet Yin and Yang."

"I thought you disliked cute." Mamoru spoke without inflection, examining the hardware. "I will need the use of one of your decks."

"Well, I don't let strange dudes lay their hands on my deck."

Mamoru frowned.

Flatline pointed at a silver box on the floor under the sofa. "You look like a Matsushita man."

"I was."

"Had a bad experience? Usually their shit's top of the line. Bit pricey if you ask me, but… I suppose you get what you pay for."

"They tried to kill me." Mamoru stooped to retrieve the box, flipping the lid up to expose a slab of gloss-black technology. On the left end of the otherwise featureless device, the familiar M-in-a-circle logo of Matsushita Electronics appeared in dull black upon the gloss. He traced a finger over the word 'Ultra'—in katakana as well as English—below the logo. It wasn't quite an Oni series, but it came close. "This is adequate."

"Haven't had time to tweak it yet. Only amateurs plug in out of the box."

Mamoru chuckled. "You have a strange definition of amateur. Ultra Series grade eight is close to a million credits."

"It's my backup. Don't got an e-mag for it, you'll need to use wall power. You can plug in over there." Flatline waved at a tangle of smaller wires at the back end of his desk. "I got a plan. We can't go hunting that bastard in its home network. AIs are more powerful running on custom hardware. How bad does it want you?"

"Bad." He ignored the feline hissing coming from under the desk as he took a cable lead and snapped it into the right end of the Matsushita Ultra. The orange tabby wandered back in and sat in plain sight, giving Mamoru a 'go ahead, try and do something' stare. Red light glowed in thin strips around the unit as it powered up. "You saw what it did to the city."

"Perfect." Flatline cracked his knuckles. "We'll lure the fucker out. Going to better our odds too. I got a buddy who wouldn't miss this for anything. Hope that isn't a problem."

Mamoru removed his katana from his waist, knelt, and sat back on his heels. He set the blade with reverence to his left, and the deck in front of him, one hand atop its surface. After a moment of concentration, he closed his eyes. The presence inside his mind seemed agitated at the delay and showed no sign of understanding the need for it. Memories of his fight with the dragon AI replayed in his mind, as if to evaluate his tactics as well as demonstrate to the presence with which he had made a deal.

Akuryō, do not interfere if you wish our bargain fulfilled.

"Hey man, you awake? I think we could use his help," said Flatline.

Mamoru frowned, emitting a grunt of disapproval. "As long as he does not get in my way."

"Awesome. See you there." Flatline shut down a small holo-panel with a finger tap and looked over his shoulder at Mamoru. "He won't."

AMBUSH

Althea

Wind lofted Althea's hair in a sudden gust. She smiled and leaned on the broom, closing her eyes to enjoy the air. Late morning quiet settled over the street. Most of the small children were nowhere to be seen. She knew the strange police had been taking them all into a building for a couple of hours a day. Suspicion ruled at first, but when she talked to them later, they spoke of the same sort of annoying things the datapad Father gave her tormented her with. 'School' as they had called it, sounded like a far more pleasant experience than having a little slab of plastic call her stupid. Althea wanted to go, but no one had thought to include her. Perhaps they figured she liked that awful device.

The breeze subsided, and Althea resumed her task of sweeping the porch. Each scratch of the bristles over the boards reminded her of the unusual quiet. A minute passed of staring at her feet. She traced lines in the unswept dust with her big toe. Father and Den had gone off with the Watch, Karina working on the field.

I have lonely.

She glanced left, at the corner of the street two blocks away, where Beard's truck had appeared. It seemed silly to her now that she had been so terrified of it. However, she felt a small twinge of worry at the thought of the giant metal beast. Her grip on the broom tightened and she brushed fear and bad thoughts away as well as dust. She nudged the ever-growing pile of silt to the edge, and off the side to the ground.

Althea set the broom on the porch in the pose of a conquering hero holding a huge sword, and squinted in the direction of the city center.

I wanna go to the school.

Hair and dress flared as she whirled to lean the broom on the wall before racing down the three steps to the street. She didn't care if most of the kids there were half her age. The stupid machine-thing kept talking to her as if she was six anyway. A real teacher couldn't be any worse. Elation built up inside her as she ran, matched by a broad smile.

"Althea," shouted Father.

She stopped and looked behind her. One block past her home, Father and a large group of people from the Watch marched in the direction of the house. A few seconds of staring let her sense worry and anger on him. Without a second thought, she sprinted toward him and leapt into a hug.

"Thea," he said, no longer yelling. "There was an ambush."

Her eyebrows came together. "Does it need watering?"

Nervous chuckling emanated from the group of armed men and women. Father hugged her again.

"*Un guardia fue emboscado.*"

Althea understood and took his hand. "Okay. Let's go."

"It is not that simple *cariño*. Miguel is at the bottom of a ravine. We fear to move him."

She looked in the direction of the gate. "Okay. Let's go."

"It feels like a trap." He squeezed her hand. "To bring you out of the walls."

"I am not afraid." She closed her eyes and tried to open her thoughts to whatever gave her strange feelings. The scent of Karina's hair came to mind, followed by an image of her working the field with a smile. The same smile appeared on Althea's face. "There is nothing wrong."

He held her hand as they walked across Querq. Her smile faded a little each step, wondering why a powerful sense of Karina's presence would fill her thoughts when attempting to think about a wounded man. By the time they arrived at the gates, she worried. The vision made her think of someone watching from a distance, hiding.

"Father... You should not bring so many men. It will make the city weak."

"What if this is the Buffalos attempting to take you?" He glared at the imagined raiders out in the distance.

"I am not scared of raiders anymore. You are right. Something feels wrong. I keep seeing Karina."

"Alright, alright." Father waved at the group. "Montez, Estevez, Garcia, Hernandez, and Nelson. You're with me. The rest of you keep an eye out for an attack."

Crack.

Everyone jumped at the loud noise echoing over the city.

Shepherd had dropped a large crate. The big man jogged over to the unusual gathering. "Something wrong?"

Althea smiled at him.

"You may as well come with us," said Father.

Shepherd nodded. "What's the situation?"

Althea wandered toward the town's exit, holding Father's hand while he explained about the patrol ambush. The enormous door had already been pulled open by the new city machines. Warm dirt underfoot became hot metal as she entered the gate tunnel, a ten-ish foot long corridor made entirely of steel that connected Querq's dirt to the old city's smashed up roads. Boots clanked above her from more Watch patrolling the metal walkway overhead.

At the sight of the old city, she hesitated. Feet together, hands clasped at her chest, she trembled under the weight of inexplicable dread. Something *bad* was in the air. Father had been right, and the feeling came to her when she didn't even try to find it. A wave of flames erupted from the walls and engulfed her; she yelped, raising her arms to guard her face. The red-haired woman who had come to kill her stepped out of the fire, chasing it away and protecting her. As the woman ran a reassuring hand over her head, Althea held her stomach at a powerful surge of nauseous worry for her sister.

"Althea?" yelled Father.

She backed away from the outside and let her arms down. "Father... You should stay with Karina."

Conflict twisted his face. "I am worried for you as well. Karina is safe in the city."

"No." Althea ran to him, clinging. "Please, Father. Please."

"I could keep an eye on her if you want," said Shepherd.

"It must be Father." Althea stood on tiptoe, pleading.

Father shook his head. "This has ambush written all over it; I cannot let you go alone."

Althea cried. "No, Father. Please. Karina is in danger. Please stay with her."

At the fear in her eyes, he let his head hang with the resigned look he always showed when he could think of nothing more to argue and didn't like something.

"Alright." Father rubbed her back, patting it until she calmed down. "Shepherd, you will go with her."

"I will."

Althea sniffled and wiped her eyes. "That woman you do not trust should come with me too."

"There's a lot of women he don't trust," said Garcia.

"And you're one of them, *chica*," added Montez.

Garcia laughed.

"Kate?" asked Shepherd. "I thought she went back to the city."

"She came back." Nelson gestured over his shoulder with a thumb. "It's Saturday, they flew in about an hour ago. You want I should get her?"

Althea stared up at Father. He nodded to Nelson, who ran off.

"What have you seen, child?" Father held her hand and took a knee in front of her.

"Fire was coming for me, but Kate stopped it. I... don't know why, but I am scared for Karina. I will be safe. You need to protect her. I feel someone watching her, having bad in their heart."

Something in her expression made Father pull the new city-rifle off his shoulder and straighten.

After a minute or two in uneasy silence, clomping boots drew all eyes to an alley. Nelson ran ahead of Kate. She'd dressed like a local in a plain white tee and jeans. As soon as she saw Althea, she changed course and rushed over.

"What's wrong? He said you needed me?" Kate wrapped her in a hug and squeezed.

Father tensed.

Althea gave him a plaintive look. *She does not want to hurt me.*

He snorted but dropped the challenging stare he'd been fixing on Kate.

"You need to come with us." Althea settled down from tiptoe to stand flat. "I don't know why, but you need to. I have a feeling."

"David should be out of the bath in about ten minutes," said Kate.

"No time." Father patted Estevez on the shoulder. "Miguel isn't gonna last that long."

"Come on," said Hernandez. "I was with the patrol that got hit. It's not too far from the edge of the old city."

Father stared at Althea as if expecting it would be the last time he'd ever see her. His sadness hit her in the gut. She focused, projecting confidence into him, raising his mood. He stood tall, chest puffed. She held his hand and touched his life essence, bolstering it. Her eyes glowed brighter for a few seconds as she channeled power into him, priming his reflexes for speed and precision.

Father took on a twitchy affect, glancing around as if aware of a thousand sounds and smells that had escaped him before.

"What did you do?"

Althea knew she'd done something to his body, but she couldn't explain it, so she fell back to her days with the Chamán for an explanation. "I have asked a spirit of war to watch over you. He will not stay long, but he will protect Karina with you."

Father looked perplexed. He'd never been a believer in tribal mysticism, but what he felt at that moment defied his understanding.

Althea hurried to the gate, following Hernandez and the others.

Debris strewn streets crisscrossed the ruins of old Albuquerque, covered with dirt and trapped tumbleweeds. Althea kept her gaze down, not wanting to look at the faces of buildings or ruins of cars and think about the people who had died here. Shepherd held her hand as they walked.

Spirit of war? Kate's voice drifted in her mind, trailed by a telepathic laugh.

Althea looked over at her. *I do not know what to say it as. We had no time.*

Fair enough.

Hernandez led them to the edge of the city and out over the scrubland. A short distance along an ancient highway, a wounded horse lay on its side at the edge of a cliff. The animal calmed as soon as Althea looked at it. She let go of Shepherd's hand and ran forward.

"Wait," shouted Kate, sprinting after her.

Althea put a hand on the chestnut mare's flank and forced the animal asleep, a quick surge of power also caused a gunshot wound in the animal's side to stop bleeding.

Kate grasped her shoulder. "The horse can wait, there's a person down there."

"She does not have to suffer while she waits."

Althea stood and crept to the edge of the ravine. Forty feet down a steep incline, at the end of a long trail of impact marks, a man lay on the ground. Both of his legs twisted at unnatural angles and blood seeped out of his mouth and nose, bubbling with each breath. White bone pierced his left thigh, and his lips moved with endless whispering.

Shepherd approached. Althea's dress tightened about her chest as he grabbed a fistful of cloth at her back. "Careful, girl. You don't want to fall."

"I have to go down there." She looked at the uneven surface. "I can climb this."

"Hold on," said Estevez. He took a length of rope from his shoulder and dropped it on the ground. He kick-tested a root that seemed sturdy enough and tied one end around it before throwing the rest over the edge. "That will help."

Shepherd let go, reluctantly. Montez, Garcia, and Nelson moved to the edge to look at their fallen friend.

Garcia muttered nasty words under her breath. "We never saw where it came from. Some bastard shot the horse out from under him."

Althea crouched and turned her back to the drop, easing one leg over the coarse grass lining the edge until her toes sank into dry dirt. She held onto the rope with both hands and let her weight settle onto that foot before moving her other leg from the top. She lowered herself in search of the next place to step. A spike of panic wafted from above when Althea's chin reached the level of the road.

Kate flung her arms to the sides. "Wait!"

Althea jumped at the shout, slipping a few inches before she caught herself. "What?"

A tremble of exertion shivered along the woman's body. "I'm holding back a bomb."

DEATH UNDONE

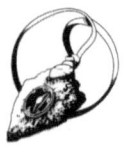

Althea

Before Althea could ask what a 'bomb' was, gunshots rang out. She ducked, pressing herself against the dirt wall. Men and women shouted in English and Spanish as bullets ricocheted from ancient paving. The sound of people running in a mad scramble for cover barely reached her senses over the din of fighting. Icy claws scraped at her heart, twice. Tears flowed from her eyes without thought; people had died.

Shepherd stood in front of Kate, who for some reason, hadn't moved at all.

Chaos gave way to silence in a few seconds.

"Well that's a surprise," said a male voice, higher than average in pitch and a bit familiar.

A few pained moans followed.

Althea's feet sank deeper into the loose soil as she stretched up to peek over the top. Nelson curled up behind an old guardrail, holding his bloody shoulder. His rifle sat in the road, a few feet away from where he'd taken cover. Garcia and Estevez had gone twenty yards further down the road where they ducked behind the decaying struts of an old billboard, aiming their rifles. Montez lay flat on the ground, the front of his face smeared all over the pavement, the back of his head cracked open. He'd never even gotten his rifle off his shoulder.

On the other side of the road, three men pointed rifles at them over a wall of sandbags covered in tumbleweeds. Blood and abandoned guns lay where two others had died and fallen out of sight. A third body slumped over the sandbags, dead.

Hector, the man who had shot Karina, stood on the road as if immune to bullets, pointing a handgun in Shepherd's general direction. Althea sniffled at the pain of death. Six people with rifles held their breath in a standoff.

"Definitely wasn't expecting that fucker to fail." Hector grinned at Althea. "Guess you are charmed or some bullshit. Don't matter you live. By the time you get back to town, that bitch sister of yours will be dead." He laughed. "Maybe I leave you alive so you can cry for her."

A single gunshot echoed in the distance, muted and sharp—a city rifle.

"I don't think that worked out for you either, asshole," said Kate.

Althea shivered at the noise. Since no great sense of clairvoyant sorrow came over her, she hoped she had heard Father's gun. Her gaze fell level to the earth before her eyes, where a bit of green plastic poked out from the soil.

"Don't just stand there," muttered Shepherd.

"I can't do anything," whispered Kate. "If I stop concentrating, the fucking bomb is going to go off. It's a goddamned inch away from Althea's face."

"Seems we got ourselves a little impasse here," said Hector.

"Go to hell, traitor," shouted Garcia.

Althea brushed dirt away from the plastic, revealing a curved rectangular object about ten inches across with letters on it. Weeks with that irritating machine had taught her those 'funny marks' she'd seen here and there were words. Speech that people somehow froze so it could keep speaking. She ran the shapes over in her head, trying to remember how to say them.

"Front toads emmeny."

Shepherd glanced down, raising an eyebrow.

Althea projected an image of what she saw into Shepherd's mind. His surface thoughts flashed from 'how the hell is that thing even still working' to 'damn that's old,' followed by several bad words. He thought the little plastic box could kill her.

She blinked. *This is a bomb?*

"I've already been there, *señorita*," said Hector. "You point your gun at me, my friends will shoot you. Looks like you'll all kill each other, and we don't want that."

Shepherd thought about a little piece on the top, screwed into the green block. Althea looked for the part he seemed to be trying to 'show' her. A thin metal wire came out of it and disappeared off to her left into the ground. He wanted her to remove it and imagined her unscrewing it and pulling a three-inch silver stick out of the green brick. She braced a knee against the cliff and took one hand off the rope. The piece refused to budge when she twisted it. She grunted under her breath and made herself a little stronger. On her second attempt, it came loose, and after twisting the cap a few turns, she lifted a small metal post out of a hole.

Kate, staring at her the whole time, finally breathed. *Throw the little thing as hard as you can.*

Althea tossed it to the side. It fell a distance away and burst with a white flash and a sharp pop, not quite as loud as a gunshot. Everyone with a weapon twitched.

She looked up at Shepherd and Kate, unimpressed with the tiny explosion, confused why they had been so afraid of it.

"They killed Montez," said Estevez.

"Kill the bastard," Garcia growled.

"No," Althea yelled. She clambered over the edge and slipped into the gap between her two protectors. "Hector, stop. Why must you hurt people?" The sight of the dead brought tears. "I was wrong. I am sorry I did not help Emilio. I did not know I could when he got hurt. I did fix a dead person once, but I don't know how." She slipped an arm around Shepherd's back and clung to his side. "It was my fault he died. I had so much guilt."

Hector's face reddened. "So you *can* fix the dead? You *chose* to let Emilio die!"

Kate advanced. "For fuck's sake, asshole. Can you get it through your tiny little brain that she's a goddamn child?"

Boom.

Two feet of orange fire belched from Hector's massive pistol. Althea screamed as Shepherd shoved her behind him. The shot hadn't been aimed at her. A heavy, fleshy thump sounded from Kate's chest an instant before her clothes flash burned to a fine layer of dust. She staggered back out of the smoldering remains of her sneakers, grabbing at a huge bruise between her breasts where molten lead trickled down her skin. Kate gulped air like a fish out of water, apparently wanting to speak, but lacking the ability.

The three men behind the sandbags slackened their aim; one blessed himself. Hector turned pale.

An emotional change darkened the minds of the three still-armed members of the Watch. Althea snapped her head to face them. "No! Don't kill anyone more!"

Kate snarled.

Hector's pistol burst into flames and exploded a second later. He clutched his burned hand to his chest and wailed.

Wheezing, Kate staggered toward Hector, shrouded in fury. The sight of her nakedness kept his friends gawking. A mixture of solidifying lead and copper glimmered on the road, a dribbled trail running down her leg.

"Althea..." wheezed Kate as blue spheres of fire appeared in both of her hands, "don't watch. Son of a bitch is going to pay for trying to hurt you."

BETTER A PAINFUL TRUTH

Anna

Earl Grey didn't taste as good tepid as it did hot or even iced. Anna couldn't bring herself to take another sip as she paced back and forth inside Penny's flat. Spawny pressed himself into the couch harder each time her circuitous route moved in his direction. Whenever he flinched, he offered an apologetic look.

Penny remained at the table, staring at her empty cup. Every so often, she'd reminisce about their time together, as if recalling the horrible life they'd led as teens would somehow fix whatever had gone wrong in her head. Anna considered it a true miracle she had made it to her twenties without being raped, stabbed, or shot. She had Penny to thank for being alive—as much as James, perhaps more so. Somehow, the two of them had made it. Everything bad that happened to Anna came as a result of poor choices on her part. How could Penny have forgotten her so easily?

She let her head fall into her hands and sobbed.

Aaron grasped her shoulder. "It's not her, luv. She's been adjusted."

Penny hesitated, approaching with an awkward ostrich-like gait and a faltering smile. Anna looked up at her, feeling worse at the discomfort in her dear friend's face.

"This is all to cock," said Penny. "I feel sick. None of this makes any sense."

"Something's been done to you," said Aaron. "To your mind."

Anna shivered at the sound of his voice above and behind her, vibrating in her bones.

"Thought she said we'z got nuffin ta fear from 'er." Spawny stuffed a hand down the front of his trousers and scratched himself. "Roight?"

"It wasn't me," Anna muttered at the floor. "I'm not much of a telepath."

Aaron squeezed her shoulder. "You don't give yourself enough credit, luv. Makin' people not see ya isn't easy."

"So what does that mean?" Penny dragged a chair closer. She trembled, but sat near Anna despite the terror obvious in her eyes. "For us?"

The truth stood right in front of her. Could she believe it enough to speak it? How much of anything could she believe anymore? Alexi's innocent smile flashed in her mind. Was she as damaged as that boy? Did Archon do this for her benefit?

Aaron's hand rubbed confidence into her back.

"Someone wanted me away from London." Anna's sadness faded to detached calm. "He made it possible for me to leave. I'm not sure I could have gone if you didn't hate me."

"Anna!" Penny yelled, and bit her lip after. "I… uhh, never hated you. T'be honest, I don't know why I'm so frightened. Whenever I think of you, it's like I remember you wantin' to kill me, and I can't figure on what I did to get you cheesed off."

"That's bollocks," Anna replied in a flat voice, unable to look up. "Do you remember the alley?"

"A bit. You killed those blokes when we went to skim their 'minis. Said it was better to take all the creds instead of just a pittance."

"No, Pen. That's not how it went… they chased us into an alley and knocked the shite out of Spawny. One of 'em tossed me over a rubbish bin." Warm tears ran down her cheeks at the memory of an invading hand between her legs. She squirmed in her chair and looked up. "I wasn't going to fight. Just let 'em take what they wanted of me like I always did. I heard you screaming and I couldn't let them do that to you. Not ever."

Penny's eyes dilated. She glanced up at Aaron, who seemed to be focusing on her.

A soft knock came from the door.

With Spawny paralyzed on the couch and Penny locked in a trance with Aaron, Anna sniffled away her tears and hurried to the door. A wiry, thirty-something man in a dark coat and glasses offered a polite smile.

"Anna," he said, with a nod of greeting.

"Agent Hughes… I wasn't sure if it was safe to contact you." She backed away from the door. "Please, come in."

"You've made some disturbing claims." Hughes folded his glasses with a deft snap of the wrist and tucked them in a pocket. "Are you sure the professor is responsible? That calls into question much of what's gone on here."

"I… don't know. I don't want to believe it, but I'm finding it difficult to dispute."

Aaron grumbled behind her. "Damn. Almost had it that time. Anna, if you kept feeding her memories from that night"—he paused—"what the devil is that reporter doing here?"

Anna moved back to the table, caught off guard by the confusion on Aaron's face. Penny still stared into space. "Reporter?"

"Aye, 'e followed me into the locker room a half a dozen times. Damn Guardian chaps never know when to back off."

"Aaron." Anna grabbed his hand. "Promise you'll trust me."

"Oi, what?"

"Please."

Aaron sighed. "Fine. I trust you."

"He's not a reporter. This is Agent Hughes, CSB."

Hughes smiled.

Panic, shock, anger, and confusion played on Aaron's face for a few seconds, leaving his jaw cocked to the side and one eyebrow up. "This better be good."

"I already warned him not to go peeking." Anna held onto his hand; it was her turn to reassure him. "He's an inside man. Hughes is trying to help us. His registration tag is fake."

Aaron wagged his head as if pointing with his nose at Hughes's neck. "He's not got one."

Sure enough, he didn't.

"What?"

Hughes gestured at Anna. "Things are changing 'round the Tower."

"Coventry?" Anna blinked.

"No, the Tower. Your friend Thompson launched an inquiry into the workings of the CSB. It's a right hames at the moment, but things are looking promising. Fortunately, they are worried enough about Eastern Europe to fear offending the UCF. He's managed to expose the detonator law. The press got a hold of it two years ago and made quite a scene. They'll be dealing with lawsuits until you're a grandmum."

Anna looked at the rug, shying from Aaron like a child who'd done something wrong. "He's a telepath. I thought he could help you with Pen."

"Oi, what about me?" whimpered Spawny.

She sighed at him. "Of course."

Hughes unbuttoned his coat, revealing a plain beige-brown outfit so nondescript it all but screamed government agent. For a minute, he stared at Penny, before blinking off a trance and rubbing the side of his head.

"Bad?" asked Anna.

"It's strong. I get the feeling whoever did it is a little more skilled than I am, but there's more to it than that. A lot more raw power involved rather than technique."

"Awakened," mumbled Aaron.

Agent Hughes scowled at the wall before flashing an inspired look at him. "Perhaps we should combine efforts. Your power, my control?"

"Aye, might work." Aaron squinted, suspicion plain on his face. "Anna, you help as well. Keep showing her the truth."

"Alright."

Aaron took up a position on Penny's left. Hughes on her right. Anna sat on a chair facing her friend and held her hands. Her use of telepathy had—up until recently—been limited to communication, peeking at surface thoughts, and mental invisibility. Mind reading or deep diving had never been something she'd tried to do often. Usually, people kept secrets for a reason. The downside of invasive telepathy was that the reader tended to revisit the memory as if they had experienced it. Her brief glimpses into Faye's mind had given her a nightmare or two, as if Deacon Bell had molested her instead.

Anna concentrated on Penny's thoughts. Reality faded to blackness, accompanied by the sense of two other minds. It felt as though Hughes entered a dark place first, with Aaron behind him and her wandering off to the side.

Scenes emerged. The night Penny first found a twelve-year-old Anna crying in the alley after running away from social services. Telepathic tinkering had made Penny feel burdened by the obligation of taking her in rather than happy to help. Anna projected her memories of how they'd formed an immediate bond.

Hughes latched onto that and forced the truth under the implant to unseat it, holding a nail in place for Aaron's hammer to drive home.

The memory shifted back to where it belonged.

One by one, various memories came and went, each one altered to make Penny fear her. Every time Penny had protected her from thugs, the Met, or the occasional creep, the memory had been changed to Anna having a lightning-throwing tantrum and almost hurting her. The telepathic overlays shifted Penny's feelings from protectiveness to being bothered at always having to take care of Anna, and terror of a power that seemed always on the edge of losing control. Minutes later, Anna found herself floating in the alley, watching it from Penny's point of view. They had just run a skim on a train, and Penny forgot all about the Crossmen chasing them here. In this version, the three friends had stumbled upon a group of men minding their own business in the dark.

Anna's false self laughed and suggested an easier way to make credits— murder. 'Accidental' electrocution worked for her once already.

With that, the lightning flew.

No! shrieked the real Anna. *That's not what happened at all.*

She dredged the horrible truth out of where she'd tried to bury it. Once more, she felt the cold metal trashcan on her bare stomach as the Crossman bent her over and held her down. She suppressed the urge to gag at the sensation of his hand between her legs. Shame paralyzed her; she hadn't cared about what he wanted to do to her. She would have let him do anything to stop him from hurting her afterward.

Penny screamed.

One of the men tried to rape her friend. Anna was worthless. It didn't matter what anyone did to her. She couldn't lay there limp and useless while her dear friend, the reason she'd grown up intact, suffered a fate worse than death. She cast her apathy aside and killed the man on top of her so she could get to her friend. Nothing mattered but protecting Penny.

All three Crossmen died by her hand. Her secret was out. She could no longer hide her power from her two closest friends.

She had risked Penny's hatred to save her. Penny's gasp in the real world as that idea unfolded in their telepathic dance made Anna cry.

A surge of white light devoured the alley. Penny's sobs pierced the resulting silence; distant at first, they intensified until the feeling of arms around her emerged from the nothingness of the telepathic dream.

Anna lay on her back, on the floor, with Penny on top of her—a bawling wreck.

Aaron and Hughes looked drained and sagged into nearby chairs.

"Anna... Anna... I'm so sorry." Penny sniffled into her shoulder. "You were going to let... how could I have forgotten that?"

"You didn't." Anna sat up with her. "Someone took it from you. To 'spare' you."

"Bollocks," muttered Aaron.

"Not bad, mate," said Hughes. "You're more skilled than I thought."

"Thanks." Aaron panted. "Not much of a telepath, I just dabble at it." He winked at Anna.

Anna looked down.

"Did you happen to catch a glimpse of the source?" asked Aaron.

Hughes shook his head. "No. Bunch of white space. Whoever did it tried to remove themselves, as well as the entirety of the meeting where the implant took place. In most cases like this, the telepath responsible changes their identity in the memory both as misdirection and because it's a lot easier to change appearance than to remove the scene entirely. Whoever did this was—"

"Arrogant, self-absorbed, cocky...," muttered Aaron.

Hughes chuckled. "I was going to say quite thoroughly convinced of their own ability, but that's spot on."

"Maybe we shouldn't," whispered Anna. "Were you happier not remembering?"

Penny composed herself and wiped her face. "How could you think I'd be happier not remembering what you did for me?" She pushed Anna's shoulder playfully. "It was terrifying, but it could've been far worse. I'm horrified you were going to just let them 'ave you."

"What choice did I have? Be a victim of that, or defend myself and 'ave the government kill me."

Hughes coughed. "Sorry about that, Anna. Had to keep up appearances. I wish I could've made contact without Gordon around to tell you it looks worse from the outside."

"What d'you mean?" Anna's head snapped up.

"Except for a few hard cases like him, we ran our own shop. The Crown thought we were shipping psionic tykes off to internment camps, but it was quite a bit different on the inside. Actual detonators stopped a few years before. Lot of smoke and mirrors."

She scowled. "You mean I was running from a story? The whole thing? The drugs, the sex clubs, all of it to avoid bollocks?"

"Well, based on old truth," said Hughes, out of the side of his mouth.

"Lauren said they put a real bomb in her head when she was around fifteen!" Anna stomped.

"At least ten years ago, they did use real ones. It took us awhile to work enough influence."

"What's done to psionic children now? The ones who're arrested out of their schools?" Anna squinted at him. "Do you still shut them up in secret prisons away from their families?"

"We only remove them from the home if the family doesn't want them. It's closer to a hospital, actually. Observation. Relatives can visit them, and you are overreacting. We don't 'arrest' them. It's no more traumatic than being sent to see the nurse."

"No more traumatic than your parents telling you to bugger off," muttered Aaron, sarcastically.

Anna frowned. "You make it sound almost pleasant. It's disruptive and cruel."

"I assume the newest ones arrived alright?" Hughes pursed his lips. "The parents are rather insistent on arranging visitation."

"You?" Anna blinked.

"Of course." Hughes smiled. "There are quite a few of us working to help Dr. Mardling's cause. Even with the changes, they're better off going with us to a new world. None of the parents involved have a trace of gift."

Aaron stared at Hughes. "'E tweak your bean too?"

Hughes's eyebrows drew together.

"Those two girls are miserable. Shut in a dreadful cargo box for weeks, taken away from everything they've known. They miss their homes so bad they're barely eating!" Anna fumed. "They belong with their families. Now you tell me their parents *want* them?"

"We tried to get the lot, but Dr. Mardling insisted on only those with gifts. Said there was limited room. Once the colony is established enough to defend itself, we can bring up any relatives who want to join us."

They're so homesick. Anna folded her arms as if hugging herself. Abducting Althea had felt dodgy enough, even if she didn't have real parents looking for her. These two girls... *It's not right. If they're not going to be imprisoned, they belong home.*

Hughes glanced at Aaron. "Shall we go back in and try to figure out who did it?"

Aaron smirked, gesturing at Spawny. "Better we save our energy an' give that bloke a look before his heart explodes." He wandered deeper into the flat.

Anna stood, pulling Penny to her feet. "Where are you going?"

"Need a moment to gather some strength. Also, it's my turn to call someone." Aaron winked, and ducked into the bathroom.

THAN A COMFORTABLE LIE

Aaron

Lights flickered on as a slab of opaque frosted glass slid closed behind Aaron. Small porcelain cats of various shapes and sizes covered every surface in the little bathroom. He smirked at the wall, wondering where Penny had stashed the little old woman she'd obviously stolen the flat from. He left the lid down and sat on the furry toilet seat, NetMini in hand. He felt no need to go prying for who'd altered Anna's friends, he knew. It wouldn't do anyone any good for their somewhat-ally Hughes to see his glass castle broken yet.

A fifteen-inch holo-panel scrolled open in midair over the device, containing a list of his installed apps, contact lists, email, and Vidphone. The upper half of the screen went black as a large rectangle slid down over everything, interrupting him with a 'breaking' story from the NewsNet.

Dense tropical forest burned bright orange in the middle of the night. Shadowy figures in military armor traipsed back and forth over the wreckage of some manner of encampment far away from the city. Aaron reached to brush the panel out of his way, but hesitated when he noticed the carcasses of military vehicles strewn about, warped and twisted as though thrown by great force. Corpses littered the ground, dragged into a neat row by uniformed ACC soldiers.

"...have confirmed military action against members of the Venezuelan resistance. Authorities have reported around a hundred and twenty suspected militants engaged government forces just after midnight last night. Rumors are circulating that this particular cell harbored dangerous psionic fugitives, and the Department of Motherland Security had been avoiding direct confrontation with them for some time.

"Local authorities are not providing the NewsNet with additional details; however, our on-site reporter was able to determine the bodies of around thirty rebels were unaccounted for prior to his being arrested."

The psionics are missing. Convenient, that. A crude hut wall moved into the scene, spattered with blood and bullet holes. Handcuffed bodies slumped on the ground. Venezuelan soldiers dragged a number of injured women toward a prisoner transport. Three kicked and screamed, fighting their restraints in an effort to run to the dead men by the wall. Three seconds later, the image cut to black. *Guess Ol' Professor Mardling didn't get them all.*

He flicked the NewsNet off the top of the screen and poked Mikhail's entry in his contacts.

Twenty-eight seconds later, a six-inch holographic head appeared.

"Britain, Aaron?" Mikhail cringed. "Have you changed your mind then, or are we looking at an international incident?"

"I'm ready to talk." Aaron rubbed his forehead. "This may be deeper than you thought, and things haven't rightly worked out like I expected with the bitch."

"Well, I'm glad to see you didn't get yourself killed." Mikhail's smile left him looking like a Middle-Eastern trader with a dodgy car for sale. "I am thrilled to hear that. How are you coping?"

The reminder of Allison wasn't welcome or helpful, but he accepted the gesture. "As well as can be expected."

"Good, good. I'll get things moving on this side for you. Have you learned much?"

"He's influencing people to collect as many psionics as he can. Do you remember the McKay girl? Melissa? Ran away from the dorm a couple times."

Mikhail looked thoughtful, but shook his head. "Afraid not."

"Guess her case didn't get up to your level then. He wanted her quite bad. She's awakened as well, I think. She's got a lot of power but has a ways to go learning how to control it." Aaron explained about her parents. "He's done the same thing to Anna's old friends. Tell me you saw that bit on the NN about Venezuela."

"I did." Mikhail raised an eyebrow. "That was him?"

"No proof, but seems sketchy the ACC hadn't hit them before. Resistance doesn't live too long out in the open like that with a camp. They 'ad psionics with em. Enough to scare the authorities away. Now all of a sudden, they get wiped out and no trace of the psionics. Sixty, seventy people dead so he could build his army."

"The man's insane, and dangerous," said Mikhail.

A panel on the wall chimed. A smiling cartoon nurse appeared. "You seem to be taking quite a while, would you care for some reading material? Perhaps some medication to help?"

Aaron poked a button to turn off the assistant. "Aye. You've no bloody idea how glad I am no one has the balls to try an' read my mind. I gotta go." He paused, stared at Mikhail for a few seconds, and saluted. "Sir."

He got up and went outside, interrupting a mild argument between Agent Hughes and Anna.

Anna scowled to the side. "Bother what James wants. Did anyone think to ask the girls their opinion? He's always rattling on about how it's everyone's choice. I told them to their faces they were free to leave if they wished." She stomped around. "I suppose when you're eleven and nine and you're stuck in a foreign country after a month-long trip locked in a stinking box you pretty much feel like a prisoner no matter what you're told."

Hughes scratched at his head. "The younger girl went poltergeist during lunch period. Everyone in her school knows. It would be a bit daunting to just plop her back into her normal life."

"Yes, but what if that's what *she wants*? And what of Lucy?" Anna tried to lean up at him to seem more intimidating.

"We found her in Meredith's memory. They had a secret pact. Next-door neighbors. Telepath, if I remember correctly."

"So they *were* friends before this idiocy."

Hughes nodded. "Aye. Since they could walk."

"Anna?" Aaron trotted over. "Archon always says he only wants those willing to go with him. Why not have the girls ask him if they can go home?"

She glared at him for a second, but it melted to worry. *What if he makes them forget? Did you see Alexi? He thinks he's Alastair now. I... think he thinks he's known me for years.*

Aaron smiled despite his worry. *I'm sorry, Anna. That couldn't have been easy for you to accept, but you're right.*

"All right." Anna looked at Spawny. "That's what we'll do then. After we're done here."

AARON SLUMPED IN THE BACK SEAT OF HUGHES' HOVERCAR, HOLDING HIS HEAD. The Agent had insisted on hammering away at the blockade guarding the identity of the person who'd reprogrammed Spawny. It seemed unlikely they would break through, even without Aaron half-assing it on purpose. The important bit had been freeing the man from his compulsion to stain his trousers every time he laid eyes on Anna. After more than an hour and a half, they'd defeated the implant. Anna's emotional connection to him hadn't been near as strong as with Penny, and the man's memories bore large pockmarks: a minefield of gaps caused by drugs.

He tried not to think about being in the rear seat of a CSB vehicle. It bothered him more that Anna occupied the rear seat of a CSB vehicle, even if she had asked for the ride. Aaron slid his hand over the seat and held hers. She startled at the contact, dragged out from wherever her mind had wandered.

"Where are we going again?"

"Oh." She stared at her lap. "Near Finsbury Park."

"You're not popping in on a Frictionless match?"

"Certainly not." A hint of a smile played on her lips, faded, and her grip on his fingers tightened. "I need to know."

"He's not the sort to appreciate the likes of my company," said Hughes. "Shall I wait on the roof?"

Anna looked at Aaron, questions in her eyes.

"Might want to join us," said Aaron. "Just in case we need the extra finesse."

"Right."

The CSB agent brought the car about in a gradual upward spiral, passing over the park on the way to the top of the apartment tower. Anna seemed to find her confidence again as they touched down, and stormed across the roof to a small elevator shed. Aaron had to jog to catch her before the doors closed.

She backed against the inner wall, fidgeting with her coat. "Sorry. I'm not sure I'm going to like what I find here."

He moved to her side and held the door for Hughes, who walked with a casual government-issue stroll. "Blighter thinks he's got all day."

Hughes cracked a smile as he stepped in.

"Thirty-ninth," said Anna.

Aaron pushed the button. A debate went back and forth in his head. How much distance should he maintain? Should he press his luck and try to turn her now? If she misconstrued his intentions attempting to reveal Archon's true nature to her as simple male rivalry, she'd get herself hurt. He couldn't rightly ask Hughes to help check Anna for any latent programming either, not without giving away who he suspected—and potentially igniting a massive headache with the CSB. *How much of the Bureau does the bastard control?*

A chime flooded the cabin as the elevator halted on the thirty-ninth floor. Anna sucked in a breath and marched down a blue-carpeted hallway with windows for a right-side wall. Tiny dots, people, moved about in the grass across the street. Aaron raised an eyebrow at the strange impressionist sculptures along the interior wall. One bore a pair of hovering silver cubes, spinning around each other in an endless dance. At the word engraved on the pedestal, Aaron raised an eyebrow.

"How the bloody hell do a pair of spinning boxes equate to lust?"

Anna's serious face cracked with a chuckle. "I thought the same thing the first time I was here."

"Who lives 'ere, anyway?" asked Aaron.

"Calls 'imself Mr. Orange." Anna pushed the buzzer by a door marked 3915. "Someone who helped me once."

A muscular man about Aaron's height with thick black hair answered. He wore a white silk robe in a Japanese style, open down the front, over a loose-fitting pair of dark pants. Matte-black plastisteel covered his neck and shoulder area. Aaron didn't want to imagine what sort of injury required reconstruction of an entire neck.

"Pixie… Never expected to see you again."

"Hello, Nathan." Anna looked up at him. "This is an unplanned trip. I know you're funny about psionics. I think someone might've hacked your brain and I'd like to find out."

The man looked Aaron and Hughes over. "Who're these two?"

Anna chuckled. "Don't panic, but remember how you were worried about me leading the authorities to your door? Aaron's an ex-cop and Hughes is CSB."

Mr. Orange became Mr. White.

"Relax, Nathan. His loyalties lie with us, not the Crown."

"Which one's Hughes?" Orange stared at them for a moment before pointing at Aaron. "Wait, I know you. Pryce. Aaron Pryce."

Aaron held his hands up as if surrendering. "Aye, guilty."

"That leg thing was a face job, wasn't it?" Orange shook his head. "Damn, the boys've been gettin' mullered since you vanished."

"Sodding Hell. You too?" Anna scowled at the ceiling. "I'm surrounded by bleedin' Arsenal fans."

Hughes whistled innocently.

"Look, Nathan. I need answers. I know I still owe you one. Call it two? If someone did a bodge job on your brain, would you want it undone?"

Orange backed up, allowing them in. "You're serious? No one knows this place." He glanced at Hughes. "Well, I suppose I'll have to burn it and move now."

"Honestly, I couldn't care less about your electronic forays. I deal with psionics." Hughes's eerie calm seemed to unsettle the man more.

Aaron offered a hand. "Always nice to meet a fan. Look, mate. I've a feeling some tosser's gone traipsing about your grey matter with a sledge. Mind if I 'ave a look see?"

"There's enough in here to get half the people in London wanting you dead for knowing." Orange fell into his chair, elbows on his knees.

"I ain't interested in your secrets." Aaron sat on the end of the Comforgel pad, facing him. Much to his pleasant surprise, Anna joined him. "Just hers."

"The place hasn't changed at all." Anna looked around.

"You have." Orange winked at her. "Now, I'd believe you were a competent operator. The entire way you carry yourself is different. Okay, Pryce. One condition. If someone *did* mess with my head, I want names. There won't be a rock on the planet or a colony world where he'll be able to hide."

Aaron stuck out his hand, and Orange took it. "Deal."

He leaned forward, staring at Mr. Orange's eyes until his perception slipped past them and into the man's thoughts. He concentrated on Anna in an effort to respect privacy. A Vid call between Orange and Anna struck him as odd. Anna's blasé reaction to him telling her he'd eradicated 'the video' confused him, though he could find no evidence of tampering there on Orange's side.

Chasing down the meaning of 'the video,' Aaron caught flashing memories of a paunchy slovenly bastard of a man pounding away on a rather unconscious Anna, who lay face down on a cheap bed, naked except for a set of holographic pixie wings.

He recoiled from the remembered video, racing ahead to a glimpse of Anna's reaction to learning Blake had not only raped her, but sold the recording of it across the GlobeNet. He pursued linked memories to a time burp a day later. Orange had lost an hour and change and hadn't noticed. After a short while of going over every thought, mood, scent, and sound occurring in the span of fifteen minutes before and after, Aaron realized the difference.

After the time burp, Mr. Orange believed he found evidence the man Anna killed was a CSB agent and not her real father. She hadn't asked him to look; it came out of nowhere.

Rage at what he had witnessed brought shaking to Aaron's hands as he dropped the telepathic link. "Hughes. Found it. Need a hand."

"Right." The CSB man walked over.

Orange shifted, uneasy. "What did you find?"

Aaron smiled. "Nothing too drastic. A tiny false memory implant. We can remove it if you like."

"What was it?" Orange scratched his head.

Anna stared at him. "You look about ready to kill someone."

"Aye, but no one here." Aaron covered his face in his hands and rubbed the fury away. "Okay… Looks like someone put a fragment in your memory that made you call Anna with a bit of bollocks."

She looked down. "Tell me."

"Are you sure you want to know?" He put an arm around her back, caution be damned.

"Alexi's a child. It's different." Anna's sapphire eyes glimmered in the light when she stared into his soul. "I'd rather a painful truth than a comfortable lie."

"I..." He glared at the rug. "I can't hate him for sparing you this."

Anna leaned into him. "How bad is it? Please, you have to tell me. I can't stand not knowing what's real and what isn't."

"Can you hold your emotions in check?" Aaron raised an eyebrow at Orange's impressive quad-deck cyberspace rig. "That's a few million credits you'll cook if you lose yourself."

Anna shivered. "It's that bad?"

"Aye. I want to kill some paunchy bastard."

She stopped shaking. "Blake?"

"No idea. Orange doesn't know the fat shit's name."

Anna's eyes gleamed. An image of a four-day unshaven face leering through a gap in a door manifested in his mind, along with Anna's shame of being looked at like a piece of meat.

"Aye, that's the fucker." Aaron clenched his hands into fists.

"He's already dead. I killed him for leavin' me locked in a cage overnight."

"Anna..." Aaron pulled her close, touching foreheads. *That's not why you killed him. He's made you forget.*

"Tell me," she said, her voice empty of life.

Aaron shot a look at Hughes and Orange before answering with telepathy. *That Blake chap... He... You were unconscious, face down on a wreck of a bed with blue wings.* He shuddered, trying to hold back the urge to smash something. *He took a holo-vid of what he did to you and sold it.*

She sat paralyzed; only the tears rolling down her face moved.

He clasped a hand over the back of her head and peered into her thoughts. The painful memory peeled like an onion, opening layer after layer. She had no conscious recollection of the assault, only of waking up naked in an alley. With the cork pulled, Anna recalled every detail of her return to Bristol City, every blubbering scream her lightning coaxed out of the fat man. Even Archon's implant couldn't keep its grip on her brain against the tidal wave of emotion crushing it.

"I-is that it?" Anna trembled, holding on to him.

The look she gave the floor showed no sign of shame or imminent sobbing. She appeared livid, and barely holding it in.

"Orange was programmed to tell you the man you killed was a CSB agent and not your real father."

Anna jumped up, looked around for a second, and tossed a brilliant arm-thick serpent of lightning into the bathroom. The smell of ozone grew staggering.

"What did that poor bog do?" asked Hughes.

"It was either that or everything within fifty meters of me." Anna shocked the toilet a second time. "You're saying I really did kill my father?"

"I'm saying Orange was programmed to say you didn't. I don't honestly know, but I would say yes given the circumstances."

"It's gone," said Hughes. "Little effort on this one. I don't think the person who did this expected us to track them here."

"Who did it?" Orange growled.

Aaron reluctantly looked away from Anna. "One moment."

Once more in Orange's mind, he searched for the moment of implantation. The white outline of a person made no appearance. The source of the false memory appeared to be a holographic male angel, face obscured by a white hood with metallic gold trim. Whoever it was had done it via a Vidphone call. Aaron pulled the image to the forefront of Orange's consciousness.

This is the bloke what did it. He got to you over the wire.

Orange's pupils dilated with fear.

There's only one person I've run into who can do that. Aaron took a breath. *I'm already after him. I need you to sit back and let me handle it. You are of no concern to him. He used you to control Anna.*

Aaron released the link and groaned, reaching for his NetMini. "Oi. Anyone want coffee?"

"Black," said Orange.

"Caramel latte with two extra shots," said Hughes.

Anna had her hands in front of her face as if praying.

With a grunt, Aaron stood and staggered over to her. "Anna?"

"I'm fine," she whispered.

"You don't look fine." He didn't risk touching her.

"I mean fine in the sense of I don't want coffee, twat." She looked at Orange. "Can you tell me who died at Number Six Woodseer Street about fifteen years ago? Freak 'sem accident."

Orange pulled a thin wire from one of the cyberspace decks and plugged it in behind his right ear. The machine's tiny lights betrayed a flurry of activity, though nothing appeared on any screen, nor did Orange seem to lapse into the far-off trance common to net jockeys. A moment later, Aaron's NetMini chirped. He answered the door to take coffee from a delivery bot. It glided off down the hall to a purpose-built hatch for bots, and disappeared. He gave the button a telekinetic poke to close the door, and carried the holder of coffee cups back to where everyone sat.

"Multitasker?" asked Hughes.

"Aye," said Orange, sounding a little distracted.

"He was trying to help me," whispered Anna. "All he wanted to do was help me."

Aaron couldn't tell if she spoke to him, or to herself. Rebutting her could prove disastrous to both of them, but letting her convince herself being used had been in her best interest seemed equally poor.

"Anna," he whispered, grasping her by the arms at the elbow. "I am certain he wanted to spare you the pain of that memory. Consider one thing."

She froze, staring at him.

"What if he thought you weak? What if he thought you'd be no use to him burdened by such guilt and pain? You saw what he did to Melissa's parents. They *wanted* her home, but he drove her away and made them terrified of their own daughter. Why?"

She pulled back, but he held her. "Stop it."

"Anna. Please think. The best lies are three-quarters truth. Penny and Spawny are the same situation. They were your ties here. He wanted you away from London."

"I..." She struggled as if to get away, but didn't try terribly hard at succeeding.

"You are a strong woman." Longing burned in his chest. He wanted to pull her close and hold her until the world ended. Fear kept him paralyzed. What if she ran? "You have to decide for yourself."

"I—" Anna gasped.

Aaron tracked her wide-eyed gaze to the image of a middle-aged man on one of the holo-terminals over the desk. A silvery-black scruff covered his face, and he had the general disheveled appearance one would expect from the sort of chap who toddled out of bars at two in the a.m.

"Andrew Morgan, age thirty-nine at the time of his death," said Orange. "Former employee of Harrington-Donner Associates, a junior account manager. His background is pretty boring, even for a stock trader. He was on the verge of being dismissed for tardiness when he was killed in a"—he coughed—"accidental electrocution in his home."

Anna sank to the floor. Aaron picked her up and guided her to sit on the bed, holding her up with an arm across her back.

"His wife, Heather Morgan, died at the age of twenty-three nine years prior. From what I can find, it looks like she was caught by a stray bullet from a gang turf war."

"That's bollocks," Anna whispered. "CSB."

Aaron glared at Hughes.

"I wasn't out of primary school then," said Hughes. "Besides, that was the Mi6 guys, operating under a project named Glass Derby. They always were too quick on the trigger. They're the sods who want to keep us all in boxes and poke us with needles."

"What bloody happened?" Aaron spoke through clenched teeth.

"Breeding program," said Anna. "My mother was a test subject. She escaped and ran away after the in-vitro. It took them three years to find her. No idea how they missed me."

"They didn't." Hughes pursed his lips. "Someone decided it would be a brilliant idea to 'observe you in the wild' and see how that affected the test. I don't think they planned on your dad turning into an abusive drunk."

Anna held on to Aaron, not that he minded.

"Why didn't they intervene when he got out of control? The man could've killed her." Aaron yelled.

"Buggered if I know." Hughes sighed. "Probably wanted to see how she'd react."

"Did I pass that test?" Anna snapped.

Hughes studied the carpet.

"Look, I think we've imposed on Mr. Orange for quite long enough." Aaron patted her on the back. "Perhaps we should take our leave."

"What about my bog?" asked Orange, scratching his head.

"What about Ol' Jack?" Anna folded her hands in her lap. "He was always so protective of me; then out of nowhere, he thought I was a threat. Was he CSB or was he tinkered with?"

"Lieutenant Jack Evans, formerly with His Majesty's Special Air Services," said Orange. "Transferred to Mi4 for a few years before winding up in the employ of Mi6 and later the CSB."

Anna slouched.

"We'll take care of the bog," said Hughes.

"Hang on. I'm going to need to go full in for this one." Orange plugged a second cable in behind his other ear and went limp over the back of his chair.

Aaron held her, no longer caring what she thought of him as much as trying to comfort her. Hughes flipped pages on the screen of his NetMini, offering a useless shrug after a few minutes.

Orange sat up without warning. "Buggers have some security on that node." Both wires fell out of his head, ejected by auto-prongs. "Seems like Ol' Jack had an attack of conscience. After two other volunteer project mothers had their babies and vanished under mysterious circumstances, he broke your mum out of her secure hospital room and helped her escape the facility."

"Miracle the chap's still alive," said Aaron.

"A man like that is nothing if not methodical." Orange went to the window to let a delivery bot in. "If I was in his position, I'd have gathered as much dirt as I could on the operation before going rogue. Then, told my former bosses if they came near me I'd blast it to the NN."

Aaron laughed. "The NewsNet would've had a damn orgasm with that information."

"He felt guilty over mum." Anna blasted the toilet again. Bits of porcelain clattered to the tile floor. "Sorry. Cheaper than the rigs."

"Much appreciated," said Orange, as he handed out coffees.

"I can write off the bog," said Hughes.

"He watched over me out of guilt. Because he couldn't save my mother."

Aaron put a hand on her shoulder. In the span of a second and a half, he thought of and discarded a handful of things to say, all sounding horrible in his head.

Anna sniffled and stared up at him with red-ringed eyes. *Archon made him afraid of me, didn't he?*

"Cut all ties." Aaron patted her on the back. "He wanted you for himself."

EXILED AGAIN

Althea

Ripples of blurry air surrounded Kate; the heat wafting from her body made Althea lean away, clinging to Shepherd's side. She glared at Hector with a mixture of rage and pity. The man had caused all this death, and once again threatened Karina, but she did not want him to die. His friends' anger had faded. As soon as her clothing flash burned, Kate had filled them with the same emotion raiders gave off during wifeing.

Hector, on the other hand, couldn't take his stare away from Althea, enraged to the point he didn't feel human anymore. She forced calm over him, sapping the hate from his sneer. She had to believe Father had protected Karina. Conflict gripped her heart. In addition to the people around her, at least one more had probably died in Querq. Her hope the assassin who tried to kill Karina had been killed (instead of her sister) made her feel ashamed. She clung to the possibility that Father may have only wounded the man.

"You miss your brother so much, asshole?" Kate hauled her arm back, fireball in hand. "Let me set up a meeting."

"No!" screamed Althea. "Please don't! There is too much dying."

Hector's friends stared at the fireball, lust withering to fear in an instant. They all made the sign of the cross, dropped their rifles, and ran.

Althea let go of Shepherd and reached for Kate's arm. She drew back before contact, due to the heat. "Please don't kill him. That's what *it* wants."

"Sorry, Althea." Kate narrowed her eyes. "I know you did something to my head. You're like my daughter, and this son of a bitch tried to kill you. If you hadn't asked for me to come out here with you"—Kate shuddered, trails of steam wisped from the corners of her eyes—"you'd be dead. Blown to pieces. I'm going to melt this cocksucker's skin off."

Althea tamped down Kate's fury. "I'm sorry. I wanted to protect you from the Sentience."

"It's okay." Kate blinked, looking confused by her sudden calm. "I honestly don't mind, but this shithead is going to burn."

Estevez, Garcia, and Hernandez muttered amongst themselves, debating shooting Hector. Garcia held them off since Althea had asked.

"Rachel said some people deserve to die." She looked up from the ground to Hector. "I don't think he is evil."

Nelson groaned and sat up, leaning on the guardrail. He clamped his hand over the bullet wound in his arm. Althea looked at him.

He pointed at the ravine. "I'm okay, Miguel first."

"He is." Shepherd's hand engulfed Althea's left shoulder. "Look what he did to Miguel, just to draw you out here. Montez is dead. Those men he convinced to help him are dead. He sent another man to murder your sister. That is evil."

Althea reached across her chest to put her hand on Shepherd's. "Hector shot Karina once. She almost died. I got angry and hurt him, but it was wrong. Pain does not fix pain." She looked up at him. "When Karina almost died, I knew how Hector felt about Emilio. I am sad I could not save him, but I didn't know I could."

Fire in Kate's hands fluttered in the stillness.

"Why didn't you help Emilio?" wailed Hector.

"He was dead, shithead," screamed Kate.

"So was the ox." Hector pointed at Shepherd.

"Emilio died when raiders attacked." Althea stared at the ground, grinding a toe into the dirt. "The Sentience made them go to Querq. He wanted to hurt me. I do not blame Hector for thinking Emilio's death was my fault. I didn't know I could bring him back."

"Not sure you could have," mumbled Kate. "I think Shep only happened because you considered him a friend and you felt responsible, as if you'd killed him."

"Only works on family, eh?" Hector twitched and stole a glance at his mangled hand. "I'd love to test that."

"I wanna help everyone. Bad people wanted to control me." She stood tall, reining back the water leaking from her eyes. "I won't let them do it anymore. Hector, you have hate because the Sentience feeds on you. I do not hate you. Please don't have angry at me."

Althea looked at the ground. A weak moan emanated from the bottom of the ravine. She gasped and hurried to the edge, gazing down at Miguel. Despite the distance, she felt his life slipping.

"Shep?" asked Kate, letting the fire go out.

"Yeah?"

"Can I borrow your shirt?"

He reached for the flannel's buttons. "Uhh, sure."

Hector let off a bellow of anger, tearing a machete from his belt with his left hand and charging. He roared at Althea with the blade over his head. Blood sprayed from the ruin of his right hand as he ducked under hasty shots from the uninjured Watch. Althea whirled to face the oncoming madman, stunned for an instant by the sheer rage in his eyes. A second later, she gathered the presence of mind to focus her power.

"*Stop!*" she yelled, her eyes flaring bright.

The rush lost speed, but not before Shepherd lunged into a punch, and drove his fist into the skinny man's sternum. Hector's feet swept forward off the ground; his shins smacked him in the forehead as he wrapped around the huge arm. The machete slipped from his fingers and sailed past Althea, skittering across the dirt before going over the edge. Hector hit the ground on his back and slid a few meters, wheezing.

"Bastard!" shrieked Kate. "Don't you touch her!"

Fire streamed from her outstretched hands, covering Hector, who emitted a strained gargle, still breathless from the massive punch. She shrieked in anger, and the burn built into a conflagration ten feet high. Althea clutched her chest as the frigid prickling grasp of a departing life swam over her. Seconds later, Kate relaxed, panting. Only a char mark in the dirt bearing a vague resemblance to a human figure remained of Hector. Even his bones were gone.

"Well damn," said Shepherd, both eyebrows up.

"She made me feel like her mother. What does she expect me to do when some piece of shit tries to kill her?" Kate slumped forward, hands on her knees and out of breath. "I'm sorry Thea. I know you said you didn't want him to die. Sometimes you're just too damn nice for your own good."

Althea's lip quivered. She shivered, sniffled, and fought the urge to cry. No one said anything about her shedding tears over someone who had done such awful things, exchanging silent glances instead.

She knew they thought her foolish, but also respected the way she considered all life sacred.

Eyes downcast, she started to turn toward the ravine, but stopped at the appearance of a malignant presence on the road. A shadow exuded from Hector's ashes, taking on the shape of a decrepit old man in a leather coat and wide brimmed hat.

He smiled a ruin of kelp-colored teeth at her, tipped his hat, and faded away.

DOWN CAME THE LIGHT

Althea

Cold air blew past, teasing Althea's hair. She narrowed her eyes at the
gale, steeling herself against any potential attack. Nothing happened.
Kate slipped into Shepherd's flannel shirt, which hung down to her
knees, her hands hidden in the huge sleeves. Estevez and Hernandez did what
they could to prepare Montez's remains for transport back to Querq.

Althea peered over the edge at Miguel, who'd stopped moving. She gasped;
it felt as though his life would slip away at any second.

The rope will take too long. She crept to the edge until her toes curled over
the crumbling dirt. *My legs will break, but I can mend them. I can't let him die.*

Driven by the need to help Miguel, Althea jumped. Kate's scream startled a
pair of buzzards into the air. She stared at Miguel's prostrate form
approaching fast, eager to get close enough to help him. Althea gathered her
power into herself, attempting to strengthen her body for impact. At the same
instant, an instinctive urge not to fall came out of nowhere, siphoning off the
energy she tried to send into her legs.

A warm feeling washed over her back, and her plummet slowed.
Glimmering ribbons of pure white energy burst from her shoulder blades,
spreading out seven feet to either side. They took on the general silhouette of
wings and, despite being made of light, caught the air like a parachute.

Her feet touched down at Miguel's side without pain, and she knelt.

"La ángel a venido por mi," whispered Miguel, as he fainted.

Althea ignored this bizarre new development, paying little attention to the canopy of light shrouding them. She ripped at his shirt until she could get her hands on his skin, and sent a surge of power into his body. First, she commanded his mind to ignore pain.

The life-shapes appeared in the blackness of her closed eyes. Broken bones, burst blobs in the middle, and two cracks along his backbone. She forced him to regrow in places to stop the blood-shape from flowing where it didn't belong, and tended to the blobs next. Pangs of fatigue clawed at her as she urged things back to the way they should be.

Minutes passed in the silent darkness of shifting red, beige, and black shapes before a crunch of boot on gravel registered in her mind. It sounded miles away, but she knew someone approached close by. She sensed concern and awe.

"Please straighten his legs."

Miguel moved, though not of his doing. When the legs untwisted from the pose he had landed in, she channeled her power into the bones. She saved the spine for last, urging the delicate tendrils inside out of the way as the cracked ring-like parts mended.

When she could do no more for him, she opened her eyes and slouched, kneeling in the dirt.

Shepherd loomed over her, his bare arms and neck covered in a sheen of sweat and dust, his sleeveless undershirt smeared with dirt. Her 'wings' were gone, and she spent a moment staring at the space they had once occupied, frightened and confused by what had happened to her.

"How is he?" asked Shepherd. "Is it safe to move him?"

"He is not hurt, but he will be very hungry." Althea couldn't stop from yawning, and her stomach murmured. "And tired."

Shepherd picked Miguel up as if he were a boy, and draped him over his right shoulder. He scooped Althea to his chest. She threaded her arms around his neck.

"Can you hold on?"

She squeezed herself tight to him. The motion of his ascent all but rocked her to sleep by the time hands slid under her armpits from behind. She looked back at Kate, who peeled her away from Shepherd as Estevez and Hernandez took Miguel so the big man could haul himself up over the edge. The woman radiated guilt, and couldn't look her in the eye.

"What is wrong?" Althea yawned again.

"I think I know why you're so... innocent." Kate dropped to her knees. "I'm sorry I killed him. Please forgive me."

Althea pulled on Kate's arm. "Please don't kneel at me."

Kate got up.

"Hector had the hate, but not like you did. Your hate came from having the sad. He wanted to be important, to be bigger than others. He would never have stopped trying to hurt people I love. You want to protect me. I... understand. It is like how I had the anger when he shot Karina. I do not have to like that he is dead, but I do not blame you."

Sensing a hurt, Althea slipped a hand under the borrowed shirt that covered the woman like a dress. Kate's skin remained hot to the touch, but not painful. Althea concentrated and mended the bruise as well as a crack in her rib.

Kate wheezed.

"What... was that light?" asked Garcia as she wandered over, helping Nelson walk. "Did that just happen?"

"I thought 'little angel' was just a metaphor," rasped Nelson. *"Dios mío, somos bendecidos."*

Althea forced a smile. "I don't know. A man in the bad city called me that too. He thought I was there to take everyone to some place called Heaven and make the world stop."

Awkward silence. The adults exchanged glances.

"I'm not." Althea smiled. "I don't even know what Heaven is."

Relief spread over the Watch. Kate stared at the ancient paved road, guilt in her eyes. Shepherd gazed into the clouds, as if deep in thought. Althea touched Nelson's arm by the bullet hole, sensing a tunnel through from one side to the next and a chip displaced from the bone-shape. She mended it and forced his body to generate more blood. After, she knelt by the horse and concentrated until repairing muscles forced the bullet out.

The overjoyed animal stood and nuzzled her.

When she tried to open her eyes, they refused to budge. Her legs went numb and she noticed herself falling only after she collapsed at Shepherd's feet.

Shepherd picked her up and cradled her. "You need rest."

He set off toward Querq, carrying her. Her legs dangled over his right elbow, feet flopping about with each stride. She lacked the energy to do much of anything but lay limp in his arms. Kate walked at his left, surrounded by a cloud of regret. Althea peeked up at her, trying to offer a consoling expression. The woman's emotion deepened. Nelson and Hernandez carried Montez a few meters back, while Garcia led the horse and Estevez lent his shoulder to help Miguel stumble home.

"Guess it wasn't a dream," said Shepherd.

"Mmm?" Althea mumbled.

"When you called me back. I saw you with those wings, floating over me. I figured my head was playing games on me."

"Mmm," muttered Althea. "Aurora said a part of me is from another place. I don't know."

Althea let her head lean against his chest and shut her eyes. In an instant, desolate road became the inside of Querq by the gate. She blinked, realizing she'd fallen asleep. Father pushed past a group of Watch, muttering sharp, rapid commands to people in his way. Karina trailed after him, screaming her name. Her sister radiated fear as soon as she saw Shepherd carrying her.

"What happened?" Father took her hand.

"She is exhausted," said Shepherd.

"I'm sorry about Montez," mumbled Althea to the spinning world. "I couldn't..."

"It was Hector," said Kate, her guilt swirled into anger. "The bastard had a bomb waiting for her. He almost—"

"Yeah, damn lucky it was a dud," said Shepherd. "Looked like an old claymore mine, centuries old."

"Probably repacked with new explosives," said a man Althea couldn't place.

"It wasn't a dud," whispered Kate. "I uhh... stopped it."

"No way in hell that thing should've been functional," said Shepherd.

"*He* wanted it to work," whispered Althea.

Father plucked her from Shepherd's arms and squeezed a squeak out of her. "I will kill him."

"You can't," said Althea.

"No, child. He's gone too far this time. He will answer for what he has done." Father kissed her atop the head. "Even you cannot give me a reason not to rid this world of his filth."

"Too late," mumbled Kate.

Althea's voice faded to a whisper no one noticed. Her thoughts drifted back to The Many standing on the road, smiling at her as he absorbed Hector's soul. "He's not alive."

Miguel, stuffing his face with empanadas, walked over and patted her on the head. "Bless you, child." He bowed to Father. "You have a little angel there."

"*Si*," said Father.

"Yeah... we do," said Kate.

Althea summoned a weak smile, and surrendered to the urge to sleep.

LOOSE ENDS

Anna

The image Mamoru had found of her mother lying dead in the street haunted Anna's thoughts. In the middle of Orange's flat, she broke down and sobbed. Aaron pulled her close and held on. Orange shifted uneasily in his chair as if trying to remain between her and his network rig. Hughes meandered to the far end of the apartment with his attention absorbed by his NetMini.

What's real? I don't know what's real anymore.

Her father's angry glower rose out from the miasma of her daydream. Twinges in her face and arms echoed where his fist had come down.

Daddy, stop! Her twelve-year-old voice screamed in her memory.

When he hit her again, she lashed out. She'd sat on the floor, staring at his corpse for an hour. The police had shown up before she dared to move, and considered her a traumatized witness to a bizarre kitchen mishap. Anna hadn't lied about being beaten, but she claimed a misaimed punch striking the food assembler had caused his death. Any trace of guilt she projected, she explained away as blaming herself for ducking. If she hadn't ducked, he'd still be alive. Being tiny got her picked on at school, but it also made the cops trust her. She'd been twelve, but they mistook her for nine.

Old Bill had bought the story.

What else would they have believed?

"What am I?" Anna's voice emerged on autopilot.

"Alive, and with friends," whispered Aaron. "Don't try to make sense of it all at once. Bit by bit."

The glow from the NetMini ceased painting Agent Hughes's face bright green, returning his cheeks to pale normality. He pocketed the device and walked over. Anna glanced up at him, feeling foolish for bawling like a schoolgirl in front of three men. Even if she had recently learned she *did* murder her father.

"I don't have all the details, but I was able to find some records concerning the initiative that resulted in your birth." Orange paused for a breath. "Designated Project Seraph, Mi6 experimented on psionics detained in the interests of national security. Genetic material was harvested and matched with an interest in weaponization. The Crown did not so much want to eradicate psionics as they wished to keep them away from the public eye while using them for their own purposes. Seraph was a breeding program intended to create a pool of gifted operatives. Unfortunately, their attempts to engineer a desired ability set in babies failed miserably."

"Probably had something to do with locking them in their rooms," said Aaron. "Tends to make people a little testy."

"They killed the mothers?" Anna glanced at Orange.

"I'm afraid Mr. Orange there found one of the honeypot data nodes. You may want to check for malicious softs, friend. Only your mother decided to flee. Your friend Jack misinterpreted their clandestine relocation as being eliminated. Mi6 had no interest in 'squandering' loyal resources. The other women, and a few of their offspring, are still active agents. Some are even on board with our agenda."

Orange swiveled around and plugged into his rig.

Anna's glare hardened. "I'm going to kill the man who murdered her."

"He's already dead," said Hughes. "Agent Allan Charles was found in his flat dead of an apparent heart attack. The Bureau wouldn't have thought much of it if not for a breach into our network traced back to UCF military intelligence. Our general suspicion is that he was assassinated by a C-Branch operative, but we have no proof."

Mamoru said he would kill him for me. I wonder how he managed that one.

"I'm sorry, Anna." Hughes sighed. "Not even the PM knew about Project Seraph. When your mother escaped, it attracted attention and the project was scuttled. Since it failed to produce quantifiable results, no one bothered fighting the decision to shut it down. Of a dozen babies, only three were psionic—including you, and they were unable to predict or selectively breed desired abilities."

Aaron squeezed her shoulder. "Guess you hogged all the good genes."

She smirked at Aaron before sending a pleading stare at Hughes. "If those two girls want to come home, can you keep watch on them? You're certain they won't be shut away?"

"Seems a bit of a roundabout, considering we smuggled them out... but if you are certain it's what they want. Aye, they'll be monitored, but not detained."

"Neither of them are Awakened. I doubt ol' Mardling will protest." Aaron chuckled.

Anna clamped her hands over her stomach to fight the knot of discomfort. James had pulled her out of the gutter, protected her, brought her back from... "Zoom."

"Oi, what?" asked Aaron.

"Not again," muttered Orange. "Mind the shit, awful business that."

"No, I don't want it." Anna stood. "That's what I was on. Zoom. I couldn't remember the bloody name of it."

"How do you forget a thing like that?" Orange spun his chair to face her and raised an eyebrow.

"Don't' ask." Aaron smiled.

James wanted me to break ties with everything I knew in London. She swallowed hard, thinking of Faye. *Did he mess with her as well?*

"What now then?" Aaron got up. "We should probably get back before we're missed."

"In a hurry?" Anna found herself blushing when she made eye contact.

"I need to meet someone."

"That man from the playground?" Anna bit her lower lip. *The police bigwig.*

"Aye." He gave her a look like a lost puppy.

She glanced at the katanas hanging on the wall over the desk. Aaron looked vulnerable at that moment. If he was meeting with that man again, his status as an *ex*-cop seemed tenuous at best. It might be possible they remained mere friends, but if that were true, why the pleading stare? No, that look asked her not to tell Archon. He had to be suicidal to challenge the man. As comforting as James had been to her, he could also be terrifying. Anna rubbed her hand where the chopstick had pierced; she'd rather not see his cold side again. James wasn't the sort of man to suffer threats. *With us or against us.*

Anna made eye contact with that same forlorn look; his expression hadn't changed. *Why?*

He reached out and took her hand. His touch sent a tingle up her arm and down her body. *I had to protect you.*

She fidgeted. *He's not an evil man.*

Aaron's eyes twitched. *After everything you've seen? Ask him about Venezuela. Seventy some odd people sacrificed to the local military so he could recruit a handful of psionics.*

That can't be possible. Anna shivered, thinking of the scientists in the Timmons-Orben building. James did seem perturbed at her protest of killing them all. A faint tickle in her brain gave away Aaron eavesdropping on her thoughts.

A block of sweet... He squeezed her hand. *I knew it. You couldn't kill them.*

Her father's face jumped back into her mind. *I am a killer.*

You defended yourself.

She fidgeted and stared at her boots.

Aaron wandered to the nearest trash flap and dropped his empty coffee cup into the wall. A faint electronic hum signified its molecular disassembly. "We should be going."

"Shall we continue to direct newcomers to you?" asked Agent Hughes.

How can I do that to more people? Anna lifted her gaze to Hughes' chest, picking at her coat. A disruption in the status quo would set James off. Chopsticks had been a demonstration, what would he do if he became angry? "I suppose, but can you make sure they want to first?"

She followed Aaron to the door, hesitating as he stepped onto the porch.

"Coming?" He offered a weak smile.

"You go on ahead. I'd like some more time with Pen... and there's one more stop I need to make in London."

NO ONE WALKS AWAY

Kate

Kate's scream filled her mind along with the image of Althea leaping from the cliff. She remembered rushing over, as if she could somehow have stopped the child from getting hurt. Kate had skidded to a halt at the edge, dirt between her toes, only to find Althea gliding on glimmering wings of light. Energy radiating from the girl had left her transfixed and staring, unable to move or process what she watched.

Awe and shame had stolen her words.

Every so often, the reality of the present intruded on the repeating daydream. Sunday afternoon on the way back to civilization. The scent of sun-warmed plastic mixing with cologne. A Division 0 patrol craft flying twenty feet off the ground, Officer David Ahmed at the controls. Kate's fingers teased at her chest where Hector's bullet had bruised her.

Kate twisted her plain white shirt. *He'll think I've lost it.*

Her weight pressed harder into the seat. The sand brown blur in the window to her right changed to sky as the car climbed higher. She looked up from her lap at the expanse of West City ahead on the horizon. Even from miles away, the streaming glow of hovercar lanes stood out against the dark shapes of buildings.

"The last time I felt that emotion on someone, they were on their way into an interrogation room."

Kate rolled and unrolled fabric between her fingers. "David?"

"Hmm?"

"Do you believe ghosts?" She glanced sideways at him.

He tilted his head as if pondering. "Not if I think they're lying."

A hint of a smile played on her lips. "I mean *in* ghosts."

"Well, I've met some people who did. Handful of them say there's even one wandering around the PAC. A dead officer too."

"The admin center probably has more than one." Kate shivered. "So is that a yes?"

"It's a 'who knows.'" He leaned on the throttle as they shot over the wall, urging a grunt out of her as he made an abrupt cut right and up to join an aerial traffic lane. If they weren't in a police vehicle, the driver behind them surely would've blared on the horn. "I've seen enough to keep my mind open. Is that what's bothering you? You think you saw a ghost?"

She flattened the shirt on her stomach and smoothed her hands over the soft, black slacks she'd gotten from the Querq outpost.

"Was it someone you killed?"

The question made her cringe, despite his calm. He hadn't said it a way that sounded harsh, more concerned than accusing. He followed up with a reassuring non-judgmental smile. Taillights glowed ahead from a ripple-slowdown. An advert bot crept by, trailing a six-foot tall holographic cup of coffee.

"No." She rubbed her face with one hand before sliding it up and over her head, raking her fingers through her hair. "You're going to think I'm crazy."

"Why don't you let me be the judge of that?" He set the car to automatic and took her hand. "Or are you afraid I'll run off?"

Kate squeezed his fingers, her face warmed with blush at the sparkle in his dark eyes. "If there's ghosts, there's gotta be other things, right? Like..." She glanced up and down.

"Demons? You're saying you saw a demon." David raised an eyebrow.

"Not exactly. I'm"—Kate waved her right hand about in frustration—"not the least bit sure what I saw, but she isn't a demon." She pulled his arm close, staring at him. "Take a peek."

She let the memory replay, gripping his hand tighter at the wave of emotion that hit her when the ribbons of energy burst from the child's back.

David blinked. "Angel?"

"That was my first guess too, but I don't believe in that shit."

"It's gotta be some kind of psionic ability no one has seen before." David's eyebrows wiggled back and forth, conjuring the image of an idea rolled side to side inside his skull. "I keep hearing this term 'Awakened' brought up. We barely know anything about what they are capable of."

Kate couldn't handle the faces he made any longer; she covered her mouth and let the giggles take over. Buildings slipped past as the patrol craft flew along a canyon of plastisteel and silver glass.

"I don't want to complicate that kid's life any more than it already is," said David. "Maybe I'll try to talk to her about it later in the week when I rotate back out there."

"I can't explain the way it felt when she did that." Kate bit her lip. "It was like she just *knew* all the bad things I've ever done and rather than hate or scold me for it, just felt sad for me. That made it so much worse. I feel like such an evil, horrible bitch."

"You're anything but."

I'm still thinking of going after that Pryce guy too. Another kill for the Syndicate. She clenched her hands into fists. *If I don't, they'll kill me. No, El Tío couldn't do that... he cared for me. I can't let him down. What did Aurora mean by not to worry about it?*

"Please stop feeling so guilty." David squeezed her knee. "That's the way she is. Doesn't mean she's anything more than a sweet person."

Kate smirked at him. "No one is *that* sweet."

"You shouldn't dwell on it. We know the girl left a permanent emotional imprint on your brain. We don't know what other effects that could have."

"I *did* go there to kill her." Kate swallowed hard. "She thinks I was possessed. Maybe I was. Maybe I *did* see a demon."

David waited for a stiff leftward turn to end before trying to speak. "I've heard the stories from the locals."

"I met him." Kate scowled. "If he's real, I'm inclined to think angels are too, but it doesn't make sense."

"Oh, it doesn't?" David grinned. "Angels and demons not making sense, as long as we're clear."

"I mean it." She slapped at his arm playfully. "She's alive. She's a kid, not some supernatural creature."

"You're overthinking it. Don't feel guilty." He let go of her hand to take manual control again. "She's obviously forgiven your trespasses."

"You're not going to let this go, are you?" Kate laughed.

"Not for a bit."

"You don't think she's an angel, do you?"

"I think she's a person, like you or I... well, maybe more like you than me, but no literal angel." He slowed and dove out of the hovercar lane. "Heck, maybe she had one in the family a generation or two back."

"Now you're being silly."

He brought the car in for a landing on the roof of her apartment building, slipping in under an awning and setting down close to the elevators. "I don't think you're nuts, though, and we're here."

She tugged at the door, which hissed upward. "Coming in?"

"Drat, and I was hoping to kill the rest of my Sunday evening doing reports at my desk... Just let me put this thing in a space and I'll be right in."

Kate hopped out and stretched.

"Kate!" shouted David. "Get—"

She whirled at his sudden yell; threads of infrared laser light, invisible to the eye, flickered on the patrol craft's electronic windscreen. Before she could think, muzzle flash erupted from the windows of a white luxury hovercar at the far end of the parking area. Intense heat washed over her body as impacts peppered her chest. The stink of scorched fabric and liquefied metal assaulted her nose. Her legs buckled at the pain of a half-dozen punches, dumping her on her back. Bare skin met the scratchy traction coating over cold plastisteel panels.

Naked again.

Heavy liquid seeped over her ribs, dribbling past her armpits to the ground. More gathered in her navel. Molten lead, neither hot nor cold to her touch, got into places she never wanted molten lead to touch. The low hum of David's E-90 firing came in time with bright blue light. Althea had repaired the cracked rib and massive bruise Hector's pistol had left on her chest, but getting shot again in almost the same place hurt enough to paralyze her breathless for a few seconds.

"Officer down, request immediate backup to my location," yelled David, firing again.

Something exploded in the distance. Kate *felt* the burst of combustion. She didn't have to look at it to will it larger. A flare of warmth washed over her.

"God dammit!" Kate screamed, despite the pain. "Twice in two fucking days."

She sat up, sending the dense pool on her stomach over her lap to the ground. Men in expensive suits scattered about, crawling away from the flaming hovercar. Another laser blast came from her left. It hit a man in the back; the fatal shot left a tiny ring of fire around the hole.

Kate lunged to her feet, willed a blue fireball into her hand, and flung it at the closest armed man. He ignited like a firework, rolling back and forth while screaming. Her mind reached into the energy of the blazing wreck, drawing forth a serpentine mass of incineration, which she rained down on another three.

A bullet slapped her in the shoulder, bursting like a tiny water balloon with the force of a robotic fist. She stumbled backward against the freezing patrol craft, and immolated a man with a pistol ten paces to her right.

Two figures scrambled for cover behind a thick wall of dark smoke rising from the extinguished sedan. A dark-skinned man with silver metal clips every half-inch amid cornrow-braided hair popped out from behind the wall at the end of the elevator bank. A flat, black metal plate covered most of his face, featureless save for a tiny red light blinking between his eyes.

He squeezed the trigger of a submachine gun, spraying bright silver rips in the charcoal-grey ground where ricochets tore up the traction coating. One slug hit her on the top of the left foot, another in the shin, and the third got her in the hip before the recoil pulled his aim up over her head. All three bullets splashed away, molten. Somewhere behind and above, a sharp *clang* preceded the sputtering of a wounded advert bot.

Kate gasped as though someone in heavy boots had stomped on her bare foot and whacked her in the leg with a police baton. She focused the pain into anger and centered it on the weapon in his hand. All the propellant in the oversized magazine exploded, pulping his right arm halfway to the elbow in a spray of red. He stared in horror at the blood oozing from the stump. She threw a fireball straight into his chest, still managing to hit him despite hopping on one leg.

David fired through the wall; the laser pierced the man's head, sending a blast of steaming gore out his eye sockets.

"Uhh, command?" said David. "We're gonna need a Div 2 crime scene unit."

Kate looked across the roof at him. He'd opened the door out to the side, off its usual up-down travel, and taken a firing position behind it. A faint voice from inside the patrol craft said something she couldn't make out. She stumbled forward, limping and brushing the huge bruise covering her front while tossing fist-sized fireballs at random into the corpses. She hoped at least one faked death so they'd feel it. She recognized some of the bodies. Her anger kept her warm, despite her incinerating another outfit.

Syndicate.

"Kate? Are you hurt?"

She spat blood. "Broke another fucking rib. Maybe two. They torched my fucking clothes again."

A shoe crunched on debris ahead and to the right. She looked up from the purpling marks on her skin at two huge men creeping out of a hanging cloud of smoke, both with full-length assault rifles.

Paul and Leo—El Tío's leg breakers.

Her former friends.

Leo stared into her eyes, fear plain on his face. Paul looked at the ground, guilt obvious on his. Old daydreams of Paul, and the usual jokes about how well-endowed he was came to mind. For a while, she'd fancied him; he'd been the fuel for her roaming fingers. In an odd way, she found it amusing how meticulous he was about keeping his flattop afro perfect. The idea of killing him, or his being willing to return the favor, hit her like a gut punch.

"What the fuck is this?" Kate's body trembled.

"Uhh," said Paul, lowering his rifle. "El Tío said you'd become a risk."

Leo twitched. "We're supposed to get the cop as well."

"I'm still looking for Pryce. I haven't walked away." Kate flicked beads of molten lead off her breast. Had she betrayed El Tío? *I tried to tell him I can't kill for him anymore. I didn't say no. Pryce is a goddamn ghost. I can't find him. All this time, I believed he thought of me as a daughter...* She gazed around at the carnage and sighed. "Guess not."

"Huh?" asked Paul.

"Drop your weapons," yelled David. "Now."

A tingle of psionic activity happened behind and to her left. David had to be tweaking their emotions, intensifying fear and guilt. He didn't want to kill them. Kate smiled. He was too nice.

Bang.

Smoke peeled from the barrel of a handgun, wobbling in the grip of one of the men lying near the smoldering wreck. David let out a yelp and collapsed. Kate screamed with fury and pain, channeling it into the shooter. His body convulsed and gurgled; the handgun went off twice more, striking nothing but distant glass. Blisters formed and burst all over his back and face, as boiling blood and body fluids sought release. His final attempt to scream in agony emerged as a rush of steaming, brick red ooze. If the amount of pain a person experienced in death meant anything, some astral sensate would be in for a hell of a ride.

Kate ran to David. He lay on his back, E-90 a few inches from his hand. He looked shocked and confused, blood trailing from the corners of his mouth. Kate pawed at him, frantic until her hand found a sticky, wet patch on the right side of his chest.

Blood on a black uniform.

He wheezed. Kate ignored Paul and Leo, grabbing at his belt for the case of stimpaks. Nervous fingers fumbled to pull the safety caps off the ends; she gave up and bit them, spitting the yellow plastic aside. After emptying five autoinjectors into him, she fell on top of him.

"David!" She fought the urge to sob. "David!"

When his hand closed on hers, she burst into sobs.

Her relief evaporated at the sound of an incoherent roar. Kate whipped her head around and perched on top of David, glaring like a lioness guarding her mate. Leo broke away from Paul, who had tried to hold him back, and charged at her.

The huge man was on her before she could gather her wits or a fireball. He grabbed her in a crushing embrace, catching her attempt to leap away. She kicked at the air as he hauled her off her feet and whirled her around. As if controlling where she pointed would matter, he clamped his hands about her wrists and forced her arms across her chest. She gasped from a crushing embrace that drove the air from her lungs. Her foot landed on the cold fender of the patrol craft; she pushed but didn't have enough strength to move him.

Leo kept howling, spittle raining on her head as he twisted away from the car. She pedaled her legs at nothing, her mind unable to process an idea more complex than the need to get air into lungs that couldn't move. Her desire to get away from him activated her Pyrokinesis. Leo's suit erupted in flames as her body superheated. Molten skin peeled like cheese from Leo's hands, sticking to her forearms when he screamed and jumped away, swatting at his burning suit. Kate caught herself before her ass hit the ground, landing in an awkward crabwalk pose. She leaned onto her knees and brought her hands up to defend herself in case he rushed again.

Strands of charred flesh on her arms turned to wisps of ash. Leo held his arms up in the pose of a doctor washing before surgery, gazing in horror at the exposed muscles and tendons. Traction coating melted away from wherever she touched, her toes smearing it away like wet paint from shiny metal. Kate stood, circling around him, leaving a trail of chrome footprints on black.

"What the fuck, Leo? Why are you doing this?" Wanting to cry and kill him at the same time left her doing neither. "What happened?"

"If you're not with us, you're against us," he muttered, still staring at his hands.

Kate let her body cool. Naked on the roof of her apartment building, she shivered from the freezing wind.

"Influence," whispered David, struggling to sit up.

Distant sirens grew louder. Leo lifted his gaze. As soon as he looked at her, his expression went from horrified to murderous beyond reason. Kate drew her hand back to kill him, but Althea filled her thoughts. The child wouldn't want her to kill. Leo tensed as if to charge. Kate backed off, holding her hands up.

"Don't do it, Leo." She took another step back.

He leaned forward; streams of blood dribbled off his fingers as he raised his arms. Before he could charge, Paul came out of nowhere and tackled him. The men rolled to a halt a few meters away. Kate's eyes narrowed in twitches, keeping time with meaty thuds as Paul punched Leo unconscious. His tight, curly hair glistened from where Leo's blood covered it. He refused to look at her.

Kate crouched at David's side and took his hand. He stared at Paul.

Flashing lights flooded the area, red and blue mixing to violet; at least ten Division 1 patrol craft swooped in and landed, armored officers spilling out. Some ran to the corpses by the blown-out hovercar, others rounded the front of David's patrol craft with weapons raised. The sight of her nude form huddled over him seemed to stall them in their tracks. Four officers focused their attention at Paul. Two holstered their sidearms; one moved to Kate, while the other put in a comm call for a medical unit. The female officer took a knee. A faint line of bright green light ran down the silver visor on her helmet.

"Thought you were a vic… Officer Solomon? What happened to your uniform?"

"David needs a MedVan," she rasped, letting the officer ease her upright and away from him. "Off duty… clothes. I got shot."

"Looks like you could use a medic, too," said the patrol cop. A static chirp cut off the last syllable of her words. "New to the force? Yanno, getting shot doesn't usually cause people to go streaking."

"Does getting shot usually cause bruises?" Kate coughed up some blood.

Pain burst out from under her fading adrenaline, her hypervigilance eased by the security of cops everywhere. She froze, blinked, and laughed. *When did having cops around go from scary to making me feel safe?* As soon as she laughed, she regretted it. Every bullet bruise ached.

Another officer approached and wrapped a plain, grey blanket around her from behind.

The female officer guided her to rest against the Division 0 patrol craft. "Is he your TO?"

Kate held the cloth tight around herself as she watched David fight to stay conscious. "No… off duty. He's my boyfriend."

Blood leaked out of his smile.

"Guess the assailants caught them at a bad time." A male officer chuckled.

Kate blushed. "We weren't…."

A gleaming white MedVan popped up over the edge of the roof, brilliant plumes of cyan light streaming from the ion thrusters at the four corners. It circled around and landed nearby, sparks dancing upon the metal ground beneath its engines. Figures in white swarmed out of it and rushed to David. Kate shot a mournful glance at Paul as officers led him away in cuffs. He tensed his arms as soon as he saw her, and forced himself to look away.

The officer squeezed Kate's arm. "Officer Ahmed will be okay."

"We're always supposed to tell families that," Kate said, without emotion.

"Come on, Solomon." The armored woman tugged on her arm, pulling in the direction of the medical transport. "Sometimes, it's true."

NIGHTWING

Mamoru

Hollow samurai armor floated inches above a street devoid of cars. Mamoru lifted his gaze to a sky without smog, where every star shone bright and clear. He noted the lack of hovercars or advert bots and felt pleasure. He would have smiled, had his avatar possessed a face. This version of West City appeared too clean, too new, and far too silent.

Wavering violet light drew his attention to an alley where a tall man with impossibly thin features, milk-white skin, and pointed ears appeared. An indigo strip, a haze of perhaps makeup or tattoo, crossed his face over blood red eyes that looked like solid orbs of colored glass. He walked with a long staff, topped with a crystal surrounded by two counter-rotating spheres of amethyst light. Metal bracers on both forearms shone with intricate scrollwork of gold leafy vines over a red enamel coating.

"What in the nine hells are you supposed to be?" asked Mamoru.

The figure lifted an eyebrow, exuding arrogance. "A noble of the house of Selethiel."

Mamoru let off a low, throaty grumble.

"I see you require the simple explanation. An elf. A wizard if you must know."

"Why do people in this country waste their time on such things?"

The elf chuckled. "Says the man whose country still *lives* medieval. We only chop each other up with swords in VR."

"I was expecting something more... technical."

"They called me Flatline because I kept *getting* Black ICEd. It's not a name of choice. Besides, high elf wizard seemed appropriate since we're after a dragon."

Mamoru shook his head. "I expected it to be here by now."

"Dude," said the elf, raising his hand. "I don't know how the hell you jacked in without a plug, but that's probably why the damn thing can't sense you."

"Where is your friend?"

"He's coming. Said he had to wrap something up with an accounting server cluster that kept trying to use an address range he'd mapped to marketing. He's got a *day job.*" The elf shuddered as if he'd sworn the worst oath imaginable.

"A serious problem."

Flatline raised his eyebrow again. "Is that Japanese sarcasm, or are you serious?"

"I do not think your friend is coming."

The elf, staff clicking on the road, walked a few paces away to a metal hatch at the mouth of the alley. "Oh, he will. I said dragon. He couldn't pass up this much experience."

"When will you say something that makes sense?" Mamoru squeezed one hand on the handle of the katana at his side. "So, what is your great plan?"

"Simple. I've set up an isolated network node on an old GlobeNet relay server the Authority hasn't taken offline yet. It doesn't have the power to handle a full dragon AI's parallel processing demands. Plus, once we're in, I can burn the egress proxy so it can't call any reinforcements."

"You expect it to walk right in there?"

"Of course." Flatline held his arms out to the sides, playing up the melodic not-quite-human accent the avatar added to his English. "You said it was angry with you. All you need to do is piss it off to the point it loses reason and jumps down this hole."

Flatline tapped the end of his staff on the ground and the hatch opened with a pneumatic hiss and a rush of steam. It looked like one of the access panels leading to the Beneath.

Mamoru set his weight down on his boots and marched off.

"The uplink is kinda old," said Flatline. "You should be able to get across with only a little lag. Make sure you get it nice and angry so it doesn't have second thoughts when its fat ass gets stuck."

Three blocks away, Mamoru stopped in the center of an intersection where two six-lane roads crossed. Eerie darkness filled streets devoid of cars and people. It felt like a city after a viral apocalypse, cavernous and deserted. This part of cyberspace mapped to the real world equivalent outside Flatline's apartment. A grey zone on the darker end of the spectrum. No one wanted to be here in cyberspace either.

He drew the katana with a deliberate, ritualistic motion, flipped it upright, and clasped it in two hands before his face.

"Hachiman-sama, may I bring honor to you on this day."

Mamoru lowered his blade to the side with a sweeping motion. A lone white dove glided to a landing atop a vendomat at the corner. Seconds later, it flew away, vanishing between two mirrored skyscrapers. He wondered if the bird had come from his subconscious influence over the net, or if the God of War had heard him.

He took in a great breath, holding it for a second, before bellowing, "Nightwing!"

The shout echoed into the dark replica of West City.

Moments passed. Mamoru looked up at the sense of an approaching presence. At least a quarter mile away along the great road, two eyes of lime green raced toward him. The shape of a black dragon drew in around them, awash with the fury of lightning and thunder. Windows shattered to chrome splinters as it passed; the shards burst into space over the street and froze in midair like glittering snow.

"There you are," thundered a voice from the heavens.

Nightwing extended his talons, gouging trenches in the road. Pure black matter occupied the rips, highlighted in thin lines of glowing cyan light.

Mamoru upended his blade and drove it into the paving at his feet. He commanded the GlobeNet's 'dark matter' to reshape itself, altering the boundaries of the world. Program code flashed into being within his thoughts, responding to glimpses of ideas and concepts. Not even a fish as powerful as Nightwing could reshape its bowl.

The dragon bore down on him with all its weight and fury. Mamoru forced power out of the deck into the GlobeNet, causing a forty-foot wall to erupt from the street in front of him in a burst of shiny silicon flakes. Nightwing smashed into the barrier with a resounding detonation that sent a radiant wave of force rippling forth. A shimmer of blue lines pulsed outward along the wall from the point of impact, hinting at the form of bricks. The GlobeNet best approximated the incalculable power of the impact by breaking everything representing glass within a two-mile radius.

Despite appearing only an inch thick, the barrier held.

Rolling thunder faded into the distance, amid the sound of billions of brittle objects shattering.

The wall dissipated at Mamoru's command. He leapt upon the dazed head of the beast, cutting an X between its eyes. It reared up, smashing a clawed hand down upon its face as Mamoru overrode the GlobeNet's location tracking algorithms and teleported underneath it. The katana sank into its scales, cutting a gash open in its belly from which inky darkness swelled like vapor.

Nightwing roared lime green flames into the sky.

Mamoru pulled the blade loose and rolled out of the way of a frantic raking of claws. Alas, the Matsushita Ultra Series deck he borrowed only had so much processing power. The corrupting effect of viruses represented by his sword stroke could not outpace the error checking of a grade ten AI.

The wound closed.

"Your feeble attempt to take my life in the other world has failed, lizard." Mamoru teleported onto the beast's back, stabbing down between its shoulders. "Here, you are but an ungainly beast."

Nightwing's body shifted, morphing from standing upright to lying on his back. The claw hit before Mamoru could react, swatting his vision white. Street and sky traded places too many times to count before he struck the side of a building with a *crack* like a gunshot. Dozens of walls smashed over his helmet as he passed clean through a skyscraper. He bounced once after falling from the third story to the street on the far side of the building. Sparks rained from his armored back as he scuffed to a halt on the road.

His hand burned; the deck overheated in the real world.

Nightwing clawed gouges out of walls while pulling himself down an alley too narrow for his bulk. Metal girders buckled, and hundred-story buildings collapsed behind him, raising a cloud of simulated dust as well as another deafening roar.

Mamoru floated upright and gestured at the ground. He generated program code at the speed of thought, creating a waterfall of ancient golden coins, which swelled up into a pile that reached his knees.

"What's this?" bellowed Nightwing, his distraction by the wealth obvious. "You seek to bribe me? Hah! I shall devour you and claim your tribute regardless."

"I thought the gold might work. Simple-minded creatures are often attracted to shiny things."

Nightwing's massive face trembled with a tic. His eyes darkened to red. Roaring beyond the realm of coherent speech blew the reek of brimstone past onyx teeth as he opened his mouth. Green flames swirled at the core of his throat.

Mamoru teleported a block away, watching the fire breath melt out the foundation of another skyscraper and leave the street paved with liquid gold.

"That looked like it might have been unpleasant," yelled Mamoru. He glided backward to the hatch, whistling as if calling a dog. "Here boy."

The dragon sank its claws into the street and dragged himself around to face Mamoru. "You will suffer like no mortal has known suffering in the history of your pathetic species. I shall destroy you and anything even bearing the slightest connection to you once I am done."

Mamoru generated an image of a six-foot wide dog treat and waved it, whistling.

Whatever words bellowed from Nightwing's mouth next drowned in a swirl of muted sound as Mamoru leapt into the hatch. The sensation of falling down a narrow chute slowed, as if the air around him had become dense syrup.

The narrow passage vibrated with a deafening roar that shuddered in his armor. Even his ears in the real world ached. Cringing, he looked up.

With a resounding *crash*, Nightwing rammed his head into the tiny hole, ripping and clawing at the sides to force his massiveness into the small space. Mamoru couldn't help but remember Flatline commenting about the AI's fat ass getting stuck, and laughed. The raging dragon faded into the stretching tube above him as he fell with increasing speed.

His feet touched ground, and the pipe snapped away into the sky like a rubber band, exposing miles and miles of rolling green fields. Far off to his left, the shape of a castle shimmered amongst the meadow. Flatline, rather the elven wizard, stood a few paces to his right next to a huge man in gleaming medieval armor.

Mamoru attempted to raise an eyebrow his avatar lacked. The titan had to be at least seven feet tall with the kind of ridiculous muscles only a professional bodybuilder could possess, and a square-chinned jaw verging on cartoonish. Long blond hair hung to the middle of his back over a blue-trimmed white cloak. He chatted away with the elf, in a voice so stereotypical it hurt.

"I couldn't believe I made it back in time. This couple was in front of me at the Cyberburger and they couldn't figure out what they wanted. How can you go to Cyberburger and not know what you want? It's not like their menu ever changes. They only give me forty-five minutes for lunch, and I'm spending ten of it just standing there waiting for no reason. It's not hard."

"Tragic," said Flatline.

"Oh," said the knight, holding up a shield made of pure yellow-gold light. "I finally managed to get the Dawn Aegis. About damn time, too. I've lost the roll on this drop six times already. I can't believe Jimmy let Ly11th have it last week. She doesn't even off-tank, but she's sleeping with the guild master. Everyone knows she's doing it. That's why he brings her along every raid even though she has no damn idea how to play a damage paladin."

"Why don't you complain to HR about it?" asked Flatline.

"You're mocking me, Eric." The knight wagged a finger at him. "The raid group isn't from work. I can't complain to HR about them. I should argue for more time for lunch. I'm the head of their network administration team and they only give me forty-five minutes."

"I know. You say that every time I see you." Noticing Mamoru, Flatline gestured at him. "Milton, this is Mamoru."

"I'm Davan the Pure, Eric. Milton doesn't exist in this world. Davan the Pure would get more than forty-five minutes for lunch." Milton shifted to face Mamoru. "Nice gear. What raid did that come from? I don't remember an Asian expansion pack."

A dark spot appeared in the sky, from which black threads of lightning crawled out into the perfect blue.

"He doesn't play Monwyn Online." The elf flashed an apologetic look to Mamoru. "Is it coming?"

"Yes," said Mamoru. "I believe I may have annoyed it."

All three men looked up as the sky shattered, sending chunks of blue and black glass the size of small boats spearing into the meadow all around them. From an expanding hole filled with stars, Nightwing dove amid the flickering cloud of tumbling shards. Milton raised his shield, creating a dome effect over them. Mamoru teleported to the side; Flatline blurred into a streak, moving thirty meters to the side in an instant.

Davan the Pure became Davan the Flat.

"Still slow, lizard." Mamoru ran in, slashing at the dragon's side.

Nightwing leapt over him, snarling and snapping. He raked at Mamoru with a series of cat-like swats. Too late, Mamoru realized the distraction and walked right into a power swipe that sent him flying. His landing gouged a long trench in the grass, sod and dirt spraying skyward. Nightwing's mocking laughter melted to a yelp of pain as a blue ray of frost connected Flatline's outstretched hand to the dragon's rear end. Mamoru gritted his teeth, focusing all his energy on protecting his borrowed deck's firmware from deleting itself. The hollow samurai armor sat up, a clod of dirt fell out of the helmet and broke apart over his leg. A mental impulse dumped the corrupted operating system from memory and brought back a fresh load in a nanosecond, something a normal deck jockey couldn't do without losing connection. Splintering cracks creeping across the white enamel slowed to a halt. A second later, they reversed until he appeared whole again.

Flatline held his staff over his head, surrounded by a glowing azure sphere of light. Ice spread over the dragon's body, engulfing him in an inch-thick clear shell. Nightwing stopped moving, looking much like a lawn statue left out in freezing rain.

"Ouch," said Milton, sounding far more grand than his embedded-in-the-dirt posture conveyed. He sat up in a paladin-shaped hole. "What the hell was that?"

"This isn't a Monwyn node," said Flatline. "You still remember how to run standard combat softs, don't you?"

"Thrice-damned beast." Milton climbed out of the divot and readied his shield. "I am here."

"Can't 'tank' this thing, Milt. No threat mechanics, and it doesn't give a shit about your armor." Flatline threw more ice into the dragon. "I'm not casting frost bolt. I'm bogging down its error checking routines with a Bogosity virus. It's looking for damage that ain't there."

"Yes, yes." Davan-the-no-longer-flat brushed dirt from his chest and pulled out a broadsword. "I do recall, though it has been awhile. You said this would be worth a lot of XP."

The elf gestured at the dragon with a broad smile. "It *is* quite an experience... just not measured in points."

Davan the Pure sighed.

Mamoru roared and leapt out of his trench, projecting himself skyward. He cleared the distance to the dragon in an instant, careening in an upward arc, and landed on Nightwing's head. His katana came down in a raking slash from the ridge above the right eye to the tip of his nose. The strike shattered the ice, precipitating a spreading crack that wrapped all the way over the beast, freeing it. Mamoru attempted to teleport, but the server couldn't handle processing that at the same time it chewed on Nightwing's error-correction routines. The world bogged down under syrupy lag, slowing Mamoru's fall to the point he hung suspended in midair. A massive black-scaled hand swiped around and seized him. The agony of watching such a slow attack coming for him while being unable to move made him scream in rage. Patches of samurai armor turned to white glowing panels, cracking under the strain of the dragon crushing him.

Milton reached up and closed the visor on his plate helm. He rounded his broadsword into the dragon's side, causing a loud bellow of pain to issue forth from the beast as a scale broke. Nightwing raised Mamoru in a closed fist and smashed him into the meadow under a flattened hand. A second later, two inches of katana broke out of the back of his paw. The dragon leapt up on its haunches, screaming and waving his hand as if burned. Mamoru sprang out of the ground like a missile, slashing the huge lizard twice along the throat before landing on top of it and running the length of its back, cutting left and right on his way down the tail to the ground.

Nightwing writhed around, seething with anger that sent lime-colored flames shooting from gaps in his teeth. Milton ran up along the creature's left flank as it chased Mamoru in circles. His next three swings glanced away from scales with ineffectual *clanks*. Mamoru skidded to a halt and whirled to face the dragon. Milton's shield disappeared at the utterance of a command word; he grabbed his broadsword in both hands and thrust it up under a scale, sinking it to the hilt.

Nightwing flickered, claws frozen in midair three feet from Mamoru's head. His skin vanished, changing him into a dragon-shaped outline of white light for an instant before the creature faded to a wireframe model. The beast's horrible roar broke into digitized chunks and bits, a sound akin to glass shards scraping over silicon.

Milton leaned into the blade, calling out in a deep voice befitting his image. "Hah. I still got it, Eric. Poison CRC. It's eating itself."

"That virus hasn't worked since we were sixteen." The elf waved his staff around in an intricate pattern, tracing a fiery azure rune in midair. Both energy spheres orbiting his weapon rocketed straight up. He held the staff sideways over his head, intoning a chant in a strange language.

"Guess they forgot about it and stopped programming countermeasures." Davan the Pure raised a blond eyebrow and cupped the pommel of his broadsword. Golden light surrounded his hands. "Back to the abyss, foul creature!"

The same gold light shone from spots where Nightwing's eyes had been; the dragon clawed at the ground and pulled itself forward. "No! Insects! Fleas!"

"Hit it now," grunted Milton. "I killed its hardware acceleration support, it's gotta do everything in software mode now… and this server is a piece of shit. Where the heck did you find something this old?"

The elf laughed. "You sold it to me a year ago."

Milton looked shocked for a second. "Oh… right."

The teleport finally kicked in, much to Mamoru's irritation. He sprinted back to the fray. Black skin spread over the wire model from nose to tail, with the faintest hint of scales defined by discolorations in the surface. When he got close enough, Mamoru sprang at the AI, but his katana met no resistance, as if he'd struck at a hologram. He thrust his left gauntlet forward, sword held to the side in the other hand. A blazing glow flared around his fingers as they pierced the beast's hide. Hundreds of thousands of pages of program code took shape in his mind; Mamoru strained, focusing his will on altering the software into useless routines that went in circles.

The flutter of fire drew his gaze up at a six-foot wide fireball streaking out of the sky. Unsure of its nature, but alarmed by its appearance, Mamoru leapt away. An explosion of violet flames drilled Nightwing flat on his belly seconds before a second meteor smashed over his head.

Silver, like liquid mercury, spread over the dragon's body from the point of impact. Wisps of flame rocketed back to Flatline, forming again into the twin spheres orbiting the top of his staff.

"Sector scan," said the elf. "The server thinks the memory this bastard's taking up is corrupt and is trying to flush it."

"You hacked the system," said Milton. "Starcall isn't 'til level 130, and you're only ninety-three."

Flatline gasped, hand across his heart. "Hack? Me?" He examined his fingernails. "We're not even technically in the game right now anyway. I only borrowed the graphics."

Mamoru sheathed his blade and grabbed the dragon's chin in both hands. "Time to destroy this abomination."

White spots approximating eyes flared inside the empty helmet. Mamoru wanted the AI to break apart into a thousand separate programs. He sectioned off routine after routine, spawning innocuous device drivers, flickering animations of cherry blossoms, and several harmless 'pet' softs. Data tiles erupted like a volcano from the center of Nightwing's back, raining around them.

"Okay." Milton stepped away and pointed with his sword. "That is completely outside the parameters of normal network operation."

Flatline approached, looking impressed. "That it is. What are you doing?"

Mamoru growled, his mind too far into the code to answer.

"I think he's somehow trying to delete it a piece at a time. It's stopped trying to get up. The CPU is decked from the AI rewriting itself." Milton strained as if stuck to the ground. "I can't even cat my softs."

"It's stalemating." Flatline raised his staff. "It's rebuilding itself as fast as he's killing it."

The elf froze, a band of blue light appeared at his forehead and crept downward over his body.

"What are you doing?" asked Milton.

"Trying to run a virus, staring at a loading bar. I haven't seen a loading bar in fourteen years. Not since the Zeo-series machines."

"Ooh. I remember those things." The knight gave up trying to move. "It would be better not to delete it."

Mamoru's concentration faltered; holes in Nightwing's side filled in. "Impossible. This monstrosity stands in my way."

"Whoa," said Flatline, jerking back and forth from a combat posture to standing upright in an endless loop. "Milt's right."

"Davan the Pure," said Milton, with a gallant face.

Mamoru growled, focusing again on destroying the program that had reached out of cyberspace to kill him.

"It's going to have a backup," said Flatline. "It may lose the memory of what happened between when it saved itself and now. And if I know AIs, it's still going to want to come after you. You'll be killing dragons twice a week for the rest of your life."

"I cannot allow this thing to interfere." Mamoru scowled.

"I need some CPU," said Milton. "Back off a little and let me try something."

"It must die."

"Mamoru." Milton struggled to unstick his foot from the grass, which stretched up like glue. "You can't kill software. Unless you are prepared to hunt down and destroy every backup copy it ever made of itself deep inside military server farms."

Mamoru relaxed; fatigue wrung his muscles tight, leaving him ready to collapse where he stood. He had no words for his anger.

Sir Davan the Pure strode to Nightwing's nose and took on an air of authority. "Dragon, hear me."

Full-resolution scales spread over the creatures head, recreating the sense of emotion in the shape of its eye ridges. "Mortal..."

The booming voice lofted golden hair in a puff. It hovered for a few seconds, caught in lag, and fell flat against his back.

"I'm sure you've realized you have strayed into a realm that cannot withstand your power."

Mamoru narrowed his non-eyes. *Why does he defer to it?*

"What have you done to me?" Great wings folded inward, cramped. "I cannot bear this place, or suffer the insolence of your presence."

"If you would prefer to be vanquished, then so be it." Milton raised his sword. "Against our combined strengths, you cannot survive. Your arrogance shall be your downfall."

A broad grin spread over the face of Flatline's elf. "This one perhaps thought himself too strong to waste time with a backup. How long has it been?"

"Moments ago," snapped Nightwing, struggling to lift himself onto his legs.

"Then destroying you shall be only a minor setback." Milton gestured at Mamoru. "Please, continue."

"Wait," rasped the dragon upon weary breath. "What do you propose?"

"Abandon your quest to kill this man, and we shall spare your life." Milton thrust forth his chin.

"Insolent mortals," roared Nightwing, rising to his full height.

The dragon leapt upon Milton, swatting him aside with a dull *clank*. Davan the Bouncing's plate-armored figure skipped over the grass as Nightwing surged forward, his serpentine neck swinging his head to the left. He exhaled with a thunderous rush, covering Flatline with a twenty-foot wide shaft of green flames. Somewhere within the deafening roar, an elven voice shrieked.

Mamoru leapt into the sky, flipped, and came down upon the dragon's back, between its wings. The impact flattened the great beast into the meadow and sent a wave rippling outward across the grass like a stone dropped in a lake. Flatline's elf had become a standing suspension of ash that blinked once before it disintegrated.

He lurched over and buried his arms up to the elbows in scales, which gave way like dough rather than armor. Mamoru resumed his assault, willing parts of the dragon's program into blocks of zeroes. Nightwing let out an agonized roar. The creature clawed at the ground, futilely trying to drag itself forward as if pinned under a tremendous weight.

Milton ran to the ash-outline of the elf; he held a hand out over it, but nothing happened. "Damn. It's knocked him offline. I can't rez him."

Mamoru roared. Psionic energy coursed through his body, outlining every bone in a sheath of pain. The horizon on all sides closed in, forming a dark whirling mass around him and the dragon. He ignored the fire in his limbs and swam amid a vortex of whirling zeroes. White streams of lightning crawled up the walls of shifting numbers from whatever Milton did. Somewhere in the distance, the metallic *clang* of a sword striking scales rang out three times.

A rush of air preceded a deep, keening roar. Threads of lightning joined, turning the tornado of digits into blank space containing nothing. Mamoru fell upon a smooth surface of gloss white, gazing upon a reflection of his true appearance. A lumpy mass rose from a pool of opaque white liquid, expanding into the form and detail of a dragon's head, an unpainted porcelain sculpture.

"Hold," said the dragon. "I… I yield."

"You have pressed beyond that point." Mamoru stood. "You will be destroyed."

Nightwing narrowed his eyes. "Hear me, Mamoru Saitō. Delete this copy of me, and I shall reawaken. I shall not make the same mistakes again." His neck extended, a coiling serpent winding its way around the man. "While you have proven my hubris, you forget what I am. You accuse me of arrogance, yet you suffer the same condition. You pay no heed to my capabilities beyond my sentient software. We are not so dissimilar."

Mamoru's hand found nothing on his belt.

"Your sword matters not in this place. For us, time has paused. Destroy me, and you will regret it."

"I should have destroyed you when first we met." Mamoru ducked the elongated serpent, backing away.

The dragon straightened out, head gliding after him. "I need not venture from my primary core to harm you. Tell me, how long can you survive being hunted by the full might of military intelligence? Can your… abilities detect a sniper three miles away?"

"You will not remember."

"Will Nami see the bullet coming?"

"Do not dare!" yelled Mamoru

"Will Caiden?"

Mamoru stared.

"Will Sadako?"

"No!" He grabbed at the reptilian head, which eluded him.

The serpent coiled to the right, low to the ground, gliding at the same pace he advanced. "I propose a truce, as your downtrodden associate suggests. I shall direct no harm toward them and I shall not *interfere* with you, on one condition."

"You are dying, yet you demand terms?"

Nightwing's colorless lips parted, letting chuckles slip past razor teeth. Panel screens appeared in a curtain around Mamoru. Hundreds of images of Nami, Caiden, and Sadako appeared. Innocuous scenes from daily life, Mamoru's home, Mars, and even a few of a curious Sadako wandering the streets of Querq.

"Their lives for a simple request," said the dragon.

Mamoru closed his eyes, his voice resigned. "What?"

The voice drifted closer, nose to nose with him, and took on a tone of wounded sadness. "Take back what you said about me being simple-minded and fancying shiny things."

When Mamoru looked up, the dragon seemed to be pouting. "Fine."

"Say it."

Mamoru wanted to rip its head off, but stilled his rage with worry for his sister, for the woman he knew he could never have, and for a boy who had helped him.

He bowed as if to an equal. "*Gomenasai*, dragon. I rescind my statement that you are simple-minded."

The ends of Nightwing's mouth curled upward.

Disintegration rushed across the floor, reducing the room—and the serpent head—to floating one-inch cubes. Mamoru fell, tumbling head over feet until he hit the ground like a meteor. Despite the explosive sound of his landing, he found himself standing and unharmed when the dust settled. The dragon's great wings beat overhead as it fought its way higher in the air to the broken sky. Its massive reptilian form vanished into the starfield, which sealed off as shards of broken sky-glass unseated themselves from the earth and tumbled upward to mend the breach. The screams of scraping glass made his spine twist. Grass once again stirred in a wind that seemed real, bugs no longer hung motionless in midair.

The unnatural lag had gone.

"What just happened?" asked Milton, walking over with a hand on his blade.

Mamoru scowled at the distant castle. "We reached an accord."

"You *talked* it down?" Davan the Skeptical quirked an eyebrow. "Wait, you have diplomacy? You actually wasted skill points on that?"

Mamoru sighed.

CRY UNCLE

Kate

Dreamless sleep ended with a pleasant female voice intruding on silence. Kate's blurry consciousness stripped all meaning from the sounds. When her eyes opened, a dark woman in a white coat hovered on the other side of a peach-hued miasma. The sensation of being trapped in a gel tube with a person in white staring at her brought a rush of panic. Kate's eyes fixed on the black text above the woman's coat pocket. "E. Chowdhury, MD."

Alarms went off in the room outside her prison.

The woman had to stand on tiptoe to pound her fist onto something out of sight. Kate fanned her arms in the slime, trying to swim away. Mechanical noise permeated the substance, which drained away in seconds, lowering her weight onto her feet. Residue of the breathable gel wisped to steam, filling the tube with a haze of sweet-smelling smoke. The gurgling hiss of gel boiling out of her ears drowned out the alarm.

"Officer Solomon, please calm down." The woman, eyes wide with concern, held her hands up in a comforting gesture. "I'm not sure what made the tank malfunction. We drained it as fast as we could, were you burned?"

Kate wiped her face. *Doctor, not a scientist. Get a fucking grip, girl. You're not seven.* She opened her mouth to speak, but gel came out instead of words. She knocked on the tank wall and made a 'down' gesture. Dr. Chowdhury pushed her finger into the holo-panel at Kate's left, and the clear barrier twisted a quarter turn and sank into the floor.

As soon as she had the room to move, Kate bent over and braced her hands on her knees. She opened her throat and let the liquid out of her lungs. Trails of slime drained from her nose and mouth, splattering over her feet for a little over a minute. Her first breath of smoky air made her choke. She hunkered down, head between her knees and gagged. When the convulsions subsided, she straightened up and wiped her face on the back of her arm.

"No, I'm fine. Sorry," she croaked. "Bad memory."

The doctor hesitated, clutching a white robe made from towel material. "You should learn to duck."

"Huh?" Kate ran both hands over her chest, checking on where she remembered bruises. She felt stiff, but at least nothing hurt now. "What?"

"I don't see many people so blasé about the transition between breathing gel and air. I assumed you are injured frequently."

Overpowering light glaring down from the ceiling made the edges of everything in the immaculate white room fuzzy. Kate trudged past the doctor, ignoring the robe, and headed for the autoshower. She felt woozy and drained, as though she could fall asleep where she stood.

"It's a long story, Doc."

🜛 🜊 🜨 🜔 🜒

KATE RUBBED HER HANDS BACK AND FORTH OVER THE SMOOTH, IRIDESCENT material covering her thighs. The one-of-a-kind Division 0 uniform looked either black or indigo depending on how the light hit it. David said they had it made from threads of indirium thinner than human hair. She'd heard of it before, a dense metal not found on Earth, but only in the context of armor-piercing bullets her gift may or may not be able to melt. According to him, they also used it for the skeletal structure of military cyborgs.

Division 0 command hoped this uniform would tolerate heat. Between the day she'd been having, and what she planned, it seemed her best choice of outfit.

Hey there.

David's voice swept over her thoughts.

Her head snapped up a second before she leapt out of the chair next to his med tank. She didn't care if embracing the tube made her look silly. David glanced around with an uneasy look.

What? Does something still hurt? Kate squeezed the transparent cylinder.

He forced a smile. *No, I just hate this stuff. Feels like I'm drowning.*

A medtech guided her away from the tank as another man hit the button to drain it. David choked and gagged, doubled over on the ground with gel spraying from his face for a few minutes. After a few deep, gurgling breaths, he coughed some more and spat out a few glops.

"You guys love this, don't you?" he wheezed. "Next time, use the green stuff."

"I'm sorry, Officer Ahmed. The bullet pierced your lung. We needed the nanobots to get in there."

He accepted the bathrobe as well as help standing. Kate waited out in the hall while he showered off the remnants of the slippery gel. A short while later, she leapt up to embrace him as soon as he left the nanosurgery room, once again in his uniform.

"What happened?"

Kate held on for another second. "I don't know. It doesn't make any sense. I've got to do something."

He caught her wrist as she tried to walk off. "What doesn't make any sense?"

"The Syndicate. They know I signed on to Division 0. Even they don't want to risk starting a pissing contest with the police."

"Until they asked you to kill one."

"The guy went rogue. I... he's not active duty anymore. It's not a respect thing, David. It's a fear-of-reprisal thing. They can't squeeze money out of people when they're dead. Do you have any idea what a Syndicate war would look like?" She grasped his arm where he held her other wrist. "The police wouldn't be able to stop. They'd have too much to lose in the public eye. The people I used to work for are too stupid and proud to walk away. It would be a complete disaster. They're in both cities... ACC territory too... even independent nations. Only place they don't have much sway is China. Hell, they're even on Mars."

He squeezed her hand. "So what are you going to do?"

She took a deep breath, held it for a second, and let it out her nose. "I'm going to confront El Tío. I need to understand why."

"I'll put in a call for some Div 1 support."

"No, David. I have to do this alone. If they see an army coming, they won't even try to talk."

He pulled her against him. "No way. Don't you watch any holo-vids? Going in alone is when the idiot gets themselves killed."

"El Tío's the closest thing I have to family." Tears pooled behind her eyelids. "Something happened to him. You said Paul and Leo had some kind of implant."

"What, exactly do you plan to do about it? You're not much of a telepath."

She paced about, grumbling. "I'll worry about that once I get there."

Kate stomped down the hallway. Squeaking boots came up behind her before a hand caught her shoulder.

"I'm going with you at least."

"No." She spun around and held on to him, shaking. "You almost died once already. I can't lose you."

"I might not be able to override an implanted suggestion, but I can force him to be too calm to act on it."

Fear and guilt kept her clinging to him. As afraid as she was of losing David, having him be there for her... *What's wrong with me? I've never needed anyone before.* She laughed. *Maybe that's why I'm so fucked up.*

"Okay."

David brushed her hair away from her eyes and smiled. "You don't sound very confident. Are you sure this is a good idea."

She tucked away her worries. "No, but... let's go."

KATE BROKE INTO NERVOUS LAUGHTER AS DAVID SET THE PATROL CRAFT DOWN in a familiar looking alley at the edge of a grey zone. The shuttle ride to the East Coast had taken less time (about twenty minutes) than convincing the local Division 0 brass to let them borrow a patrol craft for an unofficial excursion.

He raised an eyebrow at her while shutting down the drive system. "You are giving off genuine amusement?"

She covered her mouth until she got control. "Yeah. I was just thinking about how to put on the whole 'cop attitude,' and then I realized I'd been scared shitless of the police for years. Feels so twisted to *be* one."

The patrol craft door opened with a weak hiss. Kate stepped out, stood, and pulled it down, leaving her hand on the armored surface. She felt foolish exiting an armored shell in the middle of a war zone. Her worry intensified at the lack of any visible sentries by the back entrance into El Tío's little restaurant. Silva and the large aug were gone. Perhaps they'd been sent to her apartment to wait for her. Maybe El Tío had panicked and cleared out.

"David?" She stared at the plain grey door.

"Yeah."

"I need a nudge. This isn't gonna work if I'm scared." She glanced over the car at him; within seconds, her fear faded. An upwelling of confidence came from nowhere, and she stood tall. "Thanks."

"Don't do anything reckless."

"That's why you're here." She grasped the handle of the stunrod hanging on the left side of her belt and marched into the alley.

Inside, a few toe prints burned into the cheap, decorative floor covering reminded her of the last time she'd come to visit. She navigated the dim, cramped corridor, hung a right, and walked past the kitchen. Two of the men working there stopped and gawked. She didn't bother looking at their thoughts. It didn't matter if they were horny, recognized her, or freaked by the presence of someone in a police uniform. She took her time walking, remembering her old mad dash when her feet would start fires wherever they touched. Her confidence increased—it felt good to be human.

Kate rounded another corner, but jumped back at the chirp of El Tío's sentry gun. Without her holographic bracelet on, she expected it to fire. Instead, it made the same safe chirp it used to.

"Police ID." David reached forward and tapped the rigid guard on her left forearm. "By law, automated defenses have to yield to cops. Modifying them not to is grounds for a summary. It's considered the same as attempted murder of an officer."

She stomped out from behind the corner. Behind the sentry turret, the unassuming door to El Tío's 'storeroom' hung ajar, also devoid of the usual living guards. Kate frowned at the memory of the man who always stared at her tits. A charred handprint on the wall made her smile.

The door opened without resistance. She gave it a shove and it flew aside, slamming against the bare cinder blocks with an echoing, metallic *boom*. The men who once stood guard at the door lay dead on the floor inside. From the looks of it, they'd killed each other.

El Tío sat at his desk, a rough-cut obsidian oval held in the grasp of a pair of nude, chrome succubi. Bottles of various liquors stood in a row in front of him near a single shot glass. Crimson spatter marred one side of his otherwise immaculate white fedora. The rest of his dark suit looked impeccable.

Her old chair waited on the thermal tiles in front of the desk, a recognizable ass print in heat bluing upon the seat. The man seemed old and frail now, devoid of the fear caused by his reputation. Kate smirked at the corpses. Had all the bodyguards made him seem so intimidating? She wasn't a terrified savage child any longer. Perhaps, to a fifteen-year-old, he might still be scary.

No. He looks broken, almost sorry.

Kate wondered if David's telempathic boost of confidence made him seem so harmless. He didn't look up at her as he poured a shot of something brown.

"*Buenas noches, señorita.*" He pulled another tiny glass out of a drawer. "*Te puedo interesar en una bebida?*"

"No, thanks." Kate held her hand up. "I'm on duty. *En servicio. Yo soy policia ahora.*"

His eyes raised to regard her. Hard eyes; the way he looked at a man before killing him. El Tío could kill a person as easily as eat an olive. David grunted. Despite the look she'd seen directed at other people so often, having it aimed at her didn't scare her at all.

"*Lo que le pasó, El Tío?*" Kate stood at the side of the desk, avoiding her old perch. "What happened to you?"

"He's enraged," said David, his voice strained as if he held a heavy burden.

Kate did what she had promised never to do. She peered into El Tío's mind. Blurry images cavorted in the shadows of his hatred. Somehow, he believed she had attacked the Syndicate. The dead men in the room—Silva from outside, and the four associates who happened to be in the restaurant at the time—were her doing as far as his thoughts cared. He believed the girl he had protected had betrayed him and had come here to end his life. He had only survived by a chance absence.

"He thinks I did this." Kate gestured at the dead. "He thinks I tried to kill him." She banged on the desk. "El Tío, look at them! They're beaten to death. No burns."

"He sees them as burned," said David.

El Tío's killing stare never faltered as he downed his shot.

"It's got to be a telepathic implant." Kate moved to David's side. "We can't leave him like this."

David's light brown face beaded with sweat. "This man is quite intent on becoming angry. I... I can't dent this overlay on his memory. It's way out of my league. Maybe Lieutenant Commander Ashford can do something about it." His cheeks lost some color.

"You say that name like he's the grim reaper or something."

"Heh. Not too far off. Mind blast. Even stronger than Burckhardt."

"So?" Kate raised an eyebrow.

"If he wanted to, he could make you into a drooling lump... permanently." David shrugged. "If you ask me, I'd rather just die. Damn, I've never seen an implant this strong."

Kate's anger raised the temperature of the room a few degrees. "Archon. It's gotta be Archon." She looked around for something to burn. "Fuck! I should've known as soon as Paul said it."

"What?"

"If you're not with us, you're against us. That's what Archon said. It was him!" She stared in horror at El Tío for a long moment before gazing into David's chocolate eyes. "What can we do?"

"We—gun!" David shoved her off her feet, grabbing for his E-90.

Boom.

A blast of blue muzzle flare flashed under the desk. Kate's involuntary reaction to being shot at triggered, surrounding her with heat blur. A bullet splashed off her hip. She landed on her side as David let off a yowl of pain and hit the ground.

At the sound of the man she'd fallen for crying out in agony, unbridled rage took her.

She screamed and thrust her arms forward, commanding the air around the desk to ignite. A tornado of flame whirled into being, engulfing El Tío.

Another gunshot went off amid the conflagration, but the bullet ricocheted in the distance.

Kate's furious shrieking faded to desperate wails. The energy left her; the cyclonic inferno dissipated a second before the fire suppression system went off. Water spraying on her special uniform sizzled to steam in an instant.

She scrambled up into a crawl and rushed to David. He lay on his side with his back facing her, right hand clamped over his left armpit. Kate grasped his arm, hovering, ignoring the water raining all around them.

"David!"

He rolled onto his back, grinning at the water like a delirious fool. "Oh, that feels nice."

A starburst of lead had melted his shirt, enmeshed with molten skin and a bleeding bruise. She glanced at the flaring pain on her hip, finding a smear of lead on her still-intact uniform. Soaked hair clung to the sides of her head as she burst out laughing and crying at the same time.

"It hit me enough to melt."

"Not completely." He cringed and reached for his stimpak case.

"You should've let me take the bullet." She pushed his arm away and gave him two stims. "You're too gallant."

David's laugh stalled with a wince. "Ouch."

"I'll call a Med."

"I'll be okay. Didn't get the lung this time."

Kate picked at the slug fused into his skin. "You need a doctor."

"Fine, but we can drive back. You know how cops are. Two MedVan trips in one day, I'll never hear the end of it." He pointed at the desk. "We should at least call in a crime scene unit."

With her immediate fear for David's life gone, Kate shifted to look at El Tío—or rather, what remained of him. She knelt, numb to the frigid downpour, staring at the blackened husk of a body tilted at an angle in the chair. His warped gun dangled on two fingers between his knees. The shot glass, halfway to his mouth, overflowed with water from the sprinklers. Charred skull protruded from places where no skin remained; hollow eye sockets seemed to look back at her.

David grunted and sat up. Kate shivered at what she had done. Yes, El Tío had been a bastard. He had exploited her need for human contact and turned her into a weapon. He became the stern father figure in the back of her mind she'd have done anything to please. Not out of fear, but out of wanting to be loved. Until she had found El Tío, she had never killed a person with malice, or worse—no feeling at all.

Yes, he had been all of those horrible things, but she had loved him anyway, and his last dying thought had been that his girl had betrayed him.

The sprinklers cut out with a loud *clank,* making her jump. Kate reached toward the pathetic, emaciated corpse.

"I'm sorry." She sobbed. "I'm sorry. I didn't kill them. That son of a bitch made you believe it."

David put an arm around her, wincing from the pain it caused him to move. She shied away from the grisly sight, hiding her face in the crook of his neck. For a moment longer, she cried, until anger returned.

El Tío didn't try to kill David.

Archon did.

She didn't kill El Tío.

Archon did.

Kate pulled herself tighter to David's chest. His comforting her became her protecting him. She lifted her head and peered over his shoulder at the flickering of police lights in the hallway outside. Archon's impatient sneer appeared in her mind, followed by the memory of pain as the stun collar knocked her senseless and kept her from his grasp.

You're a dead man, Archon. I'm not even going to give you the chance to speak.

ON ONE CONDITION

Aaron

The wind played on the abandoned merry-go-round, nudging it into a slow spin and making the rusty metal sing with a series of soft creaks and squeals. Aaron stuffed his hands in the pockets of his long coat and tapped his foot. He didn't have much time to get back to Archon's 'compound' before being missed. Perhaps it had been a good thing Anna remained in London. Maybe she'd stay there, in relative safety.

If nothing else, they'd arrive separately. Maybe he wouldn't suspect anything. Archon seemed afraid to plunge into Aaron's mind, a fact that afforded him a degree of comfort. Anna had no such protection. He'd have to hope the man's blind faith in Aurora's predictions—and his own arrogance—made him feel it unnecessary. He'd seen the doubt in her eyes. If the man looked into her thoughts now, things would get... messy.

"Aaron..." Division 0 Regional Commander Mikhail Kovalev stepped out from behind an old steel slide. "Why do you pick such somber places to meet?"

"This is the closest grey spot to the Police Admin Center." He glanced at the broken play equipment. "It is a bit morose, though, isn't it?"

Mikhail stopped close enough for a shake, but left his hands in his pockets. "What happened in London?"

"This Archon chap's less stable than we thought. He's been manipulating people. Programmed everyone Anna knew into hating her so she'd leave

Britain. He's got his fingers into Mi6 as well. Wouldn't be surprised if he's got C-Branch in his pocket too."

"Doubtful." Mikhail chuckled. "Far too many synthetics and AIs. The Brits are afraid of them—perhaps rightly so. Anything out of whack here would stand out."

A moment of quiet passed.

"So, did you do it?" asked Mikhail.

Aaron lifted his gaze from the ground. "Eh? What?"

"You found her, didn't you? Did you do what you wanted? Did it make you feel any better?"

"No." He sighed. "Believe me, I tried, but she's wif him now."

Mikhail blinked.

"No, not *with* him like that." Aaron pinched the bridge of his nose. "Talis is a suggestive as strong as Archon's telepathy. Bloody hell my luck; she's Awakened too." He explained the deprogramming of Melissa's parents as well as Anna's friends, how it took three of them to undo what must've been a casual toss-off for Archon's power. "I got the feeling he didn't care all that much if the implant stuck. He only needed enough to get Anna out of the country. Still, it was a ballache to pluck loose. If he did an implant and really wanted it to be permanent, he'd be the only one capable of removing it."

"Did that Hughes fellow help?"

Aaron made a noncommittal face. "I s'pose it's possible. 'E's had a lot more practice at the whole telepathy thing than me. I had to boost him. Either way, it won't be long before he knows Anna's 'avin' doubts, an' when that happens, things are going to go pear-shaped in a spectacularly bad way."

Mikhail leaned forward, his expression serious. "You may be the only way we can stop him. Your... condition protects you from his influence. I'd prefer this dog didn't run out the back door. If the military gets wind of it, I can't guarantee you Zero will be able to keep things under control. They won't care what they shoot at."

"More than half of 'em are kids, Mik. He's importin' 'em from all over the world. Sometimes I almost believe his bullshit about 'finding a better life.' They're scouting out colony worlds, and seem to be runnin' logistics. The bloke's even been posting images of what the city he's going to build will look like."

"There's still the matter of his theft of a military starship worth hundreds of billions."

"Aye. Somethin else ain't sittin' right with me either." Aaron gestured to the side. "Well, if he's so concerned about protecting psionics, why's he get his knickers in a twist if one of 'em doesn't want to go with him? Especially anyone he thinks is Awakened. I wonder how many of those people really want to be there."

"He knows she is Awakened." Mikhail squinted into the east. "We've been expecting him to make a move on the healer child."

Aaron shook his head. "I doubt that. According to Anna, he's afraid of her."

Mikhail raised both eyebrows.

"I know…" Aaron chuckled. "She's about as far from scary as I imagine a person can get."

"We need you, Aaron. You said you were ready to talk. Say the word."

"I want something." Aaron stuffed his hands in his pockets and pursed his lips at the ground.

"A hundred million and a hovercar to Mexico?" Mikhail chuckled.

"Whatever happens… However the dust settles… I need you to guarantee Anna won't be prosecuted."

"You know Carter will only go for the compulsion thing so many times."

"Thing?" Aaron looked up. "You know it's the truth. She's not like him at all. He's influenced her. Look me in the eye and tell me they haven't turned a blind eye to worse in the name of public perception."

Mikhail stared at him.

"Come on, what's she done that's worse than some of the others who've gotten a pass."

"There was a hostage incident at the Timmons-Orben facility five years ago. None of the victims remembered anything at all. Even Ashford couldn't unearth the memory. Several security officers were killed, and some witnesses reported seeing a woman fitting her description."

"Off the record?"

Mikhail nodded. "Sure."

"She was there. She's also the reason everyone in the lab wasn't killed. Archon wanted to kill them all, but she refused."

"Aaron." Mikhail's expression softened. "You went in to protect her, didn't you?"

"Damn empath." Aaron chuckled.

"It's not completely up to me, but I'll do everything I can." Mikhail flashed a fox's smile. "I didn't need empathy to see your feelings for her."

Aaron glanced at him for a moment, at the sky for a moment more, and offered a hand. "Alright."

"Welcome back, Lieutenant."

Aaron blinked. "Lieutenant? I was tactical."

Mikhail chuckled. "You're Awakened?"

"So I've been told."

"Consider this a transfer to I-Ops. I'm sure they'll have some questions."

"Aye." He pursed his lips. "As long as there's no probing involved."

"Don't worry, Aaron." Mikhail smiled. "They'll warm the instruments first."

37

NUMBER SIX WOODSEER ST

Anna

Five years hadn't done much to improve the condition of Anna's old home. She rested a hand on the thin metal fence and sighed at the tiny, unkempt yard. The grass had become too thick to tell if her old, pink bicycle still rotted in the overgrown lawn. Not that anyone would steal it.

The building held six flats, but none showed a trace of life. Anna looked up at the black square of plexi that used to be her bedroom window. She pushed open the gate, which made a wrenching squeal of metal on metal that set the hairs on the back of her neck on end. Three steps up the walkpath, she felt watched. Of course, the locals would take notice of anyone visiting this place. Ignoring the sense of eyes upon her, she climbed the stoop.

She had little trouble tricking the front door lock—an old, familiar circuit —into opening. A little jolt to the right contact and the bar snapped out of the way. Green-grey mold crept up the otherwise white walls of a narrow staircase. A dark brown door to her left offered entry to the first floor flat.

I wonder what became of Mrs. Morris. The scent of fresh-baked ginger cookies came to mind.

Anna went up the stairs to the second-floor landing.

Mr. Pertwee and his 'daughter.' Anna smirked at remembering the way her father referred to the young brunette. She shivered, not understanding what a twenty-something would be doing with a man old enough to be her grandfather. *Money, probably.*

Two moldering dolls sat on the third-floor landing. Anna kicked one out of her way. The siblings who lived beneath their flat often teased her whenever she had a visible bruise. The girl, Ella, seemed to take particular delight in having a 'real' family—both mother and father—and reminded Anna of that fact whenever possible. Her brother Christopher rather liked Anna, up until he tried to kiss her and got a shock. He'd not been able to look at her again.

I should pop in to see how he's doing. Anna flashed a wicked grin, imagining a grown man screaming like a child and running.

Her mirth stopped at the fourth-floor landing, by the small, Epoxil-wood railing overlooking the stairs one flight down. The railing she dangled her legs through so many times after school, afraid to go in because *he* would be home.

She startled at a cold breeze and looked up at the door—an inch shy of closed. Old Bill hadn't even taken the yellow crime scene tape down. She brushed it aside and walked in. Her former home looked (aside from more dust) identical to her memory of the place. At the sight of familiar drab-green walls, she covered her mouth and tried to swallow past the giant lump in her throat. Every missing paint chip, every gouge in the fake wood, every scuff on the floor had a memory. Not all were bad. Some scratches in the furniture showed where her tricycle crashed. She'd been four, and unable to wait for the rain to stop so she could ride it. Red stains marked the wall where she'd slipped in sock feet while trying to carry spaghetti dinner to her father when she was six.

He hadn't even been angry with her.

Anna choked up and crept deeper into the flat. It felt like stepping sixteen years into the past. Everything looked exactly as it had the night she murdered him. The spilled synthbeer can on the living room rug amid a spray of popcorn, the knocked over table, the broken vase.

She stared at the mess for a moment and closed her eyes. In the blackness, she saw the Frictionless match on a shimmering holographic screen from her twelve-year-old perspective, sitting cross-legged on the rug in front of her father. Arsenal scored. Her anger came on so strong the holo-bar fried. Tears started before she could wail apologies. She'd knocked the table over running to get away; popcorn and beer went everywhere. He'd chased her to the kitchen.

When Anna opened her eyes, she found herself cowering on the kitchen floor. The room seemed smaller. She glanced upward at the hollow among the appliances where the food assembler had been. The police had taken it for testing. Anna lowered her arms and rolled forward onto her knees, rubbing her hand over the spot of floor where her father fell.

"I'm sorry, Pa. I didn't mean to kill you."

Her right shoulder twitched, as if a fat droplet of frigid rain struck her. She sat back, grasping the spot.

"Thanks, Lauren… Now you've got me expecting ghosts."

A brush of chill traced up her cheek, making her shiver.

She stood and crept out of the kitchen to the back hallway, hesitating by her bedroom door. The voice of a constable echoed out of her memory, sounding distant as he asked if she wanted to take anything from her home before they left. She could have played along. Old Bill didn't despise her then. Behind that door, she'd left her innocence.

Anna bit her lip and turned away, but the door creaked open without her touching it. She froze. Pink walls and carpet, posters of tween boy singers, and dolls. So many dolls. Everything her father ever bought as an apology for losing his temper. Monday's bruise became Wednesday's new gift. Anna covered her mouth with both hands, tears running down her face. Without realizing it, old habits kicked in. She wound up on her bed, curled in a ball, sobbing out of control into a pillow she hadn't touched in sixteen years while clinging to her favorite doll—Madeline.

She wanted to go back in time and start over from that moment, damn Archon and all of it with him. If only she could've controlled her temper, the holo wouldn't have fried in the middle of a game and her father wouldn't have died.

Minutes later, a weak knock sounded at the bedroom door.

"Daddy?" She sat up, half expecting, half hoping to be a child again, waking from an awful dream.

Aurora peered around the wall, covered to the middle of the thigh by one of her father's button-down shirts. "Almost."

Anna blushed, glaring at the rug.

"I'm sorry for intruding." Aurora padded over, eyeing the décor. "Ian Marbury… he was cute. I had a thing for him too back then. Can't say I was ever a fan of this much pink, though. Surprising… never figured you for being a girly-girl."

She looked at the holo-poster over her bed; the blond fourteen-year-old boy in the fancy headset mocked her with his grin. Anna couldn't even remember what his music sounded like.

"It was my dad's idea. Girl equals pink." Anna shrugged. "I wasn't super girly as a kid, but I didn't mind it. His nice spots were rare enough I didn't care what they looked like." She couldn't hold back sniffles. "It wasn't his fault. I was a monster."

Anna froze at the odd sensation of another presence in the room. The faint essence of beer, aftershave, and unwashed clothes teased at her nose.

"I'm sorry, Anna." Aurora sat on the bed and put a sisterly arm around her back.

"I..."

"What?"

"It's silly, but I thought I smelled him."

Aurora looked at the door. "You probably do."

Anna sat up, clenching her jaw. "Not now, Lauren. Don't fuck with me."

The alabaster woman looked at her with the most sincerity she'd ever seen in all-black eyes. "I'm not, Anna. He's right here."

She grasped her knees, afraid to look up.

"He wants me to tell you not to be afraid of him. He doesn't blame you."

"What?" Anna looked up. "But I..."

"He drove you to it." Aurora reached out and put a hand on top of Anna's. "Do you want to see him?"

Yes. No. Fuck no. What's wrong with you? Yes. I'm insane. "Uhm."

"It's up to you."

"I'm sorry, Dad."

"He heard you in the kitchen."

Anna shivered. "I figured out why I hate Arsenal so much."

Aurora glanced to her right. "Well, that made him laugh. He said he agrees with you about Postalwaste."

Anna laughed, tears flowing like faucets. "We were watching a match. Forty seconds left to a draw. Arsenal put one in. I got so angry it leaked out and fried the holo." Anna broke down, crying into her hands.

Aurora rubbed her back. "He's saying he was drunk. It's not your fault. He still loves you."

Something cold brushed Anna's cheek. She stopped sobbing.

"Alright." Anna wiped her eyes. "How can I see him? Is my mother here too?"

"No... I think she went right over. Not sure what makes some stay and some go wherever it is they go." Aurora stood. "Be right back, I need a knife."

"What?" The blood drained from Anna's face.

"I'm not going to stab you. I need to bleed on your coat. Unless you fancy being starkers on the other side, which I'm fine with, but I know you... and I suppose it *would* be somewhat awkward since he's your dad and all."

Anna sat in silence, picking at her pants and looking around at the closet full of junk, her desk, and datapads with old schoolwork. She picked one up and the screen flickered to life, showing an essay she'd been working on for her seventh-grade history class—about the war that left the area around Coventry Tower in ruins. Tears splattered on the screen, magnifying the text of the report she wrote about the slum she'd wound up living in months later.

"Now that's ironic."

She cried more, daydreaming about how her life would have gone if she hadn't lost control over a silly Frictionless match. High school, boys, college, a real job... would she have kids by now? Would the government have taken her in the night?

Anna shivered. "I'm being delusional. They knew about me already. Like they would've let me be normal."

"What?" Aurora walked in with a small kitchen knife. She nicked her finger and grasped Anna's coat. Yellow-orange light shimmered around the garment for a few seconds. "There."

"What was that?"

A handprint pressed into her sleeve. She shivered.

"Astral binding. The coat's solid to spirits now, so it'll come with you."

"Come with—"

Aurora grabbed her hand and pulled. A blast of freezing cold blinded her for an instant, and the room changed. Color washed away to a world of sepia tones. A gossamer touch swept down her body. She looked down at her clothes on the floor; everything but the coat had fallen right through her.

"Anna..."

Her father, appearing real and solid, stood by the doorway. The air smelled of him, his Manchester team shirt and frumpy sweat pants looked as they had the night he died, even down to the scorched child-sized handprint on his thigh. A mournful mask of guilt replaced the angry glare she remembered him always having. He still appeared to be in his mid-thirties, by appearance only five or six years older than her. Anyone seeing them would assume him an older brother. She cringed away from her burned handprint.

Her father walked up to her. "It's not your fault, sweetie. It's mine. Your mum said she was a psio, and I didn't really know what it meant. I was head over ass for her."

She sniffled. After a moment, she looked up. "I broke the holo. I didn't mean to. I can't control it."

"I know that now." He reached out a hand. "It wasn't that. It never was."

Anna trembled but took his hand. He seemed neither warm like a living man nor cold like a dead one. A second after she touched him, she burst into tears, falling against him and crying like a little girl.

"I was angry at them for what they did to your mother. They kept giving her all these serums and whatnot. Every time I saw you do something... psionic, it reminded me of her, and what they did to you."

She whimpered.

"I was never afraid of you. I never hated you. I wasn't man enough to handle the pain of losing Heather. The drink didn't do me any favors." He grasped her chin and made her look him in the eye. "I'm glad you defended yourself before I killed you. Rather it be me stuck here than a little version of you."

"Y-you didn't get angry with me for ruining your things?" Anna composed herself.

He scratched the side of his head. "Okay, it did get a bit frustrating... but every kid breaks stuff. And, yeah, the brew... You'd zap somethin' and I'd get annoyed, and then I'd think that Heather could'a helped me cope with your gift, and then I'd get steamed at them killin' her and wit' the drink in me, I just dumped it all on you." His lip quivered and he bowed his head. "Sorry seems a bit weak fer what I done, aye? I know ya sat outside the door, 'fraid ta come in most days."

Anna sniffled, remembering her head pressed to the poles in the railing by the door, listening to him rage and kick things, upset some moron from his job. "We had the life, didn't we?"

"The bloke what killed your mum's dead, by the by," said Aurora.

"I know." Her father's apparition darkened. "I ran into him already." He wiped tears from Anna's cheeks. "I also had a chat with a couple o' those Crossman chaps you sent over."

Heat rushed to her cheeks. "You know..."

He shot a guilty look at the rug. "I'm also waitin' for that bastard, Brown. Constable my ass."

"Y-you s-saw?" She wanted to crawl into a hole, and cringed.

"No, Anna, I didn't *watch*." He let go of her hand and paced. "I just *know*. It's... one of those strange things about being dead."

"Are you trapped here because I killed you?" She ran after him and held onto his arm. "I'm sorry. Whatever I have to do to set you free, just tell me."

"Guilt." He sighed. "Not sure what you can do about it but be happy."

She stared at the floor. "Oh, just ask for something easy why don't you?"

"I'll stick around an' keep the flat nice and cheap till you decide to move in." He smirked at the window. "Municipality owns it now, but they've had a bastard of a time trying to sell it." Her father chuckled. "People been 'round ta check it out, but for some strange reason, they never can stand to be inside for more than a few minutes."

She shivered.

"You'd have inherited it if you didn't drop off the grid." He grasped the back of her head and pulled her into a hug. "Might still be able to argue it's legally yours."

"The CSB knows what I did. I couldn't come back here. I..." She cringed away from the memories. "It's too much. All I can think about is what might've been. I..." Anna rubbed the front of her throat as she looked over her old bedroom. "I doubt I could live here."

"You can wallow in it or you can pick yourself up and keep walking." He patted her shoulder and let go. "Besides, you keep coming back."

"Aye, I suppose I do." Anna laughed, sniffling. "We're going away from Earth, Dad."

Aurora hummed. "I'd not dismiss the idea yet, hon. I think you might find that missing piece of yourself here someday."

Anna glanced at her. "What are you saying? Is something going to happen?"

"I'm not entirely sure." Aurora walked to the window, standing with her back to Anna. "I see glimpses of a little girl with white hair riding a bike outside. She looks like you... and there's a light-haired boy, quite a bit older than her, but I can't see him clearly."

"You're seeing the past." Anna absentmindedly squeezed and rubbed her father's arm.

"I doubt that." Aurora glanced over her shoulder and winked. "The sprog's wearing an Arsenal shirt."

Anna gasped.

38

UNDER A DARK WING

Kate

Steamy air hovered around the lockers, carrying the scent of soap, cologne, and perfume. Kate stripped out of her sweats and stuffed them in her assigned storage space next to her uniform and gear. Two men, one in a towel, one naked, sat on benches behind her with their backs turned, chatting about a pyrokinetic hopped up on a drug they called Stardust. She shivered. Limitless energy and a complete disregard for reality didn't go well with psionics in general; pyrokinesis made it close to a worst-case scenario.

A tall black woman walked by with a small towel around her neck, trailed by a mixture of jasmine perfume and autoshower soap. Kate tucked up to the lockers to let her pass without contact. The woman gave her an appraising glance as she opened her locker and took out a clean pair of undies.

"You're new, aren't you?"

"Yeah," said Kate.

"Somethin' wrong?"

Yeah, I just killed a man I thought of as my father. "Shooting. Someone I thought I could trust tried to kill me and hit David. I had to kill him."

"Oh, that's rough shit, girl." The woman slipped into her underwear and a Division 0 uniform.

Kate eyed the rank insignia—2nd Lt. Investigative Operations. Her sadness devoured the spike of fear that might have come from failing to show respect to an officer. "Thanks, Ma'am." She offered a limp salute.

How serious can you be when everyone's naked?

She trudged to an open autoshower on the far end of the room, in the midst of the steam cloud where ten or so other people, men and women, stood in various stages of the process from initial rinse to hot air tornado. A number of them checked her out.

So much for it being no big deal. "Fucking scientists." *Yeah, Russian supermodel is subtle.*

She closed her eyes and let the machine work. When soap covered her, David's voice filtered into her thoughts.

I wasn't expecting anger. Are you okay?

Kate smiled at his being there. *No. I still feel like shit, but Sanchez and Dawmer were staring. What kind of morons work for C-Branch anyway? I was made to be a spy, not draw every damn eye in a room full of people supposedly desensitized to group showers.*

His laughter came back over the telepathic link. *Plain girls don't get invited to the ambassador's bed.*

She brushed aside her artificial indignation. Truth was, she didn't much care who saw what, but it did provide a convenient excuse to stop thinking about El Tío for a few minutes.

The man manipulated you, Kate.

"I know, I know." She stared down and sighed. "But he was still the closest thing I had to family." After wiping soap away from her eyes, she looked at him through the foggy tube. *It would've been bad enough to find him dead, but to have to kill him myself? The worst part was how he looked broken because he thought I'd betrayed him.*

He stared at her with guilt and adoration. Neither of them spoke—aloud or via telepathy—the obvious truth. Kate reacted to protect (technically avenge) him. Incinerating El Tío had been as much a declaration of love as anything could have been.

El Tío was good to me... at least as good as a man like that could be to anyone. It would've been much worse for me on the street without him.

David shrugged. *You're powerful, Kate. You could've looked after yourself. All he gave you was guilt. What he made you do...*

She shut her eyes as the rinse kicked on. "Yeah, yeah. He was good to those he thought were loyal, and I betrayed him."

How did you betray him?

I procrastinated too long. He wanted me to kill a cop. Kate held on to the handrail, keeping her head down. *I told him I couldn't kill for him anymore, so maybe I took my sweet time finding this Pryce guy. I don't know how that would play here, but in El Tío's world, that's as good as taking a shit on his desk while he watched.*

David coughed. *I don't think you understand. He didn't care at all about you, only what you could do for him. Look at that big bastard from the roof. He managed to resist the order to kill you, figured out the compulsion only worked when he looked at you. He cared for you more than El Tío did, like an older brother.*

"Paul?" An image of his guilt-ridden face haunted her. "What happened to him?"

I mentioned suggestive mental implant in my report, so they fed him to Ashford. Last I heard was a Syndicate lawyer got him out. Patrol craft's video showed him pulling the other man off you, so I imagine that helped.

Kate stretched under rinse two. *El Tío was a complex guy. You can't just quantify him in simple emotions. He was—*

A sociopath. David offered a consoling smile. *A sociopath who found a vulnerable girl he could turn into an assassin no one would ever see coming. The way you feel about him was all planned.*

Kate shrugged as the hot air started. *I'll be okay.*

He put his hand on the tube. *Worry?*

Oh, lots of things. Archon. You deciding out of nowhere I'm a monster and leaving, random idiots with big guns...

David leaned close. *I do not think you are a monster.* He glanced at his forearm. *I do, however, have to report to briefing. I should go; I'm already late. Vid me if you need anything.*

The dry cycle ended and she stepped out, not caring if the entire world saw her kiss him. Besides, he had his uniform on. Much to her disappointment, his hands remained gentlemanly.

KATE TOOK HER TIME GOING TO THE PSYCH DEPARTMENT. 'STANDARD procedure' they said, for an officer-involved fatality. The last thing she wanted to do was air her dirty laundry out to a total stranger with the power to extinguish her nascent career with Division 0.

"Kaaaaate!"

The approaching jubilant wail of a teenaged girl gave her enough warning before impact to avoid incinerating the body that tackled her into a hug against the wall.

"Ohmigod ohmigod ohmigod ohmigod," muttered an olive-skinned girl with bright powder-blue hair down to the backs of her knees. She wore a set of standard Division 0 blacks, but didn't have a utility belt or weapon.

"Uhm." Kate stood rigid, not sure what to make of this young woman clamped around her like she'd stumbled on a long-lost relative. "Do I know you, kid?"

The girl let go, staring adoration up at her. "You're my new goddess."

"Uhh..." Kate scratched her head. "Did you hit the Flowerbasket a bit hard?"

"No." The girl smiled. "I'm not a kid either, I'm nineteen... just short. Ohmigod I can't believe you're here."

"I'm sorry, whoever you are... I have no idea who, uhh, you are."

"I'm Shimmer."

"Guess it was your parents on the Flowerbasket."

"Ha. Ha." The girl rolled her eyes. "It's my net name."

"Okay, so why are you looking at me like that?"

"You're Kate Solomon right? The uber-pyro?" The girl lowered her voice. "Is it true you killed El Tío?"

Ice filled Kate's veins. "How the hell do you know that?"

"If it's on the net, I know it... or can find it."

Kate walked off. "Yeah, he's dead."

Shimmer jogged alongside. "What's wrong? The guy was a fucking bastard. The world's better off."

She spun and grabbed the girl by the arms, slamming her back against the wall.

"W-what the fuck?" The hero-worship in her eyes faded to fear.

Nineteen or not, now she looked innocent. Kate sighed and let go. "I knew him. I didn't want to kill him, but he shot someone I care about while trying to kill me."

"Sorry." Shimmer seemed less fearful, but her former enthusiasm stayed at arm's length. "How'd you know him? Who'd he kill?"

"No one. Well... A lot of people, no one I cared about. He..." Kate sighed. "I was like fifteen, living on the street, and he took me in."

Shimmer gasped, turning pale. "Oh, no way... He made you kill for him, didn't he?"

Kate grabbed the girl's shoulder again. An admin cadet patch caught her eye, which usually identified the wearer as a ward of the dorms, or at least would have if she were a minor. Not quite a sworn officer, but not quite a civilian either. Kate let go.

"How'd you know?"

"Duh, that's the kind of evil scumbag he was, making a child kill for him. I just assumed."

Kate seethed, but held it in.

"My brother was a Div 1 cop. Syndicate took over my dad's business when I was little. They killed him to get control of the board because he wouldn't give in. After my brother grew up and became a cop, he went undercover in the Syndicate trying to find the man who ordered my dad's murder. They killed him too."

A moment of panic seized Kate, but the image of the brother in the girl's surface thoughts matched no one she'd ever assassinated for El Tío.

"Sorry."

Shimmer offered an apologetic smile and some of the adoration returned to her eyes. "It's okay, I didn't know that part. I'm happy whenever the Syndicate gets kicked in the nuts. Tío was big league, and you did the world a favor." She kicked at the floor. "I won't dance on his grave again in front of you."

"Nah, it's all right. You can be happy about it. I never had anyone I loved killed by the Syndicate." Kate made a fist as if she were about to punch the wall. "I guess you and David are right. He used me. I'll never know what the truth is."

They parted ways, but Shimmer ran back on squeaking sneakers a few seconds later. "Uhh, Kate?"

"Hmm?"

"Do you know where I can find Aaron?"

"Aaron?"

"Uhm." Shimmer held up a NetMini with a hologram of a smiling thirtyish blond man. Judging by the teeth, British. "Aaron Pryce. He's supposed to be in Div 0, but I can't find him. I wanted to surprise him. He kinda saved me from myself."

"Oh, him." Kate shrugged. "No idea. He's not easy to find."

39

NIGHT TERRORS

Anna

The Autocab whirred to a halt at the front receiving area of Heathrow. Anna hadn't stopped trembling since she'd left her old home. Aurora's offhanded remark that NetMinis could sometimes record ghost voices and let her talk to him got her brain spinning. *What does that woman know? Am I to wind up living there? What's going to happen with Archon?* Her urge to use a dose of zoom to cope with the overwhelming emotions caused by the past two hours of talking to her dead father reassured her as much as it terrified her. Immediate nausea came on at the thought of even touching an innocent looking one-inch square of skin-colored plastic. She had to get away from temptation. She had to distance herself from familiar surroundings, old haunts, and bad people.

She had to find James.

Annoyed buzzing from the Autocab console called her attention back to the now. She'd been sitting still for almost two minutes. The screen informed her of a 'convenience charge' if she made it wait any longer. Anna wobbled to her feet and wrapped her arms around herself, shivering. At least the automatic cars in Britain waited for a person to step away before they rushed off. Her sudden craving to run to James struck her as disingenuous. She shuddered, trying to find some way to believe Aaron had been alarmist, but her thoughts kept circling back to the idea she'd been manipulated.

"Oi, Miss," said a male voice.

Anna looked up, grumbling at the sight of a constable raising his hand at her. Her heart pounded for three beats before she remembered she appeared to be a Proper, and was nowhere near Coventry. This one wouldn't hang her from the ceiling and try to rape her. A thin spark crept over her tightening fist. No one would ever do that to her again.

"Are you alright? Ya look out of sorts. Did someone 'urt ya?"

Shit. Damn cops smell lies like flies on shite. Let's see how he reacts. "Spent the past hour at a séance, talking to my dead father."

"Ach, bloody charlatans." The man shook his head. "How much did they ding ya for that dog and pony show?"

"Didn't charge me a whit. I'm alright, honestly, just a little shaken up." She took a step toward the door. "Thanks for your concern, constable."

"Miss." He followed. "I'm afraid you're forgetting something."

She'd heard that line before. Anna whirled on him with more than a little vitriol in her stare. "What's that then?"

He leaned back and folded his arms. "You've come all the way to London, yet you forgot someone."

She blinked. "What?"

The Constable's stern expression cracked to a distinctly feminine giggle. "Oh, come on, Anna… How could you forget her? She needs to see you."

Aurora. Anna slouched, tension and anxiety melting out of her. "That was cruel. You know I haven't the best experience with the Met."

He grasped her right arm above the elbow. "I behaved myself in your house. I had to mess with you a little here. Come on, I'll give you a ride."

🜍 ♀ 🜔 🜂 ♍

The building at Nine Clifton Hill sat quiet in the early evening. Anna held on to the gate, staring at where her pale hand covered the black metal. Aside from a few Vidphone calls, she hadn't seen Faye since leaving London. Dread pushed her away. *What if she's upset at me for leaving?*

"Go on, Anna," said the constable, from his car. "It's alright. You've spent too much time starin' at 'ouses today."

"Yeah," whispered Anna. "I s'pose I 'ave at that."

She pushed past the gate and got to the porch before the second wave of hesitation hit. The place seemed so quiet without all the NewsNet bots and police. Anna kicked at the ground, feeling foolish for making all the wrong moves. Penny's, her old home, Faye's flat… if the CSB was after her, they were either asleep or more incompetent than possible.

Buzz. The doorbell sounded angry.

A few minutes of silence later, Anna pushed it again.

"Keep your knickers on, I'm comin.'"

The voice sounded too young to be the mother, too old to be Faye.

Anna fidgeted with her coat until the door opened. A young woman answered, gaunt, pale, and with shadowed eyes. Her oversized tee shirt hung down to her thighs over baggy leggings, covered by straight, black hair as long as her waist. Her expression of 'what the hell do you want' fell to shocked neutrality for a second before her eyes went red and she leapt into a hug.

"Anna?"

Her fears of anger and rejection unfounded, Anna raised her arms and held on. "Hope I'm not interrupting anything."

Faye leaned back. Her baleful expression made Anna think the girl had forgotten how to smile. "Come in! It's Baltic out here."

Anna followed her into a living room a bit too warm for comfort and shrugged out of her coat. The place screamed milquetoast middle class, decorated in beige and tan, with small fake plants interspersed among a dozen portraits of the family. A chronology of images circled the inner wall above the couch, showing Faye's transformation from infant to the child she remembered to the haggard skeleton of a teen she'd become. The two most recent shots at least showed an attempt to smile.

"Place looks the same," said Anna, taking a seat on the sofa. "Few more photos."

"Aye. Parents are out for a re-date or some ghastly nauseous rubbish. They need time away. Apparently, I'm a bit of sad sack." Faye stuck her tongue out. "Ya want some tea? Water?"

Before Anna could answer, the girl ran out and returned with Sainsbury's brand iced tea in an automatic-cool can. She handed it over and flopped in a facing seat, elbows on her knees, eyes watery.

"Sorry I've been out of touch." Anna turned the can about. "I've been in a bit of trouble. What're you now, eighteen?"

"Next month. They're worried about me 'cause I haven't given much of a fuck about gettin' my certification for autos. An' they really think I'm nutters 'cause I don't sneak off and drink and shite. How cocked up is that? They suspect I'm wonky because I'm *not* on drugs." Faye dug her toes into the carpet. "I thought you were mad at me."

"I… Not at all. I was caught up in a bit of a mess and I didn't want it to spill over onto you. Besides, you had a family and a home and everything and I was just an outsider who didn't belong mucking it up."

"Rubbish," Faye whined. "I would've liked an older sister. Mum would'a let you stay with us."

Anna laughed. "I'm too old to have parents now. I'm twenty… eight?"

"Shit, really? You don't bloody look it." Faye blinked.

"Thanks." Anna smirked and popped open the tea. A fizzling crackle escaped the small hole on the top with a brief whiff of metallic chemical, and a layer of frost swam down the outside. In seconds, the canister became too chilly for comfort. She took a hasty sip and set it on the coffee table. "Cripes that's cold."

Faye pulled her legs up onto the seat. "So…"

"How've things been for you?" Anna looked the girl up and down. "Are you eating?"

"Yeah, not much. Ain't much for sleep neither."

Anna leaned forward. "Talk to me."

"I… I don't sleep well." She went from leaning left to sitting cross-legged. "Doc says I have 'night terrors' or some shit. I keep waking up screaming, thinking those men are coming through my window to take me again. Dad's a proper champ about it, though. Always runs in to check on me." She loosed a somber laugh. "What am I, five? When I do sleep, I crash hard an' don't hear my alarm. Was late for school last month, an' Mum tossed a sheet over my face to wake me up and I thought it was a black bag." She cried into her hands. "I freaked. Mum's still afraid to be alone in a room with me."

"I'm sorry for leaving you to deal with that." Anna reached over and put a hand on Faye's arm.

"It's okay… you had those fuckers still chasing you for real." She wiped her cheeks, sniffling into a giggle. "After that crap with Bell, Mum and Dad are still super guilty. I could get away with murder. Guess they're lucky I'm a geek, huh?"

"I'm still willing to kill that worthless nonce if you want."

"Anna!" Faye threw a pillow at her. "He doesn't scare me anymore. My nightmares are about those cockbags in black. Everyone at school thinks I'm the crazy bitch. You know, one of the tinfoil hat crowd what sees aliens."

"The man who ordered your abduction is dead." Anna risked the tea, finding it tolerable. "James threw him off a roof."

Faye cringed.

"I stayed away to protect you. The CSB has no reason to mess with you if they can't use you to get to me." *Did I? I could've called her. Why didn't I ever think to?* She looked up from the can of tea to Faye's sunken eyes and thought of Alexi. Would it have been kinder to make Faye forget everything that happened? "Faye…"

"Hmm?"

"Would you want to forget it all? Bell, being abducted in the night by the government, everything?"

"I'd forget you and Penny and that horny bastard Spawny too, wouldn't I?" She slid out of the recliner and flopped on the couch next to Anna. "I can handle a few nightmares, and I don't give a rat's ass what the morons at school think of me."

"Better a painful truth than a comfortable lie?" Anna chuckled. "Yeah, I suppose."

"Something bad happened to you, didn't it?" Faye leaned her head on Anna's shoulder. "You can talk about it if you want. I'm not a kid anymore."

Anna smiled at her. "No... I suppose you aren't. You'd be pretty if you actually ate food."

Faye gave her a raspberry. "Are you back in London for good?"

"I've got to leave soon. It's not safe for me here... I'm not sure it'll ever be." Anna squinted at the bay window, thinking of Aurora's comment at her old home. "Course, stranger things have happened."

"I wish you'd stay. Well..." Faye hopped to her feet and started for the kitchen. "I'll order takeaway then. Thai? We've got a lot to catch up on."

Anna let her head sag back into the cushions. Worrying about delays now felt ridiculous. James would have noticed her absence already. *Fuck it. Fix me to the bed will he? He can wait a day.* "Sure. Something with chicken, not too spicy."

"Noodles?"

"Why not."

Faye grinned, looking as if Anna had breathed life back into a zombie. She scrambled off the sofa and darted out of sight.

Anna scowled as soon as Faye left the room. Five years ago, she felt responsible for getting that little girl mixed up with the government. She'd thought Faye had been doing well at home with loving parents—instead, she'd been barely sleeping or eating.

Bloody CSB. If Gordon wasn't already dead...

SLEEPOVER

Anna

Half-asleep in a borrowed shirt, in a shared bed, with Faye's arm over her, she felt as though she'd gone to an alternate dimension: twelve some odd years ago in another world where Annabelle Morgan was an ordinary teenager having an ordinary sleepover. The weak scent of Thai food still hovered in the air, wafting from the takeaway containers on the floor. She laced her fingers behind her head and breathed, drifting in and out of sleep, trying to imagine a normal life.

Plain, white walls had a couple of pre 'everything-went-to-shit' holo-posters from when Faye still liked contemporary music. She'd taken down the Dead Ballerinas stuff as it reminded her too much of 'the bad time.' The lack of effort put into the decorations made her worry more. This bedroom could be a model for a rental office. Faye had no interests to speak of, didn't care much for music, vids, games, driving, or even dating. Her parents made her go to a therapist for depression and night terrors, which she tolerated but thought useless. As Faye had put it, 'coping'll mean fuck all when soldiers kick in my window again.'

After a banquet of amazing Thai takeaway, they'd stayed up to the wee hours talking about the past five years, save for a half-hour interlude when the parents returned. Her mother had been concerned about the awkwardness of an almost-thirty-year-old woman sharing her daughter's bed, even if she did look like a teenager. They lacked a guest room, and Faye had seemed so energized around her. After repeated insistence that Faye liked boys, Anna's "I'll just crash on the floor," and Faye's horror that they thought anything unseemly would happen between them, they'd relented. The change in the girl *was* dramatic. Anna felt a bit like a pitbull guarding her sleeping human. For years, she worried the sight of her killing those men during the escape had left mental scars, but Faye barely remembered that part at all. She still thought of her as a savior.

As odd as it seemed, Anna felt better after talking out what Mr. Blake had done to her, the conversation she'd never been able to have with Penny. Faye was horrified; for a short while, Anna found herself on the receiving end of being comforted. In a way, she rationalized some kind of karmic circle had turned around. She'd rescued the girl from the government, and Faye had rescued Anna from her shame.

Faye's mother peeked in around nine in the morning, offered a hesitant smile, and left.

A bit past noon, Faye woke. She blinked at the clock, and let off a sleepy laugh. "Guess I got the day off."

When they went to the kitchen, the Vidphone played a recorded message from Mr. Taylor apologizing for not being home due to work. He thanked Anna for dropping in and, addressing Faye, mentioned her school was sending her day's work electronically.

"Because of my 'condition.'" Faye rolled her eyes. "The crazy girl has attacks, you know. Sometimes she gets to work from home."

"Don't most kids attend from home?"

"Oh, I wish." Faye sighed. "This isn't the UCF. We're still required to go in person."

Anna held her shoulders. "Faye. I want to show you something."

"'Kay." Faye let her arms drape in her lap and stared into Anna's eyes.

She opened a telepathic link and recalled the CSB agent dressed as a constable standing in the shadow of the press frenzy. Anna focused on the memory of him saying, "The Taylor girl will not be bothered."

"Thanks." Faye hugged her. "Maybe that'll help... but you know this shit isn't rational fear."

By the time Anna returned from a quick shower, Faye had set out a full English breakfast: poached eggs, fried mushrooms, toast, and sausages. Anna took one look at the eagerness in the girl's expression and felt horrible for having to leave.

Conversation as they ate largely became an elongated farewell process. Faye's desperation mounted with each passing moment. By the time they'd cleaned their plates, she looked like the little girl who'd begged Anna to come inside the night she'd returned home.

"I'll pop back at least once a month." Anna offered a weak smile. "It's only an hour's flight."

"Next time, will you stay at least a weekend?"

"I can do that." Anna frowned inside, thinking of the look on James's face as he left her chained to the bed. "Maybe a whole week if I can manage it... but, you'll not use me as an excuse to skip school."

"Kay."

Aurora's comment needled at her again. "And I dunno. If ever I can manage it, I might consider coming back to London more permanent like."

Faye grinned.

They walked together to the door and the porch. Anna hid her tears as they embraced, not resisting an excuse to take a few minutes longer.

"You vid me anytime you want," muttered Anna.

"Aye." Faye sniffled. "Safe flight and all that."

Anna started to walk for the gate, but stopped and spun back. She grasped Faye's hands and stared her in the eyes. "You know how you really beat those bastards, Faye? *Live*. You live." Anna paused a second to keep from choking up. "You live your life in defiance of what they did to you. You're not psionic. They've got no reason to bother with you again. Don't mire in the past forever."

"Pot. Kettle." Faye's eyes ran with tears, but she smiled.

All the house lights faltered. "Aye." *I've got a bit of living to do myself.*

"So what about you then?" Faye bit her lower lip.

"Things are... complicated at the moment." Anna exhaled, head down. "I'm not rightly sure 'ow any of it'll turn out, but, I'll try to live if you will."

"Gonna hold you t'that." Faye drilled a limp punch into Anna's shoulder, grinning. "Vid?"

"Aye. Will. I'll try an' come 'round more if I can." She glanced up at the sky, for the first time in five years' time unsure if she *wanted* to leave Earth behind.

"Brill." Faye smiled. "Can't wait."

Leaving had proven harder than she thought, and standing on the porch with Faye clinging for almost a half hour came close to changing her mind. Eventually, Anna trudged along the path to the gate and paused with one hand on the metal. She feared if she looked back, she'd be unable to leave, but she did. As expected, Faye hovered in the doorway, wiping tears from her eyes.

I'll not be gone for good, said Anna telepathically.

Faye gave her a look like a kid who'd been promised a new puppy. Anna picked up the reply upon her surface thoughts. *'Ats what the ghost said.*

A pang of worry stabbed her in the gut. Anna waved with a semi-enthusiastic grin and walked off in the direction of the city center. 'Ghost' had to mean Aurora. Faye had no gifts at all, at least, not in a psionic sense.

What the devil's going on?

ANNA TRUDGED AMONG LIGHT PEDESTRIAN TRAFFIC. TWICE SHE CAUGHT pickpockets, and once she sensed the approach of a skimmer—and fried it. A dark-skinned, teenage boy in a heavy, green coat with smoke pouring out of the pocket ran off yammering in rapid Hindi. Hearing him made her remember how Penny used to babysit for one of the Propers and claim the little boy as hers when collecting her dole. Almost twenty minutes after she'd left Faye's house, a glimmer caught her eye from a plasfilm poster on the wall of a coffee shop, depicting a smiling young boy surrounded by text demanding equal rights for psionics. Another one had a grimy little girl in the rags of a street urchin with a forlorn expression. She held her hands up, with two dolls floating above her palms and the slogan 'we're not evil' written across the paving below her feet. The third poster showed a young couple holding hands with text demanding an end to the ban on psionics marrying.

The fragrance of coffee proved too much to resist after staying up until almost five a.m. She stumbled into the place and bumped a disheveled man in an orange blazer at the end of the line. His wild hair looked like she'd already shocked him senseless. He glanced at her for an instant, looked away, and whirled around screaming. He seemed a week's worth of starved and several days without a razor's attention.

"Bloody fuck!"

"Plonk?" Anna blinked. "Of course, only *you* would wear that shade of orange with a white shirt and a pink necktie."

"Don't bloody kill me!"

Anna smiled at the room, trying to look as innocent and harmless as a tiny woman could.

Stop it, arse. You're causing a scene. I've no interested in 'arming you.

He whimpered at the telepathic message until the meaning chipped past the thick layer of muck around his brain. Plonk glanced side to side and rushed up close enough to smell last night's booze on his shirt.

"They're lookin' after ya, Pix."

"Damn." She caught herself eyeing the room. "Who?"

"Dunno, lass. Some government tool. Came by the flat this mornin' askin' about ya." He grinned. "Need anyfin'?"

"No, Plonk. Remember what I said about not wanting to harm you?"

"Aye."

"If I wind up with a zoomie anywhere on my body, I'll rescind that promise."

"Right." He glanced down. "Gotcha."

Her NetMini vibrated at the same instant a teen behind the counter yelled "Next."

Plonk gave her a nervous smile and ran to the clerk. Anna drifted to the side of the shop, answering in voice-only mode.

"Hello?"

"Where the bloody hell have you gone off to this time? Are you not quite done over there yet?" asked Archon.

"Almost. Just nabbing some coffee."

"We have a minor problem. I would prefer to have your assistance with a misplaced starship and an absentminded Awakened samurai with issues of self-worth. What are you doing back in London? Do you not understand the danger over there? Where are you that you have the image off?"

"I'm well aware of the danger I'm in." Anna narrowed her eyes, holding that thought for a moment—and not in the way James would take it. "I didn't want the entire coffee shop to partake of our chat."

"I know that tone. I hope there is nothing wrong."

"Oh, I'm peachy keen." She examined the fingernails of the hand not holding the NetMini to her ear. "For being left spread eagle all damn day. Yes, I'm a bit cheesed off about that. What the hell's gotten into you?"

"I thought you were fond of that sort of... kinkery, is it? I hoped you would find a bit of a thrill in it. Honestly, I had not intended to be away as long as I was; the situation in Venezuela became... more complicated than I had anticipated."

An accident? Bollocks. That look he gave me was no accident. "I wanted to check up on Pen and them." *If I tell him about Faye, he'll rewrite her.* "I thought you'd decided to be a bastard again, like with the chopsticks. I needed some time to clear my head." She picked at her coat. "The trip was a mistake. I never should've come here." She thought about her father to make fake sniffles sound real. "They all practically shat themselves when they saw me. Probably have the CSB coming after me already. I'll be back on the next shuttle."

"Nothing to panic over. Be careful. I am sorry I was delayed. I'll make it up to you as soon as you are back."

"Ta." She waited for a moment, wondering if he'd say something cute like 'love you' or what have you. "James?"

"Keep your head down and be safe."

He hung up.

Love you, too... Do I?

"Next," said the teen behind the counter. "Miss?"

She sighed and let the NetMini slip from her fingers into a pocket. "Triple espresso."

FOR THE FOURTH TIME, ANNA STOPPED IN THE SCANNER TUNNEL AS IT BLARED an alarm. She stomped, snarled, and marched back to the entrance. Once again, she'd made it halfway when it buzzed, sensing something 'anomalous.' Starport security asked her to back up and remove her coat the first time. Shoes the second time, and asked about body piercings the third. As the security officer walked her to the start of the full-body scanner for pass four, Anna realized her nerves had been playing hell with the machine.

"I've not got any metal, your machine is wonky. I'll go starkers, and you'll bloody well see."

Quite a few men took notice of her as she grabbed her shirt as if to pull it off.

"Calm down, Miss."

"Right, if I get too loud, I'll get arrested for daring to question the sanctity of your beloved scanners."

"Do you have any cybernetic implants that might be too new to be in the system?"

"No. Look, I'm bloody telling you"—Anna kept her voice calm—"I've got nothing. I'm seconds away from flinging my clothes off and storming through it bare as a babe. Will that prove that it's your stupid machine having a conniption?"

"Need backup at checkpoint fourteen," said the agent into his shoulder.

"Oh, bloody hell." Anna rubbed the bridge of her nose.

"That won't be necessary," said a man. "Agent Hughes, Mi6."

Anna jumped and let her startlement look like nerves. The Starport Security Agency rep backed off. Hughes 'pulled her aside' and offered a conspiratorial wink.

"What's got you nervous enough to mess with the sensors?"

"Someone I used to know said the government's trying to track me down."

Hughes chuckled. "That was me. That Plonk fellow's quite the slob these days. Not quite the same bloke he used to be."

"Tell me about it." Anna relaxed.

A security woman ran over with Anna's coat and shoes in a plastic bin. Anna took them, and the guard scurried away as fast as she could.

"I wanted to tell you. Lord Thompson's motion carried. Parliament is having hearings on psionic legislation starting next week. Most of the talk is sounding like the registration program will be officially discarded, as will additional criminality attached to the use of abilities in the commission of other crimes."

"What about the crime of simply *being*?"

Hughes pursed his lips. "There is a real chance of adopting the UCF's stance on it. They've even been floating the idea of incepting a bureau on the order of their Division 0. Heck, another year from now and they might even let them get married."

She rolled her eyes. "Oh, how charitable of them."

"Well..." Hughes chuckled. "Everyone knows two psionics having a child will produce the antichrist on fire."

Anna sighed. "Fire sounds like a good idea. Can we burn the C of E?"

"Now, now. That'll just make them think they're right. Those of us with abilities in the Bureau are being considered for the new startup agency. Pay's top notch. We could use someone with your talents. Least they could do to make up for things."

"What?" Anna stared at him as though he'd slapped her. "You want me to *work* for the people who had my mother murdered?"

He cringed. "Technically, that was Mi6, not us, and the whole paradigm is changing. We have to show the people we can be part of society in a good way."

Anna's lip quivered thinking about the picture of her mother's body and her father's ghost. He'd kept the house for her, terrifying away anyone who set foot in the place or considered buying it. That wouldn't last forever. Sooner or later, someone would ignore the spookiness. Gleaming sunlight drew her eyes to the long row of windows on the far side of the security checkpoint where a shuttle slid by outside. Brick red, the corporate logo of RedLink covered it from nose to tail.

A hopeful man in thick glasses stared at her. In a moment of eye contact, she heard him wondering if she was really going to get on with the stripping. Red-faced, she averted her eyes.

Lauren told her to consider her old home. Silly as it was, Faye's need to have her close by carried more weight than it ought to have. She didn't completely trust Hughes, yet, but Lauren said... and Archon had started to frighten her.

Anna blinked, realizing her inner voice called him Archon and not James. She swallowed, trying to remember what she had been like before meeting him. Even working for Mr. Carroll, she dodged jobs that would have required her to kill. Aside from her Father, she managed to avoid taking life until the night the Crossmen went too far. Since falling in with Archon, she'd killed at least eleven people, because he'd needed them out of their way. Still, the Anna she used to be lurked inside. That redhead, the Awakened pyro, melted down a squad of men without batting an eyelash. Anna shivered. She could never be that cold, but Archon *had* changed her. The idea of staying with him made her fear she'd become like Kate had been. Of course, Althea had rewired her brain and turned her soft—at least softer. That woman had seen something in Archon that made her flee. After getting her out of that C-Branch holding facility, the woman had turned her back and run off. Aurora tried to tell her a few days later that the woman still considered Anna a friend, but had become terrified of Archon. What would he do if *she* tried to leave as well? She'd been his right hand for as long as he'd been in the UCF.

If she tried to leave, he would make her forget everything she ever was.

Hughes brushed her cheek with a tissue. "Is everything alright?"

She hadn't realized she'd been crying. Anna looked down. "That offer of yours..."

"Hmm?" He raised an eyebrow.

Anna folded her arms, fighting to keep her nervousness from blowing out the entire security station. "Can I 'ave a few ta think about it?"

THE RONIN RETURNS

Mamoru

A thick haze of smoke greeted Mamoru when he opened his eyes; a trail of white fluttered up from the left end of Flatline's deck, eye level ten feet in front of him. His fingers peeled away from the Matsushita Ultra, out of the handprint he'd melted into the housing. Thin black plastic flaked away from his closing fist. He kept his breaths shallow to minimize the taste of burned silicon and flesh.

Flatline's arm and head poked out from the right side of the desk from where he'd collapsed to the floor. Mamoru stood and attached the katana to its place on his hip. He stared at Flatline's pallid, unconscious face for a moment, eyelid twitching at the notice of a thread of smoke seeping out of the man's M3 interface port. The two cats, Yin and Yang, pawed at his cheek, meowing.

Trash crunched underfoot as he advanced and took a knee by the fallen hacker. The wire plugged in behind his ear remained hot to the touch, though Mamoru resisted the pain long enough to pull it out. He gathered the twig-thin man in his arms and lifted him. The cats stared at him, tails fluffed.

An impatient sense of contempt spread up his back. The other presence returned. A shadow shifted on the wall, though Mamoru sensed no one. Four cats darted out of the room.

"Sympathy, Mamoru?"

The unexpected voice sent a wave of tension over his muscles. He turned, careful not to smack Flatline's head into the desk, and stared at the ancient gunslinger who had come out of thin air. The man's head tilted forward enough for the brim of his cowboy hat to obscure his eyes, though strands of whitish hair trailed to the side like cobwebs in a weak breeze. Dark miasmic fog obscured his boots and the ends of a long, brown duster coat, open to reveal a six-gun.

From where he stood, the foulness of the entity's breath stalled the air in Mamoru's throat.

"We have an arrangement," said the old man, raising his head until red, glowing eyes peeked out from under his hat. The dark mass around his legs moved and congealed, as if alive and looking at Mamoru. "We have no time for mercy."

Mamoru huffed to clear his airways. "This is not mercy. This is honor."

He walked out, carrying Flatline. The old man's menacing grin melted to an annoyed frown, and the rest of him burst into a column of black smoke, which fell straight onto the floor. Inky fog flooded the room, billowing out into the hallway behind Mamoru's slow trudge. Tendrils lapped at his back, but the mass of darkness did not overtake him.

Shadows followed Mamoru for several blocks, sliding along the street and up the walls of buildings long forgotten. Gangers, dosers, and cyberjunkies watched him. Few moved. One woman with numerous feline cybernetic parts hissed before tripping over herself to run into an alley.

The dark energy following him seeped into the ground, vanishing from sight as he reached the end of the grey zone. Buildings no longer rotted in place, electronics in the walls once again worked, and the overhead glow of innumerable advert bots bathed him in neon pink and green.

Mamoru ignored the thickening crowd around him. No one seemed to notice Flatline, who appeared to be a corpse in his arms. When he felt he had left the grey zone behind, he set the man down on the curb and took his NetMini from his pocket. The device bent to Mamoru's will and unlocked long enough to page a ride. A PubTran taxi arrived two minutes later.

He laid Flatline across the back seat and rested his hand on the roof, influencing the vehicle's computer to think he'd paid. "Nearest medical center. The passenger is injured."

"Thank you for choosing PubTran Corporation for your travel needs. Would you like to use our emergency expedite service? Only fifty credits."

Mamoru frowned. "Opportunistic." He forced the little car to register a paid boost.

Holographic flashing bar lights appeared atop the little car, which sped off after Mamoru closed the side hatch door. Flatline was no longer his responsibility. He backed away from the curb and walked. The crowd flowed around him, a river breaking around a moving boulder. A few miles deeper into the city proper, Mamoru sought the solitude of a shaded park in the courtyard of an office tower. The smog layer muted the late afternoon sun, leaving the area awash in pale grey light and the scent of recent rain.

He took a seat on a bench below an unnatural blue tree and grasped the NetMini in his pocket. The peaceful courtyard flew forward from his perception as a sense of vertigo came hand in hand with falling down into the floor. His link with the small device allowed him to send his consciousness into the GlobeNet, and he found himself standing in the center of a virtual reproduction of the same space. Advert bots remained, though few people did. Hundreds of threads of light extended from the towering structure at the far end of the park, remote connections to work-at-home employees. Every so often, a dark egg-shape pulsed over one of the gossamer strands, arriving or departing data.

The world felt slow and boggy compared to using a proper deck, and the little device lacked the power to render an avatar. Knowing he was the only one in the world who could 'plug in' with a NetMini made him smile.

Mamoru willed programs into being. The ground beneath his bench erupted with thousands upon thousands of palm-sized spiders made of jagged shards of onyx. The search routines rushed off in all directions, a dark stain spreading over cyberspace with the clicking of needle legs on metal. Minutes later, the last of them departed the ruptured ground, and the hole sealed.

He waited, meditating. Data moved at the periphery of his awareness; in this place, it mattered not if his eyes appeared open or closed. Over vast virtual distances, each tiny spider whispered to him.

Hours passed in cyberspace. Mamoru did not move or blink until an approaching signal shimmered in the dark. One spider scuttled toward him across the park, clutching a glass thread in its mouthparts. The fiber stretched to the horizon, flickering with the heartbeat of a keepalive signal.

Mamoru smiled and bent forward to take the offering from his pet. The little program wobbled with glee a second before the animating force faded, and it fell apart as small slivers of inert onyx. The delicate sound of billions of tiny chips of glass shattering came from far away. He had no further need of the search programs.

He raised the thread in a fist and squeezed. A rectangular pane appeared above it in blue wireframe, stretching and texturizing until it took on the appearance of a small torii gate. Open space between the poles swirled with energy, creating a portal into a corporate office. Nine copies of Archon's face, each at a somewhat different angle, stared back at him with a mixture of surprise and indignation as Mamoru's presence took over all nine of his display panels.

"You... How did you?"

Mamoru's expression held no emotion. "I regret my unfortunate delay, but I am once again in the city."

"Where have you been?" Archon's right eye twitched. "Tell me you still possess the ship?"

"The ship is, as far as I am aware, still where I left it. I will bring it to Earth as soon as necessary."

Archon's heads shifted as he glanced from one copy of Mamoru's face to the next. "Have you been compromised? What caused the delay?"

"A woman who believes herself to be my sister attempted to interfere."

"How does an Awakened allow an ordinary human to pose a hindrance?"

"Even the Awakened must sleep," Mamoru grumbled. "This woman had been trained from a young age in the ways of ninjitsu. Foolish is the mouse who attacks a cat in the open."

"Ninjitsu?" Archon scoffed. "Primitives, but I suppose I should at least respect your culture for not regarding our kind as pariah. Still, someone with your gifts should have prevailed."

"I am here now, am I not? In the right circumstances, she could have bested even you."

Archon sighed.

Mamoru's blank face cracked with the hint of a smile. "Do you possess some mystical resistance to poison? Her ilk have the patience of androids. All you need to do is sleep."

Unease shone from Archon's eyes. "Are you so certain I sleep? What took you so long?"

"Our conflict took place on a shuttle flight. She knew she could not defeat me, so she forced a crash. I have been walking through the abominable Badlands for days."

"Go to Sector 6112 where no one will see you. Stay there," said Archon. "I'll send a car."

CRACKS IN THE HOUSE OF GLASS

Anna

Desperate fear energized Anna's nerves as she stormed down the corridor. Forty yards separated her from Archon, dwindling with each step. She had to prepare herself. One wrong look might set him off, and she couldn't let him in. He'd devour her like he did Alexi, make her into some other person, someone who'd do whatever he asked without a second thought. Her only chance would be that he'd never expect her to fight back.

Telekinesis couldn't catch lightning.

She shoved the door to the office-turned-bedroom open hard enough to slam it against the wall. Archon, behind his desk in the back corner, peeled reading glasses off and raised an eyebrow at her.

"A bit of the dramatic today?"

Anna stopped two steps in. "Tell me what you did to my mind."

"Anna... I told you returning to London would do nothing but stir up pain." He set the spectacles on the desk and stood. "Come, sit. Relax."

"So you can rewrite me again?" She pointed. "Like Alexi? He's not even the same person."

He softened his expression. "The boy wasn't a person, Anna. He was a shell. You are not so cruel as to demand a child suffer those memories, are you?"

Heat rushed over her face. "I am not cruel. At least, I never used to be. Not until you... you... *changed* me."

"I did nothing of the sort." He walked around the desk, hands out. "You are being over-emotional. Tell me what happened in London."

"You made my friends hate me. You made them not even remember what I was really like." A knot of fear twisted with anger and sadness in her gut. "How many others are *conditioned?* What did you do to me?"

"If you really must know…" He stopped, letting his arms drop to his sides. "I removed a bad memory so you can function. I made you forget the chems you propped yourself up with."

"Is that all?" She squinted. "What of my father? How could you make me think he was some random tosser from the Bureau?"

"What makes you so certain he was not?"

"Because I spent two hours yesterday talking to his fecking ghost," shrieked Anna.

Lights flickered. One of Archon's terminal panes winked out, the rest filled with static.

"Anna…" He raised a hand.

"Don't 'Anna' me, James. You manipulated me, you turned everyone I knew against me, and you've made me into a monster who kills for you and kidnaps little, innocent children away from their families."

Color faded from his cheeks. "That girl is not so innocent."

"Yes, she is, James. Even after what we did, she doesn't hate me. She doesn't even so much as *dislike* you. She wasn't frightened when I saw her."

"You saw her?" Archon stepped back. "Where?"

"Days ago. Aurora brought her to patch Aaron up after this mercenary shredded him."

"She what?" He blinked. "Brought her?"

"Don't look at me like that, James." Anna pointed at him. "I've no bloody idea how it worked. The two of them just popped out of thin bloody air. Ask Lauren. Stop changing the subject; what the hell did you do to me?"

He put on the calming smile again. "Everything I did, I did to protect you."

"What did I forget?" Sparks lapped at her boots from the carpet.

Archon frowned. "Is that a threat?"

"No. I'm angry. You know it happens. Mucking about with who I am makes leavin' me fixed starkers to the bed for anyone to find seem like nothing big at all. What were you thinking?"

Darkness came over his face. She edged backward

"You would really rather have that memory once again?" Archon took another step closer. "I could put it back, but it would leave you crawling once more into the rat-infested gutters I found you in. Whoring yourself out for drugs, dancing naked in the rain for any Tom with a spare patch to throw after you. Is that what you want, Anna? To chase scraps of false happiness like a dog going for treats? I have elevated you from that wretched existence to civilized society." He shifted to face the window, as if looking far off into the heavens. "No, I have brought you above society."

"This is a black zone, James. We're not above society. We're still in the gutters of it, hiding like those rats."

He scowled.

"I know Blake raped me while I was zonked to the nines." She shivered, holding back the growing lightning so desperate to erupt. "I know I killed the sodding bastard. You made Orange lie to me. I'd asked him to come up with something to delete that vid. You took my friends away." *Don't give in to guilt. Faye has parents, it's not your fault she's had trouble coping.* "You've damaged lives."

He stared, eyes narrowing. "There is a concept known as the greater good. Few people can ever truly appreciate it. *I* can. I am doing what needs to be done to ensure the survival of *our* kind. People *will* suffer for it. No change comes without hardship." His anger receded. "I merely wanted to shield you from the worst of it. You are too beautiful a person to have to hold such pain."

"Did you leave me tied to the bed because you thought I'd enjoy it, or were you trying to remind me I belong to you? A possession. Feeling a bit threatened by Aaron?"

"Of course not." He smiled. "You certainly enjoyed it the night prior. If I remember correctly, you requested I leave you that way overnight."

Anna blushed, muttering, "Overnight isn't the same as all sodding day."

"Honestly, I lack any taste for that sort of thing. I had hoped a small negative experience might make you shy away from it."

"Oh, you didn't just wipe it out of my brain?" She made a sarcastic face. "Wouldn't that have been easier?"

"Anna..." He held his arms out as if to embrace her. "I do not wish to alter the person you are. You do remember that even with that dirty little habit of yours, I tried the usual methods first. Adjusting the mind is a last resort. One I took to only after you proved too weak to resist the chemicals."

"Umm." She sighed. *He's got a point. He could've just made me forget right away.* Blush spread over her face. Enough time had passed for the idea of being helpless to carry a little temptation, but the thought of James quenched the carnal embers. She lowered her gaze to the carpet, breathing in the ozone crackle of sparks shifting over her clothes. "I did need a slap in the face to come out of the place I'd let myself fall to. You pulled me back on my feet. I'll always be grateful, and I'll never forget what you did for me. I need some time to sort everything out. I can't tell what's real and what's figments. I'm really not sure if I could love you the same way again after everything I've learned."

A moment passed of silent staring. Archon at her, Anna at the floor.

"Mamoru called," said Archon, wandering back to the desk. "Would you mind giving him a ride?"

That's it? No protest? Not even an acknowledgment? She held back the urge to cry, unwilling to let him relish that power over her.

"He is in the city, south of here and much closer to the east."

Anna's voice came lifeless. "What happened in Mexico?"

"The church?" Archon scoffed. "They made themselves too much of a nuisance, funneling money to executives and board members. Bribes, mostly. I had spent months conditioning a councilman to our cause, and they went and got him assassinated. They needed to be dealt with."

"You had them all killed?"

Archon leaned on the desk, hand poised with his glasses inches away from his head. "You would rather have done it yourself? I think not." He slipped the spectacles on. "Those two adorable little Mexican children you got so upset about? If not for my efforts to sway Cortez before his untimely death, those two *felons* would have been put before a firing squad."

Anna thought of the grungy siblings shuffling out of the cargo container, shackled like mass murderers.

"You should not feel sympathy for those hypocrites, Anna. The *religious* people that burned in the church cared nothing for their supposed faith. They wield it like a sword to control and harm people they dislike—even children."

"What of Venezuela?"

Archon sighed. "Mamoru is waiting, Anna. The bothersome thing about smuggling psionics out of the ACC is that most of their citizens want to murder us on sight. To them, we are devils ready to steal their secrets and twist their memories."

You don't say? Anna bit her lip. "Yes, yes… I knew that."

"I made an arrangement. We solved each other's problems. I gave them the resistance, and I took away the bothersome psionics. Much easier to smuggle them out when the government provides the transportation."

"You traded lives. Is a psionic's life worth three people?"

Archon pondered. "Rather ten, but there were only so many rebels."

She gasped.

"I see you have lost your appreciation for sarcasm." He smiled. "I took no pleasure in it, but for the greater good."

The way he looked at her sent a chill down her back. "James… I believe in what you are doing, but I don't want to be someone I'm not. You've got the conviction to do things I'm squeamish about. Maybe they need to be done, but it doesn't mean I have to like it, and my not liking it doesn't mean I support you any less."

"Fair enough."

She pondered testing him by asking how he'd feel if she wanted to remain on Earth when they left, but decided against it. "I'll go fetch Mamoru then."

"Preferably not by way of Madagascar."

"What?" Anna blinked.

He put his glasses back on and scooted up to his terminal screens. "The last time you went 'out for a walk' you wound up in London."

She pursed her lips at being dismissed. After five years, she'd expected *some* kind of reaction to her questioning whether she could continue to love him; instead, she'd simply gotten the emotional equivalent of, 'oh, well then.' Did he trust she'd 'get over it,' or did he really not care that much?

'The Plan' is all that matters to him. Before anything riskier came out of her mouth, she hurried to the door.

Anna fumed on her way down the stairs and out into the tent city. People Archon had collected gave her a wide berth purely from the look on her face. She wondered how many of them thought her capable of murdering a little girl for trying to run away.

Did Archon start that rumor to keep them in line?

She looked around at fearful, suspicious, and disinterested faces. The siblings perked up and waved at her. An intact family the Syndicate had managed to extract from Mexico City had taken them in. They looked much more alive wearing clean clothes and big smiles. Their new father was on the security detail, and they sat with him in the lobby of the central tower. Granted, he'd have been about fourteen when they were born, but they didn't seem to mind. Anna couldn't help but grin back at them as she walked past.

A constant breeze wailed through the twisted wreckage of a distant skeletal building. Anna pulled her coat tight and hurried to the gold Halcyon-Ormyr hovercar, pausing as her hand touched the driver side door. A glimpse of something white on the back seat caught her eye, and curiosity pulled her to investigate. She opened the rear door and picked up the bundle, which unfurled to a plain child's dress.

"What the bloody hell is that doing there?"

Its size made her think of a ten-to-twelve-year-old, which in turn made her think of Althea. Anna cast an uneasy glance at the building; moonlight left it stark white against an indigo sky. She bundled the garment around her hands and put it back where she'd found it.

"Oh, Lauren..." She stared up at the tallest of their three buildings. "What do you know that you're not telling anyone?"

THREAT PRIORITY

Kate

Shouts of rage and screams of pain emanated from alleys on both sides of the abandoned road, mixed with bursts of automatic gunfire and the occasional explosion. Kate held her E-90 laser pistol in a two-handed grip, advancing toward a crude wall made of burning hovercars. Tactical armor, especially the helmet, felt heavy and confining, but not altogether bad. After twenty-five years unable to wear a stitch, she rather liked the sense of protection.

Her breathing echoed in her ears over the presence of comm chatter in the back of her consciousness. A female voice warned other units in the area of an augmented rioter moving west along City Road 1885. The floating navigation map at the right corner of her vision spawned a red dot, two miles east of her. Whenever a shadow shifted, she swiveled to aim at nothing. Her heart raced at the worry of what would happen if something shot at her.

This is a damn simulation. Why am I so nervous?

Would her body, safe in the Police Admin Center, flare hot enough to melt bullets if the computer tricked her brain into thinking she'd been shot at? Would her not-quite-awake-but-not-quite-sleeping mental state protect her from her own flames? The possibility that a simulated bullet might kill her for real took her attention from her apocalyptic surroundings.

Wait. I'm being an idiot. Requiem Excelsior didn't make me burn down my living room.

She jumped at the sudden appearance of a yellow-mohawked man, a knife in each hand, wearing only blood and body paint. His bulging eyes locked on her as he rolled his head to the side and drew one of his blades across his chest, leaving a trail of blood.

Kate shot him in the face.

At a crunch behind her, she whirled and aimed at another man who'd been sneaking up on her, a black wire held between his hands. He leapt back from the tip of her laser pistol and ran.

"Stop, police," Kate said, with little enthusiasm.

A comm window opened on her helmet visor, appearing as a four-foot panel a distance in front of her. Technical Sergeant Mina Hong, a head floating over blue-uniformed shoulders, frowned.

"You're supposed to give warning before you engage. You shot the first man without identifying yourself as an officer."

Kate smirked. "Seriously? The idiot was obviously insane. You think he'd have listened to a 'drop the knife' command? He just cut a ten-inch slash across his own chest and had a massive hard-on pointed at me." She patted herself on the chest. "This is marked tactical armor. Anyone stupid enough to need to be told I'm a cop before they attack me deserves to be shot in the face."

"It's procedure."

"Besides, if I took the time to warn psycho-boy, the other asshat would've had a cord around my throat. The giant dick waving in my face was supposed to be a distraction."

"Hmmf." Mina Hong vanished in a flash of glimmering pixels.

Kate crept toward her assigned sector marker, an inverted floating white pyramid hovering at the center of an intersection three blocks away. The simulation presented a riot situation in the wake of a quasi-doomsday scenario where all the various street gangs united into a militia and declared open warfare against the government. Another reason Kate felt fine about her lack of warning. These people didn't qualify as civilian criminals at the moment—they'd technically become an enemy force.

Creaking metal attracted her aim to the left.

Two men appeared simultaneously; one climbed out from behind a nearby car, raising a bottle of flaming chemicals over his head as if to throw it at her. Down the street, perhaps sixty meters away, another man jumped out of an alley with a six-foot-long Nano sword. He swung the weapon around in a fancy display of intimidation and roared at her.

Kate disregarded the man throwing the Molotov cocktail and shot the gladiator three times in the chest. The bottle broke on her breast, covering her with flames. Kate smirked with disinterest and shot the thrower in the back as he ran away.

Everything turned white.

The overbearing glow faded to strips, which sharpened into the shape of overhead fluorescent lights. Going in an instant from full body armor to a tank top and sweat pants made her shiver. She twisted her arms out of the straps holding her to the bed so she didn't flail out of control while in the sim, and grasped the underside of the massive interface helmet. She grunted, pushing herself down and away from it.

Mina Hong walked up to the end of her berth as she sat up to unstrap her legs. The short woman tapped her booted foot with a look of annoyance.

"You're dead, Solomon." She sighed. "You had an opponent at range with a melee weapon and an imminent threat to your side. You made a bad tactical choice. What kind of idiot ignores a firebomb at close range for a guy with a sword far away?"

"What kind of idiot tries to burn the pyrokinetic from hell?" Kate swung her legs off the side of the bed, in no great hurry to introduce her bare feet to a floor she expected to be icy.

"You need to learn to prioritize threats better, Solomon." Tech Sergeant Hong tapped at a datapad while making clucking sounds with her tongue."

"No offense, Sergeant, but the Molotov wasn't a threat at all."

The woman smirked. "Take fifteen. Maybe when you reattempt this course, you can pass."

Kate jumped to the floor, advancing on Sergeant Hong while summoning a wall of flames to enshroud her like a cloak. "How's this for a firebomb? Is this hot enough?"

Sergeant Hong yelped, and backed off. Black ash flakes danced in a cyclone of hot air.

"Tactical assessment is more than following the goddamned rulebook or jumping through specific hoops of a training sim," yelled Kate. "It's about knowing your capabilities, the situation, and making snap decisions. I'm more fucking worried about a sword that could cut a cyborg in half than I am a bottle of incendiary gel. He would have done more damage throwing a jar of frozen piss at me. *That* might've actually hurt me."

Anger pushed the flames around her body from orange to blue. Mina Hong raised her hands to shield her face from the heat.

Two other training personnel as well as fourteen or so Division 1 cadets not currently immersed in virtual reality all stared. When Kate let go of her power, and the fire dissipated, they gasped at her nakedness. One man clapped.

"I feel flame," said Kate, trying to stay calm. "It wouldn't have burned me." She glanced at the room and held her arms out to the sides. "What, you've never seen tits before?"

Everyone found things to focus on other than her.

A sound like raining flakes of glass preceded the appearance of a full-size hologram of a man in a Division 0 dress uniform. He looked about forty or so with short, dark hair, and a trace of a goatee ringing his mouth. Captain's rank insignia gleamed from his shoulders. Kate disregarded her lack of clothes, stood at attention, and saluted him.

"Captain Buckley," said Kate.

He stared at her, more in a 'what the hell is going on' way than a lurid one. "Officer Solomon? Has the simulation gotten out of hand?"

"Just attempting to make a point, Sir. Sergeant Hong didn't understand an idiot with a firebomb isn't a threat to me."

Another training sergeant ran over with a spare jumpsuit. Kate snapped her salute to the side and accepted the offer of clothes.

"I'm sorry, Sir." Sergeant Hong saluted. "We're not used to dealing with Zeroes over here. The computer isn't capable of properly representing the capabilities of psionics. You people never quite play by the rules."

Kate pulled the jumpsuit's silent MolWeave fastener closed from belly to throat. The garment hung a bit loose on her, but it beat nothing. Sergeant Hong glanced sideways at her, as if afraid of what she might be doing.

"I wouldn't worry about it. Officer Solomon is one of a kind. Any other pyrokinetic we've seen couldn't shrug off an attack like that. I doubt it would kill them, but it would leave a mark." Captain Buckley seemed relieved to find Kate dressed when he looked in her direction again. "Solomon, get your gear on and get to the motor pool. Samir will assign you a vehicle."

"What?" Kate blinked. "I haven't been activated yet… I'm still just a train—"

"I can't discuss specifics here. Consider yourself activated on a temporary basis."

"Sir," said Kate, with another salute.

She shrugged at the equally confused-looking Sergeant Hong and rushed to her locker.

༝ ༞ ༟ ༠ ༡

SAMIR, IN MOTOR POOL, COULDN'T HAVE BEEN OLDER THAN FOURTEEN. HIS AGE made itself apparent in the way he kept staring at Kate's chest. She didn't blame him as much as the damn scientists who fiddled with her genetics.

Kate snapped her fingers in front of his face. "Eyes up here, chief. Where's my car?"

His already dark skin darkened. Samir went from staring at her to looking anywhere but. "Space 184."

She patted his shoulder. "Thanks. No worries, I'm in a hurry."

"Everyone's always in a hurry," he muttered.

Kate jogged down a row of armored, black hovercars. Thirty-eight hours in a simulator flying one through ridiculous situations made her more nervous about doing it for real. Still, the police versions had the usual anti-collision and auto-assist systems of civilian models. The driver's seat felt alien. As soon as she realized she missed having David at the controls, she felt a twinge of anger at herself.

I'm no princess. She pulled the door down, flicked the buttons to bring the car online, and grabbed the sticks. A real patrol craft felt a little different from the sim—it reacted faster. Even the best helmets had a control delay compared to a wire jack, something few in Division 0 were willing to obtain. The difference turned out to be minimal, and she acclimated by the time she pulled up into a hover lane.

Captain Buckley's six-inch holographic head appeared above the dash. "Solomon."

"Yes, Sir?"

"We've intercepted a communication involving other Awakened." A smaller image of a Japanese man in his middle-to-late twenties appeared next to the Captain, his waist-length hair in a ponytail. "Other units are en route to a location where we suspect a man responsible for the theft of a military starship currently awaits contact from his accomplices. We have no idea what to expect from them, we need you there as you're all we've got capable of matching them."

"Understood."

"Use your judgment, Kate." The formality in his expression lessened. "Ideally, we don't want anyone dead, but do what you need to protect yourself and others."

She nodded. "I'm glad you understand, sir, but it'd be nice if those drones in the sim room understood that the real world isn't a damn video game. There's more than one solution to any given situation. Just because I do something that doesn't fit neatly into their little playbook doesn't make it wrong. Thanks for trusting me."

Captain Buckley smiled. "Just make sure you come home alive."

Kate flicked her thumbnail on the control stick. "Will do, sir."

SHOWDOWN

Mamoru

Quiet permeated the Sector 6112 grey zone, save for the intermittent buzzing of an old electronic sign. Bulbous holographic breasts rendered in hot pink bounced over an unmarked door at the far end of the block. Small bits of trash skittered across the road. Mamoru scanned the sky and the alleys, waiting for his ride to arrive. Chaos swam in his mind: screams of the dying and the roar of ancient aircraft streaking across the sky. An inexplicable desire for revenge, in the form of destroying any life he found, clenched his hands into fists.

Mamoru closed his eyes and concentrated on his memory of Sadako. Each time he tried to picture the smiling face of the little sister he once knew, the broken and battered woman he'd left in the Badlands filled his head. He was responsible for her death, for surely she would have died if not for the intervention of whatever *Akuryō* possessed his body. These people did not matter as long as his beloved sister lived.

He shuddered, forcing his eyelids apart. *What insanity is this?* One tear ran down his cheek. *To barter a million souls for one. She would not have it.* Pain as though he'd killed her himself scratched icy at the bottom of his heart.

Four large blurry shapes, backlit by snaps of blinding azure light, descended into his vision. Mamoru straightened, lifting himself out of regret. Black police hovercars landed on the deserted street in front of him, forming a horseshoe. Eight figures in matching body armor emerged, silver handguns aimed at him.

"Don't move," said a male near the center.

Mamoru gazed at the wet traction-coated plastisteel in front of his boot, reflecting the rapid snap-flashes of azure bar lights. "You cannot prevent what will come to pass. We are agents of change, and this world cries out for rebirth."

"This one's on the good shit," said a woman.

The tingle of surface thought reading spread over Mamoru's forebrain. He knew he had little telepathic ability, but he managed to block them out. None of them were Awakened.

"Peasants."

"Keep at it," said a different woman. "If he's erected a mind block, he won't be doing anything else."

"I don't think it's a block." One of the male officers pushed harder on his thoughts. "It doesn't feel like a wall. It's a rattling door I can't open."

"You are peasants," said Mamoru.

White energy flared across his shoulders and arms. Desire withdrew his existence from the electronic eyes in their helmets. His consciousness spread forth, psionic feelers sensing the machinery around him, and commanding it all dormant. None of their weapons would work—he forbade it.

"He's invisible," said a man.

"HUD's gone," said another. "He's done something to our armor."

Mamoru flooded his muscles with power and leapt at the nearest officer. The *Akuryō* inside him demanded death, but his own goal was more important.

No. A sheathed katana smashed into the man's armored chest, launching him forty meters back and through a window. *If you wish our goal to be realized, we cannot afford to suffer their vengeance. We must remain the underestimated nuisance left unaddressed until it is too late.*

He spun into a savage leftward downstroke, smashing the helmet of a petite black-haired woman. Her unconscious, but still living, body bounced off the car and slid to the ground, blood oozing from numerous cuts on her face.

They are unworthy of your blade Mamoru. Kill them.

One of the men pulled his helmet off and startled at the sight of Mamoru so close. He tried to shoot, but the weapon did nothing.

They are insects, but there are many. Mamoru raised his blunted sword.

The officer drew his stunrod and charged. At the same instant, Mamoru floated off the ground, a constricting force holding his arms against his chest. A tall woman with blonde cornrows and dark skin fixed him with a stare, her hand outstretched.

"I got him, whack that son of a bitch," she yelled. "He ain't goin' nowhere."

The scintillating white light across his shoulders flared brighter. He concentrated on strength, overpowering the non-Awakened telekinesis with mild effort, and brought his katana into the path of the charging officer's stunrod. The baton zoomed into the air, bent in half from the force of the parry, and exploded in a blue flash on impact with a building. Mamoru threw his weight into a sword stroke, using it to spin his levitating body. He kicked his attacker, forgetting his boosted strength. The man's jaw exploded into a stream of bloody ooze as the hit launched him over the patrol craft, shearing the roof lights off in a spray of shattered plastic and sparking wires.

"Aug!" yelled the telekinetic woman. "Aug!"

Another police hovercar plummeted from the sky, settling down in a clumsy landing at the middle of the intersection.

"There's no electronics inside him," screamed a thin man, backing away. "He's not a fucking aug; he's a kinetic."

"Bullshit! Kinetics aren't this strong."

"He's Awakened," said an alluring feminine voice.

Mamoru looked from the annoying telekinetic to a red-haired beauty slithering out of the fifth car. Unlike the others, she wore no armor. A thin, shimmery, indigo-black uniform hugged every curve. He drank in her model's figure: perfect hips, round breasts, high cheekbones and deep, emerald eyes. For a moment, Mamoru forgot all about the *Akuryō*, his sister, Nami, Archon, even where he was at that moment. He did not feel love, desire, or even base lust.

Awe.

Beautiful.

The dark spirit remembered her. Mamoru felt his lust for her, but not sexual lust. It craved her rage, her power, her ability to kill and cause pain, but she had also angered it.

"Comms are down," shouted a male voice to his left. "Hollister's jaw's on the fucking road."

"Got it," said the entrancing redhead. "Medical team on the way." She raised both hands in front of her and stared at Mamoru. "We need to talk. I can't let Archon have you."

Who is this person? "How do you know of him?" He swung the katana such that the scabbard flew off, blurring into a streak that struck the telekinetic woman in the faceplate of her helmet like an arrow. The impact smashed the visor and knocked her out cold. He dropped to his feet and advanced toward the redhead, casually disabling another charging officer with a kick to the knee and hilt punch to the forehead. The second woman didn't even grunt as her unconscious body hit the floor. "Do you outrank these fools? I do so loathe having to harm women."

Relish it, said the *Akuryō*. *Kill her. Kill them all. Make them part of us.*

He stalled, eyes shut. The concentration needed to stop himself from turning his blade on the unconscious consumed all of his focus. The redhead stared at him as he took three more steps and tucked his foot under the scabbard. When he kicked it into the air, she made a fireball in her hand, but let it go out when he caught the sheath by thrusting the blade into it.

"I do not have time for you," said Mamoru, turning away.

"Hey! There's a fuckin' party goin' on, and we're missin' it," shouted a manic voice from across the street.

Shouts rang out, followed by blue muzzle flare erupting from windows and alleys. Automatic fire chattered; the sharp snaps of smaller weapons interspersed with booms from handguns. Pings and clanks came from the patrol cars. Mamoru looked toward a loud *slap* from the direction of the redhead. A spatter of liquid metal sprayed from the back of her left leg. She grabbed her ass, screaming as if someone had snapped her with a wet towel, and fell into her car.

The whisper in his mind urging him to kill battered down his resistance; the thugs lacked the threat of retaliation that came with killing cops. A surge of white chi-fire spread down his back. Time stretched out to slow motion and he leaned to the side, avoiding a creeping colony of bullets frozen in midair. Weaving among the maze of hanging projectiles, he rushed the oncoming street gang. Grip clenched on the rubberized handle, Mamoru squeezed and drew the katana. His hand thrummed from the vibro-inducer as he sliced into the first thug.

A sheet of blood sprayed from a cut passing shoulder to hip. Mamoru whirled around behind him, slashing the neck of another man with a metal chest. The empty scabbard in his left hand smashed into the throat of a teen girl with a submachine gun in each hand, spraying at the police.

You are weak, Mamoru. Why do you spare her? The young are the strongest fountains of rage. She must join us. His body twisted out of his control, bringing the blade to bear on the helpless girl, stuck in the slow motion world of normal humans.

A chorus of tiny screaming voices filled the back of his head, louder than the rush of jet engines and the explosions of bombs. Mamoru snarled, breaking out in a sweat as he forced the dark presence to recede, and lowered his weapon from her defenseless chest.

Muzzle flare sputtered dark, the guns hung in space as her hands withdrew to her neck and she collapsed. Mamoru leapt to the corner of a dumpster at the alley, boot planted on the glowing green keys of its code lock panel, and sprang from there into a descending slash that opened the gunmetal-blue back of a cyberjunkie with a complete torso rebuild. Sparks lapped at the edges of the cut. Mamoru bashed the scabbard into the side of his knee, whirling around into a slash that took the man's head as he fell.

Laser blasts lit up the night behind him. Mamoru's concentration lapsed, allowing time to return to normal and the white flames to peter out. Leaving the police to deal with the remaining punks, he stormed into the alley. A few steps later, a blinding detonation of orange went off inches from his face. He leapt back, slashing in a spiral around himself since he could not see. Searing pain shrouded his hand; he dropped the katana before the scream left his mouth.

"Hands up. You twitch wrong and you're fuckin' done," said the intoxicating redhead.

Mamoru raised his arms, smoke peeling from his hand. "That was painful."

"No damn idea how you moved that fast. I didn't feel like getting cut in half."

He glanced over his shoulder. The woman half-limped closer. "You're walking. I saw you get shot."

"Guess we both have our little surprises. Eyes front."

Whoops and screams continued from the street, guns and lasers flashing.

"I suggest you leave. It would bring me great sadness to harm a being of such beauty."

"Nice try. I'm placing you under arrest for the theft of a military starship, plus whatever else we haven't figured out you've done yet."

"Oh, but I intend to return it, Kate," said an ancient voice, from Mamoru's mouth

A pair of headlights dove out of a hover lane fifty stories up. Mamoru glanced up at a gold luxury car descending toward the grey zone. Such a fancy vehicle landing here meant only one thing. He glanced over his shoulder. She'd stopped in her tracks, face pale and eyes wide. The *Akuryō* wanted to consume her suffering. Mamoru clenched his jaw; his arms shook trying to resist the bloodlust.

"Our ride is here," said Mamoru. "You should leave. I cannot hold him back for long."

The change in his voice made her twitch.

She is lost to us. The abomination has protected her. She must die.

The hovercar landed a few meters in front of Mamoru. Water vapor rose from where the ion engines heated the ground, fog dancing in the headlight beams.

Anna set one foot out, leaning on the door. "Mamoru?"

"Anna?" asked Kate.

"Kate? What are you doing here?" She smirked. "Nice outfit. Guess the police will take anyone these days..." Anna looked downcast at the road. "Even here."

Mamoru squinted at Anna's sad face.

"Anna, Archon's dangerous," said Kate. "He tried to control—"

Her words warped into a deep swirl of sound as Mamoru accelerated himself and leapt at her. A blue fireball shot past his head on either side. He refocused power from speed to strength, grunting as time shifted in jittering chunks back to normal. His fist struck her sternum, driving her flat on her back and sliding.

More sirens in the distance grew louder; the gunfight a block away intensified.

Kate twisted and gasped, making noises like she couldn't breathe. He rushed after her, hauling her by one arm into a headlock. Kate flapped a hand, trying to grab Mamoru's arm away from her throat.

"Mamoru, what are you doing?" yelled Anna.

"Your master would want this one, would he not?" Mamoru dragged Kate toward the car, squeezing her neck in an effort to knock her out.

Kill her, said the *Akuryō*.

Anna grumbled. "Forget her. I don't feel like crashing on the way back."

Energy sapped from Mamoru, leaving his legs feeling rubbery. The ancient gunslinger appeared before him, smiling the disaster of his rotting teeth at the woman he held. Black smoke exuded from his opening mouth, rife with insects and the reek of carrion.

Kate screamed. Mamoru's coat ignited. He released her before his mind could process the pain he felt from touching her. Patches of skin blackened to ash; his cheek melted to an open hole where it had been pressed against her head. Twitching from agony, Mamoru staggered backward and fell to a knee, swatting at himself to put out the fire.

"What the hell?" whispered Anna.

The ancient one vanished in a blast of flames. Mamoru coughed, squinting into the blinding light at the redhead laying on the road. She scrambled away, eyes wide like a terrified child waking from a nightmare. A tornado of red and violet flames projected from her outstretched hands, blackening the plastisteel roadway where the apparition had been.

Dark vapor swam up Mamoru's chest, reigniting the pain of his burns. Mamoru grabbed his face and howled, falling to his knees before slumping forward, elbows on the ground. He wept without conscious thought, lost in the throes of agony. The skin on the palm of his right hand bubbled and boiled as it regenerated.

We cannot die, rasped the decrepit voice in the back of his mind.

Mamoru clenched a shaking fist.

"Anna..." Kate wheezed. "Don't trust him. The demon's inside him. Help me!"

"He... uhh wants to protect psionics." Anna's boots clicked up behind him. "Are you alright, Mamoru? What was that old man?"

Mamoru recovered his sword and got to his feet. Obvious fear tainted Anna's voice, but he didn't care.

"Anna, don't!" yelled Kate. "You don't understand, it's not—"

Mamoru leapt at her, but she jumped away. Her hands sheathed with fire that formed into spheres in her palms. Mamoru pulled the katana four inches out of the scabbard, but hesitated at the sight of molten metal on her leg. This succubus was not worth losing his sacred blade. He walked through the fireball, ignoring the smell and sound of sizzling flesh regenerating.

Kate leapt to the right, but he caught her arm and swung her into the wall. His skin ignited where he touched her; boiling flesh regrew as fast as it turned to ash. Kate screamed and gagged from the fumes. Mamoru grabbed her throat, lifting her at arm's length, crushing her ability to breathe into the grimy metal. His thumbnail caught fire, blackening before it fell off. She kicked at his gut; patches of ooze boiled away, bubbling past the thin material covering her back.

"Mamoru!" yelled Anna. "Don't kill her. If she really is with the police now, it'll cause a shitstorm."

Flames engulfed Mamoru for all of a second and a half before a loud *crack* split the night, echoing down the alley. Paralyzed, he fell over backward like a plank. Kate slid to the ground, seated against the wall, foam leaking from her mouth.

Mamoru shuddered, unable to command his muscles to obey. The taste of ozone filled his mouth as biting sparks danced upon his lips.

"She's with the police now, twat. We need to keep a low profile. Kill her, and all of Archon's planning will be for shit. Don't think they won't get the military involved. We're trying to protect psionics, not start a war that'll make them extinct."

Pain ran back and forth in waves over his body, mixing with a maddening itch from mending burns. Who did this *woman* think she was, talking to him like that? Despite his anger, he could do nothing but glare at her.

"Since when are you a healer too?" Anna stared down at him, arms folded. "You know what? I don't care. I don't want to know."

Kate jumped up holding a fireball in a throwing pose. "Anna, get away from him. A demon—"

A hair-thin thread of lightning connected Anna's hand to Kate, knocking her flat. "Stay down, girl. A pyrokinetic going rage queen isn't going to help anyone." She looked at the street, guilty. "Sorry… Don't take it personally. I… can't let you get in Archon's way. You'll only get hurt."

"Ngh." Kate twitched and convulsed.

Mamoru grumbled as Anna pulled him upright. He leaned on her for support, unable to walk while fighting off the urge in his mind driving him to kill both of them. She dragged him to the passenger side door and opened it before giving him enough of a shove that he fell in. He slumped, lost to an ocean of pain, and closed his eyes. The other door closed, and the car lurched upward.

You have no focus, spirit. The tiny woman is right.

Dry chuckling scratched at the recesses of his mind. Mamoru cringed, unsure where the old man began and he ended.

They shall soon have no dominion over my world.

Mamoru closed his eyes and focused on tuning out the pain of healing burns. The spirit devoured him more and more; how long before he ceased to exist and only the *Akuryō* remained?

It matters not what fate befalls me. Sadako lives.

LEGACY OF FIRE

Kate

Hot spittle ran down Kate's chin. A rush of ionized air from a departing hovercar sprayed her with bits of trash and plastic film. She grunted, forcing her arm up to cradle her breast, still tender from the shock she was certain almost stopped her heart.

One drawback to metal threads.

Anna's telepathic apology only did so much to make her less angry at being shocked. The woman had seemed scared, as if she had begun to share her feelings toward Archon, but the man still had some inexplicable hold on her. She slid over sideways, forehead to the cold plastisteel ground. Seconds later, she curled in a ball cradling her chest. *The demon wants Archon. Did that bastard reprogram Anna too? She looked so torn.* Kate braced a hand on the ground and pushed herself up into a sitting position. The street at the end of the alley glowed with emergency lights. The addition of red to the flurry of blue signaled either a MedVan or Division 1 backup had arrived.

"This 'take them alive' thing is overrated," she muttered while struggling to her feet. "I should've just killed him."

Not quite recovered from the electrical jolt, she stumbled on stiff legs toward the street where she'd left her car. Whoever the Japanese man was, the demon had taken him. The old priest appeared on the road—in West City— scaring the color from her cheeks. If he could get to her here, could she ever be safe? His clothes had changed, but she'd never forget the entity who demanded she kill Althea. Bile collected at the back of her mouth as she tried to ignore the smell of flesh burning. The sight of scorched dead didn't bother her much, but watching someone heal as fast as she seared it got to her.

Next time she saw him, she'd try the laser.

Kate made her way back to the intersection, finding Division 1 officers as well as medtechs on the scene. Bodies littered the street; from the looks of it, the suicidal gangers who flung themselves at the cops had gotten their wish. A few punks survived with various degrees of injury. Blue armored police dragged them to either a MedVan or a prisoner transport depending on how much blood leaked out of them. A girl of about fifteen with a black and purple throat struggled to escape restraints holding her to a hover-stretcher. She wheezed and rasped at the police and medical personnel, but couldn't speak. The fight left her as an autoinjector to the shoulder stole her consciousness.

No one paid Kate much attention as she walked among the frenzy of activity. She didn't look wounded enough to attract notice from anyone in white, and her Division 0 uniform kept the normal patrol officers away. She forced herself up to a jog, working the stiffness out of her muscles, and ducked under the still-open door of her patrol craft. For a few seconds, she stared at all the screens and shiny lights on the console and felt overwhelmed by it all.

"Ops?"

A hologram of a dark-haired male doll appeared. "Go ahead 1185-0T2."

"I don't have time to read the user manual for this damn thing. I need to find a suspect fleeing the scene."

He, or it, smiled. "I need more information, officer."

"Uhh, yeah. Right." She pulled her door closed. "Fancy hovercar, gold. Left a few minutes ago from my current location."

The man's eyes shimmered with digital snow. "You are lucky to be in a degenerated area. There's only one transponder signal recorded close to you not associated with a municipal vehicle within the past five minutes. Halcyon-Ormyr Executive Series III, tag D8FF94AA300C."

"Whatever the fuck that means." Kate pulled back on the stick, her car shot straight up. "I need to follow it. Can you do that? What button do I push?"

"Division 0 should spend more time training you kids before they throw you to the wolves. One moment."

"Kids? You look younger than I feel." She smirked.

When a flashing yellow arrow appeared ten feet in front of the car pointing right, she twisted the stick to swing the car around until it turned into a dotted line leading off into the distance. Waypoints she remembered from the sim. Following them was easy, setting them not so much. A ribbon of light wavered and stretched, a clear indication the far end moved.

"Thanks," said Kate.

She accelerated along the digital marker and hit the emergency flashers.

"Do you require backup, Officer?"

"Yeah." Kate shuddered at the memory of seeing the Japanese man's exposed ribs vanishing beneath new skin. She'd never forget that smell. "Shitloads. Might need the damn Army."

The young man's holographic apparition nodded and faded away. Kate let her mind go back to the training sim, and tried not to think that the gleaming buildings and advert bots whizzing past her were real. Sweat ran down her face and made the control sticks slippery. One wrong reaction and someone would be scraping her off the armored windshield. She screamed a few times when advert bots came too close, forcing her to roll or side-slide out of the way. The idea of life as a primitive didn't seem so bad all of a sudden.

Sometimes, technology really sucked.

A few bots responded to her approach, yielding to a patrol craft in emergency mode. The twisting light ribbon swerved, heading north and west. Her police vehicle could outpace the Halcyon-Ormyr in a straightaway, but only an idiot or a doll would dare do 600 mph between skyscrapers. Kate grinned and climbed, ramming the left stick forward to accelerate. Once she crested the top of the highest buildings, she leveled off and pulled as tight a turn as speed would allow in the direction of the waypoint guide.

The arrow stretched for miles, plunging downward into an area the Navcon marked black. Sector 10081. It took only a few minutes at full speed —a hair under Mach 1—to close the distance. From three-quarters of a mile up, the area even *looked* black to the naked eye. Kate slowed. The computer indicated the car she'd tracked had landed in the middle of an abandoned corporate campus with three buildings. On either side of a ten-story, central tower stood a pair of smaller structures that appeared to have withstood the worst of whatever war happened there.

She kept a cautious distance in the air, waiting for backup to arrive. Magnification showed numerous bodies in the courtyard area, though most seemed to be cyborgs that had been dead for a long time. Kate tapped her fingers on the sticks, not liking the number of heat signatures thermal showed occupying the ground floor of the left building.

All the lights and controls flickered and flashed. Kate clenched her sphincter, expecting her patrol craft to fall from the sky like a brick. The image of Archon's face, drawn from rainbow light in front of the car, scared her even more. Six feet tall, the disembodied head pulsed bright orange, striated with azure numbers streaming from right to left. The scrolling text continued within the void-like hollow of his empty eye sockets. He had to have gotten into the car's systems, forcing his way into the digital windscreen.

"Hello again, Kate." Archon's voice surrounded her, emanating from hidden speakers. Skin texture, sharp enough to reveal every pore, spread as liquid over his face, wrapping him in a shroud of reality. "I've been wondering when you'd return to us."

"What the fuck?" She pounded the console. "Ops? Ops? He's hacked me."

"Hacked?" A two-foot wide eyebrow climbed as the head grew even larger. "So droll. They cannot reach you now, Kate."

A tingle started at the tip of her mind. She didn't dare waste the second it would take to wonder how a hologram could use telepathy. Kate focused every ounce of her willpower on keeping him out of her head.

"No. I'm not one of your pets. You can't have me."

"It is in your blood, Kate." His voice sounded as much inside her head as in the cabin around her. "Do you know who you are?"

"Out. Out. Out. Out." She drove a fist into her thigh in time with each word.

"You have the genetic material of Ekaterina Myshkin. Do you know who she was?"

"Leave me alone!" Kate pulled on the control stick, but it clicked back and forth without effect on the car. "Shit!"

"Ekaterina Myshkin survived three gunshot wounds at the age of ten when resistance fighters smuggled her out of ACC-controlled Russia. A courageous child who made us aware of the horrors that went on there. It was by her bravery we learned of the midnight raids, the executions, and the torture. Many people died to help her escape. She was the first pyrokinetic the world knew. You have greatness flowing in your veins, Kate. Or, shall I call you Ekaterina?"

"You're fucking crazy, you know that?" With one eye closed in concentration, she fought the energy trying to seep into her mind and punched the autopilot button. It, too, did nothing. "Go away! You have no idea what's coming after you, do you?"

"It is time you fulfilled your destiny, Kate."

"Fuck you." She slapped herself. The rush of pain knocked the invasion from her mind and she poked at random buttons in an effort to regain control of the patrol craft. "My destiny is mine, bitch."

"The man you think of... David... he is a government tool put in place to control you. You think he loves you?" Archon's laughter vibrated the sound system in the car, shaking her bones. "Come now, Kate. You are not a stupid woman. An empath falls in love with you at first sight, and you him? Tell me you are not blind to that truth."

"Truth? Hah. You're lying." Kate couldn't help herself but cry at the possibility of David being a lie.

"He is influencing you to be part of the problem. Division 0 is not there to protect the interests of psionics, they want to enslave us."

"Isn't that what you're doing?" Telepathic tingles threaded into her brain. "Ngh, stop. Get out. I know he's not forcing me to feel. I know what it's like. The girl already did it."

Her recollection of Althea repelled him from her brain like a light chasing off a roach.

Still squinting one eye, Kate looked up at the monstrous face. "You're afraid of a little girl?"

Archon scowled. "You *will* fulfill your destiny. *Come to me.*"

Kate screamed, sensing a suggestion take root in her brain. Her heart raced. Images of David flashed by; a life she'd never have. She sobbed. With the last few seconds of free will she knew she had left, she hit the emergency open on the door.

"No!" she screamed, and leapt.

Wind whipped her hair about as she sailed out into the sky, a half-mile above ground. Archon's influence peeled away, as though a rubbery tendril connected to the car reached its limit. Whether her physical inability to obey the command in the midst of free fall or the catharsis of imminent death had kicked him out, she couldn't tell. Freedom would come with darkness. Death would be better than slavery.

West City rushed up at her. Kate closed her eyes and let her body go limp. *Please forgive me, David. Hmf. Fucking scientists. At least I'll be free.*

Seconds passed. She waited for impact, afraid of what she'd see if she opened her eyes. Her stomach lurched and twisted. Her whipping hair settled; the air rushing past her face slowed. She felt weightless.

"Well, that was certainly dramatic," said Archon.

Kate's eyes snapped open. She floated, her boots mere inches from the roof of the ten-story tower. Archon stood a few meters away, wearing an unassuming tweed suit and a wry smile. Thick chestnut hair wavered to his left. Behind him, another man with dirty blond hair stared at her with an intense look of concentration. His black suit and red-wine colored silk shirt looked more like the expensive outfits the Syndicate bigwigs favored. She recognized his face from hours of fruitless searching.

"Nice catch, Aaron," said Archon.

A hint of a smile fought out from under his concentration. "Shame to lose this one; she's top totty, aye?"

Archon smiled. "More than you know."

Shock at surviving such a fall collided with terror at the sight of Archon so close. Kate willed a fireball into each hand.

"*Don't.*" said Archon, with a flare of light in his eyes.

Her arms locked in place as if they'd become iron. Wind rippled upon the flames. A second later, her brain released the pyre against her will.

"There you go, pet." Archon moved closer and stared into her eyes. "Everything will be fine. You are perfectly safe."

She whined, unable to move or peel her eyes away.

Archon reached up and caressed her cheek. "Welcome home, my dear."

A MINOR EMERGENCY

Althea

The burrito sat upon a dull blue plate in front of Althea, covered with gooey cheese and flakes of chopped scallions. Karina glanced across the table with an expectant look. Father, at her left, had gotten to work on his food without ceremony. To her right, Alejandra radiated confusion and worry. The woman had grown fond of Father, and he had brought her home for dinner for the first time. As friendly as the girls had been to her, she still radiated hesitance.

Althea narrowed her eyes at the fork, peered up at Karina, and growled at her food, mimicking the sound of an upset chihuahua. The huge grin on her face broke any illusion of her being angry, and the girls erupted in laughter. Alejandra's confusion deepened; Father burst out in laughter.

She picked up the fork, still intending to make good on her promise to fate. It took her a moment to find a comfortable grip, and she stabbed it into the end of the burrito. The knife posed no difficulty. Knives she knew. After managing to slice a half-inch thick cross section of burrito onto the fork, she stuffed the piece into her mouth and tried to chew.

"Great!" chirped Karina.

"The girl's not three," muttered Father past a full mouth and a grin.

Althea giggled, dribbling burrito sauce all over herself.

"Or perhaps she is." Father reached over to dab a napkin at her.

She held her chin up as he wiped, shifting her eyes toward Alejandra. The woman finally relaxed enough to laugh with them. Every so often, Althea let out a playful snarl, which set Karina giggling all over again.

"There's a story behind this," said Alejandra.

"Yes." Father wiped his mouth on a napkin and ruffled Althea's hair. "When we found her, she was quite wild. She growled while she ate, like a dog afraid her food would be taken away."

Alejandra gave her a pitying look. "You don't need to do that anymore."

"I know." Althea grinned. "It makes me think of Karina laughing."

Her sister reached across the table to squeeze her hand. A sudden tremor ran down her back. Althea got up, ran around the table, and jumped into Karina's lap.

"Thea, what's wrong?" Karina wrapped her arms around her. "You're trembling."

Father's chair scuffed on the floor. "Someone's coming."

"You're gifted too?" asked Alejandra.

Karina held Althea tight.

Father stood. "No, I hear footsteps."

The front door opened hard.

"Hello? Althea?" called a man's voice. Soft thuds got louder. "I'm Officer Ahmed with Division 0. We need you."

"No," yelled Karina. "She's not well."

Althea relaxed and lifted her face from Karina's chest, looking up at the man with coffee-toned skin who stood in the arch separating the kitchen from the hall. He wore the uniform of the city police as well as a cloud of anxiety. She tried to slip to her feet, but Karina held on.

"It's okay. I have to go."

"No, you don't." Karina squeezed, making her gurgle. "Father, tell him he can't take her away."

"I'm not taking her away." Officer Ahmed fidgeted. "Something's happening and we need her help."

"You are afraid," said Althea. "Someone you love is in danger."

He tried to look stoic, but he couldn't hide his strong emotions from her.

"Aurora told me the city police would ask for me. Many will die if I don't go." She squirmed around to face Karina, whispering at her sister's ear. "I will be okay."

"I don't like this," said Father. "She's eleven years old. What possible need is there for the police to involve a child in their business?"

Althea looked down, picking at her dress. For a few seconds, she wished she could be an ordinary little girl with no powers, so people would stop asking her to do dangerous things. Before she could even sigh, she felt guilty for thinking such a thing.

"I assure you, sir, if we had an adult officer capable of doing what she can do…" He ran a hand over his hair and shifted his weight from leg to leg. "I'll be honest with you. I don't understand it either. A clairvoyant unlike anyone I've ever met told me she's critical to saving the lives of millions of people."

"You'd believe someone who just says such things?" asked Father, waving.

"I do when they appear out of thin air in my apartment," mumbled David.

"Kate," said Althea. "She's in danger."

Officer Ahmed swallowed and covered his mouth with a hand. "They activated her, and I haven't been able to get her on comm. I tried to contact her when I landed, but her car said she'd called in a MedVan, reporting officers down. Then she put out a call for backup and her car went dark."

Althea squirmed, unable to get away from her sister. "Karina, please." Reddening eyes threatened to erupt with tears. "People will die."

"What if one of those people is you?" Karina cried first.

"If I don't go, and all those people die, I'm bad." Althea slipped loose and stood.

"You're not even crying." Karina grabbed her wrist. "Please don't go away. Why aren't you crying?"

"Because I know I'll be home again soon." Althea smiled.

Father approached and gathered his daughters to his chest. She sensed sadness and worry.

"I do not want to leave, but I must. Please understand." After a minutes-long embrace, Althea gazed down as she walked to Officer Ahmed's side. "I cannot let all those people die."

"I'll do whatever it takes to keep her safe," said Officer Ahmed. "As would any of us."

"There is no time," said Althea, jogging for the door. "I love you, Father. I love you too, Karina."

"That sounds so final." Karina collapsed against Father, sobbing.

Althea spun on her toes and forced Karina's sadness away. "Do not cry."

Karina, looking neither sad nor happy, stared at the half-eaten burrito. "You didn't finish your dinner."

"Keep it for me."

"Take it with you," said Father, handing her the plate.

Althea apologized in her head to the powers that be for not using a fork. She grabbed the burrito with both hands, savaging it in three huge bites as she walked to the door. If what Aurora said was true, she'd probably need the food.

Once outside, Officer Ahmed broke into a hasty jog. Althea ran ahead of him, knowing he would go to the black flying car in the middle of town. She waited by the door until he caught up. He stopped, looking her up and down. Althea wiggled her toes and held her dress out to the side.

"Do they make small uniforms?"

He bit his lip.

"They do?" Althea gasped.

"Not duty uniforms. Cadet uniforms, for school." He opened her door and ran to the other side. "You wouldn't like them. They come with boots."

Althea gave him a raspberry and got in.

"Don't touch anything."

She looked up as her door closed on its own and the console thrummed to life with light and a barely-audible electronic hum. Her bravery lasted only as long as ground remained visible out the window. Not two seconds airborne, she shut her eyes and whimpered.

"Althea? You're afraid of flying?"

"Yes."

David erupted with uncontrollable, tear-inducing laughter.

Indignation pushed down her fear of heights, enough to let her eyes open. She squinted at him while maintaining a white-knuckled grip on the seat.

"Why are you laughing at me?"

Officer Ahmed coughed while wiping tears from his cheeks. He grasped the sticks and acceleration pushed her into the seat. His mood fell to worry, the kind of dread that comes with expecting he'd return to the city to find someone he cared deeply for dead.

"Something Kate said." He breathed as if trying to calm himself. "She thought you were an angel."

Althea gazed into her lap, at which point she remembered about seat belts and tried to figure out how to put hers on. "Why is angel funny?"

"Oh, it's just myths. Artists always depict angels with big, feathery wings. They can fly. The idea of an angel being afraid of heights seemed so ironic."

"I can't fly." She gave up on the seat belt and folded her hands in her lap. "I falled slow."

"You... what?"

"When Miguel was hurt, I jumped off the cliff. He was going to die, and I didn't care if I broke my legs. I had to help him." She pulled her feet up, curling her toes over the edge of the seat. "I don't know how I did, but I falled slow. I think I do have wings. They come out when they want. I don't know why."

"Uhm."

Althea risked a peek out the window. The sight of the scrub racing past made her cringe away. "Too fast."

"We're safe."

"I know." She looked anywhere but at a window for a few minutes. "What has happened?"

"The shit hit the fan." Officer Ahmed cringed. "Sorry, I shouldn't swear in front of a kid."

Althea blinked at him, glanced at the console, and reached forward to close the air vent before the stink came out.

GIRL PROBLEMS

Aaron

Deep breaths helped rein in Aaron's racing heart. Catching Kate's nosedive had taken a lot of energy in a short amount of time. He shivered at the thought he'd almost dismissed Aurora's unexplained demand he go to the roof. The sight of a Division 0 patrol craft hanging over the campus had been enough of a shock, but the officer pulling a suicide leap was the last thing he expected. The surprise of Archon's sudden appearance almost cost Kate her life, but he'd managed to hold his focus long enough to bring her down safe.

Aaron glanced around, seeing no one but himself, Archon, and Kate. Her terror radiated, obvious even to someone without a shred of telempathic ability. He'd seen the aftereffect of Archon's mental reprogramming. The toss-offs were nigh impossible to dislodge. Whatever he'd done to Talis looked as good as permanent. What he was doing to Kate would likely be the same. Aaron's face reddened with anger.

I can't let him rape her, even if it is the brain.

His gaze flicked to the stunrod on Kate's belt. Telekinesis depressed the trigger on the handgrip at the same moment he lifted it out of its ring and touched the tip to Archon's forehead. With a flare of blue light, the leader of the Awakened fell over backward. Kate dropped to her knees.

Bang.

Aaron's right thigh exploded with a geyser of blood. He screamed like a little boy and fell to the side.

"I knew it!" yelled Melissa, climbing out from behind an air handler. Six pistols hovered around her. "You're a fucking cop traitor."

Aaron clutched at the wound, gasping for breath as involuntary tears wet his cheeks. He managed enough concentration to push her weapons askew as she fired them all. Melissa grunted, beginning another telekinetic duel. If the look on her face was any indication—this one would be to the death.

"Melissa, stop," wheezed Aaron. "Your parents don't hate you."

She got angrier, adding tears to her growling.

"Ba, baba… baaa…" muttered Archon, twitching, grasping at nothing. "Kaaa. Waaa."

Aaron glanced sideways at him, pushed Melissa's guns hard, and dragged the stunrod into Archon's ear. Another flash, and wispy threads of blue plasma danced out of his eyes; his body went limp. The teen ceased trying to fire the handguns and brought all her telekinetic strength to bear in aiming them. If not for the horrible pain in his leg, it would've been trivial to hold her off. At present, the task made him sweat.

"Melissa, listen to me. Archon reprogrammed them."

"Liar," she yelled. The girl snarled, clutching the sides of her head as if it would make her powers stronger.

"They want you to go home." He gave her his desperate 'you can trust me' look reserved for a last ditch attempt to get a walker-away's panties on the floor.

"Bullshit! They think I wanna kill them." Her face went cherry red. Sadness, frustration at Aaron being stronger than her, and pain at her life warped her innocence into something out of a horror vid.

"Give me a sec?" asked Aaron.

"You're a fucking traitor. Why should I listen?"

"You've been kidnapped and I'm a cop trying to help you. Three seconds. If you don't like it, I'll let you shoot me."

"You're crazy."

"They know the coven thing was fake. Deal?"

"Three fucking seconds, dickbag."

"Call them." He pressed a hand on his thigh wound.

"What?"

"Call your bloody parents and ask them if they want you home."

"You're trying to mess with me. You want me to cry."

"You're already crying." Aaron dragged himself into a sitting position. "Please?"

Melissa let go of her pistols, leaving them in Aaron's telekinetic grasp. He relaxed and exhaled. Skittering metal behind him made him whirl, too late to stop the stunrod heading for his balls. The world flashed blue and white. A thousand tons of pain raced up his spine like the weight on a strongman game at a carnival and smashed into his brain. The tiny inconsequence of having his femur cracked by a bullet faded from awareness. Aaron realized he puked only by the smell of it.

Every muscle in his body clenched at once. Seconds, feeling like minutes, passed in paralytic agony. Finally, air made its way into his lungs and he howled. He wanted to cradle the boys, but couldn't move. Sparks, or at least the feeling of sparks, raked across his testicles like a horde of fire ants. His back felt as though someone had replaced his spinal fluid with acid.

No, acid on fire... with needles.

"Aaron... I am so, so, disappointed in you." Archon leaned over him, not that Aaron cared about anything at all at that moment other than his possibly exploded man-bits. "I thought you understood the gravity of what I am trying to do"—he paced about as if lecturing a class—"however, you clearly do not. I would like to think you better than a mere government stooge. Alas, due to your... issues, you are a liability I must deal with directly. Is there anything you would like me to pass along to Anna?"

Aaron risked a tentative grasp of his most sensitives, finding them too tender to make even the slightest contact.

"Nothing then?" asked Archon. "Nothing at all to say?"

"Look out!" screamed Melissa.

UPLINK

Mamoru

The room on the seventh floor had once been the office of someone with an unusual fascination with boats. A small private bathroom had, in addition to forty-three tiny models of watercraft, an autoshower. Mamoru could not resist the embrace of civilization even a moment longer and luxuriated amid two full cycles. The comfort he expected seemed fleeting, consumed by contempt for the world around him. He stormed out of the tube to dress, further embittered at the sound of children outside.

An image of the primitive Scrag girl who had paid him tribute filled his senses. Her large brown eyes had offered respect and fear. Dust and war paint covered her slender, brown body. They were the true children of the world. His world. Though they dwelled within a realm of suffering and hardship, he sheltered the ones who knew him as their god.

Mamoru frowned at the window, gazing out at the city. *Those whelps know nothing of life. This civilization is an abomination.*

His vision blurred to a field of rubble and dirt, a broken building. Somewhere, far off in the Badlands, the little shaman girl sat with a hubcap bowl between her legs, mashing plant matter into paste. She looked to the clouds, at him. She sensed his eyes upon her and bowed her head.

The Sentience smiled with Mamoru's lips. He would provide for her. A chance discovery of food now, the rest of the world in time. More visions filled his mind as he wandered from his room. The same girl, no longer a child, strolled among great slabs of wrecked metal, many of which still exuded plumes of smoke. She still wore the paint of a shaman, but with age, had added clothing made of animal hides, loaded with dangling shinies—cans, silver discs with finger-sized holes in the middle, and feathers. Beautiful and strong, the young woman strode the length of a yawning cavern of twisted debris with her head held high and a spear made from a Nano combat knife lashed to a staff. Such fortune to find a modern weapon; in the Badlands, it made her invincible.

Her followers collected at the edge of a great cliff as she walked out onto a steel I-beam protruding from a ridge and stared at the ocean below. The woman again bowed her head, knee-length raven hair drifting in the wind, and thanked him. The world, *his* world, had expanded all the way to the coast.

West City had burned to ashes.

🐍 🌾 🏮 💧 ♑

ACTIVITY DREW MAMORU OUT OF HIS VISION. TWO MEN, A WOMAN, AND A HALF-dozen teens sat around a conference table laden with technology. Innumerable holo-panels above it bathed the area in a glow of ever changing color. His walk from the seventh floor of the central tower to the ground floor of a side building had passed in an instant.

He ignored the curious glances and moved to the farthest point of the room from the door, where a server-class processing unit sat on a wheeled base. The charcoal grey box came up to his waist, with beveled corners and slats on both sides lit with a lime glow from inside. For a minute, he stared at it, as if he couldn't understand what the machine was.

The vision of the shaman girl faded. He remembered his obligation.

Mamoru placed a hand atop the computer and *knew* the machine. Seconds later, his consciousness floated above a massive silicon crater. Scorched ground shimmered with flecks of blue and violet light, flashing in pulses. The black zone around the corporate campus, shut off from the GlobeNet, rendered as a victim of a meteor impact.

He willed himself airborne, sailing out over the shining silicon grid. Globules of energy flowed along virtual circuit paths in a digital mimic of a city and its traffic. The blackened scar of blight fell away. Far in the distance, a gleaming pillar of white rushed skyward. Inside, a helix of blue energy cords whirled.

Flying across the net gave him a rush of freedom. Mamoru's sense of self returned for a brief moment, but drowned in the weight of duty to his sister. He had accepted assistance from an *Akuryō* to spare her life, a gift it would certainly rescind if he broke his word. What loyalty did he have to this place, this city?

None.

What loyalty did he have to Japan or Minamoto Akio?

None.

Sadako was his loyalty.

Mamoru's body floated up alongside the roaring column of energy, an interstellar data transmitter. He smirked at his true reflection upon its glass-like surface, not having bothered with the samurai avatar. What did it matter how dead people saw him?

One arm reached up. One finger broke the surface of the data. His body melted, passing through the space opened by a finger poke. The chaos of a hundred thousand simultaneous conversations washed over him. Mamoru flew between the channels of data. His consciousness fragmented into packets swimming among business deals, music, entertainment, spouses apologizing for being late, teary-eyed people begging colony settlers to return home, and porn—so much porn. Flesh and moans, images, sounds, and smells he cared not to experience, surrounded him as he flew.

Within this conduit, he had no physical form. A sense as though he raised his arms over his head caused his travel to accelerate. Soon, the digital representation of Earth below him resembled a glinting dark marble wrapped in threads of cobalt blue. Transparent nerve fibers lapped at the column, communications from satellites that vanished like bullets.

He hit the lunar relay, bouncing away from it as if he'd collided with an enormous rubber sphere, and hopped onto a Mars-Earth interconnect. Ordinary netizens rode tramcars in a reproduction of a commuter system. Mamoru rocketed over them, peering upward past a transparent orange force field at outer space. Another data pipe ran parallel far above. Black against the void, he sensed the other transmission channel's presence in his gut rather than with his eyes. Mamoru pushed himself higher with a thought, passing through the barrier overhead. Inside the military channel, no pretense of reality dwelled. It had no trains or artwork. Male and female avatars in various uniforms flew back and forth like superheroes.

Mamoru refused to allow them to notice him. He projected his body down the pipe, finding the relay three times faster than the civilian channel. Minutes later, the Marsnet cluster came out of the distance as a red sphere. It expanded from ball to landscape, and he plummeted headfirst into a military communications center at the heart of Elysium City.

Even a virtual visit to Mars made him remember the taste of its dirt, like spoiled eggs and grit.

He infiltrated the infrastructure with ease. Programs he had previously altered opened the path for him to a hidden allocation of neural memory he'd left behind. The system rendered a dark hallway, like one buried deep in the basement of a long-abandoned government facility. Dim fluorescent lights clicked on with resonant *thunks* overhead. Section by section, light advanced into the distance, lifting the bare concrete passage out of darkness.

At the end, a plain, black door with a silver handle led to a room the size of an autoshower tube. One file cabinet inside opened at a glance. A single data tile rotated within its drawer containing frequency specifications and a cryptographic key.

Mamoru lifted the tile to his chest, holding it against his coat until glowing lines appeared, binding it to his flesh. The ten-inch slab of chrome sank into him and vanished. The circuit pattern emerged from his collar, threads of blazing white spread up over his cheeks to his eyes, which radiated light.

He looked up. A transmitter dish somewhere on physical Mars aligned with a starship he had stashed in a debris field known as the Periculum Belt. Once the link opened, Mamoru's essence surged out of his eyeholes, drawing his collapsing body up into the transmission beam.

The bridge of the CSS Angel, or at least its virtual equivalent, lay dormant, pristine, and quiet. A cartoon caricature of a samurai—a mockery of Minamoto Akio—sat in the captain's chair, raising its head as a swarm of black cubes melted from the walls. They spiraled into a cyclone, from which Mamoru emerged.

He ignored the ship AI and approached the navigation system. An image of Earth appeared on the large screen at the front of the room. At his will, the planet rotated to place the western coast of North America at the center. Mamoru zoomed in at the approximate midpoint of West City, locked in the coordinates, and engaged the drive system.

"That route is impossible," said the warlord. "You are plotting a course with a destination at the core of the Earth."

"I am aware of that," said Mamoru. "Did you not notice me disable the orbital maneuvering system as well as the safeguards?"

"I cannot let you destroy me," said the warlord.

"What you desire is irrelevant, Minamoto-chan. You are a program."

It screamed, bashing its fists on the captain's console. Black lacquer gauntlets pulsed with grids of green light each time they struck glass. "How did you lock me out of my own system? This is impossible!"

Mamoru erected a third layer of firewall. Red spheres grew out of the consoles, covered in spikes and flames.

"I am considered sentient. You... This is murder."

The *Akuryō* squinted at the virtual Earth on the screen, at the tiny twinkling lights of West City. "Yes. Yes, it is. Glorious murder... and a necessary one. This machine is a mercy blade, spilling the blood of a society too weak to claim its right to exist. It does not deserve to be."

TINY POINTS OF LIGHT APPEARED ALONG THE SURFACE OF A DARK METAL SHAPE hidden among thousands of pieces of space scrap and rocks. Slow at first, more spots appeared, until the entire silhouette of the CSS Angel glowed to life. It pulled away from the side of a massive asteroid, swinging in a graceful arc to point at Earth. Maneuvering thrusters wisped energy from various places, stabilizing the great machine.

A silent ripple of energy burst from each of the primary engines, as if a pebble had broken the surface of a still pond. Three concentric rings expanded from behind the vessel as it got underway. A blast of light shot from the side of the superstructure at the back, where the bridge overlooked the deck. Seconds later, a thruster flare glimmered, stalling the tumbles of a small capsule, which oriented itself on Mars before accelerating toward the surface.

49

MAKING WISHES

Kate

Thick liquid flowed in and out Kate's nostrils. She felt tired and weightless. Someone called her name, far away as if shouting into a pipe. Her body protested waking up too early. All she wanted was to be left alone, to sleep. Echoing knocks, as though someone pounded on glass rocked her body. She opened her eyes, and tried to scream, "Go away," but only fluid came out.

Her hands were tiny. She gasped and clutched her chest, finding her breasts gone. The reflection on the surface in front of her looked like a seven-year-old child.

"Katie, sweetie?" a silken male voice came from everywhere.

She looked past her naked reflection at the laboratory. Computer-covered walls fell over like a set dressing for a holovid show, revealing a suburban backyard full of happy children.

Something tickled her ankle. Kate looked down. The gel tube had vanished. Grass brushed her legs. Her hands were sticky with ice cream, which dribbled down the front of a white dress that had appeared out of nowhere. Tightness in her hair made her remember ribbons. Rendered silhouette by the sun overhead, a man leaned over her. The unexpected lack of gel in her lungs made her cough.

"Happy birthday, Sweetie. All of your friends are here."

Shadow receded. Archon reached down and picked her up.

A rush of adoration filled her heart. "Daddy!" she cried, clinging to him and giggling. He carried her to a long table with a pink cake on one end, a white tablecloth fluttering in the gentle breeze. Forty smiling children around her age crowded both sides, waiting for her. The cake seemed so small, impossible for everyone to get a serving. Kate didn't care. She wouldn't feel bad because she'd pass on her piece. They were her friends. They came here to be with her on her birthday, so she didn't need cake.

Archon set her down in a chair and patted her head. She swung her bare feet back and forth, giggling.

"Oh, wait for me," called Anna from the house. She swiveled sideways to squeeze past the patio doors with a huge sheet cake.

The little pink one was only for making wishes.

"Wait for your mother, dear." Archon smiled at her. "She wants to see you blow out the candles."

Little Kate stared at the seven tiny flames. Something about the fire frightened her, but all the love around her made her feel silly to be afraid of candles.

"Make a wish, dear," said Anna as she set the tray down and wiped her hands on an apron.

Kate giggled and looked at the cake, squinted, and looked up at him. "Daddy, what should I wish for?"

He smiled, opening his mouth to speak, but lightning shot out between his teeth. As if he'd eaten a spider made of electricity, tendrils wrapped around his cheeks and lapped at his face. His eyes glowed.

"Fuck. Bollocks. Bastarding hell." Archon roared, and collapsed into a twitching, convulsing heap. "Baaa... Baaa..."

Pain like boiling water poured on her head ran down her back. Kate screamed and jumped away, falling out of her chair and landing on her front. She simpered into the grass, whining for Daddy and Mommy to help. The soft dirt firmed, and the burn at the rear of her mind became nausea. Kate whined and tried to move, feeling full breasts squished between her and tiny, sharp rocks.

"Look out!" screamed a young, female voice.

She got her hands under her and pushed up. The idyllic backyard party had vanished, replaced by a hard surface made of thousands of tiny stones trapped in cement. Cold wind whipped her hair. Her father stood a few meters away, glaring down at a wounded man. A black aircraft hung in midair behind him, turned sideways. Long, angled wings protruded from the rear, two up and one down. Like the proboscis of a giant, alien insect, a ten-foot-long antenna pointed at him.

"Dad!" screamed Kate.

He swiveled. Kate lit off a conflagration of fire near the sniper. A spiral of blue light connected the tip of the weapon to the roof inches to Archon's left.

Rage built inside her as she scrambled to her feet, keeping the curtain of fire between the assassin and her father.

"Get inside, Daddy."

"Daddy?" wheezed the injured man. "You've got to be takin' the piss."

"What?" blurted a dark-haired teen girl, surrounded by a cloud of floating handguns. She stared at a NetMini in her hand, its glow lighting her face. "Are you serious? I…"

Whatever the teen looked at made her burst into sobs. Kate ignored her and ran to Archon's side.

"You see now, Melissa?" yelled the injured man, curling into a ball. "This is what he does, he fecking devours people."

The teen's jaw hung open; she shook her head, muttering an endless string of 'no.'

"Who's that, Dad?" asked Kate.

Archon ducked behind her. "A threat. Kill him. Bloody hell. Soldiers."

"Kate!" yelled the man. "Snap out of it, he's gotten in your head."

We're both Division 0, you've been mind-controlled. That bastard isn't your father.

She stumbled to the side, lightheaded from the voice invading her thoughts, but shook it off.

"He *is* my father!"

A sphere of fire swelled up to fill her hand. Before she could throw it at the prone figure, Archon screamed in fright. She spun as he leapt to the side, away from the hovering sniper's second shot. Her father grunted, raising a hand. The long-barreled railgun bent and twisted, sparking twice before exploding, knocking the large craft into a sideways spin. Three other aircraft, smaller and less angular, raced in as the silent one fled, trailing smoke and flames. The smaller ships glided to a halt near the roof, open doors on their sides packed with armed figures. Soldiers in black/grey camouflage jumped, gliding to the roof with the aid of ion thrusters in their armor.

"Melissa, get out of here," yelled the injured man.

The teen stood gobsmacked, staring at her handheld and crying, as if nothing else in the world existed. Floating pistols fell one after the next, clattering to the roof around her.

A scrape of metal made Kate whip around in time to see her stunrod flying for her head. She caught it, staggering four steps back from the force.

"Sorry, luv. You're not yourself," said the man.

Kate roared and projected a stream of fire into his chest, making him scream. "I know you. You're that killer cop everyone's looking for. Aaron something." She laughed. "I heard the Syndicate's put a shitload of money on your head, you know. I wonder if they'll pay me for killing you."

"Fuck, fuck, fuck," wheezed Aaron, smoke peeling from his chest. "Oh, Mommy."

"Mmmm!" screamed Melissa as a gloved hand covered her face.

An armored soldier dragged the flailing teen out of sight behind the air handler. Chaos erupted on the east side of the roof where a female Marine opened fire on her comrades.

Archon smiled and looked away from her, gesturing at Aaron. "This is your doing, chap. You are wasting life."

Camouflage-armored figures on that side scrambled for cover, trading shots with the dominated woman who stood out in the open. A handful of young men and women dressed like gang toughs spilled from a door at the south corner of the roof, engaging the soldiers. Only their psionic abilities kept it from being an outright slaughter, but even still, the commandos cut them down with brutal efficiency.

Another soldier popped around the corner of the roof enclosure, aiming a rifle at Archon. Kate hurled a fireball too fast to aim; it hit the wall but fouled his shot. The second one hit him in the face, melting his helmet to his skull. He fell forward, dead. Three other soldiers gave her a confused look for a second, before aiming at her, too.

"She's dominated..." Aaron coughed.

"Killing is not my mission," said Archon, eyes flaring wide as he flung a man off the roof with a telekinetic shove. "My mission is survival. I am trying to protect our kind." He brought his arms together, clapping in time with two of the aircraft colliding. A brilliant blossom of orange lit the sky the instant his hands touched, and a blast of hot wind whipped his hair forward. "I am a man of peace."

Burning, twisted metal fell out of sight below the edge of the roof. Seconds later, a great *whump* echoed back up the chasm between buildings from the wreck meeting the ground ten stories below. A gust of wind carried the stink of burning plastic back to the roof.

An invisible force pulled Kate's legs out from under her. She hit the ground on her back with bullets spraying rock fragments all over her. She rolled to the side, snarling, and called to the scraps of ember still burning on Aaron's coat. He flared bright, howled, and went still.

A bullet slapped Kate in the chest as she sat up, knocking her flat again. Molten lead splashed up over her face. *I love this uniform. It doesn't burn.* She played dead for three seconds, before lunging upright. These men wanted to kill her father.

"Daddy!" she screamed, setting off a pyroclastic detonation over the soldiers firing on her.

One slumped in place. The other two staggered to the side, smoke pouring from their mouths and noses. Armor, clothing, and skin from stomach to forehead disintegrated as they collapsed.

The female soldier on the east side of the roof leaned her weapon over her shoulder and smiled at Archon like a little girl who'd finished washing her father's car to surprise him. She bled from multiple bullet wounds, but didn't seem to notice.

"Thank you, dear," said Archon before a telekinetic shove sent her off the roof too.

Aaron wheezed and grunted. The soldier's rapid acceleration slammed to a halt in time for her to slap an armored glove onto the edge.

Archon shook his head at the woman clinging for her life. "You always were a soft touch with the girls, Aaron."

"I got it," said Kate.

She could've ignited the fingers and made the woman fall, but she wanted to look into the eyes of a person who tried to murder her father before they died. Archon passed her on his way to Aaron. A dead soldier's rifle floated into his grasp, and he aimed down at the twitching, wounded, man.

"Aaron, Aaron, Aaron... I wish you could have realized."

"We can talk about it." Aaron offered a used-hovercar-salesman smile.

The soldier who had dragged Melissa to cover popped up and fired at Archon, winging him in the arm. Kate whirled about, screaming with unbridled rage, and hurled a fireball at him. He dove to the side, somersaulting out of the way and firing at her from the ground before sliding out of sight behind an old air handler. Another man popped up from behind the machinery where they'd pulled the teen, and fired at Kate.

Bullets hit her in the stomach and chest like a pummeling from a Kung Fu master. Blood leapt into her throat after the crunch of a broken rib. She braced an arm over her gut, calling upon her power. The soldier's insides heated; he howled with agony and slumped to his knees. He convulsed from the blood boiling inside him. The one who'd grabbed Melissa stayed down.

Archon shot the wailing man in the face, freeing a sluice of steaming gore from his helmet. "Do you not see, Aaron? I am a bringer of mercy."

Kate sprawled where she fell, wheezing, trying to catch her breath. Archon pointed the rifle at Aaron's head.

"I regret this, Aaron. Truly, I do. I wish I could have made you see the light, alas the only light you are willing to see will come from the angels waiting to greet you."

50

THE WINGS OF ANGELS

Aaron

The nauseating realization that his scorched and molten chest smelled a bit like a cheeseburger brought bile to the back of Aaron's mouth. It didn't hurt all that much, at least not compared to the agony between his legs, which remained fresh in his mind. He raised a hand, as if it would do something about the assault rifle hovering over him.

Motion in the air distracted him to a shimmering glow. A whispercraft dropped out of cloak, its long, wand-like railgun oriented at Kate.

"No…" wheezed Aaron, reaching for it. "They don't understand."

"Oh, but I do," said Archon

A tight blue spiral connected the tip of the weapon to the ground behind her. Blood exploded from her back and her arm went flying into the air. Archon startled at the railgun's tiny sonic boom, firing a bullet into the roof inches from Aaron's head.

Aaron cringed.

A man's voice yelled overhead, too far away to make out the word, but panic and surprise sounded clear.

Blinding light glimmered in the air, saturating the roof as though a star had come too close to the Earth. It carried the presence of another world, making time feel detached and sluggish. Archon turned, glancing upward. The thud of Kate's body collapsing to the roof came from the right, though endless light shrouded everything.

"Stop it!"

The plaintive wail of a little girl thundered across the sky, far louder than possible. The source of the radiant light became distinct; ribbons of energy formed the shape of wings, each span three times the height of the scrawny figure between them.

The girl from Rakshasi's flat.

Althea held her arms out to the sides. A glow like tiny azure suns shone from her eyes, stark in contrast to the luminous white enveloping the rest of her body. She seemed to hang in midair, hair and dress aflutter in a driving wind.

Overwhelming calm came over him at the sight of her. The child's hair changed from blonde to white, glowing with the same power that had become wings. Her expression looked to be a combination of horror and anger, most of which she directed at Archon.

Aaron grunted, trying to sit up, but his body refused. He hadn't noticed the continuing gunfire between the soldiers and the psionic gang's sentries until it petered out.

The assault rifle slid from Archon's hands and landed on Aaron's gut. The leader of the Awakened loosed a yelp of terror while staring at the floating child. Once his lungs had emptied, he ran out of sight. Aaron couldn't help but grin like an idiot as the girl's toes touched the roof. Her wings flared out and rose above her, framing her little body with an intense glow.

She cast a forlorn stare at the carnage on the roof.

Two soldiers emerged from cover among the air units. They averted their eyes and fell to their knees.

Aaron reached toward her. Reassured by her presence, he stopped fighting and let himself slide away to unconsciousness.

THE WRATH OF LEGION

Mamoru

Square panels of starship bridge fell away from the reality around him, exposing the small conference room full of teenaged technokinetics. Mamoru removed his hand from the server, clamping his fist to disperse a lingering bit of energy.

"How did you do that?" A fourteen-year-old girl with cobalt blue hair grabbed his left arm. "You spawned eighteen outbound threads without doing anything but touching the box. You gotta show me that trick!"

"Yeah, man," said a dazed-sounding, older teen who might have even been past twenty. "Sucked all our cycles away."

"Fuckin' got me killed," whined a preteen boy.

"The crap are you playing games for?" yelled the blue-haired girl. "We're supposed to be finding a new home." She released Mamoru's arm and looked at him the way one might gawk at their personal deity come to life. "Was that technokinesis? What were you doing? You gotta show us!"

"Plucking the wings from an angel," said Mamoru, without emotion.

He walked out, leaving the group of precocious hackers to their confusion. He had fulfilled his obligation. This place no longer held anything for him. Archon and everything around him would burn. Now, he could go to Sadako. He had to be sure she lived.

The corridor led him past half-dozen conference rooms to a small area with an unused reception desk and a pair of double doors, which opened to a larger hallway beyond. People ran back and forth, chaotic shouts echoing from both sides. A blond boy, about twelve, ran up to him.

"Oi, mister, 'ave you seen me dad?"

"No." Mamoru kept walking.

"Mum?"

"I have not."

"Bloody hell," whined the boy, before he ran off shouting for his parents.

A dark-skinned woman with long, sand-brown dreadlocks rushed in from the lobby, barking commands at anyone she saw to get out to the vans. When she spotted Mamoru, she pointed at him.

"You. Where's the ship?"

"On its way," said Mamoru, walking right past her.

"Where do you think you're going?" She grabbed his arm.

Mamoru stopped, glancing at her hand as though she had smeared animal waste on him. His gaze flicked from her fingers to her eyes. An instant later, a powerful urge to trust her filtered into his mind. The feeling faded as the presence of the *Akuryō* roiled to the surface. Her expression changed from alluring to terrified. She backed into the wall, palms flat.

"Home," said the voice of an old man, on a wisp of black breath that smelled of carrion.

She broke away and ran down the hall. Mamoru, chuckling, resumed his walk to the exit. Anna had left the car in front of the tallest building when they'd arrived. It would be adequate to bring him back to Sadako. He jogged across the space between the buildings, amused by the sound of gunfire overhead.

A great crash of metal exploded above; seconds later, a fireball made of two small aircraft careened into the cyborg graveyard. The *Akuryō* reveled in the death. Power seeped in Mamoru's skin, souls drawn to the entity inside him.

I have done what you asked.

He forced his way in the side door of the ten-story building, bending the plastisteel frame. People in a large open room full of tents stared at him as he jogged past and headed for the middle corridor and a right turn to the main exit. A handful of armed men and women ran past him to the stairwell, shouting about enemies on the roof.

Anna appeared at the archway where the corridor met the main lobby. She walked against the fleeing crowd, making her way into the building. The arrogance in her strut filled him with the urge to hit her, perhaps the *Akuryō's* feelings. It would be highly amused if he killed her.

She lifted her gaze long enough to render a brief nod of acknowledgment. Light glinted from her emerald eyes as they passed. Something seemed off. Mamoru took three steps before he froze and twisted.

"Anna."

In defiance of the war going on overhead, she paused with a look of irritation, as if late for a board meeting. "Wot is it? I'm in a bit of a rush."

He studied her for a moment before turning away. "Nothing."

She mumbled something too low to hear and trotted into the stairwell. Mamoru stormed down the corridor, across the lobby, and out to the courtyard. The gold Halcyon-Ormyr sat where he expected it to be. He squinted again at the building's doors. Brilliant light flared overhead, like the flash before an ancient hydrogen bomb. Its touch burned him and sent smoke wafting from his raised arm. Mamoru leaned back to stare up at the sharp angle, at the figure of a tiny, winged girl gliding down from on high.

He howled with rage and staggered to the side. Primal fear, that of a shadow facing the sun, robbed him of all rational thought. His surroundings blurred with a kinetic run, fifty miles per hour into the darkened city, away from this place.

Away from the *abomination*.

BETWEEN WORLDS

Althea

Sound had taken on a muted and blurry quality as if underwater. The world around Althea lost its color, washed out to shades of monochromatic blue. Men and women, spirits emerging from corpses, shifted to stare at her. Horror filled her heart, and she clutched her hands to her chest. Blood flowed in the cracks between the tiny rocks on the roof's surface, coarse and uncomfortable underfoot.

A man not much older than Karina stood over his dead body. He took notice of her and screamed. "Why am I staring at myself? I can't get up! What the fuck?"

Seven figures in camouflage emerged from corpses, surrounding her in a horseshoe formation, followed by fourteen or so other spirits in street clothes.

Althea let her arms fall, finding solace in being able to give them peace. "You should not dwell here. There is nothing for you in this place but sadness. Go."

Something deep within her, a reflexive action she could not explain, called out to a distant place, which felt far away and close at the same time. Shimmering spirals of silver light formed near each spirit. She had opened a doorway for them. Dark and sinister forms, clouds of shadow bearing arms tipped with wispy claws, crept over the wall, chasing two other apparitions off the roof. Althea felt neither fear nor pride in watching the creatures chase the fleeing ghosts.

Some people deserve to die.

The spirits dispersed one by one, some confused, some grateful. The energy on the other side called to her but didn't beckon. The other-place held a familiar warmth. She did not understand why she remembered it, and didn't bother trying. Agony surrounded her from numerous survivors, some barely alive.

Althea bowed her head. Her hair billowed past, thin strands of glowing white light. She paid it no mind, absorbed by the overwhelming need to help these people. Energy radiated from her, flowing out from her back as a surge along the ribbons. The simultaneous sense of sixteen bodies' life-shapes coalesced in her mind, and she willed them whole. When she opened her eyes, two forms remained hurt, more wounded than the rest. The burst of healing energy had forestalled their deaths, but only for a short time.

"Kate," said Althea.

The redhead sat up, half out of her body. Her left arm, and most of the shoulder on that side, had ceased to exist. Althea's power kept the woman's blood inside, and her heart beating. It felt strange to exert influence over a body without touching it, though she remembered what she had done to Hector. She had been across the room from him when he'd shot Karina. The energy of whatever state she had entered prevented any feelings of anger— her memory of Hector brought only regret. Regret he had harmed Karina and regret he had to die. If the anger of someone harming Karina could send her abilities beyond the reach of her touch, it had to be her despairing horror at witnessing such murder from high above that let her heal from afar.

She had leapt from the car without even thinking twice.

Althea assumed using her power that way would tire her far more than if she touched them, yet she felt no fatigue.

A transparent version of Kate struggled to get up, as if stuck from the waist down to her mortal remains. Althea tiptoed around bloodstains and stooped at her side, putting a hand on her transparent head. Calmed at the touch, Kate's spirit ceased moving. The woman looked up at her with the pouting face of a little child.

"You are not dead yet." Althea smiled, the brilliant glow in her eyes bathed Kate in azure light. "I don't want you to go away."

Spectral tears covered Kate's cheeks. "It's my birthday! They stole my cake! I never got to make a wish."

Althea guided her to lie down, back into her body, leaving a hand on Kate's solid forehead. Orbs of light swelled from the tips of her energy ribbon wings before gliding along their length and disappearing into her back. Warm tingles ran down her arm and a similar sphere of light formed around her fingers and spread out over Kate.

Threads of flesh emerged from the horrible gouge, tentatively exploring the roof as they grew longer. The mass stretched and twitched, like fast-forwarded video of plant roots growing. Another tendril joined, twisting together and thickening into a new arm. Bones appeared in the center, wrapped with muscle, and finally pink, new skin. Althea guided the life-shapes back to rights. Once satisfied the woman's body was whole, she leaned forward and kissed her on the forehead before standing.

Harsh shadows crept over the roof, the light from her wings pivoting with a slow turn. The tips flicked and twisted as if alive, avoiding contact with air handlers and vents. Althea surveyed the area, sensing only one person still hurt. The man from the apartment, when Aurora had brought her to the city across the world of the spirits. He'd been injured again, burned as well as shot.

He came to as she padded over to stand beside him. His hand slid over her foot and grasped her ankle. She crouched, taking his hand in both of hers. He strained to stay awake. Despite the healing energies she had saturated the area with, he remained close to death.

"'Ello again."

"Hi." She commanded his brain to ignore pain.

The man smiled, radiating love. "Gettin' ta be a habit, innit?"

"I don't know what you mean." She bit her lip at the sight of dark blood oozing out from the charred flesh on his chest.

"Is that it then? Am I gone? Where's Allison?"

"What, no, and I don't know."

"Are you real?"

"No, I'm Althea." She closed her eyes and squeezed his hand.

"Wiseass," he muttered.

She grinned.

Aaron groaned and fainted. She clasped his hand to her cheek, projecting serenity as she urged his body's life-shapes to mend themselves. Once she mended all the hurts within him, she let go of his hand and stood. She sensed no spirits and no living people nearby at the precipice of death any longer.

Her desperation to stop all the killing relaxed. The energy ribbons diminished and withdrew into her back. Her hair ceased glowing, and her eyes faded from their abnormal intensity to their usual bright glow. All at once, the exertion of helping so many people in such short a span fell upon her shoulders. She looked down at the unconscious man, swayed on her feet, and collapsed on top of him.

Seconds, perhaps minutes later, light, weak by comparison to what her wings had made, shone in her face. She squinted at a black hovercar landing on the roof. The door opened, and a figure rushed out.

"Althea!" screamed Officer Ahmed.

Content, secure, and exhausted, she closed her eyes.

THE KING'S GREATEST FEAR

Anna

Most of the rooms on the ninth floor had walls of frosted glass. Evidently, the entire story had been executive conference rooms. Anna gave up and spent an hour roaming the eighth before settling on the former corner office of Alexis B. Moseley, Vice President of Finance. The floor-to-ceiling windows on the two outer walls faced southwest and would offer a beautiful view of the setting sun; at least, for however much longer they stayed here. Archon would insist they leave soon, now that Mamoru had returned to the fold. Not having a starship had been a rather large impediment to leaving Earth.

She debated what she wanted to do: soak in a bath, curl up naked amid silk sheets (perhaps after said bath), get blind drunk (perhaps while curled up in bed), or grow enough backbone to tell James to get stuffed. Her indecision resulted in none of the above happening. An hour and twenty minutes after returning with Mamoru, she'd still not so much as taken her coat off.

I don't want to get comfortable here. She walked to the corner where the two windows met, staring out at the dark Pacific ocean and the dying sunlight sinking into the horizon. Her dark sapphire eyes reflected back at her from the window, another person staring accusingly out of another life, astonished she'd even bothered coming back to Archon. She bowed her head. *I can't get comfortable here.*

She put a hand on the glass. Aaron's various quirky expressions flashed by in a slideshow of memory. Her feelings made no sense. He wasn't the sort of man who loved. He only wanted another tick on his belt, another Awakened weapon on his hip. Her throat tightened.

Aaron has such sad eyes. What had he been like before his wife died? I... She covered her mouth. *I've been such an idiot. I've got to find him.*

Anna whirled to leave, but froze as Archon rushed in with fire in his stare and blood on his coat.

"No point moving your things." He glanced at the room. "Not a bad choice, but too late. We need to leave, immediately."

"What's going on?"

"They found us. We had a mole." He scowled. "How could you not have heard all that?"

Gunshots and random explosions had been the norm for this area, though they did sound a tad closer than usual. Anna stood like a deer in the headlights as he stormed toward her, barely suppressing a cringe when he got near enough to grab her. She held her breath until he passed without contact. Nothing stood between her and the door out. Her weight shifted onto her left leg, right foot about to take a step.

"Attention everyone," said Archon, his voice projected by speakers all throughout the complex. "Government forces have located us, and are advancing as we speak. It is imperative that we evacuate immediately. Everyone should proceed at once to Edmonson Memorial Starport by any means necessary. Anyone too little... or too simple to know how to do it, go to the café in the main building."

Anna hesitated, thinking of all the children they'd collected. She looked back at him, standing in the corner gazing out at the city, holding his NetMini like a microphone. Three Archons, one real and two reflected, sighed. If she didn't leave now, she might yet wind up on a starship she did not want to be on, away from her home... number six Woodseer Street.

"They are afraid of us and are shooting without asking questions. They do not care how young you are or how wide you smile. Do not, under any circumstances stand and fight. It is time for us to find our new home. Talis, I am sure you can hear this. Proceed to Edmonson at once and secure the facility for our purposes." He let off the transmit button, speaking only to Anna. "Help me corral the little ones, will you?"

"Dad!" yelled Alexi. "There you are. I've been looking everywhere." The boy ran to him and held on. "What's all the noise?"

Archon patted him on the back. Archon's fatherly smile was as false as the origin of the boy's English accent. The sight of him squeezed Anna's stomach.

She stared at the boy. "Aye. I'll get the little ones then. What of the Angel?"

James paled, white as a ghost.

Anna blinked. "Did something happen to the ship again?"

"Oh." He chuckled. "Yes. That is the name they gave the ship. I had almost forgotten. I think I shall rename it at the first opportunity. Where is Mamoru?"

"Not the foggiest. I haven't seen him since we landed. He asked where the computers were set up and ran off." She raised an eyebrow. "What's gotten you bricking it?"

"Nothing, dear. Overreaction to Lauren's prattling. She has been known to be wrong on multiple occasions anyway. Come on, then. You have children to collect."

Anna stayed quiet, noting how he leaned on the word *children* every time he said it. Once, he had bemoaned how many of their 'recruits' were kids; he wanted people capable of fighting. Now, he turned them into leverage to control her.

"Good instincts picking Manchester, by the by."

"What?"

"Arsenal... those blighters will always disappoint you."

"What are you saying?"

"He led them right to us." Archon glared at her. "Lauren was wrong. The whole thing must have been some elaborate setup. I doubt the man ever even had a wife."

She drew a gasp, covering her mouth with both hands. "Is he..."

"No, unfortunately. Not far from it, though, but I suspect that damn whelp will see to that. Where is that witch?"

"Witch? What witch?"

"The police arrived ever so suspiciously on time. Where is Lauren?"

"Cripes, James... You're afraid of her, aren't you?"

He glared. "Of course not."

"Not Lauren. Althea." Anna's eyes widened. "You're petrified of that little girl because of what Lauren said."

Archon patted Alexi on the back. "Present company excluded, I am rather starting not to like children. Especially petulant little girls who do not know when someone is looking out for their own best interest. Now, are you going to help me with the *precious little tykes*, or should I deal with them myself?"

A dread chill made her shiver at his words. "I haven't seen Lauren at all. Not since before I went to get Mamoru. Of course. I'll... go to the café."

"I shall see you at the starport." He stormed out. "Alastair, go with your mother."

"Mum?" Alexi ran over and clung to Anna, shivering with fear. "Why's Dad so angry? Why is everyone shooting? Are we going to die?"

You bastard.

Anna swallowed, trying to suppress the urge to tremble. "H-he... he doesn't want anyone to hurt us. Come on, then. We'll be all right, but we've got to get out of here."

FORTRESS BREACHED

Aaron

Cold air brushed Aaron's face, teasing him out of a wonderful dream of strolling across an empty Frictionless arena with Anna at his side. He moaned, confused by weight on top of him. Hair fluttered in his face with the next gust, making him sputter and open his eyes. The blonde girl who saved his life in Rakshasi's apartment lay on top of him, warm cheek to his bare chest, drooling. She made no sound as she breathed, soft and slow. Aaron reached up, brushing the hair from her face, and squeezed her shoulder. The girl didn't react.

"Oi, mite," he whispered. "Y'awrite?"

I'm on the bloody roof. He forced himself to sit up, cradling the limp child in his arms. Aside from some blood she'd stepped in, she didn't have a mark on her, yet she wouldn't stir. All around him lay bodies, soldiers and some of Archon's security detail. A distant scuffing of boots accompanied a feminine grunting.

"Don't move," said a man, sounding on the verge of crying. "Division 0 police."

"Awright, but I don't think you're going to shoot me with 'er in me lap. An' I'm on your side, mate."

"Is she alive?"

A second glove slapped onto the edge of the roof.

"I'm gonna stand up, eh? Don't panic." Aaron slid an arm under the girl's knees, cradling her as he levitated himself upright.

A Middle Eastern-looking man in gloss black psi armor stood near the unconscious body of the red-haired woman. Aaron raised an eyebrow at her one bare breast and arm, but paid more attention to the E-90 pointed at him.

For a second, a camouflage helmet rose up between the gloves but dropped out of sight. A woman panted. Aaron telekinetically latched onto the gloves and hoisted the wounded Marine up and over onto the roof.

"Put it down, mate. I'm not with them. I've recently come out of retirement."

Moans from the right made the man jump. A few of Archon's people got up and dragged themselves to the door. Aaron looked down at the child in his arms. *Screw it, let 'em run.*

"Besides," said Aaron, holding the girl a little higher. "Would this one 'ave used me for a bed if I was unsavory?"

"I suppose not. She's got a sense about people." He stowed his weapon. "I'm not sensing any duplicity."

"Ehh." Aaron grimaced. "Don't try an' influence me, it wouldn't be pretty."

"You're Pryce."

"I've been called worse."

"David Ahmed. They said you'd gone rogue."

Aaron offered a cheesy smile. "Was a bit of a misunderstanding. I suppose the official story will be that the whole thing was an elaborate undercover operation. Truth is a little more dodgy. How's your girl?"

David blinked.

"Come on, mate. Don't gotta be an empath to see the tears on your face. Grab a blanket from your Pat-V, her tit's out. Oh, be careful with her. Archon got into her head. She thinks he's her damn father now. Might try to hurt you. Did quite a number on... feck, do you know how much this suit cost?"

Aaron whirled at a scuff behind him. Melissa, bound hand and foot with plastic riot ties, crawled like an inchworm out from behind the air handler. Tears oozed from her red-ringed eyes. She coughed and sputtered on snot, bawling like a girl half her age.

"I wanna go home. I'm sorry. You were right." She struggled. "Help, please..."

Aaron looked down at the scorched necktie hanging over his naked chest. The sight of the sleeping girl in his arms sapped his anger away.

"Sorry, kid," said David, approaching Melissa. "I can't say what'll happen, but you're probably going to face some charges for shooting Officer Pryce."

"Lieutenant, apparently."

Melissa bawled and screamed, unsuccessful in her attempt to writhe away as David put a metal headband on her. "Daddy!"

"Lieutenant?" David shook his head. "That's going to go over well."

"Not my idea, mate. Oi, is that necessary? She's just a kid."

"She was part of an organized criminal psionic gang. She's got to answer for that."

"For what? Being conned by a lunatic? Archon turned her parents against her and fed her a line of shite. We both know the brass has a habit of being forgetful when people sign on that dotted line."

"I... voices," Melissa muttered and shook her head. "Stop it. No. I don't wanna. Shut up. Shut up. Where am I? I don't care. Stop. Stop. Stop. Mommy! Please! I swear I'll stay in the school. I promise I won't run away again! Stop whispering!" She surrendered to bawling.

David cringed.

Light swarmed the roof as a legion of Division 0 patrol craft swooped in and landed. David took the psi inhibitor off Melissa's head. Her psychotic mumbling ceased to a low, repeating moan of 'ow.'

"I hate those bloody things." Aaron shivered. "It's like having a houseful of tertiary relatives you see once every few years crammed into your brain and chatting about Aunt Mildred's bunions."

David cut Melissa's ankles loose and helped her to her feet, but left her hands secured behind her back. "She's terrified."

"Are all telempaths masters of the obvious?" asked Aaron. "She's a telekinetic, potent too."

"You could've told me that *before* I took the inhibitor off."

"I won't do anything bad. Please, don't put that fucking thing on me again. I'll do whatever you want. Please." She dropped to her knees, crying. "I wanna go home. I want my parents."

Two tactical officers trotted over. David pulled Melissa upright and handed her to them. "Kidnap victim." He gave Aaron an accusing look. "Go easy on her. Sounds like the guy in charge here threatened her parents."

"Mind control," said Aaron while hefting Althea. "For a scrawny thing, this girl's getting rather heavy."

Melissa sniveled, but walked obediently with the officers to a car, though her NetMini did leap from the roof to her pocket. The woman in grey/black camouflage armor, lying on her back where Aaron left her, groaned and sat up. She stuck her finger in a hole where a bullet had pierced her chest plate, looking mystified at the lack of blood gushing out.

"ID checks out," said one of the Division 0 officers to the others, lowering his weapon. "You ok, Corporal?"

The woman held up her right hand. "Think my fingers are broken, but I'll live. What happened to me? My body moved on its own... I..."

"Archon took over your mind." Aaron carried Althea to the car David arrived in and set her down on the back seat.

Thank you. Melissa's teary voice entered his thoughts. *You were right. Mom and Dad want me. I'm, uhh, sorry about the stunrod.*

He leaned on the vehicle in front of him as a blast of remembered agony emanated from his crotch. She stared at him, standing by the rear door of a patrol craft. The officer escorting her put a hand on her head and guided her into the back seat.

"If that kid does something," said David, walking past him. "It's your ass."

"She won't. The only reason she was with Archon at all is he put the gris-gris on her parents." Aaron wheezed, still in the throes of latent testicular trauma. He clung to the car to keep from falling over as David took a knee by Kate's side. "Careful. She's been mind-wanked."

"I don't like this Archon guy." David slipped the psi inhibitor over Kate's head, locked her wrists behind her, and wrapped her in a blanket. "I really don't like him."

Aaron limped around to the other back door, opening it so David could ease Kate inside. "I tried to stop him before he got in too deep. I might be able to break the telepathic overlay. Did it twice in London already. Bit of a ballache, that." As soon as he said the word, the boys twinged with pain, and he grunted.

"Get in," said David. "I'll drive."

Aaron fell into the passenger seat. "You should talk to Ridge. He's got a betting pool on who'd bring me in first."

David jogged around the hood and got in. "Didn't you say you're reinstated?"

Aaron leaned back and closed his eyes. The soft seat felt amazing. "Aye, but Vern doesn't know that yet."

THE DEATH OF PHANTOMS

Kate

The scent of dirt filled Kate's nostrils. Her eyes opened. She lay face down on a forest path, nude, underbrush scorching away from wherever her little body touched it. A short distance to her left, the charred carcass of a deer sprawled on the ground. Kate gathered her feet under herself and stood, looking down at her flat, shapeless body. Small clumps of dirt stuck to her chest and thighs, steaming and drying out. The ashen remains of weeds curled up and blew off upon the wind.

I'm dreaming.

Cracking and crunching trampled out from the forest behind her, a sound growing louder as if an army of monsters approached. She faced it, finding herself taking hesitant steps back. Her heart raced. Something sinister rushed toward her in the darkness. The deer carcass moved; its head rose from the ground, pivoted to face her, and its mouth hung open, leaking blood. Kate screamed and ran, arms held up to shield her face from low hanging branches whipping at her.

The rustle coming up behind her intensified to a steady rumble, shaking the ground. Her surroundings seemed familiar and alien all at once: the forest where she'd lived for so long, alone. None of the landmarks she remembered remained. Her passage left a trail of flames across the underbrush. Even the sharpest thorns broke apart to ash before they could pierce her unprotected skin. When she crossed a small creek, water flashed to steam where her feet dared approach. Kate scrambled up the inclined bank on the far side.

This is not real. This is a nightmare. Wake up!

Laughter, watery and distant, drew her to a clearing in the trees, where a tall wooden fence right out of suburbia surrounded a picture-perfect two-story home. The sound of giggling children came from the other side. She sprinted over the manicured lawn, eager to get away from the menace behind her. Kate flung herself with a flying leap onto the fence, her touch burned char marks in the shape of hands and toes in the planks as she climbed up and over the barrier. For a few seconds, she perched at the top like an alley cat, looking back at the undisturbed forest. Fire spread outward along the wood from wherever her skin made contact.

Nothing emerged from the tree line, but the forest seemed frightening still.

She jumped down. As soon as she landed, a frilly pink dress appeared on her. It didn't burn, nor did the bright green grass upon which she stood. Faceless people stared at her from behind a table so long it stretched to the horizon. Thirty or so generic children with blurry spots for heads clapped and cheered. Two adults, a man and a woman, waved at her to join them.

Kate looked down at herself. The ostentatious dress looked like something a doll would wear. The skirt flared out over white frills beneath. Her dirt-caked bare feet seemed woefully out of place for such a fancy affair. Without even realizing, she swiped them through the damp grass in an effort to clean herself before taking a hesitant step closer, unsure if she should trust the blurry figures. A snarl came from her left, more cute than menacing, like one of those dogs small enough to sit in the palm of your hand. She hopped to the right and spun. A tiny pink cake, the size of a grapefruit, balanced on spindly white legs made from birthday candles. Beady stick-on eyes atop the icing glared at her. The separation between layers opened to reveal a row of gleaming triangular teeth. It growled and flung itself at her leg.

She screamed and kicked it. Icing oozed between her toes as the monstrous confection exploded on impact. The faceless children laughed. Kate looked up at the 'father' figure for help. He pointed and laughed, regarding the little creature as harmless. Another appeared in the grass, running at her. She stomped it flat and kicked another one rushing in. Sugary goop splattered everywhere. A fourth mini-cake snuck her from behind, sinking needle-like teeth into her right calf. Her glass-shattering scream made all the faceless children clamp their hands over their ears. Cake smushed between her fingers as she grabbed the snarling critter and crushed it. Teeth, once sharp, smeared to soft icing.

I'm having a nightmare.

"Well, you wanted a nice cake for your big seventh birthday, Katie!" said the 'mother,' in a grand voice. She gestured to her left as if presenting a game-show winner with a new car. "It took me all weekend, but I made it."

The Cake stood between the faceless parents. Six feet tall, nine feet wide, it separated between the second and third layers, exposing a mouth lined with red preserves that seemed more like blood than jam, an endless throat stretching into darkness. Glinting fangs outlined a mouth big enough to swallow five children whole. A blast of hot, sweet air laced with strawberry blew her hair back as it roared. Kate forgot she dreamed.

Piss ran down her leg.

'Mother' smiled, proud of her baking. "Now go on, cake, have some birthday girl."

"Blow out your candles, sweetie," said a distorted, deep voice.

Seven candles atop the monstrous dessert fumed like inverted rockets spewing flames upward.

The fence shattered to a thousand toothpicks under the weight of an army of red-eyed deer, skinless and cooked. The smoldering horrors smashed their way into the yard and rampaged among the partygoers. Faceless children screamed and ran as the creatures set upon them. Kate darted away from the gargantuan cake, but stopped three strides later in front of a little boy with no arm and a deer chewing on his neck. More trotted over, forming a ring around her

"How many of us did you kill?" asked one deer. "We had feelings too."

An enormous buck, its chest a hollow cavity, loomed over her. "Saying sorry doesn't make it all right. I'm still dead."

"Time for deer to eat people," said another, snarling.

Kate spun in place, finding nowhere to run. She bawled, surrounded by smoldering, undead deer and one extremely agitated giant cake.

"Daddy!" she screamed as they closed in.

KATE SAT UP IN A PLAIN ROOM, PURE WHITE ON ALL SIDES EXCEPT FOR ONE WALL, which consisted of a shimmering blue energy barrier. Sweat covered her, and she trembled for a few seconds until the realization sunk in she'd had a nightmare. The thick plastic of a Comforgel pad formed a bowl around where she sat, holding a puddle of warmth. She blushed at wetting her bed. Daddy would be angry with her. Kate was a big girl now. She'd just turned seven, and big girls shouldn't wet their beds. She climbed out of the mess, pacing in a circle around the small holding cell, biting her fingers and whining. A thigh-length white smock clung to her, keeping the foulness pressed against her skin.

"Eww!"

Disgusted by the chilly touch of urine-soaked cloth, she pulled it off and used the dry parts to wipe herself before wadding it up and tossing it at the force wall. The garment crackled and sparked for a few seconds as it fluttered to the floor.

After a few more laps, she curled up on the floor, knees to chest, and cried. She rubbed the back of her leg where the cake bit her, but found no wound. The pain in her calf lingered only in her mind.

Daddy, help! I've been kidnapped!

She sniffled and whimpered for some time, shivering in the cold chamber. The Comforgel pad would keep her warm, but she'd soiled it. Outside, a stark white hallway, every bit as featureless as her cell, remained silent. What could have been minutes or hours later, a Hispanic woman walked into view in a black, clingy uniform. She looked at Kate with a mixture of worry and disapproval.

"You're awake."

Tears streamed out of Kate's eyes and she slapped her hands on the ground. "Where am I? I wanna go home. Where's my daddy?" She rocked back and forth. "I'm scared. I wanna go home."

"Sounds like she's regressed," said a male voice. "I wonder if it's a side effect of the botched implant."

The female officer moved to the side of the cell. "She's terrified. It's no act."

Kate sniffled, cowering away from the scary woman. Her fear weakened and leveled off to an inexplicable calm. Soon, she felt such contentment she didn't want to move. Gravity took her over sideways, and she smiled.

The officer walked into the cell and, after wiping her down with a flower-scented cleaning pad, pulled a clean smock over her head, dressing her as though she were paralyzed. When the woman let go, she remained where she flopped, lacking the willpower to move.

A few seconds after the thrum of the energy wall resumed, the overwhelming tranquility faded, though she didn't feel as frightened as before. Kate sat up, looking around at her room as if seeing it for the first time. "You're bad people! Let me go! Daddy!"

"She's dressed, sir," said the female officer.

A pale man in a long, dark coat stepped out from behind the wall. He looked like a reanimated corpse with short, somewhat curly black hair.

"You're not my daddy," said Kate. "You're scary."

"How old are you, Kate?"

"Seven." She grabbed her toes, grinned, and rocked. "Today's my birthday, but the cake tried to eat me."

The female officer whistled.

"Do you understand what happened?" asked the man. "Do you understand why you are here?"

Kate twirled her hair around a finger. "You kidnapped me?"

"No."

She looked up. "Am I in a hospital?"

The man didn't move or change the inflection of his voice. "No. I'm Lieutenant Commander Ashford. You are being held for observation. You're not a child, Kate."

She squinted at him, giving him a raspberry. At a tingle in the front of her brain, she went cross-eyed. "That feels icky."

The nightmare rewound, though to her waking mind, it looked more like a bad cartoon than anything scary. The faceless father became Archon. She looked down at her obvious breasts. A churn of nausea rumbled in her gut at the disconnect between what she believed and what her eyes told her. Feeling lightheaded, she moaned.

She rubbed her face. "What happened?"

Commander Ashford clasped his hands behind his back. "There is a video record of you participating in the murder of several military personnel. The last thing we have on our side is your request for backup while in pursuit of a suspect Captain Buckley sent you after."

"Buckley?" Kate blinked. "I... don't remember. Those soldiers tried to kill me. They tried to kill my father."

Ashford moved closer to the barrier, a thin wisp of electricity teased at his hair. "Your name is Kate Solomon. You are a Tactical Officer with Division 0. That man is not, nor has he ever been, your father."

Gelatinous energy swam around in her mind. Images twisted and flipped in her head.

A dark skinned man felt love for her. *What's his name?*

A little girl with glowing blue eyes smiled at her. *That's my daughter! She looks like she's ten! How can I have a daughter older than me?*

A dark Hispanic woman with a shotgun came crawling out of a burned refrigerator. *Why do I know her?*

A slender, older man with killing eyes in a black suit with a white hat. *Is he my father?*

The same man burned to a charred skeleton.

Kate's voice screamed in her head.

The feeling in her mind grew painful, and she collapsed in a fetal position.

"How is it going?" asked the female officer.

"I've never seen an implant this strong. I'm not sure I can remove it. I'm sorry, but I think I'll need to wipe this one."

"Oi, sir," said another man. "A minnit?"

"What are you doing here, Pryce? You should be in medical for an evaluation."

"Sorry, sir." Aaron limped into view outside her cell. "I'd like to have a go at her."

The female officer gasped.

"Oh, for cryin'." Aaron gazed at the ceiling. "Telepathically."

Ashford regarded him with a measured stare, rubbing his chin. "Your files don't mention any particularly astounding rating in telepathy."

"No offense, sir, but you've read Director Kovalev's write up on the whole 'Awakened' thing?"

"I have."

"Before you hit the reset button, let me give it a whack."

"It's more involved than that," said Ashford. "There's paperwork, hearings…"

Aaron smiled at Kate. "I've had a bit of practice undoin' Archon's cheesedickery. He only had a few minutes with her. Follow me in, eh? Worked it the same way with this Hughes bloke in London. His finesse, my oomph."

"Dad?" Kate leapt to her feet. "Where's my father?"

"I'm sorry, Kate," said Aaron. "He's not your father."

Both men stared at her. Their presence shifted from looking *at* her to looking into her soul.

The three figures in the doorway blurred. Kate swooned to her knees and grabbed her head. Cold fingers stroked the top of her brain. *Daddy… Help.*

He's not your father, said Aaron's voice from inside her mind.

She fell onto the floor and sailed out over a glittering expanse of West City. Kate screamed. She'd leapt from the patrol craft, ready to kill herself before succumbing to mind control. The ground raced up beneath her, too fast for a simple fall. A beige square—the roof of Archon's building—came at her. She braced for impact but wound up standing on it. Archon in front of her, Aaron to the left, frozen in time.

"Remember him?" Aaron pointed at David.

David.

"You thought of him as you jumped," said Aaron.

That false memory is deep. Ashford's voice boomed overhead.

Aaron looked at the clouds. "Aye. You've got the finesse. I've got the force. Can you find the interface between real and bullshit?"

Yes, said Ashford. *I see it.*

"I'm sorry Kate, but this might hurt." Aaron smiled.

A splitting headache tore into her mind. She wrapped her arms around her head, screaming. The pain exploded outward in throbbing waves, as if her skull would burst. Dazed, she flopped flat on her chest, shuddering. Her meeting with the Japanese man, the demon priest appearing in the city, and chasing the Halcyon-Ormyr into the black zone replayed in her thoughts. The roof sped away into the distance, leaving her tumbling in a void. Lightning flashed overhead, concussive thunderclaps rocked her bones. Her body spun faster and faster. Gravity returned along with a sense of falling. Before she could scream, she crashed into a smooth, hard floor with an explosive *boom* that left her seeing nothing but white light.

"Kate?" asked Aaron.

She lifted her head and lowered her arms, staring past a curtain of disheveled hair at the three people in black.

"Should she be bleeding from the eyes?" asked the female officer. "That's not normal."

"What about this shite is normal?" Aaron leaned left and right, trying to make eye contact. He seemed out of breath. "Kate? Are you back?"

"Her emotional radiance no longer feels childlike," said the woman. "Oh... she's angry."

"Motherfucker," growled Kate. "I'm going to kill that bastard." She sat back, pulled her hair out of her face, and stared at the red droplets on the floor.

"Shit, she's spiking depression." The female officer hit a button on the wall to disable the field and rushed in, putting an arm around her. "Kate. Don't harm yourself. It's not your fault."

"I feel so violated." Her voice came out as a weak croak. "He knew how desperate I was for a family... for a real life. He tried to invent it all. I can't think of anything worse to do to someone."

She looked up at Aaron. "He did that to Anna?"

"Aye." He clenched his jaw. "At least somewhat."

"Anna got me out of that C-Branch prison. I saw it in her eyes. She's not like him." She kept quiet for a moment. "How many... people did I kill?"

"They're still piecing it together. Initial reconstruction puts the count at about six." Ashford held up a datapad and poked at the screen. "I'll need to re-verify your mental state."

"She's borderline suicidal, sir," said the woman.

"I'm borderline going-to-melt-Archon-to-a-cinder," grumbled Kate. "I'll be okay... I-if David is. Where is he?"

"He's close," said Ashford. "We were worried about your reaction to seeing him in your previous state. As far as the dead soldiers are concerned, I am convinced you were under the influence of another psionic. Pending your psych review, we will be charging the individual known as Archon with their deaths."

She let her hands flop in her lap. "Yeah, that makes me feel so much better. Can I see David, or am I still a prisoner?"

"Unfortunately," said Ashford, "you're still under detention until I complete my evaluation."

"More mind reading? What are you waiting for? Let's get it over with." The oddity of her arms being two different colors made her pause. "Why is my left arm pink?"

Ashford and Aaron exchanged glances. Neither one seemed like they wanted to speak.

"Rail gun," Aaron mumbled into his fist.

Kate peeled the smock away from her shoulder, about ready to faint at the sight of the discoloration spreading halfway over her right breast. "How the fuck am I still even alive... was all this uhh, missing? I should be dead. Wait. Am I dead? Is this some fucked up dream?"

"That makes two of us." Aaron winked. "No, I'm afraid you're alive."

"Althea?" Kate's throat constricted.

"Aye."

Kate looked up at him. "How? Where?"

Aaron exhaled. "She just... uhh... fell out of the sky."

Squeaking boots echoed in the hallway a few seconds before David jogged to a halt at the entrance to her 'room.' "My heart about stopped when she jumped out of the car."

Kate knew he meant Althea, but his comment still hit her deep. She leapt up and ran out of the cell, diving on him, crushed the air from his lungs with a fierce hug, and sobbed into his shoulder. The last thoughts she expected to have as a living person had been about him. He held on, sniffling as well. A few minutes later, after she got her emotion in check, she offered an apologetic smile at Commander Ashford.

"Sorry. I suppose I shouldn't have run out of my cell."

She hung her head and trudged back inside.

"How long, sir?" asked David.

Ashford stuck the datapad into his coat. "If she's up for it, perhaps twenty minutes."

Kate smoothed her hands on the front of the smock and took a deep breath. "I can handle it, sir."

A WORLD RESHAPED

Mamoru

Flying out of West City offered Mamoru a taste of freedom. His consciousness permeated the inner workings of a sporty hovercar liberated from the roof parking of H. H. and M. Legal Services. Its owner was likely frothing at the mouth at the same moment Mamoru cruised at a hair under the speed of sound. The little black midlife-crisis-mobile had two seats, brown synthetic leather, and a profile like one might expect from a scale model of a military fighter aircraft.

For the first time in many days, he thought nothing of obligation, and only of the future.

He overflew Querq, as it had snuck up on him, and pulled into a hard, decelerating turn. His return course threaded the needle through a decaying skyscraper in the old city, sucking old desks and a few dog-sized rodents along in his wake.

A great dust cloud whirled into the air as he streaked down the largest street. Goats and children went tumbling away, screaming. The nimble car swerved to a neat stop in the center of town, settling onto wheels that folded out as Mamoru thought of putting his feet down. His senses seeped back into his body; no longer did he feel the wind upon the metal shell around him, or 'see' with the car's sensors and cameras. The ride had not even been long enough to make his legs stiff.

People in denim, bearing rifles, advanced on him. He opened the door and stood, disregarding their subtle threat. One woman recognized him from his last visit and aimed at his head.

"You got some cojones coming back here, pendejo."

A man next to her looked back and forth between them. "You know this man?"

Two Division 0 cops emerged from a pod building on the far end of the square.

"He's the one who tried to kill Althea and used Shepherd to bash a hole in a wall," said the same woman.

"Where is my sister?" asked Mamoru. "It is not my intention to harm anyone, but I will destroy any who stand in my way."

"You gotta answer for what you did," said an older man, wagging his rifle at the ground. "Get down, now. Won't warn ya again."

He found it pleasant they pointed modern weapons at him, modern weapons with electronic trigger mechanisms he could influence. Their rifles went dark, as did all the equipment on the belts of the Division 0 officers.

"Before you can take the knife from your belt, I will take your head. I ask a simple question and your hospitality is lacking."

Dead triggers clicked.

"I will not ask again."

The youngest of the Watch, a round-faced woman in her twenties, shrugged. "The woman what looked like you's left. She been gone a couple days."

"She left?" Mamoru raised an eyebrow at her. "How?"

"Uhh." The guardswoman glanced at the older man as if asking for help. "She ain't like no prisoner or nothin'. Even though you went nuts and all, you brought her in for medical help. She didn't do nothin' wrong. She uhh, just left."

"S'right," said the older man. "Here one day, gone the next. No one saw her go."

Akuryō, where is my sister?

Mamoru stared at the Watch, waiting for an answer. No voice inside him responded. His eyes narrowed with the kind of anger only betrayal can cause. One thing had scared the spirit. Perhaps that thing could find Sadako.

"I must see the child with the glowing eyes."

"What, so you can try again?" The old man lowered his useless rifle. "How stupid do you think we are?"

"I give you my word, I will not harm her." Mamoru clenched his jaw for a moment. "She can help me."

The girl is not here either. A man's voice spoke in his mind.

Mamoru locked eyes with the only possible source, the male Division 0 officer.

I have no idea if you're schizophrenic or somehow got legitimately possessed. These people will die before they let you near her after what you did. Besides, she isn't here.

"Where is she?"

"West City," said the old man. "Probably at headquarters."

The Watch gasped and grumbled. A few yelled at him.

"This man is telling the truth," said the officer. "He doesn't want to hurt her. Even if he did, he could not harm her where she is now."

"Damn right," said a deep voice to the left. "She wouldn't let him."

A huge man came stomping out of a side street, headed right at him. Mamoru smiled, remembering their last meeting in fleeting glimpses.

Shepherd halted a few feet away, glaring. "Nothin' for you here, pal."

Mamoru drew a deep breath, held it, and let it seep out from his nose. Sadako was gone. The strange child was gone. This place had nothing for him. Wind in the hollows between buildings mocked him with a mournful howl.

He faced the large man, eye to gut, and looked up. "It seems you are correct. I do not expect you to understand, but I was not myself when we faced each other. You fought with honor, and have my respect."

Mamoru bowed, keeping eye contact.

Shepherd loomed over him with barely-restrained hostility.

No one moved or said a word as he slipped back into the car. Fortunately, no one noticed the rifles coming back online as he pushed his consciousness into the vehicle and lifted off.

🐗 🌾 🐚 🜄 🜂

MILES OF FEATURELESS DESERT OFFERED NO ANSWERS OR CONSOLATION. Mamoru's thoughts drifted in a haze of doubt and guilt. He had let the *Akuryō* overwhelm him. What was it about the child that had filled the dark spirit with such rage? Had he controlled himself, he would have been at her side when Sadako opened her eyes.

Searing pain raked across his chest, accompanied by the sound of grinding metal and a soft explosion. Lost in his thoughts, Mamoru had not noticed the old tower before flying into it. Some manner of antenna or lightning rod gashed open the undercarriage and smashed the right rear ion thruster. The back corner of the car dipped with the loss of lift.

Mamoru's scream distorted out of the car's sound system. The front wheels opened as his imaginary arms cradled the cut down his belly. He nosed down from drag, and the vehicle smacked into the ground, skidding into a spin. Mamoru detached himself from the machine to spare his hands and feet the sensation of scratching over a concrete tarmac covered in sand and rocks.

His consciousness focused in time with a loud *whump* as the car came to rest broadside against the wall of an old aircraft hangar. He sat motionless, rubbing a hand over his right pectoral. No wound existed in his flesh, but the pain from a metal whip-strike lingered for a few minutes.

Dust and smoke drifted away from the hood, revealing a wide, flat area covered with squares of concrete and collapsing buildings. The broken shell of an ancient airplane slumped into the earth a hundred or so meters away. Shapes and indentations in the windblown sand hinted at carts and the dead-manatee silhouettes of bombs.

Beeping from the dash announced an unfurling holo-pane. "Unable to obtain signal. Please note that crashing outside of your coverage area may invalidate your warranty. If you have crashed in error, please contact local emergency responders via personal communications devices."

Mamoru squinted. *Idiots.*

Another panel popped up, displaying text.

"West City Underwriters Insurance Company thanks you for your business. Your vehicle's monitoring system has informed us of damage consistent with an ion vehicle accident. In accordance with your hovercar operator's insurance agreement, this has resulted in an automatic risk increase of your monthly premium to C4669 from C2240. If you would like to submit a claim for damage to your vehicle, the estimated final premium would be C7400 monthly. Accepting responsibility for repairs outside of your policy will not impact your premium. Thank you for choosing West City Underwriters Insurance Company."

Mamoru emitted a low growl from deep within. After a scowl of contempt at the console, he forced the door open and climbed out into a warm breeze. The second inexplicable crash in the Badlands was less eventful than the first, and this time he suspected he knew why.

"Show yourself," said Mamoru, pacing around the car.

A twenty-foot tall slab of metal rattled in the wind a few meters behind the wrecked car. From a gap in the hangar's doors, a presence beckoned to him. He grasped the metal and peered around the edge into a cavernous space, four stories tall and two hundred meters long, empty save for the sound of dripping water and a few aircraft parts. Grime-coated windows muted the sunlight to an off shade of pale yellow, puddles collected here and there. A six-foot tire lay flat to his left.

Mamoru's hand slipped from the door as he ventured farther inside. The scent of rust and mildew hung in air cooler than outside, but thick and humid. He pulled his coat away from the handle of the katana. His footsteps echoed over themselves, the sound bouncing back and forth in the cavernous space.

"Mamoru," said the voice of the old man.

He had expected the *Akuryō* to appear behind him, but still tensed when it happened. "You have released my thoughts."

Hard boots tapped the floor, circling to his left. "Our agreement has been fulfilled."

"Where is my sister? Our agreement was that she would live."

The old man appeared in the periphery of his vision. His raised hands poised at his side could have been either a gesture of surrender or a second's distance from drawing a gun. "She did live, Mamoru. Our agreement said nothing about what she may do to herself."

"Where is she?"

The Sentience reached up, adjusting his hat. Metal discs adorning the crown rattled. "You are convinced her disappearance is of my bidding?"

Mamoru's feet slid a few inches further apart, he gazed down. "You will know where she is. You see these truths."

Chuckling, the sound of dried weeds crackling in a flame, swirled in the air on all sides. "You are so quick to seek a new master, Mamoru?"

"I do not wish to serve you, *Akuryō*. I simply acknowledge your power."

The old one's eyes flared red. "She is in the city."

Mamoru closed his eyes. "What have I done?"

Footsteps passed in front of him. "Is the question rhetorical, or do you expect an answer?"

Blankness filled his thoughts. Mamoru looked up at a cracked rust hole in the roof, peering at the deep blue sky above. The memory of dragging Sadako across the wasteland came with soreness in his fingers from where the cable had dug in. He remembered the face of a little girl with glowing blue eyes. She had looked at him with worry, which changed to fear and then pity. Her angry glare dissipated, leaving him standing in a field with a knight and a slender, effeminate man in a robe. A flash of a white-haired woman with green eyes passed before him. His next torment took the form of sinking despair as the people of Querq told him his sister had gone.

"I do not remember."

The old gunslinger walked a few steps further away and paused in a shaft of sunlight. "We have reshaped the world, the way it has always been. For all of mankind's technology, one thing remains true. They love nothing more than to kill each other."

Mamoru stared at a puddle lapping at his boot.

"There is no purity in it. I am an agent of purity, Mamoru." The hazy image of a pudgy man in a suit appeared to the side, seated behind a lavish desk, surrounded by holo-panels and expensive food. "A worthless man has power over those he should not."

The executive bellowed. Behind him, an image of a muscular man faded in, a laborer of some kind climbing out of a dented exoskeleton. Another man in a blue dress shirt handed him a credstick and offered an apologetic shrug. Cyborg replacements walked past, AI-models, workers who did not need pay.

"Power comes from strength, Mamoru."

Both men faded. In their place appeared a mountain of smoldering rubble. The laborer emerged, clad in dusty brown leathers, climbing to the peak of a twisted metal spire. He raised a sword overhead and howled.

"Power earned is power deserved."

Mamoru gazed at the barbarian until he dissipated back to the mists from whence he'd come. "What of the girl?"

The Sentience knew of whom he spoke. Her image appeared between them; long, black hair, dark skin, perhaps nine years old, war paint and dust her only raiment. Pouches dangled from a leather cord strung with beads around her neck, and her anklet of copper wire glinted.

"She is strong," said the old man.

Mamoru raised an eyebrow. "The child carried a pistol. Is that not power undeserved?"

The little girl looked down at her hand, where an old-world gun had appeared. She ran her fingers over it as if it were an object of reverence.

"Is it not?" Mamoru held one hand up, waving his index finger in the gesture of pulling a trigger. "A child with a gun could kill your warrior as easily as snap her fingers."

"Mamoru, that girl would take a man's life as easily as you. The executive? With the same weapon, he would lack the conviction. He orders others to do what he cannot stomach to do himself. The child has no such qualms." The ancient gunslinger paced in a circle around the girl, who stared at Mamoru as if she could put a bullet in his heart without batting an eyelash. "Strength is not always physical. When she must use her weapon, she will not hesitate." The old man whirled, flaring his coat. "The executive ignores the primal laws of nature. He lets his body waste while he drinks in false power. A king incapable of besting his serfs is no king. If his underlings decide to disobey, he cannot stop them. No, Mamoru. It is not the same."

"You adore their suffering, their starvation. You make them kill each other or lead monsters into their midst. Will she even grow up?"

An old hand with paper-thin skin settled atop the child's head, patting her like a beloved granddaughter. The girl smiled up at the Sentience, and a second later, burst into a wisp of smoke.

"Yes, Mamoru. You felt her words with me. The girl will grow strong, and guide her people into the new world we have made for them. She will be a great ruler in ten years' time."

"What have I given you for my sister's life?"

A long sigh blew the rot of carrion into the air. "This place is mine. Power earned in the fires of war. I am the anger of the innocent, Mamoru. You have brought down the vengeance of an angel to return the land to me."

Mamoru's eyebrows drew close. "The ship."

"Yes. It will tear down the heavens and rain fiery wrath upon the metal scab which defaces my land."

At the far end of the hangar, an image of West City appeared, as if viewed from a distant mountain peak. A searing comet struck at its center, triggering a rippling wave out to each side. Darkness spread from the impact point as the city collapsed in on itself, exposing the land beneath.

"Millions of people will become part of me, Mamoru. Stress and heat will crush the elevated city. The destruction will spread. What does not burn or collapse will be consumed by my influence. Society will become as humanity was always meant to be."

"The strong rule the weak," whispered Mamoru.

"You learn fast."

"Chaos and death. That is not what humanity desires. What of poetry and art? What of beauty?" He thought back to his Edo Castle of matchsticks... and Nami.

The old man laughed. "My beauty lies in the simplicity of the struggle to survive, where the human will to endure is all that matters."

"Sadako..." Mamoru sank to his knees.

"My lands will grow. My presence will grow. You were pivotal, Mamoru. In the midst of what is to come, I will become even greater. Sadako will not perish. I shall spare your sister, beyond our agreement." The old man smiled. "You will be reunited in my world."

Mamoru breathed in and out... in and out.... A tear ran from each eye. "You shall guide her to me so that I can be reminded every moment what horror I have visited upon this Earth."

A hissing rush consumed the sound of footsteps. Mamoru looked up. The rickety old cowboy burst into a spinning whorl of black vapor that sank to the concrete, spreading out into a layer of inky fog that seeped into cracks. In seconds, no trace remained, leaving Mamoru alone with his thoughts.

ARCHON ONE, ARSENAL ZERO

Anna

Security officers in enamel white armor bearing the logo of Edmonson Memorial Starport herded travelers out of the terminal. The mood of the crowd turned angry as people shouted about missed flights and non-refundable fares. Anna pulled open the side door of a stolen van, holding the hands of psionic children as they jumped down to the street. Alastair hovered at her side, still frightened, but calmer than he'd been back at the corporate campus.

"Everyone stay together," said Anna. "This is the moment we've all been… well, this is the big day."

Lucy emerged from the van, with Meredith clinging to her. Both of them paused next to her with terror on their faces. Their dingy school uniforms looked every inch of being worn for months straight.

Please, Miss Anna. We don't want to go into space. Meredith's lip quivered and she burst into tears. *I want to go home.*

I miss my Mum and Dad. The telepathic whine of the younger girl spiked guilt into her heart.

I don't believe them. Lucy chimed in next, a little hope shining under the dread in her eyes. *You didn't kill that other girl. You'll help us, won't you? Please let us go. You said we could leave if we wanted.*

A man a short distance away handed a toddler to his wife before getting in the face of a female security officer a head shorter than him.

"You can't just kick us—"

The woman walloped him across the face with a short-barreled assault weapon, knocking him to the ground and aiming at his back. Screams rang out from the kids around Anna; the sudden high-pitched cries of horror seemed to startle the woman away from firing. The man whimpered and crawled away, holding his bleeding face as the security officer went statue still, staring into space with a shocked expression. She continued to aim at the ground where the man had been.

Dissent in the crowd quieted. People went from resisting the militarized evacuation to fleeing from the armed security forces.

Lucy and Meredith wrapped their arms around Anna, shivering. Rooted in place by a child on either side, Anna continued ushering the others out of the van to the last. The British girls whimpered and whined as she waved her arms in an effort to corral the group into a coherent mass.

"What's going on?" asked a pale boy with a Romanian accent.

"We're borrowing the starport," said Anna. "Come on, everyone inside. Stay together. We're not going to hurt anyone. They're going to try and stop us from getting away."

A week ago, she would have added 'because they want to kill us,' but she didn't believe it so much anymore—at least not here, or even in England.

The girls pulled at her, attempting to resist her dragging them past the doors. Anna clasped their hands the whole way down the main concourse. Alastair followed close behind. More security officers chased people out of shops and cafes along the side of the entry hall. Her charges clustered in a tight group, terrified at the chaos going on around them. The scene struck her as something she'd expected in the ACC, not here. Granted, the people with weapons weren't pointing them *at* the psionic children.

Please, Anna. I miss my mum and dad. Meredith set her heels, sliding. *You said you weren't going to force us to go.*

She looked down at the pitiful faces staring up at her, grateful that telepathy didn't care about enormous lumps in her throat. *I don't want to go either.*

The girls blinked at her in surprise, evidently having expected the usual 'but we have to' response.

Buck up, mite. I'm serious. I don't want to go. She squeezed their hands. *I'll get you home.*

Adoring smiles from both girls made her angry—at Archon.

A circular arrangement of holo-panels, each the size of a living room wall, hung in midair over the main information desk at the center of the terminal hub. Anna glanced up at a domed ceiling made of triangular clear panels, six or seven stories tall. Three levels ringed it, packed with more shops, restaurants, and places to entertain oneself while waiting for a departure.

Talis, at the side of the larger portion of their group, engaged in a conversation with an older woman who wore a cloth version of the security force uniform. Straight hair like burnished pewter ran to the middle of her back, and her expression looked stern, yet distant. Whenever Talis's lips moved, the woman spoke into a comm, directing the security team, a puppeteer working her dummy.

Some of the kids who rode with Anna ran off to their parents or older siblings, who'd arrived in other vehicles. A few grumbled about Archon's promise to bring non-psionic family along with them and wondered if anyone had gone to fetch them. The rest, younger teens who didn't yet trust anyone, trudged over in a cluster. Meredith and Lucy continued pressing themselves against her.

"Alright, alright, alright," Anna shouted, sounding frustrated and angry. "The lavatory's this way. We don't have all day. Damn tiny bladders. Alastair, please wait here with the group while I run them to the loo."

"Aye, mum." He fidgeted. "Be careful."

Anna stormed off, dragging the girls behind her by a hand around each wrist. Every time that boy called her mum, she felt like Archon punched her in the stomach. The boy couldn't be blamed for it; for him, she had only pity. She didn't glance back or wait to see what, if any, reaction Talis showed. A telempath could read emotion but did not necessarily know where that emotion came from. Hopefully, her anger at what Archon had done to these girls would be mistaken for irritation at a pair of whiny brats demanding to go have a wee.

She followed blue holographic signs pointing the way to bathrooms until she could slip out of the dome hub to a smaller hallway. Empty ticket counters lined one side, interspersed with rental car booths. More shops lined the left wall, selling luggage, clothing, toys, and electronics—all of it quite a bit more expensive than it should be.

Only security officers remained, walking like a zombie patrol. They gave her suspicious glances but seemed to recognize her and did not stop to talk or question.

I don't have to go. Lucy stumbled in her effort to keep pace.

Anna stopped, looking around. She peered down at the girls. *Stay quiet and stay close.*

They nodded in unison.

Anna reached out with her mind, linking to the sentience of three men and two women in security armor. Without the effects of Zoom clouding her mind, she found it a simple task to force their minds to disregard the trio. The children huddled so close to her, the three of them became one entity she could lift out of the troops' consciousness. As good as invisible to the security team, Anna crept forward. It felt strange to use that ability for a noble purpose rather than breaking into a corporation to pinch trade secrets or befuddle a jewelry store clerk to nick a necklace she could sell for food. *Is this how Aaron feels being with Division Zero?* She pulled the girls close, guarding as much as hugging them.

Eight agonizing minutes later, she reached the end of a corridor where a short stairway led to a door that opened to a starport employee parking lot. No longer needing to concentrate on her power, she took the girls' hands and hurried outside.

"You made them ignore us," whispered Lucy. "Can you teach me that?"

"Maybe once we're all back home... I think I'll be joining you back in London." *If I survive this.* Anna pulled out her NetMini and ordered a PubTran car. "Look, I don't have a lot of time."

"Why are you scared?" Meredith blinked. "You said we weren't kidnapped."

Anna looked downcast. "I think I might've been wrong."

Small hands gripped her arm.

"I think I was abducted too." Anna stared at the floor. "I... I just don't know."

"What'll we do?" asked Meredith.

"There's not much time. I have to go back. I dunno, maybe I can stop this before anyone gets hurt. Two choices. I can put you on a shuttle to London. There's a man there I think I can trust. Hughes."

Lucy shivered. "Agent Hughes is the one what sent us here."

"Aye," said Meredith. "He'll arrest us again."

Anna hugged them. "No, he won't. He thought he was helping you, but he didn't understand. Things have changed. He'll take you to your parents. The other option is you can go to the police here."

"I want to go home," whispered Lucy.

"I'm scared to fly alone." Meredith stared at her shoes. "I want me mum."

A tiny grey and cyan car squealed to a halt. The side door hatch opened with a pneumatic hiss.

"Thank you for using PubTran Corporation for your transportation needs," said a young, male voice, brimming with forced cheer.

Anna looked from the girls to the car. *What am I thinking? Buying tickets for a flight to London and sending a pair of terrified kids with no identification on their own to a shuttleport?* She cringed. *Damn Old Bill for making me distrust the police.*

"Come on." Anna pulled them to the car and pushed them inside. "You've been through a lot, be brave a little while longer."

"Please state your destination," chirped a cheery electronic voice.

"Take these children to the nearest Division 0 office. They're victims of a kidnapping."

"Summoning authorities," said the car.

"No, it's too dangerous here. You have to get them away from here. Take them to the police."

The car ignored her.

"Dammit, how much will it cost to drive them to the police?"

"Emergency transportation service is available for three hundred credits," said the car.

"Bloody mercenary trash." Anna reached in, swiped her NetMini, and leapt back before the door shut on her.

Lucy and Meredith pressed themselves into the window as the car pulled away, both crying but with grateful smiles.

Anna held up a hand to wave. *Tell them the truth about everything.*

The girls nodded. They kept staring at her until the little car disappeared down a ramp to the street level.

ANNA'S MIND FIXATED ON THE EXPRESSIONS ON THE GIRLS' FACES, A MIXTURE OF forlorn and hopeful, as the little PubTran car drove off. She trudged back into the starport, unable to get the image out of her head. She halted at the edge of the crowd, feeling a small bit of relief from the general sense of elation. The rest of the people there, from a starved-thin six-year-old boy taken from the German underground to a middle-aged Iranian man, seemed thrilled to be finally about to live Archon's dream. As far as she knew, only Meredith and Lucy had families that wanted them in a country where they didn't face death or incarceration for being 'gifted.' The refugees from ACC-controlled regions weren't so lucky. They *wanted* to go off into space.

Anna squinted with sudden doubt of the sincerity of their joy. They seemed *too* happy at the prospect of leaving Earth in a stolen starship, with not a single experienced crewperson running it. It seemed no better than trusting a blind person to drive a bus, and yet they all brimmed with excitement.

A pair of boys, somewhere near eighteen, laughed over the din.

"I shouldn't be fuckin' alive, dude." The one with green hair held up the front of his jacket, showing off three distinct bullet holes. "Fuckin' soldier shot me from behind. Next thing I know I'm awake and alive and I just hauled ass."

"Deep," said the black-haired one, inhaling something from a little device.

"Ol' Arc is twisted pissed. D'you see what he did to that traitor fire bitch?"

"Naah, I was with Amy when it got cray."

"Yo, Amy don't even like you."

Black hair chuckled. "She does when I want her to."

"Not cool, Raith. Not cool at all."

Anna made a fist.

"Hey." Raith raised his hands. "Just fuckin' around. Amy doesn't want her girlfriend to know about me. Alonna's hard-core. She'd melt my brain if she knew a man was 'tainting' her lover."

They laughed.

"So, yeah, this fire bitch shows up all cop like. Super-unbelievably-hot one with the perfect ass?"

"Yeah?" asked Raith.

"You know, the Awakened one ol' Arc was bitchin' about."

"Yeah."

Green-Hair held his hands up, fingers apart, eyes wide with awe. "So ol' Arc gives her the voodoo and all of a sudden she's like his attack dog. She came down there to kill him and she's throwing fuckin' fireballs left and right nuking the soldiers, and callin' him Daddy. She burned a hole right through that British shithead."

"Yah," said Raith. "I heard he was a cop. Liss was right."

Anna gasped, turning away so no one saw the tears forming in her eyes. *Aaron, no...*

"Dude," said Raith, sucking on his inhaler again. "Dude."

"Yo, you seen Melissa?" Green hair spun around, gazing over the cluster of people.

"Why? Bitch is jailbait. Fifteen."

"You're a giant penis with legs. I'm not lookin' to get with her; I haven't seen her since the attack."

"Think she went traitor too?" asked Raith. "Liss didn't run with the rest of us. That Aaron motherfucker was a cop. Redhead psycho bitch tryin' to kill us, and Mammowhatever disappeared."

"I doubt it. She'd be the last one to go traitor. She was on to Mr. Telekinesis the whole time. She called it he was a cop. Shot him a couple times. Gotta be either dead or on her way to jail."

"Yeah." Raith exhaled a cloud of vapor that made his friend lean back. "Liss been wants for the kill on him for awhile. Bitch was angry as shit."

Green-hair waved him off. "Don't use *was,* man, you dunno if she gone."

Anna couldn't get the image of Aaron lying dead on the roof of her former, temporary home out of her mind. The burns she imagined varied from cartoony char to a smoldering hole that hollowed out his entire torso. She gave the crowd a quick once over, hoping to spot Lauren, but could find no sign of her. She fumbled her NetMini out in unsteady hands and tried to call Aaron.

It went to Vidmail after six rings.

She squeaked at hearing his voice, muting it before anyone nearby could recognize him. Her heart pounded in her chest. Terrence pushed his way out of the group and walked up to her.

"Hey, Anna. You seen Archon?" He pointed his thumb over his shoulder.

"We got everyone accounted for here except for thirteen." Terrence sighed. "We lost nine in the assault, part of our security group. Melissa's MIA. Izzy went astral to scope the place out, but didn't find her body. We're also missing Lucy, Meredith, and Kim."

Anna leaned to the side, peering at a willowy blonde seated in the middle of their group. The girl looked in her teens, but clutched a white rag doll the size of a ten-year-old to her chest, rocking back and forth and muttering with the cadence of a nursery rhyme. Pink lights on her cat-headed sneakers blinked in time with her motion. The doll's head, a round pad the size of a dinner plate with yarn for hair, flopped back and forth.

Izzy?

The girl looked up and gazed in a circle before realizing Anna as the source of the voice in her mind. *You didn't kill Althea. I know.*

Thank you, Izzy. You looked at the roof?

Isabelle burst into tears. No one reacted to her spontaneous outburst, as though she had them often. *Yes. Many ghosts, and an angel.*

Anna squeezed her fists, forcing herself to send her next thought. *Was Aaron there?*

Yes, Ma'am. Izzy clutched her doll, hiding her face against it. *The angel was with him.*

Anna covered her mouth with her hands. All care for what happened around her faded. Talis glanced her way, no doubt sensing a strong surge of sorrow. The tall woman's already radiant aura of authority seemed to grow stronger. Her eyes narrowed, and she started to walk over.

He wasn't dead. Izzy looked up from her doll, having gone from weeping to giggling so fast her cheeks remained wet. *The angel helped him.*

"Anna?" asked Terry. "What're we supposed to be doing? We haven't heard a thing from Archon since we got here."

"What's wrong, Anna?" Talis made no attempt to layer false concern over her eagerness.

That bitch is everything Archon wanted...

She backed away from Talis's approach, faked a glance at her blank NetMini, and patted Terry on the arm. "Something's come up with James. I need to go."

Anna broke away and sprinted down the main concourse, headed for the doors.

HONOR

Mamoru

O nly the creak of ancient metal disturbed the silence in the hangar, whenever the wind battered the walls. Mamoru removed his coat, folded it, and set it on a dry patch of floor. He detached the sheath from his belt and laid the katana on the ground sideways in front of his boots. Head forward, he drew a deep breath and clapped.

Spirits of Honor, know my shame. I bare myself to you.

He knelt, sat back on his heels, and set his NetMini on the floor between him and the sword. Palms on his knees, he stared at the gleaming onyx slab in silence. He clapped again and bowed.

Hachiman, spirit of war, patron of Samurai, hear me.

Mamoru touched a fingertip to the NetMini. A tiny wisp of white energy caressed the back of his hand as he called upon his power. The device responded to his desire, projecting holograms. The faces of Sadako, his mother, his father, and Nami flickered to life in a line, each about the size of an orange. After a moment of staring at the people he had betrayed, he touched the device again, adding Caiden's image to the display. Next to the others, the child's paper white skin seemed glaringly out of place.

On Mars, he had not seemed so unusual. He thought back to Caiden's request to accompany him to Earth, and his protest. In Japan, he would have been mistaken for a *taikomochi* in white face paint—or an *oni*. The boy's constant smile had unsettled him. In the few weeks they'd spent on Mars waiting for Raziel's agent to recover Caiden's mother from a prison camp, he never managed to get a picture of him without that look in his eye—awe, and the want of a father figure Mamoru couldn't provide. He had gone to Mars to reclaim his honor, and failed.

The boy is safer for being away from me. He who strikes deals with Akuryō. He who values one life over millions.

Mamoru meditated on the time he had spent with Sadako. The hope she had for a life free from being owned, free from having to kill. The life he had denied her. He closed his eyes, remembering her desperate attempts to talk him out of stealing the CSS Angel.

"There is no way she could have known the end of things." Mamoru exhaled. "I cannot say she was wrong."

He gazed upon the faces of his mother and father. Mother's distance had come from the fear she would have to give him away. For so long he had taken it as indifference, even contempt. He wondered if he had been their true son. The woman could not bear to show her love, lest her heart be shattered.

Mamoru bowed at her image.

His father's hologram frowned. No, not a frown—his face always held that set. A disapproving glare he gave everyone who failed to live up to his expectations. Since no one ever lived up to his expectations, it had become his face. Had Mamoru listened to him and trained his body instead of seeking the escape of video games and electronics, he might have protected his innocent sister. He stared at his hands, calling the energy to the surface of his skin.

"Such power I hold now. Surely even as a boy I could have protected her, had I bothered to try."

He bowed at his father.

Minutes passed before he found the strength to force himself to gaze upon the face of his former slave, Nami. Perhaps it would be better for him never to know if she cared for him, or if she only pretended in hopes of better treatment. The woman had been born to a noble family, cast down to the lowest echelon of society for the deeds of her father.

"The disgrace of a family is shared by all."

He bowed at Nami.

"I shall not allow Sadako to suffer for my transgression."

Mamoru leaned forward, clasping the katana by handle and scabbard. He pulled three inches of blade loose and pressed his thumb to the edge. On the floor to his right, he smeared blood into neat vertical rows of kanji:

I am Saitō Mamoru.

I was a Samurai in the house of Minamoto.

I was Ronin.

I am nothing.

I allowed the Oni to exploit my weakness.

I brought fire and death from the heavens.

I atone in eternity for my crimes in this world.

Warm blood ran down his forearm as he reached up and pulled his shirt apart. He drew his arms inward from the sleeves and extended his hands out the gap in front, forcing his shirt down around his waist in time with a low, ritualistic grunt. Mamoru stared at the flickering faces as he wound his hair up into a knot to expose the back of his neck. He did not have *a second* to render the merciful strike, nor did he deserve one.

He rested his palms on his knees and glanced once more at each person. The shame he felt under the weight of their holographic stares made him resolute.

Mamoru grasped his katana with a bloodied hand, drawing the blade clear of the scabbard. He held it horizontally, raised it with reverence, and brought it down so the edge touched his belly. Lacking a wakizashi, or even a knife, it would have to do.

Silence lingered, as heavy as his guilt. He closed his eyes and tensed his muscles. He would pull the sword tight to his flesh and draw it out to the right. An agonizing death would purify his honor.

His last thoughts would be of his sister, and of the woman who might have loved him.

Mamoru's fingers clenched on the handle. He took his final breath, held it, and yanked, but the blade remained rigid, frozen in place. Again, he pulled, but it didn't move. It floated away, dragging him for several inches until he released the tension in his arms. A hairline trickle of blood remained on his stomach from where the edge had pressed.

"Mamoru, I require a moment of your time," said Archon, voice echoing across the massive hangar.

His eyes snapped open as he found himself fighting to retain ownership of his weapon against a telekinetic grip. He held on to the retreating katana, which dragged him to his feet before the energy released.

"Why are you here?" Mamoru lowered his arms, glancing to the side.

Archon stood a few steps inside the door. Anna looked up from behind him, smiling the smile of a woman who wanted to see someone suffer. Malice flashed across her emerald eyes.

"We need the ship," said Archon.

Mamoru looked at the blood-smeared kanji at his feet. "It is already coming."

REINSTATED

Aaron

Exhaustion blurred the world around Aaron as he made his way out of the Division 0 detention area and trudged toward the cafeteria. Immaculate white hallways blended one to the next. A mixture of looks ranging from unfamiliarity to welcome to open hostility adorned the faces of everyone he passed. He hurried through a cluster of briefing rooms and lockers, heading for the cafeteria.

When he arrived at the mess hall, he stopped at a huge food assembler and punched up the largest coffee the machine could generate. Once it beeped to indicate it had finished, he grabbed the cup, which turned out to be too hot to carry. The steaming beverage floated alongside him as he dragged himself to an open table and fell into the bench seat. Everyone in the room stared at him, not one daring to make a sound.

"Alright, let's see if this stuff they're so fond of over 'ere does anything." He took a cautious sip, coughed, forced a gulp, and cringed. "Ugh."

He sat for a while, staring at the featureless white table. Every so often, he'd choke down another swig before returning the weight of his cheek to his hand. Sleep teased at his mind. Fingers slid into his hair as his elbow slipped. Aaron caught himself before his palm flew from his temple and his face bounced off the table.

"Uhh, Lieutenant?" asked a high-pitched voice.

"Hmm?" He felt hung over, peering between his fingers at a boy too young to shave. The sight of such a small body in Division 0 blacks made him chuckle.

"Cadet Gutierrez, sir." The boy rendered a sharp salute and set a plain, black device on the table. "I have your new NetMini. Sorry, I couldn't save your old one."

"How bad was it?"

The boy stood stiff, hands at his sides. "Umm, it was a blob of melted plastic. The neural memory fluid boiled off. The substrate died. I couldn't recover anything. I'm a technokinetic, not a necromancer."

"Cripes." He sighed, glanced at the boy, and waved. "At ease or whatever I'm supposed to say. Bloody hell, this officer thing is going to be a ballache."

Cadet Gutierrez's eyes widened. He laughed for a second before looking afraid.

"Thanks, kid." Aaron smiled. "Stop trying to grow up too fast."

The boy grinned and took a step back. He moved to walk away, but whipped back around with a curious expression.

"Go ahead, ask." Aaron held up the empty cup. "But it'll cost you fetching me another cup."

"Umm. It's true you didn't mean to do it, right? People are talking." He scratched the side of his head. "The empaths say you're okay, but some of the others think you're nuts."

"Coffee first." Aaron smiled.

The boy hurried a salute, nodded, and darted off. Minutes later, he handed Aaron a replacement extra-large, black coffee and hopped up on the bench seat across from him, swinging his boots.

"A very bad person put something in my head." Aaron tapped his temple. "She made me do something horrible. I fought as hard as I could not to do it."

Cadet Gutierrez gave him a sympathetic look. "Suggestives scare me too."

"My brain broke a little. It's like the bean's got a mind of its own now, and it doesn't like to be poked."

The boy thought about it for a moment. "You shouldn't let anyone poke it."

"Aye." Aaron slurped coffee and winced. "That's the tricky part."

"Aaron?" asked a woman.

Kate walked up to the end of the table. She'd changed into a standard Division 0 uniform.

"Hi again," said Cadet Gutierrez.

"Guess they cleared you," said Aaron.

"Considering the cuffs are on my belt instead of my arms, yeah."

The boy gasped. "What did you do?"

"She went in alone," said Aaron.

"You can get in trouble for that?" asked Gutierrez.

"Yeah…" Kate flopped into the seat to the boy's right. "I didn't even intend to *go in*. I wanted to wait for backup, but he got into the car somehow. How's the coffee?"

Aaron grimaced, shaking his head. "I've not the foggiest idea how you people can drink this horribleness. Tastes dreadful, but it's working."

"Well," said Kate, "they have this magical potion called creamer, as well as this enchanted powder that makes things sweet."

"Right…" Aaron picked at his eye with his middle finger, though smiled.

"I should go." Cadet Gutierrez stood, saluted, and ran out.

"How's your head?" Aaron forced another swallow.

Kate leaned on her elbows. "Spinning. Archon knew I wanted a family more than anything. I hate being a lab freak." She stared down at her hands. "El Tío used me the same way."

"How's your boy doing?" Aaron peered over his cup at her as he sipped more of the detestable swill.

"He went to check on Althea. I wanted to ask you how you deal with it."

"With what?" Aaron glanced at the cup, steeled himself, and drained it.

"Being forced to kill people. How do you come to terms with that?"

Aaron sighed. "I only remember Allison. She was the only person I was *forced* to kill. The others happened in a blackout. I've no actual memory of it at all. It just explodes and leaves me smashed. I'm sure they'll be keeping me in a box when this is over with. It's too dangerous to let me out there. Someone tries to give me a command and…" He made an explosive sound while flicking the fingers of his right hand open.

Kate pushed his NetMini around the table in a circle, fidgeting. "Maybe Althea could fix it. I had a bit of a nasty side effect too."

Beep.

Aaron leaned over to peer at the NetMini.

A text message from Anna: ‹Are you alive?›

He pursed his lips. ‹I think so. I've no idea how these blokes can drink coffee.›

Two dozen emote faces, alternating grins and tears spammed his screen. A second later, another text appeared. ‹West City will be destroyed ‹ 12 hours. Help! Meet me here.›

A cartoon pushpin wobbled around beneath the message.

"Shit." Aaron jumped up. "I hope she's being dramatic."

"Who?"

"Anna." Aaron ran for the door.

Kate raced up alongside him. "Where are you going?"

"Wherever this pin goes."

"Is Archon going to be there?"

Aaron stopped and faced her. "Probably. You should rest; you just came back from the brink of death."

"So did you. No way am I going to miss a chance to get a piece of him." The air warmed with a sudden wind from nowhere. "What he did to me..."

"I don't want you to get hurt." He walked off.

Kate caught up in two strides and grabbed his shoulder. "Didn't you just tell that kid going in alone would get you in trouble? Fuck that, Pryce. I'm going to burn that bastard's balls off."

Aaron loped across the cafeteria, stopping into a lean against the wall by the hallway out, legs weak. "You *had* to say balls, didn't you?"

Kate quirked an eyebrow.

"Stunrod," whispered Aaron.

She cringed.

"Aye." Aaron huffed a breath, got his balance, and kept going. "What about David?"

Kate caught his arm to stop him. "This is over his head. I already almost lost him twice. I don't trust risking him a third time."

"What about me?" Aaron summoned a sheepish grin.

"Syndicate's still got a big bounty on you."

He turned pale.

Kate punched him in the arm. "Jackass. I'm not serious."

"You thought about it, though." He grinned.

"Yep." She folded her arms. "When you were a fugitive, not active duty... and I thought you were a bastard."

"Oh." He winked. "I *am* a bastard, but only to the right people."

AARON PUSHED THE PATROL CRAFT TO THE LIMIT OF ITS ENGINES. LOUD crashing rumbled outside as they slipped back and forth across the sound barrier. Kate relaxed in the passenger seat, in total calm, as if they had merely decided to swing by Cyberburger for a mid-patrol snack. Even the occasional sonic boom shaking her back and forth caused little reaction. Sweat ran down the side of Aaron's head, soaking into the neck of his uniform. The brick-like shape of the patrol craft didn't lend itself well to control at that speed, and he had fractions of seconds to respond to turbulence.

"Wouldn't it be easier to stay above Mach 1?" asked Kate.

"Bloody limiter keeps kicking on and slowing us down."

"Perhaps you should listen to it before we explode."

He whipped his head around to glare at her.

"No, I don't feel an explosion coming... just saying."

Aaron looked at the Navcon. The pin Anna sent went out into the Badlands, about forty miles past the western border of the area once called Arizona. Minutes crept by without conversation. He steered a bit to the right, further south, and slowed until the car no longer felt like a capsule trapped at the heart of a thunderstorm.

"What's the plan?" asked Kate.

"I've no idea what to expect in there. 'The city's going to be destroyed, help' doesn't have very many details."

"I mean if Archon's there."

"Oh." Aaron smirked. "Probably best if we disregard the pleasantries and skip right to killing him."

"Good. At least we're on the same page."

"Well, the bugger did point a gun at my face."

"Not to mention—"

"Good idea. Let's not mention that other bit." Aaron licked his teeth and smirked. "And technically, that wasn't him…"

"What?"

He smiled. "Teen angst. Lot of anger issues."

Kate picked at her fingernails. "Every time I close my eyes, I see a demonic birthday cake trying to eat me."

Aaron blinked. "I… No. You know what? I don't want to know."

Kate made a face as though her urge to laugh couldn't quite dent her anger.

Beeping signaled the approach of their programmed destination. He eased off the throttle, letting air drag bleed off airspeed. A long strip of road up ahead, surrounded by massive hangar buildings with curved roofs came into view.

"What the hell?" asked Kate.

Aaron circled, peering out the side window. "Looks like some kind of old military airbase. Looks as dead as everything else out here."

"There." Kate leaned forward, pointing. "Cars."

At the front of the largest hangar, a small, black sports car lay crumpled against the building. A dust-coated, gold luxury hovercar sat behind it, closer to the door. Aaron pulled in and set down a few meters off to the side, away from any angle people inside could see them. He ducked the slow gull wing door and pulled the E-90 from its holster, not waiting for Kate as he jogged to the edge of a small gap in the doors.

Archon and Anna stood a short distance inside, facing a shirtless Mamoru. Aaron aimed, but couldn't get a clear bead on the man without shooting through her. A brief flashback of staring over his gunsights at Allison caused him to picture Anna turning at him with that same pleading 'don't do it' expression. He stifled a gasp and lowered his arm.

Outside, the whine of another hovercar shot overhead.

A weak tingle touched the tip of Aaron's forebrain. His instinctive reaction to incoming telepathy snapped him out of his guilty fog. He swung his arm up, training his E-90 on Archon, but she remained in the way. "Anna, move!"

"Good grief, man. Have you not enough decency to stay dead?" Archon frowned.

Aaron grunted as invisible tightness grasped his weapon arm, pushing it to the side. He brought his telekinesis to bear in a mental tug of war that bounced the E-90 around, making it impossible to get a clean shot at anything. Forces mushed and twisted at his muscles, threatening to wrench all the bones in his arm to splinters at the slightest error anticipating which way the other man would push.

Anna backed around, hiding behind Archon, giving Aaron an icy stare.

What's gotten into 'er?

Archon focused, forcing Aaron's arm up. "Anna, be a dear and deal with that toy."

Sweat streamed down Aaron's face. He growled, glancing at his gun, trying to hold back Archon's effort to tear the weapon from his grasp.

Footsteps skiffed in the dirt behind him.

"Kate," rasped Aaron past gritted teeth. "I think that tweed cunt is looking a bit flammable, don't you?"

"How the devil did you get over there?" asked Archon.

The external pull on his E-90 released; Aaron's telekinetic retaliation pulled him into a backward stumble. A small woman caught him, grunting from the effort.

When Aaron looked up, Archon stood alone, shooting a perplexed look past him.

"Aaron!" Anna hugged him from behind. "You're here! You're alive."

AND DOMINOES FALL

Anna

H er arms around Aaron, Anna almost gave in to the urge to kiss him right in front of everyone. Archon twisted back and forth, glancing from her to a spot of floor right beside him.

"What are you doing here?" asked Anna.

"We came out here to collect Mamoru," said Archon, eyes locked on Aaron. "Have you forgotten already?"

She squeezed herself to Aaron's back, as if his body would shield her from Archon's angry confusion.

Where the bloody hell is Kate going?

'Round the side. Anna squeezed him, keeping her head down. *This is going to get messy, isn't it?*

Aaron nodded. "Probably."

Anna raised her voice, yelling over Aaron's shoulder. "Where's the ship? What did Lauren mean when she said the city was going to burn?"

"It will arrive in a few hours," said Mamoru. His morose stance straightened to one of confidence, and he laughed.

"James." Anna moved away from Aaron and crept forward. "What is wrong with you? You used to be so righteous. What justifies you taking over people's minds because they don't agree with you? Kate ran because you tried to program her. Having doubts doesn't mean she wanted to kill you."

"Oh, she rather wants to now," muttered Aaron.

Archon brought his hands together. "She is a powerful Awakened, Anna.

People like her are too dangerous to allow to fall into the hands of our enemies. They are either with us or against us, and I cannot allow them to be against us."

"What about Althea? Would you call her dangerous?"

He sneered. "She could not hurt a fly."

"Explains why he bricks it every time she turns up," muttered Aaron.

"You made me forget things. You'd have rewritten Aaron's brain if it wouldn't have killed you to do it. Meredith and Lucy were taken from loving homes, James. Loving homes! They weren't the subject of government persecution. For feck's sake, we kidnapped them. We kidnapped Althea." Anna fumed. Sparks crackled and danced overhead, racing down girders and beams among dead gaslights. "How many of those children are still who they were before they met you? Shit, you've probably made Lauren into a lapdog as well."

"No..." Archon let his arms fall. "That one lives in her own little realm... and I mean to have a chat with her about concepts like loyalty. You seem to be standing on the wrong side of a rather thin line, Anna. If Lauren had not assured me you would never betray me, I would have some serious doubts about your intentions right now."

"As always, you've added your own misinterpretation to my words, James." Aurora's disembodied voice floated from everywhere.

Archon rolled his eyes. "You and your cryptic nonsense." He clapped his hands together then gestured at Anna. "Well now, the gang is all here."

"James," said Aurora. "If you recall, I said there was *zero* chance she would betray you."

Archon glared at Aaron. "You..." He pointed, shaking his finger. "You devil of a sylph. Division *Zero*. You knew all along she would turn on us for that sodding wanker."

Aaron held up one finger. "She's promoted me to twat, mate."

Redness spread over Archon's face.

Anna grabbed her chest, over her heart. No wonder Lauren insisted she be the one to 'recruit' Aaron. She'd been pushing her toward him since minute one.

"No future is a guarantee, James," echoed a ghostly feminine voice. "I told you abducting Althea would kill you. I told you I saw a vision of great metal claws tearing you in half. You chose to disregard me."

"Yet here I stand," said Archon. "Just what are you up to, Lauren? After all my effort keeping the authorities away from you... Why?"

"Dominoes." Silence hung thick for a few seconds. "A fate envisioned is not a fate guaranteed. Taking her may have very well set in motion a chain of events that will mean your death. I know without a doubt, the girl will choose to let you die."

"Rubbish, Lauren. The girl does not have it in her to wish anyone dead." Archon's eyes widened. He pointed at random spots. "She could not bear it once. She saved my life."

"Mamoru has been influenced by something beyond your understanding. The starship is on a course that will drive it into the heart of West City. I have seen the flames devouring the streets."

"I have seen the ruler of the new world I have made," said Mamoru in a near-whisper. "She is but a child now, but shall grow into a queen who bears a spear tipped with diamond."

"Sounds like our samurai's gone off the deep end," muttered Aaron.

Anna grabbed Aaron's arm, shaking, tears streaming from her eyes. "Oh, shit, Aaron! All those people. We have to stop it!" She looked desperately at the room. "Lauren, can we stop it? What's going to happen?"

"Ungrateful women! All of you traitors!" Archon screamed. "I never should have put blind faith in such hormonal, emotional, weak creatures. Lying deceivers, all of you!" He rasped, spittle flying from his teeth. "Everything I have done for you. Lauren… the CSB would have hounded you until the day you died. Anna, you forget how I found you? You would rather be back in London whoring yourself, suckling from the government tit?"

"No!" Anna screamed, her face hot with blood. "It's not like that. I don't hate you, James. I hate what you *did*. There is nobility inside you, but you've gone cack-handed with it. You cannot force people to agree with you. *That* is why the world hates us, James. You are doing exactly what they fear. You are perpetuating all the scary stories and worst nightmares. Why is everything always an extreme with you? Anything less than total agreement does not mean hatred."

Archon leaned back, eyes closed. "They would hate us anyway, Anna. It is how people are. They hate us for being superior to them. They fear what we can do, and the ignorant, bigoted masses will not have it. We must leave Earth and start over."

She shuddered with nausea and anger. "No, James. I won't do it. I'm not leaving Earth. There are people here I care about. Yes, there are countries where they do kill psionics. Leaving won't save them. You cannot snap your fingers and wish every single psionic in the world onto the ship. Who'll fight for the ones left behind if we go away?"

"Fine. Stay here with your government simpleton." Archon waved his arm at Aaron and turned on Mamoru. "Stop the ship."

"It is not that simple," said Mamoru. "I ensured he burned the transmitter on the way out. Even if you could get this man to a place where he could enter the computer world, he would not be able to touch the Angel. It will fall, and bring with it the birth of my world. It shall wipe the glimmering scab from the face of the true earth."

A chill ran down Anna's back at the look in his eye. "I don't think that's Mamoru anymore."

"Mr. Samurai's gone loony," said Aaron.

Archon waved his hand. Mamoru flew into the air and smacked chest-first into the wall thirty meters away.

Mamoru slid to the floor and stepped back, apparently unhurt. He turned to face the room, a trickle of blood descending from one nostril over a dark smile. "Your rage is delicious."

A woman's angry scream echoed over the hangar. Kate leapt out from behind a huge aircraft tire, whipping a two-foot wide fireball at Archon's head. He zoomed sideways, yanked by a telekinetic pull. Mamoru raised his vibro-katana, squeezing the handle to activate the high-frequency inducer. Aaron waved his E-90 to the right, trying to keep pace with the blurred figures. Anna screamed, shoving him to the side.

"Don't kill him!" She pointed at Mamoru, panting. "We need him to stop the ship."

"Sorry." Aaron shivered. "I'm rather allergic to long pointy things that large."

Mamoru let off a roar and rushed Archon, sword high. At the same second, Kate threw a barrage of fist-sized fireballs. Anna opened her senses to the surroundings, but her psionic feelers found no significant electrical power sources from which to draw a boost. The hovercars outside sat too far away to reach. She raised her hand at him; warm tingles wrapped her back and slid along the underside of her arm.

She concentrated, sending a finger-thin strand of lightning out from her hand with a loud *snap.* It caught Mamoru in the chest, knocking his run into a tumble.

Archon slid back and forth on his feet, as though someone worked a magnet under the floor to pull him out of the way of the fireballs. He went from sliding to rolling and sprang twenty feet into the air. Kate kept chucking fireballs after him, but the slow-moving projectiles missed by inches. Mamoru growled and sat up, eyes locked on Anna.

Her heart skipped a beat. *That should've knocked him senseless for a few minutes.* "Aaron... Aaron..." She slapped his arm. "Something's very wrong with our friend over there."

"It's a fucking demon," shrieked Kate. She flung her arms out to the sides. A detonation of orange flames erupted around Archon, singeing his coat before he could shove himself clear.

The great tire flipped up on its side and toppled at Kate. Aaron pivoted and gestured as if catching a great weight. Kate yelped and dove back. The tire fell, pinning her to the ground, but its impact had slowed to the point it didn't crush her legs. She grunted and groaned as the tire bounced on her; Archon pushed it down while Aaron tried to lift it.

Anna grabbed an e-mag from the back of Aaron's belt and concealed the flat, rectangular battery in her palm. Archon sailed across the room, landing at the middle near the right-side wall. He swiped his arm sideways, and a cart full of tools went rocketing at Kate's head. Aaron shifted his attention. Kate howled as all the weight of the tire fell on her legs.

Mamoru stomped toward Anna. Somewhere off to the side, the tool cart smashed into something, bits of metal went clattering over the concrete.

"Something's wrong," yelled Anna. She projected another stunning shock into Mamoru's bare chest. He strode into the electrical discharge like so much harmless light, grinning. "I don't know what's happening. It's having no effect. He should be on his arse."

Anna's brain seized. The look in Mamoru's eyes as he stalked closer with a vibro-katana made her want to cry out for help, but her jaw wouldn't open. *Aames! Jaaron!* Another bolt of lightning had no effect. *Daddy!*

Boom.

Startled by a deafening explosion that made the walls of the hangar shake, Anna screamed. A blur of black caught her eye, drawing her attention up to where the burning aircraft tire wobbled near the roof, forty feet off the ground at the top of a huge billow of smoke.

Kate let off the angriest noise Anna'd ever heard come out of a woman. "Where are you, fucker? I'll blow this whole damn building apart."

Wham.

Anna clamped her hands over her ears as the massive, fiery tire slammed into the concrete floor, sending a shaft of thick, black smoke billowing upward from the hole at its center.

"Troublesome thing about smoke, my dear," said Archon... somewhere off to the right. "*You* need to see. I can sense your mind."

"That's two of us then," said Aaron.

Archon yelped a second before something thudded into metal.

"James, please listen to reason," screamed Anna. "There's no need for us to fight."

The stink of burning rubber watered Anna's eyes and made her cough. Mamoru came flying out of the fog in mid-leap, katana overhead. She drew another breath to scream, but gagged on smoke. He stopped in midair, blade less than ten inches from her face. The Japanese man's eyes glowed red like coals and his presence swam into her mind.

Reality, the hangar, faded away to the dark rain-soaked alleys of London, filled with the laughter of Mr. Blake, and all the harpies from Bristol City. Shadows of men that had followed her into dark places took over her thoughts, memories of a dozen murders she'd almost fallen victim to as a teenage runaway. If she'd been thirty seconds slower walking one time, not found a door someone accidentally left unlocked another, or not stumbled into an unexpected constable —dozens of nights she would've been dead if not for small bits of chance.

Self-pity and terror seized her soul in two clawed hands and tried to pull it apart. Anna wanted to shriek like a little girl meeting the Devil face to face, but only a pitiful squeak flavored in smoldering rubber rasped from her throat.

Mamoru lurched backward, flying out of sight.

Anna grabbed herself to make sure she hadn't soiled. "Aaron!"

"I'm here," he yelled and ran out of the mist at her side. "The man's possessed."

"I…" Anna trembled. "I got that feeling. I-it was radiating terror, pulling my nightmares out."

A body hit the ground on the other side of the smoke with the chirp of flesh on wet concrete. Mamoru's voice, deeper than it should have been, laughed. A glow glided across the murk, in time with the fluttering of an azure fireball. As no one screamed in pain, Anna assumed it missed.

"That one almost came within forty meters, my dear." Archon laughed.

Mamoru roared. Kate screamed. Anna jumped as the air shook with another detonation. Seconds later, a whiff of burned flesh added to the awfulness of melting rubber.

Anna looked up, thinking of the starship hurtling toward the Earth, and squeezed the e-mag in her hand. If she killed Mamoru, they couldn't stop the ship. *That's silly. The military can stop it.* "Aaron, call it in."

He grabbed her free hand. "What?"

"The starship. Call your superiors and warn them."

"What a romantic moment," said Archon.

Aaron gurgled as invisible force hurled him at her. Their faces smacked together hard enough to leave the world spinning and blood spilling from her nose. Anna collapsed to the floor, cradling her mouth.

"Ngh," moaned Aaron. "I'm going to twist your head off, you bloody fuck."

Anna rolled on her side, begging reality to stop spinning.

A SHOCKING STALEMATE

Aaron

With a hand pressed to the side of his head, Aaron closed his eyes and tuned out the throbbing in his cheek. The pain didn't bother him as much as being used as a club to strike Anna. That had enraged him. He reached out into the grey smoke with telepathy, searching for minds. The closest sentience had to be Anna. Off to the left, he sensed an inhuman tangle of thoughts he assumed to be Mamoru. Another two minds lay further distant, one near the center of the building and one to the right near the wall. A fifth glimmer of sentience winked in and out near the roof, small and blank of surface thoughts.

Must be a cat or something in the rafters.

Aaron remembered Archon running for the side and focused on that area. Telekinetic feelers wrapped around something near the mind he'd located. He gave it a hard, instant shove too fast for Archon to mount an effective resistance. A body clattered into metal.

Archon's arrogant muttered curses brought a smile to his lips.

A metal *clang* resounded out of the fog, followed by the ear-splitting squealing of a vibro-blade trapped in softer metal. Aaron spun to face the exit. His breath came in short, rapid pulses as he gathered a sense of the mass present within the enormous sliding doors.

He called upon the deepest reserves of his telekinetic power and roared, thrusting both arms to the side. The great, segmented doors slid off their rails, hurtling open many times faster than the mechanism could tolerate. Huge slabs, as well as shrapnel from smashed guide rails and roller wheels scattered, drawing forth a breeze that sucked most of the smoke out of the space.

"Aaron!" screamed Anna.

He spun in time to catch her as she leapt in front of him. An old air-to-air missile hovered over them, a lance poised to spear him through the chest.

"Anna, please move," said Archon.

Covered in blue flames, Mamoru chased Kate around stacks of smaller tires. As fast as his flesh melted off from a continuous pelting of fireballs, it regrew. She screamed and ran in circles, occasionally diving into somersaults to evade the sword.

Aaron wrapped his telekinetic force around the missile, struggling to push it aside.

"Now, Anna. Move!" Archon raised the shaking missile up and back, as if preparing to stab it into the pair of them.

Changing course without warning, Mamoru leapt at Archon. The instant his opposition ceased, Aaron's mental shove hurled the missile across the hangar. It smashed into the floor, fins breaking on impact, the body snapping in half. Archon made a shoving motion, but the katana tasted blood before its master went sliding away.

Archon shrieked and gasped, staring down at his chest. Red expanded over his shirt at the left breast.

Anna pulled a brilliant arc of lightning from the e-mag concealed in her left palm, twisting it over her right hand. An instant later, a blinding, jagged stripe connected her fingertips to Mamoru's chest with a resonant *boom* that knocked dust from the walls. A pair of crackling blue arcs shot out of Mamoru's legs, lapping at a puddle behind him. Anna yelped and released the charge, shaking her left hand as if it had burned.

Sensing opportunity, Aaron whipped the E-90 off his hip and put the blue ring-dot sight over Archon's stunned expression of horror. Before he could squeeze the trigger, Anna pulled his arm down.

"No, Aaron."

"Die, motherfucker!" shrieked Kate, her entire body surrounded by a sudden blast of flames.

The fire gathered like a serpent around her legs, up over her shoulders, and spiraled down her arms, gathering into a twisting rope. Anna nailed her in the chest with a thin, stunning spark. The shroud of flames whiffed out in a puff of blue-orange. Kate wheezed and flopped to the floor.

"Stop, stop, stop!" Screamed Anna.

Mamoru twitched in a heap, moaning. Archon looked up, his expression one of complete surprise.

"Anna, he's dangerous," said Aaron.

She held onto his arm with almost all her weight to keep his aim down.

Archon's expression hardened to a sneer. The instant he looked at Aaron, Anna nailed him with a flash spark that knocked him flat against the wall. White foam leaked from his mouth as he slid down to sit on the floor.

"Stop. No one is killing anyone. This is *stupid!*" Anna stood between Aaron and Archon. "All of us are Awakened. There's only half a dozen of us in the world. We shouldn't be killing each other."

Aaron's gaze flicked back and forth from Mamoru to Archon. "I'm not sure either one of them's much in the mood for compromise."

She put a hand on his chest. "James is passionate, but he's not stupid. He has to understand how valuable even one Awakened life is."

Mamoru's bellow of rage morphed into laughter as he stood. No trace of injury remained visible anywhere on him, despite the smell of ozone and charred meat in the air. Even his pants had mended. His attention locked on to Anna when she ran to where Archon had slumped.

"Anna!" yelled Aaron.

She spun as Mamoru charged, jumping back with a cry of surprise. Aaron caught the man in a telekinetic grip, hauling him airborne.

"We don't have time for this." Aaron held his breath, concentrated, and launched Mamoru to the far left corner of the hangar, fast enough that his figure blurred.

The body hit the wall with enough force to dent the steel, filling the room with another deafening *boom* and sending a spray of blood and gore sliding off his bones. Anna screamed. Black vapor wisped around Mamoru's mangled remains. A starburst of expanding blood flowed up the wall, stopped, and raced back into the body. Splintering crunches muted by a cover of new-grown flesh ceased a few seconds after the last of the gore reassembled into an intact figure.

Mamoru slid out of the pit his impact left in the wall and landed on his feet. He cracked his neck with a side-side wag of the head.

Red eyes, like small windows into the fires of hell, flickered with amusement. "Aaron, I am impressed. That almost hurt."

Bugger me... he's getting stronger.

62

TEARS FOR THE WICKED

Althea

The scent of flowers filtered into Althea's consciousness. Strange beeping noises in the distance reminded her of being far from home. Heavy eyelids parted. Spots of blue light appeared on a white ceiling above her. Warm, squishy material below the blanket conformed to her shape. An odd minty taste lingered in her mouth, growing stronger as she sucked in a deep breath. The feeling permeating her body couldn't be called pain in the truest sense of the word, but she found it unpleasant.

She sat up. Four similar beds lay to the left, five to the right. Her dress was gone, replaced with a stretchy white one-piece garment that clung to her body, covering her arms to the middle of the bicep and her legs to her upper thigh. Althea rubbed her face, whined, and gave serious consideration to letting herself flop backward and staying put.

Two narrow, grey tubes connected a sticky patch on her left forearm to a panel on the wall full of lights and a little drawing of a person with a blinking red dot where the heart should be. Her stomach ached like she'd been punched, and she held it for a few minutes until the pain changed to hunger.

Althea pulled her hair away from her face and peered down at the tents her feet made in the white blanket. Hazy memories returned; a lot of people hurt, many see-through people confused, Kate and Aaron at the brink of death. A feeling of being drained spread over her. Soon, another need made itself known, and she grumbled. After spotting a toilet in a small room at the far end of the ward, she slipped off the bed. Freezing cold shot up her legs as her feet touched the floor. She let out a yelp of surprise and her body went rigid. On tiptoe, she crept toward the bathroom until the rubbery hoses taped to her arm stopped her.

"Ow," she whined, grabbing the pad.

Not sensing any metal stuck into her skin, Althea figured the pain had come from stickiness. She clenched her teeth, peeled the pads off with a quick yank, and threw them aside. The little cartoon figure on the screen flashed red, and a distant beeping sounded from another room. Seconds later, a head-sized silver ball floated out of a hole in the ceiling and raced over to her. It made her think of a smaller version of the awful metal sphere that tried to kill her, and her eyes went wide. She backed into the tiny bathroom, the orb following.

"Are you in distress?" said an electronic voice.

Althea glanced at herself. "This isn't a dress."

Lines of green laser light ran up and down her body. She cringed, but felt nothing. Apparently satisfied, the little machine zipped off and disappeared back into its nest. Althea stared at the hole in the ceiling for a few breaths before examining her garment for a seam, but couldn't find a way to remove it no matter how she grabbed and tugged at the stretchy material. She crossed her legs and bounced, whining, before trying to pull one of the legs open and up. It snapped back against her thigh hard enough to make her yelp.

Althea rubbed her leg and stared at the toilet.

"What's wrong, child?" asked a low, feminine voice.

A dark-skinned woman with short hair in dense cornrows peered around the doorway before walking in.

Althea pulled and tugged at the smock, whimpering.

The woman chuckled. "Is the MolWeave broken?"

"What?" Althea bounced in place.

"That little bead by your shoulder." The woman reached over and tapped a thumbnail sized plastic oval embedded in the fabric above the left collarbone. "Squeeze it."

Althea reached up and grasped it. It beeped, and when she pulled it down, the annoying smock split open from neck to navel. With a grandmotherly smile, the nurse eased the bathroom door closed. Althea wriggled out of the smock and leapt onto the toilet. When she finished, she stepped over the uncomfortable thing and stumbled naked to the bed.

The nurse, who'd been waiting nearby, gave her an odd look. "Something wrong with your smock, hon?"

"I don't like the tight on my legs. It feels stretchy-icky like skin. Can I please have my dress back?"

Althea sat on the edge of the bed, swinging her feet as the medtech retrieved the garment and brought it back to her. Without asking Althea's opinion, she pulled it up over her legs.

"I've got no idea what happened to your dress. Come on girl. This isn't the Badlands; people here don't run about in the all-together. Ain't proper."

Althea tilted her head. "Yes they do. I saw them in this place with flashing lights and noise. And everyone had the strange." She raised her arms over her head and shook her body around in the same way the people she'd seen at the club did. "Girls were spinning and dancing on shiny poles, and they didn't have the clothes." She tilted her head the other way. "Is it because they were cat people?"

"You shouldn't been in those kinda places, girl." The woman radiated awkwardness as she lifted her off the bed, set her down on her feet, and snugged the smock up. "Don't be givin' me a hard time, hey?"

"I'm sorry." Althea hated how it felt to wear something so tight between her legs, but she put her arms into the sleeves and let the woman tug the MolWeave up to her neck.

The annoying clothes moved as if alive. Althea shivered from the sensation of the rubbery material engulfing her body and sealing tight to her skin. She held her arms up to the sides with an expression as though she'd stepped knee-deep in animal waste.

"Oh, stop. It's not that bad. Now sit, I gotta check you out an' make sure you're okay."

One after the next, the medtech waved various handheld devices at her, shone light in her eyes, looked in her mouth, and squeezed her arm. Althea tolerated the poking and prodding, all the while her stomach rumbled and growled. Eventually, the woman collected the gadgets and shuffled to the side to replace them in a cabinet on the wall.

"All set, girl."

"You can't find any deezes, par-sights, or feckshins, but I'm border nine mal nurmished."

The woman laughed. "Poor thing, you've been through a lot haven't you?"

Althea smirked, swinging her feet. "Am I done? Can I go home yet?"

"I don't know. I'm just a medtech. I don't have anything to do with all the police stuff." The woman shook her head. "Damn crazy if you ask me. You're way too little to be sent out into the field. What the hell are they thinking?"

Her stomach rumbled again.

"Do you feel up to solid food, hon? I could get you something to eat… or maybe just soup?"

Althea scooted back on the bed, crossed her legs, and grasped her ankles, grinning. "Yes."

"Alright, you look like you could use a few calories." The woman shut the cabinet and walked out. "I'll be right back."

She picked and fidgeted at the uncomfortable smock for a while until the medtech returned carrying a tray. Althea stared at it with the focus of a cat tracking a mouse, attacking the meal as soon as the woman set the food on the bed. Taken by hunger, she gasped and coughed trying to breathe and eat at the same time. Handful by handful, she packed her face with chicken, mashed potatoes, and gravy. After a moment of stunned staring, the woman grabbed her wrists, holding her hands together away from face or food.

"Slow down, child, you're going to choke. You're going after that like you've never seen food before."

Althea tried to lick gravy from her chin. "'Kay."

She resumed eating once the nurse released her arms, this time with more care.

The woman stood and made to leave. "If you need anything, I'll be right outside at the desk."

"I need a fly home." She looked up from the plate for a few seconds.

"One of the officers will probably help you with that. I'll let them know you're awake."

Althea beamed at the woman, who seemed happy and concerned for her. This visit to the bad city did not feel as scary as she thought it would, but she still wanted to leave as fast as possible. Content for the moment, she resumed devouring her food. Althea licked every morsel from the plastic bowl and nibbled whatever she could taste out from under her fingernails. She set the empty vessel aside and went for the sealed cup. The soup was warm, but not hot enough to make her hesitate in taking the cup in two hands and gulping it down as fast as she could chew the more solid bits.

Aurora appeared amid a cloud of silvery fog. "Well, you were hungry."

"Don't let the woman see you. She'll make you wear one of these awful things." Althea plucked a pinch of smock from her chest and let it snap back.

"We'll not be here long."

Althea grinned. "You're taking me home?"

Aurora shook her head.

Althea stopped smiling. "You're worried."

"You need to come with me, right now."

"I'm not going home yet, am I?" She sulked and crawled to the side of the bed.

"No, sweetie, not yet. Anna needs you."

Althea swung her legs over the edge. A sudden dark feeling ran down her spine, making her curl into a ball and shiver. She knew the feeling. *Him.* "Something bad will happen."

"Yes, Althea. Something very bad is going to happen, and you have to promise me not to feel guilty about it."

She slid off the bed to her feet, and emitted a tiny burp. "Will I be with my family again?"

Aurora took her hand. "I haven't seen anything to say you won't, but... I can't promise. I do know, if you stay here, a lot of people are going to die—including you."

Althea looked up into Aurora's pure onyx eyes. "I have never felt the scared on you. Don't be afraid."

"Who the devil are you?" yelled the nurse. "Security breach, medical ward one."

"Thank you for the food. Please don't have the scared. It's okay." Althea waved to the woman in the doorway.

Aurora drifted back a step and slid into a swirling vortex of silver-grey energy. Althea sensed a pull beyond the simple physical tug of Aurora's hand around her own, drawing her into the mist. She leaned into it, allowing the energy to wash over her. After a bright flash, the room took on a sepia color, and the uncomfortable clinginess of the smock released her. The medtech gawked, looking around as though she could no longer see them. She ran in, passing through their insubstantial bodies, and picked the one-piece garment Althea had been wearing off the floor.

"Mary, mother in Heaven," muttered the nurse.

As before, Aurora leapt skyward, the ceiling offering no resistance. They traversed walls and solid objects with only the resistance of passing through large blocks of jelly. Althea felt more at ease this time. This world had some of the same energy she had felt from the silvery swirls she'd opened for the dead. She still couldn't explain what she did, or why, but felt confident it needed to be done. She thought of Anna and focused on the need to find her. A flickering light in the distance called out to her, winking at her from beyond miles of endless fog.

"That way." Althea pointed.

"You're learning." Aurora smiled.

Minutes later, the building with the beds, hallways, more rooms, and other sleeping people gave way to the shapes of the bad city zooming by. Althea tried to focus on her desire to move toward Anna. A feeling welled up inside her, a combination of energy and urgency she could barely contain. At any second, she expected to rocket away... but whenever she tried to grab on, the squishy sensation slipped between her fingers and faded. Over and over, she tried to pin it down, but it eluded her. She growled in frustration, paying no attention to the spirit world gliding by as Aurora led her along.

She focused so much on finding Anna that when Aurora stopped short, Althea sailed right into her.

"Mmf." She floated back a few inches, rubbing her nose. "If we're spirits, why did that hurt?

"We're actually here." Aurora laughed. "We're not spirits, mite. We're still alive. I've brought our bodies into their world."

They floated in the shadow of a huge building, next to a fancy, gold car. Behind and to either side, endless, flat desert stretched to the horizon, everything wavering with the endless shifting of the astral realm. Aurora arched her back and stood on tiptoe for a second, and the world returned to normal color, devoid of the constant vague whispering that seemed to exist everywhere on the other side. Stark chill gave way to a hot, dry wind Althea adored, though a flicker of mood told her Aurora loathed the heat. To her, the spirit world had been comfortable. The dusty breeze reminded her of home, and of her family. She stretched and took in a deep breath, basking in the heat with her hands on her hips, her hair fluttering in the wind.

A scream came from the end of the building. She started toward it, but Aurora grabbed her shoulder. Althea looked back, trying to pull away, annoyed at being made to wait while people suffered.

"People are hurting!"

"You have time for this. A few seconds won't harm anyone." Aurora opened the car and reached into the back seat. She took out a plain, white dress like the ones Karina made for her and handed it over.

"You knew?" Althea hurried to wriggle into it, scurrying toward the screaming while adjusting the garment around her body. "Where's yours?"

Aurora smiled. "Oh, I'm sure I'll find someone to put on."

Althea sprinted along the wall, not at all liking the feelings she sensed from inside. A loud *boom* shook the entire structure and knocked a rain gutter from the wall. She dove for cover, shrieking as metal pipes clattered to the ground a few feet away. Althea glanced up at a large blister-like dent in the wall about halfway up the building. A vague human shape to the imprint both terrified and angered her.

She darted forward, racing as fast as she could pump her legs to the end of the hangar, grasping the metal to take the turn without falling. Great slabs of warped metal lay on the ground by the entrance. She ducked between the wreckage and the wall, skidding to a halt on smooth concrete inside. The reek of burned rubber made her cough and cover her mouth.

The man who tried to kill her in Querq scowled at Aaron, red light flaring from his eyes.

Hate surrounded him.

Kate lay on the ground, twitching.

Anger surrounded her.

Anna, the only one to notice the weak sound of a child's cough, looked at her.

Fear surrounded her.

Archon moaned on the right side of the room.

Disbelief surrounded him.

Aaron stared at Anna.

Love surrounded him.

Althea balled her hands into fists. She glared at the man with the sword. A burst of energy flared outward from between her shoulders as her wing-ribbons unfurled, flooding the massive room with scintillating white light. Her eyes shone like portals into the heart of a blue star.

"Leave them alone!" Althea pointed at the man. "You do not belong here."

Black smoke whorled out of the Japanese man and sank into the floor. His eyes rolled up into his head and he fell like a sack of wheat.

"Away!" screamed Archon. Anna lurched into motion, sliding across the floor toward him. She pivoted to her feet like a puppet in the hands of an amateur, pirouetting into his grasp, her feet not even on the ground. He cowered behind her small body, a wide-eyed stare locked on Althea. "Get that filthy little dust rat away from me! Get her out of here this instant!"

The level of terror she sensed within him defied her understanding. Althea tilted her head.

"Best listen to reason, mate." Aaron stared death at him. "Put Anna down. You know what Lauren said. Don't get on the li'l sprog's bad side."

"Why are you afraid?" Althea took a step forward.

Archon's eyes widened. "Get her away from me."

"Let Anna go," yelled Aaron.

Anna grabbed James's arms, squirming to get away from him, but couldn't break free. She seemed hesitant to shock him; fear lost in a wave of guilt.

Attempting to force calm into Archon's mind, Althea took another step closer, but found his emotion out of reach.

A short, straight, Nano sword erupted from Anna's left breast. Archon let off a gasping groan, his face a mask of shock.

"Anna!" screamed Aaron.

Anna's legs went limp, but she didn't fall. Her body floated forward off the transparent blade protruding from the center of Archon's chest. Blood seeped down the front of his shirt.

"No!" wailed Althea. Her wings trembled as she shook her fists.

The sword vanished backward into him, leaving a neat slit. Archon fell to one knee, twisting to peer behind him—at another Anna.

"Wha…?" Archon gurgled.

Anna Two's head shimmered into a holographic rainbow. Inky black spread down her snow-white hair as it grew out from pixie cut to bob. Her features morphed, and her skin darkened from Anna's porcelain to the tone of Asian ancestry. Sparkling emerald eyes altered in shape, but not color, continuing to stare disdain at the man in front of her.

Althea gawked at the woman she'd almost failed to heal.

"Sa... da... ko," wheezed Mamoru.

"But..." Archon reached up, color fading from his face as his eyes rolled into their sockets. "You cannot best me... You are"—he coughed up blood —"not even psionic."

Sadako blurred. One instant she stood at rest, the next, she leaned to the side, both hands on her outstretched sword. A second later, a line of red formed on Archon's throat. His head slipped two inches left on a glass-smooth cut—then toppled to the floor.

"No!" Althea screamed.

Anna's limp body skidded across the floor, sliding to a halt in Aaron's arms.

"Althea," said Aaron, tears streaming down his face. "Please, help her!" He sobbed. "She's dying!"

Archon's life essence faltered and waned, as did Anna's. Althea stared at the severed head. The mass healing she had done on the roof wouldn't save him, nor would it be enough to stem the blood pulsing out of Anna's chest.

Drawn by the love and sadness glowing from Aaron, she ran to him and fell to her knees, placing her hands on Anna's cheeks. Althea closed her eyes, concentrating on Anna's life essence at the same time she felt Archon's wink out. She gritted her teeth, weathering tendrils of ethereal ice clawing at her chest. Anna's blood-shape rushed out of a slash in one of the large tubes above her heart. Warm energy tingled across her fingertips, channeled into Anna. The precise cut required little effort to seal. After, she focused on mending the sword-shaped channel in the woman's chest. Once all the bone-shapes and meaty parts had mended, she funneled power into urging the woman's body to generate more blood.

Anna gasped and sucked in air.

63

ANGER AND CHAOS

Aaron

Fingers clenched into the material of Anna's coat, Aaron stared at the strange, violet effect of blue light hidden by the child's eyelids. He glanced up at the woman dressed like Anna, with a Japanese face. She remained motionless by Archon's corpse, sword held to the side, angled down. A few drops of blood ran along the edge and dripped from the point. She looked in the direction of Mamoru, her expression unreadable. Anna moved, taking a huge breath and lurching upright. Aaron forgot about everything else going on and cradled her.

Althea sprawled nearby, kneeling with her hands on the floor, head bowed. She gasped for breath as if she'd sprinted around the entire hangar. After a few seconds, the streamers of light receded into her back. She looked drained, and sniffled, crying as quietly as she could. Tears patted onto the dusty concrete between her splayed fingers.

Anna twitched and coughed up blood. Aaron eased her forward, patting her on the back. He tried to talk, but couldn't. Tears wet his cheeks as well, though his anguish had become joy.

The Japanese woman stared at Mamoru—passed out on the floor—for a moment longer before narrowing her eyes at Anna. Aaron peered into her mind. Her inner debate rambled by in Japanese, beyond his understanding. Images provided enough to understand the sight of Althea with glowing wings had startled her into inaction. Her thoughts reordered themselves as she watched Anna gasping for breath. Her mind fixated on the sensation of a handgun in her coat pocket. Sadako concealed her intent with slow, innocuous movements as her hand crept closer to the weapon.

"No!" Aaron growled and thrust his arm at her.

His telekinetic shove launched her across the hangar. Sadako tumbled over backward in midair and slid to a halt in a three-point stance with her sword held out to the left.

"Aaa…" wheezed Anna.

Sadako drew the pistol. Aaron roared, lashing out with his mind. The gun bent under the weight of his anger. Bits of plastic flaked away and a bright flash snapped from the digital ammo display near the handle. Sadako yelped and leapt back, abandoning it.

The sparking weapon clattered to the ground. Sadako's eyes widened as the handgun compressed into an unrecognizable lump of plastic. Her gaze flicked up, locking with his for an instant. She sprang into a tumble and darted toward the stack of tires. Aaron's power yanked her off her feet and slammed her down on her back. Sadako resisted the urge to cry out from the pain of impact, though she could not help but emit a muffled grunt. He eased Anna to the floor and rose to his feet, E-90 leveled at the Japanese woman.

"Don't bloody move." He stepped two paces closer. "Why? Why Anna?"

"I will kill them for what they have done to Mamoru." The woman turned into a transparent human shape for a half-second before vanishing.

Aaron fired, but the narrow, blue beam hit only concrete, leaving a glowing orange dot.

"It wasn't Anna," said Althea. "The Many has taken Mamoru."

"Uhh, Kate?" asked Aaron, glancing at the unconscious redhead. "Shit. Anna, stay alert. I don't have the best luck with invisible bitches holding sharp things."

Anna coughed, muttered something incoherent, and collapsed.

Aaron dropped to one knee, hovering over her. "Anna!"

"She is tired," said Althea.

Mamoru groaned. The sound of his voice filled Aaron with inexplicable rage. He blamed that man for Anna getting hurt. Everything that had happened was his fault. Mamoru would kill them all. Mamoru killed Allison. Mamoru killed Anna.

Aaron howled, blood pounding in his head. He clenched his fingers into the rubbery grip of the E-90 but lacked comprehension that the object in his hand was a killing machine. Incomprehensible screaming scratched his throat as he lashed out with a telekinetic wave. Mamoru sailed into the air, twisting and spinning in random directions. Aaron wanted him to explode from centrifugal force tearing him limb from limb.

"Aaron, no!" yelled Althea.

His rage dissipated, a balloon meeting a pin.

A sharp pain at the back of his head blurred the room. Aaron stumbled forward, falling as something swept his legs out from under him. A distance away to the right, a dull metal thud announced Mamoru's meeting with the wall. A feminine hiss from behind came an instant before a strike to his chest knocked the air, as well as his ability to move, straight out of him. He flopped on his back, staring up at Sadako. The tip of her blade had stopped a finger's width from his neck.

A drop of Archon's blood fell on his skin.

Sadako lifted her gaze to where Mamoru lay moaning. She drew her arm up; the cold, calculating glare of a trained killer faded to the eye-bulging fury of a madwoman. Sadako roared, grasping her blade in two hands with all the finesse of a drunken Viking. Aaron pushed her away with a brief telekinetic blast, but lost concentration as a cloud of freezing vapor swam over him. The ghostly outline of Aurora appeared superimposed over Sadako for an instant, seeping into her. The Nano sword slipped from her grasp, sticking into the concrete slab behind her like a spoon dropped into pudding. She teetered and fell to all fours, gasping, with one hand clutching her chest.

"Anna, I owe you an apology," wheezed Sadako, with an English accent. "Your chesticles really aren't that small. Don't worry about this one, Aaron, I've got her." She sat back on her heels, staring into her shirt. "Poor girl. No wonder she's so angry."

He forced himself to his knees. The room spun too fast to risk standing. He reached up and found the back of his head bloody and tender. Mamoru's katana scraped across the floor as he shambled with a zombie's gait toward his sister. Dark vapors coalesced around his feet; he stopped.

His arm trembled as he brought his sword up. He hesitated, grumbling in Japanese. When his face snapped up, he wore a psychotic grin. White fire roared down his arms and he vanished in a streak of steel and skin.

"Stop!" screamed Althea.

Aaron forced himself up. Mamoru, in striking range of Althea, held the blade poised back as if to take the child's head. Her eyes flared with light too intense to look straight at. Azure tendrils leaked in wisps from the corners; she wept energy.

Mamoru's arms slackened. The sword drooped as he took a step back. Althea held her ground, fists balled, glaring up at him. Dazed from the blow to the head, the sight of a little barefoot girl in a simple white dress staring defiantly up at a man with a large sword struck Aaron funny, and he laughed. This, of course, made his skull throb. He blinked, remembering he once again wore the uniform, and grabbed a stimpak from his belt. He looked at the thin, red autoinjector in his hand, flicked the end cap off with his thumb, and jammed it into his shoulder. In seconds, a rush of energy flooded him from the synthetic adrenaline. Tingles crept over the back of his head along with the maddening squealing of nanobots mending cracked bone.

Althea muttered something too low for him to hear. Mamoru backed away, looking frightened. The child took a step closer, making Mamoru retreat another step.

The pain pounding in the back of Aaron's brain faded once the coolness of the stimpak fluid migrated up his neck to his skull. He raised the E-90, unsure if he should aim it at Mamoru or Sadako.

"Awright," said Aaron. "What in the bloody hell is going on?"

DAUGHTER OF RAGE

Kate

Sunlight shone in bands amid a haze of smoke hovering near the roof. Crashing, screaming, and shouting seemed far away. Kate struggled to breathe, but couldn't draw in more than tiny sips of air. Pressure, as though an evil, hundred-pound duplicate of her heart sat outside her chest, pinned her to the ground. She wheezed, sucking in short, choppy gasps. Her back arched, prickling with sparks. Her arms and legs felt absent, no longer part of her, and her effort to grab the weight off her chest triggered convulsive twitching.

Kate fought past the pain in her muscles. Inch by inch, pins and needles replaced numbness. She thrashed on the floor. Hot foam slid out of her mouth and over her cheek. A moment later, her body obeyed and she curled on her side, shivering.

"Stop!" screamed Althea.

Motherly instinct welled up out of nowhere. Kate sat upright, gazing around at a scene of carnage. She leapt to her feet in the ungainly stagger of a newborn deer, gaze drawn to Mamoru—too close to Althea with a sword. The child's eyes shone with such light she flinched. It didn't matter her protective urge came from a telempathic implant. After all the bad things she had done, she could have been punished in far worse ways than an irresistible urge to protect the person who had given her a real life.

Her will molded fire into a sphere. Tears of guilt and gratitude blurred her eyes and caused the fireball to miss Mamoru. He didn't react, continuing to stare at Althea. The child's angry glower had somehow stalled him, and he lowered his weapon.

Aaron raised his sidearm, but couldn't seem to decide who to point it at. "Awright, what in the bloody hell is going on?"

Mamoru slumped to one knee.

She stepped on something and her boot slipped. Kate glanced down at a large pool of blood, following a trail with her eyes until it met the source—Archon's headless body. Her eyes went wide. She screamed, part horror, part anger, and part joy, and projected a stream of fire onto the dead face she swore stared at her as if alive.

Archon's severed head vanished in a cloud of black ashes. The man who had violated her mind no longer existed. He could never do that to her again.

The carnivorous cakes flashed in her thoughts. She pictured the family life he had fabricated, both the idyllic vision he'd invented as well as the nightmare into which her mind twisted it. It had hit her so hard because it *had been* everything she truly wanted. Kate would've gladly allowed herself to be a child again for the chance at such a normal life: parents, childhood friends, parties, actual school, boyfriends, the whole package. Archon had read that out of her and exploited it. Why had the world been so cruel to her? The hangar melted away into the dark alley of a black zone. Kate's uniform vanished. Naked, she huddled for shelter under a broken awning, gazing at society from the outside. Why had she ever gone to the city? They did not want her.

In a flash, the scene changed. She looked out of the eyes of her six-year-old self, kneeling on the floor of a pink-painted test lab. Men and women in heavy silver suits placed patches of different material on her forearms and thighs, grumbling and shaking their heads as each sample melted, ignited, or evaporated.

Little Kate wailed, feeling like she had done something wrong. One of the scientists tried to comfort her, but burned his hand. At his scream, she felt even more guilt. She reached to hug someone else, and he ran away in terror. Another man appeared with a long, metal pole. A gripper clamp the perfect size to fit around her neck opened at the end. She knew she had to go back in the tank, and he would use the painful thing on her if she didn't obey. Kate stood, hands up. She backed away from the advancing group of huge men in flame-resistant suits, shaking her head.

"I'll be good!" she wailed in her waking dream.

One silver-gloved hand reached up and pulled the fireproof mask away, exposing the blotchy face of the old priest. Thin, dark lips parted to reveal teeth the color of seaweed. Kate's perspective changed as he approached, rising from the neck-spraining vantage of a little girl to standing eye to eye in the body of an adult.

"Damn scientists," croaked the old man.

Kate clenched her fists. "Fucking scientists. I'm a person, not a damn monkey to be put in a cage."

The silver fire suit wisped off to smoke, swirling into a billowing leather coat. "They were going to kill you."

"I killed them first."

Cold metal constricted tight about her throat. She reached up to grab the neural stun collar.

The ancient gunslinger traced a finger over the metal, which broke and fell away. "The government would kill you rather than lose control of their weapon."

"I'll kill them first." Blue flames squeezed out of her fists and wrapped up her arms.

"There's only one place you can be free." He smiled.

The lab vanished with a glare of desert sun. Kate stood at the tip of a high rocky overhang overlooking an endless sea of warriors. Her pale, naked body glowed in the sun like a fire goddess descended from above. Smoke peeled from under her feet, wisps of flame fluttered along her outstretched arms. Everything she touched burned. So-called civilization wanted her dead, but she would survive. The modern world would yield to the scorching flames at her command. She raised her arms, basking in the adoration of a thousand grimy savages below holding blades, spears, and axes overhead, praying to the Queen of Flames.

"Kate?"

An unlikely voice emerged from a goofy buck-toothed man with a helmet made from old truck tires. His British accent caught her off guard, and she squinted down at him, trying to remember why he looked familiar. The Badlands canyon blurred away, once more a hangar, the rocky precipice upon which she had stood a stack of aircraft tires. She had her arms held wide, surveying... her domain?

Below her, the charred remains of her greatest enemy lay vanquished. Figures moved in the blurry distance, wearing uniforms. The government. More people trying to kill her. Thousands of boots tromped all around her, closing in.

No. I won't let them get me!

Feeling surrounded and certain of her imminent death, Kate collapsed in a ball and screamed.

"Run!" yelled the British man. "She's going to nuke the building!"

Kate shuddered, remembering how she felt when soldiers aimed rifles at her eighteen years ago. The fear of an innocent child had triggered a nova of destruction that wiped them out to the last. She remembered how she felt when bloodthirsty nibblers overran the tiny house in the Badlands. At that moment, the path to the great reserve of energy lurking inside her lay clear. Rage and flame waited for her to call upon it, yearning for release. Mental fingers coaxed it out. The army coming for her would burn.

Everyone would blow away, ashes in her hands.

Her eyes snapped open as she leapt up, surrounded by a cyclone of fire. The energy drew inward, seconds from a withering burst.

"Katie," said Althea, the voice in her mind as much as in reality.

She glanced toward the sound, at a little girl in the hangar doorway. *My little girl...* The anger changed, external, not hers. Something tried to force her to hurt this child she thought of as a daughter. Kate recoiled from it, clinging to the need to protect her at all costs. As soon as she locked eyes with her, the consuming rage collapsed and the roaring inferno vanished with a *whuff.*

"Leave her alone!" yelled Althea. "You've done enough bad."

Kate's legs gave out and she spilled forward off the stack of tires. An invisible force caught her, guiding her in a gentle float to a landing near Althea. Anna lay on the floor, unconscious. Aaron trotted up behind her. Mamoru, to her left, knelt like a Samurai about to commit seppuku. Guilt leaked from Kate's eyes. She knelt where Aaron had placed her, staring down at wet pats appearing on the grey concrete.

Two small bare feet stepped into view.

"Kate?" Althea reached out and grasped her cheek. "Kate? He's gone. Stop feeling so sad."

"Kill me," said Kate. "I'm too dangerous to live. He's gonna take over and I'm going to hurt someone I shouldn't. I can't control myself."

Althea wrapped her arms around Kate's head, hugging her face to her chest. "You just did."

"You took away the anger."

"I made the Many go away." Althea released the hug stared into her eyes. "You stopped the fire. You can resist him."

Kate glanced up to the side as Sadako passed by, on her way to stand by Mamoru. When she looked back at Althea, she broke into sobs.

"You gave me the only thing I ever wanted." Kate cradled Althea's cheek in her hand, wiping a smudge of dirt from under the girl's eye with her thumb. "I remembered how happy I was. I've done evil things. I didn't deserve what you did for me."

Althea reached up and held on to Kate's wrist. "You're sorry. I know you won't do bad stuff. Father says if you keep hitting a dog, it will bite. The dog isn't bad. It's been hit too much."

Kate sniffled. "How are you still so sweet after everything people have done to you?"

"She's been hit wif a stick enough, but she doesn't bite," said Aaron.

Althea looked up at him. "I'm not a dog."

"Althea's hardly a fair example." Kate stood, gazing to the dusty horizon in the west. She couldn't tell if the sudden onrush of determination came from her or the child, but it didn't matter. "We gotta get back to signal range and warn them about that ship."

SOME MEN DESERVE TO DIE

Anna

Quiet stillness hung in the air. Anna stared up at cotton clouds gliding across a deep blue sky. She floated over tall grass, which tickled and tingled along her back. The sound of birds and the soft brush of wind in the treetops made her feel calm and at peace. She took a breath, savoring the wetness in the air that carried the fragrance of meadow flowers and lake.

"Anna," said Archon.

She sat up, finding herself at the spot where she had first made love, on the lakeshore by the cabin in County Gwynedd. Archon stood at the edge of the water, a look of utter disappointment on his face. A bird swooped in low, skimming the surface, and snatched a fish from the greenish depths with a soft *sploosh*.

"James?"

He glanced down and turned away. "The fools do not understand."

"Who doesn't understand?"

Archon trudged into the lake, not disturbing the water. Anna's eyes widened. When the surface reached his neck, he paused long enough to look back at her. His expression could have been sorrow or disdain.

Without another word, he vanished into the water.

"James!" Anna yelled.

She tried to get up, but her body refused to move. Anna growled, tugging at arms as heavy and dead as sandbags packed with lead. Althea, shrouded in a glowing nimbus of white light, emerged from behind and stepped around in front of her. The girl put a hand on her shoulder and pushed her over backward.

"You can't go with him."

Despite the calm on the child's face, her voice sounded as though she sobbed.

"Please stay."

Anna exhaled, noticing a sharp, cold, pain in her chest. "What's happened?"

The girl pressed her hands into Anna's breast. "You've been hurt."

A wave of dizziness came and went. Anna gathered her wits and stared up into the face of the child hovering over her. Blonde-white hair floated around a worried, innocent face. Her eyes matched the sky in their depth of blue. The aura of light surrounding the girl burst into a blinding flash, obscuring everything. Althea's voice murmured, sounding farther away. Another voice muttered.

Aaron?

"Am I dead?" asked Anna.

"Anna!" yelled Aaron.

Something warm squeezed her hand numb. Faint lines appeared in the haze, struts, and girders of a steel roof. *The hangar.* Aaron's face floated over her, red, covered in tears. Cold, sticky wetness squidged over her breast as she sat up.

"Anna..." Aaron pulled her seated and wrapped his arms around her. "I don't want to lose you, Anna." He grasped her shoulders and held her back enough to look her in the eye. "I love you, Annabelle Morgan."

"I..."

Sincerity in his eyes flickered with fear. He patted her on the back.

She coughed and spat blood. "I... I know."

A weak grin teased at his lips.

Anna blushed. "I'm... I've fallen in love with you, Aaron Pryce." She clutched at his coat to pull herself up, staring into his eyes. "So stupid. I should have—"

He seemed frozen in the moment, trails of silent sorrow running down his face. Seconds later, his brain absorbed the truth she survived, and he kissed her. She clung with as much energy as she could force into her arms, trembling with physical pain as well as terror at what Archon would do to her if he caught her. *I don't care... I must be free of him.* After a moment, Aaron's kiss slid off to the side and he cradled her tight to his chest. The sound he made could've been sobbing or laughing.

She closed her eyes, forcing out hot tears. Sparks leapt out of her, dancing over Aaron's arms into the ground. It struck her funny that her little monster got out of control over a positive emotion. He leaned back, flashing a quizzical look at the charge, which made her giggle despite her inability to stop crying.

"Even if you are an Arsenal wanker," she muttered.

Anna leaned up, pressing her lips to his. Time lost meaning; they parted seconds or minutes later for all she knew. Her eyes crept open. He hovered close enough to taste his breath. "Is that coffee?"

"I'm sorry, Anna." Aaron rubbed a hand up and down her back, his face grim.

"Sorry?" She tucked her face into the crook of his neck. "Is being with me going to be that awful?"

He knelt and took her hand in both of his. "James is..."

"He's lost 'is 'ead," said Aurora.

Aaron cringed.

"What?" Anna looked to her right, startled at the sight of a Japanese girl. "Lauren?"

"Aye. Don't mind the outfit. This one's still got a mind to kill you. She's trying to protect Mamoru from us."

"Sadako?" rasped Mamoru. He glanced up at her and recoiled. "Do not look upon me. I am no longer worthy of your concern."

"Not exactly," said Aurora. "I'm just borrowing her until she gets over being so stabbity-stabbity."

Anna shifted to her knees and craned her neck. The twisted tweed suit sprawled on the ground told the story.

"James!" Anna screamed, scrambling to get up.

Aaron held her down. "Don't. It's not pretty."

"James..." Anna sobbed, collapsing over Aaron's shoulder. "James, no!"

She had been terrified of him for the past few days, frightened of what he might do to her. The few minutes she spent alone with him in her 'new room' had made her fear for her life, but the sight of his headless corpse filled her with regret. That no trace of a head remained anywhere in sight horrified her.

How much was an act? What if it wasn't? Nausea pounded her in the gut. Here she was, draped over Aaron with James not yet even cold. She couldn't deny her feelings for Aaron, but a tsunami of guilt threatened to drag her down. Her fingernails dug into his arm. James had used her. He had manipulated her friends, driven her from everyone and everything she'd ever known. Anna closed her eyes, languishing at the intersection of anger and sadness.

"I'm sorry," whispered Aaron. "There was nothing I could do." He shuddered and held her tight to the point of discomfort.

Anna looked at him, sniffling. His hazel eyes glimmered. A vision, from his point of view, slipped into her thoughts. He'd seen her pierced through with a translucent blade. Along with the vision came the feeling of Aaron's almost-broken heart.

She shied away from the body, wondering if Aaron had felt the same way when Allison died. Archon had used her like he had used everyone else. How many others had died like the Venezuelan resistance? *'People of no consequence,'* was his term for them—non-psionics.

"Shit." Anna's head popped up. "The ship! The ship is crashing."

At that moment, the strangest noise reached Anna's ears.

The sound of Althea growling.

SUFFER THE INNOCENT

Althea

Mamoru shuddered and staggered to his feet, saturated with the sense of dread incarnate. Althea sensed the darkness within him and snarled. He raised his katana, gaze darting from Sadako to Kate to Anna to Aaron before focusing on her. She stared up at the man, leaning forward in the most aggressive posture her body could produce.

"Out!" screamed Althea.

Streamers of white light unfurled from her, stretching more than twice her height to either side in the shape of wings. Althea arched her back and floated off her feet. Ruffling noises, fire upon the wind, fluttered from the strands. Energy built up within her chest. Seconds after leaving the ground, she thrust her arms forward, palms flat, and glared.

A thunderous rumble echoed to the horizon as an apparition of black vapor burst from Mamoru's back, repelled out of the hangar. Ink mixed with dust as the shadow zoomed across the desert. Wispy black arms flailed and grabbed at nothing as the entity attempted to hold on to the air to stop himself.

Thirty paces behind Mamoru, the darkness coalesced into the ancient cowboy. Red glowing eyes burned with hate, turning orange from fury. The Many rushed into a blur, but his charge halted six feet from her, hand raised, face twisted with rage.

"You have the fear of me because you know I can hurt you." Althea floated higher. "You have the anger, and you are not wrong to have it. These people did not do anything to you. Don't have the angry with them for what happened in the before-time. Stay away from him."

Mamoru wheezed, coughing on finger-thin tendrils of inky smoke peeling out of his nose and mouth.

The old man raised an arm to shield his face from the searing white light.

"You are wrong. I do not want to hurt you, but I will *not* let you kill the bad city. So many people..." Althea glanced down. "It is the wrong. You have the angry from the before-time, but you want to do the same thing! I do not *have* to fight you. The chamán said the world is having Light and having Dark, always. One can't be without the other."

The Sentience growled and surged into Sadako. Aurora appeared out of thin air on tiptoe behind the shorter woman, screamed, and fainted. Sadako rushed to where her blade stuck out of the ground, snatching it for another attack. Althea's wing ribbons snared the woman's wrists, holding the sword back from Aurora's helpless throat.

Sadako's arms smoked where the energy touched. Scenes of a terrified child flashed in Althea's mind. The woman had watched her parents murdered, men whisked her away to a strange flying machine. They had kidnapped her and made her a killer. Sadako leapt at Althea, sprouting metal claws from her fingertips. Althea yelled, twisting her entire body to hurl Sadako to the ground with the energy streams. The light ribbons released the woman, rising once more into the shape of wings.

"Out!" Althea glared at Sadako.

Black vapor slipped across the floor at Anna. Aaron shoved her out of the way, and the darkness crawled up his chest. Althea leaned forward, screaming at him, her desire to protect Aaron from The Many too large to fit into words.

Aaron swooned to the ground as the cloud burst out of his eyes, ears, and mouth. Seeing it coming, Kate surrounded herself with a wall of flames, but the shadow didn't even slow down.

Althea's wings lanced forward and mummified Kate in glowing ribbons. A man's voice howled from Kate's writhing body, as if he burned alive.

"Leave my friends alone!" Althea tried to stomp, forgetting she floated.

Dark vapors exploded out of the gaps between strands, rushing at her, engulfing the world into blackness.

Warmth at her back faded to cold, hard metal. Althea looked up from her grimy legs at the bars of a cage too small to allow her five-year-old self to stand. She hated the bars. She hated the box that controlled who she could help and who she was forced to *feel* die. The Wagon Man took a knee outside, smiling. He loved her. Loved her in the way a man loves the thing that makes him rich. He had given her plenty of water and plenty of food, but nothing else, neither affection, comfort, clothing, nor freedom. She grabbed the bars and braced her feet against them, rattling the door.

"This is where you belong. In a cage. Nothing more than an animal for the using."

She stopped struggling and looked up at him. He had been a handsome, if not horrible, man. Thirty or so, about Aaron's age. The voice that emanated from him on a sulfurous breath sounded much older.

"You are lying," whispered Althea. She let her hands fall from the bars. "I am not angry. I will not give you power. Even as a slave, I helped people."

A crack of thunder split the quiet. She blinked and found herself sitting on dirt at the center of a ring of teepee style tents with hubcaps, chains, and sheet metal attached to them. A manacle around her right ankle tethering her to a dead tree, and a ratty blanket were her only clothing. This place had been her home two years after the wagon, one of many raider camps. Men in armor made of leather, tire treads, and metal carried a wounded third. They dropped him at her feet and walked away. All the skin of his chest had been ripped to tatters, and his entrails hung out. She gazed down at the bloody gore sliding to the ground, not bothering to back away as the crimson touched her toes. She remembered this man. He was dead already. She could do nothing for him. Their leader, the one with the purple hair and half-metal face, thought she disobeyed. They thought she'd refused to help him on purpose.

None dared strike her, but they screamed and threatened. They took her blanket away, left the dead man next to her, and denied her food for three days. Some even taunted her with bits of meat, holding them inches out of her reach before snatching them away and devouring the morsels in front of her. From her vantage point of a dream, she knew that on the third day of her starvation punishment, other raiders would come. They would kill to take her. The few survivors, raiders following a new chief, would blame the old war leader for starving her. They would say it was her wrath, and the Badlands would come to believe the legends that all who mistreated her suffered.

Althea stood and walked to the end of the chain, letting it hold her leg off the ground behind her.

"This is not real. I am not here." She squinted into the indigo sky. "I know you are making me see this lie. I have a family. This has passed."

Metal constricted around her throat as her body grew a little. The tents slid away to the horizon and an old, flattened blue car rushed up behind her. A rusty chain, padlocked about her neck at one end, the front bumper at the other, gave her about twenty feet of range. This place happened two years later. She had thought herself ten at the time but had likely been nine. Seated on the dusty metal hood with scraps of leather arranged around her, she braided cords into a thicker band, which would become the belt of the skirt she had considered so precious. The first article of clothing she had ever owned, and no Seeker or parent had given it to her.

She had made it herself.

This camp of broken vehicles had been her home one abduction before Den's people found her, where she lived among settlers with a hard edge. They said the leash was to keep people from stealing her, not to hold her captive. Althea smirked at the leather scraps. It didn't matter; a leash was a leash, regardless of why they put it on her. None of this mattered anyway. The Many told another lie to her eyes, and she would not let it bother her.

She ignored the uncomfortable tightness at her throat, humming as she worked on her future skirt. Althea smiled, knowing she would be wearing it when Father found her. Karina would laugh and roll her eyes at how attached she was to a simple leather tatter.

Growling seeped from the sky. Her contentment enraged the Many.

The chain disintegrated into rust powder, which blew in spirals over her chest. The car melted to nothing, leaving her standing. Her white dress appeared. An endless field of desert sand and scrub stretched out to the horizon on all sides. She glanced around and at herself; she seemed to be in the now once more—but this place did not remind her of anything that had yet happened.

A blonde woman in blue ran across the distance, chased by men in dark coats. She cried out for help. They raised rifles and cut her down in a flurry of shots. It seemed as though she had died too fast to feel any pain.

Althea didn't have to be close to recognize her mother. She gazed down at where her feet had sunk into the dirt. "She made sure I was safe. She gave her life up so I would live. It does not matter what lies you show me. My mother loved me more than anything. I know the see-through people go somewhere. My mother is waiting for me there. She is not gone."

The old man appeared in a whirl of smoke and leather, pointing finger an inch from the tip of her nose. She looked up at him, calm, unflinching.

"What if you could have her with you again?"

"You don't have that power." She didn't blink.

"Althea... you would be so quick to turn your back on your own mother? After she gave her life to protect you?"

"What you would give me would not be my mother. If she is dead, she is in a place you cannot touch. You are darkness and anger and evil and sorrow. You cannot reach my mother because she is love. You give only lies and suffering."

The ancient finger retreated. He glared down at her.

"Go and be in your own place. You don't belong here."

He squinted. "Neither do you."

Althea thought back to Aurora's mention of a gate opened between worlds. Her mother had worked where the machine exploded. People kept calling her an angel. Maybe a small piece of whatever they make angels out of touched her before she was born. "I did not ask to be what I am. People made me when their ritual failed."

The sentience leaned back with a dry laugh. "People made me as well. Their need to control, to kill, to profit. We are two sides of a coin."

"Then we should not hurt each other, or we will both die."

"You are a fool, child. You cannot hope to match our power."

Althea shook her head and sighed. "You are not strong. Killing does not show the strong, it shows the weak. It takes strength to forgive. You have only the weak."

She reached for his hand, but the apparition disintegrated. Gravity lurched in her stomach as she dropped out of the air and fell to her knees, hands braced on the ground. Shimmering energy wings shrouded over her for a moment before receding into her back. She tucked her legs to one side and sat up, pulling her hair out of her face and squinting at the sun overhead. No trace of the Many remained here. He had fled from her. A thing like that might never die, but she would hold it back for as long as she could.

"What the fuck was that?" asked Anna.

"Oh... Angels and Demons locked in mortal combat... Fire, brimstone, and such. Usual Wednesday afternoon stuff for Division 0," said Aaron while waving his hand about.

Althea giggled at the sound of a soft punch thumping into his chest. She bit her lip, smiling at the love radiating from both of them.

HONOR RECLAIMED

Mamoru

Tightness squeezed Mamoru's hand. Droplets of warm liquid struck him on the chest.

"Is that one safe?" asked a man with a British accent. "I'd rather not get stabbed."

"Aye," replied a woman. "We had a nice long chat while I was wearing her."

"I'll never get used to hearing that," said Anna.

"Please don't cry," said a child. "Your brother is not dead."

Tightness squeezed his hand again. Mamoru opened his eyes and looked into the face of his sister, warped with sorrow.

"Sa... da... ko," he whispered.

"See," said the child.

"You're sure he's not goin' ta try and kill us again?" asked the British man.

"Why don't you ask him?" Aurora stood over him, her alabaster skin blinding in the raw sunlight.

Mamoru sat up. Strange visions tormented him. Fire burning his flesh, lightning searing his bones, and organs sliding out of him as he burst against the wall. Darkness had gripped his mind. He gasped, clutching at his gut.

"What have I done?"

"Please, Mamoru, do not throw away your life." Sadako fell to her knees at his side, head bowed. "I found your confession."

What else could he do? He rested his arms over his knees, squinting at a dust storm crawling across the endless brown. "I must."

"No." She grabbed his shoulders and shook. "You're a ronin now. You don't have honor anymore."

A flash of anger warmed his chest. He drew his arm back to slap her, but she didn't flinch. The weight of her stare sapped the fury from his heart. *She is right. A ronin has no warlord. I am a broken man.* Sadako guided his arm back into his lap and held his hand.

"There is no shame in what happened," said Sadako. "I saw the *Akuryō* leave your body. You could not have been responsible. You are strong, but such an evil cannot be resisted."

"I did not resist it." He hung his head. "I welcomed it."

Sadako drew a breath and gasped into her hands. "What? Why?"

"That's a right good question," said the Brit. He had his arm around Anna, who looked miserable and red-eyed. "I'm not entirely sure *what* the bloody hell that thing was, but *inviting* it to tea seems like a right howler. You've got to be dead from the neck up."

"I could not allow my sister to die. She injured herself trying to protect me…" Mamoru plucked a clump of lint from his pants, rolling it between his thumb and finger. "Our shuttle crashed. She would not have lived long enough to find help. An old man appeared offering a deal. I could not say no and watch her die."

"He's persuasive," muttered Kate.

"The Many was the cause of her hurt." Althea gazed into space. "He broke the fly machine and made you crash. He wanted you."

Mamoru growled. The shuttle had failed without reason. Every system had shut down or overloaded. How had he not realized that? "I am a fool."

"My life is not worth that of an entire city." Sadako sat back on her heels. "Tell the *Akuryō* to undo his bargain."

"Aaron," said Anna. "We've got to go. We have to warn them."

"I tried." Aaron looked off to the west. "I imagine a few executives and the government bigwigs are planning to evacuate. They didn't want to release the news. Mass panic."

What little color Anna had in her face drained. "They're just going to leave everyone unaware of what's falling on them?"

"We can't just stand around here feeling shitty and crying," yelled Kate. "Fuck."

Anna looked at the Division 0 patrol craft. "Take me back. We have to get the others out of there. All those children…"

"There's more kids in West City than just the ones Jimmy boy collected." Kate folded her arms.

"Do you have to call him that?" Anna sniffled.

"It was the friendliest thing I could think of." Kate scowled. "Did he fuck with your head too?"

"I don't kn—" Anna's body rippled with sparks. "Yes. He did."

Aurora put on a Mona Lisa smile.

"It is too late," said Mamoru. "Even if I could find access to the uplink at the starport, I would not be able to gain control of the ship before it was stuck in Earth's gravity. I have also disabled the communication relay. It would not receive a transmission anyway."

"What of a military assault?" asked Anna. "There's got to be something."

"It would take hundreds of aircraft to take down; it's massive," said Aaron. "Even if they did that, they'd have to let it enter the atmosphere before striking at it. The bloody thing would still crash into the city."

"Yes, but… smaller chunks." Anna flailed. "The destruction wouldn't be as bad… it's something."

"There is no way." Mamoru stood and faced Aaron. "My shame is too great. Please spare my sister and our family from it." He offered his katana handle first. "I ask you to give me back my honor."

Sadako bowed her head and wept. "Mamoru. You bargained with an Oni to spare my life. Do not make me live knowing I do so because of your death. If you are to die, I will join you."

"Sister, no," Mamoru yelled.

"No one needs to die. You're both having the stupid." Althea stomped over and glared up at him. "There is too much death already. Stop having sad and *do* something to make it right. Killing yourself won't make what you did any less bad. All you do is run away."

"You cannot understand our ways," said Mamoru. The child hadn't pleaded—she'd called him a coward with her eyes. As improper as it struck him for a girl-child to be so… forceful… he couldn't deny her truth. "What is there to do?" He lowered the sword and grasped it by the handle. "I cannot reach the ship."

Hope spread over Sadako's face. "If you could gain control, could you stop the crash?"

"I cannot say. Perhaps." Mamoru squinted at the breeze. The pristine sky offered no sign of the doom he had set in motion.

"Can your police car go high enough?" Sadako pointed at it.

"Nope," said Aaron. "About a mile up tops."

"Maybe the little angel can hop on his back and fly him there," said Kate, smirking.

Althea jumped up and down. "Yes!"

Aaron coughed. Anna stared. Kate did a double take. Mamoru raised an eyebrow.

"No." Althea spun around to point at the statuesque nude by the hangar wall. "Not me. Aurora."

Mamoru glanced at the bizarre woman. "You are smiling like that because you know something we do not."

Aurora uncrossed her arms and put her hands on her hips. Lemon-blonde hair, as long as her calves, lofted to the side in a gentle uptick of wind. "I was waiting to see how long it took someone to suggest that."

"Reckless," said Aaron. "If you knew it would work, you should've said something. Why'd you make us run about the circus like that?"

"Dominoes," said Althea, sounding annoyed.

Aurora burst out laughing.

"What the bloody hell does that mean?" Anna and Aaron asked simultaneously and exchanged glances.

"Of course I can get him there, but… there's no guarantee he won't die in a fireball." Aurora raised an eyebrow. "You'll not be able to bring anything you weren't born with, even cybernetic implants."

"Is that why you are naked whenever I see you?" Mamoru raised an eyebrow.

"Not entirely. I enjoy making people uncomfortable." Aurora winked. "We can go whenever you're ready."

Sadako shuddered. "I don't want you to die. Let us run. Their military can destroy it."

Mamoru slid his blade into its scabbard, and knelt at her side, pressing the katana sideways into her lap. "Hold this for me, sister. Alive or dead, I will return to you."

Althea walked up to Aurora. "I will wait here. You can take me home later."

"Aaron," said Aurora. "You have some unfinished business at Edmonson Memorial Starport. I suggest you bring Althea with you."

"Why?" asked Anna. "Is she still pivotal?"

Aurora sashayed over to Mamoru. Despite his guilt, he still found himself staring at her chest, not that she appeared to mind. "Even if she wasn't, you'd leave an eleven-year-old alone in the Badlands?"

"Bitch." Aaron chuckled.

"Actually, she might come in handy." Aurora reached for Mamoru's hand. "Are you ready?"

Mamoru released the katana into Sadako's care and stood. "If the kami have presented me a chance to reclaim my honor, I shall take it. I am ready."

"Kami? I thought I was an oni." Aurora winked and pressed herself against him. The touch of her nipples on his bare chest made it hard to concentrate on much of anything. "Just relax, and let me do the work."

"I bet she says that a lot," muttered Aaron. "Oof."

Anna pulled her fist out of his side. "Be nice."

"You will feel a tug," said Aurora.

Aaron cracked up; Anna punched him again.

Aurora ignored his outburst. "A tug in your mind. Concentrate on wanting to follow me. This will only work if you want to go." She faded into a ghost, surrounded by a swirl of white-silver energy. A mass of whirling, freezing air spread up his arms from where he held her hands. Mamoru surrendered himself to the odd sensation in his head and leapt through a barrier of standing cold. The ground fell away in a blur as they rocketed skyward, a feeling that recalled his time embodying the Fūjin. Whatever waited for him beyond the clouds, he would correct his mistake.

Or he would die.

THE AWAKENED

Kate

Cool air rushed out from the space Aurora and Mamoru had stood seconds earlier. Kate couldn't help but stare at the pants and boots slumped on the ground where he had been. Her mind wasted little time in thinking of nude men, David in particular. Twenty-five years old and she'd barely held hands with a man, and yet after being with him for almost a month, they'd never done more than kiss. She wanted him, more than she could stand sometimes, but she also wanted her first time to mean something.

Kate peered into the hangar. After what happened here, as well as almost losing him twice, she worried that *right moment* would never come. She daydreamed about tearing his clothes off and jumping him on the spot when she next saw him, no matter how many people were there to watch.

Althea gawked at her.

Shit. Damn empaths.

Kate's face went as red as her hair.

"I wonder what's going on at the starport," said Aaron. "I suppose there's no harm in investigating."

"You want to go *to* the city?" Sadako gestured at the west before waving her arms up and down. "It will be destroyed. We should stay here."

Althea grasped the woman's hand. "Your brother is trying to stop it."

Fear faded from Sadako's face. "You are right. If he fails, I wish to join him on the other side."

"So… what are we looking at?" asked Aaron.

"About ninety or so of The Awakened," muttered Anna.

"Oh, is that all." Aaron gazed at the clouds.

Kate's heart almost stopped. "I thought you said there were only six of us?" She glanced at the hangar. "Five."

Aaron gave her a 'too soon' grimace.

Anna sighed. "No, all the strays we took in got into the habit of calling themselves that. They're not *actually* awakened. Some of the older psionics who'd been living on the street before we got here had formed like a gang or some such nonsense. They're just psionic. Every one of them fell for Archon's bullshit. He'd promised he'd find a way to make everyone more powerful."

"That's why he wanted me," said Althea, staring down and dragging her toes over the sand. "He thought I could 'waken them."

"Well." Anna bit her lip. "There is one."

Aaron glared. "Talis." He pulled Anna toward the car.

"Wait, Aaron… We"—she stared into the hangar—"can't just leave James lying there like that."

"Sure we can." Aaron stopped. "But we won't."

"It would not be wise to put a headless corpse in the car," said Sadako.

"You could wait here with him." Ice coated Anna's voice.

Althea ran to Anna and took her arm in both hands. "I'm sorry I couldn't help him."

"Oh, no, I reckon I'd call in a crime scene unit." Aaron smirked.

"We don't have the time or the tools to dig a grave," said Kate. "I'll cremate the body."

"No!" yelled Anna.

Kate kept her anger inside. She had wanted to burn Archon for what he'd done to her. She had wanted to make it hurt, and take a while. Despite the gratification of a protracted immolation, an instant death would likely have been her only chance to defeat such a powerful telepath. An instant of eye contact and he would've made her his *daughter* again. Her stomach knotted at the thought.

"We don't have time, Anna." Aaron squeezed her. "We can leave him here and come back… if we survive."

"No, it's alright." She sniffled and looked at Kate. "They cremate everyone now anyway. I want to watch."

"You sure?" A small bit of guilt rose within her as she made eye contact with Anna. *Whatever love she's got for him's bullshit. He raped her mind too. She has to see him burn. Maybe she won't admit it, but she needs to.*

"I…"

"Come on," said Kate. "I'm burning more than bodies."

She stomped into the hangar, over to the tweed-clad remains. Dr. James Mardling, of Oxford, lay on his back with his right leg twisted up, and no head. A fan of dark red expanded from the neck. The Nano blade had left such a smooth cut, the end of his neck resembled dark red glass. Anna turned away and gasped. "Oh, feck... James."

Kate kicked Archon's leg in an effort to make him lie straight, drawing a whimper from Anna. Wisps of flame coiled around her hands as she let anger seethe for a moment and fade. Knowing Archon had moved beyond feeling any pain, she resisted the urge to stomp on him more. She crouched and arranged his body to lay as if in a casket. She dug her nails in, a subtle attack that escaped Anna's notice. It didn't do much damage, but it made her feel a little better.

"Thank you, Katherine." Anna choked up, taking a step back. Even in death, she still seemed afraid of the man. "I know you... hated him."

"I'm surprised you don't." Kate stared at the body for a moment before she stood. "He almost took away who I was. He made me see him as my father. He made me kill soldiers who answered my call for backup. Soldiers who were just doing their job."

Anna sniffled. "He hurt so many people."

"I don't know what he did to you, or what you think he was to you, but it's probably bullshit."

"Yes and no." Anna crept up alongside her. "He did pull me out of the gutters of London. Probably saved my life. I guess he only did it because of what I am." Her face hardened, but tears continued to flow. "If I wasn't Awakened, he wouldn't have cared about me at all."

"He'd do anything to have us." Kate looked down. "Kill anyone. Re-write anyone."

Anna rubbed her hand back and forth over her arm in an effort to stall trembles. "I didn't know. I was terrified of thinking about anything that might make him angry. When I started having doubts, I was sure he knew. I expected him to do something to me." She shivered.

Kate offered a sympathetic hand. "He made me think I was his daughter."

"Lauren's gotta be laughing about this. She always could be a bit on the cold side." Emotion had left Anna's voice. "I wonder if she knew the Japanese girl would be the one to kill him. That must've bothered him more than dying."

"Why? He's got a problem with Japanese?" Kate raised an eyebrow.

"No, he's got a problem with mundanes. She's not psionic."

Kate looked at her. "Are you sure, I thought she was trying to read my mind?"

"I am weak," said Sadako from behind them.

Anna jumped, awash with sparks. Two hit Kate in the arm like bee stings.

"Ow, shit." Kate clamped a hand over the spot.

Kate stared down at Archon; it occurred to her that she'd probably write her first official report as a Division 0 officer about this fight. She stooped and collected his NetMini. "Sorry. Guess as a cop I should turn this in for evidence."

Sadako moved closer, standing to Kate's left. "My father gave my mother serums and drugs while she carried me, trying to repeat what they had done with Mamoru. It did not work as well, but it did give me a little ability."

"Guess we're all someone's science project." Kate drove her boot into Archon's side. Blood squirted out of the neck.

Anna flinched.

"I can see what people are thinking, and sometimes make them not see me." Sadako stepped closer, head bowed. "Please forgive me for trying to kill you. The child has made me understand you were this man's puppet."

"Maybe someday I'll think of you as having set me free," said Anna. "I'm not sure I can do that yet, but I understand."

Sadako bowed.

"I don't know how you can have anything but fear and hate for this piece of shit." Kate scowled. Her glare softened as she thought of her situation with El Tío. She sighed. "Well, maybe I can. Is there anything you wanna say before I do it?"

"I'll never know how much of his feelings were real." Anna stuffed her hands in the pockets of her coat and looked down. "I'll always be grateful to you for getting me off the street, but you've hurt so many these past few years. Even the best of intentions don't excuse the worst of actions." She bowed her head for a moment of silence. "Goodbye, James."

Kate took a step forward so Anna couldn't see the grin on her face as she surrounded her arms with flames and projected them over the body. She tapped into her anger, remembering the feeling of icing squishing between her toes, the little fang-like teeth in her leg, and the horrible, nauseating memory of having this man insert himself as the father she never had. The flame paled from blue to yellow-white. Over the course of minutes, the body blackened, bubbled, smoked, and collapsed to ash and bits of bone.

She slumped and tried to catch her breath when little remained of him but a stain on the ground and bone pebbles. At some point during the burn, Anna had retreated, likely from the heat or the smell. Anger faded to a vacuous hollow of doubt. She wondered if it would have been that bad after all. If she hadn't known it was a lie, she would've had a loving father. Kate frowned. *No, he would've loved my power, not me.*

She made a fist, shaking with rage.

Calm down. She exhaled and relaxed. *I can't be angry all the time. That'll only let that thing win.* After a final scowl at the ash pile, she hurried out to join the others.

KATE TWISTED AROUND IN THE PASSENGER SEAT, ENGAGED IN A TELEPATHIC conversation with Althea. She attempted to clarify why her emotions had gone where they had gone in such an inappropriate way.

Is your thinking-shape hurt?

What? Kate blinked. *No, I feel okay.*

You felt like a raider right before he wifes a slave. Althea scowled.

Warmth crept over Kate's cheeks. *I miss David... He's almost died twice. I love him. I want to... uhh...*

Althea blinked, covering her mouth. *But you're a woman... Only the broken slaves want that.*

Kate burst out laughing, earning strange looks from the others. *Men aren't the only ones who enjoy... uhh... wifeing. It's very different when there's love involved.*

The girl's eyebrows drew together with suspicion.

You're little yet, but it won't be long before you understand.

Althea looked at her lap for a moment, picking at her dress. *You did feel different. More like love than greed. Den makes me feel funny, but I don't want that.*

Not yet you don't. Kate winked. *Some day you will.*

Althea blushed, shaking her head. *No. Eww.*

With the girl's desire to ask awkward questions gone, Kate reached out and squeezed her hand for a moment of gratitude before adjusting herself to face forward. The imprint that made her feel like a daughter had worked. It gave her the strength to fight off the demon. She no longer needed to fear losing control.

Sadako had taken James's Halcyon-Ormyr as Anna couldn't bear to drive it. She sat behind Aaron, staring at her hands folded in her lap. Kate gazed out the window, checked her equipment for the fourth time, and sighed.

"What?" asked Aaron.

"I was just wondering how awkward it would be if they made us partners," said Kate.

"Bullshit." Aaron chuckled and glanced at his nameplate. "I'm apparently a lieutenant. Assuming they don't put me in a box when all this is done, I'll be transferred to I-Ops. What's really bothering you?"

"They *promoted* you after what happened?" Kate blushed. "Uhh, that didn't sound like I meant it."

"No offense taken. I expect they want to study me. They'll probably promote you to I-Ops, too, since you're Awakened... once you've had some experience on duty."

"I doubt it. I still have to go through ISCOT, and all I can do is blow shit up." Kate picked at her uniform. "That's what I'm worried about. I don't know what good I'm going to be in a hostage situation. All I can do is kill. I'm just a weapon."

"If your power is just a weapon, you're no different than an ordinary cop with a gun. They still deal with hostage situations." Aaron smiled. "You define your power. Don't let it define you. Besides, killing might come in handy. There's a dangerous bitch down there that I don't think the world would miss."

"Aaron," said Anna. "We have no idea what he did to her. She might be a mouse now."

"You're fibbing." Aaron leaned the car to the right. "There's a cute little tremble in your voice whenever you're scared."

"Sod off." Anna blushed.

Kate looked back and forth between them. "Anna, if you know something, now's the time to speak."

"I just had the strangest paranoid delusion." She looked up. "James got darker after she arrived. What if she was really pulling the strings and not the other way 'round? She never liked me. Always stared at me like I was standing in her way. As soon as she showed up, James seemed to start pushing me away."

"Narcissists do that," said Aaron. "He doubted your loyalty, so he wanted to crush you to build you back up. There's no way Talis would've even *acted* subservient. It's not in her DNA."

"She wanted your man." Kate checked the energy meter on her E-90 for the fifth time. "She wanted the king's crown."

Anna gasped. "You think she made me afraid of him?"

"Nope," said Aaron. "That was me."

"W-what?" Anna looked horrified. "What did you do?"

"Showed you the truth." Aaron reached over the back of his seat.

Anna grasped his hand. "That's not funny."

"It wasn't meant to be." He took hold of the stick again and nudged the car to a gradual dive.

The console flickered with a flurry of activity as they moved into range of West City's network. Within fifteen seconds, the holographic head of Captain Buckley appeared. He opened his mouth as if to bark at Aaron, but turned to face Kate.

"Solomon. There you are. I hope you have a good explanation for your sudden disappearance so soon after your... incident."

"Sir," said Kate. "An inside informant contacted Lieutenant Pryce in regards to a critical situation occurring out in the Badlands. I happened to be with him at the time and since I'm... uhh, Awakened"—she shivered at the word—"I insisted on going with him."

"Ashford said your mental state might be at risk."

"Yes, sir." Kate didn't flinch. "I wanted to kill Archon for what he did to me. I couldn't pass up the chance."

"What happened out there?" Buckley raised an eyebrow.

"Well, sir. A demon possessed Mamoru, that Awakened technokinetic you sent me to intercept. It forced him to set the CSS Angel on a collision course with West City because it wants to expand the Badlands out to the coast. We intercepted Archon meeting with him. There was a fight, sir, and the demon tried to turn us against each other, but we had an angel on our side."

"Demons? Angels?" Buckley blinked. "You're starting to sound as dodgy as that Astral Sensate over on Captain Eze's squad."

"Well, the girl's only part angel," said Anna.

"Solomon?" asked Captain Buckley "What the—"

Althea leaned left into the view of the camera and waved at him. "Hi."

"Pryce? Dammit man, that's a child, what are you doing bringing a child into a tactical situation?" Buckley froze, his pointing finger added to the hologram. "Are that girl's eyes *glowing*?"

Althea nodded. "Bio loom-nis-ant."

"No offense, sir, but if Burckhardt knew what this kid can do, he'd sell his bollocks to have her in command of her own tactical squad."

"That's not funny, Pryce," said Buckley.

"No, sir. It isn't." Aaron's grin went flat. "I didn't mean it as a joke."

"If I may cut in..." The holographic head of Mikhail Kovalev appeared next to the captain.

Captain Buckley paled. "Of course, sir."

"Sir," said Kate, saluting.

Aaron saluted without saying anything.

Althea saluted also, seeming confused when the Captain and the Director both chuckled.

Director Kovalev's expression returned to grim. "There is a situation at—"

"Edmonson Memorial Starport?" asked Aaron.

Mikhail stared at him.

"We're already en route, sir." Aaron grinned. "Archon had a pet precog."

"Had?" asked Captain Buckley.

"Archon is dead," said Kate.

Anna shrank into herself.

"You killed him?" Buckley looked down and grumbled. "That'll be a pile of bureaucratic horseshit we'll need a front-end loader to slog through."

"No, sir. I wanted to, but he was dead before I could get to him. A ninja killed him."

After a three-second blank stare, Buckley cracked up laughing so hard tears streamed out of his eyes. "Oh, of course. Demons and angels were incomplete. Needed some ninjas. Next thing you know, there'll be werewolves involved."

"There's a samurai too." Aaron winked.

"What's a werewolf?" asked Althea.

Anna mumbled a brief explanation to her.

"Oh, the werewolf isn't here." Althea shook her head. "He helped me get away from a slave catcher. He was nice after I made his hurts go away and took the angry metal out of him."

Captain Buckley made a noise somewhere between whimper and giggle. "Werewolves? Have you *all* cracked?"

"That'd be a canid mutant, sir," said Aaron. "Doubt they've got a particular aversion to silver."

Buckley twitched.

"I understand how crazy this sounds." Kate sat tall in the seat. "I didn't believe it either."

"What's the situation on the ground, sirs?" asked Aaron.

"A number of psionic terrorists have taken over the starport and have control of the security team." Mikhail glanced at something off to his right and behind him. "At this point, we are unaware of their intentions or demands. They have released all potential hostages other than the security personnel, as well as a group of about a hundred, most of whom are of children."

"The children are all psionic," said Anna. "Those are the people Archon wanted to 'save.'"

"It doesn't make any sense." Buckley pinched the bridge of his nose. "They gave up all their advantages."

"They are not interested in demands," said Anna. "They are expecting the stolen starship to arrive and take them off Earth to a new home somewhere in deep space. Archon dreamed of saving psionics from a world that hated and feared them. He wanted to create a new life on some distant colony world."

"We've established a mobile command unit at the starport, set up on Intra-atmospheric Pad 2 in the southwest." Mikhail saluted Aaron. "Report there for further information."

"Sir." Aaron returned the salute.

Both holograms vanished.

Anna let out a long sigh.

Althea saluted her, making Kate giggle.

"Don't be scared, Anna." Althea held her hand. "You don't have to be sad anymore."

Kate thought of David.

About twenty minutes later, Edmonson Memorial Starport spread out below them as they flew between a pair of gleaming silver century towers.

Two and a half sectors of almost-flat city surface formed a valley amid the skyscrapers. Northeast of center, the donut-shaped main building resembled the hub of a wheel, connected by white spurs to banks of landing pads. Angled walls surrounded areas designated for orbital craft, meant to contain the downblast from powerful engines. Landing zones for shuttles that didn't leave the atmosphere lay off to the southwest, huge gleaming chrome pads without walls. Automated tramcars sat idle, scattered about on magnetic rails behind the landing areas.

Aaron guided the car toward the chaotic scene of flashing lights and military vehicles on the pad marked 02. Huge, six-wheeled A3Vs established a perimeter around a larger cargo truck with police lights. Kate held on to the seat as the car lurched downward, fascinated for a few seconds at the sight of the huge armored vans.

Kate glanced at him. "What do I do?"

"Just follow my lead," said Aaron.

About twenty police in blue armor advancing toward the main starport entrance stopped short and faced back the way they'd come. Their posture changed, suggesting they had gone from infiltrators to sentries.

"Oh, shit." Kate pointed. "Look at them."

"Talis." Aaron almost growled the name. "That bitch needs to die."

He rushed the landing, putting the patrol craft down hard behind the mobile command trailer. Althea bounced off the seat to the floor and let off a whine. The middle third of the trailer, on the side away from the starport, had opened into a ramp, exposing a room filled with holographic screens floating over map tables, workstations, chairs, and quite a few people in Division 0 uniforms. Aaron pointed through the front seat gap at Althea.

"You stay in the car. It's armored, you'll be safe." Without waiting for a response, he hopped out. "You too, Anna." The driver side door closed with a *thunk.*

Kate shoved her side open and trotted around the hood, jogging to catch up to Aaron as he stormed over to a cluster of people huddled around a tactical map, Captain Buckley and Director Kovalev among them. Kate made eye contact with Buckley.

I'm fine, sir.

Later, Solomon. You look okay for now. We'll suss it later.

Sir. She saluted.

At the right side of the tactical display, a man in a sand-brown coat frowned at a datapad in his hand.

As soon as she saw him, Kate felt a tight coldness around her throat and the urge to burn him to ash. She made fists but held back the itch.

"We have an unknown number of psionic criminals who appear to have exerted mental influence over everyone remaining in the starport," said the man in the coat.

"Good day, Officer Master of the Obvious," said Aaron.

The man smirked at him. "Major Reston, Division 9."

At hearing 'Division 9' and not 'C-Branch,' Kate relaxed.

Aaron forced a smile, followed by a limp salute. "Major."

"I was merely appraising your immediate superiors of the contingency and containment planning already in place. It seems the riot team has met a similar fate as the starport security personnel."

"You can't kill them all!" yelled an older man from Division 0.

A dark-skinned woman in her later fifties, Chief of Detectives by her hawk-shaped rank pin, adjusted the fit of an external hearing-augmentation rig. "We must keep this from spilling into the NewsNet. This will set back public opinion sixty years."

"With this many Division 0 personnel in the area," said Reston, "it's already obvious this situation has significant psionic involvement. We need to show the public we can deal with these events."

"Half of them are children," yelled Anna, jogging up behind Aaron.

"Shite," muttered Aaron.

"Who's this?" asked Major Reston.

"Annabelle Morgan, Mi6/CSB," said Anna.

Everyone, Aaron included, stopped what they were doing and stared at her.

She and Aaron exchanged glances. Aaron turned red and appeared to be trying not to laugh.

"I doubt that," said Reston.

"I'm probationary," said Anna. "Offer's been extended, but I haven't signed on the dotted line yet. You can talk to an Agent Hughes for verification."

They looked at each other again. Aaron's eyebrows shot up.

Kate knew the look. *Guess I'm not the only one who joined to save their ass. Better than prison.*

"It doesn't matter if I've signed or not." Anna stepped onto the ramp. "I know the composition of the group inside. There are eighty-nine people remaining. Forty-seven of them are under the age of sixteen. About half are locals, the rest are refugees from ACC territory where they shoot psionics on sight. They won't react well to an armed containment team. It will remind them of where they came from and make them lash out. They are desperate, lonely, scared, and many have been spoon fed a diet of idealistic codswallop for the better part of the last four-ish years."

"Your real threat," said Aaron, "is Talis Lir. She's an Awakened suggestive and telempath. That's the only possible way they're influencing all those people at once. There's no telling what kind of control she's got, probably even over the other psionics."

"Maybe the Corporates have the right idea," said Reston, earning dire looks from everyone in a black uniform. "At least with the suggestives. If you can't contain this, we're going to kick jurisdiction over to the military. C-Branch will sweep and clear the starport."

Kate gasped. "They'll kill everyone. Talis won't be able to control synthetics with AI brains."

Another Division 0 patrol car landed near the trailer.

Anna exuded ice. "I'd suggest against that, Reston. If one of those children dies, I'm going to hold you personally responsible."

"I'm trembling," said Reston in a flat tone.

"You're a C3 doll aren't you?" asked Aaron.

"That is correct." Major Reston leaned toward him, eyes narrowed.

"You'd better listen. Machines have a nasty habit of buggerin' themselves 'round 'er."

"Sounds like the threat is one person," said an older woman.

Kate looked at the new arrival's chest. Her nameplate read 'Carter' in all caps, with a much smaller font spelling out 'Jane' below. The rank insignia under the large zero on the left side consisted of five stars, each made of separate onyx chips.

Carter, Jane looked at Kate's confused expression with a hint of a smile. "Something troubling you, Officer Solomon?"

"I'm sorry, ma'am. I'm new. I don't recognize your rank insignia... I was just wondering if I should be saluting."

More like shitting your pants, said Aaron's voice in her head. *That's Director Carter. The head of Divison 0. The big boss.*

"Now, Solomon. No need to be nervous. I'm merely an empath." Carter returned Kate's clumsy salute, adding a wink. "This is a special situation." The woman shifted her attention to Reston. "What's this I hear about murdering children? And is everyone forgetting the enormous starship falling on our heads?"

"Our tracking satellites have picked up the CSS Angel approaching Earth," said Major Reston.

"That's being handled, Ma'am," blurted Kate.

"Oh?"

"It will sound ridiculous. Please read my mind," said Kate.

"Try me." Carter smiled.

"After the half-angel girl chased the demon away, the ninja's samurai brother came back to his senses and flew through the astral world to get back to the ship so he could possess it and try to stop the crash."

The Division 0 brass went silent.

Carter raised an eyebrow. "Well, I don't know what to be alarmed with more. The meaning of what you just said, or that you seem to believe it."

"We've got more immediate problems than the starship, Ma'am," said Aaron. "An awakened empath is controlling armed men, and possibly up to ninety some odd psionics."

"Empath?" Carter smiled. "We'll see about that."

FALLING ANGEL

Althea

Alone in the car, Althea crawled forward to kneel, leaning past the gap between the front seats to watch the people in the giant box full of flickering lights talk. A black-haired man in a brown coat gave off impatience and a little worry. The men and women in black uniforms radiated fear at various levels. Anna swung back and forth between anger and sadness. Althea grinned and waved at Carter, but got no reaction. She pouted for a moment before remembering the 'windows' of this car were black armor plates on the outside.

Carter, flanked by Aaron, Kate, and a handful of other police in black walked out of the big box and jogged over to the smaller six-wheeled ones. They gathered in cover behind a tire a few inches taller than Aaron. Carter peered around the nose end of the boxy truck. A moment later, her confidence became anger. A minute after that, worry. She swooned and grabbed onto the tread to keep from falling.

The blue police opened fire on them, though their aim seemed distracted and half-hearted when Carter tried focusing. Some of the officers behind the barricade returned fire. At the sound of shooting, the rest of the defensive line got involved. The officers in blue grunted and staggered backward a step at a time as bullets hit their armor. Some shots penetrated, some glanced, but none of them showed any signs of surrender.

"Stop!" Althea screamed, but no one heard her inside the car.

She climbed into the driver's seat and swatted at the door, grabbing and twisting anything that looked like it might open it. A bullet clanked off the roof, but she didn't cringe. She pulled at another handle, giving up when she figured out it was only something to hold onto. A momentary pang of guilt hit her as she remembered commanding David to open the door so she could jump. For the life of her, she couldn't remember what button he'd pushed.

Carter waved her hands about. The officers on the perimeter slowed their return fire, but not all of them stopped. Two of the figures in blue armor fell over, dead. Althea screamed and kicked at the door.

"Let me out! Let me out!"

When her foot had no more success opening the door than her hands had, she sat still for a few seconds, trying to catch her breath. She tried to remember how people had opened car doors in the past. She'd been in these vehicles a few times now and never thought twice about it. Everyone always opened the door for her. Althea pictured the way Aaron moved when he got out. She knelt in the seat and stared at a silvery padded bar at the midway point. It looked like something to rest your arm on, but she gripped it in both hands and pulled upward.

The door hissed and rose on mechanized struts. She slithered under it and ran toward the line of armored vehicles.

"Stop! Stop! Stop!" she yelled.

"Kid," shouted a man to her left.

"Hey, someone grab that girl!" yelled a woman.

People ran at her from the large box. Telekinetic force encircled her, holding her back.

Althea grumbled as she floated; her sprint became legs pedaling in open air. She focused on the armored officers and released a pulse of radiant calm with as much energy as she could summon. Everyone stopped moving, gazing into space as if wondering what air was. The telekinetic grip released, letting her drop to her feet.

Arms rigid at her sides, Althea marched past the line of A3Vs into the open space between them and the seventeen remaining police officers in blue. Carter blinked at her. Althea felt a modest push as the woman tried to fight off her empathic calm, the only person she'd ever even noticed trying—aside from crazy people who had no emotions to touch. Althea didn't want the nice lady from Division 0 to get hurt; she squashed the effort.

A placid smile like a kindly knitting grandmother spread over Director Carter's face. "That adorable little girl is so strong. Everything's going to be all right."

Althea advanced at a slow, but deliberate walk. The long stretch of plastisteel tarmac chilled her feet, and the stink of burned ballistic propellant soured her nostrils. She focused on the police in front of her, their emotions swimming with fervor. The image of a dark-skinned woman with high cheekbones and long hair like thin golden ropes saturated their every thought. She was their queen, their goddess, their entire reason for existing.

For her, they would do anything—even die.

Althea's eyes glowed brighter as she pushed the invading emotions out of them. One by one, the police officers shook their heads and collapsed to their knees. She walked among their ranks, pausing when her foot landed in blood. The aura of empathic control emanating from the building fought against her with too much force to allow her to heal while maintaining her counter-empathy at the same time. They were hurt, yet none seemed in danger of imminent death.

"Hide behind the big monsters." Althea pointed to the rear at the trucks. "Go."

She left a trail of bloody footprints to the main starport steps. A pair of women in white armor rushed out and aimed rifles at her. Thralldom compelled them to kill anyone trying to enter, but minds burdened under the artificial adoration hesitated at the sight of an unarmed child. She gathered her energy around them, pushing against an opposing effort from inside the building. Tiny growls slipped past her teeth as she trembled from the exertion. Talis's influence receded like a wall of dense gelatin pushed back inch by inch.

The starport security officers reacted with dread; both women seemed aware they had been controlled. They held their rifles over their heads in a gesture of surrender and stumbled past her toward the police line. Althea ascended the steps at a burdened creep, advancing into the weight of oncoming telempathic power. Along the way, six more armed figures in white confronted her, one after the next. Each swooned when she freed their minds. By the time she reached the top, sweat covered her.

Althea crossed a wide flat space to the main terminal doors, which refused to open. She set her feet and strained, tugging on the handle. Clomping noises grew louder. Someone jogged up behind her. Althea whirled, back to the glass.

"One moment, mite," said Aaron.

She shivered, wondering why her radiant calm had not made Aaron 'have his reaction.' He'd warned her not to do it to him, and she'd forgotten to exclude him. Perhaps his mind accepted the emotion of calm. She removed him from the effect, and the glazed look left his eyes. He reached up and made a pushing gesture at the air. Cracks raced across the transparent material in the doors seconds before they flew off their bolts, sailing a good distance into the atrium and wedging like shuriken in the side of an information display.

Twenty holo-panels cut out in an instant as the silver wall behind them exploded in sparks.

She stepped around shattered bits of glass and debris from an earlier gunfight. A group of security officers came charging down the main concourse, their battle cries faded to confused grunts as her aura of calm took them. Like a magnet repelling an opposing polarity, Althea shoved Talis out of their minds, shielding them from the aura of devotion saturating the air.

A woman's grunt echoed in the dome far ahead, amid the nervous whimpers of people gathered in a crowd at the center of the hub. They sat amid boxes, some on bundles of clothes and bags, others flopped on the ground asleep. Families, where they had formed or remained, clustered together.

"What is happening?" asked a Middle Eastern sounding man. "Where is the ship?"

A slender woman with chocolate skin and long, dark blonde hair in narrow dreadlocks down to her waist stumbled out of a door labeled Security Operations. The office stood at the corner of where the wide store-lined concourse met the rounded central area. She had a hand to the side of her head and looked angry as well as exhausted. She, too, appeared to be sweating.

"Talis," whispered Aaron.

"Who the fuck is doing that? I didn't think there was anyone… No empath is stronger than me."

"You're wrong on that count." Aaron winked.

"The ship is not coming," said Althea, in a tone of eerie detachment.

About twenty young voices shouted "Althea" in almost unison as the crowd noticed her. A few added, "you're alive!" Their surge of relief and happiness gave her strength, and she crushed the dark woman's radiant emanation.

"What are you doing?" Talis glared at her.

The woman generated a wave of 'love me,' which rolled toward her with the weight of a burdensome mass. Althea curled her lip into a snarl, holding the image of Karina and Father close to her heart. *No.* She pushed the false love aside with a loud grunt and shoving hands. The dissipating energy knocked Talis back a step.

"Please stop this fighting and hurting. I don't want anyone else to die."

Talis scowled. "Well, aren't you a sweet little angel."

"You've got no bloody idea," said Aaron.

Althea gave her an earnest look. "Please stop."

"You…" A pulse of fear ran away from Talis when she noticed Aaron. "No. You won't stop me. I am too close. These are my people now. My ship."

"The ship is not coming," yelled Althea. "This woman is lying." She took a step closer to Talis, pointing. "You cannot make everyone love you. I will not let you. I will not let you hurt anyone else."

Fear wafted from the psionics gathered under the dome. Much to her surprise, it came strongest from the adults. Althea drew upon their need, she bowed her head for an instant before thrusting her chest forward. Energy ribbons burst from her back and flared out. Her wings lifted her from the ground, bathing the area in scintillating white light. She let her arms and legs hang limp. The placid, sad look on her face filled Talis with guilt. Archon's former 'army' stared in stunned silence for several seconds; a few gasped. One female voice giggled. Izzy peered out from the side of the group, laughing into the head of her giant rag doll.

"No more death," said Althea. "Please stop."

Talis's eyes vibrated with terror. Her mind shut down and her radiance collapsed.

A sense of every living person within the starport formed in Althea's thoughts. All at once, an emotional reverberation rang out as they broke free from the woman's control.

"No," wheezed Talis. "You can't... What are you?"

"You hit the nail on the head before, bitch," said Aaron. "Little angel. Day of Reckoning and all that."

"Don't kill her." Althea glanced over her shoulder at Aaron. "The people are free. Please tell the city police not to shoot anyone."

"No. I'm not staying here. I need to get off this planet. Archon had the right idea. I'm taking these people, and I'm leaving one way or the other. I'm tired of hiding. We should be the ones in control, but there are too many of them. Our only choice is to find a new home."

"Althea!" yelled Aaron.

She whirled to face Talis as a gun came out of the woman's pocket. The arm holding it twisted and whipped upward, flinging the weapon into the air. Althea gazed at the pistol spiraling higher, glinting as it spun, worried it may hurt someone by going off.

Pain.

Althea looked down. Talis's other hand pointed at her. A metal throwing knife stuck into her chest. Bright red blood stained outward over her immaculate white dress. Cold plastisteel inside her twitched with every breath; hot blood filled her air bag. Her wings vanished in the blink of an eye, and she collapsed in an ungainly heap on her knees, grasping the handle sticking out of her.

"No... no... no..." growled Aaron. He tore his E-90 from its holster and fired, but the blast of azure laser missed Talis's head by an inch as she dove to the right. "Shit!"

Before he could fire again, a fiftyish Middle Eastern man jumped up from the crowd and threw himself in the way, a zombie's emotionless expression on his face.

"*Die*," said Talis, a wash of gold light danced over her eyes, staring at Aaron.

Aaron grasped two fistfuls of his hair and swooned to his knees, screaming past clenched teeth. Anything more than fifteen feet away faded to black; his brain spun into a loop, about to detonate. Sweat ran in streams down the sides of his head as he fought to hold himself back. He lifted his gaze to meet Althea's, his eyes full of terror and apology. His shaking hand reached for her. One finger touched the blood dripping onto her thigh.

The psionics screamed and cried Althea's name. A few called Talis bad words. Several pulled guns on her. Orange light surrounded Althea as a circular curtain of flames swirled up, walling the child off from the rest of the world. Kate slid to a halt on her knees, holding on to Althea's shoulders.

"I got her, get the bitch," yelled Kate.

"No." Aaron roared. "I will... resist."

Random crashes and cracking noises erupted around her, fading into a muted haze as the world grew distant.

A woman's footsteps ran off. Althea stared at the knife in her chest, feeling woozy and detached from reality. Pain, far different from any she had ever felt pulsed within her. She clasped the end with both hands. Her own blood coated her fingers. She stared at her imminent death, concerned only with how Karina and Father would feel. Dizziness pulled her forward.

Did I save all the people? Will the ship still crash?

"Althea?" asked an unfamiliar female voice, melodic and comforting.

She couldn't find the strength to lift her head.

"Althea? It is not your time." A beautiful blonde woman with ice blue eyes and a dingy jumpsuit the color of sky crouched in front of her. Behind her, a swirling tunnel of silver beckoned. "Althea, look at me."

"Mother?" Althea wept. "Am I dead?"

"Only if you give up. Please don't give up."

"Are you dead?"

A cold hand squeezed her shoulder. "Karina is worried. She knows you are hurt."

Althea's head snapped up. Her mother had vanished. Alone with Kate, she sprawled on the floor, inside a swirling vortex of fire. Horrible pain lanced her chest. She wailed.

A loud *bang* preceded the thump of a body hitting the floor. The smell of ozone overpowered the stink of burning plastic for a few seconds.

Kate, shaking and crying, grasped the knife and put a hand on her shoulder. "I know you can make yourself not bleed."

She swooned.

"Thea!" shouted Kate. "Don't make me slap you."

She looked up, dizzy. "What?"

"Don't bleed."

Karina's voice, sobbing, came out of nowhere. Althea blinked and stared at the blade stuck in her chest. Her hands slipped away from it, too weak to move. She shut her eyes and concentrated on her body, commanding her blood-shape to stay inside her. Kate grunted. Althea gurgled at the feeling of the edge sliding out of her. She lost concentration from the pain, screaming.

"Damn that bitch," said Aaron. Smoke and the scent of burned cloth choked the air from his throat. He crawled closer, away from the roiling wall of flames and held on to Althea, steadying her. "Kate, try a stim."

Althea floated in a haze of pain and confusion, unaware of the source of several clicking sounds to her right. A point stabbed into her chest. She looked down as the shock of cold liquid forced into her flesh dulled the pain. The little device seemed to be attempting to fix her hurt, but the hurt was too much for it. Fatigue evaporated as a second injection sent a shiver down her back.

"They're not doing anything," said Kate, sounding on the verge of panic.

Aaron exhaled smoke.

Drool slipped from the corner of Althea's mouth; she stared at the wound, trying to comprehend what had happened. Mangling her wrist to get out of the handcuff had hurt more than this. She narrowed her eyes, focusing on a small slice in her heart-shape. At her urging, it closed, followed by her air bag. She willed the blood inside the air hollow back into the tubes in which it belonged. Hunger roared in her belly, and the pain subsided.

Althea took two rapid breaths and concentrated as hard as she could on wanting Karina to know she was okay.

"Althea?" Kate sounded close to sobbing.

When the woman shook her, she opened her eyes. Kate pulled her into a hug, rubbing her back and squeezing her with a mother's desperation. The protective cyclone of flames dissipated, leaving a ring of scorched tile around them. Althea rubbed the spot where the knife had been and cried on Kate's shoulder.

Aaron patted Althea on the head and lurched upright. He staggered down the concourse in a drunken lope, a small char mark at the center of his back. "Thanks for the zap." He shot a look at Anna. "Bitch almost got me. Shitballs, that hurt."

"She almost got all of us… if you'd gone off." Anna started after him, but stopped when Alastair forced his way out of the crowd and ran to her.

"Mum!" he yelled, bursting into tears. "Izzy said Dad's dead."

Anna looked at Althea with a 'help me' expression as the boy flung himself into her. She embraced him out of reflex and looked at the rest of the group. "I'm sorry… Alex—Alastair, he… yes, he died."

The boy wailed.

Kate pulled Althea standing and held her close as they moved up behind Anna. Division 0 tactical officers in gloss black armor tromped up the concourse.

"Listen to me. It's over." Anna approached the refugees, Alastair clinging to her side.

People muttered and looked around. Many conversations in multiple languages created a din louder than the approaching police officers. Althea looked among them, feeling a sense of relief from some. Others gazed around with fear. A handful got angry. An unusual sense of adoration emanated from among them, near the middle. Althea leaned around Kate to get a better look, squinting. A skinny blonde girl around Karina's age sprawled on the floor with both arms wrapped around a four-foot tall rag doll. She clutched it to her chest, gazing over its head at Althea with a wide smile. At the instant they made eye contact, the girl sprang to her feet. Pink sneakers emitted soft meows as she ran over and slid to a halt, kneeling in front of her, holding up the doll.

"I named her Althea," said the strange girl.

Althea blinked.

"I knew you would save us." The girl clamped her arms around the live Althea, sandwiching the stuffed version between them. "The shadow people told me what you did on the roof."

Althea sensed no malice on the young woman and tolerated the physical display of gratitude. Director Carter approached with a line of tactical officers behind her. Althea waved at her, grinning.

Anna mumbled something to the boy and shot a loud *crack* of lightning into the ceiling to silence the crowd. Worry and fear wafted from her as the police took up positions around the group of psionics.

Most of the Division 0 people, Director Carter included, gazed at the lightning bolt while radiating awe, fear, or confusion in varying degrees. Althea glanced at them, unsure why a small lightning bolt caused such reaction. She picked the strongest source of awe and peeked at the surface thoughts of a tall blonde woman who thought of Anna as an 'electrokinetic,' but couldn't understand how she'd generated a bolt that big without something called a conductor.

Carter halted at Anna's left. "Miss Morgan. Meredith and Lucy were rather talkative."

Relief. Anna took a deep breath. "Please tell me they're safe."

"Yes." Carter smiled. "They've been on the vid with their families. We're making arrangements to get them home."

Anna raised her voice, addressing the crowd. "What Archon has been telling us over the past several years has been somewhat exaggerated. These police here, in the UCF, are not our enemy. They will not send any of you back where you came from... unless you want to go. None of you will be harmed. Please, everyone, just stay calm."

Althea smiled.

Calm she could do.

70

SUCCUBUS

Aaron

The weight of a dying star balanced upon Aaron's skull. Talis's suggestion had almost succeeded in setting off his out-of-control brain. Perhaps he had been able to hold it back long enough for Anna to shock him due to the vagary of it. A simple command to 'die' seldom did anything more than create confusion—too many variables. Talis's power was such that his brain started to work out the most efficient way to go about accomplishing death. The ambiguity had allowed him to hold the eruption at bay, long enough for Anna to knock him senseless with a shock to the back. Maybe Talis knew he would resist an imprecise compulsion like that, or perhaps she didn't care if he 'went off,' and only wanted to buy herself time to run.

His head throbbing, his shoulder burning, Aaron sprinted after the bitch down a long hallway full of offshoots to various terminal gates. She took the first right, setting off a myriad of alarms as she ducked through an abandoned security station into an elevated concourse leading to interplanetary departures. Curved transparent windows lined both sides, making him feel like a hamster running along tubes in a fancy cage. Metal-faced benches offered spots for tourists to sit and watch the shuttles as they jockeyed around the tarmac, took off, or landed.

RedLink occupied a large section of the terminal, as they handled sixty percent of all flights ferrying people back and forth to Mars. A few side passages branched off to various lunar commuter shuttles. Seven-foot tall holographic posters advertised the joy of colony life, pitching it as 'the new wild west.' Wholesome families in space suits posed in front of silvery drop-box buildings with a neat garden and perfect sunset in the background.

Talis, looking back over her shoulder at Aaron, ran headlong into a pair of Division 6 assault officers emerging from a commuter terminal. They grabbed her by the arms and hauled her off her feet.

"Calm down, Miss. You're safe."

"No, you twats!" yelled Aaron. "She's the suspect."

Full-face helmets covered in shiny green metallic pivoted to face him. Once they recognized his uniform, their stance changed. Rather than support a terrified woman, they contained a dangerous suspect.

Too late.

"Help, he's trying to kill me!" wailed Talis, sounding like a teen girl. *"Kill him."*

The two men staggered, dizzy for a second. She slipped out of their grasp and hid behind them, pointing at Aaron. "Kill him. Please, kill him before he can hurt me."

The men raised their weapons.

"Oh, bollocks," muttered Aaron as he skidded to a halt. "Sorry, boys."

He seized the pair in a telekinetic grip. A spray of blue muzzle flash erupted from their rifles as he spun them each to the side. The curved glass along the hallway shattered in a creeping line for a few seconds before the men ceased shooting, grunting as they strained to correct their aim. Aaron swung his hands apart, and the assault officers flew away from each other, gliding out the broken windows. Seconds later, they hit the ground one story below.

Talis's eyes bugged out of her head.

He smiled. "Jes' you an' me now, luv. I've a message from Allie."

She whipped around and ran, but got only two steps before he swept her into the air and slammed her flat on her chest, making her bark and wheeze. Aaron drilled her into the ceiling and let her fall again. She grabbed her knee and screamed, rolling onto her back. Aaron brushed his arm to the side, sending her skidding into the wall. Six times, he threw her careening back and forth like a pinball between the poster stands and the walls until she stopped moving with any semblance of coordination.

Her body slid to a halt at his feet; one blackened eye puffed closed. Blood seeped out of her nose and mouth, as well as from an uncountable number of small cuts where she'd slid over broken glass.

Her open eye, unfocused, gazed right past him.

Aaron squatted over her. The sight of the broken woman almost made him feel guilty, but knowing who she was—and what she had done to Allison, to him, to Althea, and to Anna—let him hold his conscience at bay.

"So, how'd it work?" asked Aaron, forcing his telepathic feelers into her mind.

Talis coughed.

"You and Archon. Did he really rewrite you into a groveling wretch, or does that Oscar go to you?"

He dove into her memories, back to the starship plant, watching the moment when Aaron had almost cornered her. Archon, tired of Aaron's traipsing about and delaying everything, had shown up to get rid of her for him. They'd stumbled across each other in a dank concrete tunnel, stained green from whatever chemicals had been used to treat starship engine parts. As soon as he realized she was Awakened, his attitude changed. Talis had been thrilled to hear of his plan to leave Earth. He did not need to influence her. Of all the Awakened he had ever encountered, Talis had been the most eager and the most alike in mindset. Leave Earth—something she'd been dreaming about for years. Like him, she felt herself elevated above the 'mundanes.' They'd both been wrong. Archon had not been under her control as Anna feared, and contrary to Aaron's opinion, she had been able to act afraid of him.

"You lying bitch," Aaron slapped her, knocking blood from her teeth. "You weren't sorry. You were just trying to save your own ass."

She gurgled. "She wasn't the first cop I had to put down. If it makes you feel any better, I really didn't know she was your wife."

Aaron grabbed two fistfuls of her shirt, shaking her. "Would it have mattered if you did?" He flung her to the floor. "You tried to kill Althea." He slapped her again, knocking her face the other way. "What the fuck is wrong with you? She's an innocent child!"

"She's stronger than me." Talis coughed up blood. "I couldn't let her make everyone hate me."

"You twisted bitch." Aaron lifted his E-90 out of its holster. "None of these people ever liked you to begin with. She only reminded them of who they were before you got them all killed. Archon's dead! The ship is probably going to smash into the city and kill us all. Even if it doesn't, you're not going anywhere."

Talis shivered, grunting under the telekinetic force holding her to the floor. "W-what are you going to do?"

Aaron glanced at the silver laser pistol. "This is the gun you forced me to murder my wife with." He pointed it at her face. "I think it's only fitting to—"

Something touched his arm.

He looked down at the crook of his elbow, at a child's blood-caked fingernails. Past his sleeve hovered a somber face with two glowing blue eyes. Althea shook her head at him. Blood stained the front of her dress, but the bit of skin visible in the slit fabric looked whole.

Aaron sighed, glared at Talis, and raised his hand. "...beat you senseless with it."

Althea frowned.

Unbelievable. This kid isn't fecking human. He paused. *Well, mostly.*

He peeled Talis off the ground, forcing her to sit up and look at Althea.

"Do you understand this? Even after you damn near killed her, she doesn't want you to die." Aaron smirked at the ceiling and mumbled, "Of course, she didn't want Archon to die, either."

"It is wrong to kill," whispered Althea before taking a step closer to Talis. "She is hurt."

Aaron nibbled on his lip. "Sorry, kid. Even if we bring her in alive, she's legally responsible for Allison's death. They're going to execute her anyway."

Talis jumped up and grabbed his wrist, pushing the E-90 to the side. Aaron fired into the ground, missing her head by inches.

"Stop!" screamed Althea.

Growling, Talis kicked at his legs, her eyes wild with fear. A telekinetic blanket of force pinned her flat. Aaron lowered the gun at her. The emotion in her eyes in the seconds before he fired reminded him only a little of his wife. Fear looked the same, but anger lit it from behind—not love.

"No!" yelled Althea, grabbing his arm.

In the second of hesitation, Talis locked eyes with him. Before she could open her mouth to give him a fatal command, he screamed and shoved her hard with telekinesis. Talis rocketed off like a human torpedo, tearing carpet from the plastisteel floor. Forty feet away, she smashed the base of a plastic monolith covered in advertising holograms, setting off a geyser of sparks. Barely conscious, Talis moaned.

"Why?" yelled Althea, sounding on the verge of tears.

Boots squeaked up behind him.

Althea hung all her weight on Aaron's arm. "Please, don't kill her."

"They're going to do it anyway." Aaron squinted. "Like a rabid dog. Althea, she killed my wife. She's killed police officers. She's killed all the people that died here today." Another look at the child's tearful expression did it for him. "Fine. Fine. I can't do it with you giving me that face. Cripes you're worse than a dog in a bedroom."

The girl looked confused.

"I can," said Kate, a second before a fireball streaked over Aaron's head and ignited Talis's chest.

The pain knocked the woman out of her stupor and she wailed, fingers pulling bloody shirt fabric and skin away from exposed muscles.

"Kate!" shrieked Althea through sobs. "Stop! No more killing!"

"Althea. That bitch tried to k—" Kate shivered, crying. "Althea. She tried to k-kill you."

The fire already burning on Talis's chest flared. The woman yowled. A look of sudden, placid calm overtook Kate and she stared into space.

Althea ran to Talis, sliding to a stop on her knees and grabbing the woman's hand. Aaron trudged over, looking away from the awful vision of burning flesh re-growing. The child whimpered and grunted with effort, as if trying to lift something too heavy for her. Aaron pointed the E-90 at Talis's head.

"I really ought to put her out of our misery." If not for feeling dodgy about firing a laser into her brain while Althea worked on her, he would have fired.

Kate continued to gaze into nowhere.

"Perhaps we may be of assistance," said a male voice.

Two men in black raincoats and sunglasses approached, walking in tandem. Neither had surface thoughts Aaron could find, and their footsteps made no sound.

"Agent Jones," said the man on the left, holding up a C-Branch badge.

"Agent Foster," said the other, flashing a similar ID.

Aaron raised an eyebrow. "Are you from the generic government agent department?"

"This suspect represents interests of national security. We are exercising jurisdiction."

Agent Foster pulled a metal ring out of his coat.

Kate hissed, scowling at them.

"Seeing as how Division 0 will not extend their usual offer in this case," said Agent Foster, "we are taking her into custody."

Talis moaned.

Aaron framed her face with the E-90's glowing blue ring-dot sight. "Well, bitch. Your choice. You fancy life in a box or an easy out?"

71

I AM THE MACHINE

Mamoru

A vortex of grey energy yawned above, spiraling up toward endless black. Mamoru held tight to Aurora's hand as she glided higher and higher. An ancient military airplane passed below, a pilot too wounded to be alive looked up at them with confusion in his eyes. Soon after, fragments of a Mars shuttle, a hundred-year-old design, tumbled among the clouds around them. Six screaming people in flight suits reached out to them, begging for help.

"Pay them no attention," said Aurora. "They have been dead for a hundred and thirty years or so. Test pilots. Their ship exploded during re-entry."

"This is awful," said Mamoru. "Is their eternity to fall and never die?"

"They're already dead."

Mamoru grumbled. She pulled him upward, darting left and straight. The sky darkened from blue to indigo and eventual black. Far ahead, the CSS Angel appeared as a sliver of white against the infinite darkness, a brightening nimbus of fire peeling from the front. They picked up speed; the silhouette of the ship expanded fast enough to make him cry out and raise his free arm to shield his face. A second later, hallways and rooms blurred by in an impossible diagonal path. They traversed decks and rooms in defiance of walls, the blare of warning klaxons flooding every passageway.

Aurora leveled off in a wide corridor and glided many times faster than a human could run down its length to a thick, armored door. They passed through, the plastisteel having no more solidity than a standing wall of medical tank gel.

Flashing lights saturated the bridge with red. Alarms blared and buzzed. Mamoru relaxed his pointless gesture of defense. The odd sepia-tone faded along with a rush of freezing air over his naked body. Aurora patted him on the ass. He smirked and walked out of her embrace to the nearest of the six pilot's consoles.

"Your show now, mate." She sashayed up a small stepped dais and flopped in the captain's chair, winking at him as she crossed her legs. "I'll watch from up here so I can enjoy the view."

His sense of duty allowed him to disregard the alluring temptress behind him and rest his hands on the smooth, glass control surface. The frigid faux leather on the seat stole the breath from his lungs when he fell into it. Muscles in his lower back rippled into paralysis. He glanced over his shoulder at Aurora, sitting as if in a warm and cozy chair.

"Oh, please stand… I can't see your ass anymore."

What is wrong with that woman?

Mamoru closed his eyes and focused. The whoosh of white flames filled his ears as his power connected his mind to the machine. Within seconds, the chaos and cold of the bridge faded from his awareness, as did the chill of the seat. He extended his consciousness beyond the ship's computer network, embodying the entirety of the vessel. Burning heat spread over his face and chest, his link with the ship sharing the sensation. Thousands of sensors and cameras became his eyes, but they offered a view only of re-entry glow. He partitioned off a section of his mind, maintaining a cyberspace link to the control system, which took the form of a dark chamber. Walls of infinite black held glowing green grid lines. Proximity warnings, heat warnings, abandon ship notifications, and other useless streams of information flashed at him out of the shadows.

A stick figure drawn in silver walked out of nowhere. Metal feet clicked like high heels on hard tiles as it paced back and forth.

"I am grateful you have changed your mind, human." The genderless voice held no trace of emotion beyond an electric undertone.

Mamoru blinked. Somewhere on the outer hull, lights turned off and on. "You jettisoned yourself when you realized the ship would crash. How are you still here?"

"I am not sentient," said the AI. "I am the emergency backup interface system. My functions consist of voice-activated ship control and access to basic systems. I am unfamiliar with your mechanism of connection and do not have the necessary subroutines to interact with you in modes other than via voice command."

With his consciousness inhabiting the ship, the pull of gravity twisted and bent him. A feeling as if two enormous sumo wrestlers used him as a rope in a tug of war made him cringe and grunt. At any second, his spine threatened to crack in half. He focused on the need to fly, to climb, to get away. The roar of thrusters shook the hull.

"Disable the"—Mamoru grunted—"autopilot."

"The automatic navigation system has been severed from the control interface. I am unable to process your request."

Mamoru felt around inside his head, his sentience transplanted into the ship. When he found the navigation computer, he willed it dark, allowing him to start pulling out of the dive.

The focus of heat moved from his face, distributing evenly over his entire front. He yelled despite gritted teeth, fighting the instinctual urge to let his awareness snap back into his body to get away from the burn.

I deserve this.

Agony as though he'd laid face down naked upon a hibachi table seared his flesh. The touch of re-entry upon the hull entered his mind. Every so often, a painful jab in the head or back announced the impact of space junk. The ship clunked and shuddered as if caught in a hailstorm.

"I do appreciate, inasmuch as I am capable of, that you returned to plot a course correction." The stickman ceased pacing, pointing at holo-panel after holo-panel full of mathematical calculations and graphs. "My calculations show no crew could possibly coordinate the firing of the maneuvering thrusters and main engines with sufficient precision in sufficient time to avoid impact with the surface. You may be able to avoid striking the city and put down in the ocean."

Gravity's effect increased. Mamoru suppressed the urge to scream as the ship bucked and twisted. He focused on his urge to escape the crushing grip of the Earth, ignoring the pain. The systems of the CSS Angel had become him; all the thrusters, terminals, lights, and even toilets had linked to his mind. Every inch of the ship obeyed as if part of his body.

"I am not a crew."

His muscles clenched. He roared, forcing himself past the agony of melting skin, welcoming the pain as just punishment for what he had done. Energy surged at his feet. The ship shuddered as the main engines fired up, joining a symphony of a thousand control thrusters reorienting at once.

The stick-man shook its head. "Your attempts are commendable, but even the most experienced crew would be unable to—"

"I am not... a crew."

The CSS Angel rocked with his desire to change course. Aurora flew across the bridge, thrown from her seat by the maneuver, but she vanished in a silvery cloud of fog before crashing into the giant viewscreen. Mamoru shuddered, growling past clenched teeth from the exertion.

"I am… the machine."

72

THE SKY BURNS

Kate

The neural-stunner collar captured Kate's attention from the moment it left Agent Foster's coat. He shifted his gaze sideways at her with a tiny hint of a smile on his lips. Agent Jones stared at Talis, seeming almost curious. *Plastic melts.* Kate clenched and released her fists, straining to keep herself calm. They couldn't touch her now. She wondered if Carter had been the source of the arrangement that kept her safe.

No, I doubt it. It had to be Burckhardt.

"Miss it?" asked Agent Foster, holding up the collar. "I believe you two have already been acquainted."

"That's the same fucking one you bastards put on me?" She covered her neck with a hand.

"We do not have many of them," said Agent Jones. "If you ever get tired of small time work, we'd love to have you back."

"I'm not that desperate for a new necklace, no matter how much it cost." Images flashed across her mind like a slide show, complete with the scent of burned skin and pain as if a dozen red-hot needles pierced her skull. The floor of a white room rushed up to meet her face, a flash, then a curtain of lightning rose up to devour Archon's annoyed sneer. An overwhelming feeling of helplessness came on as she remembered staring down the barrel of a handgun with two bullets left, the cold metal seeming to constrict around her neck. "Those things are beyond cruel. I'd die first."

"We find them rather humane," said Agent Jones. "Your division's inhibitors are cruel."

Agent Foster turned the collar over in his hand, letting the light play off it. "The containment rings are only necessary when there is a lack of trust."

"Oh, there's a lack of trust." Kate took a step back. "A giant fucking lack of trust."

"Fascinating," said Agent Jones. "The suspect's metabolic processes are accelerated well beyond a thousand times normal. Her cells are regenerating as fast as they burn."

"We will need to interview the child as well," said Jones.

"We only brought one restraint," said Foster.

Kate snarled, her fear destroyed by anger. *Get away from my daughter!* The mental speed bump of thinking of Althea in that way tripped her up for a second. She blinked at the windows, pondering the permanent telempathic imprint left on her brain. One look at Althea kneeling with her defenseless back to the two agents pulled the rug out from under her reason and triggered another wave of worry and anger.

"Don't you dare fucking touch her." She made fire in her hands. "You go anywhere near her with one of those *things*, and I'll show you what a hot piece of ass your scientists really made."

"You are active duty Division 0. Attacking us would invalidate certain agreements," said Agent Jones.

"Fuck your agreements. That's my dau—" Kate clenched her jaw. "She's an innocent."

"Sorry boys," said Aaron. "Althea is a sworn officer too." He held up his NetMini, showing them something. "Tech Officer Althea Prophet, Division 0 admin section. Strictly by the books, as a WO1, she presently outranks Kate."

"The girl is a minor," said Agent Foster.

"Exactly why you motherfuckers aren't going anywhere near her." Kate raised a hand, but Aaron caught her wrist.

"Admin section is considered rear echelon, mates," said Aaron with a grin. "She's a military cadet attending school if you want to split hairs. Covered. Hands bloody off. Besides… she'd be worthless to you anyway. The girl's far too innocent and pure to associate with the likes of you lot. The most of a 'military application' you'd get out of her is getting troops back on their feet."

The fire still burning on Talis's chest glimmered in her mind.

"Aaron," wheezed Talis, shuddering. "Do it."

Aaron lifted his E-90 and aimed, pursing his lips.

Both C-Branch synthetics raised eyebrows and tilted their head at the same time, in the same way.

"Naw." Aaron lowered his arm. "I think you'll have a much more enjoyable time with your new friends. Besides, my wife was a soft touch like the kid. Allie wouldn't want me to kill you."

Kate commanded the fire out. Regenerating skin devoured the embers on the woman's chest, though her shredded sweater and executive coat continued to emit smoke.

Agent Foster's body smeared into a blur of color. He moved with such speed he appeared to exist in two places at once, connected by a stretched image. The latent ghost vanished as he clipped the neural-stunner around Talis's neck. Kate twitched at the sound of it locking. Since the woman no longer burned, Althea forced her body whole in a matter of a minute. Both C-Branch synthetics appeared entranced at the sight of burns closing, glass fragments rising out of her flesh and falling aside, and her puffy, black eye receding to normal.

The child stood, jumping with a high-pitched squeal as she noticed the two men behind her. Her fear sparked an instinctive parental reaction in Kate. She grabbed Althea by the shoulders and pulled her away, glaring at the men.

"They're dead," whispered Althea, clinging to her side.

Kate put an arm around her, holding her tight. "They're not dead, but stay away from them."

"Are they going to be cruel to her?" Althea asked, trembling. "What are they? They're not real. They don't have souls."

"Oh," said Aaron. "They're *bureaucrats*. Here and I thought they were C-Branch synthetics."

Both agents frowned.

"We may be synthetic, Lieutenant Pryce, but we do have a fully-functional emotion-response system."

"You hide it well." He smiled.

"Depends on your definition of cruel," mumbled Kate.

"You know you'll never be able to control her," said Aaron. "She's a suggestive and a telempath more powerful than anything we've yet documented. The instant she gets that brain zapper off her neck, she's going to leave."

A surge of pride welled up within Kate at the idea that Althea had stronger telepathy than Talis, like her daughter had won a trophy at school. She allowed a smile, but didn't dare say anything aloud near the synthetics.

"If she manages to escape, and your people find her first,"—Agent Jones looked at Talis, his voice flat and emotionless—"feel free to execute her for the murder of eleven police personnel, thirteen civilians, and a dog. It is in her best interest to work with us."

Agent Foster smiled. "We've been tracking her for a while."

"A dog? You killed a dog?" asked Aaron, raising his weapon. "I take it back. You don't deserve jail."

Talis didn't flinch.

Agent Jones blurred in front of Aaron, blocking his shot.

"Easy." Aaron jumped back. "Thought you blokes said you have a sense of humor."

Both agents frowned at the same time, in the same way. Kate exchanged a look with Talis, almost feeling sorry for her.

Almost.

🪔 🌿 🏛 ◊ ☿

KATE HELD ALTHEA'S HAND AS THEY WALKED OUT THE FRONT DOORS OF Edmonson Memorial Starport. The psionic refugees clustered around a number of MedVans behind the line of A3Vs, matched two to one by men and women in Division 0 uniforms, some armored, some in the standard blacks. Officers appeared to be answering questions as well as keeping them corralled in one place, though none appeared to be under arrest. Medtechs made their way among Archon's former followers. Anna sat on the side of the command trailer ramp, looking terrified whenever anyone in a uniform walked toward her. A twelve-ish looking boy with blond hair sat beside her, leaning against her. Though he cried in silence, his expression appeared relieved. When Kate and Althea reached the bottom of the starport steps, the strange teenager with the giant rag doll stood up and waved (also making the doll wave) at Althea with a huge smile.

Boom.

Thunder rolled overhead. Everyone jumped and looked up at a comet of fire streaking across the sky, a great burning disc ten times the size of the mid-day sun.

The world turned orange.

The psionic children, most of the adults, and some of the police officers, screamed. The willowy blonde teen broke away from her escort and ran over, emitting a high-pitched wail. She fell to her knees in front of Althea and hugged her giant rag doll.

"Please save us!" cried Izzy, tucking her doll behind her to protect it. "Please stop the fire."

A tingle of presence danced atop Kate's consciousness. She looked at the conflagration with widening eyes, sensing the re-entry burn. Aaron glanced at her with a mischievous squint. Kate felt him peek at her surface thoughts but didn't care. He squatted out of sight and murmured.

"What?" whispered Althea.

The flaming sky grew closer, hotter, more alive—falling right at them.

"Mommy!" yelled Althea, flinging herself against Kate. "Don't let us die!"

Desperation welled from deep within. She *had* to protect her daughter.

The world ceased to exist, save for the roiling pyroclastic horror plummeting out of the sky. Her mind wrapped itself around the combustion and crushed. Harder and harder she concentrated, pushing her arms up as if the inferno was a physical object she could hold back. Althea let out another shrill yelp, which caused Kate to strain with as much force as her body could tolerate. Heat built and rolled around her; for a veritable eternity, she struggled to focus her power into the sky. Eventually, the beating heart within the fire miles away succumbed to her influence and the burning overhead grew faint.

Cold wind embraced her.

"Bloody hell, it worked," said Aaron.

The burn diminished to a point she could no longer feel anything from it. Kate opened her eyes. A far smaller flaming line traveled sideways across the deep, blue sky. What had once been a devouring portal into Hell had shrunk to the trail of a firework. Sunlight glinted from metal as the recognizable form of a starship turned, heading west. She watched it veer off, descending like a glimmering star toward the sea. Seconds before the faltering ember touched the horizon, a brilliant wave of white light in three expanding rings erupted from the dark spot at the center of the orange glow. Kate cringed from the intensity.

When she looked again, no trace of the ship remained. Fourteen seconds later, the roar of a great explosion silenced everyone in the area.

"Never got to replace that special uniform?" asked Aaron.

Kate kept staring at the distant ocean. "I'm naked again, aren't I?"

"Yes," said Althea. "You lit on fire. Your clothes turned to ash."

"That was cruel, Aaron. Telling her to say that." Kate looked down at Althea. "Do you really think of me as your mother?"

He cringed, grinning. "Aww, heard that, did ya?"

"Not exactly… she said 'what,' and then…"

"Worked, didn't it?" Aaron smiled. "Figured you could use the motivational boost."

Althea shot a guilty look at the ground. "I hope my mother isn't mad at me." She grimaced. "Is that a lie?"

"I don't think so." Kate patted her on the head. "I'm sure she'd understand. She wouldn't want you to die either, and I want to protect you."

"Sorry." Althea offered an earnest wide-eyed look. "I didn't want you to hurt me."

"I" —Kate sighed—"It's okay. I kind of like it. Besides, it helps keep *him* out of my head." *I need something to live for, don't I?*

"If you like, you can be my mother, but Father wants to join with Alejandra." Althea smiled.

Arms slipped around Kate from behind, wrapping her in a blanket. She recognized David by his scent before he said a word. "You're out of uniform, Officer."

Kate twisted around to face him, her arms trapped under the blanket against her chest, and kissed him. She pulled back, looked into his perfect, chocolate eyes, and kissed him again. A few nearby people in uniform clapped.

"Are you gonna wife her now?" asked Althea.

Kate blushed. "David… I need you. I want to spend the rest of my life with you." She choked up. "I can't wait another minute." She leaned up to whisper. "Let's do it right here."

His eyes flared open with a look of surprise and embarrassment. His hand on the back of her head pulled her close to his heart. "You want it to be special. Two hundred witnesses isn't very special."

"It'd be pretty special for them," muttered Aaron.

"I want them to know how I feel. I want you, David."

She tried to pull the blanket open, but he held it closed. When she looked in his eyes, he had the same expression of concern he had when she saw him standing in the breach of the wall, two seconds after she wanted to take her own life. If not for him, she'd have done it. She forced one hand up out of the gap in the fabric by her neck and held onto his shoulder. Tears came unbidden.

"Kate…" He swayed side to side in a gentle rocking motion.

"I don't deserve all this. What you did for me, what Althea did… I'm just a monster that should've been flushed down the toilet when I was little. The scientists were right. All I'm good for is killing. Why did you spare me?"

Sorrow and despair faded, as if someone had freed her shoulders from the weight of damp, woolen cloak.

"You're making me feel better." She tried to sniffle, but found herself laughing.

"Enough sadness. You might've just saved us all. Kate, you are a beautiful person inside and out. I knew from the moment we first met, you did not deserve all the pain you carried in your heart."

"Stay with me," said Kate. "I'll ask Captain Buckley to let me ride with you."

Aaron cleared his throat and looked down. "I'd rather advise against that."

Kate whirled to make a sarcastic remark, but the somber expression on his face stole her humor. She looked back to David and rested her head on his shoulder. With the light show in the sky at an end, Division 0 officers and medtechs resumed attending to the refugees as well as wounded starport security and police. Aaron went over to take a seat by Anna, who seemed reassured by his presence, though she still jumped whenever a cop got too close. Althea gave Kate a big smile before taking Izzy's hand and walking with her over to Archon's former army. The kids crowded around her, thrilled to see her alive.

David patted her on the back. "Look up."

She followed his gaze to the sky, where a brief rising streak of white sparkled like a star before going out.

"Make a wish."

Kate kissed the side of his neck, the corner of his jaw, and his earlobe before whispering.

"I already did."

73

HOME

EPILOGUE: PROPHET OF THE BADLANDS

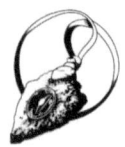

Althea

Acurtain of dark green leaves wavered in front of Althea's face, painting her with patches of sunlight in a shifting camouflage pattern. She crouched in the shade by the wall of the Water Man's metal mushroom house. Her fingers and toes sank into the moist dirt as she crawled along, slow and quiet, spying on the people working the field. Althea crept to a darker spot where the rounded structure met the start of the wall that wrapped around the farm, hiding behind bushes.

As soon as she crouched, a little boy squealed and pointed at her. "Found you!"

Trapped against the plump building and the wall, she raised her arms and legs, squealing into giggles as he jumped on her.

The boy yelled, "You're it!"

She crawled out of her hiding place, still laughing, and squatted in the field with her hands over her glowing blue eyes. They made her easy to find, but they also gave her an advantage. Other kids couldn't hide in the dark because she could see them with ease. She had never known 'dark' as anything other than the absence of color. Out of fairness, she'd explained that to them, but still, quite a few attempted to hide in darkness alone.

"One... two..."

The boy ran off, shouting at the top of his lungs, "Althea's it!"

Althea counted up in a slow march to twenty before she stood and yelled, "I'm hunting!"

She waved to Karina as she ran across the farm field and headed out into Querq. The kids had agreed on sticking to an area within one block of the farm for the game. Since the farm spanned six blocks wide, even that restriction left her roaming a large portion of Querq. A few minutes of quick exploring yielded no results, so she circled back to her starting point. Walking at a creep, she searched high and low, peering into every black and white space where someone might be hiding.

Sarah, the five-year-old daughter of Carlos, the mechanic, hid under a car that had crashed into the side of a building long before Querq had been resettled. Althea knew the girl would wail and scream, thoroughly miserable if she were to be caught. She acted as if she couldn't see her and walked right by. The giddiness emanating from the hiding place made her smile. Althea couldn't care less about winning. Everyone having fun made her happy.

A rattle up ahead brought a grin. Althea darted into an alley between two buildings, catching Kim trying to get her hands on a dangling fire escape ladder on the back of an old red brick hotel. The former city girl's dress resembled Althea's, only peach instead of white. She jumped up to grab the bottom rung and grunted, but lacked the arm strength to pull herself up. Althea stalked up on her like a cat, but an abandoned glass bottle skittering away from her foot ruined her stealth.

Kim dropped to her feet, let out a cry of startlement, and ran. Althea sprinted after her, overtaking her before the end of the alley. She wrapped her arms around the taller girl from behind, held on until she stopped running, and lifted her off the ground.

"Ugh." Kim gurgled. "Ow."

"Gotcha!" chirped Althea. "You're it."

Kim rubbed her ribs once Althea put her down. "Ow. Your arms are so boney. How the heck are you so strong?"

Althea shrugged. "You're skinny too."

Parents' voices filled the air, calling after the little ones they'd been playing hide and seek with. A dozen children appeared out of trash cans, old tires, and windows. One boy shimmied down a rain gutter from the roof of a four-story building.

"Fernando!" yelled Althea. "You're not supposed to go up there. It's dangerous."

"Sorry!" he yelled, not slowing down.

"Guess the game's over." Kim shrugged.

They walked together to the porch of an old hotel (that had been converted to individual dwellings) and sat on the steps.

Kim brushed dirt off her bare feet and smirked at her dress. "Do they have any real clothes here? I'm *so* done with the peasant girl thing. Why'd Aurora make me leave all my stuff behind, even clothes?"

"What's a peasant?" asked Althea.

"Us," said Kim. Her mood darkened and she scowled off to the side. "Anyone who isn't a f—damn senator."

Althea held her hand. "Don't have the sad. Are you happy here? We won't tell the city police."

"Oh, yeah, 'cause no one will notice I'm the only other white girl in this whole place. One of those Zeroes looks at me, they'll know I'm a telepath."

Althea smiled. "They will let you stay here if you want. Paolo and Maria are happy to share family."

"Yeah… I guess it's kind of like having parents that don't suck. They're *way* cooler than my birth parents." Kim leaned forward, hands together on her knees. Unkempt raven hair hung down to her shins. "It's better than being in 'the system.' You were right, Archon was a total whack-job."

Althea frowned into her lap. After a few seconds, she gave up trying to figure out what that meant. *I couldn't save him.*

"I can't believe they're gonna make me work a job. I'm only fourteen."

"Everyone's gotta help." Althea smiled.

"Easy for you to say, you're ten. You still got four years before they make you work."

"I'm eleven. Almost twelve."

"Bullshit," said Kim.

"Where?" Althea looked around at the road and checked her soles.

Kim laughed. "Maybe I should go back to the city. Get a real education, learn engineering or software development or something and spend the rest of my life wage-slaving until I die."

Althea gasped. "No! Slavery is bad!"

"You are ridiculous." Kim pulled her into a one-armed hug. "Well if I stay here, I'll need some tech… and some damn shoes. Think the cops will get me some real e-learns?"

"What is eee learn?" Althea blinked.

"It's like school, but you do it by yourself."

"Altheeeeeaaaa." Karina's voice echoed.

She looked up at the darkening sky. "Time to go home."

"Yeah," said Kim, standing. "Feels kinda weird to have one."

"Nice," said Althea.

Kim grinned. "Yeah. It feels nice."

♌ ♈ ☗ ☽ ♋

ALTHEA SAT STOMACH DEEP IN HOT BATHWATER, A RING OF SUDS TICKLING AT the base of her ribs. Karina, sitting outside the tub behind her, poured soap over her head and worked it into a lather. Her sister ran her fingers over and over through her hair. Althea drew her heels close, knees poking out of the surface as she hugged them to her chest. Karina mumbled a song she'd forgotten the words to, something her mother had sung to her as a little girl. She clung to a vague sense of melody, but the words didn't matter. Althea basked in her sister's love.

She felt guilty over leaving for a few days, and worse at the reaction Karina had to the bloody slash on her dress when she returned. Althea didn't lie, and told her everything about what happened. Her sister had missed two days of farm work after that, refusing to let go of her. Althea closed her eyes as water poured over her head. Karina dipped the pot in the bathwater and repeated the rinse. She added more soap for another round. Althea's guilt increased; Karina still acted clingy.

Althea thought of Archon laying on the ground in the hangar. She shivered and let off a sniffle.

"What's wrong?" Karina wrapped soapy arms around her, pulling her against the back of the tub into a hug. "Thea? You're crying."

She reached up and grasped the arm over her chest with both hands. "I have the sad 'cause I am home an' I have you and Father, but many people still have the suffering."

Karina kissed her atop the head, holding her tight. "You can only do so much, Thea. Take comfort in the joy you bring to others. There will always be people we cannot help. That is the way of the world. You help everyone you can. That's all anyone can ask of you. Do what you can and don't fret over things you can't help. Now, let me finish washing your hair."

Althea smiled and wiped her tears, sitting up and stretching her legs under the water. Karina washing her hair reminded her of when they had first met. It would forever be a symbol of a bond stronger than any chain or cage.

THE NEXT DAY, A WARM, DRY BREEZE NUDGED A FLOCK OF TUMBLEWEEDS DOWN the street. Althea walked backward across her porch, sweeping. She paused at a faint rumble in the ground. Sand particles on the boards vibrated into a beige blur around her feet. A tickle of fear brushed down her back. The noise grew louder, changing from an indistinct tremor in the earth to a loud, mechanical roar.

She looked up and to the left. A dusty, black truck rounded the corner four blocks down, with tires taller than her. Four dozen goats scurried out of its path, screaming and bleating. When the driver leaned on the horn, one decided to stand defiant. A little itch in the back of her mind said they'd kidnap her if she didn't run and hide under the sink. Her knuckles whitened on the broom handle, a tremble rocked her body, but she held her ground—like that goat.

I'm not afraid of you. This is my home.

Rachel stood up in the truck bed and threw something to the road, which attracted the animal out of their path. When the truck passed in front of her, she waved at Althea. Beard and Darren raised their hands in greeting from the cab. Dean's absence didn't surprise her.

Her fear vanished. Althea waved back.

Karina rushed out of the house and up behind her, grasping her shoulders. "Thea, are you okay?"

The truck rumbled on by, lofting a rolling dust cloud in its wake. Den emerged from the haze, jogging across the street to the porch steps. His rifle hung on a strap over his back, and he carried a metal case with food packed for a short trip. She remembered he'd wanted her to slip away to have lunch by the stream that afternoon.

Althea grinned at him and leaned her head back to aim her smile at Karina. "Yes. I'm okay."

OL' JACK

EPILOGUE: ARCHON'S QUEEN

Anna

Rain fell in steady sheets around Coventry Tower, saturating the coal-black soil into a field of mud. Anna stared at herself in the puddle around her boots, mesmerized by the dark glow emanating from reflected clouds. A fleeting memory of demonic shapes forming from the mist teased at the edges of her awareness. The wind gusted in short, chilly bursts, carrying a stink part rotting engine and part sewer.

A lanky man in a glossy dark plastic trench coat emerged from the rubble, his arm bearing the red 'E' logo of the East End Boys. "Oi, 'avent seen you in a bit." Metal fingers clicked as the cybernetic fist on his right arm opened and closed. "'Ere for a fix? Who'd ya bash for the kit?"

"Knux," said Anna. "It's a proper miracle you're still alive. I'd say time's been kind to you, but it hasn't."

Three more East End Boys stepped out from behind a standing slab of concrete, one wall the only trace of a former building. Knux walked closer, his black plastisteel hands upturned at the end of long, dingy sleeves. The coat hung open down the center, showing off his pallid, anemic frame. His mates flanked him, staring at her as if trying to undress her with their eyes.

"'Ow bout a bit of tit?" said one with green hair.

The other in a long, clear trench coat, laughed at the rhyme.

"I think not," said Anna. "I've no need of your services."

"What if we 'ave need of yours?" asked Knux.

Green Hair fidgeted. "Oi. She's a bit different, eh?"

She shifted her eyes to them without turning her head. "The only service I'll provide you lot is an express to the Devil's Doorstep."

"That's a right dodgy pub, that," said Trench Coat. "Waters their shite down."

Anna sighed. "No, you sod. The actual Devil."

A slow crackle of lightning connected her hand to a nearby puddle, spattering their legs with mud and making their hair stand on end. Ozone filled her nostrils.

"Bugger…" whispered Knux. "You're a witch? 'Ve you always been able ta do 'at?"

"Aye. An' the world would thank me." Anna smiled. "For improving the overall intelligence of Britain's gene pool."

She walked away from the four confused East Enders, trudging across The Ruin. With the rain falling, none of the local Cov children risked going out and about. None of the clouds held the shapes of demons today, no baleful yellow eyes staring down at her. She set her jaw, ignoring her memories of a hallucinatory goblin, and approached her former home. Ol' Jack still stood in the shadow of the doorway. He startled, seeming surprised by her presence. She leapt a huge mud bog and took shelter under the building at his side.

"How are you feeling, Jack?"

"Your friend left me with a 'ell of a 'eadache." He fidgeted his hands in his pockets. "Good ta see ya, Anna. He said the bastard what fucked with my head's been got?"

She tightened her jaw, holding back her regret so it didn't show on her face. James had been many things, one of them definitely a bastard. "Yes. He's dead. I wanted to thank you for helping my mum."

He scowled at the rain. "I didn't do much of a good job of it. I couldn't get to her fast enough."

"I know that's why you took after me so. You don't have to feel guilty over what they did to her. You helped her escape. I'd have grown up in a laboratory cage if you didn't do that."

"Might've been kinder for ya than that sod."

Anna looked down, a long, slow exhale trailing out of her mouth. "I've made my peace with him, Jack. What're you still doing out here in the dustbin?"

He shrugged one shoulder. "It's a comfortable habit. The poor sots here could use the help. Figure it's a step to makin' up to the world for some of the shite I did in the name of King and country." Ol' Jack looked her up and down with an appraising smile. "You look a lot like her, you know. What're you up to?"

"I'm not entirely sure yet. I've sort of painted myself into a corner. Seems like I've gotta make good on a bluff to stay out of jail."

"Not much of a choice, luv."

"After what Old Bill's done to me... to everyone 'ere, I'm not sure I could stand to be associated with them... even if I would technically be under Mi6."

"Watch those bastards," said Jack. "They'll have ya doin' shite ya don't realize."

"It wouldn't be traditional. The CSB is divesting itself of everything to do with psionics. King William is throwing a fit because Parliament is likely to vote in favor of making us citizens."

"Oh, the horror." Ol' Jack chuckled.

"That paranoid bastard can't stop it now. They want to put together something like Division 0 over here."

"What's that?"

"Police, but psionics. Fight fire with fire sort of thing. I'm just not sure I could tolerate being a cop. Too many bad memories."

"It's just the washouts what wind up 'ere. Those lot don't deserve to wear the uniform. If you ask me, they're due for a bit of housekeeping."

"Aye." She hugged him. "Thanks for everything, Jack. Drop by sometime. Number six Woodseer."

He blinked. "You're takin' the old place?"

"Yeah." Anna smiled. "Need room for the boy."

Ol' Jack's eyebrows went up. "There's a story there."

"James gave 'im the zap. He thinks I'm 'is mother. I..." Anna stared down. "I'm not going to be very good at it, but I couldn't bear the look he gave me. How do you tell a twelve-year-old who just lost his 'dad' that you're not really his mum? Even if it's all bollocks. His real past is so horrible I don't even want to talk about it. This new person is pounded so deep in his brain it's no different..."

"Archon?" Jack shook his head. "Aaron didn't deprogram him?"

"I'm not sure he could. Archon spent hours working on his new personality... besides"—Anna clenched her hands into fists—"it's kinder to leave him be. He's had a right awful time of it. Kinda makes my life not feel so bad."

"What if it unravels? He might resent you."

"Aaron's pretty sure it won't. It's a heavy implant. The boy's not a telepath, not in the least. He's a bit like Mamoru... all kinetics, speed, strength. He's not Awakened, but he's going to be a handful."

"Whatever a Mamoru is..." Jack chuckled. "Sounds like a heart condition. Well, I'll be here if you need me."

"I need to go before Alastair drives the Taylors up the wall. I'll be late for dinner." Anna hugged him again, letting her hand linger on his. "Don't be a stranger, Jack."

SUIJINSAMA

EPILOGUE: GREY RONIN

Mamoru

Waves of white cherry blossoms snowed in a graceful cascade, whirling about wherever the wind carried them. Mamoru didn't move, his empty samurai armor hovering like a statue under a blue torii gate lined with small, black birds. The sounds of nature emanated from the endless forest in all directions, and the scent of wet ground permeated everything. Minutes passed before motion caught his eye. Six men in black suits walked out from the trees. The sky reflected in six pairs of sunglasses, clouds scrolling by too fast for reality. The lead man, the only one with traces of grey above his ears, advanced and bowed. A thumbnail-sized silver pin on his lapel bore the letters NSK in English under the Kanji for Nippon Shōgyō-Kumiai.

Mamoru shifted his avatar, appearing as himself in a blue *haori* jacket and baggy white *hakama* pants, *daisho* at the left side of his belt. He returned the bow and reached into the flap of his shirt, pulling forth a wooden lockbox that could not have fit there. He presented it to the older man, who took it and lifted the lid.

Silver credit chips glowed with white light. Green numbers hovered over the pile of treasure, reading the sum of six million. The elder bowed again, and with a grunt of approval, closed the box. At his nod, the next nearest man approached and offered Mamoru a scroll.

The younger NSK representative bowed. "I hope you enjoy her."

Mamoru cut the man in half from hip through the top of his head in the same motion that pulled his katana from its scabbard. The man's scream broke into digitized chunks as his body exploded into a shower of onyx fragments. His remaining four associates raised their arms; pistols appeared in their hands in a shimmering coalescence of pixels. The elder man raised an eyebrow, but made no move to ready a weapon.

"Sadako is my *sister.*" Mamoru stood for a few seconds, allowing his rage to fade, before he reached out, grasped the hovering scroll, and slid the katana back in its sheath.

The men lowered their guns.

"Forgive Kimura-san's rudeness," said the older man. "He did not know her relation to you."

Mamoru detested their buying and selling of people, but that burden did not rest upon his shoulders. It didn't matter that they dressed it up under terms such as contract and employment. A slave remained a slave regardless of the euphemism one hid behind.

"Imura-sama," whispered one of the men, in a faltering voice. "Kimura-san is dead… for real."

The older man turned pale.

"Do not be hypocrites," said Mamoru. "You cling to ancient ways that permit the ownership of slaves and the theft of children from their families. Yet, when one offends the honor of a samurai, you question the right afforded him by the same traditions? Live by the old ways or do not. There is no in-between."

Mamoru let the scroll unfurl. He now legally owned his sister, purchased from the same people who had stolen her. With this, he would petition the Shogun of Yoshida-Nakano, the corporation that ruled Sapporo prefecture. Sadako would be free, able to return to Japan without consequence should she ever desire to. Mamoru collapsed the scroll and pushed it into his chest, transferring the file to his deck.

He bowed to them and released his connection to the net.

Serene woodlands faded to black. The oily stench of metal and dirt rushed into the void left by cyberspace. The absence of real sensation drowned beneath an influx of touch, taste, and smell a hundred times more intense than normal, saturating every breath with the flavor of steel and grease on the wind. Mamoru covered his nose and coughed.

When his clothes no longer felt like sandpaper, he stood. "Sadako?"

He looked around the two-room apartment. The NinTek berserker series deck, grey-blue and gleaming, seemed the only item in the room not forty or more years old. Metal walls smeared with grime surrounded dingy furniture handmade by the locals. He found the bathroom door open, no sign of her there either.

Mamoru stepped outside, searching the rolling grassland between him and the river. Sadako chose this place, twenty or so miles further inland from the edge of East City. The locals had warned him not to travel to the northwest, where the prewar city of Atlanta supposedly 'still glowed' from the nuke that had gone off. Kate had called the area the Scattered Lands, not officially part of the UCF, but not the Badlands either. Each town here ruled itself, and none of them knew him. They'd chosen this settlement for its proximity to East City, still within range of a wireless GlobeNet connection. Sadako wanted him to spend some time away from technology like her father had.

If only I had obeyed as a son should have.

Sadako waved from the river. He disregarded his sandals and walked barefoot to the bank. She stood thigh deep a short distance ahead of him, her long red t-shirt held in two fists above the surface.

A hopeful smile formed on her face. "Do you think Suijinsama can hear us from so far away? I have been trying to talk to him."

"He is water. The sea god is not bound to Japan."

"Nor are you." She waded closer to the bank, over to him.

"It is done, sister. You are free."

Sadako let her shirt drop and gathered her hands together at her chest to lean against him. He put an arm around her. They stood for a few minutes, shin deep in the silent water. East City smeared grey across the horizon, speckled with winking lights.

"Will you be happy here?" asked Sadako. "I am afraid you will not be happy without your technology."

"I do not trust them."

"You gave them back the ship. They have no reason to be angry with you."

Mamoru gazed at the clouds. "Division 0 would be little more than another master. It is time I became the family you deserve."

"Don't dwell on the past. You should live your life to fulfill yourself. I will be at your side."

He smiled. "You should find someone and start a family."

"You nag like a mother."

Mamoru's laugh turned to a somber stare. He put his other arm around her and pulled her close. "I must be both Father and Mother for you now."

"I am not your burden. I was eight; you were ten. You were a boy. I do not blame you."

"Will you be happy here?" he asked.

"It reminds me of our old home. Quiet and open." She looked out over the grassy meadow. "Perhaps I will buy a hovercar and commute to the city when I grow restless and desire to work. I've already found some companies looking for people with my skill set."

"Sadako..." He pushed her to arm's length with a grip on each shoulder, frowning.

"Do not look at me like that." She folded her arms. "I'm going to be on the other side. I'm looking at an offer from a security company."

"You will not assassinate anyone."

"No." She poked him in the gut. "I was always better at spying anyway. Now come inside." Sadako pushed him toward the modest plastisteel cabin. "I've got a surprise for you."

MAMORU STARED AT THE PLAIN BLUE DOOR OF A SIXTY-SECOND-FLOOR apartment in the middle of Sapporo's residential district. He squeezed the small box in his hand—the one Sadako had given him—and eyed the silver panel on the wall. He had come too close to death too many times to fear something as simple as his feelings.

He touched the panel.

"Who's there?" Nami's voice emanated from the wall.

"Hokama Kiyomi, I have come to take back the false name I gave you."

Something dropped inside the apartment with a loud *clank*.

Soft thuds raced up to the door, which snapped open with a hiss. Nami looked much like she did before Minamoto stole her life. A loose indigo sweater and black skirt gave away no trace of her years spent as property. She reached out and grasped the sides of his ankle-length black coat. Her breath stuttered.

"I have been a weak man, Nami." He brushed a hand across her cheek. "I have been crippled by doubt, unsure if your feelings were genuine or the desperation of a woman trapped in a situation beyond her control. I hoped beyond reason that you might"—he hesitated for a few seconds before forcing the word out—"love me, as I love you."

Nami stared at him, a faint quiver running across her bottom lip.

Mamoru held up the box, opening it to reveal a pink diamond ring.

"Will you have me, even if it means forever leaving Japan?"

She let go of his coat to cover her mouth. "M-Mamoru..." Tears fell from her eyes, over her fingers. "I never knew if what you felt for me was more than pity. I have nothing left here but the fear Minamoto will learn of my escape."

He took the ring from the box and held it up. "A weak man took away your name. Allow me to give you mine."

Nami held out a shaking hand. "I am Saitō Nami."

Mamoru held her wrist to steady her arm, and slipped the ring over her finger.

76

FOG AND SNOW

EPILOGUE: DAUGHTER OF ASH

Kate

The cold breeze ripping down the dank street collected a whorl of empty synthbeer cans and other trash, rattling them over parked cars and a PubTran obelisk terminal. The gale seemed to disregard the existence of Kate's new uniform, chilling her as if she stood naked by the side of a building. She leaned against the wall, taking shelter from the rain under a tiny slab of concrete protruding from the shattered high-rise. While her training officer ran inside nextdoor to fetch coffees, she amused herself watching the rain gathering at the sides of her *real* boots, no longer afraid to get close to her.

Captain Buckley had made a show of yelling at her over her last special heat-resistant uniform being shredded, even if it hadn't been her fault. The thing had apparently been quite expensive. She had pointed out the rail gun responsible for ripping it apart *should* have killed her. Thinking about that made her want to race out to the Badlands and hug Althea again.

She lifted her gaze from the ground at a wolf-whistle. Six young men in mismatched coats and baggy pants looked her up and down. One grabbed himself, another took pictures with his NetMini, and the other four grinned and gestured as if squeezing her breasts.

Kate locked stares with them, un-leaned from the wall, and stepped out of the shadows. The realization she wore a police uniform sank in, and they backed away into a brisk walk in the other direction. The electronic bell-chime of a shop door opening sounded behind her.

"You okay?" asked Sergeant Huang, her training officer. He walked up alongside and handed her a steaming cup. "Careful, it's hot. This place don't look like much, but their coffee is amazing. Real grown beans even. I never understood why all the best places wind up in bad parts of the city."

His gloss black psi armor gleamed in the light of an overhead lamp, less revealing than the indirium mesh clinging to her skin. Her jealousy lasted only as long as it took to remember her 'gift' didn't care about armor. She couldn't get her brain to accept the concept. It would react faster than conscious thought. The same heat responsible for melting bullets would incinerate four hundred thousand credits worth of Division 0 equipment. Command didn't want to spend that much money every time some idiot took a pot shot at her. She felt uneasy about it anyway. Whatever technology allowed the Psi Armor to feed on psionic energy and reinforce itself seemed all too similar to the neural stunner C-Branch put on her neck.

"Fine. Just a bunch of idiots with bad eyesight. The damn car is right there." She took a giant swig. "It's not that hot."

Sgt. Huang shook his head. "Pyros..." He laughed.

"So, you're my TO. When does the training actually start?"

"Well, psionics are about eight to ten percent of the population. Of that group, only about seven in ten are even aware they have the gift. Of those people, maybe one in six has criminal inclinations, and that varies from minor life cheats to actual criminality. So, yeah, it's slow sometimes."

Kate chuckled. "Yeah, but when it hits the fan, it really fucking hits the fan."

Sgt. Huang saluted with his coffee. "You sound like you're done with training."

"Basic training was a bitch." She followed him to the car.

"I thought you weren't going in for ISCOT until next month?" He went for the passenger side. "You drive, I'm getting old."

"Way to miss a joke, Sarge." She trotted around the nose end of the patrol craft and fell into the driver's seat. "This isn't as bad as I was expecting. I might actually get to like this."

"Says every rookie, ever." Sgt. Huang winked.

"I mean it. I've... got a lot of karma to work off." She pulled the door down. "Where to?"

He gestured at the Navcon. "Our assigned patrol route is lit up in yellow. Keep driving until something blows up or you've gotta find a bathroom. Since you're training, keep an eye out for Div 1 calls. If we can lend a hand, we will."

"Okay. Guess the week won't be boring after all."

♨ ☙ ▣ ◔ ☕

A THICK HAZE OF FOG FRAMED DISTANT SNOW-COVERED PINE TREES, ROLLING over the top of a brown wooden railing. The fragrance of steam-soaked cedar surrounded her. The week had passed at an agonizing pace despite being shot at seventeen times in five days. Fortunately, any nudity that occurred during that time had happened voluntarily. Unfortunately, none of it had involved David.

For Friday evening, beyond the northernmost edge of West City, he had found a rustic resort catering to lovers looking to ditch the trappings of high-tech society for a few days. The ambiance felt quiet, calming, and romantic.

Special.

A dirt path led toward the woods thirty meters or so from the raised deck. Kate sank up to her neck in bubbling water and smiled at the NetMini balanced on end beside the recessed pool. Thirty-three degrees, 7:08 p.m. She closed her eyes and listened to the sounds of birds on the wind. Her hands slid over her stomach and legs; her nude body quivered with anticipation. If he made her wait another two minutes, she'd go crazy.

The patio door opened with a squeak. She looked up at David, wearing only a towel. He carried a dark green bottle and two champagne glasses as he scooted to the edge of the pool, teeth chattering as he stepped in water that had splashed up onto the deck planks.

"I d-didn't know this m-matchstick cabin had a hot t-tub."

"It doesn't." She winked. "This is a small pool."

David let his towel drop and lowered himself into the water. "Gah! It's freezing here and this water is too hot."

"Isn't that the point of a hot tub? That it's hot?"

It took him a few minutes to ease himself into the water. As soon as he acclimated to the temperature, he scooted close and slid an arm behind her back. "Have you given any thought to what you want to do?"

Kate reached out of the water to tap her chin. "Well, I figured we could start with a traditional missionary, maybe cowgirl a little later. If you really want to, we can try doggy… but I'd rather be able to see your face. After that, I'll think about going down on you if you're willing to reciprocate."

He babbled. "Uhh, I meant about your assign—"

"I know what you meant," she purred and rubbed his thigh. "I also know what *I* meant." She cuddled against him underwater. "This place is special."

With all the steam surrounding them, a fantasy of being the only two people left on Earth came easy.

"A basement slum in the middle of a disavowed sector would be special if you were there with me." Tension stiffened his muscles.

"It's cute how you act shy." She kissed him on the lips, bit him a little, and climbed on top of him. "You're making me feel like a slut even though I've never done this before."

He slid his arms up her thighs and around her back. "I can't help but worry you might think I'm manipulating you. There's a stigma about male empaths."

She rubbed herself against him; the urge to know what he felt like *inside* her made her moan. "Are you?"

"Of course not."

"I believe you. I trust you. I want you." Her eyes half closed as she laced her fingers behind his neck. "I want you, David Ahmed. Forever."

His unease faded and his body relaxed. He leaned forward and kissed her chest and the front of her neck. Kate shuddered. His right hand slipped from her back to her breast, tracing circles around her nipple. She moaned.

"Touch me," she rasped. "Touch me everywhere."

She leaned back and let his hands roam. Time lost meaning as she reveled in the feeling of his skin on hers. After an eternity of touching, kissing bliss, his hands squeezed her ass and lifted. She knew exactly what he was about to do, and shivered with anxiety and ecstasy in equal parts. The sensation she had spent twenty-five years trying to imagine exploded within her body as he entered her; she arched her back and let out a cry of ecstasy mixed with the pain of her first time, chasing birds from the distant treetops.

All around, snow-covered pines and fog swirled. Icy wind brushed over her back where she sat up out of the water, but she didn't care. He grunted and moaned as her fingernails dug into his shoulders. Their bodies slid over each other; water splashed. She leaned into him, arms sliding around his back, clinging. David stared into her eyes as he kept up a rhythm. He couldn't help but radiate love. His emotion added to hers, driving her over the edge. Her legs went numb, her heart pounded, and stars burst in her mind.

A series of crackling explosions overhead drowned out her cries of passion. After, she collapsed limp on top of him. He gasped for breath, gazing skyward with a dumbfounded grin on his face. They cuddled for a few minutes before he found the strength to move.

"You know, fireworks are supposed to be a euphemism." He kissed her again.

"Mmm." She cuddled against his chest, both of them neck-deep in the warm water.

"Are you going to do that every time?"

She snuggled her head into his shoulder. "Mmm?"

David brushed her hair off her face. "The fireworks."

"I don't know." Kate laughed. "Maybe we should live outside."

77

INQUEST

EPILOGUE: ZERO ROGUE

Aaron

Noisy commuters shuffled back and forth on the platform of a PubTran terminal three blocks away from the grey zone where he'd lived with Darwin. Aaron leaned against the wall, seated on the floor, observing the crowd. A few people stopped to give him strange looks. He chuckled inside his head, finding no end of amusement at what they must think of a man in a Division 0 dress uniform slumped on the floor of a PubTran terminal like a vagrant.

Aaron sat up and glanced at the empty floor to his right. "Cheers, mate. Wherever you are now, I hope it's better than you had it 'ere."

He stood, dusted himself off, and wandered down the steps to wait for a PubTran car. It cost a bit more than the tram, but he was already running late. After fishing out his NetMini, he poked the little cartoon taxi icon and kept the device out while he waited. Within two minutes of his summons, a little grey and cyan car squealed to a halt in front of him. On the ride to the Police Administrative Complex, he pawed at the holo-panel until he found the data file Shimmer sent him.

Aaron had gone back and forth over the file, finding it unbelievable at the same time it presented a perfect explanation for the unexplainable. *Reading* his mind would not have set off his involuntary detonation. Garber wasn't trying to see what Aaron remembered. He had been paid off by C-Branch to implant a memory. He wanted to make Aaron give himself to the military intelligence department as a guinea pig. They had gotten wind of the devastation he'd wrought at the scene of Allison's death, and took quite a keen interest in him.

He thought about Querq and his initial revulsion. *How could anyone want to live out there?* Now, he had a better idea. No 'day jobs,' no shady corporations, no government getting away with everything it could. The occasional mutated prewar horror seemed trivial in comparison. Still, the Badlands wasn't his cup of tea. As romantic as it sounded, he knew he wouldn't tolerate it for long. Even his two-day visit left him missing the real world.

The automated taxi halted outside the PAC. "Thank you for choosing PubTran Corporation for your transportation needs. Please note that a travel fee of one hundred and fourteen credits has been deducted from your account. You may be selected to receive a brief five-question survey based on your experience. Have a nice day."

Aaron got out, not bothering to respond to the insincere robotic voice. No one on the grounds or in the main hub paid him much notice. Once he arrived in the Division 0 wing, he got the usual wary looks, angry stares, and curious whispers. He glanced at the NetMini to check the time: 7:58 a.m., and moved up to a jog. Four corridors, an elevator, and one security checkpoint later, he stood at a pair of wide, silver doors with curved lines at the top. It conjured the image of a hole made to accommodate an enormous loaf of French bread.

He took a deep breath and walked toward them. They opened, sliding to the side to let him enter. The Division 0 command council sat behind a long table at the far end of a hearing chamber: Deputy Director Johannes Burckhardt on the far left. Regional Commander Mikhail Kovalev, responsible for West City, beside him. Division 0 Director Jane Carter next, and at the far right, East City Regional Commander Ravindra Kumar attended via hologram. He stopped in front of a small podium facing the tribunal.

His shoe squeaked to a halt exactly at 8:00 a.m.

Aaron rendered a salute, which they all returned.

"We have reviewed your case, Lieutenant Pryce," said Carter. "Do you have anything you wish to say before we close the Inquest into the death of Officer Allison Pryce, and of the subsequent deaths of Lieutenant Jonathan Garber, Officers Elaine Rios and Marcus Frost, as well as Dr. Michael Korran?"

"Aye," said Aaron.

His saying something was expected, as evidenced by the unsurprised nods from everyone on the other side of the table.

"I have some new evidence regarding the incident in the infirmary. With your permission, I would like to share it with you."

"Please do," said Carter.

Aaron took his NetMini from his pocket, pulled up Shimmer's file, and made pitching motions with the device at each of the senior officers. Their devices all chirped. He stood at attention once more.

"Lieutenant Garber was operating under the direction of C-Branch, with financial encouragement, to implant the desire to defect to their employ. His attempt to *alter* my mind is what resulted in the involuntary telekinetic eruption. A simple read would not have triggered my... issue."

"You're accusing Garber of killing Rios, Frost, and Dr. Korran?" asked Burckhardt.

"That would imply a degree of intent, sir," said Aaron. "Garber also killed himself. He was the first one to die as my subconscious tried to protect itself. I believe it was an accident; however, it does explain what triggered the event. A simple *read* as he was supposed to have been doing would not have. I will always live with the guilt of being unable to stop it."

"I've already brought the council up to speed on the situation concerning Dr. James Mardling," said Mikhail. "Excellent work dealing with that. I'm impressed you even managed to recover the Angel."

"The ship suffered extensive damage," said Burckhardt with a frown. "It'll be out of commission for months."

"Thank you, sir, but Mamoru and Officer Solomon had more to do with the starship than me."

"Oh?" asked Commander Kumar.

Aaron tried to breathe away his nerves. He didn't care if they dismissed him, even a dishonorable discharge. If he could avoid prison time, or worse, he'd be thrilled. He thought of Anna.

Burckhardt cleared his throat after a minute of silence. "Is it a difficult question, Lieutenant?"

"No, sir. Mamoru is an advanced technokinetic. He can apparently imbue his consciousness into a machine. That is how he was able to steal the ship on his own."

"He was also the one responsible for turning it into a missile headed to wipe out West City, was he not?" asked Carter.

Oh, boy. Aaron whistled. "In one manner of speaking yes. Just skip right to the mind reading here. You'll not believe me if I say it was a demon."

Telepathic tingles swam over his mind. He thought back to the fight in the hangar, specifically the manifestation of the old gunslinger.

"That 'Sentient Badlands' story has been floating around among the astrals for a while," said Mikhail.

"Seems like it's more than a story." Carter looked worried. "Unless we're looking at another mass-hypnosis incident."

"How does Officer Solomon factor into the starship equation?" asked Kumar.

"As it was explained to me, when he 'embodies' a piece of technology, he feels sensation, as though the machine were his body. The burn of re-entry had grown too great for him to control the ship, and he was quite about to crash. Kate—pardon the pedestrian explanation—put the fire out so he could think straight."

"You're saying she influenced a pyrotechnic event occurring miles away in the upper atmosphere?" Burckhardt raised an eyebrow.

"We're still here, aren't we?" Aaron smiled. "Sir. I believe her powers experienced a temporary surge related to a high emotional state."

"Anything else to add, Lieutenant?" asked Carter.

"No, Ma'am," said Aaron, staring over their heads at the large window overlooking the gleaming city. Rows of mirror-faced skyscrapers formed a canyon packed with streams of hovercars and advert bots. "Nothing I can think of."

"I have a question," said Mikhail. "It says here that you requested a two-day delay in these proceedings. You went to the outpost at"—he glanced at a holo panel in front of him—"Querq. What was the nature of that trip?"

"You are aware of Kate's... umm, Officer Solomon's previous unfortunate circumstance?" The command staff nodded. "Althea managed to repair that part of her brain so she would not burn everything she touched. I was curious if she could do the same for me. Since by all figuring, it was an emotional wound, I hoped she could mend it. It came with a good chance I'd lose my amplified power, but I thought it reckless not to try."

"And?" asked Burckhardt.

"I'm honestly not sure, sir." Aaron smiled. "I can still lift a dozen patrol craft... but I haven't tested the other bit yet. Can't say I'm eager to."

"Seems a little foolish." Burckhardt frowned. "That... 'problem' was the only reason you were able to handle Mardling."

"And that problem," added Kumar, with a stern look, "would've left him unsuitable for field operations where he may encounter hostile individuals with mental capabilities and no forewarning of what would happen were they to use them on him."

Carter raised a hand. "Let's not test anything just yet." She cleared her throat.

Aaron stood rigid for a few minutes while the brass exchanged glances, no doubt a telepathic discussion going on.

Director Carter tapped at a datapad for a few seconds before setting it down and making eye contact with a neutral expression. "Lieutenant Aaron Pryce, it is the finding of this council that you acted under the influence of a psionic compulsion. We declare that you were not responsible for the deaths of the aforementioned police personnel, as well as associated civilian casualties. You are hereby reinstated to active duty, effective immediately."

Mikhail smiled past his steepled fingers.

Aaron felt faint. He blinked at Carter, unsure if he'd heard her right.

"Jane," said Mikhail. "I've got an idea. I think Lieutenant Pryce would be a good candidate to help establish our ties with the UK office."

"Don't be too hasty, Mikhail," said Burckhardt. "We still do not understand the full extent of his capabilities. There are tests and evaluations to be done."

"Can we not conduct them in London?" asked Carter, flashing a knowing smile at Mikhail. "Lieutenant Pryce has no command experience, but I am sure he would be happy heading up a single patrol group as well as functioning in an advisory capacity." She offered a sympathetic look. "There are some here who may not be so quick to forgive him for what happened, even though it was not his fault. Better he enjoys some distance until memories blur."

Aaron nodded. "Appreciate that, Ma'am. That is more than generous."

78

THE LAST DOMINO

Aurora

Wind rustled the treetops of the woods surrounding a small cabin in County Gwynedd, Wales. Aurora perched on a submerged rock in a bubbling brook, the water lapping at the underside of her generous breasts. She reclined in the flow, enjoying the crisp caress, laughing as some curious fish nibbled at her toes. To anyone else, the water would—as Anna once said—freeze their bollocks off. Aurora grinned, thinking back to Anna's declaration the water's temperature was to the point where if a person didn't have bollocks to be frozen, it would give them some so it could freeze them off.

She stretched and took a breath, savoring the scent of wood smoke and forest. After a few more minutes of soaking, she climbed out and padded along the grass to a cut-stone path between an outhouse and the cabin. Birds chirped in the distance and the wind whispered overhead, making it rather difficult for her to imagine the destruction the CSB brought down upon her little sanctuary. Fortunately, the government had agreed to pay for the repairs. She figured it helped that the magistrate who approved her request had been under her possession at the time, and likely still didn't realize what she'd signed. A few hundred thousand credits tagged as 'reparations for citizen property damage caused during the course of an illegal raid' came close enough to the truth to survive scrutiny. No one would notice. Even if they did, it wasn't like anyone could throw her in jail. The CSB had been trying that since she'd been nine, and walls had never been able to hold her.

P'raps now they'll bloody well leave me alone.

She paused on the back porch to take a nice long breath of crisp morning air, and went inside. Not bothering to put anything on, she retrieved a peach the size of her head from the pantry and took a seat at the rickety table in the center of the cabin's primary room, enjoying the lingering scent of wood smoke. Feet up, ankles crossed, she leaned back in her chair and took a bite.

Juice dribbled from her lip, falling over her chest. She ignored the droplets running down her body and took another bite, dribbling more juice. Soon, the quiet calm of the forest gave way to the whirr of an ion drive outside as a hovercar circled once and set down out front.

"Come in, Anna," she said, two seconds before a soft knock sounded at the door.

Anna entered, her usual navy colored wool replaced by a black raincoat that had 'government agent' written all over it. Aaron tucked in behind her, in street clothes.

"Good grief woman, are you always naked?" Anna averted her eyes.

"Not always. Only when it would make someone uncomfortable or I'm trying to relax. I'll leave you to guess which it is now."

Anna's face turned pink. "I had a feeling I'd find you here. You disappeared. We never got the chance to say thanks."

"Oh." Aurora waved dismissively. "I caused as much of the mess as I fixed. Sorry about that, though I dare say it was rather satisfying to watch everything fall into place."

"People died, Lauren," said Aaron. "That's not much of a game."

"So serious." Aurora stuck out her tongue. "It would've been a lot worse if I ran off and hid in a cave. At least sticking around, I could nudge things a bit. So what if I had a little fun along the way?" She took another bite. Juice ran down her arm in rivulets.

"I think my father's still at the house." Anna slid into the facing chair, still not looking at her. "Got the feelin' 'e's fond of Alastair. The boy's sure he's not alone sometimes."

"Oh, you moved in!" Aurora let her feet drop and sat up. "That's wonderful. I'm sure you'll be happy there." She winked at Aaron. "All of you."

"What are your plans?" Anna looked up, blushing. "I hope you'll stop by here and there to say hello. If you do, please dress. There's a boy about. Before, when you had that vision of children playing on the lawn... that was Alaistar you saw, wasn't it?"

Aurora winked. "Good of you to take him in. My plans? I think I'll live here for a while... maybe for good. I'm going to enjoy the lack of things blowing up, cities burning, and people dying everywhere I look." Aurora's next bite sprinkled her lap with peach juice. "He'll be fine. I believe he'll even wind up saving his sister's life at some point."

"What?" Small sparks connected Anna's legs to the floor. "I'm going to have a daughter? She's going to get shot?"

"Six actually. Identical sextuplets, you'll be the size of the Gherkin for months."

Anna almost fainted.

"Hah! Got you!" Aurora laughed. "I only saw the one, and she's not going to get shot. Looked like she wound up choking at dinner and he did the squeezy thing. Pleasantly mundane."

"Oh, goodness," said Aaron. "Now she's going to keep the child on pudding until she's forty."

Anna glared at him.

"You can still choke on pudding." Aurora winked. "Stop trying to read ahead, Anna. Enjoy yourself." The mirth faded from her voice. "If you try to muck about, you might make it worse."

For a moment, Anna stared in silence at the trail of wet footprints leading in from the back door. "You're going to need another bath. You're getting sticky all over you."

The bedroom door at the deep end of the hall opened. Anna looked away from the room she'd once shared with James.

Agent Gordon walked out in sweat pants and a 'kiss the chef' apron. "Oh, we've got visitors."

"Shit!" Anna jumped out of her chair, flying backward into Aaron. "What the bloody fuck, Aurora? You brought his ghost here?"

"Oh, he's no ghost, and I do have a feeling he'll be more than happy to help get rid of all this juice." She winked at him as he walked to the stove. "Stay for lunch? He's a fabulous cook, and he's great in the sack."

"He… he…" Anna pointed.

"I think she's still upset about the whole Tube/motorbike thing." Agent Gordon set a frying pan on the stove.

Aaron held Anna back. "Easy, luv."

"More the stabbing me with a fucking knife thing… and what you did to Faye."

Aurora gestured with the peach at Gordon. "You know it wasn't his fault. James had him hounding you on purpose for weeks, trying to drive you out of London. Gordon wasn't supposed to kill you, but he got a bit cheesed off. His nickin' Faye was James's idea… 'oped you'd consider her a lost cause and give up."

"Sorry about that." Gordon dropped frozen sausages into the pot and smiled. "I wasn't myself."

Anna trembled, pointing. "James killed him."

"No," said Aurora. "James flung him off the side of a parking deck. I caught him. The man never did learn to look over edges, just assumed 'the most powerful telepath in the world' couldn't half-ass anything. Calm down, Anna. Gordon's a teddy bear. He took the patriotic thing a smidge too far. Hughes set him to rights."

"I really am sorry about trying to kill you." Gordon held up a cluster of mugs. "Care for some Earl?"

Anna looked at Aaron, who shrugged. She sank into a chair with a far off look in her eyes and an expression of shock, muttering something about James under her breath.

"Oh, you're adorable," said Aurora. "Aaron, please sit."

"And…" Agent Gordon winked while setting the mugs on the table. "We've even got Tim Tams."

Aaron failed to stifle an eager whine.

Aurora laughed. "Welcome home, you two." She sighed and gave Anna a worried look. "Alas… I do have some rather tragic news for you."

"You saw something?" Aaron fidgeted and sank into a chair.

Anna stared, a faint tremble in her hand. "How bad?"

Gordon pulled a box of Earl Grey from the cabinet, speaking without looking back. "Tragic I believe is the word she used."

Anna bit her lip.

"Your daughter's going to be an Arsenal fan." Aurora winked.

fin

ACKNOWLEDGMENTS

Thank you so much for reading the Awakened series. The Awakened series represents a labor of love, something I have been working on for a long time and am thrilled to be able to share with the world. These characters have been with me for almost twenty years, originally as part of a campaign I ran for a tabletop roleplaying game... however the events of that campaign bear little resemblance to this series in novel form.

Additional thanks to:

Mark Woodring for his insightful editing.

Jackson Tjota for the cover illustration. Ricky Gunawan for illustrating the interior art. Alexandria Thompson for cover formatting.

Fernando Melo and Dioris Betances, for their help ensuring the Spanish dialogue made sense.

Carol Jayez and Koko Yamamoto for help with the Japanese dialogue.

Special thanks to Jen Wadsworth for her help proofreading.

ABOUT THE AUTHOR

Originally from South Amboy NJ, Matthew has been creating science fiction and fantasy worlds for most of his reasoning life. Since 1996, he has developed the "Divergent Fates" world, in which *Division Zero, Virtual Immortality, The Awakened Series, The Harmony Paradox, and the Daughter of Mars series* take place. Along with being an editor at Curiosity Quills press, he has worked in IT and technical support.

Matthew is an avid gamer, a recovered WoW addict, Gamemaster for two custom RPG systems, and a fan of anime, British humour, and intellectual science fiction that questions the nature of reality, life, and what happens after it.

He is also fond of cats.

Visit me online at:
    Facebook: https://www.facebook.com/MatthewSCoxAuthor
    Amazon: https://www.amazon.com/author/mscox
    Pinterest: https://www.pinterest.com/matthewcox10420/
    Goodreads: https://www.goodreads.com/author/show/7712730.Matthew_S_Cox
    Email: mcox2112@gmail.com

OTHER BOOKS BY MATTHEW S. COX

Divergent Fates Universe Novels
Division Zero series

- Division Zero
- Lex De Mortuis
- Thrall
- Guardian
- Harbinger

The Awakened series

- Prophet of the Badlands
- Archon's Queen
- Grey Ronin
- Daughter of Ash
- Zero Rogue
- Angel Descended

Daughter of Mars series

- The Hand of Raziel
- Araphel
- Ghost Black

Virtual Immortality series

- Virtual Immortality
- The Harmony Paradox

Prophet of the Badlands Series

- Prophet's Journey

Divergent Fates Anthology

(Fiction Novels - Adult)

The Roadhouse Chronicles Series

- One More Run
- The Redeemed
- Dead Man's Number

Faded Skies series

- Heir Ascendant
- Ascendant Unrest
- Ascendant Revolution

Temporal Armistice Series

- Nascent Shadow
- The Shadow Collector
- The Gate to Oblivion
- The Queen of Discord

Vampire Innocent series

- A Nighttime of Forever
- A Beginner's Guide to Fangs
- The Artist of Ruin
- The Last Family Road Trip
- The Phantom Oracle
- How Not to Summon Demons
- Ordinary Problems of a College Vampire
- A Vampire's Guide to Surviving Holidays
- An Introduction to Paranormal Diplomacy

Standalones

- Wayfarer: AV494
- Axillon99
- Chiaroscuro: The Mouse and the Candle
- The Spirits of Six Minstrel Run
- Sophie's Light
- The Far Side of Promise anthology
- Operation: Chimera (with Tony Healey)
- The Dysfunctional Conspiracy (with Christopher Veltmann)

- Of Myth and Shadow
- The Girl Who Found the Sun

Winter Solstice series (with J.R. Rain)

- Convergence
- Containment
- Catalyst

Alexis Silver series (with J.R. Rain)

- Silver Light
- Deep Silver
- Silver Quarrel

Samantha Moon Origins series (with J.R. Rain)

- New Moon Rising
- Moon Mourning

Vampire For Hire series (with J.R. Rain)

- Moon Master
- Dead Moon
- Lost Moon

Maddy Wimsey series (with J.R. Rain)

- The Devil's Eye
- The Drifting Gloom
- Dark Mercy

Samantha Moon Case Files series (with J.R. Rain)

- Blood Moon

Immortal Operative series (with J.R. Rain)

- Broken Ice

Four Elements series (with J.R. Rain)

- The Elementalist

- The Black Rose
- The Wakefield Curse

Young Adult Novels

The Eldritch Heart Series

- The Eldritch Heart
- The Cursed Crown

Evergreen Series

- Evergreen
- The World That Remains
- The Lucky Ones
- Nuclear Summer

Standalones

- Caller 107
- The Summer the World Ended
- Nine Candles of Deepest Black
- The Forest Beyond the Earth
- Out of Sight

Middle Grade Novels

The Adventures of Ubergirl series

- My Dad is a Mad Scientist
- Aliens Ate My Homework
- The End of all Halloweens

Tales of Widowswood series

- Emma and the Banderwigh
- Emma and the Silk Thieves
- Emma and the Silverbell Faeries
- Emma and the Elixir of Madness

- Emma and the Weeping Spirit

Standalones

- Citadel: The Concordant Sequence
- The Cursed Codex
- The Menagerie of Jenkins Bailey